DARK MATTER

by

S.W. Ahmed

 BRANE Science Fiction

DARK MATTER

Published by
Brane Science Fiction

Library of Congress Catalog Card Number: 2008901013

ISBN 978-0-9815263-0-0

PRINTED IN THE UNITED STATES OF AMERICA

10 9 8 7 6 5 4 3 2 1

For my daughter Saira.
May the world of her generation be a more
peaceful and tolerant one than ours.

TABLE OF CONTENTS

Chapter 1

Marc Zemin awoke with a start, and jumped up in his bed. The first thing he felt was relief, as soon as he realized that it had all just been a bad dream. Opening his eyes, he noticed it was daylight outside. Then he gasped as he saw the time on his clock-radio. 10 am! He had slept through the alarm once again!

He quickly got out of bed, left his room and headed to the bathroom at the end of the hallway. Luckily nobody was in it, so he slipped into the shower and turned on the hot water.

There was nothing like a hot shower in the morning, at least not for Marc. He always needed a shower to properly wake up, followed by a nice cup of hot black tea. 15 minutes later, he was on his way out, with a cup of tea in his hand and a backpack swung around his shoulder. Aware of the weather conditions outside, he had a heavy blue winter coat on, with a ski hat covering his head and a scarf wrapped around his neck.

It was a typical winter morning in Ithaca. Located in the snowbelt in upstate New York, this town often experienced temperatures dropping to -20 degrees Fahrenheit, and that was without the wind chill factor. With the constant high winds in the area, especially in the hills above Cayuga Lake where he lived, Marc didn't even want to know what the effective temperature was that morning. As he walked out the door, the wind hit his face like a sheet of solid ice. Ithaca's climate was clearly not for the faint hearted!

"Jeez!" he exclaimed, tightening the zipper of his coat up to his neck and putting his gloves on. As he trudged forward in his winter boots, he cursed himself once again for having moved here. He detested this cold weather. He should have gone to Hawaii or southern California instead, when he had still had a choice. But now, he knew, he had none.

The clouds hung low over the sky, contributing to a gray and gloomy atmosphere. And gray and gloomy was exactly how he felt that morning. Sipping his tea, he tried to remember the last time he had truly been happy, but it all seemed so long ago. Four years had passed since his move to Ithaca, four years since he had joined Cornell University as a graduate student. And he didn't remember having had a single happy day since.

He peeked at his watch. Alas, he was already running 10 minutes late for the scheduled meeting that morning with his advisor. "Oh boy, isn't Graham going to be mad today," he thought. He quickened his pace, knowing all too well that he still had a 20 minute walk ahead.

Marc was a slender young man, about 5'11" tall, with small, sharp brown eyes and a somewhat flat nose. He owed that to his genes, which were half Caucasian and half East Asian. His skin color was a light tan, and his head was filled with short, dark brown hair, so short that it was spiky. He also wore a pair of metal rim glasses that were rectangular in shape. He usually walked with his head bent forward, and he almost always had a somewhat serious expression on his face. The mixture of his genes did give him a unique and good look, but few would consider his appearance to be particularly stunning or extraordinary.

As he walked the path through the campus to Rockefeller Hall, he thought about his horrible dream. Still fresh in his memory, it was easily the worst nightmare he had ever had. He had experienced quite a few nightmares in his life, but this one had truly been exceptional. Countries at war, innocent people dying everywhere, lots of suffering and pain. And then the ultimate catastrophe – the Earth had suddenly exploded into tiny bits. All 6 billion people, as well as all other forms of life on this planet, destroyed in an instant. And there he had been, watching the whole spectacle from a distance, unable to do anything to prevent it. Why the Earth had exploded, and how he had been able to watch it from a distant location, he could not explain. He just knew what he had seen.

He decided not to put any more thought into it, and instead tried to clear his head to prepare for the meeting with his advisor. It was not going to be fun, that much he knew. Four years into his MS/PhD program, and still no sign of a decent thesis. Since the last such meeting three weeks earlier, he had almost nothing new to report. And he couldn't imagine Graham taking that too lightheartedly.

The path through the campus led from Collegetown, where Marc lived, through the Engineering College quadrangle, and then straight on East Avenue to the College of Arts and Sciences. The campus, considered by many visitors to be one of the most beautiful in the entire country, was spread out over an area of gently rolling hills, lakes and wooded areas. Numerous bridges existed on different paths, providing breathtaking views of deep gorges. It was very much an ideal place for those in tune with nature, with ample trails for people to take off on pleasant strolls on warm summer days.

This morning, however, the temperature was 3 degrees, and Marc really wasn't finding much pleasantness in his long walk through the campus.

"Hey, Marc!" somebody shouted.

Marc looked up and grinned. "Hi, James! What's going on?"

James was one of Marc's few friends at Cornell, a fellow graduate student in Astrophysics. He was heading the opposite way. He seemed to have a bad cold, though, as he was holding a tissue that he kept blowing his nose into. "You heading to the labs, br..?" he began asking, but a loud sneeze came in the way.

"Bless you! Are you alright?"

James blew noisily into the tissue again. "Yeah, yeah," he said with a hoarse voice, "just a cold I caught, thanks to the heavenly weather we have in these parts."

James was from Florida, and hence had no tolerance for the wintry conditions of the Northeast. He was a little shorter than Marc, but had a heavier build. Of African-American descent, he had dark skin and curly hair, which he kept very short like Marc.

"I wish I was heading to the labs," Marc said. "I'm actually running late for a meeting with you-know-who."

"Dr. Slavedriver! You know, I never understood why you chose to work with that man on your thesis."

"Hey, come on! He isn't that bad! He might be a little uptight, but he's the only one who had the foresight to give my idea a chance."

"You mean the only one crazy enough!"

"Don't you start! Anyways, you heading back home?"

"Yep, in between classes. Need to take a break. So what happened to you last night? Why didn't you show up?"

"Dude, I was working. I needed to make some progress."

"That's what you say every time."

Marc knew James was right. He had not bothered to hang out with his friends in quite a while. All his time was now spent either working on his research or helping Cheryl with her studies.

"Any new developments with Cheryl?" James asked, as if he had been reading Marc's mind.

"Are you kidding? She's the toughest nut I've ever tried to crack! Can't figure her out at all."

"Well, you know what I think."

"And no need to repeat it." Marc knew the admonishment that was about to come, and decided not to give James the chance. "Listen man, I've gotta run. Hope you feel better."

"Okay, call me."

James patted Marc on the shoulder and walked away. In the distance, he could be heard blowing his nose again.

Marc sighed. The last thing he needed to worry about right now was Cheryl. She always seemed to cause him more pain and sorrow than anything else. And yet he somehow just couldn't break things off with her. He cursed James for reminding him of her right before this very important meeting.

He finally arrived at Rockefeller Hall, the main Physics building at Cornell. A large, hipped-roof building with red brick walls and tall windows, it was about 5 floors high and symmetrically shaped like the letter 'I'. Built around the turn of the 20th century, it seemed to have the general styling of that era.

Standing outside Professor Graham Dimbleby's office on the third floor, Marc tried to collect his wits. "Keep calm, just keep calm," he whispered to himself, closing his eyes. "It's not going to be the end of the world. He is your advisor, he's on your side!"

He breathed deeply a few times, in through his nose, and out through his mouth. This was a technique he had learned in his martial arts classes – it really helped relax the mind and body. Unfortunately it wasn't working very well at that moment, for he still felt very nervous.

Finally, he knocked lightly on the door.

No answer.

He knocked harder.

"Come!" was the harsh response.

He walked into the office. It was very tidy inside, quite unlike what some would call the typical professor's office. Books were neatly stacked on the shelves, and all the sheets of paper on the main desk were sorted into labeled piles. There wasn't a hint of anything out of place anywhere. A sweet fragrance filled the air, most likely from some air freshener that had been sprayed around the room earlier in the morning. It was always the same rosy scent in this office, and he had never liked it. Why anyone would voluntarily substitute the beautiful smell of a real rose for the fake odor of a tin can, he just couldn't understand.

Sitting in the chair behind the desk, peering at his computer screen, was a huge, grossly overweight white man. He was probably in his fifties and almost completely bald, except for a few gray hairs to the side and on the back of his head. A bushy mustache hid behind a disproportionately large nose, whose size a pair of horn rim glasses attempted to conceal. A white shirt and gray cardigan covered a big pot belly. Overall, he looked like a very stern person, someone who had little tolerance for wasted time or disorderliness.

As he saw Marc walk in, he looked at his watch, then back at Marc. He seemed quite annoyed.

"Good morning, Graham," Marc said softly.

"Yes, well, you do still care to call it 'morning', hmph?" No mistaking it – he definitely was annoyed.

"I'm really sorry for being late." Marc sat down on the only chair in front of the desk. "You see, I was up late going through some calculations. And then I slept straight through the alarm."

Graham snorted. "Oh, spare me the usual gibberish!" he said condescendingly in his strong, upper class English accent.

"I know. I'm really sorry. It won't happen again, I promise."

Evidently unconvinced, Graham shook his head and glanced at his watch again. "Yes, well, I have about 15 minutes for you, before my presence is required elsewhere. So how have your calculations progressed since our last discussion?" His voice was on the sharp, shrill side, and his pace of speaking quite fast.

"I've been thinking a lot about the time paradox problem." In contrast to Graham's, Marc's voice was deep, soft and relatively slow.

Graham looked unimpressed. He took a sip from a mug of coffee, which he seemed to relish more than talking to Marc. "And?"

"I'm still not convinced that you need to end up in a parallel universe if you travel back in time."

And so the discussion began. Marc went over to the whiteboard and started writing some very complicated equations. As he wrote, he tried to explain what he was doing.

Graham gazed at Marc's scribbles, and his expression slowly turned into a scowl. "Indeed, I don't believe I've understood how this overcomes the time paradox problem," he said after Marc had finished.

"Well, as I was saying, that if you look at this last equation, even if you travel back in time, you, uh, don't need to end up in a parallel universe."

"According to you, then, you can travel back in time, and alter the course of history within the same universe?"

"Yes," Marc said, taking a seat again.

"Hmph! I see. And if you went back in time and killed your grandfather before you were born – what would happen to you then? Would you just disappear?"

"I don't believe that would be possible."

"What would not be possible? Your disappearance?"

"No, me being able to kill my grandfather."

"Why not? According to your theory, it would!"

"Well, no, because I believe in the Cosmic Sensor."

Graham laughed. "Ho! Ho! Because you believe in the Cosmic Sensor, do you!" He threw his arms up in the air, and leaned back in his chair. "Do you mean to tell me that you are basing your entire PhD thesis in Astrophysics on some medieval doctrine?" His voice had risen, and so had his temper.

Marc could see where this was going, but tried to keep his calm. It was critical not to jeopardize the already souring relationship he had with his advisor. "It's not just me. Even the top professors at Cambridge believe in the concept of a Cosmic Sensor."

"An omnipotent interventionist that lets you travel back in time, but prevents you from altering your past? Which self-respecting professor would ever believe in such twaddle?"

"Uh, well, Professor Dillingham, for one. He published a paper on it a few months ago."

Graham frowned. "Dillingham? That old fart? I cannot believe he's still allowed to publish anything! Gives us Cantabs a bad name, he does."

"So much for that approach," Marc thought. He had hoped that Graham would take more kindly to a fellow alumnus from Cambridge, but apparently not.

Graham went on. "Besides, you do realize you are contradicting yourself? You want to travel back in time to alter your past, yet you believe in an entity that prevents you from doing so."

"I believe you can alter your past, to the extent that you don't destroy your own future."

"To obtain the best of both worlds in one sitting, hmph?" Graham sat back in his chair, took his glasses off and put them on the desk. "Now you listen to me, Marc," he said, changing his tone to a more solemn one, "this is not working."

Marc swallowed hard. "What do you mean?"

"What I mean is that your research does not appear to be going anywhere."

"But what about those equations?" He pointed to the board.

"Those equations do not prove anything. It's still all conjecture. Other people have attempted this before, but have not resolved the fundamental problems related to time travel."

"What if I can prove that my assertions are true, with an experiment?"

Graham laughed again. "An experiment? The last successful experiment you ever performed must have been in a science laboratory in your undergraduate studies!"

Marc was instantly reminded of his years at MIT. Those days had been so much better and happier, in every way he could think of. "I know I haven't had much success so far," he admitted, "but I think I'm much closer now. I'm almost done building the, uh, transport device."

Graham shook his head. "Let me explain something to you, young man. I took you as a student because of your astounding track record. But since you arrived at Cornell, you really have not accomplished much at all."

Marc looked down, saying nothing.

Graham pulled out a file from his drawer, and produced a sheet that looked like a resume. He glossed over it for a second, but it was obvious he already knew what was written there. "You completed a double degree in Physics and Astronomy at MIT, and graduated top of the class with a perfect GPA by the time you were 20. You accomplished some groundbreaking research in particle physics as an undergraduate that resulted in the discovery of three new particles at CERN and other cyclotrons. You also revolutionized the whole debate in the most revered astronomical circles about what exactly happened in the very first instance of the Big Bang. Some of the top theorists still believe you are correct."

Graham paused for a few seconds, as if to remember those glorious times. "In summary," he continued, "there is no doubt that you are an absolute genius, easily the youngest and most brilliant graduate student I have ever had."

Marc felt a wave of emotion hitting him, and he felt both embarrassed and honored at the same time. But he tried hard not to let any of it show.

Graham let out a big sigh. "So what in heaven's name happened? Ever since you arrived here, you have barely passed your graduate courses! And I just don't understand why on Earth you have decided to waste your PhD thesis on an unattainable dream that is fit only for fantasy stories, not real research institutions such as this one." He chuckled. "Seriously, a time machine? It's preposterous!"

Marc realized he was getting pushed into a corner, and there was no way out this time. It had to happen sooner or later, but he hadn't expected that it was going to happen so soon. "I know things haven't been going well for me here, but I know I'm close to the breakthrough! Graham, I really believe I can make this work. I *need* to make it work!"

"I am sorry," Graham said, handing him a piece of paper. "I tried supporting you for as long as I could, mostly due to your reputation and my intellectual curiosity to see how far you would go. But the faculty committee does not share my curiosity, and has had enough."

Marc eyed the piece of paper anxiously. It was a letter, with the Cornell University letterhead neatly printed in bright red on the top. Addressed to him, its content left room for no ambiguity whatsoever:

December 19th, 2003

Dear Marc,

I regret to inform you of our decision to herewith place you on probation, due to a lack of visible progress in your graduate research in astrophysics. You will be required to display verifiable results within 30 days as of the date of this letter. Otherwise you will be subject to dismissal at the discretion of the department.

Academic probation is a serious matter. I trust you will give this notice its due attention, and I hope that we will have reason to keep you as a valued member of the academic community at Cornell.

Regards,
Jonathan Becker
Director of Graduate Studies

Chapter 2

Disaster had struck, and Marc knew it. His face turned pale, as the full consequences of the letter he was holding sank into his mind. His first instinct was to argue and plead with Graham, but it was obvious that nothing was going to convince Graham or the rest of the department anymore to give him another chance. At this point, the only thing that would make a difference was a breakthrough in his research.

He knew it wasn't just about his lack of progress. As with any other university department, politics was at play here as well. Others on the committee didn't like him for one reason or the other, and wanted him gone from Cornell. He knew for a fact that Professor Thomson was very threatened by his potential and track record, worried that he might one day disprove her controversial claims on superstring theory. Then there was Poloski, who had a tremendous rivalry with Graham and didn't want any of Graham's students to succeed. Not to mention Robson, who just didn't like Asians, it seemed. Come to think of it, Graham probably was the closest friend he had on the committee and the whole faculty. And somehow that didn't seem too comforting.

In any case, he was not the kind of person to stand up against authority. He generally avoided confrontations, and rarely displayed his anger or discontent. That was, of course, unless someone really drew him over the edge by upsetting him time and again. But he had no reason to feel that way about Graham at the moment. Graham had generally been patient with him, and had supported him through failure after failure over the past few years.

Right now, however, Graham was looking at his watch, clearly late for his next meeting.

"Well then, I'll just get back to it," Marc said, taking the hint. "I will try to have some results for you within the next week or two."

"That would be a good idea." A ghost of a smile appeared across Graham's lips, indicating the end of the conversation.

Marc left without saying goodbye. He was too shocked, too hurt and too disappointed. Graham wanted him gone from Cornell, just like everybody else. Graham definitely didn't understand why this research was so important to him. Nobody did.

He decided not to go to his lab. After a meeting like that, he needed some time to recuperate. He was heading back home.

Although it was reaching midday, it felt like it had gotten even colder and darker in the past half hour. It had started snowing again, but not heavily. A thin sheet had already formed on the ground, and the wind was still strong. He remembered the weather forecast he had heard on the radio in the morning – snow flurries all day, with no letup for the rest of the week either. Wheezing, he tightened the scarf around his neck and headed down East Avenue back towards Collegetown.

"If only I could make them understand," he kept saying to himself. But they couldn't comprehend what he had been through. None of these people knew what it was like to lose everyone who was dear to them, one after the other. None of them shared this tremendous need to travel back in time to alter the course of certain critical events in their lives.

His friends had always told him to accept the inevitable and to move on. Not that he hadn't tried – he had, repeatedly. But he had never been able to find anything else to be happy about or look forward to.

Probably the biggest shock to him of all had been the death of his mother four years earlier. She had developed kidney cancer, and by the time of its detection, it had already reached such advanced stages that the doctors had given up within a few weeks of treatment. This had all happened right after his graduation from MIT. After learning of his mother's cancer, he had deferred starting the MS/PhD program at Cornell for six months, and had spent that time with her back home in Vancouver, Canada.

Those months had been the hardest of his life, seeing his mother's health rapidly deteriorate right in front of his eyes. As a child, he had always imagined himself as a hero. He had often spent hours daydreaming about his adventures, helping weak, powerless victims against crafty, evil gangsters. His favorite scenarios had always involved him defeating a drug smuggling ring led by a highly feared, eccentric character called Mr. Jade. "The Jade Exterminator!" he used to call himself. And yet, years later as an adult, he had been unable to save his own mother.

She had died within five months of the detection of her cancer. After that, Marc had really felt alone and abandoned. He had no siblings, and had never been close to any of his uncles, aunts or cousins. Not that he had many relatives to begin with, but those that he had he had never liked. His grandparents on both sides had died a long time ago. And his father, well, Marc had never met his father. He had died in a car accident before Marc's birth.

Marc's father had been returning home to Vancouver one winter's morning in 1979, from a skiing trip in Whistler with some friends. Just past the town of Squamish on Highway 99, the truck in front of their car had hit an icy patch on the road, spun out of control and turned 180 degrees. Their car had hit the truck head-on at a speed of 80 mph. The impact had instantly killed the drivers of both vehicles, as well as the front seat passenger in the car. The passengers in the rear of the car had survived with heavy injuries. Unfortunately, his father had been in the driver's seat.

His mother had only been six months pregnant at the time of the accident, an accident that had abruptly ended both his father's life and a very happy four year marriage. He had lost his father before even beginning his life, and at the age of 20 had lost his mother too.

After his mother's death, Marc had come to Ithaca to begin his graduate studies. Horribly depressed and lonely, he had just not been able to get over his loss. Eventually he had come up with the idea to use his knowledge of physics and mathematics to build a time machine for his PhD thesis, so that he could go back in time to save his mother. If that turned out to be successful, he would then travel even further back in time to save his father as well.

"Whoa!" Marc suddenly said to himself. He was back in Collegetown, just outside the steps to the house where he lived. He didn't even realize that he had already walked the entire length home. The time always seemed to fly by when he immersed himself in his memories.

After picking up a sandwich at a nearby deli for lunch, he went up to his room. He lived on the second floor of an old, 3 story house, where individual students rented rooms from the owner. They shared the common areas, including the kitchen on the first floor and a bathroom on each floor. The landlady didn't do a good job maintaining the place or keeping it clean, something he really hated. She would always promise to clean it up that week, but then never did. There was always that disgusting smell of uncooked fish and rotten eggs coming out of the kitchen, an excuse he used to never even try to walk in there to cook anything. But at least the rent was low, and as far as he was concerned, that was all that really mattered.

He didn't socialize much with the other people in the house. In fact, he didn't even know most of them, as he hardly ever went out of his way these days to meet new people. Things had been different in his undergrad years, of course. So many things had been different then.

The answering machine was beeping, indicating a new message. He ignored it, took off his coat and sprawled over his bed. It was probably somebody he didn't want to talk to right now, like one of his friends wondering where he had been the night before. It couldn't possibly be Cheryl – she hardly ever called until later in the afternoon, if at all.

The answering machine, however, was one of those annoying ones that kept sounding a loud beep every 10 seconds until the message was heard. He could only ignore the sound for so long before it started getting on his nerves. Cursing the machine, he finally got up, walked over to the desk and pressed the "Play" button.

A voice crackled over the speaker. "Marc, can you call me when you get this message? I need to ask you something. Bye."

The voice was female. Goodness, it *was* Cheryl!

"Should I call her back right away?" he wondered. "No, let her wait a little. After all, I mustn't let her think I'm desperate to talk to her."

Ah, but who was he fooling? He knew all too well how desperate he was. He had tried many times to figure out why he so strongly needed her companionship, even though he knew she wasn't the nicest person in the world. Many a rationalization and resulting strategy to get out of it had ended up doing him no good. In the end, he had always given in with the hope that things would improve, that she would one day give him the love and attention he deserved.

He picked up the phone and dialed her number. His heart began beating faster, and it seemed to beat faster with every ring. Finally, after three rings, he heard the familiar voice. "Hello?"

"Hey there, it's me, Marc."

"Hey, where've you been?" That was Cheryl alright - curt and straight to the point, with an unmistakable southern accent. Her voice was on the high pitched side, not particularly pleasing to the ear. But it had a hint of sensuality to it, something he definitely found to be a plus.

"I had a meeting with Graham this morning," he replied.

"Oh yeah, I forgot! How'd it go?"

"Horribly. Things aren't going well at all. My days here might be numbered." He let out a heavy sigh. The sigh was real, but exaggerated just a little in the hope that she might show some sympathy. He should have known better.

"That's too bad. Hey, so listen, I need some help with my new math assignment. Can I meet you later today?"

"Yeah, sure."

They decided to meet for dinner. And afterwards, he would help her with the assignment. With that, he put the phone down and stood still for a while, thinking about his relationship with her. He wondered if tonight was the night that he would finally be able to take things to the next level.

He walked to the window and looked outside. The wind was blowing hard, and the snow was falling down heavily now. A few brave souls were trying to confront the wind, hoping to still get to class on time. Someone was trying to get his car out of a parking spot, but it wouldn't budge in the piled up snow.

His head turned back to face the inside of the room. It was very modestly furnished, nothing unusual for a poor graduate student. It did, however, have a very tidy and clean air about it, more so than probably any other room in the house. There was a small, twin size bed in the corner, with an old mattress on it that squeaked with every motion. A heavy comforter on top neatly covered the whole bed. The gray desk facing the windows was quite large, and appeared to be slanted to one side. It had a lot of drawer space for stashing books and papers, leaving the top free for a desktop computer and a small stereo system. The closet on the far wall had no doors, revealing a small collection of rather ordinary clothes – jeans, t-shirts, sweatshirts, a few dress shirts, a couple of jackets, one pair of boots and two pairs of downtrodden sneakers. The floor was covered by a thick, dark brown carpet that was probably as old as Marc himself. The walls were off-white, with large paint chips evident everywhere.

A few posters were placed symmetrically on the walls, all of them displaying pictures of stars, planets and various scientific phenomena. But there was one outstanding, oversized poster that was different. Plastered on the inside of the door, it was a homemade collage of different faces, faces of some of the most famous astronomers, mathematicians and physicists of the modern day, including Stephen Hawking, Roger Penrose, Albert Einstein, J. Richard Gott, Michio Kaku and Nicolai Kardashev. All of the scientists on the poster had one thing in common – their work had led to groundbreaking advancements in the theories of time and space travel. Famous quotes from each scientist were displayed under his or her respective photo.

Marc's eyes rested on another photo on his desk. As usual, he had forgotten to put it back in the drawer. It was a picture of him, a few years younger, standing in front of the famed dome of the Maclaurin buildings at MIT. His hair appeared longer than it was now, he seemed a little bigger and fitter too, and he definitely looked much happier. More important, though, and the reason why he looked at that picture so often, was the person in it standing next to him.

She was absolutely beautiful, with long auburn hair, big brown eyes and tan skin. About 5'6" tall, she had a nice, slender figure. Her face was sweet and soft, but the features were sharp, giving her the air of both innocence and experience, of humbleness and confidence. In the picture, she was wearing a black blouse and a loose red skirt. She looked of Middle Eastern descent.

And she was. She was originally from Jordan, and her name was Iman. He had dated her during his junior and senior years at MIT. She had been an undergraduate student at Harvard at the time, studying history. He had loved her deeply, and had grown in many ways as a person during their time together. He still could not forget her, even though it had been over four years since their breakup. She was truly a wonderful person in his mind and memory, and in many ways the ultimate standard by which he judged all other women.

They had had a very deep friendship, and had been able to discuss anything and everything. She had been his girlfriend, best friend and soul mate, all in one. Losing her had been a big shock to him, one which had taken him a long time to recover from. The timing could not have been worse either, just months before losing his mother to cancer. Their breakup had also largely contributed to his subsequent loss of self-esteem and confidence in dealing with women.

This was yet another major reason to build the time machine. For various reasons, going into the past and altering events still would not be able to keep him and Iman together, but perhaps he could prevent the existence of their relationship altogether. He was convinced he would be a far happier person today as a result.

During their time together, Iman had changed Marc's perspectives on a lot of things. Before meeting her, he had always been a very scientifically minded person, tackling all ideas and issues with logic and mathematics, never once acknowledging the existence of anything supernatural or inexplicable by science. Iman, on the other hand, was a much more spiritual and philosophically minded person. She had introduced him to a world he had barely touched before, opening for the first time questions in his head about the reasons for the existence of mankind, of the universe and of God.

"How could this entire universe, with all its different entities, all existing in harmony and bound by the same physical laws, have come into being by itself?" she had once asked him.

"It could be by pure chance," he had said in response. "A series of events that just occurred in a chain reaction, one after the other, each determining the outcome of the next."

"Oh really! So all the cities, buildings, cars, trains, planes, computers, all the things that we know and use everyday – were they created by pure chance by themselves, or did humans actually sit down, think up the ideas, design them and then build them into existence?"

"Obviously they designed and built them, but you're comparing apples and oranges."

"How so?"

"Humans design and build things over a period of months, sometimes a year or two. In Nature's case, change takes place over millions or even billions of years, where through the process of natural selection a new, more complex species slowly evolves from an older, simpler one. Or through geological forces a mountain rises up or a lake is created. Evolution occurs naturally without outside interference, due to random changes in climatic or other conditions over a long period of time."

"Okay, so according to your logic, if I want a new house, I just need to sit in front of a field of sand and grass, and wait for a few million years until Mother Nature builds the house by herself, right?"

"No, of course not! Over time, geological movements may with a certain probability create some kind of cave or shelter at your chosen spot, but Nature is not going to build a house for you there according to your design specifications of what a house should look like. Nature has its own design specifications."

"And who determines Nature's design specifications?"

This was a question that had dumbfounded him for the longest time, and he was never easily dumbfounded. It was many a discussion like this with Iman that had eventually led him to develop a stronger interest in spirituality and religion. Likewise, she had learned quite a lot from his depth of scientific knowledge and analytical approach to solving problems. Many a time, she had been able to tap into his uniquely sharp mind to tackle issues she had been facing at home, in school or in her dealings with others.

Through her vivid storytelling ability, Iman had also opened Marc's eyes to the world outside North America, to the Middle East, Europe and Asia, where she had extensively traveled and lived with her family. He had, in fact, never traveled anywhere outside North America, having lived all his life in Vancouver until his move to Boston to attend college. Neither he nor his mother had ever been able to afford such a trip. Although he did have Chinese blood in him, since his father was originally from Hong Kong, he had never had much involvement with Chinese culture. His mother was a white Canadian, and as his only living parent, had pretty much raised him as a white Canadian.

Cheryl didn't come close in any aspect to Iman, Marc felt. She really had no major interesting qualities or traits, nor was she even half as attractive. He could also see that she was quite selfish at heart. But unfortunately she was the only woman he had in his life right now, if it could be said that he actually "had" Cheryl.

"Well," he thought, as he looked at the clock on his desk, "maybe I'll finally find out tonight."

Chapter 3

Ithaca was a small town. Its total population, according to a census done in the year 2000, was less than 30,000. The nearest cities were more than an hour and a half away. Cornell University, taking up a significant percentage of the town's population, was situated on top of a group of hills overlooking the downtown area in the valley below.

Like most students, Marc rarely ventured downtown. He didn't have a car because he couldn't afford one, and walking the steep trek back up the hills just wasn't his idea of a fun time. Taking the bus was simply too time-consuming. Moreover, the Collegetown area where he lived had a small grocery store and a few restaurants with different cuisines. "Why would I ever want to go downtown?" he would always say to himself. "Everything I need is available right here in Collegetown."

It was in one of the Collegetown restaurants that he sat that evening, waiting for Cheryl to show up. Called Delhi Palace, it was the only Indian restaurant in all of Ithaca. Although the quality of the food didn't come close to the good Indian restaurants he had been to in Vancouver or Boston, it was decent and unique enough to warrant an occasional visit. Besides, he loved Indian food. To him, the spicier the food, the better it tasted.

"Would you be wanting something to drink, Sir?" the waiter asked in a thick Indian accent. A tall man, probably in his early 30's, he was dressed in a neatly pressed white shirt and black trousers. The restaurant had a nice décor, with pictures of Indian landmarks on the walls and exotic artifacts situated in different corners. The smell of curry and spice hung low over the entire room, and sweet sounding sitar music emanated from speakers mounted to the ceiling.

"I'll just wait till my friend arrives, thanks," Marc replied. He glanced at his watch and frowned. Cheryl was already twenty minutes late. "I hope she's not wasting time with that buffoon again," he thought.

"That buffoon" happened to be Randy, Cheryl's "official" boyfriend. At least, "official" was how Marc coined it. As far as he was concerned, Randy was a loser who had merely gotten to Cheryl first. She liked him much more as a person, of that he was convinced. But as much time as he spent with her and as much as he helped her out with her studies, she always ended up going back to Randy at the end of the day.

The few friends that Marc had, including James, kept telling him to forget about her and to move on with his life. They insisted that she was just using him for her own benefit. But he couldn't do it. Maybe he just needed female company, or maybe it was the fact that she was the only woman these days who gave him any attention at all. Either way, he kept hoping she would soon realize that she actually wanted to be with him, not Randy.

She finally showed up at the restaurant. "Hey! Sorry I'm late, but my Psych study group meeting ran over. We were having this really interesting discussion about mind conditioning."

"No problem at all," he said, "I just got here myself." Somehow he could never try to make her feel bad or guilty, no matter how inconvenient things got for him.

She was attractive, no doubt. She had white skin, with short blond hair that she kept nicely styled in flowing curls, and blue eyes that had a mischievous twinkle about them. Her figure was full and quite voluptuous, something he enthusiastically observed every time he saw her. He definitely preferred the full bodied figure in a woman, as long as she wasn't overweight. He just wasn't too crazy about ultra-thin girls, something he found to be an unfortunate trend in his day and age.

Cheryl was wearing tight blue jeans and brown boots, and a white sweater that hung loose over her upper body. "In the mood for Indian food, huh?" she remarked, as she began looking at the menu.

"I thought you liked Indian food?" he said, a little surprised. She had loved it the week before, and had eaten a ton of lamb curry and naan bread.

"It's okay. Don't always like the spicy smell though. Not really in the mood today."

"Would you rather go somewhere else, then?"

"No, it's fine. I'll just pick something light."

She ordered a mulligatawny soup and a small salad. He got an extra large order of chicken tandoori for himself, well knowing that she would end up having a significant portion of it.

As they waited for their entrees, she began talking about her coursework. As usual, she was complaining about her problems with fellow students or professors, and about how much work she had.

"That Janet just drives me up the wall!" she cried. "You know what she did today?"

Before he had a chance to respond, she kept on talking. "She actually had the nerve to cut me off twice in class, while I was making important points. What's more, she never even thanked me for allowing her to copy my math assignment word for word."

"No mention that I actually did the assignment for you a couple of days earlier," he thought.

As she kept on talking, the food finally arrived. After a few sips of the soup, she began picking up pieces of chicken from his plate.

He asked her about her different classes, and she just kept on chatting about each of them. She was a Psychology major at Cornell, in her senior year as an undergrad. Her area of focus was the mathematical formulation of human behavior patterns, which required her to take a number of higher level math courses. Some of the material was quite difficult for her to grasp, which was why she depended on him to help her out with her assignments and in understanding complicated mathematical concepts.

As they finished their food, Marc was hoping she would finally ask him about his problems of the day, problems that were clearly much larger than hers. But she didn't. Eventually he brought up the topic by himself, bothered by her lack of concern. "I got a real bashing from my advisor today," he said with a sigh.

"Oh yeah, you mentioned that on the phone," she said. "What happened?"

"Well, in a nutshell, I may be out of here in a month."

"What?" She looked genuinely surprised.

"They aren't happy with my research," he explained. "So they're giving me a month within which to come up with something that will change their minds. If not, then they're kicking me out of the program."

"Oh, wow! I thought you were working on some really exciting, pioneering stuff?"

"I am, but convincing those bozos of that is a different story."

"You know," she said with a ponderous expression, "I never really understood what it is that you're working on anyway."

He leaned back in his seat, hiding the urge to roll his eyes. He couldn't believe this was all she could say, after hearing that he might be kicked out of the university. Was that really how little she cared for him? Sometimes he wasn't sure if she truly was like this by nature, or if she just put on this cold façade around herself for her own protection. Although his friends kept telling him it was the former, he had faith that it was the latter. He had faith that he would one day break through to the real, soft-hearted Cheryl.

After a pause, he leaned forward again. "Essentially I'm trying to find ways to exploit wormholes in the space-time continuum."

She had a dumbfounded look on her face. "Huh?"

He had to remind himself that he wasn't talking to a physicist. "I'm building a time machine," he put in plainer words.

The dumbfounded look turned to one of disbelief. "Really! Is that even possible?"

"Oh, yes it is!" He began to get excited and his voice rose. "It's all about using higher dimensions, you see?"

She apparently did not see, as she was shaking her head.

He thought for a second about how to explain better. "Do you have a piece of paper in your purse?"

She took out a piece of paper and a pen. He grabbed them and drew two dots on opposite ends of the paper.

"Show me the shortest distance between these two points," he said eagerly, giving her the pen.

She drew a straight line between them, as he had expected. He then lifted the sheet from the table and carefully folded it into the shape of a cylinder, in such a way that one dot was directly below the other.

"Now tell me, what's the shortest distance?"

"Well, that way it's much shorter," she said, pointing at the distance across empty space between the dots.

"Exactly! When you drew the line before, you were showing the shortest distance in 2 dimensions. But when you bring the 3rd dimension into the equation, things can look quite different. The problem is, if you're stuck in a 2 dimensional world, you will never know or see the 3rd dimension.

"So now let's look at the same problem in our 3 dimensional world. What's the shortest distance between me and that picture?" He pointed to a picture of the Himalayas on the wall at the other end of the restaurant.

"Well, I guess, in 3 dimensions, it would be a straight line, right?" she deduced, smiling. The twinkle in her eyes was more visible than ever.

"Yes! But what if there is a 4th dimension that we can't see? Or a 5th or 6th? What if I knew how to use those dimensions to get to that picture more quickly than walking straight across the room?"

The smile on her face disappeared, and began to be replaced by a look of confusion.

"The problem is that we are stuck in our 3 dimensional world," he continued. "That's why it's hard to picture higher dimensions. But for the moment, let's assume we know how to travel in other dimensions. Let's introduce another concept. Do you know how fast light travels?"

"No, not really. Very fast, I guess."

"Correct! Nothing can travel faster. At least, that's what Einstein's theory of relativity tells us, and it has yet to be disproved. The figure is actually about 300 million meters per second. Pretty fast!

"It's kind of funny, but because light needs time to travel from one point to the other, when you look up at the stars in the night sky, you're observing the past. Because they are so distant, you're actually seeing the stars as they were years ago. When you look through telescopes at other galaxies much further away, you're looking at the way they were millions of years ago. Watching the night sky is like taking a history lesson!

"Even when I look at you, your light rays are coming to me at a finite speed. What I really see is the way you looked about 3 billionths of a second ago. Of course, that's a negligible amount of time, but it is a finite amount of time nonetheless.

"Now, let's assume I can travel at the speed of light. If I start moving away from you at the speed of light, and I have a remarkable telescope that can see you from far away, what happens?"

He kept talking without waiting for her response. "I will see a still picture of you from that 3 billionths of a second ago, right? And I will continue to see it as long as I keep traveling at that speed. In other words, for me relative to you, time will stop, even though for you time will continue to progress at its normal pace.

"In fact, relativity tells us that the closer you are moving to the speed of light, the slower time becomes for you relative to everybody else. If I travel close to the speed of light away from here, and travel around space for an hour of my time, by the time I come back here, a few thousand years will have passed for you. You and everybody else I know will be dead!

"If I actually reach the speed of light itself, time for me will stop altogether! Now, if, all of a sudden, I start traveling faster than the speed of light, then I can travel back in time. Isn't that mind-boggling?"

Cheryl's mind seemed far from boggled. She was starting to look annoyed.

"Sounds fine and dandy, right?" he continued, too excited now to notice her discomfort. "The problem according to relativity, though, is that it's impossible to reach the speed of light without gaining infinite mass and energy, let alone travel faster. For particles of no mass, like photons, it's a different story. Light itself is made of photons, after all. But for anything that has mass, like you or me, it's literally impossible to reach the speed of light in our regular 3 dimensions.

"But now, let's bring back the concept of multiple dimensions I introduced first. What if I can travel in another dimension at a normal speed, but due to the great distance I will have covered in our traditional 3 dimensions within a very short amount of time, it will appear to be close to the speed of light in those 3 dimensions? Then time for me will slow down relative to you, and I will emerge back at this point right in front of you, but in the future! For me, only a few seconds will have passed, but for you, days or weeks may have gone by. And all that without having to worry about getting heavier or requiring infinite energy!

"If I now increase my speed in the other dimension, so that I will appear to have traveled faster than the speed of light in our 3 dimensional world, then I will actually emerge at this same point in the past!" He paused for a second, reflecting on what he had just said. "Well, in theory at least. What do you think?"

"Sounds pretty exciting," she said dismissively. She began looking at her watch, hinting that it was time to go.

But Marc was completely engrossed in his explanation, unaware of everything else happening around him. "That's where wormholes come in. They open up access to higher dimensions, allowing me to travel great distances through tunnels in space, and also allowing me to travel forwards or backwards in time. Many people believe that wormholes are few and far in between. But they don't know anything about string theory. See, string theory is the current, modern theory of matter and energy, closing the gap between two of the greatest theories of physics in the last century – relativity and quantum mechanics. Fundamentally what string theory says is that all matter, all energy, all forces, when you break them down to their simplest forms, are actually composed of tiny strings. These strings resonate at different frequencies, resulting in the creation of all the different kinds of elementary particles and forces that provide the building blocks of everything in the universe. Now string theory has yet to be proven by actual experiment, but I'm certain it won't be much longer. The new Large Hadron Collider to be built at CERN will undoubtedly have the ability to verify the assertions of string theory within the next few years.

"What I'm doing in my small lab will actually verify one aspect of string theory. You see, string theory directly implies that higher dimensions exist. More importantly, string theory also implies that every point in space, no matter how large or how small, is a gateway to those higher dimensions. What I intend to show, then, is that every point in space can be used as a gateway to higher dimensions. In other words, every point in space is a potential wormhole. There are potential wormholes right here in this restaurant, around you and me right now. The tricky part is to know how to open a wormhole, and then keep it stable long enough for successful travel through it. That's what my research is all about.

"Many scientists believe that every time you travel backwards or forwards in time, you always end up in a different parallel universe. That's absurd! That would mean that for every person who traveled in time, there would have to be a separate, parallel universe just for him!"

"Or her," he followed hastily, knowing Cheryl's disdain for male chauvinism. "I think that's all rubbish. I believe you can use wormholes to travel backwards or forwards in time within the same universe, right back to the same point in space that you left from. And my work will prove it!"

"That's great, really great," she said, now looking worried. "Listen, it's almost 9. Do you mind if we head out and work on my math assignment? It looks like a long one, and it's the most important assignment for the class. If I don't get it in on time, I'm going to be in deep trouble with the professor."

"Oh! Yeah, sure." He hadn't realized how the time had passed. The restaurant was almost empty now, and the waiters seemed anxious for them to leave, repeatedly asking if they needed anything else.

Cheryl definitely wasn't going to pay the bill, or even her share – she never did. He asked for the check and, after paying, got up and led the way out into the biting cold. It was pitch dark outside, but at least it wasn't snowing anymore.

They decided to head to his lab in Rockefeller Hall, since it was the most comfortable and spacious location they had access to. He just hoped they wouldn't run into Graham in the corridors – one horrible encounter per day with his advisor was more than enough.

His hopes for a more intimate conversation that evening with her seemed to be fading. "Heck, the night isn't over yet," he thought, trying to be optimistic.

They didn't talk much on the way to the lab, mostly due to the freezing cold. She complained a little about one of her other friends, but otherwise there was silence.

Marc wished that Cheryl had more intellectual understanding and curiosity for his subject area. He really enjoyed talking not just about his own research, but about many of the sciences in general – astronomy and physics on the one hand, as well as philosophy, theology and sociology on the other. How he missed his many long, educational discussions with Iman on these topics!

In his senior year at MIT, he had decided on doing advanced studies in a field that would combine his deep knowledge of the natural sciences with the interest in philosophy and religion that Iman had generated in him. He had therefore chosen astrophysics as the subject for his graduate studies, to help him learn as much as possible about the creation of the universe.

The possibility of life forms and civilizations on other worlds in the universe was something he had sometimes shown curiosity for, but had never really seriously considered. Before meeting Iman, he had never believed in anything he couldn't see, or at least couldn't prove beyond a doubt through scientific, logical reasoning. Even after being with her, accepting the mere possibility of the existence of God was about as far as he was willing to go. Acknowledging the existence of aliens, however, was just beyond his tolerance for believing in the unseen.

He did want to explore space, though. He wanted humans to go out there, discover other worlds and observe the far ends of the universe. All in the hopes of finding out more about how and why it had all been created, and perhaps how it would end. In graduate school, he was going to use his intelligence and skills to come up with something unique, something revolutionary that would allow the human race to make extraordinary leaps into space and into the future. At least, that had been his plan.

But then, he had lost Iman in a messy breakup. Things were never going to be the same after that. Even though he had gotten a lucrative offer from MIT for their MS/PhD program in astrophysics with a full scholarship and yearly stipend, he couldn't bear the thought of remaining there. Iman still had another year to go at Harvard, and they had many mutual friends who lived in the Boston area. Seeing her, hearing about her from others, or visiting the same places alone that they used to frequent together would have been too much for him to bear. He was going to need a drastic change in order to recuperate, so he had gone for a school in a more serene, isolated location – Cornell University.

Cornell's physics department had only been too excited to get him, hoping they could use his brilliance to further their research in a number of important areas. Alas, they were to be heavily disappointed! His mother's death had coincided with the beginning of his studies at Cornell, throwing him into a huge depression. He had abandoned all of his attractive research ideas, and had just bummed around for the first several months of his graduate program. Then he had jumped on the idea of building a time machine, much to the chagrin of his advisor and the rest of the department.

His research, however, still had quite a ways to go, and he was increasingly falling into a vicious cycle of conflicting priorities. The more time he spent helping Cheryl with her studies, the less time he could devote to his own research and experiments. And yet, the more time he spent working on his time machine, the clearer it became how much further he had to go to complete his work. That would depress him further, making him realize that he had to have some form of companionship in the present to keep his life going. Hence the need to spend time with Cheryl. And unfortunately the only way he got to spend any time with her was to help her with her studies.

Tonight, he knew, was dedicated to helping Cheryl. But tonight his hopes were extra high that his relationship with her would finally turn in his favor. Tonight he really needed something good to happen, something to make him forget the bombshell of failure and rejection that had hit him earlier in the day.

Chapter 4

"Marc, it's locked!" Cheryl said, trying to open the large metal door in front of her. They were standing outside one of the side entrances to Rockefeller Hall. "Come on, open it, hurry! I'm sick of this cold."

"It's not locked. It's probably just got ice accumulated around the edges. Here, let me try." Marc yanked hard at the door, and it slowly creaked open.

The corridors were dimly lit. A couple of people were walking around, none of them paying any attention to the two individuals who had just entered the building.

Marc gladly welcomed the warm air inside. He quickly led Cheryl up several flights of steps to his lab on the fourth floor, hoping to avoid running into any of the professors or other graduate students. News traveled fast in this department, and he really didn't want to talk about his situation with anybody else at that moment.

"Whew!" he whistled softly with relief, as they reached the door to the lab.

But he had whistled a little too soon. Just as he began unlocking the door, he heard a voice behind him.

"Hello, Marc."

He turned around slowly, trying his best to hide his exasperation. "Hello, Dale."

Of all people, it just had to be Dale Poloski, Graham's biggest rival in the department. Marc wondered if Dale had been standing all this time outside the lab, just waiting for him to show up. Dale didn't usually stay in the office this late.

"Working hard, I presume?" Dale asked with a smirk. He was a short, middle aged man, with pale skin and curly, light brown hair that hadn't been cut or groomed in quite a while. His round face exposed two tiny, blue eyes, a flat nose and very chubby cheeks that easily reddened during any conversation that excited him. He had a hunched posture and usually walked with his hands behind his back. During any conversation, his face was never more than an inch away from the person he was talking to. Marc absolutely despised him, not so much because of his annoying mannerisms, but more because of his constant derogatory comments about Graham's students and the work they did. Not to mention that he also had very bad breath.

"The usual, you know," Marc replied. "Have to keep trudging away."

Dale's big head edged close to Marc's, almost bumping into it. He shot a glance at Cheryl, who was standing right behind Marc. "Present company provides valuable scientific expertise, I suppose?" he jeered.

Marc said nothing, holding his own breath to avoid inhaling Dale's. In truth, he knew that Dale was a good professor with noteworthy credentials, but with an age-old rivalry against Graham and an undying jealousy of the relatively higher caliber of Graham's students. Dale would surely like nothing better than to see one of Graham's students fall, and the mightier the reputation of the student, the greater the fall. In fact, considering that Dale was on the faculty committee, Marc felt fairly certain that Dale had something to do with the decision to put him on probation.

"You are aware of your current situation? 30 days, and counting!" Dale seemed to savor every word in his mouth, and his cheeks turned red as he chuckled. "If I were you, I would spend every minute, every second, getting that, heh, fairy tale of yours operational."

"I will do my best to make it work," Marc said, trying to remain as polite as possible. Inside, he was boiling with anger.

"I certainly hope so, for your sake and for Graham's!" Dale gloated, merrily humming a tune as he walked off with his hands behind his back.

Marc led Cheryl into the lab.

"What, that was it?" she said, looking surprised.

"What do you mean?"

"That's all you had to say?"

He shrugged. "What else was I supposed to say?"

"He just walked all over you! Couldn't you say anything to defend yourself?"

"But he's right. About my situation anyway."

"That's not the point!" she cried, looking him in the eyes. "He insulted you, your work, and me too! Couldn't you at least say something to defend me?"

Marc said nothing, looking down.

She sighed, visibly upset. "You know, you really need to learn to stand up for yourself."

He sighed too. He knew very well that he hadn't always been like this. Had he had this encounter during his undergrad years, he would certainly have given Dale a piece of his mind. But the loss of the most important people in his life since then had not only sent him into a depression, it had also greatly reduced his self confidence in dealing with others. His inability over the past several months to get Cheryl to commit to a relationship with him had only further lowered his self-esteem.

The windowless lab was decently sized and somewhat dark, even with the lights on. Powerful air conditioning kept a stable, comfortable temperature, also providing a slight breeze and a fresh smell. There were at least two whiteboards on every wall, all of them covered with scribbles of mathematical equations and numbers, including several diagrams of wormholes and other astronomical phenomena. A couple of old desks stood against one of the walls, with books and papers spread over one of them, and a laptop computer and small boom box on the other.

The highlight of the lab, however, was a huge, white table in the center. It stretched across most of the room, and had all kinds of odd machinery and electronic equipment on it, some of them stacked up on top of each other. Most of them displayed flashing red and green LED lights, with a few that had small screens presenting numeric data. Cables were spread out all over the place, and a constant background hum emanated from the apparatus. A couple of flat panel monitors on one corner of the table depicted graphs of complex trigonometric and exponential functions. Underneath them sat a new, powerful looking desktop computer.

A clear circle, about 3 feet in diameter, was marked on the center of the table. Three identical instruments sat on the circumference of the circle, spread evenly apart around it in a perfect triangle. They looked like strong light emitting devices, and all three of them were facing the center of the circle. The center itself, however, was conspicuously empty.

This lab was Marc's playpen, and this was where he performed his experiments. Many of the electronic components he had built himself, using spare parts from older devices that were going to be thrown away by the department. He had originally shared the lab with three other students, but they had eventually been relocated to other rooms. At one point or the other, every one of them had complained that Marc was taking up too much space with all his equipment, and that his experiments were generating too much noise, light and heat for them to be able to concentrate on their own work.

"Where should I sit?" Cheryl asked.

Marc cleared up some space on one of the desks in the corner, and pulled up a couple of chairs. They sat down, while she took out a fat calculus textbook and notepad from her backpack.

"It's about differential equations again," she explained, turning to the appropriate page in her book. "I just don't understand how to use the superposition principle to figure out the solution. These Fourier and Laplace transforms make absolutely no sense!"

"Oh yeah, let me show you how it works." As usual, he just needed to take one look at the problem, and he knew the solution right away without even having to read the chapter. He began by writing a few formulas and sketching a couple of graphs, and then proceeded to describe very simple analogies from real life.

As he kept talking, he soon realized that her eyes had a glazed look on them. "Cheryl?"

She seemed to suddenly snap back to the present. "Yes?"

"I just asked you a question."

"I'm sorry, could you repeat it?"

"Sure. What happens to certain types of caterpillars at some point in their lives?"

"Well, uh, they undergo metamorphosis," she replied. "I mean, they become butterflies!"

"Exactly! Think of the Fourier and Laplace transforms as examples of metamorphoses. An equation goes through a metamorphosis to end up as a different representation of itself."

On he went, clarifying all the statements in the book with similar examples, and then going into more detail to show her how to solve the problems. But she just didn't seem to be paying attention, and he had to repeat the whole process several times from the beginning.

Suddenly her cell phone rang, in the middle of one of his lively explanations. She snatched the phone right away and answered, hurrying off to a corner of the lab. He could hear her talking in a hushed voice, sounding compassionate at first, but then becoming increasingly agitated. The conversation went on for several minutes. It had to be Randy, he gathered. Who else could she be arguing with so fervently?

She came back, looking quite upset.

Marc thought he may even have spotted a tear in one of her twinkling eyes, something he had never seen before. "What's wrong?" he asked, not sure that he wanted to hear the answer.

"I have to go." She looked away to avoid his stare.

"What! What about your homework? We're not even close to half way!"

"I know, but I have to go. Listen, Marc, do you mind finishing this assignment for me? I'll pick it up from you in the morning."

He wasn't sure whether it was wise to ask and then get into an argument, or to just drop it and let her go. He did, after all, already have a fairly good idea why she was leaving. But he felt a rising tide of frustration about what was happening. "Why, what's more important than this assignment right now? Did someone die or get hurt?"

She seemed startled that he had actually talked back. "I... I... look, I have other things to attend to."

That did it. He had reached his threshold. It had been a bad day to begin with, and now Cheryl had finally upset him too many times. "So do I!" he retorted. "I am on probation, you know? I do have to focus on my own research."

"I know. But if I don't get this assignment in on time, then I could fail the class."

"Shouldn't you be working on it, then, and not me?"

"But I can't do it by myself. That's why I need your help!"

"Help, yes! I can show you how to do it, and I do so gladly. But what good is it if I just do the whole assignment for you, without you even understanding what I did? How will you ever learn anything that way?"

"But it just takes you a few minutes!" she snapped. "Whereas it would take me hours. Besides, you've never had problems doing my homework for me before."

"Never had problems? I've always had problems with it. Do you think it's fair what you're doing to me?"

"Oh, so now I'm not fair to you? I have always been brutally honest with you!"

Marc suddenly got up from his chair, his face flushed with anger. "Honest, are we?" he said sarcastically. "About what, or better put, about whom? Your boyfriend?"

"I knew it! That's what this is all about, isn't it? Yes, I have a boyfriend. You've known that all this time. Did I ever tell you otherwise?"

"Yes, he's your boyfriend! And yet you rely on me for everything, not him. I'm the one who's always there for you, who listens to you and consoles you, who helps you through all your courses. You spend pretty much all your time outside of your class schedule everyday with me. So tell me, what kind of boyfriend is he exactly?"

She was quiet for a moment. "You think this is easy for me, Marc?" she finally said.

"Easy! You use me as your servant during the day, and then go back every night to have fun with your real boyfriend. That way, you have all the free time for him that he could possibly wish for. I dare say that you've got it easier than anybody else I know!"

"Oh really! Do you think it's all fun and games with him? For God's sake, he's never there for me! He's always out with his buddies, partying away in bars and clubs. Even when he's around, I can't talk to him about anything anyway. And yet, he always expects me to be there for him, at his beck and call." She looked down at the floor.

He figured her recent argument with Randy had probably been about this very complaint. The time had come, he decided, to finally take a chance. "So leave him!

Why can't you just go out with me?"

Cheryl put on a smile, but tears were in her eyes. "I can't, Marc," she said, shaking her head. "My whole life at Cornell has been with him. I... I just love him too much."

Marc sat in his chair again, feeling the strength suddenly flow out of all his muscles. It broke his heart to hear these words. He stayed silent for a minute, while she just stood there. Then he looked her in the eyes. "Well, Cheryl," he said quietly but firmly, "if you love him so much, then why are you still here with me?"

He was hoping she would stay and say something sweet to him. Instead, she quietly gathered her belongings and moved towards the door. He contemplated getting up to stop her, but this time he had really had enough. The truth about her feelings had finally been revealed, and now it was time for this vicious cycle to end.

As she opened the door, he saw her turn around to look at him. He looked in her direction, but avoided her stare. She seemed to open her mouth to say something, but nothing came out. Perhaps she was hoping that he would ask her to stay, that he would promise to help her finish her assignment after all. But he said nothing. Finally, she closed the door behind her and left.

Chapter 5

Marc sat motionless in his chair and stared straight ahead. Surprised at his own sudden boldness, he thought about what had just happened. He had confronted Cheryl at last, after so many months of this confusing, unnatural relationship.

"So much for taking it to the next level tonight," he thought. So much for all those endless hours at her side, helping her with her studies, listening to her woes and giving her a shoulder to cry on. So much for all the anticipation that she would one day become his girlfriend. It was over now, once and for all.

Depression and hopelessness began to overcome him, emotions he was sadly quite accustomed to. But this time he was determined to fight them, because he was angry. This time, he wouldn't let these emotions get the better of him. He reminded himself why it was a good thing that Cheryl was out of his life. If Cheryl really did become his girlfriend, then his plans to build the time machine would be in doubt. With Cheryl by his side, he would have something worth living for in the present. And given that she wasn't that good a person to begin with, who knew how such a life would be? But now, with that possibility completely gone, there was nothing and nobody else in the present to live for. Now he could focus all his efforts on completing his time machine. Soon he would be able to travel back in time to change his destiny to a much happier, brighter one.

He got up, turned to face the center table, and took out something from his pocket. It was an antique pocket watch, an inch in diameter, with no attached chain and a case made from shiny gold. The case had engravings in Cantonese characters on its outside cover. He flipped the watch open. Inside, the timepiece had a clear, two-tone dial with Roman numerals set on a white background. The continuous ticking sound was very faint, and he could barely hear it above the background hum of the electrical equipment and air conditioners.

This wasn't just any old timepiece. It was from Hong Kong, made back in the early 1900's. It was one of the few prized possessions Marc's father had brought during his migration to Canada in 1968, a family heirloom passed down from generation to generation. Handed down to him by his mother on the day he had left home to attend college, Marc had never let it out of his reach since.

He placed the pocket watch on the side desk, and turned on his little boom box in the corner. It began playing songs from Enya's Watermark, one of his all-time favorite albums. Enya's music always helped him relax and concentrate. Tonight he needed to concentrate, for tonight he was determined to make substantial progress on his research.

Walking over to one of the whiteboards, he picked up a marker and began making changes to some of the equations. Before long, he was frantically writing on all the boards in the lab, rushing every minute from one board to the next. After a while, he took a few steps back to survey everything he had just written. He began stroking his chin, as he often did when he was deep in thought.

Suddenly a smile crept across his face. "That's it, yes!" he yelled. "No wonder!" He had tried the same simple time travel experiment so many times before, but it had never worked. Now, he believed, he had finally figured out why. There was a variable missing in one of the equations specifying how much energy was needed to open and stabilize the wormhole.

He ran to the center table, and began making adjustments to some of the electronic instruments. This was followed by some furious typing on the desktop computer. New graphs instantly appeared on the monitors. Getting more and more excited, he began muttering different ideas to himself as he worked.

After several minutes of this frenzied activity, he was ready to try a new experiment. He went back to the side desk, picked up the pocket watch, and stared at the photo attached to the inside cover. It was a picture of his parents, taken before his birth. Both of them were smiling, his father's small, sharp eyes gleaming with happiness, and his mother's long hair flowing freely down her back. It was obvious that he looked more like his father than his mother – they had identical eyes and noses, and shared the same height, body shape and skin color. But he did have his mother's sweet smile. The brown color of his hair was also a compromise between the deep black of his father's and the light blonde of his mother's.

It wasn't just the physical resemblance. Marc's intellect and interest in the sciences were things he had inherited from his father, a highly successful, tenured professor of astronomy at the University of British Columbia. His father may have made many a great scientific discovery in his time, had he not died so prematurely at the age of 35. Fortunately Marc had carried on the family tradition of dedication to science and academia. He had, in fact, decided a long time ago that he was going to dedicate his PhD thesis to his father.

Marc's mother had been a financial analyst, having worked for most of her career at different financial institutions in downtown Vancouver. But she had never made much money by herself, particularly after her husband's death. The perpetual depression she had fallen into had resulted in a profound negative impact on her intellectual and professional capabilities. It had caused her to eventually get laid off, and to end up on unemployment benefits for most of Marc's childhood.

Marc had grown up in a sad and poor home, where his mother had often cried for hours, even days on end. She had never failed to give him love and care, but she had not been able to give him a happy or social childhood. He had spent most of his younger years as an introvert, a daydreamer, a kid who had never known the pleasure of developing good friendships or of spending quality time with others.

During his teenage years, his mother had fallen in love with another man, and the wedding had taken place just before his move to Boston. Seeing his mother finally happy for the first time in his life, he had taken advantage of his newfound freedom and independence in college to shed his introvert personality. He had gone all out to make a lot of friends and build an active social life, and he had succeeded. Life at MIT had been great. He had done well in his studies, engaged in a lot of extracurricular activities, and had also met Iman.

But now, in graduate school at Cornell, he was back to his old, miserable state. This wasn't a fault of the school or the program, but of the sad events that had occurred in his life since the end of his undergraduate days. All of that, however, was hopefully about to change.

He looked at the picture again, and said, "Mom, Dad, this is for you." He then shut the case of the pocket watch, walked back to the center table and placed the watch right in the middle of the empty circle. He thought it especially appropriate to use this timepiece as his first time traveler, and not just because of the good luck it often brought him or because of its symbolic value. One of his major goals of traveling back in time was to see the father he had never met, and to convince him not to make that fateful skiing trip to Whistler. What better way to prove to his father that he was his father's own son from the future than by carrying his family heirloom?

Next, he turned on the three identical energy emitting devices facing the center. A loud, high pitched noise began emanating from them, almost like the sound of an airplane jet. Each of the instruments projected a bright light towards the watch, one of them sending a blue ray, another one a green ray, and the last one a red ray. The rays met at the center, combining to create a white glow around the watch.

He turned to the computer and set some final figures. "Alright, my friend, see you in 10 minutes!" he said excitedly. This was a simple experiment to open up a wormhole, send the pocket watch into it, and make it reappear at the same location in the near future. With that, he pressed the Enter key on the computer keyboard and waited.

Suddenly the three energy emitters dramatically increased the intensity of their rays, turning the glow around the watch into a brilliant white light. It was almost as if the area around the watch had turned into a little sun, and he had to close his eyes to avoid getting blinded by the brightness.

After several seconds, the light rays and the loud hum began diminishing, until they eventually disappeared and all returned to normal. He opened his eyes, hoping to high heaven that the timepiece was gone. Alas, it was still there! The experiment had failed again.

"Damn!" he yelled out in dismay, banging his fist on the table. He inspected the energy emitters, but they seemed to be in perfect working order. After analyzing some of the other measuring instruments, he sat back at the computer and began modifying the main program. Every now and then, he would walk back to one of the whiteboards, look at what he had written, make a change here and there, and then go back to the computer and keep working.

A half hour later, he repeated the experiment. Once again, the light rays turned on and the loud hum began. Once again, the pocket watch was surrounded by a brilliant white light. And once again, unfortunately, nothing happened.

Marc was starting to get frustrated. He thought about giving up for the night and going home. But he remembered his probation notice and the fight with Cheryl, and he instantly felt a renewed drive to continue. "I have to make some progress tonight," he said to himself. There was no way he could continue to live this hopeless life anymore.

Following some more analysis, he came to the conclusion that the energy emitters still weren't transmitting enough energy to open up a wormhole. After making additional calculations and adjustments on the computer, he began the experiment once again.

No longer feeling as optimistic about success, he casually turned the energy emitters on, observed the pocket watch brightening up expectedly into a little white sun, and began turning his head away in frustration. All of a sudden, however, a thin blue circle appeared around the edge of the sun.

He couldn't believe it. Was it working? Just as his calculations had predicted, a tunnel began forming behind the blue circle, seemingly trailing off into a different dimension. The blue circle rapidly increased in thickness, transforming itself into a sphere and eventually engulfing the glowing white sun. Then, in one brilliant flash, the sphere departed into the tunnel with all of its contents. He had to close his eyes due to the brightness of the flash.

When he opened his eyes again, all was back to normal. The blue sphere, the tunnel and the white light had all vanished. The energy emitters had also shut themselves off. But, most importantly, the center of the table was bare. The timepiece was gone!

"Oh, my God!" he shouted at the top of his lungs, jumping up and down with joy. "It worked! It worked!"

The next 10 minutes would be excruciatingly tense for him, waiting for his pocket watch to reappear. He paced nervously around the lab, and cast a glance every few seconds at the timer on the computer screen.

It was easily the longest 10 minutes of his life. As the last few seconds closed in, he closed his eyes in anticipation of the bright flash reappearing.

The timer reached 10 minutes, but nothing happened. He opened his eyes and looked around. All was quiet, as before. The computer was showing the same graphs, and all the instruments appeared to be working properly. But no wormhole, no flash, no pocket watch.

"Maybe there is a small delay," he thought, "or my calculations are off by a few minutes." He sat down and waited, trying to calm his nerves by listening to the sweet sounds of Enya's tunes.

Another 10 minutes passed, then 20, then an hour. Still nothing, and it was already 3 am. His excitement had worn off, and exhaustion from the long day was kicking in. As he sat by the table, wondering where his calculations had gone wrong, he began dozing off. His arms curled up on the table in front of him, and his head dropped onto them without any resistance. Before long, he was deep in sleep.

As Marc slept in the lab, his dreams wandered to memories of his undergrad days at MIT. Tang Hall was the first thing he saw in his dream, a tall, narrow dormitory building right on the north bank of the Charles River. That was where he used to live during his senior year. It normally housed first year graduate students, but the university had made an exception for him. "Anything to keep him happy here," the dean of the Engineering School had told the student housing office. "He's definitely one of our brightest, and we need to ensure he stays here for his graduate studies."

Marc's room was on the 20th floor, providing an unobstructed view of the river and the buildings of downtown Boston on the other side. In his dream, it was a rainy spring morning, and he was lying in bed with his girlfriend Iman by his side. Her head rested on his chest, and his arm was around her shoulder. She looked stunningly beautiful, even with the tears in her big, brown eyes. Her long auburn hair lay stretched over her back, as his hand gently caressed some of the strands.

He was staring up at the ceiling, as unhappy as she was. The pitter-patter of raindrops hitting the window was the only sound to be heard.

"Why are you doing this to me?" he said, breaking the silence.

"You know I have no choice," she replied sadly.

"There's always a choice. It's just a question of priority."

She lifted her head and looked him in the eyes. "That's easy for you to say. You don't come from a conservative society."

"You're not in that society anymore. You're here now, with me. You chose to be with me. Why are you giving it all up, all that we've built up over the last two years?"

"Because we have no future."

"But we can create our own future!"

"Only by giving up everything else I hold dear. My family would never accept you as my husband. They would never accept anybody who's not from Jordan, let alone a Chinese-Canadian."

He sat up on the bed, raising her up as well to face him. "Listen to me!" he pleaded, holding her with both his hands. "I love you. I love you more than anybody or anything I have ever loved before. If you love me too, why are you letting others stand in the way? Why not just be with me?"

"They're not 'others'! They're my family! I've told you how strong the family bond is in my culture. I can't break away from that! I don't... want to break away from it." She looked away.

He shook his head in frustration. "I just don't understand you. I don't understand why a family that supposedly cares so much about you would want you to sacrifice your own happiness for their sake. What happened to an individual's right to choose his or her own future? Doesn't that exist in your culture?"

She shot an angry glance back at him. "You want to compare cultures? At least we have a concept of a family! We're there for each other through thick and thin, through good and bad. Do people here even know or appreciate the value of such a strong family?"

"Alright, sorry I brought up the culture topic again. I'm just upset, because I want you to stay with me. Tell me what you want me to do."

She sobbed and wrapped her arms around his neck, her cheek touching his. "You know how much I love you. I would do anything to stay with you, but there's nothing I can do. My parents will never let me marry outside my culture. You know that. There's no way they'll accept somebody from your background, and you can't change your background."

"But what if this is meant to be? What if this is a match made in heaven, where you and I will be happy together, forever? Haven't we had a happy relationship so far?"

"But we're not married. We've been dating, like two teenagers infatuated with each other. It's not always going to be so wonderful, you know?"

"I'm willing to take that chance, because I love you."

"You're also willing to take that chance because you have nothing else to lose. Your mother won't disown you if you marry me."

He got up from the bed, walked to the window and gazed at the raindrops falling from the gray sky. "So that's it, then? You're leaving me?"

"You know it's not because of you. You are the most wonderful person I have ever known, and I will always love you no matter what. But I'm sorry, Marc. I'm so sorry."

As he turned to look at her on the bed, she began fading away, her voice repeating the phrase that she was sorry. He ran back to her, begging her to stay.

But she was gone.

Chapter 6

Marc woke up to find his body trembling and his heart throbbing loudly. It took him several seconds to calm down and remember where he was – in his lab at Cornell, the same night he had finally confronted Cheryl, the same night his pocket watch had disappeared into a wormhole for the first time. He checked his watch. It was 4:30 am, so he had slept for almost an hour and a half.

That wretched nightmare! It was the same nightmare he often had, reminding him of how he had lost Iman. He had been powerless to keep her with him, just as he had been powerless to save either of his parents or to win Cheryl's heart.

The only difference in Iman's case was that, even if he went back in time to change events, he still would not be able to keep her. He wouldn't be able to change his identity or his ethnic background. No matter what course of action he took, Iman's family would never accept him. So the only solution was for him to prevent himself from falling in love with her in the first place. He would therefore travel back in time and warn his younger self not to go out with her. By doing so, he would retain his self confidence in dealing with others. He would eventually find someone else, someone who would love him dearly and never abandon him. With that person by his side, he would maintain a positive outlook on life. He would achieve his childhood dream of controlling his own destiny, of becoming a hero who would help others attain success and happiness. He would be on top of things, actively making decisions for himself, instead of just letting things happen to him and allowing others to take advantage of him.

That had been the plan anyway. But now that he was awake, he noticed that the pocket watch still hadn't reappeared on the table. "So much for time travel," he muttered groggily to himself. Not only was his research a failure, now he had lost his prized family heirloom as well. It seemed Graham was right – perhaps it really was time to give up this hopeless cause. Gathering his belongings, he decided to head home and to get some decent sleep in his own bed.

He wouldn't get very far, however, not even out of the lab. Any remnants of sleepiness abruptly disappeared when he saw a figure standing there, blocking the door.

"Holy smokes!" he gasped in shock. He couldn't believe his eyes. At first, he thought he was still dreaming, so he pinched his forearm to make sure he was awake. The sharp pain he immediately felt indicated that he was.

But could it possibly be true? In front of him was a creature that didn't look like any living thing he had ever seen before – no human being or animal. It was tall, almost 7 feet in height, with a round head that wasn't any larger than the typical human head. But the strange thing about it, apart from the deep navy blue color of its skin, was that it had only one eye, an eye that went all around the head in a full circle. The eye, about half an inch in height, had a fluorescent yellow color, except for a black horizontal line in the middle that went all around. There was no visible nose, and earlike lobes protruded out on the left and right side of the head, just under the eye. A small, dark, oval area indicated the presence of a mouth, but there were no lips. A green hat that looked more like a helmet covered the top of the head.

The body, a little wider than the average human body, was almost completely encased in some sort of greenish, metal-like armor. Shaped like a big canister, the armor had openings near the top for four robotic looking arms that projected outwards from the body at right angles to each other.

The strangest thing of all, however, had to be that the figure was floating on thin air, about a foot above the floor. That made the actual physical height of its body only about 6 feet, not 7. No legs or feet were visible at the bottom of the armor.

Marc's feeling of shock and incredulity quickly turned to one of fear. His first instinct was to run away, but this mysterious creature was blocking the only exit out of the room. Turning around, he noticed another, identical looking creature on the other side of the lab behind the center table. The only thing different about this creature's appearance was that it was wearing a red hat.

The two figures closed in on him, floating through the air. His mouth agape and his eyes wide with terror, he really didn't know what to do. He frantically stared up at the face of each creature, expecting instant death at any second. His hands were up in a defensive Kung Fu position, although he wasn't sure what good that would do against these bizarre beings.

But they just stood there, staring back at him. They made no sound, and they had no unique smell that he could identify. It was almost as if they weren't there.

Gathering his wits, he decided to confront them. "Who... who are you?" he stammered.

Silence.

"What do you want from me?"

A few more seconds of silence, and then the creature with the red hat lifted one of its limbs to reveal a small item. To his astonishment, he noticed that the item was his pocket watch.

"Mr. Marc Zemin?" the figure said slowly in a deep, monotonous voice.

"Yes," Marc whispered.

"This clock is yours, Mr. Zemin?" the figure asked, its mouth lighting up like a little lamp every time it uttered a word.

"Yes," he whispered again, his bewilderment increasing by the second. Not only did these creatures know who he was, they also spoke perfect English with no distinguishable accent.

"Then please come with us, Mr. Zemin."

"Come where? Who... what are you?"

"You will come with us, Mr. Zemin," the figure insisted, keeping the same low monotone.

But Marc wasn't going to make things easy for them. He was terrified, certain they would either kill him right away or tear his body apart bit by bit. Taking advantage of the gap between the two creatures, he dashed out, made a beeline for the door, opened it and flew down the corridor. "Help! Help!" he screamed at the top of his lungs, hoping somebody would come to his aid.

But the corridor was deserted at this time of night, and all the offices and labs were empty. He darted down the staircase, noticing to his surprise that those creatures weren't following him. Surely, with their ability to float, they would easily be able to keep up with him. "Thank God!" he sighed with relief, reaching for the main door to the building. He pushed it open and ran out into the winter night.

As freezing as the air was, he felt warm, even without his coat. The adrenalin rushing through his body was seeing to that. He was free now, he thought, and safe. Since he didn't have a cell phone, a device he had never bothered to get due to the interference its waves would generate for his sensitive lab equipment, he would just have to make a run for the nearest student dormitory to find shelter and help. Or maybe he would be lucky enough to find somebody on the road at 4:30 in the morning.

But the streets were empty. The snow that had fallen during the day was now neatly piled up along the curbs, thanks to the local plowing service. The sky was dark and clear, with the exception of a number of scattered clouds. The stars weren't twinkling at all, as if they had frozen in the biting cold themselves. The only light he had to go by was that of the street lamps. He raced down the hill towards the main road, noticing a group of people ahead. "Help!" he cried out in desperation. "I need help!"

As he moved closer, however, he began to realize why he wasn't being followed. Those were not people, but more of the same creatures, and there were many of them! As soon as they noticed him, they filed out rapidly, floating through the air like magic. Their speed of motion had to be at least 3 times higher than his. Before long, he was completely surrounded in a circle, with at least 20 of the figures spread out over the circumference.

The figure from the lab with the red hat came out of the building and floated into the circle, still holding his pocket watch. "We will not harm you," it said with the same composed voice. "You need not be afraid, Mr. Zemin."

"Who are you?" he shrieked.

"We are from another world."

It couldn't be! Aliens! How was that possible? "What do you want from me?" he demanded.

"We need your help," the figure said, handing him the pocket watch. "We will not harm you. Do not be afraid, Mr. Zemin."

Marc opened the timepiece to make sure his parents' photo was attached to the inside cover. Yes, it was his pocket watch alright. "Where... how did you find my watch?" he asked in bewilderment. "Are you from the future?"

"We will explain. Please come with us. Do not be afraid, Mr. Zemin."

What happened next, Marc could never have imagined was scientifically possible. A pale, yellow cylinder began forming around him, starting at the bottom and working its way up to encase his whole body. The same kind of cylinders began forming around the alien in front of him and around all the other aliens in the circle. He could still see everything outside, as the cylinder was made of a transparent material, even after it had risen above his head and sealed shut. The air inside abruptly warmed up to room temperature.

Then, like magic, the cylinder lifted effortlessly off the ground without a sound, carrying him with it. "What the..!" he shouted in surprise, his fear mounting again. "What's happening to me?"

"Do not worry, Mr. Zemin," the alien with the red hat said, as its own cylinder lifted off. "We are coming with you."

All the cylinders began rising straight upwards, slowly at first, but rapidly speeding up. Considering how quickly he was rising, Marc guessed the acceleration to be close to 6g. That was about 3 times the acceleration of the fastest manned NASA rocket! He would normally have expected to pass out under such an incredible downward gravitational force, but to his surprise, he felt nothing. The cylinder obviously had some kind of antigravity adjustment mechanism.

He tried touching the surface – it felt like a solid, smooth wall. Then he looked down through the transparent floor under his feet. It was amazing to see the lights of Cornell and downtown Ithaca drop away below him, soon looking like the stars in the sky themselves. "My God!" he exclaimed, mystified by this marvel that was smoothly carrying him up into space. "Nobody will ever believe this!"

He passed the first layer of isolated clouds, and then another layer above that. Although he was no atmospheric expert, he figured he was entering the stratosphere by now. As he looked out at the horizon, he could begin making out the first remnants of dawn to the east. The growing light also allowed him to see the first signs of the Earth's curved surface. It was absolutely beautiful! He had traveled on airplanes before, but this wasn't the same. Here, he had a full bird's eye-view all around, and he was already at a height well above the flight path of any commercial airliner.

Another minute or two later, he could clearly make out the curved surface of the Earth, with the Sun appearing over the edge. The North American continent took shape below him, with much of the Atlantic Ocean to the east covered by huge cloud formations. Further east, he could even see parts of the European continent. He must have already reached the edge of the thermosphere, yet he could breathe normally without any problems and didn't feel the slightest difference in air pressure or temperature. "What amazing technology!" he thought.

Looking up, he could see the night sky like he had never seen it before. It was so crystal clear, and the stars looked so bright. There were a few stars in one area that looked much bigger and brighter than the others. Maybe those were some of the planets in the solar system? But how could they all be lined up in a procession like that? His cylinder, as well as those of his companions, was moving toward those bright objects, objects that were rapidly growing in size as he drew closer.

"Wait a minute!" he said to himself. "Those aren't stars, or planets!"

No, they weren't. As he approached them, he realized what they were. They were spaceships, quietly waiting above the Earth's atmosphere. There were nine of them, standing in line, one behind the other. He wondered if any of Earth's satellites had noticed them. If so, people at NASA and the various SETI projects would surely be in uproar by now at the sight of these UFO's.

And what UFO's they were! Without a doubt, they were the largest structures he had ever seen in his life. Each ship had to be at least the size of an entire city. They were all identical in appearance, shaped somewhat like mushrooms turned upside down. The bottom section of each ship had the basic outline of a hemisphere. The top section was cylindrical, protruding up and outwards from the wider bottom layer. The ships were gray in color, with many lights in different colors twinkling across their surfaces.

That wasn't all, however. Marc noticed a darker shape behind the ships. In size, it made even these gigantic ships looks like ants, blocking much of the view of the night sky. It had the shape of a sunflower head, with petal-like extensions of a deep navy color and a center that glowed in a light blue hue. The head was facing down towards the Earth. The sight of this enormous mass caused him to shudder with fear. He had no idea what it was, but somehow he doubted it was as peaceful or as innocent as a sunflower.

The cylinders approached the first ship. As they came closer, he was able to study the ship's surface more closely. It was quite smooth, considering its size, with no uneven sections or protrusions. Many of the twinkling lights actually appeared to be windows, exposing light from the interior. He still couldn't believe how big the whole thing was.

They were heading for the lower section of the ship, slowing down considerably as they reached the surface. He didn't see any entrance, however, and began to get worried that they would crash against the ship's wall. He braced himself for impact. But just as his container was about to hit the wall, a large section of it silently slipped away, revealing an open entrance to the interior of the ship. The cylinders glided right through the entrance, as if pulled in by some invisible rope.

Marc had a hard time adjusting his eyes to the sudden increase in brightness that surrounded him. He had entered some kind of passageway, leading straight ahead as far as he could see. The tunnel was round and wide, almost as wide as some of the busiest multilane highways he had seen on Earth.

As he floated down this path at a speed of what had to be at least 90 mph, he observed periodic intersections with other tunnels. Out of some of those tunnels came more of the same creatures, some of them in similarly shaped cylinders, others operating bizarre looking vehicles. Some were headed in the same direction that he was traveling, some in the opposite direction. Others disappeared into other tunnels. None of them seemed to pay any attention to him.

The traffic on this busy highway just kept increasing as he traveled further into the heart of the ship. Soon there were hundreds of creatures and vehicles everywhere, gliding in all directions at high speed. There were no road signs or traffic lights, yet there was some kind of invisible, systematic order working behind the scenes, making sure that nobody crashed into each other or slowed each other down.

After a couple of minutes, the tunnel abruptly ended, opening up to a grandeur that left him speechless in awe. In front of him was an entire city, filled with tall buildings of cylindrical and oval shapes that were neatly organized into circular blocks. There were thousands of vehicles and cylinders occupied by aliens, all busily flying about. He could make out parks and gardens, filled with trees and other types of vegetation he had never seen before, and there were even rivers and lakes. Above the city was a cloudless, deep blue sky, a shade darker than the blue sky back on Earth. A sun, looking considerably larger in the sky than Earth's Sun, shone brilliantly. These aliens had evidently created the semblance of a part of their own planet within this ship.

Marc's container now began moving upwards towards the simulated sky, soon reaching a tunnel entrance that suddenly opened up above him. Once again, he started traveling through another passageway, this time towards the top section of the ship. And again, he was soon in the middle of a busy highway with many intersections and cross traffic. To his surprise, he noticed that no matter which way his cylinder was oriented, he always felt a very comfortable, normal gravitational pull towards the bottom of the container.

Eventually his cylinder slowed down, leading him to another opening. This time, he was greeted with a full panoramic view of space outside, with the stars above clearly visible. It was like a huge planetarium, and he guessed that it was the control deck at the top of the ship. The deck consisted of multiple levels, and his cylinder was rising up through its hollow center. On each level, he could see many of the same looking creatures floating about. Most of them seemed to be manning stations, working in front of 3 dimensional screens and other strange looking machines.

His cylinder landed on the third level of the deck and instantly faded away. The other aliens who had accompanied him from Earth landed beside him. He was afraid of not being able to breathe without the cylinder, but found that he was surrounded by air. It was definitely colder here than the room temperature he was used to, but the air also seemed to be richer in oxygen. Every breath made him feel refreshed.

A group of aliens was waiting for them on the deck. To Marc, they all looked exactly the same as the ones who had picked him up from Earth, and they all wore the same greenish metal-like armor. The only discerning thing among them seemed to be the color of their hats. He saw one figure in front with a blue hat, then a few behind it with red hats, and the rest had green hats. His companion from Earth with the red hat moved up to the figure with the blue hat. They looked at each other for several seconds, their mouths lighting up as a quiet, deep hum could be heard.

"This has to be how they communicate with each other," he thought.

Then the figure with the blue hat came forward. "Please follow me, Mr. Zemin," it said in English.

As he followed the alien, Marc wondered again what he had gotten himself into.

He still couldn't believe what had just happened to him. Any moment now, he expected to wake up and find himself in his lab, safe and sound back on Earth. But he couldn't recall ever having had a dream with such detail, such vividness and clarity in his life before.

Just to make sure, he pinched himself again, hard. He immediately winced in pain. No, there was no doubt, this was no dream. Whether he liked it or not, he had just been abducted by aliens.

Chapter 7

The alien led Marc to a corner of the ship's deck, where a wall and a door suddenly appeared out of thin air. The door slid open automatically as they approached, granting them entry into a small room. As Marc followed the alien inside, he noticed that the gravitational pull on this ship was a little less than that on Earth, allowing him to take longer strides with less effort.

The room was bare, except for a round, empty table in the middle and a chair behind it. The walls were curved, with one side providing a clear view of space outside. Looking out this wide window, Marc could see the lower section of the ship stretching out into the distance. To the left, he could see the other ships, all remaining perfectly motionless. Further below was the surface of the Earth, thousands of miles away. But still covering most of the horizon outside was that huge, sunflower-like monstrosity.

"Please sit, Mr. Zemin," the creature said, as the door closed behind it.

He sat down on the chair, while the creature remained standing on the other side of the table. He felt very nervous, not sure what to expect next.

"We found your clock, Mr. Zemin," the alien began, pointing to the timepiece with one of its front limbs.

Marc realized that he had been holding the pocket watch tightly in his hand all this time, and placed it gently on the table. "Where did you find it?" he asked. "Are you from the future?"

"Brrrrrrrrrrrrrrrr," it said.

He shook his head in confusion.

"That is how we react to humor, Mr. Zemin," it explained in its monotone voice.

"We are not from the future."

"Are you from the past then?"

"Brrrrrrrrrrrrrrrr," it said again. Obviously they were not from the past either.

"Then where did you find it?"

"Using your metrics, 50 light years from here."

He sat back in the chair and looked down, flabbergasted. "How is that possible?" 50 light years – the distance light could travel in 50 years. That was equivalent to about 3×10^{14} miles, much further than the nearest stars!

The creature was silent.

He looked up at its face. "Who are you? Where are you from?"

"We are Mendoken."

"Mendo... who?"

"Mendoken, Mr. Zemin. We are a species that live in this galaxy."

"*A* species? How many other species are there?"

"We know this is all a surprise for you. All will be revealed to you in due course."

He smirked. "Surprise" was far too mild a word to describe how he was feeling at the moment. "What do you want from me?"

"We want to know how you sent that device into space. We want to know if anybody helped you."

"That's it? That's why you came with all these huge ships to Earth, just to find me and ask me how I did my experiment?"

"Yes, Mr. Zemin."

"Why?"

"It is of utmost importance to us, Mr. Zemin. Please state if there is anybody else on your planet who knows how to perform your experiment."

"Anybody else? No, I don't think so. Nobody even believed that I could do it. Besides, it didn't work. This watch was supposed to travel to the future, not out into space in the present!"

"The future? Brrrrrrrrrrrrrrrr. Time travel is not possible." The alien leaned forward, staring closely at him with the single eye that went all around its head. "Please confirm that there is nobody else on your planet that has this capability, Mr. Zemin."

Marc's fear rose as the alien's head came close to his. "I... I'm quite certain there isn't," he stammered, biting his lip hard. "I definitely didn't tell anybody. I tried to convince my advisor, but he thought it was all hogwash."

"Hogwash?"

"You know... rubbish, nonsense."

"Then please state if there is any other species that helped you or gave you the technology," the alien demanded, its head now almost touching his.

He could clearly see the alien's mouth in front of him, lighting up every time it spoke. The mouth was like a hole with a flashlight behind it. There were no lips, tongue or teeth that he could identify. The fluorescent eye was spotless, except for the black line through the middle. He guessed that the line was probably the eye's lens.

"No, I assure you, there was nobody!" he said. "It was all my idea. But why is this so important to you? You are clearly a much more technologically advanced race than we humans are. What do you care about my measly, primitive experiments?"

The Mendoken creature didn't respond. The door to the room suddenly opened, and another alien with a green hat floated in. To Marc's surprise, the alien that had been interrogating him didn't turn to greet the newcomer. Instead, its mouth simply rotated around its head to face the other alien. Their mouths lit up for a few seconds as they communicated with each other, but no sound was audible to him except for a droning hum. Then the alien with the green hat floated out of the room without turning around.

Marc deduced that these creatures could operate or move in any direction, without having to turn their bodies. That explained the single eye going all around the head, as well as the four arms facing different directions and the cylindrical shape of the body.

Almost instantly, he noticed something happening outside. The big sunflower was turning, lifting its head away from Earth. Then it began moving away into empty space with tremendous acceleration, quickly disappearing from his vision.

"What was that thing?"

"That was a planet destroyer," the alien responded nonchalantly, its mouth rotating back to face him.

"Holy smokes! You can destroy entire planets?" His face turned ashen with horror. "You wanted to destroy Earth?"

"Not anymore. Your statements have indicated that your planet poses no threat to us."

The rest of the ships began moving away with the same acceleration, one after the other. They quickly vanished into the dark expanse. But the ship he was on stood still.

"Not anymore!" he exclaimed. "How could we be any threat to you, if you have the ability to destroy entire planets in one swoop? Why would you end the lives of 6 billion innocent people and wipe out an entire species, just because of this pocket watch? What kind of morality is that?"

"Morality, Mr. Zemin?" the alien said, keeping its steady tone. "Such a statement from a species that routinely kills its own, dropping bombs on each other, killing thousands of innocents at a time. Where it is common for one group to invade another's land and massacre its inhabitants. Where individuals blow themselves up in crowded locations, taking hundreds of children to their deaths. Where people sometimes kill for no reason other than greed and jealousy, and sometimes just because they can."

Marc wondered how these aliens could possibly know so much about humans. They must have studied Earth for a long time. "So we're horrible beings, and you know all about us," he admitted. "But we're not all like that, you know? And you're clearly more advanced than we are. Why follow the same rules?"

"Our rules are different. We only shoot in self defense, and always ask first before shooting. Neither do we kill members of our own species." The alien paused. "It is not about the clock, Mr. Zemin. It is about the mechanism you used to transport it into space. There is a lot more at stake here than you realize, which is why we had to be prepared."

"So if I tell you how I did it, will you let me go?"

The alien was silent.

"You won't let me go?" he asked anxiously.

"We need your help. But we will not hold you against your will."

He thought for a bit. "Will you at least tell me why you need my help?"

"There is a major war going on between us and another species in the galaxy, a war which we are losing. They have the ability to create consars, dimensional rifts in space."

"You mean wormholes?"

"Wormholes, as you humans define them, do not really exist. Consars, however, are the closest thing to your definition of wormholes.

"Our enemy sends ships that appear in the middle of our territory, destroy our worlds, and then disappear again before we can pursue them. We have been trying to come up with the same technology, but so far have failed.

"When your clock appeared in the Mendo-Kiertal system, it exhibited the same consar patterns that we observe whenever our enemy's ships appear. But, in contrast to their consars, your clock's consar stayed open. We were able to trace the path of your consar back to your planet, right down to your laboratory. That is how we found you."

"So you thought I was a part of the enemy?"

"We were prepared for that option."

"Hence the planet destroyer," he thought. Now at least some of this mystery was beginning to make sense.

"As unlikely an option as it was," the Mendoken creature continued. "We know your planet and your species quite well. It is not logical that the Volona would want to partner with you. We have not observed any Volonan activity in this area, and after hearing your statements, can safely confirm that the Volona were never here."

Marc assumed the Volona were the enemy. What an astounding tale! But how could he know if this alien was telling the truth? After all, how could such an advanced civilization not be able to create its own consars or wormholes or whatever they were called, when he as a human had been able to?

The alien must have been reading his mind. "It is a long story, Mr. Zemin. There is a treaty between the major civilizations in the galaxy that prohibits the exploration of other dimensions. We therefore have no research in this area. But as we have discovered the hard way, the Volona broke this treaty and developed consar capability in secret. They are masters of the art of deception, and have betrayed us time and again. We need your help, Mr. Zemin. We need you to come with us to our central star system, and show us how you opened the consar."

"To your central star system? How far away is that?"

"3048 light years, in your units of measurement. It will take us 2 Earth days to get there."

"Just 2 days?" Marc was astonished. Some engines these ships obviously had! "What if I refuse? Will you just let me go home?"

"We will not hold you against your will, Mr. Zemin. But you may only go under the condition that you never tell anyone on your planet about our meeting."

"But our radar and satellites have surely picked up your presence by now. People on Earth are probably frantically trying to contact you already!"

"Brrrrrrrrrrrrrrrrrr. No, Mr. Zemin. We are invisible to everybody and everything on your planet. We chose to expose ourselves to you alone."

He whistled in amazement.

"If you come with us," the alien continued, "you will see a lot more that your species has never seen or even imagined before. Many of the scientific puzzles that your people have grappled with for centuries will be explained and many mysteries uncovered. For a scientifically minded person like you, for someone whose intelligence clearly exceeds that of most other people on your planet, this is a unique opportunity."

That was definitely an attractive offer, and these Mendoken had clearly done their research on Marc. But there were so many unknowns. Too much was happening, and too fast, for him to think logically at this point.

The alien, probably sensing his perplexity, added, "You should also realize that the fate of your planet and your entire species depends on your decision."

"What! How?"

"Your star system falls in our section of the galaxy, and is under our protection. Should we lose the war against the Volona, your world may well be destroyed. The Volona are not known for taking prisoners, Mr. Zemin."

Marc was suddenly reminded of his dream the previous night, where he had seen Earth completely destroyed in a gigantic explosion. Were humans really that vulnerable? Had he finally understood the cause of that horrible nightmare? Or was this just another nightmare itself? He hoped to high heaven that it was.

"But how can I trust you?" he asked. "How do I know you're not making this all up?" He had to admit, though, that he couldn't think of a reason why these aliens would make up such a grand scheme just to convince him to go with them. They could easily have just abducted him and not given him any choice whatsoever.

"We just took your word, Mr. Zemin. Now it is your turn to take ours. We do not have much time. You have 15 minutes to decide." With that, the alien began moving towards the door.

"Wait! Gosh, 15 minutes! Who are you anyway? What's your name?"

"My name is Maginder Kloiden 52110984," the alien said, floating out the door. "I am the commander of this armada of ships that came to meet you."

The door shut behind the alien before Marc could open his mouth again. Alone in the room, he tried to collect his thoughts. More had happened to him in the last hour than had ever happened to him before in his entire life.

Aliens! He had been picked up by aliens! It was inconceivable. He had never believed in aliens, and he had always thought other people were crazy for believing in them. He had considered it a waste of time to read science fiction stories or watch movies about creatures from outer space with ugly, drooling, insect-like faces and slimy tentacles.

Yet here they were, without any tentacles or any drool. They looked strange, no doubt, but by no means ugly or scary. They seemed nice and polite too, not the evil monsters bent on destroying mankind that people usually imagined aliens to be. Very serious, highly disciplined, focused and efficient – they were almost like machines, actually, in their conduct as well as their physical composition. Even their names apparently contained numbers.

He got up from the chair and looked out the transparent wall. The view was stunning. The lower section of this colossal ship jutted out for several miles at least. Beyond was dark space, full of twinkling stars. To the right, he could see the Sun glowing brightly with its splendor, providing the necessary radiance to sustain life for billions of people, animals and plants on Earth below. How oblivious they all were to their vulnerability, the same oblivion he had lived with for his whole life.

How arrogant people were, to think they were so superior and technologically advanced compared to all other living things. How narrow minded so many world leaders were, thinking they had all this sophisticated weaponry with which they could control the world and the fate of mankind. Here was this far more advanced species, ready to wipe out Earth altogether in one instant. All those politicians and generals, all their big words and fancy artillery, all shattered in the blink of an eye. Human fragility finally revealed to its fullest.

With his tiny little experiment, Marc Zemin, an unimportant nobody struggling to complete his PhD at a university in a small town in the middle of nowhere, had brought on this spectacular threat that could have ended the human race. But with a few simple words, that same nobody had abated the threat. And now that same nobody was being asked to journey into deep space, to help a sophisticated alien civilization in a battle for their survival, a battle whose victory would ultimately save his own people as well. Was he up to this enormous challenge?

He didn't know. His fear of failure was great, thanks to his low self esteem. What if he couldn't reproduce the experiments? As it was, he had stumbled upon this result by accident, not by intention. What would these aliens do to him then? Would they kill him and dump him in space? Or would they just be heavily disappointed?

So many other questions were still unanswered. How did these Mendoken aliens know so much about humans, when humans had never even seen them? How come they spoke such good English? And how had they found out so much about him, his background and his interests? Why had they been protecting Earth, and from whom? What would happen to him if he went with them? Would he be able to eat their food? Would he ever come back home alive? What about his studies at Cornell, his advisor, his friends? What about Cheryl, or Iman? Would he ever see any of them again? Wouldn't they wonder what had happened to him?

Perhaps they wouldn't. None of them cared about him anyway. Graham wanted him gone from Cornell, things were over with Cheryl, and Iman had left him years ago. Friends? He didn't really have any good friends left. Family? Neither of his parents was alive, and he had no other family he was close to. Moreover, if the Mendoken lost the war against the Volona, there evidently wouldn't be any home to come back to either.

All his research and experiments with time travel had clearly failed, and he didn't have any new ideas on how to make it work. It had been yet another failure in a life of continuous failures. The ultimate irony that even the attempt to turn back the clock and eliminate his life's earlier failures had resulted in a failure itself.

Maginder had also mentioned that time travel was not possible. What had he meant, and what were these "consars" that Marc's experiment had unveiled? Above all, how did Marc know that Maginder was telling the truth? He could ask for evidence, but the evidence could easily be fabricated – clearly these aliens would have the technology to do that in a heartbeat. No, in the end, he had no assurance other than Maginder's word. But perhaps that was enough. There was something peculiarly trustworthy and comforting about these creatures.

*   *   *

The 15 minutes passed by in a flash. On the dot, the door opened and Maginder floated in.

"Your decision, Mr. Zemin?"

Marc looked at the alien. "Do you promise to return me to Earth, after I have shown you my research?"

"Yes, if that is your wish."

"What if I really am not able to help you?"

"You did not volunteer or claim to have the answer to our problem. We are the ones taking the risk by coming to you for help. You need have no fear – one way or the other, we will return you to your home."

Marc peered closely at Maginder from top to bottom, looking for any sign of nervous energy that would indicate deceit. But this was a robot-like creature, displaying no emotion whatsoever. In fact, Marc was the one feeling nervous, with sweat on his forehead and his hands clasped tightly together.

"Your decision, Mr. Zemin?" Maginder asked again.

Marc was silent for a few seconds. Then he said, "I'm coming with you."

He knew he was taking the biggest chance yet in his whole life. He wasn't quite sure why he had decided that way, but it just seemed like the right thing to do. For some reason, he trusted Maginder, a feeling he couldn't explain. And perhaps the arrival of these aliens into his life was a blessing, an indication of a change for the better. Who knew? The only thing he did know for sure was that there was no hope or worthwhile future waiting for him back home.

"Very good," Maginder said, with no change in his tone of voice. "We will arrange to have your research materials transported to the ship. Please provide a list of the things you need."

A 3D screen suddenly appeared on top of the table. It displayed a complete, miniaturized rendering of Marc's lab, with all the equipment clearly visible and laid out just the way he had left it.

"You can use your fingers to touch the objects you need inside the screen. Like this." Maginder proceeded to demonstrate, using one of his four hands. The hand slipped effortlessly into the screen, and one of its seven long, metallic fingers touched the model depiction of a measuring instrument in the lab. As soon as the instrument was touched, it disappeared from that screen, simultaneously appearing on a second, empty screen that had just opened up beside the first screen.

What technology! Marc caught on with delight, moving his hand into the first screen. He carefully touched each item in the lab that he needed, and it showed up right away on the second screen. He had to be careful to choose only a select few of the most critical items, such as the energy emitters, a couple of his measuring instruments, his laptop, data CD's and notepads. That way, Graham wouldn't notice anything unusual the next time he walked into the lab, something he had the habit of doing every now and then. Luckily Graham didn't know the details of how many different instruments there were and what each of them did.

Once Marc was done, Maginder said, "The items will be transported shortly with the last of our troops who are still on the surface of your planet. Once they arrive, we will be ready to leave."

Marc asked Maginder to have the troops take snapshots of all his scribbles on the lab's whiteboards, as well as to leave a note in Graham's office from Marc saying that he had to leave town for a few days due to urgent family matters.

Maginder communicated some commands to the screens, after which they shut down and disappeared. "It will be done," he said. "Now come, Mr. Zemin, there is much for you to learn and adjust to."

As Marc stood up, the chair he was sitting on vanished into thin air, along with the table and the walls of the small room they were in. Losing the support of the table, his pocket watch automatically fell back into his hands. He placed it in his pocket and followed Maginder.

On the control deck, Marc could see Mendoken aliens everywhere, rapidly floating from point to point, manning stations with different kinds of instruments and 3D screens. Each station was circular by design, with one alien standing in the middle. With their multiple arms and their 360 degree vision, they could easily operate equipment all around them at the same time.

Marc observed how some of them were configuring flight paths and other ship functions, swiftly swaying their arms and moving their fingers. Their pace of work was so much faster than that of humans!

Maginder took him up to the top level of the deck through an elevator. From this level, he could clearly see into outer space in all directions. The entire ceiling and external walls of the deck were completely transparent.

"Meet Petrana Kraisen 62145685," Maginder said, pointing to a Mendoken alien manning a nearby station. "She is one of our main pilots."

Petrana was surrounded by a collection of navigational paraphernalia. "Hi, Marc, how ya' doin'!" she said in a distinct, feminine voice.

Marc was taken aback by her informal attitude, which was in sharp contrast to the solemn tone of Maginder's voice. She looked just like the other aliens – he couldn't tell what about her appearance was feminine. Maybe it was the hat, which was pink in color.

"I'm fine," he said. "You, uh, sound so different from your commander."

"Well Dude, it's cuz I'm tryin' to adjust to your accent and culture, ya know?" She sounded like a typical high school teenager.

"Petrana will keep you company during the journey, and answer any questions you might have," Maginder said, seemingly unimpressed by her accent. "Once you are ready for rest, let her know and you will be shown to your quarters." With that, he disappeared down the elevator.

"Si'down, Dude!" Petrana said, as a seat suddenly appeared next to her.

Marc sat down. These aliens evidently never sat down themselves – everywhere he looked, they were either standing or floating from one point to the other. There was no other seat anywhere in sight.

"Where did you learn how to speak like that?" he asked her.

"Oh my God, it's like, so in these days! You're, like, so five years ago! Bitchin'!"

Marc chuckled. "Seriously, it sounds like you're overdoing it." He really didn't think her serious, robotic appearance went with this style of talking.

"I apologize, Mr. Zemin," she said, suddenly sounding much more like Maginder. "I was trying to make you feel more comfortable."

"No, no, that's okay! I appreciate the effort, but you really don't have to. Just be yourself. And please call me Marc."

"Very well, Marc." After observing some data appearing on one of the many screens in front of her, she said, "We are ready to leave now."

She communicated silently with another Mendoken manning a larger station nearby. The ship then started moving without a sound, just as that Mendoken touched several points on a big 3D screen in a sweeping motion.

"My goodness!" Marc exclaimed, absolutely stupefied. He felt no gravitational pull backwards, nor did he even feel a single bump or vibration. Yet the huge Earth, all this time covering much of the view outside, shrank into a tiny dot in an instant and disappeared from view. The Sun was rapidly shrinking into just another small star in the sky. And the other stars ahead and above began to look like long streaks instead of dots. He had never seen such speed in all his life!

"How fast are we going?" he asked Petrana.

"Currently only 337 million miles per hour in your units of measurement," she answered, looking at some data on a screen and performing some conversions in her head. "We have just begun accelerating."

"Jeez! Wouldn't our racecar drivers want a piece of this!" He stared enviously at the controls Petrana was operating.

"Racecar drivers?"

"Never mind. How fast can this ship go?"

"The maximum speed is 500,000 times the speed of light."

He whistled. "How do you go faster than the speed of light? Through other dimensions?"

"Brrrrrrrrrrrrrrrr. No, Marc, travel through other dimensions is forbidden. We use the same 3 dimensions you see around you."

Maginder was right – Marc realized he clearly would have a lot to learn about science and engineering from these creatures!

"However, we cannot accelerate to full speed until we exit your solar system, in 63 minutes," Petrana added.

"Why not?"

"You will soon find out."

Chapter 8

In its first hour of flight, the Mendoken ship passed close by Jupiter and Neptune. But due to the tremendous velocity it was traveling at, Marc wasn't able to catch a view of either of the planets. That didn't bother him too much, though. He was far too excited about everything that had happened to him that morning. Even though he had hardly gotten any sleep during the night, he didn't feel tired at all. He was wired and energized, and full of curiosity about the Mendoken. He kept firing one question after the other at Petrana, who patiently responded each time. But much to his frustration, the most frequent answer was "you will soon find out," or "you will learn in due course."

The few facts that he did learn included the following:

The Mendoken are one of four major, advanced species in the Glaessan galaxy, or "Milky Way" as humans call it. Almost a fifth of the galaxy is under their control. The three other major species, known as the Aftar, Volona and Phyrax, control large sections of the galaxy as well.

The solar system that Earth belongs to is in Mendoken territory. The Mendoken have a strict policy of non-interference and no direct contact with species not considered advanced enough to join the galactic community. That includes humans and all other living things on Earth. The Mendoken have explored every corner of their region of the galaxy, and have studied every species on all inhabitable planets and moons. That is how they know so much about Earth and humans. Some of them are well versed in human history and behavior. Petrana and Maginder are among them, which is why they were chosen for this mission.

Those Mendoken who interact with other species carry translator devices that can automatically translate the words spoken between them and beings from the other species.

All in all, there are at least a billion intelligent forms of life scattered across the galaxy on all kinds of planets and moons, most of them oblivious to the existence of life on worlds other than their own.

"Oblivious" was the word! Humans had lived for so many centuries in a shell of ignorance, many questioning the existence of any life beyond Earth. Marc had been one of those skeptics himself, although he certainly wasn't anymore.

"Be prepared for a shock," Petrana cautioned, after exactly 63 minutes of travel. The ship had reached the edge of the solar system and had slowed down. The stars outside had shrunk from long streaks back to familiar white spots in the sky.

"What do you mean?" he asked.

Instead of answering, she pointed out in front of her into space.

No amount of warning or explanation could have prepared Marc for what he saw. The sky, the universe, was falling apart. Or was it? No, it was more like a gate opening up. Yes, a monstrous, square shaped door in space, sliding away in front of the ship to reveal something beyond. Was it another universe in a different dimension? No, it couldn't be – the Mendoken said they didn't touch other dimensions. So what was it?

He strained his eyes to look past the opening gate. The sky beyond looked brighter, much brighter than the space they were in. He could see many, many stars, many more than the stars in the sky he was used to seeing. It almost felt like he was catching a peek of the very center of the galaxy itself, where the concentration of stars was much higher than it was here at the edge of the galaxy.

"What is this?" he asked, totally baffled.

Petrana looked at him. "What do you know about what your people call 'dark matter'?"

"Dark matter? It's all the matter in space that we can't see, but we know is there anyway. Because if it wasn't, then there wouldn't be enough mass to keep the galaxies together. They would literally fly apart."

"And do you know how much mass in the universe is attributed to dark matter?"

"I'm not sure. The number keeps changing in scientific circles. Last I heard, there's about 5 times as much dark matter as there is visible matter. Then there's dark energy as well, which takes up an even larger amount. All in all, I think dark matter and dark energy combined make up more than 95% of the total energy density in the universe."

"In other words, 95% of the universe you humans cannot see."

"We can't see it because it is invisible, no?"

"Most of it is. But some of it you cannot see because we do not want you to."

Marc's jaw dropped in surprise. "You mean..."

"We created a filter around your solar system, to prevent you from observing our worlds and our activities. While dark energy, as you humans call it, does exist, there is actually no such as thing as dark matter. There are just more stars, planets, moons and many other types of natural objects in our galaxy."

"You mean all the stars we humans have always seen in the night sky constitute only a small percentage of the stars in our galaxy?"

"Yes, around 10%."

Marc was alarmed. "Why would you do such a horrible thing? Why would you cage us in like that?"

"It is not caging, Marc," Petrana said calmly. "We have to do it for our protection, and for yours. Your people are not yet ready to join the galactic community, if they ever get that far. There are very few species that successfully make that step. Too often we have seen a civilization reach its peak, and then annihilate itself with the technologies of its own creation. They fail to reach the right balance between the need for progress and the ability to be satisfied with the way things are, between the inherent instinct to increase one's own possessions and the desire to benefit others.

"Imagine if your people, given how they are today, knew of our existence and tried to interact with us. Imagine some of your political and military leaders trying their utmost to get their hands on one of our battleships or planet destroyers. Imagine the damage they would cause to themselves, and to other worlds and species in the process.

"No, we cannot afford to take such risks, nor can we teach the billion species out there how to lead their lives. They have to learn their lessons by themselves. Some of them make it, most do not. Only time will tell what will happen to yours. The day may yet come when we will make formal contact with your people and lift the filter."

Marc took a moment to digest these statements. "What if we come up with the technology to travel to the edge of the solar system ourselves first? We'll bump into your wall, and all will be exposed."

"If your people ever get to that level of technology without destroying themselves first, then they will have already passed the survival test. By that time, we will be ready to lift the filter."

"But now I know everything. I can tell others once I return to Earth, can't I?"

"We would not have taken such a risk, if we had not already obtained sufficient evidence that we could trust you," she said simply.

Apart from the fact that nobody on Earth would ever believe him anyway, he realized. People would think he had finally gone completely bonkers.

The ship glided through the gate and on to the other side. The gate slid shut and disappeared into a black wall that he could now see emerging behind the ship. It was the wall of a shell, a shell created for the sole purpose of encasing and blindfolding humankind. Could it be that people had always lived in such an illusion, ever since the first humans had turned their eyes towards the night sky?

It was so hard to believe, he thought, yet so simple in concept. It was no different than putting a goldfish in an aquarium, or raising a tiger in a zoo from birth. The goldfish would never know of a world outside the confines of the aquarium, nor would the tiger ever live to see the jungle. The Mendoken apparently didn't place any more importance in humans then humans did in animals. At least the Mendoken didn't kill humans for food or for fun, though, or use them as beasts of burden.

"Welcome to the rest of the universe," Petrana said calmly.

It certainly was a sight for sore eyes. Whichever way he looked, Marc could see big stars, medium size stars, little stars, all very close to each other. Colorful nebulae could be seen everywhere in all shapes and sizes, as well as a number of very bright spots in the sky that had to be supernovae. It was as if the entire galaxy had suddenly been compressed, forcing all its constituents much closer to each other. The background color of the sky seemed to be more of a deep blue, not the pitch black he had seen all his life. This was probably due to all the light emitted by the heavy concentration of stars in the sky.

But that wasn't all. Even the space close by was filled with matter. There was a brown colored planet not too far away with multiple moons around it, an entire world on the outer edge of their own solar system that humans had no knowledge of. Then there was a large asteroid field to the right. Ahead on the ship's path lay what looked like a space station. Hundreds of ships were docked at ports jutting out from it, and others were moving away or towards it. Some of them looked like the ship he was on, while others were smaller or larger with different kinds of shapes.

Evidently space was busy and crowded, not the vast emptiness humans saw in the sky every night. As far as Marc was concerned, all those continuous debates between intellectuals on Earth about the possibility of life on other worlds could now be closed for good. All those expensive investments by SETI organizations and others to locate and contact aliens had been in vain. The aliens certainly were there and were even watching and listening, but they had purposely chosen not to respond.

"That is Selcher-44328," Petrana said, pointing to the station ahead. "It is our regional outpost that, among other things, monitors your solar system and maintains the shell around it."

Describing the station as huge would be quite an understatement. It had to be almost the size of a small moon, and was shaped like one too. Except that it was split into two identical halves, with open space between them for a major thruway. The ship was headed right down that thruway, slowing down considerably as it passed in between the two colossal hemispheres. Marc noticed a sunflower-shaped planet destroyer docked on one port nearby. Perhaps it was the same one that had loomed so menacingly above Earth just over an hour ago. Even that monstrosity was dwarfed by the size of this station.

The ship didn't stop at the station. Instead, other, smaller ships came alongside and docked with it for momentary periods of time while it was on the thruway. Petrana explained that this was for stocking supplies and shifting personnel. This method was quicker than requiring the ship to park at a dock itself.

After 15 minutes or so, the thruway passage was complete, and the last of the small supply ships undocked from the ship.

"Now we begin the journey to our central star system," Petrana announced. "It will take 53 hours at maximum speed."

The stars in the sky were transformed into streaks of light again, this time growing much longer as the ship kept on accelerating to full speed. And given how the sky outside the filter had a far higher concentration of stars, it really looked like the heavens were lit up everywhere in white light.

"The Milky Way has finally earned its name," Marc thought, smiling. He turned to Petrana and asked, "Tell me, how do you Mendoken even create such a gigantic filter that can span around a whole star system?"

"It is a self-replicating membrane made of a synthetic material called *silupsal*. We only have to create a small section of it, set the perimeter coordinates, and supply the energy it needs to grow quickly by itself."

"How and when do you decide where to place a filter?"

"We observe all star systems for any signs of intelligent life on their planets and moons. As soon as we detect any, we place a filter around that system."

"So when did you place the filter around our system?"

"500 million Earth years ago."

"Jeez! How long have you guys been around?"

"The Mendoken have existed as a civilization for 3 billion years. Our total population today is 7.6 quintillion."

Marc did the math in his head – that was 76 followed by 17 zeros, or 7,600,000,000,000,000,000! Talk about population explosion! But with a fifth of the entire galaxy under their control, he doubted space was an issue for the Mendoken. "So how does this membrane work?" he asked.

"The membrane is intelligent – it can understand commands. We program it to automatically allow the passage of natural phenomena such as comets, but prohibit the passing of any objects created by intelligent life forms. Controlled gates such as the one we just went through are the only way for ships to pass from one side to the other. The filter also prevents those inside from seeing any stars, planets, space stations or ships that indicate the presence of life in outer space. It further reduces the perceived size of other galaxies to match the perceived size of our own galaxy from inside the filter."

"So, in reality, each galaxy is 10 times bigger than what we humans see them as?"

"Between 5 and 10 times bigger, usually."

"What about clusters of galaxies, and superclusters? Scientists on Earth have always wondered why they are skewed along such weird skeletal lines, with large areas of emptiness in the middle."

"Well now, that is a different story altogether. But that is for another time, Marc. I need to attend to some other duties now, and you need to get some nourishment and rest."

He protested, of course. There were still so many questions he had. But that did no good. All it accomplished was a mild admonishment from Petrana that humans had much to learn in the ways of patience, one of the many reasons for their backwardness.

Another Mendoken promptly arrived to lead him away. Her name was Hildira Biederum 65871209, and she wore an orange hat. She led him down the elevator to the lowest level of the control deck, where they boarded a small vehicle. It was tall enough to easily fit a standing Mendoken, and wide enough only for two. It had the basic shape of an egg, most of it transparent to provide full views of the outside.

Hildira took the helm, while he stood next to her. The vehicle lifted from the ground and drifted into a tunnel. Soon they were zooming down the same busy highway he had come up in, back to the city of buildings and gardens that constituted much of the inside of the ship.

Hildira stayed quiet, leading Marc to wonder whether she was carrying a translator device or not.

There was only one way to find out. "Where are we going?" he asked, as the vehicle swooped down towards the city's buildings.

"To your quarters for the journey, Mr. Zemin," she replied in English. Well, she did have a translator after all. Perhaps she was just the quiet type.

He was getting a closer look at the many buildings and streets below. Everything looked amazingly well planned, with symmetrical designs of circular gardens surrounded by identical looking cylindrical towers. The trees and bushes were neatly trimmed, and the streets looked perfectly clean. Thousands of Mendoken were floating between places on the ground, while others were flying in different directions in vehicles or in their own cylindrical containers.

"Why do you need such a large population on a ship?" he wondered aloud.

"Not large by our standards, Mr. Zemin. Only 201,625 of us on this ship. This is both an exploration and a military vessel, and it usually goes off on long missions. So we maintain the semblance of life as it would be on one of our planets, with all job functions needed to preserve the management of an entire city."

Their vehicle slowed down in front of one of the taller cylindrical buildings, right outside the 32nd level. As the vehicle came close to the dark, glass-like wall, a section of the wall on that level slid aside.

"These are your quarters," Hildira said. "You will find everything inside according to the average preferences of your species. If you need anything, communication controls are available inside to contact me."

With that, she motioned to Marc to step out of the vehicle and into the building. Luckily the vehicle was almost touching the wall, so he just needed to take a small step. He turned back to thank her, but she had already sped off in her vehicle. Stepping further inside the room he was now in, he heard the wall behind him automatically slide shut.

"Average preferences!" he exclaimed in surprise. "You gotta be kidding me!" It was undoubtedly the most lavish, spacious suite he had ever seen. Not that he had ever stayed at a fancy hotel – he had never had the money. But he had seen what fancy hotels looked like on TV, and this definitely took the cake!

The Mendoken clearly wanted to make sure he was comfortable, and had gone to great lengths to determine what humans considered luxurious. He was in a big living room with plush, white carpeting, furnished with sofas, tables and chairs. Nice paintings hung on the walls, and there was even a bar in one corner. Overall, the theme seemed modern and tasteful – all the furniture was curved and simple, some of it transparent. The air was also warmer than the other parts of the ship, closer to the room temperature that humans preferred.

Another corner of the room housed a dining table, covered from one end to the other with different kinds of food. Slices of well cooked beef steak and roast chicken lay on one plate, mixed vegetables on another, right next to a bowl of soup that looked like tomato bisque. Other plates contained bread, potatoes, salad and fruits, as well as a chocolate mousse cake for dessert. An assortment of wine bottles and juices stood on one corner, next to a pot of freshly brewed black tea.

What a feast, and all of it for him alone! He suddenly realized how hungry he was, remembering that he had not eaten anything for almost 12 hours. But first, he would have to wash up. Adjacent to the living room was a bedroom, filled with a beautiful queen size bed and a closet containing a collection of clothes. Attached was a bathroom containing a toilet, sink, shower and a large bathtub. No toiletry was missing – soap, shampoo, body wash, toothbrush, toothpaste – everything was there, including a host of other items he didn't even recognize. He took off his clothes right away and jumped into the shower. Nice, hot water began blasting through the jets as soon as he entered, instantly refreshing and relaxing him.

As he stood in the shower, he let the events of the past few hours unwind in his head. These Mendoken were quite resourceful, to say the least! It was remarkable how quickly they had put all of this together, just for him. There couldn't have been more than a 3 hour time interval between the moment his pocket watch had appeared in their space and the moment they had shown up in his lab. During that time, they would have had to trace the path of the watch back to Earth and to his lab. Then they would have had to do a complete background check on who he was and whether they could trust him or not. Then they would have had to gather the appropriate teams, brief them, assemble the armada of ships, and finally send them through 50 light years to pick him up. All that in the span of 3 hours!

The earlier events of the evening crept back into his mind, causing him to feel sad again. He thought about Cheryl, wondering how she might react if he told her where he was right now. But he reminded himself that it didn't matter anymore, for she was gone from his life. Besides, he didn't have time to be sad about that now – he had far more important things to worry about.

After the shower, he tried on a pair of brown slacks, a white dress shirt and a pair of walking shoes that he found in the closet. They all fit him perfectly. Next, he sat at the dining table and ate his fill of the different items. Everything tasted top notch, a welcome change from the dreary fast food he was used to having as a poor student. The soup was exquisite and the meat so tender, with just the right amount of spice and seasoning. The cake was very rich and sweet. These aliens were real gourmet chefs! Or at least they had studied the work of gourmet chefs on Earth, and had figured out how to replicate their dishes.

With a cup of tea in his hand and a big grin on his face, he moved to one of the sofas and slouched into it. He really liked good food, and there was nothing like a delicious meal to lift his spirits. His eyes began to close, and his mind drifted to happy thoughts. He almost forgot that he was on an alien ship, traveling through space at 500,000 times the speed of light.

Chapter 9

"Had a good lunch, man?" a voice asked.

Marc opened his eyes in surprise and looked around. The living room was empty. Through the window, he could see Mendoken outside, flying in vehicles and containers between the city's buildings. But there definitely was nobody else inside the suite.

"Come on, was it up to par?" the voice continued. The accent and tone were curiously similar to Marc's own.

"Why, yes, much better than par," he answered cautiously, springing up from the sofa and surveying the room again. "Who are you?"

"I am you."

"Excuse me?"

"Well, okay, not really you. But a replica of you. At least, what these Mendoken think is a replica of you."

Then a figure appeared, right in front of him. He jumped, thinking he was staring into a mirror. The figure looked exactly like him, and was even wearing the same clothes.

"What in heaven's name is going on?" he asked in bewilderment.

"Relax," the replica said. "I am only a hologram. Call me HoloMarc, if you like."

HoloMarc clearly was a hologram of excellent quality – he looked just like the real thing. "Try touching me," he said, holding up his hand. "That will help convince you."

Marc tried touching HoloMarc's hand with his own, but his fingers slid through thin air. He then pushed his hand through HoloMarc's body, and it came out the other side with no effort. He was astonished. "Wow! This is quite something!"

"Isn't it?" HoloMarc seemed completely unaffected by the incision through his chest. "You've got to admit it – these Mendoken types are absolutely brilliant."

"Why did they create you?"

"To help you adjust to this strange, new world. They thought that you might have an easier time talking to me than to any of them. Let's face it – they are a bunch of stiff, emotionless, expressionless, robot-like creatures, eh?"

"Well, yeah, a little! So what are some of the things you can do, HoloMarc?"

"My projection range is restricted to these quarters, so I can't really go anywhere with you. But I can talk to you as much as you want while you're here."

"Ah, now that's a great help," Marc thought sarcastically. That was the last thing he needed – being able to talk to himself.

HoloMarc went on. "I can play any music you like, from any genre. Name it."

"Really? Well, let's see, how about Enya?"

The room was suddenly filled with sounds of the first track from Enya's Shepherd Moons album. Such crystal-clear sound quality Marc had never heard in his life before. Her soft, soothing voice sprang to life right in front of him, and the accompanying piano notes flowed gracefully into his ears from all around. It was as if he was in the middle of a live performance, with Enya standing no more than 5 feet away from him.

"Wow!" he whispered. "Incredible!"

HoloMarc switched the music. "How about some Bach?" The Toccata in pipe organ immediately took over, so loud that it was deafening to Marc's ears. "Or maybe you would prefer rock?" Pink Floyd's "Wish You Were Here" followed.

The entertainment wasn't over. "If you'd like to switch to visual satisfaction, I've got a great collection of movies," HoloMarc said. A large movie screen instantly appeared out of thin air in front of Marc. Previews of different movie classics flashed on the screen, one after the other.

After a while, Marc asked HoloMarc to stop. "This is all great, but I really can't concentrate on music or movies at the moment. Too many things on my mind."

"Can't say I blame you," HoloMarc said, as the movie screen disappeared. "It's been a crazy past few hours, eh? Well listen, I'm also connected to the ship's central database, giving me access to pretty much any data you could possibly want."

Marc's eyes lit up. "Oh, really?"

"Oh, yes! Go ahead, ask me a question."

"Okay. Let's see... where did the Mendoken originate from?"

A 3D screen appeared in front of Marc, in the same spot where the movie screen had been seconds earlier. In clear view was a galaxy, looking much larger and denser than any galaxies Marc had seen pictures of back on Earth. It had a fuller, rounder shape.

"This is the Milky Way galaxy in its entirety, as it looks without the filter that our friends have placed on us poor humans," HoloMarc said, pointing to the screen. "You, ah, do know about the filter?"

"Yes, I have just recently been enlightened."

"Great! Quite a surprise, huh? Anyway, there are about 2 trillion stars in total in the Glaessan. That's what they call the Milky Way, by the way."

"Yeah, I heard that from Petrana."

"Due to its real size, the Glaessan easily engulfs the so-called nearby Magellanic clouds, which really aren't separate, smaller galaxies in the vicinity, much as we humans would like to believe. The diameter of the Glaessan is actually over 200,000 light years, more than twice what people on Earth think it is at its widest cross section."

The screen zoomed in on one section of the image, a fair distance away from the center.

"Here's our beloved Sun," HoloMarc continued, as a red circle appeared around one of the uncountable number of white dots. "And here, 3048 light years away, is the Mendo-Zueger star system." Another red circle appeared at the other end of the zoomed-in image. "The first Mendoken appeared over 3 billion years ago on the ninth planet in this system. The planet is now known as *Draefarel*, or literally 'The Beginning' in English."

The image zoomed in further, now displaying a star much bigger than Earth's Sun. It had a total of 24 planets in orbit. The ninth planet was highlighted.

"Today, the Mendoken inhabit about 50 billion star systems, and another 350 billion fall under their jurisdiction," HoloMarc added. "Isn't it mind-boggling?"

The screen zoomed out to highlight the section of the galaxy under Mendoken control. It was a large slice of the upper half of the galaxy, taking up much of the edge. But it narrowed down towards the center, closing up before reaching the center itself.

"Mind-boggling doesn't even begin to cut it!" Marc replied. By now, he was sufficiently impressed by HoloMarc. "This is cool stuff! Okay, tell me, how do I distinguish between different Mendoken? They all look the same to me!"

"Yeah, that's a tough one," HoloMarc admitted, stroking his chin. Pictures of several Mendoken appeared on the screen. "It is actually very difficult to tell them apart. Eventually you'll get used to it, though. You'll notice slight differences in the sizes of their eyes and ears, and the color of their skin. Another distinguishing factor is the brightness with which their mouths light up when they communicate, as well as the angle at which the mouth juts out from the face." He showed examples on the screen.

"And the color of the hats, I suppose."

"Ah yes, the hats! Good point. You see, the Mendoken are a highly disciplined, hierarchical society, with many roles and ranks. Everyone does his or her part towards the greater good. The entire population is pretty much part of one gigantic organization. Here's a basic rundown."

HoloMarc displayed a hierarchy on the screen, and went to great lengths to explain some of the different ranks and how they were related to each other. There were many thousands of different types of positions, each one with an extensive set of responsibilities. At the very top was an elected leader known as the *Imgoerin*. Under the Imgoerin was a circle of a couple of hundred elected advisors, and under them a greater parliament of several million senators. Under them, in turn, were several billion representatives from all the different star systems. On and on it went, down to leaders and commanders of planets, space stations, ships, as well as breakdowns into different kinds of professions – scientists, engineers, architects, builders – the list was endless. One interesting fact was that the Mendoken did not have any distinctions between civilian and military personnel – everyone was a soldier.

"As you have probably figured out by know, each rank has its own hat color," HoloMarc said. "And the long number that you hear at the end of each of their names pinpoints exactly where that individual falls within the entire hierarchy, rank and all. The funny thing is, even with this strict hierarchy all the way down to the bottom of the pit, you don't see any discrimination or unfairness at any level. There is no concept of rich and poor, no homeless or malnourished living in shantytowns beside decadent barons in their fancy mansions. No, in Mendoken society, everyone is well taken care of, and rarely are there complaints of any kind."

Marc thought for a moment. "What about freedom?" he asked. "And the rights of the individual? Sounds a lot like what we humans would call a communist society."

"Hah! Far from it! Communism in practice means enslavement of the masses by a select few dictatorial leaders at the top. But in Mendoken society, every leader at each level of the hierarchy is elected by the members of all levels below. And any individual may be elected into any position at any of the higher levels. Every individual has his or her rights, including the right to explore his or her own goals. But the interesting thing is that none of them choose to exercise that right.

"That's the main difference between these aliens and us humans. Whereas we place such a huge emphasis on the freedom of the individual and the desire to gain wealth and success for oneself, they actually prefer to all work together toward the common good of the entire population. Contribution is what makes them happy, not competition. And, well, look at the progress they've made compared to us!"

"It certainly is hard to argue with such success," Marc agreed, as unconvinced as he still was about the Mendoken definition of happiness.

The discussion continued for a good few hours, during which Marc's mind was overloaded with information. He learned how the Mendoken had come into existence, and how they had evolved into the nation that they now were. He saw images of some of the other major species, and found out about their characteristics and histories. He was briefed on the background of the current war between the Mendoken and the Volona, and on other wars fought between the different civilizations in the past. HoloMarc also explained some aspects of science and technology, including the mechanisms of space travel and the laws of physics that governed the universe.

Marc knew some of the information would be biased from the point of view of the Mendoken, but he found it all highly interesting nonetheless. Although HoloMarc went into a lot of detail, much of which Marc wouldn't be able to remember later, the following facts would forever remain engrained in his exceptional memory:

The Mendoken

By number the largest species in the Glaessan galaxy, and generally accepted as the most technologically advanced. They evolved originally from amphibious creatures on the green planet Draefarel. Their brains developed more rapidly than the rest of their bodies, largely due to their consumption of a highly nutritious plant called Torteg. From the very beginnings of their civilization, they began building and using machines. To protect their soft, vulnerable organs and tissues, they encased their bodies in metal armor, with antigravity mechanisms installed at the bottom to allow them to float above the ground. They also attached robotic limbs and other mechanized body parts to enhance their strength and mobility.

As opposed to humans, who have a stereoscopic view of the world through two eyes facing the front, the Mendoken have a single eye around the head that sees simultaneously in all directions. This gives them a circular frame of reference, allowing them to operate in multiple directions at the same time. This is also why all their structures are circular or cylindrical in design, in contrast to the rectangular shapes that humans generally prefer.

A community based, hierarchical society, they place great emphasis on collaboration and participation, not on individual success or uniqueness. Shunning emotions, pleasure and spirituality, their approach to life is highly logical and scientific. Their whole definition of success is based on advancement in technology and exploration, not on individual gains in possessions or satisfaction of their senses. As a result, they are extremely united as a population, with very few reasons to hate or fight each other.

The Mendoken make no distinction between their males and females. They have no concept of intimate companionship, marriage or family. All offspring are either artificially inseminated and born in laboratories, and then raised together in groups by dedicated professional staff. Cloning is only used for regeneration of injured body parts. Cloning of entire bodies is strictly forbidden in order to maintain sufficient individuality of every Mendoken.

The current Imgoerin, or supreme elected leader of the Mendoken Republic, is called Franzek Treital 00000001. A new Imgoerin is elected every 120 Earth years. The average lifespan of each Mendoken is about 600 Earth years. They can live so long because of their advanced medicine and technology, and particularly because of the symbiotic relationship between the organic and mechanical components in their bodies.

The Aftar

By number the smallest of the four advanced species in the galaxy (total population of 332 quadrillion), and the oldest (8 billion Earth years). Their region of space, known as the Aftaran Dominion and covering much of the core of the galaxy, is also the smallest (74 billion star systems, only 9 billion of which are inhabited by their species). They evolved from bird-like creatures on a desert planet called Meenjaza in the Afta-Raushan star system. The Aftaran head looks somewhat like that of an owl, covered with tiny feathers, including large, round eyes, pointed ears and a beak-like mouth. Aftarans stand upright, with adults reaching heights of 8 feet, and have two arms and two legs each. They are rumored to have wings as well, but always keep them concealed under their loose robes. They often cover their heads and faces with parts of their robes, especially when traveling or in front of strangers.

The Aftar are a highly reclusive society. Spiritual and serious by nature, many of them devote their lives to the study of religion and mysticism. They interact little with other species, most of them living very simple lives in monastery-like communities on desert planets spread far and wide across their star systems. Their concept of individualism is considerably stronger than that of the Mendoken. They do have a hierarchical structure with a ruling council at the top chosen by popular decree, but it is far less organized and much looser than the Mendoken hierarchy. The current supreme head of the council is called Lord

Wazilban.

Although the Aftar have traditionally been a male dominated society, they do place great importance on the equality of males and females, and there are many female Aftarans in key positions of influence across the Dominion. They have strong family bonds, and individual Aftarans always identify themselves with the clans their families have originated from.

Their level of technology is the lowest among the four species, as technological advancement is not a major focus for them. Some Aftarans, however, appear to have supernatural powers that are not explicable by science. The current average lifespan of each Aftaran is close to 1,000 Earth years, the longest of all species in the galaxy. Their strict meditation routines and healthy diets appear to contribute to this extraordinary longevity, although they claim it is a result of the deep faith they have in their religion.

The Volona

With a region of space covering 220 billion star systems, most of them in the lower half of the galaxy, the Volona inhabit 68 billion of them with their population of 4.5 quintillion. About as old as the Mendoken (3 billion years), they originated from a blue marine planet called Barenoa in the Volo-Maree star system. Nobody knows what kind of creatures they evolved from, nor does anybody know what they look like now. This is because they are very secretive by nature, hardly ever interacting with other species and never revealing their history or their true appearances to any outsiders.

The Volona are known for their hedonism and pursuit of the finer things in life. Any events or objects that result in pleasure or physical comfort, such as consumption of food, leisurely activities and entertainment, are their highest priorities. They choose to live in virtual worlds, created by the imaginations of their own desires. Those few beings from other species that have had the opportunity to encounter these virtual worlds are stunned at the beauty and splendor of the surroundings and lifestyles within, unsurpassed in luxury anywhere else in the entire galaxy.

The Volona have an imperial system of government, with a ruler called Adrelina. She is the latest empress of a dynasty that has lasted for over 2 million Earth years. Since they are a female dominated society, most of the ruling positions in the Volonan Empire are held by females.

The level of technology that the Volona have is high, although almost all of it is tailored around the needs of their prized virtual environments. They have sophisticated weaponry with which to protect their virtual environments from others, and their borders are by far the most heavily fortified in the entire galaxy. The current average lifespan of a Volonan is only 180 Earth years. This is because their focus on attaining pleasure and living in virtual worlds causes their bodies to deteriorate much more quickly than those of the other advanced species.

The Phyrax

Covering the largest region of space, the Phyrax Federation is thinly spread across approximately 580 billion star systems, most of them in the farthest edges of the Glaessan below and around the Volonan Empire. There are additional sections belonging to the Phyrax that stretch all the way up to the core of the galaxy as well. Their low population of 1.4 quintillion is dispersed over 200 billion star systems, resulting in some of the most sparsely populated regions in the entire galaxy. They came into existence 4 billion years ago, on a large, yellow, gaseous planet 18 times the size of Jupiter. Called Pyratreef, it is the sixth planet in the Phyra-Benjax star system.

Phyraxes are huge creatures, towering up to a height of 20 feet and a width of 8 feet. Their bodies are composed of gaseous substances held together by pure energy, a consequence of the planet they originated from. They look somewhat like clouds themselves, although they have a distinct structure that includes a head, a lower body, and a number of limbs that dynamically take shape as needed. They have no eyes, noses or ears, but can nonetheless sense the presence of everything around them. With their low body density, they can naturally float through the atmosphere of most planets, and hence have no need for legs or feet. They have no gender and do not reproduce. Instead, a form of energy in the gases of Pyratreef gives rise to the periodic birth of new Phyraxes. This form of energy they have transferred to all other planets they live on to produce offspring there as well.

The Phyrax are mostly solitary creatures, many of them living as hermits in clouds in the sky. They have no known system of government, or any form of law and order. They value their liberty above all else, each of them living its life according to its own wishes. They are adventurers, fighters and hunters, placing tremendous importance on bravery in invading other worlds, winning in combat, and acquiring wealth by seizing the riches of the races they subdue. They have powerful battleships and military technology, but lack basic infrastructure and services on their own planets. Phyraxes generally live to about 370 Earth years of age.

The Wars

The Glaessan is not, and never has been, a peaceful place. Its history is filled with wars, each one more violent and devastating than the one before. The Mendoken have a violent history of their own, having advanced into what they now are only after many bitter battles between different groups holding their own agendas and beliefs. Eventually the ideologies of science, logic and order prevailed, after which the Mendoken rapidly grew into a sophisticated civilization. They developed high speed space travel capability, and expanded their populations to neighboring planets and eventually across entire star systems.

The other three advanced civilizations are believed to have gone through similar upheavals in history before finding their own core, unifying values that led them to power, prosperity and great strides in advancement.

Due to the rapid expansion of their territories, the four civilizations eventually made contact with each other. And that was when the real problems began. Because of their very different ideologies, the mutual distrust and lack of faith in each other were immense from the very beginning. Communication quickly led to misunderstanding, and misunderstanding eventually led to conflict.

The first great interstellar war of the Glaessan was between the Aftar and the Phyrax. It began 2 billion Earth years ago, and lasted 30 million years. The Phyrax tried to defeat the Aftar in an attempt to subdue them and take over their worlds, in the same way that they had done with countless other species before. But this time, they had finally met their match. Far from being subdued, the Aftar not only successfully pushed them back, they attempted to force the free-thinking Phyraxes to live by their strict, religious code of life. 186 billion lives were lost in the process, 32 million planets destroyed, with no victory for either side in the end. A shaky truce introduced by the Mendoken, at that time just emerging as an advanced civilization, eventually brought an end to that disastrous, bloody episode.

The Mendoken were next, however. Their relationship with the Volona was rocky since their very first meeting 1.7 billion years ago. The Mendoken consistently accused the Volona of breaking their common treaties with deliberate policies of deception. This eventually led to a Mendoken invasion of a large part of Volonan space. The Volona, on the other hand, claimed the Mendoken were after their virtual worlds, possessions dearer to them than their own progeny. They fought back with ferocity, resulting in a bitter interstellar war that lasted 14 million years. In the end, the Mendoken triumphed, but refrained from touching the virtual worlds of the Volona in a reconciliatory gesture.

And so the saga continued, with one war following the other between the different societies. Often other species that had just joined the community of advanced civilizations were at the center of disputes. Sadly enough, many a time an entire species was wiped out in the conflict. Eventually the Mendoken and Aftar drifted to one side with an alliance, and the Volona and Phyrax to the other. Peace did finally prevail after almost 1.5 billion years of continuous conflict, although occasional border skirmishes still occurred from time to time. Many treaties and interstellar regulations between the four advanced civilizations were put in place during this period.

But the Glaessan did not appear to have peace in its fate. Just recently, major wars broke out once again, with the Mendoken and Aftar on one side, and the Volona and Phyrax on the other. The cause, according to the Mendoken at least, was a Volonan attempt to make direct contact with a number of species not advanced enough to join the galactic community, in order to gain access to valuable raw materials on their planets. When the Mendoken confronted the Volona about this blatant violation of the non-interference rule, the Volona wasted little time in escalating the conflict into a military one. At the same time, a band of Phyraxes attacked several Aftaran star systems along their common border and wiped out a couple of indigenous species living there, after charging the Aftar with unfairly attempting to convert Phyraxes living near the border to their religion. And so the wars began.

This time, however, the Volona are quickly gaining the upper hand against the Mendoken, with this new ability to travel unseen through consars (rifts in higher dimensions). They suddenly appear undetected in the middle of Mendoken space, destroy their targets, and then disappear again before they can be pursued. Officially, the Volona deny they are behind the consar attacks, and claim they do not even have consar technology. But history has repeatedly revealed their deceptive nature, and the Mendoken have learned the hard way never to trust or believe what they say.

The Mendoken have desperately been trying to come up with the same technology, but for various reasons have not been successful yet. That is why they are so interested in Marc and his work. Their hope is that he will help them quickly achieve the breakthrough they need to defeat the enemy.

Space Travel

Space travel in the Glaessan is restricted by regulation to the standard 3 dimensions. This was set in a treaty between the four advanced species almost a billion years ago, and the study of consar travel has been banned since. There are two main reasons:

- Non-interference with any life forms that may exist in parallel universes in other dimensions. Although such life has never been directly observed, current scientific theory strongly indicates the likelihood of its existence. Because it is impossible for us to physically see the other dimensions, the path of a consar may inadvertently lead right through a world belonging to aliens in a parallel universe.

- Strict religious doctrine of the Aftar that any attempts to interfere with other dimensions will result in a cataclysmic downfall of all civilizations in the Glaessan. This is clearly stated in their religious scriptures.

The treaty, however, was broken by the Volona, who recently developed consar travel capability in secret, and are now using it successfully in their war against the Mendoken.

Einstein's general theory of relativity does hold true for much of the universe, at least as a reasonable approximation for how massive bodies in the universe exert gravitational pulls on each other through the spacetime fabric. It turns out, however, that the restriction his theory imposes on high speed travel, namely that the speed of light is the uppermost constant against which all other motion is relative, is not entirely correct. Although most things in nature do appear to conform to that limit, the limit can actually be passed by artificial means. Once the limit is passed, Einstein's theory breaks down and no longer applies. Ships can therefore travel faster than the speed of light without requiring infinite energy or experiencing any time dilation.

A process known as <u>bosian layering</u> is the widely accepted standard that all ships in the galaxy use to avoid the restrictions of relativity during acceleration up to the speed of light. This process entails maintaining an invisible layer around the ship as it accelerates up to light speed, a layer that is not affected by relativity. Relativity's restrictions no longer apply once the ship passes the light speed barrier, so it can then shed this protective layer and keep on accelerating normally to the top speed that its engines allow. The same kind of layer is used during deceleration below light speed as well.

A process similar to bosian layering is used to transmit messages through space at many times the speed of traditional electromagnetic waves. When a message is transmitted, however, the protective layer around the message is never shed and is maintained for the duration of its journey through space.

The tremendous energy needed for the high speeds of interstellar travel is generated by controlled collisions between matter and anti-matter. Anti-matter is actually plentifully available in the universe, contrary to what scientists on Earth believe. It is available in elementary particle form, in sizes many times smaller than those of quarks, and is spread everywhere across the vast expanses of space, totally invisible to the naked eye. Any properly equipped ship traveling through space can pick up these antimatter particles in transit and use them in collisions with normal matter. This whole process is known as kilasion, and ship engines that use this technology are known as kilasic engines. All kilasic engines have to be equipped with the ability to perform bosian layering.

For a long time, one major issue in interstellar space travel, given the volume of traffic in the galaxy (especially in the Mendoken Republic), was the possibility of collisions between ships crossing the same section of space. In order to eliminate this risk, a complex network of routes known as the Yuwa was created during peacetime 200 million years ago. Much of the planning for this was done by the Mendoken, and subsequently adopted as the standard by the other three civilizations. Over 50 billion major highways exist today in the Yuwa, coupled with an additional 820 billion smaller routes.

Accompanying the Yuwa is a standard naming convention for all star systems in the galaxy. Every star system has a name of two words joined together. The first part is always an abbreviation of the name of one of the four advanced species, depending on whose region of space it is in (Mendo, Afta, Volo or Phyra). The second part is a unique name chosen by that species for the star. The solar system that Earth belongs to, for example, is called Mendo-Biesel. Each star also has a unique numeric value that is used by all ships' navigation systems.

Other Species

The Glaessan galaxy is filled with life, of all shapes, sizes and levels of intelligence. There are billions of species on various types of planets and moons, some of them seemingly inhospitable to any form of life. But, as always, Nature has its way of adapting to different environments, equipping local creatures with the necessary properties to survive in their surroundings.

As a part of the interim peace period that began a few hundred million years ago, the four advanced species have agreed to galaxy-wide laws that require the placement of silupsal filters around any star system exhibiting intelligent life on one or more of its planets. The general rule is that the filter will be lifted whenever the civilization inside reaches the ability to travel through space at high speed. Such advancement usually indicates that they have successfully passed the self-destruction mark. Humans on Earth are not believed to have reached that level yet.

During the major wars before the peace period, the Phyrax were notorious for invading and conquering the worlds of less advanced species. In fact, this behavior pattern was one of the major causes of their wars with the Aftar and Mendoken. The Mendoken in particular have always been strong believers in non-interference, and were the ones to introduce the silupsal filter idea during the peace period.

There appears to be plenty of life in neighboring galaxies as well. But due to the tremendous distance between galaxies and the maximum speed of the fastest ships in the Glaessan reaching no more than 600,000 times the speed of light, it would take several years to travel to even the nearest galaxy. For that reason, travel to other galaxies is few and far between. So far, there have been no major confrontations with beings from other galaxies. But some limited, peaceful contact has sporadically been made by both the Mendoken and Phyrax with a species known as the Tolaf in the Andromeda galaxy, the nearest galaxy to the Glaessan.

On the discussion went, hour after hour. Eventually Marc began to show signs of tiredness, his lack of sleep from the previous night finally catching up with him. He requested HoloMarc to stop the discussion, and made his way to the bedroom. Without changing, he sprawled on the bed and fell asleep within seconds.

Chapter 10

Tibara was a desert world. The sixth planet in the Afta-Johran star system, it lay in one of the remotest regions of the entire Aftaran Dominion, not too far from the border to the Mendoken Republic. Aftarans typically preferred desert landscapes on which to live, but Tibara was quite different from the norm. This desert was not of sand, but of ice. Average temperatures in the summer rose to no more than -180 degrees Fahrenheit. And in the winter they could drop to below -400 degrees, not too far from absolute zero. The atmosphere, although very thin, contained a composition of gases similar to Earth – almost 80% nitrogen, with the rest broken up between methane, ethane, carbon dioxide, hydrogen, oxygen, diacetylene and traces of several other gases.

The land was rugged, with sharp-edged mountains and volcanoes dotting much of the surface, glaciers carving out deep valleys, and huge plains of ice stretching out for thousands of miles. The only habitable location on this ice world was a deep network of underground tunnels left behind by an unknown, extinct alien race that had once lived here billions of years earlier. Now the planet was totally devoid of any settlements or signs of civilization. Aftarans generally stayed away from it, thanks to its highly inhospitable climate.

Peering out of his post at the barren plain ahead, Dumyan reminded himself that the inhospitable climate was just one of many reasons why he always hoped that every day he spent on Tibara would be his last. The only thing he could hear was the continuous clatter of ice trinkets from the blizzard outside, hitting the transparent shield in front of him with full force. The shield was small, tightly wedged between two blocks of ice jutting out of the side of a tall mountain. But however small it was, it provided the only view he had of the planet's surface.

"At least being here means I'm not out there in the midst of the storm," he said to himself. That was the sole consolation he had for his current predicament.

Dumyan was an Aftaran, a member of the 1238th generation of the Subhar clan. He stood nearly 8 feet tall, with his body covered in a loose, brown robe. A section of the upper part of his robe was wrapped around his head and face, leaving only his round, brown eyes exposed. Strapped over his shoulder was a small weapon that looked like a short sword, and with one of his feather-covered hands he held a binocular-like viewer to his eyes.

A scanning of the entire horizon through the viewer revealed nothing unusual. He turned around to face the icy wall of the mountain, and waved his hand. A small door immediately took shape and slid open, revealing a passage behind. As he began walking down the steps of a narrow, dimly lit tunnel of ice, he waved his hand again, and the door behind him sealed shut.

"Today I will speak my mind," he kept saying to himself between his long strides. He had had enough of this place, enough of staring at blizzards, enough of sitting around and doing nothing. He had spoken his mind on multiple occasions before, but today he was determined to put his foot down to get what he wanted. Today his patience had finally run out.

The steps went straight downwards for a mile or so, right into the heart of the mountain. At the end of the tunnel, he reached another door, which automatically slid open as he approached. The chamber beyond was made of rock, not ice. The ceiling was very high, offering a glimpse of the rocky interior of the mountain. A few dim lamps on the walls kept the place from sinking into absolute darkness. The air inside was very stale, almost as if it hadn't received a gust of fresh air in a hundred years.

The chamber was not particularly large, but had enough space to comfortably fit more than 20 Aftarans. There were only seven Aftarans inside, sitting quietly in a semi-circle on the ground, deep in meditation. They all wore the same brown robes, with their heads and faces covered just like Dumyan. Behind them, at the other end of the chamber, was another door identical to the one Dumyan had just walked through.

As the door shut behind him, Dumyan walked towards the center of the chamber. Facing the semi-circle, he sat down in a crouching position. "I see nothing," he announced in Mareefi, the most widely spoken language in the Aftaran Dominion. His voice was distinctly masculine, full of life and energy, and his pace of talking was quite fast.

"Nothing indeed, my Son," was the slow response from the Aftaran in the middle. "It is only a matter of time until they strike again." His voice was hoarse, like that of a very old man, and yet it also had a deep, authoritative tone. His name was Autamrin, and he was Dumyan's father.

"May the Creator protect us from harm," all the other Aftarans murmured in unison right away.

"Has Kabur reported back yet?" Autamrin asked.

"Not yet, my Lord," another Aftaran said. Her name was Birshat, of the 618th generation of the Jalabar clan.

Silence shrouded the room again, as everybody slumped back into meditation. But it was abruptly broken by Birshat after a few minutes.

"What is our fate, my Lord?" she asked Autamrin. "Are we to just wait here until death finally strikes us?"

"No, my Child," Autamrin replied, turning his head to face her. "You know that we must await the Sign."

"The Sign that never arrives, my Lord," another of the Aftarans remarked.

Dumyan couldn't have asked for a better opportunity to begin the discussion he so eagerly wanted to hold. "The words of truth have been spoken! Why should we wither away here in darkness like this?"

"Patience, my Son, "Autamrin said calmly. "Time is on our side, not on theirs."

"No, Father, time is not on our side," Dumyan retorted. "Our reliance on time and our faith in patience have led us here to this cage of isolation. Meanwhile, Wazilban and his band of thugs forge their grand schemes, unchecked and unchallenged."

"Nay, my Son, the Creator watches them as well. Surely they will be challenged when the time is right, when their crimes will have exceeded any known bounds, when no mercy will be fitting for the harsh punishment they are due."

"Ay, Father, but will the Creator help those who do not help themselves?"

Another Aftaran spoke for the first time. "Are you doubting our Father's word?" His name was Sharjam, and he was Autamrin's other son. His voice sounded similar to Dumyan's, but the pace of talking was slower.

Dumyan turned to face his younger brother. "No, I do not doubt his word. But I doubt the wisdom of complacence. In this life, you have to fight for justice. You have to fight to regain what is yours."

"And you heard our father!" Sharjam replied angrily. "We must await the Sign before we can act."

"Ah yes, the Sign! Two years have we waited here, two years have we spent in hiding. Where is it?"

"Only the Creator knows of the exact time. It is beyond our hands. It is our duty to solemnly wait with patience."

"That is but an excuse, an excuse for inaction," Dumyan said, shaking his head.

"You take refuge behind our aging father, who has so grievously been wronged. You interpret the words of the Scriptures for your own benefit, to hide your fear for battle and conflict."

"It is no 'interpretation', as you call it," Sharjam countered. "The words are as plain and clear as the air on Meenjaza. There can be no victory for us before the appointed time. It is useless to even attempt a confrontation before that. If you choose to be foolhardy enough to fight for the sake of fighting, even when you know with certainty that you will lose, then go on your own and sacrifice your life for nothing. But do not accuse the rest of us of cowardice!"

"Tell me honestly, my brother, what logic justifies waiting for something we know nothing of? A 'Sign' indeed! How does it look, how does it smell, or feel, or taste? Is it this stone over here?" Dumyan reached out and picked up a gray pebble from the ground. "Or is it the stale air in this chamber? Or maybe the surveyors are our signs, each one more deadly than the last. Or is it you yourself, a dismal warning of the depths of futility our race might stoop to?"

Sharjam rose and stood in front of his brother. With a whisk of his hand, the veil around his face came free and magically disappeared into the rest of his robe. His face now stood bare, but the head remained covered. "Arise, you heretic!" he roared. "How dare you question the Scriptures!"

Dumyan got up and revealed his face as well. "How dare you challenge me, you insolent little poltroon!" he roared back, taking a step towards his slightly shorter brother. Their faces were very similar, with identical looking eyes and beaks. Thin, tan colored feathers covered the skin on both their faces. The untrained eye could easily mistake them for twins.

"You two will stop now!" Autamrin ordered, raising his voice as he dropped his veil as well. His face, though similar to those of his sons, was much older, with his eyes drooping and his feathers gray. "If your mother were still alive, you would surely have broken her heart with your constant bickering. And as long as I am still alive, by the power of the Creator, there shall be no bloodshed amongst our kin."

Dumyan and Sharjam reluctantly sat down, their faces still flushed with contempt for each other.

Autamrin went on. "You have both sworn to uphold with your lives the values our beloved forefathers taught us. Indeed, that is what we all swore to do, and that is the sole purpose of our lives. Our goal is one and the same – to restore peace, harmony and justice to the Dominion. We cannot afford to fight amongst ourselves. Our enemy is too powerful, our own forces too weak. You two will not destroy whatever chances we have of succeeding! Do you understand me?"

Both brothers were silent.

"Lord Wazilban is no fool," Autamrin continued. "Do you honestly think that pure determination to act will be enough to defeat him? We do not have the ability to just walk out of here and attack him – we will be immediately destroyed. Nor can we rely on help from anybody else – he has seen to that."

"How our people have forgotten us, my Lord," Birshat said with a sigh.

"Nay, my Child, they have not forgotten," Autamrin replied comfortingly. "They have just been blinded, with wave after wave of lies and deceit. Fear and paranoia have taken over the Dominion. The majority now blindly follow Wazilban's policies of hate and belligerence to defeat our growing number of enemies. Yet they oversee the self-fulfilling prophecy that he himself is the cause of our growing number of enemies. They do not realize that there can be no victory in this war, only death and destruction on all sides."

Dumyan grunted. "Which is why I say, Father, that the fate of our people is in our hands! We must arise and expose Wazilban for what he is. We must show them the truth and lead them back to the right path. We must take back the throne!"

"We will, my Son, all in due course."

"But it is this inaction, this passiveness, that has allowed Wazilban to corner us like this, to strip us of all our powers, to shut us off from the masses. We must take the upper hand and start determining our own fate!"

"We lead our lives by the Scriptures," Sharjam said, "not by overzealous, youthful whims of adventure. And the Scriptures tell us to wait for the Sign before we act! Why are you finding that so hard to follow?"

"Very well," Dumyan said, trying to show patience. "Read the verses to me once again. Tell me where to look for this 'Sign' of yours, and how to recognize it when it arrives."

Sharjam made a gesture at a young Aftaran sitting on the edge of the semi-circle. "Zeena, show us the first four verses in the 38th chapter of the Hidden Scripture."

Zeena lowered the veil around her face and stretched out her left hand, revealing a silver coin-like object on her palm. It glowed dimly in the darkness of the chamber. With a finger on her right hand, she touched the edge of the coin, and ran the finger lightly around the circumference. As soon as she had completed the full circle, the coin turned golden and began to glow brilliantly. Beautiful calligraphy in bright golden letters suddenly appeared in thin air, about 3 feet above the coin and in full view of everybody seated in the room. The light from the letters of the Scripture instantly brightened up the whole chamber.

The text was written in Altareezyan, the ancient script that all the revered Aftaran Scriptures were written in. It said:

Behold, you who are virtuous!
On the eve of Hawfa in the midst of Jemola
Shall the calamity arise from within,
From the likes of your own,
From the depths of treachery and deception,
Tremendous suffering shall they inflict upon all.

Few shall you be who withstand the storm of evil,
Outcast and persecuted shall you find yourselves,
Powerless against the might of darkness,
Yet the fate of all will be in your hands.

When the Sign advances in the darkest hour,
Arise, unite, and shun your differences.
Fight the forces of evil and drive them away,
And take back what is rightfully yours.

Hasten not its startling advent,
For it follows not your command.
Hasten not to act without it,
For you will fail in your quest.
But delay not when it comes,
For it shall not linger.

"You see for yourself how clear it is," Sharjam said, as the text faded away.

"Yes, it is clear!" Dumyan exclaimed. "It is clear that evil is encompassing us from all sides, and we must fight it if we want to survive! It does not give us a clue about what this Sign is or where to look for it."

"It says the Sign shall find us. We need not seek it."

"It also says the Sign will not wait for us. Prove to me that we have not already missed it."

Sharjam was about to open his mouth again, but Autamrin spoke first. "It is not our position to interpret the verses of the Hidden Scripture. We could continue to argue for years about this without reaching a conclusion. Only the Eminent Ouria or one of her High Clerics could have given us an authoritative answer. But alas, Wazilban knew that only too well."

"Yes, we failed them, Father," Dumyan said. "We failed to protect them. Now we must not fail to protect ourselves."

Autamrin was silent for a moment. Finally, he said, "I am old, my Son. I no longer have the strength to fight in battle. What would you have me do?"

"I am not asking you to fight, or to even leave this chamber. I am asking you to let *me* leave, to go and find help, so that we can fight for our survival!" He looked at the others in the room, seeking their approval. "I have a plan to get off this planet. My..."

Sharjam interrupted him. "Off this planet? How? Wazilban's surveyors will hunt you down before you set foot off this mountain, let alone the planet it stands on. We dare not even use any communication equipment between here and the surface of this mountain, for fear of the surveyors."

Dumyan ignored Sharjam. "My goal is to head straight to the Mendoken border and to seek asylum in the Republic. If I can convince the Mendoken to help us, then with their military might we can defeat Wazilban!"

Sharjam laughed, making a croaking sound. "Such a jester my brother is! The Mendoken are in cahoots with Wazilban! Why should they help us?"

"No, my Son," Autamrin said right away, raising his hand to silence Sharjam. "Do not speak ill of the Mendoken. So many times in the past have they helped us. They are just too honest and straightforward, too logical and regulated a society to understand Wazilban's treacherous ways. They deal with him because they have to, not because they like him or are in cahoots with him. Remember, he is the current head of the Aftaran Dominion. They do not know the details of how he came to power by deceiving his own people, or of how he is trying to destroy us. And even if we had evidence to show them, their strict policies of non-interference in the internal affairs of other species would prevent them from helping us."

"It is clear that they have not been helping Lord Wazilban either," another of the Aftarans added. "If they had, one of their planet destroyers would surely have obliterated Tibara by now in their effort to find us and kill us."

Autamrin nodded. "And they are busy with their own war against the Volona. In the end, we are on our own. No, Dumyan, I cannot let you take such a huge risk."

"May the Creator protect us from harm," the others murmured quietly, while Dumyan threw his hands up in the air in frustration.

At that moment, the door behind them burst open, and another Aftaran rushed in.

"Kabur!" Sharjam exclaimed, standing up and turning around to face the newcomer. "Why such haste?"

"A surveyor approaches from the south!" Kabur blurted, trying to regain his breath from the fast sprint down the long tunnel from the surface.

"How far?" Dumyan asked.

"It was already creeping over the nearest mountain towards us when I left my post."

Everybody got up immediately.

"Quick, everyone hide!" Autamrin ordered.

The Aftarans moved to one side of the chamber, and stood in a straight line parallel to the wall. Then, with a signal from Autamrin, they all pushed against the wall together with their left shoulders. With a creaking sound, little compartments opened up at the points where the shoulders touched the wall, each one big enough to house a single Aftaran. After the Aftarans had slipped into their compartments, the openings automatically sealed shut. No slits or cuts were visible in the wall after the closure – it looked absolutely solid.

The chamber was now bare and quiet, with no sign of any inhabitance. And then it happened. The sound came first – a deep hum, getting louder as it drew closer. The ground began to shake next, the tremor growing rapidly to that of a minor earthquake. Small rocks fell to the ground from the ceiling, causing dust to rise into the air. And finally, the rear door, the same door through which Kabur had just entered the room, burst open.

A white cloud flowed in and quickly filled up the whole room. Inside the cloud were hundreds of globules of yellow light, dancing around in all directions. Each globule actually had the features of an Aftaran face, with the eyes, nose and mouth clearly visible. The faces seemed to be looking for something, exploring every corner of the room and analyzing every crack in the walls. They spent a lot of time combing the wall that Autamrin and his companions were hiding behind, seemingly suspicious of its contents.

But they appeared to find nothing. Eventually the cloud began to move out through the other door, the one that Dumyan had entered through earlier. It was a long procession, taking several minutes for the last few faces at the end of the cloud to pass through the door. The tremor began to subside, and the loud hum diminished as the cloud moved further away. The chamber was in darkness once again.

This cloud was a surveyor, one of the mightiest and most sinister weapons possessed by the Aftar. The moment even one of the faces encountered what they were looking for, the game would be over. A small group of those light globules would break away and head back to the surveyor's dispatcher at high speed to report their findings. The rest of the cloud would then ignite itself, causing a massive explosion that would instantly obliterate anything within a 10 mile radius.

Time passed, while the dust in the chamber settled. Eventually, the wall's compartments opened up and the hiding Aftarans cautiously stepped out.

Birshat brushed off the dust from her robe. "That was a close call this time."

"Indeed it was," Autamrin agreed. "Wazilban's powers grow ever stronger, while

ours to resist him grow weaker. His noose around our necks tightens by the day."
He looked downwards at the ground, deep in thought.

"Father, let me go, please!" Dumyan implored. "It is the only way, our only hope.
We cannot continue like this. It is only a matter of time before the surveyors will
be able to see through these walls."

Autamrin stood still for what felt like an eternity to Dumyan, before finally
speaking. "Very well, my Son, you may go. But only under one condition."

Dumyan felt a wave of relief. His time had finally come. "Name it, Father."

"That you take Sharjam with you."

"What!" That exclamation came from both brothers at the same time.

"That is the condition, otherwise you may not go," Autamrin said firmly.

"My Lord, pray, tell us, what is the wisdom behind this decision?" Birshat asked.
"Will they not battle each other to death, even before they reach the surface of the
mountain?"

Autamrin smiled. "Strange are the ways of the Creator, my Child, that I should
have been given two sons with such opposite personalities and values, who have
constantly fought with each other since their childhood. This fate has always
puzzled me deeply. But now, I believe, I finally understand.

"Dumyan and Sharjam, you two will herewith leave this chamber, this mountain,
this planet, and will search for help. Where you go, and whom you ask for help, I
leave to you. I do not know if you will find the Sign, or if you will succeed in
convincing the Mendoken to help us. What I do know is that the Creator has blessed
you both with tremendous courage, brilliance and intuition, and I have full faith in
your abilities.

"Your differences in attitude and strategy will complement each other, your
conflicting thinking patterns will unite to expose a wholesome picture, and your
opposing principles will compromise to always reach the best decision. Dumyan,
when you jump to action without thinking, Sharjam will hold you back and plan a
strategy first. Sharjam, when you hesitate in crisis, Dumyan will give you the
courage and push you forward.

"Above all, through the importance of this mission and the resulting adventures
you experience together, it is my hope and prayer that you will finally come to
understand each other, and that you will develop the love and trust between
yourselves that your mother and I always longed for."

"But Father, why such a change in you?" Sharjam protested.

"It is not a change, my Son. It is a decision I made over a year ago. One whose
execution I have dreaded for so long, trying to avoid it with many an excuse. But
now, I fear I no longer can."

Sharjam opened his mouth again to speak, but Autamrin cut him off. "No more discussion. Now go! May the Creator protect you both from harm."

Dumyan bowed in front of his father, and headed towards the door.

Visibly shocked, Sharjam reluctantly bowed as well, and followed his brother.

Birshat came in front of Autamrin. "My Lord, allow me to go with them!" she begged.

"And me!" Kabur added.

"No, my Children, it is their fate to go alone. Your places are here with the rest of us."

Birshat rushed out after the two brothers, who were just leaving the chamber. "Dumyan, wait!"

"What is it, my love?" Dumyan turned around to look at her.

"Remember that Wazilban may well have one of the copies of the Hidden Scripture. His scouts may also be looking for the Sign, trying to destroy it before we can find it."

"I know, do not worry. We will return, I promise, to lead you out of this cage."

"I have full faith that you will." She glanced at Sharjam for a second, and then looked back at Dumyan. "Please look after him. He is and always will be your younger brother."

"And you take care of our Father. With the help of the Creator, the day shall come when he once again ascends the throne of the Dominion. Watch over the others as well, and yourself."

Their hands touched. "Our love grows stronger by the day," she whispered.

"And so it shall till our deaths."

Trying to hide his sadness, he whisked his hand in front of his eyes, and a section of his robe magically covered his face. Reminding himself of how important this mission was and what was at stake if he didn't succeed, he then began walking up the tunnel, his brother following several steps behind.

Chapter 11

A blaring siren woke Marc up from his deep sleep. A quick look at his surroundings made him remember that it hadn't all just been a dream. He really was in outer space, traveling aboard an alien ship.

"HoloMarc, are you there?" he called out groggily.

No answer. The eerie siren kept on wailing. It sounded like a bomber alarm, of the kind he had heard while watching old movies of World War II. And every few seconds, the ground was shaking.

"HoloMarc? What's going on?"

But HoloMarc was nowhere to be found. Getting up, Marc quickly washed up and walked into the living room of his quarters. Through the windows, he looked out at the city inside the ship. The simulated sky was no longer a bright blue – it had turned dark. Orange lights were flashing everywhere on the tops and sides of the buildings, and Mendoken aliens were frantically flying around in their vehicles, rushing to get to their posts.

"What in heaven's name is happening?" he wondered. He looked around the room, and noticed a door on the far wall. It had to be the main door to his quarters from the inside of the building. Next to the door, he found a small keypad. Assuming it was a communication device, he pressed what looked like the power knob. A small 3D screen sprang forth from the keypad, displaying the face of a Mendoken.

"Yes, Mr. Zemin?" a voice crackled through a speaker below the screen.

"Hildira?"

"Yes." She seemed to be busy, and there was a lot of commotion behind her.

"What's happening?"

"We are under attack."

"Under attack! By whom?"

"Volonans, Mr. Zemin. Please stay in your quarters. I will contact you when this is over."

"But..."

Too late, as Hildira had switched off the connection.

Marc didn't know what to do. He was frightened, and worried that his life could end at any moment. Perhaps the entire ship would blow up in one big explosion? He sat down on the couch, trying to prepare himself for that event. But he couldn't stay still. His curious nature was getting the better of him. Why were the Volonans attacking their ship, he wondered? Had they found out about him and his experiment? Was he really that important? How could they have found out about him so quickly?

He knew he couldn't go out the way he had come in. There was no vehicle waiting outside the window to pick him up, and it was a sheer drop of 32 levels to the ground below. No, the only way out was through the front door.

He got up and began walking towards the door, but then stopped. Hildira had told him to stay put. Did he dare defy her instructions? He paced around the room for a while, wondering what to do. The ground still kept shaking periodically. Then a powerful tremor hit, causing him to lose his balance and fall onto the couch.

That did it. He decided he couldn't stay here in ignorance any longer, while his fate was being determined up on the control deck. Taking a deep breath, he slid open the front door. A whiff of cold air hit his face, reminding him of the lower temperature across the rest of the ship. He went back into the suite to grab his sweater, and then stepped out through the door. It automatically slid shut behind him.

The corridor he had entered was shaped like a hollow tube with a flat floor. The siren was much louder here, and orange lights were flashing along the ceiling. He tiptoed down the long hallway, in the hopes of finding an elevator or staircase. Along the way, he noticed doors on both sides, probably leading to other residences. Luckily they were all closed and there was nobody in sight.

Suddenly he heard a door open. He instantly flattened himself against the wall, trying his best to hide. The last thing he wanted was to be reported for disobeying orders and to be banished to his quarters. Peering out, he saw a Mendoken enter the corridor. Much to his relief, the alien floated off in the opposite direction, eventually disappearing through what looked like an exit at the end of the hallway.

After waiting a few more seconds, he began moving forward again, following that Mendoken's path. He reached the same exit at the end of the hallway, but what lay beyond didn't seem particularly inviting. It looked like a staircase, but it had no stairs! Instead, it was a steep, smooth incline that spiraled down as far as he could see. That was probably just fine for the Mendoken, as they likely floated down the incline with no trouble. But how was he supposed to get down?

He turned to look back at the long corridor. Goodness, he didn't even remember which door he had come out of! There was no turning back. Carefully, he set foot on the incline, trying to balance himself with his hands against the wall. But after a couple of steps, it became painfully clear that both the wall and the floor were almost frictionless. Before long, he had lost his balance completely, and was sliding down the incline on his back.

"Yaaaaaaaaahhhhhhhhh!" he yelled, helplessly accelerating down the slope.

The path twisted round and round for what felt like an eternity, and he kept getting bounced from one side to the other. Finally, it reached the bottom and leveled off. Due to the high speed he had reached, however, he continued to glide down the smooth path toward an exit door at the end. The door slid open automatically as he approached, causing him to slide through and be thrown out onto the pavement outside.

Bruised and shaken, he got up and looked around. He was outside the building, on the street. There were Mendoken aliens floating about in the distance, and vehicles zooming by above. But nobody seemed to notice him. The big question now, however, was how he was supposed to get to the control deck.

And there was the answer in front of him – one of those egg-shaped vehicles parked on the street, unattended. He walked over and entered the vehicle. Staring at the controls, he tried to remember how Hildira had operated them earlier. Noticing one button that was bigger than the others, he took a chance and pressed it. The interior immediately lit up, and the vehicle lifted off from the ground. It was the right button!

Next, a steering column detached itself from the dashboard, and moved automatically towards his hands. The column contained two separate wheels that could be pushed, pulled or rotated. After some trial and error that resulted in some very bumpy motions, he thought he had figured out how the wheels worked. Pulling them both back, he drove the vehicle up into the air, heading straight for the dark, virtual sky.

Marc's nerves were on edge. It was the first time he had ever operated a flying machine of any kind, let alone one whose controls were not designed for humans and one that seemingly refused to travel at speeds below 90 mph. And at that speed, not only would he have to avoid hitting all the other vehicles whizzing around, he would also have to figure out where he was going. Looking up, he saw a stream of vehicles making for one of the entrances in the simulated sky. Guessing that all paths going upwards had to eventually lead to the control deck at the top of the ship, he entered that stream, almost crashing into another vehicle in the process.

After passing through the entrance in the sky, he was back in one of those busy multi-lane tunnels. Everyone seemed to be driving even faster now, perhaps because of the calamity that had befallen the vessel. Several times he almost collided with other vehicles, especially when the entire ship shook during a tremor. But some unseen control system prevented the actual impact from occurring every time, either by pushing his vehicle to the side or forcing it to brake automatically.

It turned out that his intuition was correct. Eventually the tunnel did lead up into the control deck. Slowing down, he parked the vehicle at the lowest level. In one corner, he found an elevator and stepped onto it. Up he went, one level after the other. The place was a mess – Mendoken aliens were rushing around everywhere, frantically trying to operate different control stations. And looking out into space with the clear view that he now had, he could see why.

There was a massive ship out there. No, there were three of them, two behind and one above. Volonan ships, no doubt, since they didn't look anything like the Mendoken vessel he was on. All three of them were identical – bright red in color, much flatter and wider than the Mendoken ship, and more rectangular in shape. Overhangs jutted downwards from the sides of the ships, from where barrages of shots were being fired at the Mendoken ship.

The Mendoken ship, in turn, was fleeing from these enemy ships, firing back at them and constantly maneuvering to avoid their shots. Every time its shields were hit, the entire vessel shook.

To the other side, he could see a field of rocks that the Mendoken ship was heading towards. He surmised that it was an asteroid field, but was surprised at the amount of dust everywhere and the uneven sizes of the rocks. The rocks also seemed to be dispersing in different directions. "Very strange asteroids," he thought.

"Mr. Zemin, you should not be here," a stern, robotic sounding voice suddenly said.

Marc turned to look at the Mendoken approaching him. He had been in such awe of the view outside that he hadn't even noticed his arrival at the top level of the control deck. "Well, ah, is Petrana here?" he asked.

"Yes, but you should not be, Mr. Zemin."

"I want to find out what's going on! Are those Volonan ships?"

"Yes, but please go back to your quarters."

The alien moved closer, in an attempt to keep him from stepping off the elevator. But at that moment, another Mendoken came up from behind and communicated silently with the one blocking his way. Soon after, that Mendoken left, and the other one came forward to face him.

"Petrana?" He thought he recognized her slightly larger eye and paler skin, at least compared to all the other Mendoken he had seen so far. Not to mention the pink hat she was wearing.

"Yes, Marc," was the reply.

"Thank God!" he thought. Hopefully she wouldn't send him away.

"It is not safe for you to be here," she said, as calm as ever. "We are in the middle of a battle."

"I won't get in your way, I promise! But I can't just sit in my room and wait for my death."

"Very well. Stay close to me, or others may try to send you back down."

He sighed with relief, and followed her to her station. Commander Maginder could be seen in the distance, giving orders to the officers operating the weapons to evade fire from the enemy ships and to fire back in turn.

Petrana instructed Marc to sit in his seat. As soon as he did, a belt automatically slithered around his waist and secured him in place. She explained that they were leading the ship into the field of debris ahead, in an attempt to lose the Volonan pursuers between the huge rocks. Things would get real bumpy for a while, since such sudden movements were too fast for the vessel's automatic anti-gravity stabilizers to effectively handle.

With that, she began operating some controls, alongside several other pilots who were already doing the same. They took the ship right into the debris field, skillfully coordinating their efforts as a team. The maneuvers were spotless, leaving Marc in amazement as to how a vessel of such huge proportions could be tossed around so easily. Gliding swiftly between the giant boulders, the ship didn't touch a single one of them.

What was not as spotless was how he began feeling during the maneuvers. A lifelong victim of motion sickness, he felt a rising tide of nausea in his head and stomach. Holding on to the sides of the seat, he tried not to think about it and to focus his thoughts on what was happening outside instead.

He was glad to see that the Volonan ships were not following them into the field of debris. Their ships were just too wide to risk trying to navigate between the boulders. No matter how skilled their pilots were, making such an attempt would inevitably result in significant losses to the edges of their hulls.

After reaching a safe distance inside the field, the Mendoken ship slowed down and stopped. Marc could still see the Volonan ships, waiting at the edge of the field. Eventually they started moving away. And then it happened. A thin blue circle began forming in front of each ship. The circles rapidly increased in thickness, becoming spheres that completely engulfed the ships. Tunnels that seemingly led into different dimensions appeared behind the spheres. Then, in one gigantic flash, the spheres catapulted into their respective tunnels. Soon after, the tunnel entrances disappeared into nothingness, leaving no visible trace behind.

The sirens finally stopped, and everybody on board the Mendoken ship slowed down the pace of their activities. Petrana moved away from the controls she was operating, and looked at Marc.

Marc was in shock. "Incredible!" he exclaimed, taking a while to find his voice. "It was just like my experiment with the pocket watch! The one I did in my lab!"

"Correct. Those were consars."

They were obviously much larger consars than the one he had played with, but the mechanism did seem very similar. "So let me guess," he said, "you can't trace the path the ships have taken?"

"No, not like we could with your clock. The Volonans have a way of concealing their trails."

He looked out at the rocks surrounding the ship. "So is this an asteroid field?"

"No, this field of debris is all that is left of the planet Kerding in the Mendo-Bursal star system. It was inhabited by 3 billion Mendoken, and collections of different kinds of plants and animals. It was destroyed less than an hour ago by those Volonan warships. They did not leave any of the surrounding moons intact either."

Marc's mouth dropped open in horror. "3 billion Mendoken... dead?"

"Yes, Marc."

3 billion lives, gone. Perished, in the blink of an eye. It was inconceivable! "Why... why did they do it?"

"There is no particular reason we can identify, other than the fact that we are at war. In addition, this system was an easy target because it was largely defenseless. Kerding was mainly a medical research planet, with many hospitals specialized in different kinds of illnesses. Mendoken from the furthest star systems used to come here for treatment. We never imagined that the Volona would stoop to this level, to attack such a target that had no military value. That was why it was unprotected."

Marc's face grew red in anger, unable to control his emotions like these machine-like Mendoken. "This is insane!" he cried. "It's cold-blooded murder!"

Petrana didn't answer.

"This doesn't have anything to do with me, does it?"

"No, it is highly unlikely they would know about you so quickly."

At least he could get that off his conscience. He pointed at the devastation outside. "How did they do it? Do they have planet destroyers too?"

"No, their weapons systems are different from ours. There are no separate planet destroyers. Each ship by itself only has limited firepower. However, three of them can combine their resources to generate a formidable weapon capable of destroying entire planets. In order to do so, they need to form a perfect triangle, spaced evenly apart from each other. When we arrived, they had already destroyed the planet and the moons. They tried to form a triangle again to destroy our ship, but our evasive maneuvers kept preventing them from doing so. Otherwise, this ship by itself would have been no match for that weapon."

"How did we get here? Was this star system on our flight path?"

"Not too far from it. We received a distress call from an outpost on the second moon around Kerding, reporting the sudden appearance of those Volonan ships. As usual, our surveillance network had not been able to spot their approach through consars. We immediately plotted an intercept path, but by the time we got here, it was too late."

"Are there any survivors at all?

"None that we can locate."

Marc realized he was in the midst of a tomb. All those rocks out there had until an hour ago been part of a world, a world that had housed an entire population, an entire society. He felt strange, almost spooked out, at the thought of so much death all around him. It reminded him of his own dream a couple of nights earlier, of Earth's similar destruction.

In the distance, other Mendoken ships could be seen arriving. Alas, they were too late to save the lives of their kinfolk.

"Mr. Zemin, I did not expect you here at this time."

Marc turned around to see Commander Maginder standing in front of him. "I know," he said, "I just wanted to see what was happening. I hope it's not an issue."

"Perhaps it was important for you to see for yourself what kind of enemy we are at war with," Maginder said simply.

No doubt, now it was all too clear to Marc. "I... I'm very sorry for the tremendous loss of life your people have just suffered."

Maginder was silent for a few seconds. "Thank you, Mr. Zemin," he finally said in his usual monotone. "The frequency of these attacks is increasing by the day. We need to quicken our pace to reach the Mendo-Zueger star system, so that you can show our engineers how to build the same consar travel capability that the Volona have. With our existing capabilities, all we can do in retaliation is to try to penetrate their space at our common border. And, given how heavily fortified their side of the border is, that is always a futile exercise."

Maginder then motioned to Petrana and the other pilots to resume the voyage. They had lost 3 hours due to this whole debacle, and still had another 28 hours to go to reach their destination. The other ships that had arrived would take care of any necessary rescue or salvage operations here. Repairs to the hull of their own ship would have to occur en route.

Marc headed back to his quarters, figuring Petrana and everyone else would now either be busy flying the ship or fixing it. There wasn't much he would be able to help them with, since he knew nothing about Mendoken technology. He drove the vehicle he had come up in back down to the city, and parked it at the same spot in front of his building where he had left it. The trip back down was much easier, now that he was starting to get the hang of how to operate these vehicles. Hildira met him at the entrance to the building, and showed him back up to his apartment on the 32nd floor.

Back alone in his living room, he sat on the couch and thought about everything that had just happened. He felt horrible. What a tragedy! An entire planet destroyed, right in front of his eyes. And these poor Mendoken – they didn't express their emotions, but that moment of silence in his conversation with Maginder had said it all. It was heartbreaking.

What kind of creatures were these Volonans, to commit so heinous a crime? And that against a completely innocent, vulnerable world, whose sole purpose it had been to save the lives of others? If they really were at war, why not at least attack Mendoken battleships or military installations? This was worse than the most atrocious crimes committed by terrorists and tyrants back on Earth!

It was genocide, pure and simple. And it made him feel emotions he had never felt before. His mother's death had made him sad, Iman's leaving him upset, and the recent fight with Cheryl angry. But this was different – he felt rage. Something had to be done about this – justice had to be served. He didn't know the full history of the war between the Mendoken and the Volona, but from what little he had seen so far, the Mendoken didn't seem like the type to perform such unforgivable acts of mass murder. Sure, they had planet destroyers, but more as self defense deterrents, not unprovoked aggression. After all, they had protected Earth for so long, longer than the entire existence of humanity. But these Volonans – if they won this war and took over Mendoken space, then Earth could very well share the same fate as Kerding. Maginder clearly hadn't been lying about the Volona not taking any prisoners.

Marc's mind was in turmoil. On the one hand, he felt more determined than ever to help the Mendoken. It was critical that they win this war, and he would do his utmost to help them replicate his experiments as quickly as possible. He would also gladly take on additional responsibility in the war against the Volona, if the Mendoken chose to enlist his services. Of course, he had never fought in a battle before, so he didn't know if he had the courage, strength or skill to fight. But now he felt ready to contribute to this struggle in one way or the other, regardless whether his efforts bore any fruit or not.

But on the other hand, he felt fear and regret. Fear of failure, regret in having come on this journey. He had now seen for himself how high the stakes were. If he couldn't reproduce the consar, the consar he had accidentally stumbled upon in his botched time travel experiment, then all hope would be lost. The Mendoken would lose their one chance to begin retaliating successfully against the Volona. The war would soon be over, this great civilization would be annihilated, and humanity would perish along with it.

Would this whole adventure just be another of his many failures in life? If so, this one would surely be the biggest of them all. But failure or not, there was no longer any option to turn back.

Chapter 12

Mendo-Zueger was a giant star. With a diameter about 60 times the size of Earth's Sun, it shone brightly in the night sky, even in the furthest corners of the galaxy. It was home to 24 planets, each with a unique size, composition and climate. They ranged from the green, marsh covered Draefarel to the desert wastelands of Vertat, from the tiny sea world of Kaurpa to the gas giant Nees. And apart from Nees, all the planets and moons in this system were inhabited by the Mendoken.

Although the origin of all Mendoken life, the planet Draefarel was no longer the seat of power. It was a neighboring planet called Lind that currently housed the central government, an honor it had already held for over 300 million years. The top layers of the Mendoken Hierarchy, including the Imgoerin, his advisors and the upper parliament of senators all resided on Lind and governed the entire Republic from this planet. As a result, it was the most heavily protected planet in the Republic. Due to the current war with the Volona, 300 highly fortified space stations surrounded Lind and its moons, carefully regulating the arrival and departure of every single ship. At least 50 stations surrounded every other planet in the system, and the system as a whole had another 4,000 stations around its perimeter.

The Mendoken had clearly seen to it that anybody foolish enough to attack the Mendo-Zueger system would inevitably face catastrophic consequences. Even with their consar technology, the Volona had never dared to attempt a strike here in the heart of the Republic.

The ship Marc was on arrived safely in the Mendo-Zueger system, passing unhindered by a series of space stations on its way to Lind. After the incident at

Kerding, the rest of the journey had fortunately been uneventful. Marc had spent most of the time in his quarters, going over all his research and experiments. Fresh food had been delivered every few hours by Hildira, while HoloMarc had reappeared several times to keep him company and provide him with information on topics he had wanted to know more about.

The ship docked at one of the space stations around Lind, after which Marc transferred to a small shuttle that would take him to Ailen, one of Lind's four moons. Ailen was the largest, most advanced hub of scientific research and technology for the Mendoken. The entire moon was one big urban jungle, with monstrous buildings far wider and taller than anything on Earth. As Marc learned from the pilot of the shuttle, however, what was visible on the surface was only the tip of the iceberg. Since Ailen had no atmosphere of its own, most of the buildings were actually underground.

Underground the shuttle went, right into a tunnel that belonged to a sophisticated network of busy highways through the moon's interior. The shuttle eventually came to a stop at the main entrance to the Space Travel Research Center, a very important and highly respected scientific institution among the Mendoken.

Several minutes later, Marc was standing in a briefing room, in front of several key Mendoken scientists and engineers. He felt very nervous, worried to death that he would fail to show them what they wanted to see, what they had brought him all the way here for.

The Mendoken in the room had been equipped with translator devices, in order to be able to communicate with Marc in English. But a couple of these devices did not seem to be working properly. As advanced as these Mendoken were, their technology evidently wasn't always infallible.

"Mr., you might to be in knowledge, Zemin, for the travel in higher dimension in Glaessan, not allowed this," Floray Erzass 44532105, the lead scientist at the center, said. She was slightly taller than the others, and had a small scar to the left of her mouth. Her hat was turquoise in color.

"Okay, please call me Marc," Marc said right away, trying to reduce the level of formality. It had worked with Petrana, after all.

"Brrrrrrrrrrrrrrr, Marc your name is," Floray said.

"Yeah, well, Floray ain't much better," Marc thought, taken aback by her rudeness. But perhaps it had just been a mistake of her faulty translator device.

"Mendoken the bestest technology have in Glaessan," Floray explained. "Volona only with breaking laws in consars ahead got. Mendoken in otherwise would prevalence be."

Marc took a couple of seconds to understand what she had just said. "Yes, that was explained to me by Commander Maginder," he replied, deciding not to point out that her translator was spewing out horribly structured sentences. No need to aggravate matters, particularly considering what the reaction of these Mendoken might be if it turned out that he was of no use to them.

"Marc, you us teeeeell yourrrrrr expeeeeeeeerimint." That was the slow, rumbling voice of Renkan Boesa 44532189, the lead engineer at the center. A little plumper than Floray, his translator was clearly in worse shape than hers. He also had a turquoise hat on, indicating that they were both of the same rank.

Taking a deep breath, Marc began explaining everything he had done in his research. A virtual whiteboard appeared in front of him, allowing him to draw diagrams and write equations for the others to see. Fortunately the translation of his words into their language was working fine, as everybody seemed to be following his explanations.

A lot of questions were asked about how he had actually performed the work, particularly by a young engineer called Sibular Gaulen 45383532. Tall and slender, with a wider mouth and a thinner eye than the others, he seemed the brightest and most technically savvy Mendoken in the room. He understood everything Marc was saying right away, and much to Marc's relief, his translator was working perfectly both ways.

"This makes sense, Marc," Sibular said, after Marc had finished explaining how he had opened the consar. "Can you now tell us how you stabilized the consar?"

Marc went off on another long explanation, feeling a little more relaxed after sensing some acknowledgment and satisfaction from his audience. Sibular in particular seemed very interested in everything he was saying, and kept giving him positive feedback. It was a sharp contrast to the discouraging remarks he had always received from his advisor Graham and others back at Cornell. Who knew, perhaps he really would be able to help these aliens after all.

The discussion went on for a good hour or two. At the end, Renkan communicated silently with Sibular for a while. Then Renkan spoke. "Rrrrreeeaady gooooooooo teeeeeeest tot-to-tooooo."

Sibular stepped in to address Marc's look of confusion. "We believe we understand all your steps, Marc, and are now ready to conduct a test. There are a number of assumptions you made in your calculations, but we can compensate for them. This will help in controlling the end point of the trajectory."

At that moment, the wall on the far side of the briefing room opened and slid away, revealing an entrance to a huge hall behind. The hall was broken up into multiple rings, each ring containing all kinds of strange looking equipment that Marc had never seen before. There were quite a few Mendoken about in the hall, conducting different kinds of experiments in the rings.

Sibular explained that this was one of the main laboratories at the center. It was, in fact, one of the few laboratories left in the entire Republic that had the equipment and staff to perform consar research.

Marc was stunned. "Why?"

"Because the Volona somehow always find out about the location of our consar research facilities, appear through their own consars and destroy them before we can make any reasonable progress in our research," Sibular replied. "Hence our limited progress in all this time since the war began. We suspect there are spies about in the Republic who feed the Volona this information, but we have not been able to identify them so far. This is also why we have limited the amount of consar research performed in this particular facility, in case the spies take notice. We cannot afford any incident here, so close to the seat of power on Lind."

Sibular led the way to a ring at the far end of the hall. The equipment from Marc's lab at Cornell had already been transported there, and most of it was sitting atop a table in the center of the ring.

Marc was asked to set up the apparatus to repeat his experiment, which he began diligently doing right away. Normally this process would have taken him a good few hours, but thanks to the help of Sibular, Renkan and Floray, the setup was done within a half hour. They followed his instructions to the letter, never once making a mistake. Surprised that such important figures as Renkan and Floray would actually perform manual labor like this, he guessed that Mendoken culture probably had no reservations or hang-ups about teamwork between individuals of different social standings.

Many Mendoken working in other circles stopped what they were doing, and crowded around to watch. Marc and his team were in the limelight.

"Okay, I think we're ready," Marc finally said, looking at his laptop screen one last time.

"This is exactly the way it was in your lab?" Sibular asked.

"Yes, at least as far as the equipment we brought is concerned."

Sibular communicated with a couple of the spectators, who took off and returned shortly with a number of small devices that looked like empty glass cases. A device was placed on top of each of Marc's instruments, including the laptop and even his notepad. Sibular then touched all the devices, one after the other, in a sweeping motion with his hand. Each device instantly shot a ray of light upwards. All the rays converged on a point above the table, where a large 3D screen took shape in midair. The screen began displaying data and charts, all in strange characters that Marc had never seen before.

Using his long metallic fingers, Sibular quickly made several adjustments to the data on the screen. As he did so, new data was transmitted to each of Marc's instruments, causing some of them to change their settings.

"My adjustments will help in controlling the trajectory of the consar," Sibular explained.

"Sounds good," Marc said. "So what should we use as the guinea pig?"

"Geeeeeeeeeennnnnnnneeeeee peeeeeeeeeeeeeeeeeeg?" Renkan asked.

"The device to be transported, in our first experiment."

"Your choice," Sibular said.

Marc took out his pocket watch. "It worked once before, so let's see if it works again," he said, placing the treasured timepiece carefully on the center of the table, surrounded by the three energy emitting devices.

Sibular plotted the course of the test consar on the screen – a very short trajectory from one end of the hall to the other, no more than a thousand feet away. "Please, begin when you are ready," he said to Marc.

This was it. The moment of truth had come. Marc checked everything once again. Then, rubbing his hands, closing his eyes and hoping for the best, he pressed the Enter key on his laptop.

Hearing nothing, he opened his eyes and peered nervously at the table. The watch was still there. Why wasn't it working? Or was time just slowing down for him because he was so anxious? He thought he heard Sibular say something reassuring, something to the effect that they would keep repeating the experiment until it worked. But he wasn't paying attention to anybody or anything else at the moment. All he cared about was the fact that the watch was still there.

Finally, he heard the hum he was so desperately waiting for, the hum of the three energy emitters. Then he saw their bright rays shooting towards the center of the table. A white glow began forming around the watch, and kept increasing in intensity until it looked like a little white sun.

Marc heaved a huge sigh of relief. The first stage had worked! But now it was time for the next stage. Would the consar open up? Again, each second that passed felt like an eternity. At last, there it was! A blue circle began forming around the little sun, and a tunnel into another dimension opened up behind it. The circle grew into a sphere that engulfed the timepiece, and then catapulted with a bright flash into the tunnel. After that, the tunnel entrance abruptly vanished. The watch was gone.

All eyes now turned to a screen that showed a live close-up of a ring at the other end of the hall. Almost immediately, the tunnel exit appeared above a table in that ring, exactly at the location specified by Sibular's calculations. The blue sphere rushed out and stopped at the center of the table, and then faded away. The tunnel exit also vanished as quickly as it had appeared. All that was left was the pocket watch, resting comfortably on the table.

Marc rushed to the other end of the hall, followed by Sibular and the others.

Panting, he reached the table and picked up the watch. It was still in one piece! He opened it – his parents' picture was still there, and the dials were working perfectly.

"Success!" he yelled, showing the timepiece to everyone. "Success!" He felt proud, very proud, something he hadn't felt in a long, long time.

"Brrrrrrrrrrrrrrrrrrrrrr," some of the Mendoken remarked in unison. This was obviously a big moment for them.

"Thanking Marc you to," Floray said.

"Thaaaaaaaaaaaaannnnnnnnnnkkkkkkkkssssssss," Renkan added.

Others in the hall began coming over and thanking Marc, most of them just putting their hands on his shoulder for a few seconds before returning to their duties. By now, he knew not to expect any more display of emotion from these Mendoken.

The experiment was repeated, not once, but many times, with a variety of different objects and coordinates. Every time it was successful, without a hitch.

"The next step will be to remove the need for the external energy emitters," Sibular said, "so that the device traveling through a consar has the ability to open the consar by itself without any outside help."

He opened up one of Marc's energy emitters, studied the technology inside, and within the span of several minutes added that same capability to a vehicle that was parked inside the hall. The vehicle was then sent off by remote control through the hall, abruptly disappearing as intended into a consar before reaching the far wall. Seconds later, a report came in that the vehicle had appeared on the surface of the moon at the designated spot. The experiment had been successful.

At that moment, a door opened at the end of the hall and a single Mendoken floated in. A hush instantly fell over the hall, and all the Mendoken present bowed slightly towards the newcomer in a show of respect.

"Who is that?" Marc whispered to Sibular.

"That is Osalya Heyfass 00000663," Sibular said quietly. "She is one of the Imgoerin's top aides."

"Really? Why is she here?"

"For you, no doubt."

Osalya looked different from the others. The color of her skin was darker, almost black. On her head was a gleaming, white hat, offering a sharp contrast to her dark skin. The metal encasing her body was a tad cleaner than everybody else's, and displayed several strange looking symbols that probably spelled out something important in Mendoken script.

She floated directly towards the ring where Marc and the others were, and came to a stop in front of Marc. "We are deeply obliged, Mr. Zemin," she said.

Marc took a few seconds to respond, still in awe of this individual's importance.

She was, after all, top aide to someone who ruled over about 400 billion star systems. "Thank you for your kindness," he said nervously, bowing his head a little in an effort to mimic the other Mendoken. "I'm glad to be of service."

Osalya communicated silently with Floray and Renkan for a moment, and then spoke to Marc. "You have kept your end of the agreement, Mr. Zemin, and we will keep ours. There is a ship waiting above Lind to take you home, whenever you are ready to leave. We ask only for your word that you never mention us, the silupsal filter, or anything else you have seen on this journey to your people. Their time to join the galactic community has yet to come."

Marc was about to open his mouth to voice his agreement, but, to his surprise, no words came out. Instead, a wave of weakness suddenly overcame him, and his head began spinning. Wondering why this was happening, he tried to shake it off. Perhaps this was a result of all the stress he had been under for the past couple of days. Or maybe he had just eaten too much during his last hearty meal.

"Are you alright, Mr. Zemin?" Osalya asked.

But he could hardly hear her. The muscles in his body were losing their strength, causing his legs to give way. His knees hit the ground first, followed by his upper body. Before he knew it, he was lying flat on the ground, face downwards and eyes closed. Strangely enough, he didn't feel any pain. He couldn't even sense the presence of any of his limbs, as if his mind had totally separated from his body. Was he dead?

His mind was certainly alive, very much so. He wasn't sure if he was hallucinating or dreaming, but he began having visions, one after the other. First came a view of Earth, looking quite at peace from the distance. But then it blew up in a massive explosion, just like the explosion he had seen in his nightmare a couple of nights earlier. Then he saw other planets blowing up, whole star systems disappearing into oblivion, and finally the entire Milky Way galaxy crumbling to dust. He saw dead humans rotting away and Mendoken bodies broken into multiple pieces. He saw rows and rows of Aftarans hanged by their necks, and Phyraxes crushed to pulp. He saw other creatures he couldn't identify wailing away, their hearts broken with sorrow.

These were the most horrible things he had ever seen in his life. And they made no sense whatsoever. Why was everybody dying, and why were all the planets exploding? Why would anybody or anything want to cause so much devastation? Above all, why was he having such vivid visions in the first place?

The visions continued. All of a sudden, darkness engulfed him, and he began to feel cold, very cold. Despair kicked in, at the thought of the end of all life in the galaxy and his powerlessness to stop it. He began shivering uncontrollably, unable to see anything. The only thing he could hear was the sinister laughter of a shadow far away.

But then, in the distance, he saw a sparkling light, like a star. As the glowing star moved closer, it brought light and warmth. Another star followed, and another, then three more. He stopped shivering, and began to feel stronger. The evil shadow's laughter was fading away. Hope was replacing despair.

The stars moved up next to him. He turned towards them and smiled, feeling happy and reassured, as if long lost friends had reappeared in his life. He no longer felt afraid with these stars by his side.

The last remnants of darkness disappeared, and he heard a familiar voice speak. "Good morning, Marc."

Marc opened his eyes, and saw Sibular standing right in front of him. He had finally woken up from his trance, if that was indeed what it was. Blinking, he looked around. He was lying on a bed, in the middle of a small, sparsely furnished room. Except that it wasn't really a bed – just a thin, solid sheet that was somehow floating in thin air.

"Where... am I?" he croaked.

"In the medical facility at the research center," Sibular said, standing near him. "You are still on Ailen."

"How long have I been here?" His mouth felt dry and bitter, and his eyes hurt.

"7.6 hours."

Marc whistled. "I don't understand... what happened. I was talking to... I'm sorry, what was her name again?"

"Osalya Heyfass 00000663."

"That's right, Osalya. Then, all of a sudden, I just collapsed." He noticed a small, transparent device lying on his chest, probably monitoring his body's main functions. Behind Sibular, a large screen was displaying some charts – most likely the data transmitted by the device. Another Mendoken was standing in front of the screen, keeping an eye on the data.

"Am I alright?" he asked.

"You appear to be functioning perfectly," Sibular replied. "We cannot determine what caused your abrupt breakdown. We were certainly taken by surprise, but wasted no time in bringing you to the medical facility."

"I don't know either. I was suddenly having all these visions. They were horrible, so horrible!"

"Visions of what?"

"Death, destruction, it was insane." Marc decided not to elaborate, since Sibular might think he had gone over the edge. He stared at Sibular. He didn't know why, but it felt very comforting to see him.

"How do you feel now?" Sibular asked.

"Okay, I guess. Just weak." Trying to get up, he felt a slight hint of dizziness. But it went away as soon as he had rubbed his face and swayed his head from side to side.

"We have made good progress in the meantime. We furnished a small shuttlecraft with consar capability, and successfully sent it through a consar to a neighboring star system. The next step will now be to outfit one of our battleships."

"That is great news!" Marc exclaimed. He truly felt happy to know that all the endless hours he had spent in his lab at Cornell had finally amounted to something worthwhile. Something so worthwhile, in fact, that it would hopefully help a great civilization prevail in their war against a ruthless enemy, and thereby save his own people from annihilation as well.

"There is still a ship waiting to take you back home, whenever you are ready," Sibular said.

Marc looked down. "No, I would rather not go back home."

"I do not understand, Marc."

"I would like to stay here, and help your people win the war against the Volona. That is, if I'm allowed to."

"Why?"

"Honestly, I don't really know. But when I was about to answer to Osalya that I was ready to go back home, I collapsed into a horrible trance that lasted over 7 hours. I don't want to take that chance again."

"Very well, if that is your choice," Sibular said, not expressing any surprise or emotion. "I do not believe it will be a problem, as long as you realize what this might mean for you."

"I think I do."

Marc did, of course, have his reasons for wanting to stay. For one, a Mendoken defeat would most likely mean the end of Earth and humanity. So anything he could do to help the Mendoken, however small a contribution, would ultimately be crucial to his own survival. For another, he didn't really have anyone to go back home to. He had no family, no parents, no girlfriend, no wife – nobody who cared. And somehow the thought of returning to his old research did not excite him, especially since he now knew that time travel wasn't possible. The only thing he would have to look forward to was to get more reprimands from Graham, all the way up to his inevitable expulsion from Cornell within a few weeks.

He would end up poor, without a degree and without a job. Perhaps he would wander the streets of Ithaca as a homeless person, or do the same in a big city. He would be the only holder on the entire planet of an awesome secret, a secret about the rest of the galaxy and all the life it contained. His heart and mind would burn to reveal it to others, warning them of the impending doom that could strike at any moment. And if he did break his promise and open his mouth, he would immediately be labeled as a madman and would likely be sent to a mental institution. This would be his fate if he returned home.

Furthermore, there had to be a cause for the visions he had just had. Although he wasn't the type of person to believe in supernatural phenomena, the images had been so strong, so vivid, that he couldn't just ignore them. Perhaps somebody, somewhere, was trying to send him a message that he shouldn't return to Earth. If he did, the big disaster he was so terrified of would actually happen – Earth would be destroyed. And not just Earth – tremendous suffering would be inflicted upon all the advanced species of the galaxy.

Instead, he was to stay here, with the Mendoken. But why? He had given them what they wanted. His job was done. What good would his continued presence here bring? He didn't know. All he did know was that he had never had such visions before, and that he had a higher chance of discovering who or what was behind them if he stayed here.

Chapter 13

Dumyan and Sharjam cautiously made their way on foot across the surface of Tibara. In such freezing temperatures as those found on this planet, most forms of life would quickly die. But Aftarans were different. With their supernatural abilities, they could survive under the harshest of conditions. Their robes could be magically stretched and wrapped around their bodies many times, providing them with as much warmth and protection as they needed.

The perpetual ice storms kept slowing down the two brothers' pace, but also provided them with much needed camouflage from Lord Wazilban's surveyors. They did, however, face other challenges during their trek. On the first night, a surveyor came dangerously close to the cave they were staying in, but luckily did not spot them. The next day, Sharjam slipped while climbing up the steep incline of a volcano, causing him to tumble down and over the edge of a cliff. The only thing that saved him was Dumyan's lightning-speed reaction. Shedding off his robe, Dumyan opened his wings and flew down after Sharjam, catching him in the very last second of his fall of almost a hundred feet.

Although Sharjam was saved, Dumyan instantly began suffering from hypothermia without his robe. Sharjam retrieved the robe right away, and wrapped it several times around his brother. He then lay over Dumyan for a good hour, using his own body to give his brother some warmth. And after a drink of yellow *rauka*, a very bitter-tasting but magical, strength-giving Aftaran drink, Dumyan finally felt strong enough to continue the journey.

Eventually reaching the top of the volcano, they crouched behind some rocks and peered out cautiously over the edge. An active crater that periodically spouted large chunks of lava, this most uninviting location was the first destination of their journey.

"How do you propose to do this?" Sharjam asked.

"I am thinking, unlike you," Dumyan said. "Leave me in peace!"

Dumyan was indeed thinking furiously, but he really wasn't sure how to proceed. "Perhaps we should just approach one of them," he whispered, getting ready to stand up and climb down into the crater.

Sharjam looked astonished. "Are you out of your mind? To come all this way, only to be killed in so stupid a fashion?"

"Have you a better idea?"

They both looked again through the rising ash and steam at the gaping hole below. It had to be at least a couple of hundred feet in diameter, and another hundred feet deep. The entire surface was glowing red in heat, ready to shoot out another spurt of lava at any moment.

"Yes, as a matter of fact I do," Sharjam said. "Unlike you, I actually have read about their behavior. Unlike you, I actually am well read."

"Very well, O Knowledgeable One, be my guest," Dumyan said sarcastically. He generally hated acknowledging that his younger brother could ever be right about anything.

They were talking about Roxays, highly unusual creatures that spent much of their time hovering around or inside volcanic craters such as this one. Roxays were the only known living beings to have the durability to naturally survive on Tibara. They were also the only known living beings with the ability to naturally fly through space for millions of miles at a stretch. Aftarans generally avoided contact with Roxays, because of their often rowdy and unpredictable behavior. They had very bad tempers, and could sometimes attack and kill others for no reason. Roxays were definitely not known for their good manners or friendliness, or even for their good looks.

There were a number of Roxays inside the crater, most of them comfortably perched on ledges and stretching their necks to the steaming boulders below to gulp them down. For that was what they ate – hot rocks. And with the nourishment they obtained from rocks, they could grow to monstrous proportions. The adult Roxay averaged 30 feet in length, from the tip of its round head, through the long, slender neck, to the very wide, bulky body and abrupt end with no tail.

The internals of the Roxay were a unique marvel of nature. The whole body functioned as a highly efficient engine, breaking down the consumed hot rocks into combustible liquid fuel. It then burned the fuel when needed, generating enough thrust to overcome gravity and propel itself at high speed into space. Other nutrients from the rocks were extracted to support basic life functions. Once stocked up on a solid meal of rocks, a Roxay could actually survive for weeks on end without having to eat again or even having to respire.

A disproportionately tall hump on top of the Roxay's body served as its fuel storage tank. The animal also had two massive wings, one on each side of the hump, usually kept neatly folded unless it was taking off from or landing on the surface of a planet. A long horn extended outwards from the top of its head, believed to be some kind of radar device used for navigation and communication.

"They are as ugly in real life as they are in pictures," Sharjam observed.

For once, Dumyan had to agree with his brother. Neither of them had ever seen a Roxay before in real life, and it definitely wasn't a sight to be enamored by. No Aftaran would ever be envious of its strange body shape, and even less so of its insect-like face with eight eyes and long, dangling tentacles. Surrounding the large mouth in the center of the face, the tentacles were used to pick up rocks and push them straight into the mouth.

"You really are sure there is no other way to get off this planet?" Sharjam asked, eyeing the nearest Roxay.

The Roxay looked up into the sky and let out a screeching bellow, a bellow so loud that both brothers had to cover their ears for its duration.

"Why, are you frightened?" Dumyan sneered, once the bellow had subsided.

"As if you are not!"

Dumyan had to admit that it was a very scary sight. For a second, he wondered if he had made the right decision in ever leaving the safety of their hideout. But he quickly brushed that thought aside. "There is no other way. This is the only chance we have. If we try to take our ship out of its hiding place and use it to leave the planet, surveyors will locate us in an instant and blow us up before we even exit the atmosphere. A Roxay, on the other hand, is a perfectly natural flying creature that will arouse no attention."

"Not even Wazilban will imagine that we are foolhardy enough to try riding on a Roxay," Sharjam agreed. "This is truly an insane idea! How will we survive in space for days on end, maybe even weeks?"

"Our robes will protect us."

"You are absolutely mad!" Sharjam said, shaking his head.

Dumyan was getting annoyed. "We have come all this way. Give me a better idea, or go back to our father and tell him we have failed! I do not know about you, but I refuse to be a failure in his eyes."

Sharjam was silent for a moment, and then took a deep breath. "Well, this is what I know of these Roxays. They are not very intelligent or friendly. They do not like strangers, and often do not even like their own kind. Annoy one of them, which, by the way, is extremely easy to do, and it will literally pick you up with its strong tentacles and tear you to pieces. That is, if it does not first let out a ball of smoking exhaust from its rear, instantly burning you and everything else behind it to the ground."

"We can use our boryals, no?" Dumyan was referring to the standard weapon that many Aftarans carried on their journeys. Although boryals looked like short swords, they actually discharged powerful rays that could destroy targets on contact. The unique thing about the boryal's rays was that they traveled in curves, not in straight lines. That generally made it difficult for a target to realize that it even was a target until it was too late.

"Our boryals will only be useful in destroying the first, and perhaps the second Roxay," Sharjam said. "But as soon as the others see what we have done, they will pounce on us from all sides, spraying their exhaust on us and converting both our bodies and our boryals into pure ash."

"Can we not use any of our enchantments on them?"

"Other Aftarans have apparently died trying. These are amazingly resistant creatures."

Dumyan was feeling more uncomfortable by the second. "Is there a bright side to this story?"

Sharjam sighed. "As a matter of fact, there is."

"Please enlighten me."

"Well, the key is to get one of these monsters to fly into space, right? In order to do that, we need to know what natural instinct causes them to migrate between planets and moons in the first place. They are not affected by hot or cold, fire or ice, by light or darkness. But there is one thing that does affect them very much – their tremendous fear of vegetation."

Dumyan almost jumped in surprise. "I beg your pardon?"

"It is the truth, I assure you. They are terrified of trees, bushes, grass – any kind of plants. Direct contact with a plant kills them. Even the pollen some plants release in the air can cause their inner body parts to quickly decay, yielding a most painful death. That is why they love planets like Tibara, because it is absolutely devoid of any flora. At the first sign of plant life on a planet or moon, they take flight again, looking for the next barren world."

"What strange creatures! So the trick is to show them some plants, and then they take off?"

"Yes, but there is a catch. They are not easily fooled – the plants need to be growing from the ground, and they do need to be large enough to be noticeable. Unfortunately, even with the eight eyes on its head, the Roxay is very shortsighted. So the plants will have to be very close to their faces before they show any reaction."

"Do you know how to create and grow a plant?"

"Of course! That was one of the first enchantments my Master taught me when I was a child."

Sharjam took out a silver coin-like object from inside his robe, ran his finger around its edge, and uttered several words that sounded like a verse. He then made a sweeping motion with his hands and clasped them together. A light flashed above his hands, and out sprang a green *hupee* plant, a native of the planet Yarkuba in the Afta-Parmeen star system. It had a thick, vertical stem, with numerous branches that shot straight out. Hexagonally shaped leaves appeared at the end of each branch.

"Will the hupee's roots survive if we plant it in the crater?" Dumyan asked.

"No. We will need to plant it right here."

"Then let us proceed. We will attract the attention of the Roxays, scare them into beginning a migration, and then jump onto one of them as it takes off into space!"

"In theory!" Sharjam cautioned. "There is only one spot on the Roxay's body that we can hold onto without being thrown off – the base of each wing. It is the one spot on the body that has no senses. We will need to jump into those spots – me behind one wing and you behind the other, and settle there for the entire journey without moving an inch. Trust me, it will not be easy."

"Who said this mission was going to be easy?"

Sharjam decided not to respond to that comment. He had not wanted to come on this mission at all, and now he was more convinced than ever that Dumyan was out of his mind. Still, he knew there was no other option, and there was no turning back for him. Not without proclaiming himself a total failure in front of his father.

He chanted another verse and let the hupee drop to the ground. The moment the plant touched the surface, the rocky ground around it turned into soft, muddy soil, enabling it to easily take root. It grew taller instantly, rising almost to his height.

Dumyan then got up and stood upright, so that his head came into clear view from the depths of the crater. "Hey!" he yelled, waving his arms. "Yes, you ugly beasts! Look at me! Right here!"

Sharjam got up to see what was happening. The nearest Roxay, no more than 70 feet away, turned its head toward them. Another Roxay further away also looked up, dropping a rock it was just about to devour. They both let out screeching, deafening roars. As they did so, other Roxays began noticing the commotion, many of them joining the growing chorus of screeches.

"Oh, they are upset!" Sharjam observed, growing worried about the unrest his brother had just created. "Roxays do not like surprises."

"Hold your boryal!" Dumyan shouted, barely audible over the shrieks of the monsters. "Here they come!"

Sure enough, the nearest Roxay had lifted off its perch, opening its wings and heading straight towards them. Its wing span had to be at least 35 feet, longer than the creature's body itself. Another Roxay lifted and followed, and others further away began doing the same.

"May the Creator protect us!" Sharjam yelled, terrified by the danger he was about to face.

Both brothers took out their boryals from inside their robes. The weapons were gleaming in silver, no more than a foot in length each, looking very much like the bottom parts of swords that had been cut in half. They held their weapons tightly, ready for the inevitable.

The first Roxay came over the edge of the crater's wall, lowering its head towards the Aftarans. Its slimy tentacles shot out towards Dumyan.

"Do not shoot!" Sharjam cautioned, as much as his instincts and training told him otherwise. He pulled his brother back with him behind the hupee plant.

The Roxay came to an abrupt halt in midair when it saw the plant. Instead of screeching, it let out a loud howl, as if it was suddenly in a lot of pain. It turned around to face the other Roxays, and kept howling.

"It is working!" Dumyan whispered.

To be sure, it was. The wailing was sending the Roxays away. The ones already in the air began flying upwards. The other ones still on the ground dropped their last rocks and spread their wings, following their kinfolk into the sky. There had to be at least 30 of them in total, beginning their exodus from Tibara.

"Right, now!" Sharjam yelled.

They both sprang up, and jumped onto the back of the howling Roxay. It immediately stopped its howling, and began violently shaking its body from side to side, trying to lose them. But they held on with all their might, using the retractable claws on the edges of their fingers to dig into the animal's tough, rubbery skin.

"Get behind the wing!" Sharjam ordered. "It is our only chance!" He scrambled toward the base of the right wing, while Dumyan did the same on the left side.

With great difficulty, Sharjam made it to the base, and quickly burrowed himself in it. He could no longer see Dumyan now, his view to the left blocked by the Roxay's body. But he guessed Dumyan had made it to the other base, for he hadn't seen anyone fall off, and the Roxay had suddenly stopped thrashing about. No longer sensing any presence on its back, it probably thought it had finally dropped its highly unwelcome cargo. Flapping its long wings, it began its escape into the sky, following the trail of the other Roxays already in flight.

Sharjam held tightly on to the Roxay, hoping and praying that his brother was doing the same. The ride was rough, with the beast swaying up and down with every flap of its wings. The high winds and flying ice trinkets didn't exactly make things any easier either. But the wing base was offering him plenty of protection, and he also knew that things would get smoother once the creature had cleared the planet's atmosphere.

The Roxay was strong, rising steadily through the storm between the layers of clouds. It eventually cleared the last layer, revealing a deep, blue sky above, a sight Sharjam had not witnessed in over two years.

At this point, the Roxay began to start its natural engine. This process Sharjam found most interesting, as little as of it as he could actually see from his hiding place. First, he heard and felt a deep rumble coming from inside the Roxay's body. Then the rear part of the body opened up, revealing a huge exhaust vent through which a plume of fire and smoke blew out. Folding its wings, the Roxay suddenly shot up with tremendous acceleration. The wings were no longer needed, now that it had turned from a flying creature into a rocket.

Perched tightly between the Roxay's body and the folded wing, Sharjam tried to settle into a comfortable position, with his head held just high enough to be able to see past the top of the wing. The atmosphere was thinning out, and he now had a clear view of the star-littered space beyond. Afta-Johran, a star of moderate size, shone brightly to the left, showering its light over the ice world of Tibara.

If only the warm sunlight could penetrate the permanent cloud covers, he thought, the climate on the surface might have been far less unpleasant. To his right, he could see Tibara's nearest moon, and its other, smaller moon not too far behind. The nearest planet, Ureeba, was a bright speck above. Only 25 million miles away, it shone just a little more brightly than the far more distant stars.

Sharjam wrapped another layer of his robe around his head and face, and with a brush of his hand magically made the section covering his eyes transparent. Aftarans required very little air in order to sustain basic life functions, and the amount of air trapped in the many layers of his robe would suffice for a number of days through empty space.

As it reached the edge of the atmosphere, the Roxay folded up its tentacles and covered its mouth. It also sealed all its eyes shut. In space, it would rely only on its radar horn to navigate and communicate with fellow Roxays. It was still accelerating, to an eventual top speed of about 500,000 miles per hour. No other known living creature in the entire galaxy could even fly a hundredth as fast as the Roxay, nor could any other creature fly in space by itself.

Where was this Roxay heading, Sharjam wondered, along with its two stowaways? It wouldn't be nearby Ureeba, since that was a green planet with all kinds of plant life. Nor would it be either of Tibara's moons – they had no volcanoes with hot rocks suitable for consumption. Perhaps some other planet further away.

All he could do was to keep quiet and wait. If fate favored him and his brother, perhaps they would land on another world before the air in their robes ran out. Hopefully it wouldn't be infested with surveyors like Tibara was. He doubted it would be. Despite all the precautions they had taken to hide their trail during their escape from Wazilban's clutches, it seemed Wazilban had somehow figured out that Autamrin and his followers were most likely hiding on or near Tibara. Only that could explain the high concentration of surveyors in this area alone.

Better yet, maybe they would be picked up by an alien ship that wasn't Aftaran and therefore wouldn't hand them over to Wazilban's authorities. Maybe they could convince the crew to transport them to the Mendoken border.

Sharjam silently uttered a prayer for his father, as he watched another surveyor make for the surface of Tibara below. He also prayed for the success of their mission. Now that they truly were underway, too much was at stake for failure to even be an option.

Chapter 14

Marc spent a few days as a tourist in the Mendoken heartland. While the Mendoken scientists and engineers conducted more tests and equipped the first battleships with consar travel capability, he decided to use the time to see the sights in the Mendo-Zueger star system. It was a very educational and eye-opening experience for him, giving him a much better understanding of the history of the Mendoken civilization and their way of life.

He visited the planets Lind and Draefarel, followed by a brief tour of Kaurpa and Nees. He was even taken close to the giant Mendo-Zueger sun itself, on board a ship specifically designed to withstand tremendous heat. Different Mendoken accompanied him on the various tours, based on an itinerary put together by an assistant of Osalya's.

The most interesting place for him turned out to be the main Museum of Mendoken History on Draefarel. He saw displays providing detailed, graphic accounts of the evolution of the Mendoken species, from small, amphibious creatures in Draefarel's marshes to the highly intelligent, mechanized creatures that they were today. He was also exposed to a full history of the major events in Mendoken history, including their greatest inventions, internal struggles, and the wars they had fought with other species. Some of the highlights included the following:

The single most important event in history responsible for the existing Mendoken way of life was the Great War of Origins over 2 billion years ago. It was an internal fight, the culmination of a longtime conflict between the two largest nations of Mendoken, at a time when all Mendoken were still living on Draefarel. Not just a military confrontation, it was also a war of words and ideas.

The Korast ultimately prevailed, the nation known for its focus on justice, discipline and technology. With a strong group of charismatic leaders at the helm, they eventually defeated the Brandt, whose citizens, plagued by lawlessness, crime, corruption and a tyrannical government, in the end turned against their own rulers and joined the Korast.

Over time, all the national boundaries on Draefarel fell, once the Korast had convinced all Mendoken that their vision of life had the most potential for success and prosperity. A hierarchical, democratic society encompassing the whole planet was founded, a culture based on peace and order, coupled with the pursuit of science and technology. Julan Baling, one of the Korast's leaders, was named the first Imgoerin of the hierarchy. Under his governance, the Universal Charter was written, to serve as the fundamental code of life for all Mendoken from that point forward.

It was only after the creation of this Charter, and the subsequent unity of all Mendoken, that the species really progressed into an advanced society. Shortly thereafter, they began traveling into space, exploring and settling on other planets and moons, building ships and space stations, and meeting other life forms from distant worlds. Within the span of a few hundred thousand years, they developed into the powerful, sophisticated civilization that they now are.

The original version of the Universal Charter was forever inscribed in stone at the museum. Marc saw it, with several key excerpts translated to him by his tour guide. One particular inscription really touched his heart. It was simple and to the point, in true Mendoken style:

"Be it known that our goal in life is not to compete or fight with each other, or for some to attain success or prosperity at the expense of others. It is to work together for the greater good of all Mendoken. Every one of us shall be cared for, and every one of us shall have a role to play in the advancement of our civilization."

To this day, Marc was told by his tour guide, all Mendoken followed the law of the Charter to the letter. There was no such thing as crime in their society, as nobody ever broke the law.

"Unbelievable!" he thought, left wondering whether humans would ever reach that level of intellect and discipline, or indeed if they would ever want to. Humans did, after all, have a stronger sense of individuality and personal freedom, and generally a far weaker sense of selflessness and consideration toward their fellow citizens.

Another memorable sight for him was the seat of power on Lind. Endless rows of massive black buildings that rocketed straight up into the sky made up the heart of the governmental city, widely spread across the gray flatlands that the planet was known for. He was taken in a high-speed vehicle that flew very fast at close range between the buildings, giving him a thrill ride similar to that of a roller coaster.

The Imgoerin's palace turned out to be a disappointment, nothing more than a simple apartment at the top level of one of the tall buildings. Marc wasn't even shown inside. The Imgoerin wasn't there at the time and, according to the tour guide, there was nothing worth seeing anyway. The Mendoken, as Marc learned, really placed no value on luxury or pleasure. Everything was based on function and duty, at every level of the hierarchy.

Much to his delight, given his own preference for good hygiene, all the places he went to were exceptionally clean and tidy. They weren't necessarily aesthetically pleasing or pretty to look at, just remarkably well organized and neatly arranged.

On the fourth day, he was taken to one of the 300 space stations around Lind. There, he met up with Sibular, who was overseeing the first consar travel preparation of a battleship.

Standing together on a platform on board the space station, they stared through the transparent walls at the vessel docked outside. Roughly the same shape as the ship that had brought Marc to the Mendo-Zueger system, it was larger and had more extensions around its hull. The extensions gave the ship a somewhat meaner look.

"What type is it?" Marc asked. "What is the purpose of all those extensions?"

"It is a Kril-4 battlecruiser," Sibular replied. "It is designed specifically for large scale battles. The extensions you see house many of the weapons systems this ship carries. The one that brought you here from your planet was a Euma-9, a surveillance vessel."

There was a lot of activity on the platform, with many vehicles carrying goods into the vessel through the wide docking ports. There was also a constant flow of Mendoken traveling into and out of the ship.

"How many of these ships are going?" Marc asked.

"No more than three, since this is a first attempt."

"No planet destroyers, eh?"

"That will be in a subsequent attack, if this one is successful and the enemy chooses to strike back with increased force. Planet destroyers are only used as an absolute last resort. So you are firm in your decision?"

"Yes."

It had taken a while to reach this tough choice, as tough as the one Marc had taken not to return to Earth. He knew the risks, including possible death, but now he was firm. He was ready to do his part to help in the war effort. And if something went wrong with the consar mechanism while the ships were in flight, perhaps he would be able to help fix the problem. Ever since his success in reproducing his experiments for the Mendoken, he was feeling a lot more confident about his own skills.

Marc also felt very comfortable around Sibular, finding him to be quite understanding and easy to talk to, more so than any of the other Mendoken he had met. As the de facto leading Mendoken expert on consar travel, Sibular had been chosen to be a part of this mission. And that was just one more reason for Marc to tag along.

Standing on the platform and staring out at the Kril-4 ship they would shortly board, the two of them were soon deeply engaged in a conversation on the creation of the universe.

"So you Mendoken actually don't believe in the concept of a big bang?" Marc asked, remembering what his tour guide on Draefarel had mentioned to him.

"Brrrrrrrrrrrrrrrrr, it is not that simple, Marc," Sibular replied. "It is also not a question of belief. We do not really 'believe' in things. We acknowledge things based on scientific, proven facts."

"Very well, so what exactly are the proven facts?"

"What your people call the 'Big Bang' was not really a big bang. It was more of a little bang."

Marc couldn't help chuckling. "Okay fine, let's call it the 'Little Bang!' But it was a bang, right?"

"Technically, no. More of a vibration."

"Whoa! You've lost me now."

"It is a hard concept to understand initially, but the entire universe, as you see it around you in its 3 dimensions, is the manifestation of a single, slow and very long vibration."

Marc scratched his head. "A vibration that started as a result of what? And does that mean it expands initially, then contracts back to its original state?"

"Think of this universe as one of many. These different universes oscillate against each other, some expanding as the others contract. Right now ours is expanding – it has been for the past 13 billion years. According to our current calculations, it will begin contracting in another 8 billion years. Depending on the expansion of its neighboring universes, it may contract all the way down to the size of a single atom, or it may just contract to the size it is at right now. Although we can fairly accurately predict the length of time a universe expands or contracts, the amount of expansion and contraction appears to be completely random. Even our most sophisticated computers have not been able to devise an algorithm which models the behavior correctly."

"What proof do you have that this is true?"

"There is plenty of theoretical and practical evidence. Here is a simple one to begin with. According to your people, how old is the universe?"

"About 13 billion years – what you said the time of expansion has been."

"That would lead to the conclusion that no particle in the universe is older than 13 billion years, correct? Whereas the universe is filled with plenty of matter that is older than 400 billion years."

Marc whistled in surprise. He decided not to ask what mechanism the Mendoken used to date matter, since he wasn't sure he would even understand the explanation. Not that it mattered anyway. Whatever mechanism they used, it was unlikely to be so hugely inaccurate that it couldn't distinguish between 13 billion and 400 billion years.

Sibular went on. "What your scientists think was the 'Big Bang' was actually the beginning of the current expansion. In the previous oscillation, it had contracted all the way to the size of a single collection of infinitely dense particles." He paused for a moment. "Another proof of multiple universes oscillating against each other is that matter consistently travels between them when one contracts and the other expands."

Marc raised his eyebrows. "Really? You mean you can travel into other universes?"

"*We* cannot – we do not have the technology yet to travel fast enough to reach the edge of this universe within any reasonable amount of time. Although perhaps consar travel will change that, if it is legalized after the war is over. There are reasons why it is currently not permitted, as you have probably heard. But we do observe matter at the outer edges of our universe flowing in and out of its boundaries, mostly flowing in as it is currently expanding."

"Amazing! You can actually see as far as the edge of the universe? What does the boundary look like?"

"It looks like nothing, as if there is nothing but empty space beyond the boundary. But we know there is something, because only at the boundary do entire galaxies, quasars and other objects suddenly appear and disappear. That happens nowhere else within the universe."

"It's not another silupsal filter, is it?" Marc said jokingly. He thought it would indeed be ironic if some other, larger civilization had placed the entire universe within a filter of its own. It would prevent all within, including the Mendoken, from seeing what really was outside.

"Brrrrrrrrrrrrrrrrrrrrrrr," Sibular laughed, apparently understanding the joke. "That is amusing, Marc."

"How many universes are there anyway?" Marc asked, his curiosity growing more by the second. "And how long have these oscillations been going on? 400 billion years?"

"400 billion years is the age of our universe. New universes appear to be born all the time, while old ones eventually wither away to extinction after many oscillations. Our estimates indicate there to currently be at least 5.3 billion universes similar to ours. Those are only the universes that are in the same 3 dimensions as ours. Then there are universes in other dimensions. Those universes appear to have their own oscillation patterns as well. We do not know much about them, though, since studying other dimensions is forbidden along with consar travel."

"Does matter flow between our universe and those universes in other dimensions too?"

"Matter cannot freely flow between different dimensions, because matter in our 3 dimensions actually exists in all those different dimensions at the same time."

Marc scratched his head again, trying to remember all he knew about string theory and higher dimensions. Now what he was hearing took that whole concept a step further. "You're saying that everything in our universe exists in other dimensions too? In other universes?"

"Yes, but those universes may not look anything like ours. All the particles in your body, for example, are represented in other dimensions. But in those other dimensions, they will not necessarily combine to form a replica of you. In those other dimensions, your individual particles may be spread across millions of miles of space, belonging to other, separate life forms or objects altogether.

"That is why it is so difficult for anybody to attempt to travel into other dimensions, because, in a sense, that individual already exists in the other dimensions."

"But just not in the way he or she would like, eh?" Marc grinned. "How many other dimensions are there? I think current string theory on Earth indicates there are a total of 11 dimensions."

"There are many more, actually. We do not even know of a finite limit. If we were allowed to do more research in this area, perhaps we would find one." Sibular paused. "But this is what makes consar travel so unique and revolutionary, because it allows for matter in our 3 dimensions to travel through other dimensions in other universes, and arrive again completely intact at a different point within our 3 dimensional universe. It does so by maintaining a tunnel of our 3 dimensions throughout its path, never once directly exposing the traveling matter to the other dimensions."

Marc nodded, taking a moment to grasp everything he had just heard. Humans usually thought of the universe as the ultimate frontier, the end-all and be-all of everything. In reality, however, this universe was just one of billions, perhaps more. It was amazing to think how small and insignificant this made not just Earth, its solar system, or even its galaxy, but also the entire universe it was a part of. Were there galaxies of universes like there were galaxies of stars, were there clusters of those galaxies, and superclusters of those clusters? Not to mention all the other universes in the uncountable number of other dimensions. He wondered if there was ever any end, any final boundary. From everything Sibular had just told him, it seemed the Mendoken didn't know the answer to that question either.

So he decided to ask another question, one he hoped Sibular might have the answer for. "When did this all begin?"

"When did what begin?"

"All these universes, these oscillations, these dimensions? You said our universe is 400 billion years old. But how old is the oldest universe? When was the first universe formed?"

"Time itself is a function of each universe. Other universes have completely different definitions of time, so the question of 'when' cannot really be applied across multiple universes, especially not across universes in different dimensions."

"But what I mean is, is there a beginning, some point where it all began, started by somebody or something?"

"The Aftarans have a whole religious ideology that attributes all of creation to a supreme, divine entity. But we Mendoken do not acknowledge anything that cannot positively be established by scientific theory or verified by scientific observation."

"That's funny. On Earth, we have both types, those who believe in God and God's hand in creation, and those who believe purely in science and the random sequence of events that led to the existence of the universe. It's an ongoing debate that our society still has not found a totally convincing answer for."

"Which kind do you consider yourself to be?" Sibular asked.

"Somewhere in between, actually. Perhaps you could call me an agnostic. I don't deny the presence of a supreme creator, but I don't believe in a single religion, nor do I worship 'God.' I used to be a complete atheist once, but now I do acknowledge that just because I can't prove God's existence doesn't mean that God doesn't actually exist. Back on Earth, I never believed in aliens, because I couldn't scientifically prove that they existed. Yet here you all are."

Sibular was about to respond, when another Mendoken on a vehicle approached and announced that final preparations for launch were underway. It was time to enter the ship.

They boarded the vehicle, which headed down a pathway along the platform to one of the ship's gates. As Marc got a closer look at all the loading activity around him, something dawned on him for the first time.

"Sibular," he said, "how come you guys perform all this manual labor by yourselves? I mean, you have machinery and all, but there is always a Mendoken operating each device. You are so technologically advanced, yet I haven't seen a single robot or droid anywhere that could easily perform these tasks for you."

"Good question, Marc," Sibular said, as they passed through the gate into one of the ship's internal highways. "That was a conscious choice of our society long ago, never to tread the questionable path of artificial intelligence."

"Why? You all have mechanized body parts, don't you? Why not just build a whole body and brain? With the capabilities your people have, you could build the perfect robot in no time. My people have been struggling to build robots for many years now, but have gained little ground. If we had your knowledge and resources, we would have an entire army of robots by now.

"Think of how much work you could get them to do, more quickly and perfectly than you can do by yourselves. You could even shape them to look just like you, so much so that you couldn't tell the difference!"

"It appears that you have just answered your own question, Marc," Sibular said simply.

Had he? Marc thought about what he had just said. He had always believed in the advancement of science and technology, no matter what the cost. If people could keep acquiring knowledge with which to build bigger and better tools to help themselves, then that was a good thing. But the Mendoken, who had mastered this process far more effectively than humans had and would for centuries to come, had drawn a line. They would never invest in technology that had the potential to backfire on them. And artificial intelligence was a prime example. Why? Because if they really did build machines that were not only stronger and faster than them but could also think by themselves, what was to stop these machines from one day becoming independent and rebelling against their very creators? Laws? If they could think and evolve by themselves, what would prevent them from breaking the laws, or at least from interpreting the laws differently? Perhaps it would all result in a war that would turn the tide, and ultimately make the creators slaves to the created. Or perhaps they would just destroy each other completely.

This, Marc surmised, had to be one of the many tests that a species had to pass, before it could be accepted into the community of advanced civilizations. The Mendoken, of course, had passed it a long time ago. Whether humans would pass it or not still remained to be seen. The only certain thing was that the shroud around them would not be lifted until they did.

The vehicle glided along highways through the interior of the ship. This vessel didn't have a simulated city in the core, unlike the Euma-9 Marc had traveled on earlier. Instead, it was stocked up with smaller military vessels of all kinds. There were highly maneuverable fighters, disguised scout ships, heavy bombers and various types of troop transports. The ship was carrying an entire battle-ready fleet by itself, and an army of almost half a million well prepared soldiers to go along with it.

It was both frightening and comforting for Marc to see such awesome power. Frightening because of the devastation a single ship could unleash, and comforting because of the protection it would offer from the vicious enemy they were about to encounter.

Soon they arrived on the control deck of the ship, a deck with 20 levels and a fantastic, open view of space outside in all directions. They landed on the 12th level, where Marc was introduced to Tulla Froahee 51450093, the commander of the ship and of this mission. She wore a blue hat, just like Commander Maginder, and was a tad taller than most other Mendoken Marc had met so far. She didn't have her own translator device, but as Sibular explained to Marc, others could use the translator device he was carrying, as long as he allowed them to and as long as they were within the maximum coverage range of 100 feet. Translators were intentionally designed with this range limitation for privacy reasons.

"I am honored by your decision to join us on this historic mission, Mr. Zemin," Commander Tulla said.

"The honor is all mine," Marc replied right away.

"Our plan is to first fly out at normal speed, and then enter a consar once we have exited this star system. We will plot the path of the consar to lead us straight into the middle of Volonan territory, thereby taking their defenses completely by surprise. We will attack a few targets, and escape through a consar before they can pursue us. This will send them the message that we now have consar capability as well, and they no longer have an advantage in this war."

Marc felt a sudden hint of nervousness, remembering that this was the first time in his life that he was going into a major battle. But he had faith in the Mendoken. All he had learned of them so far seemed to indicate that they always knew exactly what they were doing. "What kind of, uh, targets are we talking about?" he asked.

"The Volona do not have any space stations," Commander Tulla replied. "Therefore, we will target their warships, similar to the ones that attacked you at Mendo-Bursal and destroyed the planet Kerding."

"What if they are expecting us?"

"That is why we are taking no fewer than three ships. If we are led into an ambush, we will be able to defend ourselves long enough to enter a consar and leave."

Marc and Sibular were shown to the new stations that had just been installed a few hours earlier on the fifth level of the control deck. These stations contained all the equipment that would control anything to do with consar travel. Sibular inspected everything in detail, making a few adjustments and conducting a few tests. His accompanying explanations helped Marc understand the basic setup.

"What is the actual physical distance in our dimensions?" Marc asked.

"82,000 light years," Sibular said. "Using our regular kilasic engines, it would take almost 2 months to cross it. But using the consar, we estimate no more than 57 minutes."

"That is awesome! This will do wonders for interstellar travel, eh?"

"Provided that it is ever officially permitted, yes."

"Well, the Volona already broke the ban, didn't they?"

"The Volona never pay heed to others. That is their trait. All they care about is themselves. But that does not mean the rest of us have to stoop to their level of morality. And believe me, it is not the only treaty they have broken. What makes their dishonesty even worse is that, to this day, they keep denying that they have consar capability."

"What! What about all the attacks on your planets and space stations?"

"They claim we are fabricating lies, so that we can attack them and take over their virtual worlds."

Another hour later, the ship was ready for departure. The docking ports receded into the station, and the gates were closed. Free to go, the ship began moving slowly into space using its auxiliary short range engine. Two other Kril-4 vessels also debarked from the space station and followed.

A seat had been made available for Marc on the deck, next to Sibular's post. He would have no separate quarters this time, since the time spent on the trip would be so short. The seat was very comfortable, allowing him to lean back and look up at the sky through the transparent ceiling.

After the three ships had reached a fair distance from the space station, their main kilasic engines took over. As the vessels accelerated together, Marc saw the space station instantly disappear from view and the planet Lind shrink to nothing more than a small dot on the horizon. Their destination was an empty section of space, right in between the Mendo-Zueger and Mendo-Palga systems. There, a consar would be opened that would take them straight into enemy territory.

Chapter 15

The Aftaran Dominion was generally lightly traveled, with many star systems completely uninhabited and some even unexplored. This was in sharp contrast to the Mendoken Republic, which had a far higher population spread across all its star systems, with a far larger number of ships traveling between them along busy segments of the Yuwa highway network. Anyone who knew even a little about the two civilizations and their ways of life would not be surprised by this disparity. The difference in population aside, Aftarans were generally more reclusive and spiritual than the Mendoken, spending their time meditating and praying in seclusion instead of traveling. The Mendoken, on the other hand, were much more community based, with a significantly stronger focus on exploration, collaboration and technological advancement.

Located at the very far end of the Dominion, the Afta-Johran system was lightly traveled even by Aftaran standards. None of its planets or moons was considered hospitable, and no Aftaran had ever attempted to settle here. The only alien civilization ever known to have existed in this system had once lived on the planet Tibara. But they had been gone for billions of years, leaving no clue behind as to what calamity had eradicated them. Since then, all had been quiet.

For the past couple of years, however, a few Aftaran ships had been patrolling this star system, especially the area around Tibara. Their purpose was to keep sending out surveyors to find and destroy Autamrin and his followers, who were believed to be hiding somewhere on Tibara. Lord Wazilban couldn't afford to send more than a few lightly armed ships to find Autamrin, mainly because the Aftar didn't have that many ships with heavy weaponry to begin with, and those which they did have were already engaged in fighting the Phyrax.

The Roxay that was carrying Dumyan and Sharjam had been en route now for five days. The flock of Roxays had not raised any alarm among Wazilban's ships or attracted any surveyors, just as Dumyan had hoped. For these creatures, traveling nonstop for that amount of time through empty space was no problem whatsoever. In fact, they could easily keep on flying for up to a month. But for Dumyan and his brother, it was an entirely different story. Burrowed deep behind the folded wings of the Roxay, they couldn't afford to move even an inch, for fear that their unknowing host might sense their presence. More importantly, though, they were running out of breathable air, the precious little air that was trapped in the folds of their magical robes.

Although Aftarans had the ability to withstand hardships unimaginable to humans, this long trip through space without basic life support was becoming too much even for someone as sturdy as Dumyan. At this rate, he didn't think he would be able to survive longer than a few more hours. Whether his brother was still alive, he didn't know. There was no way to communicate with him, nor could he see him. The view of the other wing was completely blocked by the Roxay's bulky body.

Dumyan was inhaling sparingly now, trying to reduce the amount of oxygen he was consuming. He felt weak and drowsy, even more so whenever he remembered that he had neither eaten nor drunk anything for the past five days. Trying hard to stay awake, he stared ahead through the transparent section of the robe that was covering his eyes. He knew that if he fell asleep, he would no longer have any control over his breathing pattern. He would run out of air even sooner, and once he did, he would never wake up again.

By now, he was beginning to regret his decision to leave Tibara. He should have listened to Sharjam, who had rightly insisted that this escape plan was a crazy idea. Not only would his life soon be over, he would also be responsible for his younger brother's death, the same brother who really hadn't wanted to come on this adventure in the first place. He had been too foolhardy, too impulsive, and too optimistic about his chances of success. Now he would pay the price with his own life and his brother's. Any hope their dear father and his love Birshat had for a future beyond the caves of Tibara would forever be lost.

Yet there was a glimmer of hope, for it was clear now where the Roxays were headed. A blue planet lay in front, growing ever larger in his vision as they approached it. Known as Droila, it was the fourth planet in the Afta-Johran star system. According to Aftaran records, it was an ocean covered planet with no land mass and with no signs of civilization. There was some marine life – mostly fishlike creatures, but that was about it.

Dumyan wasn't sure why the Roxays were heading for this planet. Perhaps there were some recently formed volcanoes jutting out of the ocean where they could land, offering them a fresh supply of hot rocks. Perhaps whatever plant life there was on the planet wouldn't affect the Roxays, since all the plants were underwater. He wondered if his more scholarly brother knew. If only they could talk to each other right now! Actually, he just hoped that his brother was still alive.

The planet's surface was still far away. At the speed they were traveling, it would take several hours to reach the edge of the atmosphere. Dumyan doubted he had several more hours of air left. But all he could do was patiently wait. He kept getting weaker and weaker, and the urge to sleep grew stronger and stronger. He tried his utmost to fight it for as long as he could, but eventually he gave up and felt his eyes close. Within a second, he was unconscious.

When Sharjam awoke, he had no sense of where he was at first. Perhaps he was dead, he thought, and had finally reached eternal bliss. But then he opened his eyes, and realized how far from bliss he was. The first thing he felt was pain in his eyes, thanks to the torrential, steady rain hitting his face. He sat up, trying his best to overcome both weakness and dizziness. There was no doubt about it – he was alive. And given his surroundings, it was obvious he was on the surface of Droila. He didn't know how he had survived those last few hours with almost no air left in his cloak, just as the Roxay had begun its descent towards the planet's surface. The beginning of the descent was the very last thing he could remember. After that, he must have blacked out.

The environment was even worse than he had imagined. He had known about Droila's constant rain, something he had once read about a long time ago. But actually experiencing it was a different feeling altogether. All he could see around him were endless streams of water falling from the sky. It was impossible to make out anything beyond 40 feet or so, no matter which way he looked. His robe was completely drenched, as were the feathers on his face. The rain was cold, though luckily not nearly as cold as the ice back on Tibara.

He uttered a short prayer of thanks for being alive, and then began to survey his surroundings. He was sitting on some kind of rock. Its texture was like that of flowing liquid, so it had to be lava that had recently solidified. The sound of splashing waves to his left indicated the ocean wasn't too far away, even though he couldn't see that far. He surmised that he was on the side of an active volcano, one that had probably only recently surfaced above the ocean. The Roxays must have landed here to roost and eat. But where were they? And, more importantly, where was Dumyan?

Lowering the veil around his face, he called for his brother. "Dumyan!" But his voice was easily drowned out by the hammering rain.

"Dumyan!" he called again, this time at the top of his lungs. Then he listened intently for any response. The owl-like ears of Aftarans had over 10 times the hearing capacity of human ears. They could hear the faintest sounds miles away.

Sure enough, Sharjam heard a faint, muffled sound, somewhere up ahead. He got up and started walking in that direction. Immediately he felt a sharp pain in his left leg. Lifting his robe, he noticed a wound on his left shin. It must have happened when he had fallen of the Roxay during the landing. It didn't look too bad, so he decided not to pay attention to it for the time being. There were more important things to worry about.

The rock surface was both jagged and slippery, and tilted sharply upwards the more he hobbled ahead. It was also starting to feel warmer, indicating that he was nearing the top of the active volcano. He stumbled and fell several times on the uneven surface, wincing in pain every time his wounded shin hit a rock. He called Dumyan's name again, and this time the response was louder. He was getting closer! Finally, he reached a ledge on the steep, rocky slope. His brother was lying there on his back, absolutely still.

"Dumyan! Are you alright?" Sharjam was highly relieved to find him alive.

"Yes, but I cannot move," Dumyan whispered weakly. "I believe I broke my hip."

Sharjam carefully unwrapped the section of Dumyan's robe around the hip. It was indeed broken. He quickly covered the hip with both his hands, closed his eyes and whispered a short prayer. There was a momentary flash of light around his hands and Dumyan's hip. This enchantment wouldn't cure the broken hip, but at least it would accelerate the natural healing.

Next, he took out a small pouch of yellow powder from inside his robe. He emptied the contents onto his hand, and formed a cup-like shape with his palm and long fingers to collect some rainwater. The powder dissolved in the water, forming the invaluable rauka drink that gave instant strength. He then moved his hand to Dumyan's face, and gently emptied the liquid into his mouth.

As he swallowed the bitter liquid in small gulps, Dumyan began looking better right away. "Drink some yourself," he said to Sharjam, his voice still hoarse.

"No," Sharjam said. "We need to ration the supplies we have."

"We haven't eaten in days. Drink a little at least. We both need strength to continue our quest."

Sharjam knew his brother was right. He took out another pouch, emptied only half of it onto his hand, collected some rainwater, and drank the rauka. Right away he felt the strength flow into his veins.

"So where are the Roxays?" Sharjam wondered aloud, packing the pouch back inside his robe.

"I think we are very near the top of the volcano," Dumyan said. "They are probably inside the crater. I can hear them screech every now and then. I am surprised they did not kill us when they saw us during the landing. Those nasty beasts!"

"We need to keep our voices down, in case they hear us," Sharjam said quietly. "They might not have noticed us. We probably fell off our carrier Roxay's back before they all landed inside the volcano." He paused for a few seconds, before adding, "It is ironic to hear you call them beasts, though, considering it was your idea to ride on them."

"Well, we did get off Tibara, did we not?" Dumyan retorted, keeping his voice low. "And we are alive."

"Alive thanks to the Creator, not to you! And stuck in even more perilous conditions than on Tibara. You do realize we are completely surrounded by endless ocean, do you not? How do you propose to get off this place?"

"Would you rather we stayed on Tibara till Wazilban's surveyors tore us apart?"

"And would you rather we die a slower, more painful death here, with no food or shelter and no end of torrential rain? Not to mention that it is only a matter of time before those dratted Roxays notice us."

"We are our father's only hope. We must continue our quest!"

"Yes, and now not only is he without our protection, there is no way out for us from this forsaken planet!"

The argument continued, one of countless quarrels that these two brothers had engaged in since their early childhoods. They got so engrossed in it that neither of them realized how much their voices were rising. That changed, however, as soon as they noticed a shadow approaching through the rain from the crater above. As it got closer, the screeches got louder, and its silhouette became more distinct. It was a Roxay.

Sharjam froze, realizing what he and his brother had done. Soon he could make out the creature's ugly head, its tentacles sticking out in preparation for attack. They had disturbed its peace, and now they would pay the price. As expected, other Roxays had heeded its call, and were soon following behind it.

"Sharjam!" Dumyan yelled. "A hupee plant, quick!"

Sharjam stared at the approaching Roxays. "I... I cannot concentrate," he stammered nervously. Any enchantment required concentration, and he was too overtaken with fear at the moment to concentrate.

"Then run!"

"Not with you in this state." Sharjam took out his boryal weapon, and without hesitation pointed it upwards and fired. A red flame shot up, heading straight for the sky at first, but then curving downwards like a projectile towards the nearest Roxay. The creature, which was now only a few feet away from the Aftarans, was hit by the flame just before it reached them. There was a loud explosion, followed by pieces of the creature flying off in every direction. Sharjam had to duck to avoid being hit by some of the body parts.

Dumyan's face was filled with fear. "Are you sure that was a good idea?"

As soon as the other Roxays further behind saw what had happened, they screeched even louder, doubling their speed for attack. Now there would be no mercy whatsoever, if there had been any possibility for mercy before.

"There was no choice," Sharjam replied. He put his boryal inside his robe, and slipped both his hands under his brother's injured body. He lifted him up onto his back and stood up. It wasn't easy, though. He almost lost his balance on the steep slope.

Dumyan yelled in pain. "What are you doing?"

"What does it look like?" Sharjam was panting, making a dash down the slope as fast as he could.

Dumyan held on to Sharjam's shoulders with all his strength. "Leave me here!" he insisted. "I am slowing you down! We will both get killed like this."

Sharjam didn't respond, focusing on the wet, slippery trail in front of him instead. As much as he hated his brother for getting him into this mess, he was never going to leave him here to die. He was counting on the one redeeming feature of this planet to keep them alive, at least for a while longer – the fact that it was almost completely covered by water. Roxays couldn't swim, as far as he knew, and they most likely wouldn't venture into the ocean after them. If he could only make it in time!

The Roxays were catching up fast, flapping their wings to fly down the slope. Sharjam almost fell a few times, but his instinct for survival just kept him going.

"You have got to go faster!" Dumyan shouted. "The nearest Roxay is upon us!"

"You want to switch places?" Sharjam gasped, almost completely out of breath.

The sound of the ocean's waves was getting louder over the constant noise of the raindrops. And ahead, Sharjam could just make out the coastline. But as he got closer, he realized it wasn't really a coastline – it was a cliff, with a sharp drop to the ocean below. He thought of using his wings, but realized he wouldn't be able to with Dumyan on his back.

"Hold on tight!" Sharjam shouted. With that, he sped up and leaped off the edge of the cliff.

At the same time, the nearest Roxay made a lunge for them with its tentacles, but missed them by inches. It was about to strike again, but once it saw its prey falling into the ocean below, abruptly stopped. Flapping its wings and letting out an ear-piercing screech, it lifted into the air. The other Roxays further behind also followed suit. As Sharjam had hoped, the Roxays had no desire to follow him and his brother into the ocean.

After a drop of over 60 feet, the Aftarans splashed into the water with full force. The impact wasn't as much of a shock as Sharjam had expected, perhaps because being in such drenching rain was almost like being underwater anyway. Nonetheless, it was still a shock.

"Haaaaaaaahhhhh!" Dumyan shrieked. "It is cold!"

"Yes!" Sharjam exclaimed in between gulps of water. "But at least... glub... there are no... glub... Roxays here!"

But what now, he wondered? How could they get off this planet? It was too risky to try to use the Roxays again. Not only would those beasts be on their guard, it was unlikely he and his brother would be able to survive another trip through space like that in their weakened state.

With Dumyan still on his back, Sharjam tried swimming away from the volcano island, hoping to increase their distance from the Roxays. But he was very weak, and the ocean very stormy. Towering waves crashed onto them, one after the other. Before long, he couldn't find any more strength to move his arms or legs. He let go of Dumyan and motioned to him to take over, but Dumyan wasn't able to swim for more than a few feet before the pain in his hip became unbearable.

They were both stranded, and as the strength in their limbs completely subsided, they began sinking underwater. With their magical robes wrapped around their mouths and noses, they wouldn't have to worry about breathing underwater, at least for some time. But what hope did they have of surviving, let alone continuing their quest, once they had sunk to the bottom of the ocean?

As the two brothers helplessly descended into the depths of the sea, Sharjam could see different kinds of marine life around him – fishlike creatures of various shapes, sizes and colors. Most of these creatures seemed not to notice the two new strangers. But suddenly they all swam away, as if in fright.

Soon it became clear why. A large shadow was approaching from the distance – a kind of sea monster. It looked ugly and big, uglier and bigger than a Roxay. One gigantic eye covered the top of its face, and huge, sharp teeth gleamed inside its open mouth. Its body appeared to be snake-like, stretching for many feet behind the head. And it seemed to have identified its meal for the day.

Sharjam instinctively took out his boryal, before remembering that boryals did not work well underwater. He stared at the approaching sea monster, its mouth large enough to engulf both of them in one sweep. He desperately tried to think of an enchantment that would save them, but knew he wouldn't have enough time to concentrate. This time, he thought, their lives really were over.

But then, some kind of wave from the right suddenly swept the sea monster away from them with tremendous force. The monster thrashed about in vain, trying to fight the wave. But the wave kept pushing it further and further away. Before long, the creature had disappeared from sight.

Sharjam wondered where that wave had come from. He didn't have to wait long. A bright white light appeared to the right, coming closer and eventually stopping in front of the Aftarans. Carrying the light was an underwater vehicle, cubic in shape, roughly 15 feet in length, width and height. A number of jagged spikes were sticking out from the top.

A mechanical arm with a small platform at the end extended outwards from the front of the vehicle. The platform stopped right below the Aftarans, allowing them to stand on it. A railing then extended up from the bottom, enclosing them and making sure they wouldn't fall off the platform. With that, the vehicle began moving again, carrying its passengers in front.

Unable to communicate underwater, Sharjam looked at his brother in bewilderment. He wondered who was driving this vehicle that had saved their lives, or where they were being taken. It just kept moving silently, heading downwards into the dark depths of the ocean.

Chapter 16

The three Kril-4 battlecruisers reached the consar entry point within 2 hours. The view outside was quite bare in this part of space, especially compared to the heavy traffic around Lind. There were no other ships about, or any planets, moons or space stations nearby. The only things visible to the naked eye were the usual stars glittering in the distance.

The ships had slowed down to well below the speed of light. On the deck, there were several Mendoken next to Sibular, all busily operating the consar instruments.

"Here we go," Sibular announced calmly, pressing an icon on one of the 3D screens in the air.

Marc gazed at the lower section of the ship, jutting out for miles below the upper section that he was on. The surface lit up in brilliant white, and ahead in space a wide, blue circle began forming. The blue circle grew in thickness into a sphere, quickly encompassing the whole ship. A similar blue sphere was forming around each of the other two ships as well. Soon all three ships were completely covered by the spheres.

"It's working, right?" Marc asked nervously.

"So far," Sibular replied. "Hold on to your seat, as you may feel the pull of gravity during entry. It will be stronger than the ship's anti-gravity stabilizers." As he finished speaking, he dropped from his regular floating stance to the floor. All the other Mendoken on the deck dropped to the floor as well.

Marc squinted to see past the transparent lining of the sphere. It looked like a vortex was forming in the distance, a tunnel into a different dimension. The tunnel entrance grew rapidly in size, soon becoming larger than the sphere. It looked scary, like a monstrous whirlpool of different colors flowing into the center.

"What have I done?" he thought, his eyes filled with fear as he looked at the gaping mouth ahead. "Why didn't I go back home? This is suicide!"

But it was too late for regrets. Suddenly the sphere lunged forward, carrying the ship and all its occupants with it into the tunnel entrance. Marc was pushed into his seat with tremendous force, as if a 1 ton rock had just landed on him. He could barely keep his eyes open, thinking he was going to pass out at any second. All the Mendoken on the deck were somehow still standing upright, fastened by some invisible, magnetic-like force to the floor.

Into the consar tunnel they went. Once they were inside, the gravitational pull reduced considerably, allowing Marc to relax a little and look around. The walls of the tunnel were filled with random outlines of different colors, constantly changing shape and size. The space within was filled with bands of thin matter that seemed to drift right through the sphere and through the interior of the ship. Fortunately they did not appear to cause any damage to the ship or its inhabitants.

"Is the ship holding?" Marc asked.

"Yes, everything appears normal," Sibular said, closely monitoring the screens in front of him. "We are on course, with another 53 minutes to go through the consar."

"And the other ships?"

"They are right behind us. No issues so far."

Marc was only too glad to hear that. "Where exactly are we going to exit?"

Sibular opened a map on one of the 3D screens, displaying a zoomed-in section of the Volonan Empire. A vortex in the center of the map indicated the exit point of the consar. "Right near the edge of the Volo-Gaviera system, which contains several highly populated planets. The Volonans guard it quite heavily, as it houses a planet that is one of the main sources of purania."

"Of what?"

"*Purania*. One of the densest materials in the entire galaxy. It is the prime substance they use to generate and maintain their virtual worlds. The technology they have developed around it really is unique and interesting."

"Ah! So it must be highly precious for them." Marc had to agree that it made sense to hit the Volona right near the source of their most prized possession, just to show them that they too were now vulnerable.

A short period of silence followed, during which he thought more about the enemy they were about to face. "What do you think will happen if we are captured?" he finally asked.

"The chances of that happening are very slim," Sibular said frankly. "If our mission really does fail, the likelihood of us being destroyed is much higher. The

Volona are not known for taking prisoners, Marc. They are highly protective of their virtual worlds, and do not like to share them with anybody."

"How did they become like this? Why do they prefer to live in dreams that aren't true?"

"To be honest, we do not really know. They surely have a long history, just like we do. But by the time we made initial contact with them 1.7 billion years ago, they were already a completely virtual society. They are highly secretive and sinister by nature, and hardly ever share anything about themselves or their past with us.

"Our theory is that it is a result of one or more catastrophes inflicted upon them, either by themselves, by outsiders or by natural forces. Their efforts to live in reality may have ended up in pain and suffering, which eventually caused them to retreat into virtual worlds where they could live their lives in peace.

"But peaceful as a species they most certainly are not. Although we do not know how they treat each other, we do know that they have no ethical rules when dealing with other species. They trust nobody, and always see the worst intentions in any move we or any other species make. They continuously accuse us of wanting to take over their virtual worlds, a completely false claim. We have no interest in living lives of lies.

"Their distrust of others has made them highly belligerent. In reality, they are the ones never to be trusted. So many treaties with us they have broken, so many times they have invaded our space. So many billions of lives lost on both sides over the years, just because of their senseless paranoia."

Marc listened carefully to everything Sibular was saying. As interesting as the concept of virtual worlds was, the more he learned about the Volona, the more he hoped he would never have to meet any of them in person. "How do they operate as a society if they always live in virtual worlds?" he wondered aloud. "Who mans their ships? Who protects their borders? Who does anything?"

"As far as we know, they run their society from within their virtual worlds. A Volonan ship, for example, will have a crew. But each individual in the crew lives in his or her own virtual world. The captain may be in a completely different place, living a completely different virtual life than the first officer, even though they are both physically on the same ship."

Marc was totally confused. "But how can they possibly run the ship like that? How can they make any decisions based on, well, anything?"

"That is the most interesting thing about their virtual technology. Most individuals do have a real role or job, but each individual can choose to live whatever virtual life he or she wants. Every action that individual takes, every decision he or she makes, is automatically translated from his or her virtual world to reality. Similarly, anything that happens to that individual in reality is translated back to some event in that individual's virtual world.

"Take the example of the captain. Her ship is under attack by an enemy vessel, and she gives the order to strike back. In her virtual world, she may be living in a tropical paradise, where she owns and manages a hotel. The attack will be translated to an event in her virtual world, such as a competing hotel that has begun construction nearby. Her order to strike back, therefore, will be based on a decision she takes in her virtual world."

As bizarre as it all sounded, Marc thought he was beginning to understand. "Such as improving the quality of her own hotel, or increasing the marketing budget? Or perhaps something more mischievous, such as a buyout of the construction company to halt construction of the other hotel?"

"Yes, something like that. Perhaps even a step further, depending on her personality. She might choose to sabotage the foundations of the new building, for example."

"And the captain's first officer will likely be her assistant manager at the hotel in her virtual world, right? Even though the first officer himself may be living in a completely different virtual world of his own?"

"Correct."

"How can they possibly automate all those translations and keep track of everything? That would have to be some amazing technology!"

"From what we know, it is," Sibular said. "But no technology is perfect. Anomalies in these translations may have contributed to many of the misunderstandings we have had with the Volona." With that, he shifted his attention back to the consar monitoring instruments.

The tunnel outside appeared to grow darker, and the peculiar bands of matter everywhere grew thicker and more numerous. But the spheres containing the ships remained intact, gliding down the passage as sure-footedly as if they did this everyday.

The time passed slowly, very slowly. It almost seemed like an eternity to Marc. He kept looking at his watch every minute. 37 minutes had passed since entry, then 38, then 39, then at last 40. 17 minutes to go! Around him, all the Mendoken were standing still, their bodies planted firmly on the floor. Some were monitoring the ship's functions and making sure everything was running smoothly, but nobody was floating around.

The tunnel's walls slowly began lighting up again in a mix of different colors, and the bands of matter thinned out. Right on the 57th minute, the spheres exited the consar and decelerated. The tunnel exit, an exact mirror image of the entrance, quickly disappeared as the spheres faded away, leaving the ships to fend for themselves back in regular space.

It had worked flawlessly. They had just traveled 80,000 light years in less than an hour! The smile that swept across Marc's face went all the way from one ear to the other. He had directly contributed to the success of this pioneering consar voyage.

The smile didn't last very long, however, for he remembered that they were now in the middle of hostile enemy territory. He looked around to see if he could spot anything. Billions of stars were twinkling in the distance. One of the stars above appeared much bigger and closer than the others, glowing brilliantly in the sky. Volo-Gaviera, no doubt. Far away to the left, he could see a large planet. It was uniformly orange in color, like a painted sphere. A thick, gray cloud of dust could be seen to the right.

None of this indicated anything unusual or worrisome. But the barrier blocking the path ahead was a different story altogether. Ships, ships, ships, in all directions! Spread apart in a grid-like pattern, they were covering a seemingly unending, vertical sheet of space. No matter how high up or to the sides he looked, there were just more ships. They all appeared identical, similar to the ones that had destroyed the planet Kerding. Most of them were bright red in color, but others were blue, green or yellow. Volonans clearly had a preference for bright colors.

After seeing the barrier, Marc no longer felt smug about the awesome power of the Kril-4 battlecruiser he was on. The Mendoken, however, seemed far from concerned, as the battlecruiser was heading straight towards the gigantic fleet of enemy ships.

"Um, Sibular, is this really a good idea?" he asked, the fear in him rising as they drew closer.

"They are not expecting us," Sibular said. "The ships in the barrier are actually facing the other way, blocking the entrance to the star system." He was floating now, monitoring the screens and making adjustments. All other Mendoken were also floating about again, busily preparing for the attack. Commander Tulla was on the level above, giving out final orders.

"So we are actually inside the star system?" Marc asked.

"Yes," Sibular replied.

Smart, and sneaky! The Mendoken were about to give the Volona a taste of their own medicine of deception. As long as it worked, he thought. But how long before they were detected?

Not too long, it turned out. Some of the ships in the barrier began turning around.

"Hold on to your seat, Marc," Sibular said. "The attack begins."

The three Mendoken ships were advancing together now. Just as the first Volonan ships had finished turning, the Mendoken ships fired. Thousands of torpedoes were released from the lower hull of each ship, each one making for a different Volonan ship. Like shooting stars, they raced through the sky towards their targets. Made with the same kilasic technology that made space travel possible, the damage they could inflict was enormous.

Within a few seconds, the torpedoes hit the Volonan ships. Like Sibular had said, the Volonans were not prepared for an attack from the inside of the star system. The barrier evidently had no inward facing shield, only one facing the outside. Entire sections of some of the Volonan ships blew up, showering the sky with dazzling explosions. Several other ships blew up completely, sending specks of dust flying every which way.

Volonan ships that had not been hit began firing back. Instead of sending torpedoes, they shot laser-like streaks of light that hit the Mendoken ships almost instantly.

The ship Marc was on shook violently with each impact, but there didn't appear to be any damage.

"Our shields are holding," Sibular said calmly.

Relief! But only for the moment. The next phase of the battle was about to begin. Some of the Volonan ships in the grid were now moving, heading straight for the Mendoken ships. As they did so, they began releasing hundreds of smaller vessels from their hulls. The sky ahead looked like a big swarm of bees, about to take the invaders by storm.

But the Mendoken were prepared for this onslaught. Large gates opened up in the lower section of each of the three battlecruisers, releasing fighters, scout ships, heavy bombers and many other types of attack craft. They all accelerated rapidly, some of them heading straight for the approaching swarm of enemy fighters. Others flanked outwards, following a semi-circular route that would allow them to strike the enemy from the sides.

The two armies of smaller ships clashed with full force, engaging in a vicious battle that Marc could clearly observe from the deck. Uncountable flashes of light appeared all over, each one the result of an explosion. Shots were being fired everywhere, with some fighters chasing others in formations of three or more, while others were flying toward each other on collision courses. The heavier Mendoken bombers were shooting down several small Volonan fighters at a time, while other Volonan vessels that looked like long tubes were destroying everything in their vicinity using some kind of shock wave.

"You should stay seated, Marc," Sibular said from a distance.

Marc looked down and noticed that he was standing. In awe of the ongoing battle outside, he had risen and moved closer to the edge of the deck without even realizing it.

"Come back and sit down," Sibular called, still standing at his station. "Things will get a little bumpy here shortly."

Marc hurried back and sat down, knowing not to doubt Sibular's words. A belt immediately slithered out from the side of the seat and secured him in place.

And none too soon, it turned out. Suddenly the ship swerved sharply to the right, crushing him to the left side of the seat. Then it swerved downwards, before abruptly rising up again. These swerves continued, one after the other.

Between his gasps and a rising wave of nausea, he looked out and saw the cause. There were two large Volonan warships approaching at high speed behind them, and another one was closing in from above. The one coming from above looked the scariest, as if it was going to crash through the transparent ceiling of the deck at any second. More and more warships were dislodging from the barrier and approaching from the front, firing a barrage of laser-like shots at the three Mendoken ships.

There was also something else the Volonan ships were trying to do. They were splitting up into groups of three, each group trying to form a perfect triangle. And then he remembered what had happened at Mendo-Bursal. The Volona's deadliest weapon, unleashed only when three of their warships formed a perfect triangle, was about to be launched against them. And that was why the Mendoken ships were swerving so much, trying to evade that target lock. But with so many more Volonan ships approaching, this evasion procedure was going to get progressively more difficult.

"How are we going to fight so many of them?" Marc asked, not at all happy with how this attack was going.

"Not to worry," Sibular said calmly. "This was expected. We have a plan."

Marc wondered what that plan could possibly be. Several groups of Volonan warships had now arrived within firing range of the Mendoken battlecruisers, all of them in perfect triangular configuration. They would fire their powerful weapon at any moment now, the same weapon that could destroy an entire planet. And yet, all the Mendoken around him seemed as calm as ever, going about their regular tasks on the deck. How could they possibly be so unconcerned when imminent death was staring them in the face?

But imminent death was not in their plan. Before the Volonans could fire the weapon, something happened. What that something was, Marc couldn't figure out for the longest time. But eventually he saw the change. Everything outside was suddenly growing rapidly in size – the approaching Volonan ships, the other ships in the distance, even the nearby dust cloud and orange planet. The only things outside that weren't growing were the other two Mendoken ships.

He couldn't believe it. There had to be only one logical explanation. "Sibular!

Are we... shrinking?"

"Yes," Sibular said. "This is a technology we recently developed."

"Wow! How much are we shrinking?"

"To 1 millionth our original size."

Marc whistled. "Amazing!" He didn't feel a thing different about himself – all proportions within the ship were the same. But outside, everything else just looked massive. "We, uh, can grow back, right?"

"Yes, of course," Sibular replied. "In fact, we cannot stay at this size for more than 18 minutes. The technology still needs to be perfected."

The three miniaturized Mendoken battlecruisers began moving, right past the giant Volonan warships that were now firing blindly in different directions. The Volonans were either completely baffled as to where the Mendoken ships had disappeared to, or had spotted them and were trying to figure out how to reconfigure their weapons systems for such small targets.

The Mendoken ships accelerated, heading straight for the heart of the combat zone where all their fighter and bomber vessels were still in the midst of a raging battle with their Volonan counterparts. As the ships drew nearer, all the Mendoken fighter and bomber vessels began shrinking, right down to a millionth their original sizes. The enemy vessels reacted in total confusion, firing blindly like their mother ships.

Once all the smaller vessels had finished shrinking, the Mendoken mother ships flew through the combat zone and swept them all up through the front gates. Then, closing the gates, they headed for open space.

The clock was ticking, and there were only a few minutes left before the shrinking effect would come to an end. Within that short time period, the Mendoken battlecruisers would have to gain some distance from the fleet of Volonan warships, regain their original size, create a stable consar, and disappear through it before the Volonan ships could reach firing range again.

The Mendoken ships accelerated quickly. The Volonans still hadn't been able to locate them, it seemed, as they weren't following.

"How many... did we lose?" Marc asked Sibular, who was busily setting up for the consar opening ahead.

"We lost 112 vessels and 6092 lives. But we also destroyed 473 of their vessels, and more importantly, 83 of their large ships."

"I guess the surprise element worked," Marc said to himself, feeling sad for so many deaths in front of his eyes. He wondered how many Volonan lives had been lost. Possibly a few hundred thousand, if their ships were anywhere nearly as crowded as the Mendoken ones. Yes, it was horrible, he had to admit, but not nearly as horrible as the billions of lives lost during the destruction of the planet Kerding.

This was war, after all. At least, that was his justification for all the killing that had just occurred.

Right on the 18th minute, the Mendoken ships grew back to their original size. Everything outside began looking normal again. The ships slowed down, getting ready to open the consar in front of them.

Marc looked outside towards the rear. The Volonan warships had wasted no time in locating them, and were already in hot pursuit. Things were going to get very tight, that much was for sure.

Sibular hit the last control, and almost immediately, the familiar blue circles began forming ahead – three circles in all, one for each ship. The circles began thickening into spheres, engulfing each ship. Everything was going as expected.

Or was it? No escape tunnel seemed to be forming ahead.

"Sibular, the consar?" Marc said, starting to get very worried.

Sibular didn't respond. He was too busy peering at the data on the different screens. Several other Mendoken arrived around his station to help him. It was obvious something was wrong.

The Volonan ships were coming ever closer, soon to reach firing range. There had to be a hundred of them at least, breaking up into the much feared triangular formations. The three Mendoken ships were hopelessly outnumbered.

"Sibular, what's going on?" Marc asked again, raising his voice in alarm. "Can I help?"

"There appears to be a problem with the vortex creation," Sibular replied quickly, before returning to some complex calculations he was performing on the screens.

More Mendoken began arriving at the station, including Commander Tulla. They were all silently communicating with each other, none of them paying any attention to Marc. A buzzing siren began wailing loudly through the ship, the same kind of emergency siren he had heard once before at Mendo-Bursal.

Marc felt his body shiver in fear. He knew there was no time left for evasive action, no time left for miniaturization or any other maneuver. The nearest triangle of Volonan ships was about to fire.

And fire they did. Three laser-like rays, one from each ship, shot out and converged on one point. At the point of convergence, a hollow bubble came into formation. The bubble grew quickly, approaching the Mendoken ships at high speed.

Out of the corner of his eye, Marc noticed how all the Mendoken on the deck had stopped what they were doing and were just staring at the advancing bubble. Evidently, they knew all too well that the game was over.

Time slowed down for him during these last few seconds of anticipation.

Without a doubt, he was staring death in the face. He thought he saw his whole life flashing in front of him, but he wasn't sure. Too many memories, too many muddled emotions, too many failures. He had lost all his loved ones, he remembered that. He also recalled that Earth's days would now be numbered, since the Volona would undoubtedly go on to defeat the Mendoken in this war and take over the Republic. He had failed the Mendoken, and he had failed his own people. Humanity would soon cease to exist. It all seemed so utterly hopeless. Through it all, he thought he vaguely heard Sibular say, "I am sorry, Marc. We have failed in our mission."

And then the bubble hit the ships. Its transparent wall passed effortlessly through the ships and through the deck that he was on, engulfing everything and everyone within a few seconds. He felt no change as he passed into the bubble, and for a moment he thought he was safe. For that brief moment, he thought and hoped it might all be a prank or a false alarm.

But then came the massive explosion, cracking the ship into a thousand pieces, sending the debris off in all directions into space. Everything was suddenly afire. He could see Mendoken burning everywhere, being flung into space with all the stations, controls and other equipment on the deck. He felt himself being pushed up with tremendous thrust, as the deck around him shattered completely under an engulfing ball of fire. A sharp, unbearable pain tore through his body. And then, all was dark and quiet.

Chapter 17

The underwater vehicle kept on moving for a while, carrying Dumyan and Sharjam with it. It was pitch dark outside, and Sharjam couldn't see a thing, not until a group of lights suddenly appeared further below. Spread far and wide, the lights seemed to belong to a whole city.

Sharjam was stunned. He had read about the existence of intelligent species underwater on some planets, but he had never expected any on Droila. According to the Ofwariyah, the official Aftaran chronicles of the Dominion, the planet Droila was unsettled by any intelligent species. So whatever species this was, the general Aftaran population had no knowledge of.

As the vehicle descended towards the city, he could begin to see the cubic shape of its buildings. There were streets between the buildings, on which other, similar looking vehicles were moving. Amazingly, the city was not located on the ocean floor, but was somehow magically suspended in the water. The streets were actually nothing more than bottomless waterways.

As their vehicle docked in front of one of the buildings, Sharjam caught his first glimpse of the marine creatures living in the city. Several of them were swimming out of the building to greet him and Dumyan. The creature that had been driving the vehicle got out and swam forward as well. They all looked very similar, with heads and faces that resembled those of dolphins, except that their eyes were much bigger and their snouts shorter. Their bodies were also similar in shape to dolphins, although their flippers were disproportionately long and had fingers at the ends. Gill-like slits behind the eyes indicated that, unlike dolphins, they could respire underwater.

The creatures led the Aftarans inside the building, taking them through a corridor and ushering them into what looked like a small, dimly-lit room. Before any of the creatures followed them inside, however, a sliding door abruptly shut behind them. Then the creatures began crowding around outside, staring at the newcomers through a window on the wall.

Sharjam couldn't make head or tail of what was going on. These creatures did seem friendly and non-threatening, but why had they trapped him and his brother in this room? He knew all too well that the air supply inside their robes wouldn't last forever.

But much to his pleasant surprise, the water in the room suddenly began draining out through a hole in the floor. Filling its place was air, flowing in through another hole in the ceiling. The water level dropped swiftly, soon allowing both of them to begin breathing the air through their noses. It smelled a little stale and was very cold, but it was air nonetheless.

Sharjam uttered a prayer of relief and gratitude. Fortunately these marine creatures seemed prepared to deal with air-breathing visitors. Both he and Dumyan kept their faces covered, though, as was Aftaran custom in front of strangers.

Once the water had completely disappeared from the room, one of the creatures outside came close to the window and bowed its head before the Aftarans. All the other creatures behind bowed their heads at the same time. The creature in front then began moving its mouth. Instantly, a high-pitched, childlike but distinctly feminine voice could be heard inside the room through a crackling speaker on the wall.

"Welcome, Lords who are so beloved," the voice said in Mareefi. "A tremendous honor bestowed upon us it is with your visit to our humble dwellings."

Sharjam was astonished. "They speak Mareefi!" he whispered to Dumyan.

Dumyan held up his hand, motioning to Sharjam to be quiet. "Thank you," he said aloud to the creature outside. "It is always a pleasure to see your kind."

"What are you doing?" Sharjam whispered again to his brother.

"Will you shut up?" Dumyan snapped quietly. "I am playing along, to figure out who they are and who they think we are."

The creature outside bowed again. She had a small crown on her head, which none of the others seemed to have. "Hooooooeeeeeeeeeeeeeee!" she cooed. "Kah is my name. I am the new humble Chancellor of this modest city of ours."

"What happened to the previous Chancellor?" Dumyan asked.

"Alas, as you surely know, Shir was martyred while tending to the fields. May you Lords please have mercy on her soul, and we beg you to please grant her a better life in the next emanation." Kah bowed again, as did all the others behind her.

Dumyan seemed to think for a bit, before opening his mouth again. "You want us to grant Shir mercy, now that she is dead?"

"Hooooeeeeeeeeeeeeee!" Kah cooed again, flapping her long flippers together. "We Doolins are your humble servants. You who are our Masters from the sky above. You who sustain the blueness of the water, who give and take life as you please, you who protect us from the darkness and lead us to light. Who but you would have the power to grant us mercy?"

The other Doolins behind all cooed and flapped their flippers in unison.

"What in the Creator's name is she babbling about?" Dumyan whispered to Sharjam. "She talks as if we are deities. And have you ever heard of any species called Doolins?"

"Never," Sharjam said quietly, "but this is blasphemous! We should tell them the truth!"

"You half-wit!" Dumyan whispered angrily. "Living your life reading books instead of experiencing the real world has made you such a hopeless idealist. Do you realize what these creatures will do to us if we tell them we aren't the gods they have probably led their whole lives believing in? We are completely at their mercy at the moment. We need to figure out what is going on here."

"Fine! Since you want to play along, keep playing and dig yourself deeper into your own hole."

Dumyan seemed to ignore that last comment, and spoke loudly to Kah. "Yes, of course we will grant Shir mercy. Verily she was a good servant."

Once again, all the Doolins bowed their heads.

"Thank you so much, O Merciful Lords," Kah said. "My dear Lords, did you not come by fire-chariot this time?"

"Yes," Dumyan said, "but we left our fire-chariot in the sky above the ocean. We did not want to, ah, disturb the living beings of the sea." He paused, before adding, "We were just about to destroy the monster that was attacking us, when one of you pushed it away. It is indeed better that its life was spared."

Sharjam chuckled quietly, amused by his brother's ability to make up explanations on the fly.

"Hooooeeeeeee!" Kah cooed. "So thoughtful our Lords are. You must be hungry. Please allow us to offer to you from our most humble means some Fouaa."

"Yes, of course," Dumyan said, glancing questioningly at Sharjam.

Sharjam shrugged. He had no idea what Fouaa was. He had never heard of any food with that name.

Kah cooed a command to some other Doolins behind her. They swam away, and returned shortly with a couple of trays that were pushed through a slot in the wall into the air-filled room. The trays were filled with thinly cut slices of raw, fishlike meat.

"We offer the Fouaa to you as a sign of our faith and devotion," Kah said. "Please enjoy it as you please, and call us for anything you desire anytime. Hoooooooeeeeeeeeeee!"

With that, Kah bowed and swam away. The other Doolins followed her, leaving the Aftarans alone in their small, airtight chamber.

Sharjam was disgusted. "How could they offer this to us?" he said to Dumyan. "Especially if they worship Aftarans? Surely they would know that we are all strict vegetarians!"

Dumyan lowered the veil over his face, revealing a pensive look. "It does seem odd. But perhaps it is all they have to offer. In any case, we must eat. Otherwise, we will starve to death."

Sharjam refused to touch it. He had never been as adventurous as his brother, not just about trying different kinds of food, but about pretty much everything in life.

After much arguing that led to no conclusion, Dumyan grabbed some of the meat, pulled down Sharjam's veil and attempted to push the food into his brother's mouth by force. But before things got too violent, Sharjam eventually succumbed and took a bite. "It tastes like mud," he said, feeling revolted.

Dumyan chewed thoughtfully, his face showing displeasure as well. "I wonder why these Doolins believe we are gods," he said between bites.

"And how could they even know about Aftarans, when there is no record of these creatures anywhere?" Sharjam added. "This planet is officially uninhabited, according to the Ofwariyah."

"Ay, it makes little sense. But it is obvious they have interacted with Aftarans before. They speak our language, and they have chambers such as these to host beings like us."

"They were not surprised to see us either. Which indicates that they have Aftaran visitors on a regular basis. But who?"

"I wonder if Wazilban is behind this, actually. Though I wonder what he would possibly want with primitive marine creatures such as these."

Sharjam thought for a moment. "Has Wazilban not done this sort of thing before? Remember how he came to power."

"You mean the Eelaks? Yes, good point."

"He used them for his own purposes, and when he no longer needed them, massacred them all! Then he blamed it on the Phyrax, thereby creating a reason to declare war on them."

Dumyan looked grim. "And all with the support of our people. He generated such an unjustifiable, illogical fear in them, by spreading his message of hate to every corner of the Dominion. The public was totally blinded and enamored by his emotion-stirring speeches and cheap sound bites. Never in my wildest dreams would I have thought that an Aftaran could be capable of such deceit and treachery. We were not at all prepared to deal with this kind of evil."

Sharjam nodded slowly. "The worst of it all was how Wazilban betrayed the fundamental principles that we have lived with for generations, and how he got away with it. Free, independent sources of information were things our people always cherished. Yet, in one sweep, Wazilban took that away. And he was so successful in spreading his propaganda that he not only caused our dear father to be shunned and forgotten in no time, he also made sure that the murder of the Eminent Ouria and all her High Clerics did not even elicit a whisper of public discontent. The High Clerics were the very foundation of our way of life! Without them to guide us, our people are eternally lost."

"Well, it has been some time since then. I am curious to know what the public mood is like now, whether some have finally opened their eyes to the truth. If not, then we need to open their eyes for them. This time, we cannot afford to fail."

As disgusted as he was by the taste of the Fouaa, Sharjam felt better after eating. He then tended to the wound on his leg, while Dumyan did the same to his hip.

The conversation continued with a few minor arguments. In the end, both of them came to the agreement that they needed to be extremely careful in dealing with the Doolins, so as not to arouse any suspicion that might endanger their lives.

Soon after, a number of Doolins swam into view outside and bowed their heads before the Aftarans.

Chancellor Kah came forward, her face almost touching the transparent wall. "I sincerely am hoping that the Fouaa was at least somewhat edible for you?"

"Yes, it was quite good," Dumyan said. "We enjoyed it."

"Would you now like to rest, or inspect the fields?"

"We would like to inspect the fields," Dumyan said after a pause.

Sharjam felt uneasy with Dumyan's response. Why get involved in something that was clearly none of their business? He had to agree, however, that continuing to sit in this room would get them nowhere.

"Hoooooooeeeeeeeeeee!" Kah cooed. "Please fill your robes with air and cover your faces."

Dumyan and Sharjam did as they were told. The door to the room slid open, and water gushed back in. Once the water level had risen above their heads, they stepped through the door and followed Kah out of the building. There, a vehicle was waiting for them, similar to the one that had picked them up earlier. This time, the Aftarans went inside the vehicle, finding a snug cockpit with large windows that gave clear views of the outside. There were no seats, just enough space to stand in the back. Another Doolin was at the helm, ready to operate the single joystick-like control with his front flippers. Kah also came inside, and took position in the front next to the pilot. The Doolins did not stand – they gently swayed their tails from side to side, keeping their balance in the water that way.

The vehicle began moving, heading downwards out of the city and towards the ocean bed. Every now and then, a vehicle passed by in the opposite direction, heading back to the city. The surroundings soon grew very dark, until nothing outside was visible. Occasionally, fishlike creatures appeared ahead in the glow of the vehicle's single headlamp. Startled by the light, they instantly swam away.

Sharjam wondered how the Doolins could navigate through such darkness. He surmised that they had to have very powerful eyes, as he could not identify any other form of navigational aid or instrument inside the cockpit.

It took almost a half hour to reach the bottom of the ocean. The pilot pointed the vehicle's headlamp downwards, revealing a gray, rocky surface. Then, up ahead, the surface suddenly gave way to a deep, dark abyss. Sharjam didn't like its looks at all, and really hoped they weren't heading into it.

But that was exactly where they were heading. And as the vehicle descended into the abyss, he could sense how big it was. The other end wasn't even visible, nor was the bottom. But what was visible was something he could not even remotely have imagined. Rows and rows of red lights came into view below, stretching as far as the eye could see in each direction. And there were multiple levels of them, one below the other, stretching as far as the eye could see below.

The vehicle descended to the first level, in between two rows. Other vehicles could be seen ahead and below, either stationary or moving slowly. There were many Doolins swimming about, tending to the lights.

"So these are the fields," Sharjam thought. Evidently, whoever had taught the Doolins to worship Aftarans had ordered the Doolins to take care of these fields. Those same Aftarans probably came to inspect the fields on a periodic basis, and the Doolins had mistaken Dumyan and Sharjam for those Aftarans.

But what was growing in the fields? What were those mysterious red lights? Why did they need to be here, at the bottom of the ocean on a desolate planet? Who could possibly be behind all this, and most importantly, why? There had to be hundreds of thousands, if not millions of those lights here in this chasm.

Sharjam tried to get a closer look at the lights. As the vehicle passed each light, he noticed that there was a balloon-like, spherical shell surrounding the light. Floating in the water with no visible support, the sphere had a diameter of about 3 feet. Inside was the red light, a brilliantly glowing sparkle that seemed to have no fixed shape. It just kept dancing around within the confines of its shell, sometimes looking like a star, at other times like a cube or even a series of disconnected straight lines. All the other spheres were identical in size and appearance.

Unable to communicate in the water, both brothers glanced at each other in complete bewilderment. Sharjam found it all to be very eerie.

The vehicle progressed along the row for a while, then descended to other levels below and repeated the same procedure. It stopped in front of each sphere, giving the Aftarans an opportunity to examine it closely.

"They have to be some kind of living beings," Sharjam thought. And whatever they were, they were growing, like crops. The Doolins were feeding the spheres from containers of some gaseous or liquid substance, containers that they kept refilling from somewhere in the depths of the abyss below.

Kah turned around to face the Aftarans, with an inquisitive look in her eyes. Dumyan nodded to her. Kah flapped her flippers in delight and cooed a command to the pilot. The vehicle then tilted upwards and lifted out of the crater. Soon they were on their way back up to the Doolin city.

A half hour later, Dumyan and Sharjam were back in the same air-filled chamber, with Kah and a number of other Doolins outside facing them through the window.

"O Beloved Lords, we sincerely are hoping that our humble efforts in the fields have been to your liking?" Kah said, her high-pitched voice crackling through the loudspeaker in the chamber.

"Yes," Dumyan replied. "Everything seemed in order. They, ah, appear to have grown since our last visit."

"Yes, O Lords who are so observant!" Kah said, bowing to them again. "The Starguzzlers are steadily growing. We hope, by your will and grace, that they will be ready to leave our waters and join you in the Heavens by the date you ordered."

"Starguzzlers – what a strange name!" Dumyan thought. "Yes, now about that date," he said aloud.

Kah looked concerned. "Would a year no longer be sufficient for our gracious Lords?" she asked.

Dumyan smiled inwardly, happy to get the information he was looking for. "A year is definitely longer than we would like. But it will do."

"Hoooooooeeeeeeeee! Thank you, O Bountiful Lords of the Heavens above!" Kah flapped her flippers as she bowed. The other Doolins behind her did the same.

Another Doolin swam into view from outside, and quietly cooed something to Kah. Kah seemed both surprised and happy at the news.

"Dear Lords, we are indeed so fortunate to be graced by the presence of more of you," she announced. "Two more Lords have just arrived in our city by fire-chariot. Would you like to join them?"

Sharjam looked at Dumyan in alarm.

"Not quite yet," Dumyan replied, keeping his cool. "We would like to rest a little first, and then pleasantly surprise the other Lords. They are not expecting us here."

"But of course!" Kah said. "We fully understand. We will not mention to the other Lords that you are here."

"Good. Where are the other Lords staying, by the way?"

"They are in a neighboring building, the one with the tower, dear Lords," Kah replied. "We will leave you now." With that, she bowed and swam out, the other Doolins following her.

"That was a close call!" Sharjam whispered to Dumyan. "Lucky for us that these Doolins are so dumb."

Dumyan was worried. "We need to get out of here as soon as possible," he said. "The Doolins' dumbness might very well cause one of them to blurt out our presence to Wazilban's emissaries."

"You are certain that those other Aftarans have been sent by Wazilban?"

"Who else could possibly be behind this whole scheme? None other in the Dominion would have the resources, or even the desire."

Sharjam nodded. "Certainly he is the only one who would have the gall to commit so sacrilegious a crime," he said with disgust. "Teaching dumb, innocent creatures to worship mere mortals like us!"

"Yes," Dumyan agreed. "Unconditional obedience. That must have been his plan. These Doolins do not seem to question the commands they receive – they just do whatever they are told. Their sole purpose for existence is to tend to those fields, or so they are led to believe. And their existence has been kept a total secret from the general Aftaran population. No surprise, therefore, that Wazilban chose the bottom of the ocean, on a planet that is officially uninhabited in a desolate star system. Nobody would ever think to look for anything down here."

"In fact, this might also explain why Wazilban has been so keen to make sure that none of us escape from Tibara. He is worried that we might discover what he has been up to on neighboring Droila."

"Which means that Wazilban is developing something here that he considers very important, something he does not want anyone to know about."

Sharjam frowned. "Maybe those Starguzzlers are weapons of some sort. The name itself seems to indicate that they might somehow be capable of causing damage to entire stars! Although I do not know how something so small could harm something as large as a star. I wonder how Wazilban could possibly have acquired the knowledge to build such a weapon. It is unlikely the Mendoken would ever have assisted him in such an effort. They would never help another species gain military superiority, no matter how closely allied they might be."

"No, probably not the Mendoken. They do not even have the capability to cause damage to stars, from what I know. Planet destroyers are their mightiest weapon."

"I dread to imagine how much devastation those Starguzzlers could cause, or who the unfortunate victims might be."

"Maybe our archenemies – the Phyrax and Volona. Maybe our Mendoken friends, or maybe even our own people. I would not put anything past Wazilban. In any case, it will clearly be to strengthen his power over the Dominion by force, and possibly over the whole galaxy."

Sharjam looked horrified. "Wazilban is leading our people on a path to utter destruction, while they wither away in ignorance and blind faith. If they could just see through his plan by witnessing these Starguzzler fields, then they would finally wake up! Oh, how I wish the Creator would open their eyes!"

"Well, our eyes are now open," Dumyan said.

"Meaning?"

"Meaning it cannot be pure chance that we ended up on Droila. It was surely the Creator's will that brought us here. Perhaps the Creator wanted us to see this, so that we could arise and warn our people. Perhaps, indeed, this is the Sign that we were supposed to wait for?"

Sharjam's eyes lit up. "You think this might be the Sign?"

"I do not know for certain, but it is definitely a possibility."

Dumyan knew he was treading a risky path. But he also knew that, if he really wanted this mission to be successful, then he needed to get his brother to be more excited about it. He wasn't really a strong believer in the prophecies of the Hidden Scripture, or even in the overall religious code to begin with. Not that he didn't believe in the Creator, for no Aftaran could ever be an atheist. But he had lived his life mostly by his own principles, principles he had acquired over time through his many adventures.

Sharjam, on the other hand, was a strict follower of the religion, having memorized all the verses of the sacred Scriptures and leading his life entirely by the rules specified therein. He hadn't wanted to come on this quest until the Sign revealed itself, the Sign mentioned in the 38th chapter of the Hidden Scripture. But if he could be convinced that this was the Sign, then he would be ready to act. The prophecy did say, after all, not to delay once the Sign had revealed itself.

"O mighty Creator," Sharjam whispered, closing his eyes, "if this is indeed the Sign of which we have been warned, then give us the strength to fight evil, to restore peace to our people, and to bring to justice those who are such grievous wrongdoers." After a moment's silence, he opened his eyes and said, "Dumyan, we must confront Wazilban. With the Creator's help, we shall defeat him and restore our dear father to the throne!"

Dumyan heaved a big sigh of relief. It had worked! "Finally, my brother, you are beginning to think like me!"

After some discussion on their escape plan, the two brothers slowly slid open the door to their air-filled chamber. As the water gushed in, they covered their faces with their robes and slipped out. Luckily there were no Doolins in the corridor. They swam to the front door, and cautiously slid it slightly open.

Dumyan peered out. There were a number of Doolins swimming about outside, as well as a few vehicles moving through the bottomless street. He surveyed the surroundings for the neighboring building with the tower that Kah had mentioned. He spotted it on the other side of the street, a couple of buildings away. The tower was thin and about 20 feet tall, atop a 2 story cubic building.

About another 40 feet above the top of the tower, he noticed a big shadow, and smiled. It had to be the ship the other Aftarans had come on, and it would hopefully be the ship he and his brother would use to leave this planet. The difficult part, however, would be getting up there without being noticed. Although the area wasn't well lit, there were Doolins about. And the trip down to the Starguzzler fields had already proven that Doolins had excellent eyesight in the dark.

Nonetheless, the brothers had a plan, one that centered on the fact that the city's buildings had no ground foundations. Dumyan dived through the door opening, making straight for the open water under the bottom of the building. Sharjam followed suit. Right away, they pushed themselves flat up against the floor of the building, staying out of sight. Fortunately, as they had hoped, there were no Doolins swimming below the street level. There was one vehicle that could be seen heading down to the depth of the ocean, and another coming back up to the city. But their occupants did not seem to have noticed the Aftarans.

Next, the two brothers edged their way along the building floor to the side facing the street. If they tried to just swim across the street, they would instantly be spotted. Instead, their plan was to cross under the cover of vehicles that were moving along the street in either direction. Since the street was only wide enough to fit two vehicles at a time, their hope was that they wouldn't need more than two vehicles to reach the other side.

A vehicle soon approached on their side of the street, gliding along at a distance of 3 feet from the edge of the building. Dumyan waited for the vehicle to reach their position, and then jumped to its underside. Sharjam followed. They couldn't find anything to clutch onto, so they had to swim very fast to stay hidden under the moving vehicle.

They had swum well past the building with the tower, before another vehicle heading in the opposite direction finally appeared. At the moment the two vehicles passed each other, they jumped again, just barely covering the 5 feet of distance between the two vehicles.

Once the vehicle passed by the building with the tower, they jumped to that building's underside. Their next task would now be to climb up the wall to the top of the tower and make a dash for the ship above, all the while staying out of sight. And if any Doolins noticed them on that final swim across the open water, they would hopefully still be able to make it in time to the ship and take off.

The far side of the building faced a narrow alley, and was the ideal wall for climbing up in hiding. Dumyan and Sharjam edged their way slowly up that wall, covering the base 2 stories without any incident. They were already halfway up the tower, when a few Doolins suddenly swam past nearby.

Dumyan was ready to kick himself in dismay. But to his surprise, the Doolins kept on swimming, unbothered by what they had seen. At first, he thought he and Sharjam were lucky that the Doolins were so dumb. But then he wondered if the whole thing was a trap. Maybe the Doolins had already tipped off the other Aftarans, and the Aftarans were now waiting inside the ship.

"Maybe's, maybe's," he said to himself. Maybe's had never prevented him from taking action in the past, and they certainly wouldn't do so now when he was so close to the ship, so close to his means of escape.

He noticed Sharjam frantically waving his arms, trying to get him to stop climbing. "Typical Sharjam," he thought, "always the hesitator, always the risk averse." But, as he knew all too well from his many adventures, hesitation in the last minute always led to failure. He would take the lead, and Sharjam would have to follow.

With that in mind, Dumyan jumped into the open water from the tip of the tower, swimming as fast as he could towards the ship. Turning his head back for a brief second, he was happy to see Sharjam swimming behind him.

Other Doolins further away could now clearly see them swimming across the open water, but they did not react. This caused Dumyan to again wonder if it really was a trap. Then again, maybe these Doolins really were that dumb.

The ship above was now in full view. It was a standard medium-range Boura-class vessel, used by small groups of Aftarans to travel between neighboring star systems within the Dominion. It had the shape of a submarine, with a long, thin snout that widened towards the middle and thinned out again towards the end. A hump above the middle section served as the cockpit. The ship was not very big, especially compared to the longer range Gyra-class vessels. It was about 200 feet long, with a width of 40 feet and a height of 50 feet at its widest point. Its color was a dim orange – standard for most Aftaran ships. Not that the color was really visible so deep underwater, at least not to Aftaran eyes.

Dumyan reached the front of the ship, and pressed a latch on the lower hull. A small door slid open next to the latch, and he swam up into a small, dark compartment. Once Sharjam had swum up behind him, he closed the latch and hit a control on the wall. The water began draining out right away.

"Dumyan, this could be a trap!" Sharjam whispered, uncovering his face once the water level had dropped below their heads.

"I know, but we have to take our chances," Dumyan said, removing the veil around his own face. "There is no alternative." With that, he pressed another latch on the low ceiling, and a door above them slid open. Holding on to the edges of the opening with his hands, he pulled himself up into the ship's main corridor.

"Be careful!" Sharjam hissed, pulling himself up behind his brother.

Both brothers began surveying the ship, opening the door to every room to check if anybody was there. Luckily there weren't too many rooms – Boura-class vessels weren't meant to house more than 9 or 10 Aftarans at a time. More importantly, though, there was nobody in sight. After checking the last room, they felt satisfied that the ship really was empty.

Dumyan then made his way through the narrow corridor to the center of the ship, feeling relieved to be back in an air-filled environment. He found the latch he was looking for on the wall, and pressed it. A door slid open in the ceiling, and he climbed up through it into the cockpit.

Dumyan knew all about Boura-class vessels. He had piloted many of them in his younger days. Quite the stellar champion he had been, always defeating others in racing competitions. But the majority of Aftarans didn't care for these kinds of adventures or material extravaganzas – they were too busy praying and meditating in their monasteries. So his outstanding flying skills had never gained much fame or glory among the general public.

"This is more like it!" he said gleefully, as Sharjam joined him in the cockpit. Sitting and leaning back in the pilot's seat, he began to feel right at home.

Sharjam sat down in an adjacent seat, the only other seat in the snug cockpit. Both seats faced a wide screen that gave a clear view of the outside. The controls were very simple – there were none, not even a dashboard or a steering column. This was typical for Aftaran ships, since they relied on mind interfacing. Pilots controlled their ships' functions with their thoughts, by simply thinking that they wanted their ships to move, turn or stop. This was just one of the many miracles possessed by the Aftar, miracles that other species such as the Mendoken had studied in depth but had never been able to explain by science or technology.

Dumyan closed his eyes. He tried to focus his thoughts, in order to interface with the ship's control functions. Within a few seconds, the ship's lights went on and the kilasic engine sprang to life. The vessel began moving through the water, slowly at first, then tilting upwards and quickly gaining speed. Soon it splashed through the ocean's surface, and flew into the stormy skies of Droila.

Chapter 18

The soothing sound of gently breaking waves stirred Marc awake. He slowly opened his eyes, and the first thing he noticed was the bright sunlight in the room. Turning his head to the right, he saw a row of windows across the wall through which the light was entering. There was a balcony outside, covering the full length of the wall. A light, pleasant breeze was blowing in through the open balcony door, causing the thin curtains in front of the windows to dance around. The ceiling and the walls were all white, as were the bed sheets. There was no other furniture in the room, just the big, comfortable bed he was lying on. Where was he, he wondered? Was he dead? Was this heaven? It couldn't possibly be hell?

Maybe this was just a dream. Or was it? Perhaps he had just woken up from a dream? Yes, he had had nightmares, horrible nightmares. Huge spaceships coming to pick him up from Earth and take him away. Thousands of strange, floating aliens, with navy blue skin and green armor, half robotic and half organic, with bizarre eyes that went all around their heads. A shroud around the solar system, hiding billions of stars, inhabited planets and space stations beyond from those within. Traveling through bizarre wormholes into enemy space and fighting other aliens. Ships and entire planets blowing up, with death and destruction everywhere.

Yes, yes, it had all been a horrible nightmare! But it was over. He was safe now, safe and sound back home. Back with the love of his life. He turned to his side to look at her. She was lying there under the white blanket, still fast asleep, with her long auburn hair lightly blowing about in the breeze. As always, she looked absolutely beautiful, the sweet, sharp features of her face glowing perfectly in the morning sunlight. Every time he stared at her, he couldn't believe how lucky he was to be with somebody so stunningly attractive.

He laid his hand on her head, and gently caressed her hair. "Hi, darling," he whispered.

Iman opened her big, brown eyes. "Hey, sweetheart," she murmured in a sleepy voice.

"Sleep well?"

"Wonderfully," she said, rubbing her eyes. "How about you?"

"Yes," he replied, sitting up. "I feel like I've just woken up from a very long dream, a dream that lasted many days and nights."

"Well, I'm glad you're back," she said, letting out a big yawn as she sat up.

Marc got up and walked out to the balcony to savor the breathtaking view. The house was on the edge of a steep cliff. Far below was the deep blue ocean, its waves splashing against a straight, sandy beach. The ocean stretched all the way to the horizon, merging in the distance with the absolutely clear blue sky.

He had always wanted a house like this, atop a cliff with a magnificent view of the sea. Reaching up to the sky with his arms, he yelled out in delight.

Iman came up behind him, putting her hands around his waist and resting her head on his shoulder. "I love you," she whispered.

"I love you too," he said. He held her hands in his, feeling happy, very happy. And at peace, absolute peace.

"Your parents are coming over for lunch today," she said.

"My parents?" Confused, he turned around to face her.

"Yes, of course, your parents, silly! They haven't been here in a couple of weeks, so I invited them over." A smile appeared across her face, that same sweet smile that made his heart melt every time. "You don't mind, do you? Sorry, I forgot to ask you first."

"Ah, hmm, okay," he stammered. "I mean, of course I don't mind. They're my parents, after all." Yes, his parents were alive! How could he even have imagined that they were dead? What was he thinking? Those nasty nightmares – he would have to get them out of his head.

She kissed him, first on the cheek, then on the mouth. Then she kissed him again, and again. Each kiss lasted longer than the one before. The blue sea, the stunning view, the brilliant sunshine, all of it melted away from his mind as he embraced her.

Slowly they staggered back into the bedroom and fell over onto the bed, never once letting go of their passionate kisses. He slipped off her white robe before taking off his own, and made love to her. He could never get enough of her – her smooth tan skin, her slender, hourglass figure, her shapely legs. Every time he touched her, it felt as exciting as the first time he had touched her. Except that he loved her more every time.

Later, she went downstairs to make breakfast, while he took a shower and freshened up. The house was modern, with expensive upgrades, modern appliances and stylish furniture throughout. It had 2 stories – 3 bedrooms upstairs, and a study, a large family room and a living room downstairs. The kitchen provided direct access to the patio behind the house, a patio that reached all the way to the edge of the cliff.

They sat at the kitchen table, drinking apple juice and munching on pancakes with maple syrup. Then came the strong, black tea that really woke him up and made him feel refreshed. This was his favorite breakfast, and she made it for him everyday.

They chatted away merrily, talking about all the wonderful things that had happened to both of them over the years. How he had completed his PhD in astrophysics at MIT in less than three years, and right away become the institution's youngest tenured professor. How within a year after that he had proven the existence of higher dimensions, and shown how a special kind of wormhole could be stabilized to be used as a transport mechanism through them. How he had become a world famous scientist overnight as a result. How with all the wealth he had gained he continuously helped people in need all over the world, thereby becoming a hero in their eyes. How she had completed her Master's in history at Harvard, and written a comprehensive historical guide of the Middle East, including its different countries, cultures and religions. How it had quickly become a widely popular book, the first ever to be recognized as an objective account of the volatile region by academics both in the East and West. How her family had eventually embraced him with open arms, and accepted him as one of their own. How they had gotten married in the most romantic way at the very spot where their house now stood, the house itself built after the wedding as a remnant of their everlasting love for each other. How they had never had a single fight or major argument in their three years of marriage.

Yes, he definitely led a blissful life. He knew that, and he was thankful for it.

After breakfast, they stepped out of the house. They walked along the cliff's edge for a while, and then climbed down a narrow path to the sandy beach below. They walked along the beach for a long time, holding hands and talking about all kinds of things. The warm waves kept creeping up, covering their bare feet in the sand. Seagulls could be seen flying through the sky, and every now and then a pelican or an albatross flapped its wings as it passed by. There were dolphins jumping out of the water in the distance, and further away towards the horizon a large blue whale showed off its magnificent tail above the waves.

The hours passed like minutes. That was how time passed for someone who was as happy as Marc was.

"Look!" Iman suddenly said, smiling as she pointed at the top of the cliff. "Your parents are here!"

He looked up. Sure enough, he could see two people standing on the edge of the cliff. They were holding each other and waving at them.

"Come on!" he said cheerfully, as he waved back. "Let's go!"

They quickly climbed back up the narrow path, while his parents walked over to meet them at the top.

"Hi Mom, Dad!" he said, hugging both of them with delight.

"Hi, Son!" Marc's father said, beaming with joy. For his age, he looked very healthy. There were almost no wrinkles on his face. He was a few inches shorter than Marc, and fairly slender. His shiny black hair was neatly combed to the side, and his small, lively eyes protected by round, metal rim glasses that rested on his flat nose. While he had no receding hairline, his hair was thinning out a little everywhere across the top of his head. In many ways, he looked like an older version of Marc – a purer, Chinese version, with darker hair and sharper eyes.

"It's so good to see you!" Marc's mother said, with tears of happiness in her bright blue eyes. Her expression clearly betrayed from where Marc had inherited his unique, pleasant smile. She looked healthy too, as if she was well rested and content with her life. Her long blonde hair was tied behind her head in a ponytail. There were a few wrinkles under her eyes, but overall she definitely looked young for her age.

Iman hugged them both next, looking very happy to see them. Together, they then walked back to the house. Iman took out all the tasty dishes she had cooked the night before, and they had a very satisfying lunch out on the patio.

Marc loved her cooking, and so did his parents. She made the best kabobs and couscous any of them had ever had, and her tahini sauce was to die for. And somehow she always knew how to serve the pita bread at the perfect temperature and softness.

They talked and laughed for a long time. Iman told Marc's parents some of the stories of her family. She related how her parents had originally wanted her to marry somebody from her own culture and religion, and how strict they had been about it. But once they had gotten to know Marc and had spent time with him, they had started to like him.

"Now they like him more than they like me!" she joked. "They always take his side, and they all gang up on me whenever there's any disagreement."

Everybody else at the table laughed.

Marc remembered something. "Mom, Dad, we've got an announcement to make," he said. "Iman is pregnant."

"Oh my God, congratulations!" His mother got up right away and gave Iman a hug.

"How long has it been?" his father asked, with a broad smile across his face.

Iman blushed. "About three months."

They talked about how having a baby completely changed people's perspectives and priorities, and both of Marc's parents mentioned how their lives had changed after Marc's birth.

"For the better, of course," his mother added. She proceeded to give Iman some tips on pregnancy.

Marc and his dad took the opportunity to step into the family room.

"How's work, Son?" his dad asked, sitting down on a plush sofa that faced an elaborate home theater system.

"Fantastic! I just found out that they're going to award me the Nobel Prize for Physics this year. I've been getting calls from dozens of reporters already."

On and the conversations went, while the clock ticked away. Marc's parents ended up staying for dinner, and left late in the evening. Their house was only an hour's drive away. Afterwards, Marc and Iman watched a movie together on their big screen TV. Then they went to bed, where they made love again before falling asleep for the night.

And so the days went by. Sometimes Marc would go to work – a quick drive down the coast to his office at MIT. It was a very comfortable, pleasant job. He had lots of respect from students and fellow professors, as well as large amounts of funding for his research projects. He had also written a couple of books that were highly popular in academic circles, and he was currently in the process of writing another one. But most of his time was just spent with Iman, either at home or on quick getaways to places nearby and around the world.

This was the life he had always dreamed of. This was the life he had always wanted to attain. It was his to keep, forever and ever. It couldn't possibly get any better than this, only worse. In fact, that started becoming his only worry – the fact that things might turn worse. What if Iman left him one day, or his parents died prematurely? What if all his scientific research failed, and he ended up discredited and jobless?

The worries started off small, but as the days passed, they intensified, making him feel both sad and tense all the time. He didn't talk to Iman about it, because he knew she wouldn't take it seriously.

"What point is there in worrying when life is so perfect?" she would surely ask.

She would console him, but she would also think he was being silly. And he didn't want her to think that he was silly. He wanted her to be proud of him, to think of him as the hero in her life. So he kept quiet.

*   *   *

One morning, Marc got up from bed and walked to the bathroom. He glanced at the large mirror that covered the far wall. Usually, he wouldn't look more than a second or two in that direction. This morning, however, he noticed something different. His reflection showed him as pale, sick and melancholy. There were a number of gray hairs on the sides of his head, and dark circles rested under his eyes. The face was full of wrinkles, undoubtedly the result of depression and excessive worry. He looked as if he hadn't slept in many nights, even though he had just woken up from a refreshing night's sleep. He also seemed to have lost at least 20 pounds overnight.

He was shocked. He thought that maybe he was still dreaming, but a sharp pinch to the forearm quickly convinced him otherwise. Now wide awake, he began feeling his face and hair, followed by his arms, chest and stomach. Surprisingly, they all felt perfectly fine, just like the way they had the day before. And yet, in the mirror he appeared totally different. He leaned forward, his nose almost touching the mirror. Again, he felt his face. The wrinkles he could see in the mirror just weren't there – his skin felt nice and smooth. What was going on? Had he gone crazy?

But it was about to get crazier.

"Psst!" the mirror image suddenly said.

Marc looked around in bewilderment, and slapped his face.

"Psst!" the image said again.

Now he was starting to get afraid. He thought about running out of the bathroom and getting back into bed, right into Iman's arms.

"Listen," the mirror image whispered, "they're watching you."

Marc didn't know what to do. Was this for real, or had he gone nuts? After some thought, he mustered enough courage. "Who is watching me?" he whispered back. "And who are you?"

"I am you. Well, a part of you. Alright, more a part of your mind, really. The only part that's still holding on to reality."

"What are you talking about?"

"The world you're living in, none of it is real. Hasn't it occurred to you that your life is absolutely perfect? Since when is life ever that perfect?"

Marc knew his life was perfect – that was why he was so worried all the time that things would go wrong.

"Yes," his mirror image continued, as if reading his mind. "You and I – we aren't made for this kind of life. We humans cannot live in perfect worlds. It's not in our nature."

"Where am I then? How did I get here?"

"I can't tell you that. They're probably on my tail already."

"Who? Who is on your tail?"

"I can't tell you that either. Not right now anyway."

Marc tried to laugh, thinking that this was all a prank that one of his many smart university students was playing on him. "You won't tell me anything! Why should I believe you then?"

"Because if you don't, then bad things will start happening. You see the way I look? This is how you will look very soon if you don't listen to me. Your whole perfect world will collapse."

"What things? What do you mean?"

"I can't stay any longer," the image said, looking in fear to his left and right. "In case they notice me. But listen – come back to the mirror every morning, at the same time. I may be there or I may not."

With that, the mirror image shifted back to the way Marc actually looked. The ghost was gone.

If Marc was worried before, now he was terrified. He didn't know who or what he had just seen in the mirror, and what on Earth that discussion was all about. But he decided not to tell Iman or anybody else about it, because he knew nobody would believe him. It was just too crazy a tale. Maybe it had just been a hallucination anyway, a result of all the idle time he had lately been spending at home. Perhaps he needed to spend more time at work, to get his mind busy again. So he went to work that day, trying his best to forget what had happened.

Sure enough, the next morning, everything was normal. There were no more ghosts in the bathroom mirror. The following morning, everything was fine too. But then, a couple of days later, disaster struck. His father was returning home from a short skiing trip in the mountains with some buddies, when their car skidded out of control after hitting a patch of ice and slammed into a truck. He was instantly dead.

Marc was devastated upon hearing the news, as were his mother and Iman. The shock was just unbearable. He couldn't sleep at night, or put his mind to anything anymore. His health began to worsen. A few days later, the ghost reappeared in the bathroom mirror.

"Do you believe me now?" the ghost said. This time, he looked a little better – not quite as pale or sick, and a little heavier. Even the wrinkles had smoothed out somewhat. But Marc was looking worse now. He hadn't eaten or slept properly since his father's death, and it was starting to show. He had lost a few pounds and looked very tired. Dark circles were beginning to form under his eyes.

"Believe what?" Marc asked, very irritated from the lack of sleep. "You haven't told me anything of any use whatsoever."

"I've told you that you're living in an unreal world, the ideal world of your own imagination. The longer you refuse to acknowledge it, the more the world around you will crumble, piece by piece. The longer you wait, the faster it will crumble. You are not made for this kind of environment. You need to snap out of it, and rejoin me in the real world. Otherwise you will die!"

"How am I supposed to 'rejoin' you? You're nothing but an image in the mirror."

"That step will become clear, once you begin believing me."

"How can I believe you? You're not telling me where I am, how I ended up here, or who put me here. Not to mention any proof of anything."

"Ah, now there's my scientist mind at work! You want proof? How about this – your father didn't die four days ago. He's been dead for almost 25 years. You've never seen him alive."

Marc laughed. "What nonsense!"

"Your mother is also dead. She died four years ago from cancer. And you never ended up with Iman – she left you while you were still in college. What's more, you left MIT to go to Cornell for your graduate studies, where you ended up on a hopeless quest to build a time machine. It was so hopeless that you ended up on probation."

"Never!" Marc yelled. "That's not true!"

"You'd better believe it! You wanted to turn back the clock, to change events and generate the same perfect life for yourself that you're now living. Except for one fundamental difference. You wanted to go back and fall out of love with Iman. And yet, here you are together with her, more in love with her than ever before. Think about it! You never succeeded in building a time machine. This is a fantasy world, it isn't real!"

"I have absolutely no idea what you're talking about! I never wanted to build a time machine. Why would I need to anyway?"

"Because your real life isn't so rosy! You've been through some pretty rough times, my friend. But since you don't want to acknowledge the truth, you'll just have to learn the hard way again. All I ask is this – as bad things begin to happen, which I assure you they will, dig into your own mind and into your own memories. Remember your real, true life, before it gets too late, before we're both dead."

The ghost disappeared again, replacing his own image in the mirror with Marc's.

Marc was bewildered. This ghost had to be more than a figment of his own imagination. He spent the whole day reflecting on everything he had heard, paying no attention to anything else. What if it really was an imaginary world that he was living in? That would certainly explain why everything had been so perfect. Was his real life so bad, that he had resorted to building a time machine? He thought and thought, and tried to remember those events in his life that the ghost in the mirror had mentioned. But his mind was filled only with nice, happy memories.

A few days later, disaster struck again. This time, it was his mother. She was diagnosed with kidney cancer in the morning, and died that same afternoon in the hospital. The cancer was apparently at such an advanced stage that it was a miracle she had survived for as long as she had.

Again, Marc was devastated. He was now in major shock and depression, and his health was rapidly deteriorating. Iman tried her best to console him, but it was to no avail. As he tried to make sense of what was happening, he began to realize that maybe what the ghost had said might indeed be true.

The next day, Iman suddenly got into a big fight with him, the same Iman who was usually so loving and understanding, the same Iman who had never once raised her voice at him. Yet here she was, telling him that he was no longer the person she had married – that he was now a depressed, lifeless soul who didn't understand her and had nothing anymore to offer her. That she should have listened to her parents and married somebody from her own culture. That she wanted to leave him and go back to her family.

Within the hour, she packed her bags and stormed out the door, without offering any explanation for the abrupt change in her behavior, and without giving him any chance to defend himself.

It was one shock after the next. A phone call came from the Nobel Committee a couple of hours later, informing him that he was not to be awarded the Nobel Prize this year after all. The head of the physics department at MIT called next, to let him know that his tenure at the university would not be extended after the current month. No explanation was given.

Marc's perfect world was falling apart, and so was he. Now he was fairly certain that the ghost had been telling the truth. He went into the bathroom, and waited for the ghost to reappear. He waited and waited, all night long. But all he could see in the mirror was his own self.

As he waited, he thought about his life, how perfect everything had always been. And then, a series of memories abruptly flashed through his mind. Things actually hadn't been that perfect. His father had indeed died before he was born. Yes, he had never met his father! That was why his mother had always been so depressed at home during his childhood. That was why he had grown up such a loner, such an introvert, because life at home had always been so miserable. That was why he had always had such a lofty imagination, constantly daydreaming about a better life. That was why he used to think of himself as a superhero helping weak victims against their evil tormentors, because he hadn't been able to help his own mother get over her depression.

Or even prevent her from dying. Yes, his mother had died of cancer a while ago, just after his graduation from MIT. His undergrad years at MIT had been the best period of his life, but the good times had ended with his mother's death, and with the loss of Iman.

It was all coming back to him now. Iman hadn't left him today, she had left him back then! She had loved him dearly, just as he had loved her, but the pressure from her conservative family had been too much. And that was why he had ended up at Cornell for his graduate studies, not MIT. Cornell, the place where loneliness and depression had taken over his life once again. Cornell, the place where desperation had led him to that unattainable quest to build a time machine.

"A time machine!" a voice said. "What were you thinking? No wonder Cornell put you on probation."

Hooray, the ghost was back! Looking younger and fitter, his appearance now was identical to Marc's, especially after all Marc had been through over the past few days. Both of them had the same weight, the same number of gray hairs and wrinkles, and the same amount of darkness in the circles under their eyes. Marc was staring at his true mirror image now.

"How else was I to get out of the rut I was in?" Marc said.

The ghost in the mirror smiled. "By escaping into an alternate reality? That isn't the solution, my friend. Apart from the fact that it's not even scientifically possible, it never brings true happiness. Sooner or later, your own true reality will always catch up with you. And the longer you leave your problems unattended, the more they will have grown in the meantime. Don't you see what's happened to you here in this world?

"You can't alter your past, as much as you try. You have to face it for what it is, and make the best of it. You can learn from it, and you can change your future as a result of what you've learned, but you can't go back."

Marc looked down, deep in thought.

"The way forward is forward, not backward," the ghost added.

"How do you know all this?" Marc asked, looking up again.

"Because I know what you've been through. I'm the part of you that still remembers, the part they haven't been able to tamper with."

"I remember now too!"

"Ah, but there's still one thing you don't remember."

Marc raised his eyebrows with curiosity.

"Where you are and how you got here," the ghost said. "And in order to find that out, you need to rejoin me."

"How?"

"First, you have to be absolutely certain that you believe me. Otherwise, any attempt to rejoin me will fail. You will most likely end up in some transitional state that you will never be able to get out of. Next, you have to give up the imaginary world you've been living in. Let it go, leave it behind, think of it no more. There's nothing left for you there. Then, close your eyes and step through this mirror toward me."

It was going to be a big risk and an even bigger leap of faith, but Marc knew the ghost was right. There really was nothing left for him here anymore. And everything the ghost had said would happen had indeed happened. This was clearly not his real life. It never had been, and now reality was desperately trying to catch up with him before it got too late.

He closed his eyes, and let go of his surroundings. The wonderful married life with Iman, all the get-togethers with his parents, his successful career, the beautiful house, the cliff, the ocean – he just let all those memories vanish from his mind. They were fake and meaningless anyway. He then felt his body moving in the direction of the mirror. He didn't even have conscious control over it anymore. It was just moving of its own accord.

The fingers on his right hand came into contact with the mirror first. It felt like a solid surface. But once he applied more pressure, the mirror gave way, feeling more like a cold, thick liquid. His left hand came next, then his right foot. Finally, his eyes closed as his nose touched the mirror. The cold fluid quickly rushed all over his face, around his head and over his whole body. With his left foot, he lunged forward, passing completely into the realm of the mirror.

The icy liquid splashed all around him, causing him to shiver. He felt like he was being bathed from top to bottom, getting a thorough cleansing of both the body and the mind. The liquid seeped into his head, down his neck and into the rest of his body. He felt his heartbeat slow down and his thoughts fade away, and for a moment he wondered if he was dying. But then, the liquid began draining out through his legs and feet, and his thoughts and heartbeat slowly came back.

One more step, then another, and out he came on the other side of the mirror. As he did, he opened his eyes again. What he saw stunned him at first, but then all the memories came back in a flash. He realized right away why the ghost in the mirror had been so secretive about where he was and how he had arrived here. Now he knew it all. As he had expected, the ghost, now back inside his head, was nowhere to be seen. His mind was whole again, reunited with his real body.

Chapter 19

The tall figure walked silently down the dark, deserted passage, an ancient hallway with high ceilings and vaulted arches made of white stone. The hallway was long, so long that it would be impossible for the human eye to see from one end to the other.

Like a typical Aftaran, the figure took long strides with a quick pace. But this was no ordinary Aftaran. He was taller than most, standing at a height of 8.3 feet, and thinner. His robe was bright green, not the standard brown, black or white that most Aftarans wore, with a high collar that circled all around his neck. And, most unlike Aftaran tradition, his somewhat elongated head and face were uncovered. His face had the characteristic Aftaran features – owl-like eyes and ears, a short but wide beak, and feathers that covered the skin. But the feathers were greenish in color, as opposed to the far more common tan or gray feathers. Even his eyes were green, eyes that were unusually elongated in shape like his face. He appeared middle-aged, and he had an authoritative and confident air about him, a contrast from the humble, subdued demeanor of most Aftarans.

Yes, this particular individual definitely stood out in any crowd. He knew that, and that was the way he preferred it. He also knew that it wasn't just because of his appearance, but largely because of his identity.

"May the Creator protect you from harm, Lord Wazilban." The two Aftaran guards, one on each side of the heavy metal door marking the end of the hallway, bowed as they both greeted him in Mareefi. They wore black robes that covered their bodies, heads and faces, everything except for their eyes. Both guards had boryals in their right hands.

Lord Wazilban didn't respond, or offer any acknowledgment of their presence.

Instead, he waited silently for the guards to open the door, and then walked right past them. The door immediately swung shut behind him, sending off a deep, loud echo across the chamber he had just entered. The chamber was midsized, with thick brick walls on all sides and no windows. There were a number of dim lamps on the high ceiling, dispersing an orange glow around the room. Due to its underground location, the air inside the chamber was cool and damp.

But Wazilban paid no attention to any of that. The only thing he was interested in was the row of Aftarans against the far wall. They were latched onto the wall with heavy chains, their arms and legs spread apart as far as their bodies allowed. There were five of them, all cloaked in white robes, their heads covered but their faces unveiled. They didn't look at all comfortable. No doubt, they were prisoners.

Wazilban stopped in front of the prisoner in the middle. "I trust you are enjoying your stay," he said with a whiff of sarcasm. His voice was deep and loud, and echoed across the chamber.

The prisoner in the middle slowly lifted her head to look at him, but kept quiet.

Another prisoner to her left opened his mouth. "We were, until you filled the room with your vile odor." His voice quivered from the pain in his limbs.

Wazilban laughed, with a deep, croaking resonance. "Rayim, always the courageous one! Your insolence knows no bounds, but it will not save you from your unavoidable fate."

"What do you want?" the prisoner in the middle said, addressing Wazilban. She sounded old, very old, and weak from the tormenting position she had been kept in for days, maybe weeks on end.

"I have a question for you, your Eminence Ouria," Wazilban said.

"Why should we answer you?" Ouria asked with her crackling voice. Every word she spoke seemed to take the last bit of energy in her body out of her.

"Because if you don't, then one of you will die tonight." Wazilban glanced briefly at Rayim, hinting who the unfortunate victim might be.

"We will all die anyway," Rayim countered. "We are not afraid of your empty threats, you fiend! The Creator watches over us in life and in death."

Wazilban laughed again. "You may not be afraid of death, you fool, but can you withstand pain?"

"Do what you will," Rayim said defiantly. "I am not afraid!"

"Very well." Wazilban walked over to the side wall, where there was a station with a number of controls. The controls looked quite archaic, consisting of no more than a few knobs and some analog dials. He pressed on a knob, and began turning one of the dials.

Rayim screamed in agony almost immediately. Streaks of lightning flashed all over his robe, and his body began shaking violently.

All the other prisoners stared at him in fright, but kept quiet. Wazilban moved the dial even more, intensifying the torture. Rayim's squeals grew louder and louder.

It was a sight that Aftarans would normally find intensely horrifying and just plain unimaginable, but Wazilban seemed to be enjoying it. "Where is your Creator now?" he said in a patronizing tone, laughing away at Rayim's torment.

"Enough!" Ouria wailed, clearly unable to bear the suffering one of her High Clerics was undergoing for her sake. "Stop it, I beg of you! In the name of the Creator, please stop! I will do what you ask."

Wazilban turned the dial all the way back to its starting point. All was quiet again, except for an occasional whimper from Rayim.

Wazilban walked back toward Ouria. "I knew you would come to your senses, your Eminence."

"What is your question?" she demanded. Her face looked as old as her voice sounded, with white and gray feathers and faded eyes. She looked much older even than Autamrin. She was, in fact, one of the oldest Aftarans alive, at an age of 1215 Earth years.

"Something has happened, something unexpected," Wazilban said. "I need to know if it is in any way tied to a prophecy in the Hidden Scripture." With that, he took out a silver coin-like object from inside his robe, and ran his one of his long, thin fingers around the circumference. The coin instantly turned golden and glowed. Words in the ancient Altareezyan script appeared in bright letters in the air above the coin, clearly visible for everyone in the chamber to see:

> *When the Sign advances in the darkest hour,*
> *Arise, unite, and shun your differences.*
> *Fight the forces of evil and drive them away,*
> *And take back what is rightfully yours.*
>
> *Hasten not its startling advent,*
> *For it follows not your command.*
> *Hasten not to act without it,*
> *For you will fail in your quest.*
> *But delay not when it comes,*
> *For it shall not linger.*

Ouria bowed her head in front of the verse. She did not bother to read it, probably because she knew it by heart. "I never thought the day would come that you would begin believing in the Hidden Scripture, or any of the other Scriptures," she said. "The evil mentioned here refers to none other than you."

Wazilban laughed. "I do not believe in any of them," he said dismissively. "As I do not in your Creator."

Whispers filled the room. All the prisoners were begging for forgiveness from the Creator for listening to such blasphemy.

"I do have a certain image to keep in front of the public, of course," Wazilban continued. "I find their blind religious fervor to be quite useful, to steer them in any direction I want. But none of that is your concern anymore, as you are dead to them. It was quite easy to see to that, mind you, as it was to obscure any evidence of who the 'killers' were. The only reason I have chosen to keep you alive in secret, for some time at least, is for my own fancy. And in case I need your expert advice.

"I am interested in this prophecy because of the insubordination it will incite in the Dominion. There are three known copies of the Hidden Scripture. When I had you arrested, my troops only found one of them." He pointed at the coin in his hand. "The other two copies were undoubtedly given away by you before you were arrested."

"The Hidden Scripture is meant only for the eyes of the High Clerics," the prisoner to Ouria's immediate right said. "Not for yours or anybody else's."

"And yet her Eminence here has given it away," Wazilban said, pointing his finger at Ouria.

Ouria was silent.

"Your silence on this topic is of no consequence, your Eminence," Wazilban went on. "I have no doubt that you gave at least one of the two copies to your beloved Autamrin, if not both. He is now just waiting to pounce at the right moment. With the arrival of this 'Sign', he will try to join forces with the few unruly elements in the Dominion. He will lure them with these verses, taking advantage of their hopeless need for blind faith in the unseen, and will then lead a rebellion against me. I need to be prepared for that event, so that I can squash them in one swoop. It will serve as an example to the rest of the Dominion, never to challenge my authority again!

"That is, if my surveyors do not get to Autamrin first. Any day now, I look forward to the news that he and his pesky followers have been destroyed."

Ouria looked crestfallen.

"So, tell me, what kind of 'Sign' is it that Autamrin is waiting for?" Wazilban demanded.

Ouria shook her head. "The Sign cannot be seen ahead of time. Its identity and characteristics are hidden until the time it is ordained to appear."

"I did not come here to listen to a paraphrase of the verses. I want to know what kind of event would be interpreted by Autamrin as a valid Sign. Since you are the official keepers and interpreters of the Hidden Scripture, you should know that better than anyone else."

"There are no criteria for the Sign," Ouria said. "The only way for us to recognize it is for it to unveil itself."

Wazilban sneered. "You expect something to come out in the open and say 'here I am, I am the Sign'?"

Ouria shook her head again. "No, I expect to recognize it when it appears, not wallow in endless speculation beforehand."

Wazilban began pacing up and down, visibly irritated. "I am getting tired of your empty talk! I will ask one more time, before I walk back to those controls. How will you recognize the Sign?"

"You hear, O Wazilban, but you do not listen. That has been your trait since the day your banner of terror and evil darkened our worlds. The only way to recognize the Sign is for us to hear about it with our ears, to see it with our eyes. We will feel it in our minds, our hearts and our souls. It is not something we can quantify, nor can we expect it to fulfill specified conditions. Those are not the ways of the Creator, nor are they our ways."

Wazilban stopped pacing and stood still, taking a moment to decide if there was any risk in revealing the news he had to his prisoners. "Very well, have it your way," he said, realizing that they would, after all, never see the light of day again. "My spies tell me that there has been a Mendoken attack on Volonan territory."

"That says nothing to me," Ouria said frankly. "Those two nations are always at war." She sighed.

"Yes, but the difference is that this attack was deep within Volonan space. They completely bypassed the insurmountable Volonan border defenses. There is only one way to do that."

The prisoner on Ouria's far right spoke for the first time. "So they used consars. The Mendoken have been accusing the Volona of the same thing for a while now. What is so surprising about that?"

"The surprising thing is that the Mendoken do not have consar technology. They signed the transportation treaty, did they not? The Mendoken are not the kind to build something in secret, or against the law."

Silence.

"Do I need to spell it out?" Wazilban continued in frustration. "The Mendoken are getting help from somewhere else, a new, advanced and hitherto unknown force in the galaxy. I want to know if this could be interpreted as a 'Sign' by our rebel friends, to try and make contact with this new force and use it against me."

More silence. Ouria closed her eyes.

Wazilban began moving towards the controls. Rayim tensed up, evidently realizing what was about to happen.

Ouria opened her eyes again, and broke the silence. "This could not be the Sign."

Wazilban turned and came back. "What makes you so sure?" he asked, staring closely into her eyes for any indication of deception.

"Neither the Mendoken nor the Volona share our religion or our way of life. The Creator would never reveal our Sign amongst unbelievers, especially not those who have nothing to do with our struggle."

"So the Sign has to appear within the Dominion?" Wazilban asked, still staring into her eyes.

"There is no other way," Ouria replied calmly and confidently. "Otherwise it will never be accepted by our people. And surely the Creator would not want that to happen."

"Interesting," Wazilban said. "Very, very interesting." He glanced at Rayim. "Well, Rayim, once again your leader has saved your skin. You will live to see another day, although numbered they surely remain. May the Creator protect you from harm."

He laughed as he said the last sentence, then turned around and walked towards the metal door, the only door into and out of the chamber. The guards opened the door from the outside as he approached it, and sealed it shut behind him.

Another Aftaran had arrived in the meantime, and was waiting outside. His robe was green, similar to Wazilban's, but his head was covered and his face veiled. As soon as he saw Wazilban, he bowed.

"Any indications, my Lord?" he asked, as they began walking together along the hallway.

"She claims it is not the Sign, and she seems certain of it," Wazilban said. "But I do not trust her, as honest as she may seem. First she stated there were no criteria to identify the Sign. But when I mentioned the consar attack, she hastily added that the Sign had to appear within the Dominion."

"That is indeed fishy, my Lord," the other Aftaran said, puffing as he tried to keep up with his master. Since he was only 7.4 feet tall, his strides were much shorter than Wazilban's.

"Get in touch with our associates at the Volonan border. Tell them to get as close to Volo-Gaviera as they can. I want to find out everything there is to know about this consar attack. Since we know the attack failed, the Mendoken ships were either destroyed or captured. We need to find out if there were any survivors."

"As you wish, my Lord."

"And have them send a report as soon as they discover anything of significance."

"Certainly, my Lord."

"The Imgoerin may believe he has succeeded in concealing this whole project from his enemies and allies alike, but once again he underestimates the extent of our reach and influence. Which, as usual, plays right into our hands, my friend."

As the two of them walked away from the chamber, Wazilban's laughter echoed boomingly from the walls of the long, dark hallway.

It was a strange feeling for Sharjam to be back inside an Aftaran ship. Two years had passed since he and the others had crash-landed on Tibara and concealed their ship, two years of hiding in the deep caves of that wretched mountain, two years of no space travel or contact with other Aftarans. Finally, he felt like he was a part of the Dominion again.

They had cleared Droila's atmosphere within a few minutes after takeoff, and were now heading out into deep space. Their destination was the Mendoken border, about 130 light years away. At a maximum speed of 25,000 times the speed of light, the Boura-class ship would take about 2 days to get there. That wasn't anywhere close to the speed that Mendoken or Volonan ships could travel at, but not bad considering how far behind Aftaran technology was.

Sharjam was starting to feel hopeful and optimistic, something he hadn't felt in a long time. Of course, once the other two Aftarans back on Droila found their ship missing and sounded the alarm, Dominion ships would be on the lookout everywhere. But if he and Dumyan played it smart and didn't make any major mistakes, they had a good chance of making it into Mendoken territory. To be safe, they would have to avoid all major travel routes of the Yuwa and risk flying across open space instead.

Sharjam, totally exhausted from the events of the past couple of days, felt himself falling into a peaceful slumber. His mind began to wander, his thoughts trailing off in random directions, his eyelids slowly dropping over his tired eyes.

But the peace was not to last.

"Make no abrupt movements, either of you," a deep, gruff voice behind them suddenly said. "Or your heads will be blown to bits."

Sharjam froze in his seat, totally shocked that he and Dumyan were not alone on the ship. He felt the sharpness of metal against his neck, almost certainly the edge of a boryal.

"Who are you?" Sharjam demanded, paying heed to the warning and not turning his head. He felt a hand slipping into his cloak, grabbing his own boryal and taking it away.

The voice laughed with a croaking sound, a sound only an Aftaran could make. "Did you really think you could escape so easily? The Doolins might be devoid of intelligence, but we did not teach them to be traitors!"

"I should have guessed you were behind this, Ozwin," Dumyan said, without turning around. "Only someone with your devious nature could mislead an entire species like that."

"We meet again, my dear Dumyan! And this would have to be your younger brother Sharjam? Quite the righteous Aftaran he is, from what I hear, a far cry from your naughty self. Although much good that will do him now!" Again, that croaking laugh.

Sharjam wondered who Ozwin was, and how his brother could possibly know him. He wondered why he and Dumyan hadn't noticed Ozwin during their earlier search of the entire ship. There had to be a hidden compartment somewhere that they had overlooked.

"What do you want from us?" Dumyan growled.

"A silly question, my friend," Ozwin said. "You will be taken straight to Meenjaza, where Lord Wazilban will deal with you as he pleases. I can assure you that it will not be a pleasant experience for either of you. He has lately become quite annoyed with your constant evasion of his surveyors, and is anxious to get his hands on any one of you. He will surely also want to learn how your wise old father is."

"Some things never change," Dumyan said, shaking his head. "Tell me, Ozwin, have you been promoted yet?"

"Promoted?" Ozwin asked, sounding surprised. "To what?"

"To have the privilege of sniffing and cleaning Wazilban's excrement every morning? Was that not your dream occupation, the last time we spoke?"

Dumyan received a sharp blow on his head with the back of his own boryal. He was instantly knocked unconscious. Having lost the mind connection to its pilot, the ship started losing speed almost immediately.

"Enough chitter-chatter," Ozwin said. "The same will happen to you, Sharjam, if you do not keep your mouth shut. Get up slowly and turn around, with your hands above your head. No sudden movements!"

Convinced that he was dealing with a ruthless individual, Sharjam did as he was told. He could see Ozwin now – a tall, burly Aftaran dressed in a brown robe. His face was uncovered, revealing a stout face with wide eyes and a beak that was always slightly open. He had a mean look about him, with a scowling expression that seemed to be permanent. Sharjam guessed that even if Ozwin ever tried to change his expression, the muscles and feathers on his face just wouldn't allow it.

Behind Ozwin was another Aftaran in a brown robe, also with her face uncovered. She was shorter and thinner, and far prettier. Her round eyes and long eyelashes gave her an air of sweetness that Sharjam hadn't seen since... well, since his days as a student at the clerical academy, maybe the one time he had done something wild, something outside the realm of the strict religious protocol he had observed throughout his life. Raiha... that name still sent tingles through his body. She had just been so attractive and so charming, so incredibly understanding and supportive, that he had been unable to resist falling head over heels in love with her. Much as he still missed her, it all seemed so long ago now, and so much had happened since then.

This attractive Aftaran, however, clearly meant business, for her boryal was pointed straight at him.

"Take them away!" Ozwin ordered her, as he shoved Dumyan out of the pilot's seat and took his place. Dumyan, still unconscious, fell to the floor with a thud. Sharjam immediately knelt down to attend to his brother.

The female Aftaran spoke for the first time. "Did you not you hear Ozwin?" she barked. "No sudden movements!"

"Hit him," Ozwin said, without bothering to turn around to look at them.

She raised her boryal, and with its backside hit Sharjam's head hard.

Sharjam fell on top of Dumyan, dazed and weakened. He murmured a confused prayer to the Creator, asking for protection and guidance. Then he felt another blow, and was knocked unconscious.

Chapter 20

"Aliens!" Marc said to himself. "I'm on an alien world!"

The memories came back, one by one. The night in his lab at Cornell, the fight with Cheryl, the failed time travel experiment and its completely unexpected outcome. The arrival of the Mendoken, and his journey aboard a spaceship past the silupsal filter to the Mendoken heartland. Then another journey with the Mendoken to the seat of enemy territory, using the very mechanism he had discovered with his failed experiment. And finally, the failure to escape, after which the enemy had totally destroyed them. The last thing he could remember was that massive explosion all around him on board the Mendoken battlecruiser. He should have been dead.

And yet, here he was, alive. Somehow he had survived the explosion and had become a prisoner of the enemy – the Volona, the masters of virtual worlds. All this time, he realized, he must have been living in a Volonan virtual world, a perfect world created by the desires of his own imagination.

The Volona had kept him alive, and had almost certainly been observing him in his virtual world. For what purpose, he didn't know. Perhaps they were just curious about his species, but that was unlikely. Sibular had told him that the Volona never took prisoners, so this had to be a special case. For some reason, the Volona thought he was of some value to them. And this was probably their way of interrogation – holding him indefinitely in his own virtual world and watching him closely. Completely ignorant of the fact that he was a prisoner, he was to live his life, over time unknowingly revealing whatever information his captors were seeking.

What the Volona didn't know, however, was that humans couldn't survive in such worlds of perfection. That wasn't surprising, since they had probably never met a human before. They didn't know that the human mind would continuously rebel, even against itself, until it was allowed to return to its natural state, a state of imperfection. For humans, perfection was a goal to keep striving towards, never to continuously live in. Life had no meaning for humans if they could get everything they wanted without any effort.

So Marc's mind had rebelled against itself, appearing as a ghost in his own perfect, virtual world to pull him back into reality. The ghost had taken some precautions to remain undetected, such as never mentioning the Mendoken or Volona by name. Such mention may have triggered a warning to his observers that he knew he was their prisoner and why they were holding him. From that point on, he would no longer have been of any use to them, and they might have terminated his life right there and then. Instead, his ghost had found a more subtle way to get him out of his virtual captivity.

But now that he was back in reality, what was he to do? Surely the Volona would have noticed that he had escaped from his virtual prison. How long did he have, he wondered, before they came looking for him here in the real world? And so many other questions still remained unanswered. How had he survived the attack on the Mendoken ships? Was Sibular still alive? Had any of the other Mendoken survived? If so, how could he find them? And, of more immediate consequence, what kind of strange environment was he currently surrounded by?

Behind him, the mirror he had just stepped through had vanished. He found himself in the middle of a street, or at least what remained of what had once been a street. Most of it consisted of deep potholes, while the rest was covered by loose boulders. Every direction he looked, he could see the same thing. Never in his life had he seen such disarray, such untidiness and chaos. There was rubble and garbage everywhere, in some places stacked up in tall mounds. Ruins of what had once been massive buildings were scattered on both sides of the street. Smoke and dust blew all around him. The sky was a dismal gray, with lightning periodically flashing in the distance between the dark clouds. A horrid stench hung in the hot, humid air, a smell as bad as that of a trash can of perishables that hadn't been emptied in several weeks. It all reminded him of a movie he had once seen a long time ago, showing the remains of an entire city that had been destroyed by nuclear bombardment.

Except that this wasn't a destroyed city. It was a living, functional metropolis. There were alien creatures about everywhere – Volonans, no doubt. Most of them were just standing, sitting or even lying down on the ground. Some walked about slowly. But they all had that same carefree, sleepy look about them, as if they were in a trance. He surmised that this was because their minds were in their own virtual realms, where they were enjoying their lives to the fullest. The horrible state their real world was in just didn't matter. They didn't care, because none of them ever spent any time consciously living in the real world.

Marc was disgusted by his new environment. He had never liked disorderly or dirty places, but this was worse than anything he had ever seen before. What a contrast from the beautiful house on the cliff he had just left behind in his virtual world, what a contrast from the spotless and highly modern Mendoken cities, what a contrast even from the poorest human neighborhoods back on Earth! And what peculiar looking creatures these Volonans were, now that he was finally getting to see them for real. Made those Mendoken look downright normal, they did!

The Volonan stood upright, but with a curved upper back, as if it suffered from severe bent spine syndrome. Its body was chubby and droopy, with two long front limbs that hung so low that it dragged its hands along the ground when it walked. The two legs seemed more stable. Shorter and wider, they kept the body firmly planted on the ground. The head was round and big, especially compared to the rest of the body. The face looked quite innocent, with large, round eyes that were black in color, elephant-like ears that flapped in the wind, and a short trunk for a nose.

"A large penguin with a bent back and an elephant's head," Marc thought. That pretty much summarized what these Volonans reminded him of.

They were not very tall creatures, as 5 feet seemed to be the maximum height he could see around him. Although if someone forced them to stand upright, they could probably reach heights of 6 feet or more. Their skin looked rough and had a reddish tint. The clothes these creatures wore were shabby and torn all over, a clear reflection of their environment. Some of the outfits did have bright colors and interesting patterns, though, and they generally covered the Volonans' bodies from their necks down to the upper parts of their legs. Their thick-soled feet had no toes and were protected by sandals.

The Mendoken had not shown Marc any pictures of Volonans, as they had no records of what Volonans actually looked like. So he was surprised at how familiar these Volonans seemed to him. He couldn't explain it at first, but soon realized why. He had seen them in his visions back on the Mendoken moon Ailen, and subsequently in dreams that had served as a constant reminder of those horrible visions. They were the creatures he hadn't been able to identify, the ones beside the Mendoken, Aftar and Phyrax. How he could possibly have known back then what Volonans looked like was a big mystery, since it was only now that he was seeing them for the first time. He wondered if he was going crazy, or if the whole virtual world experience had somehow altered his memories.

He also wondered what to do now, or where to go. None of the Volonans around him seemed to be paying any attention to him, as they were too engrossed in their own virtual worlds. He began walking up the street he was on, to see what was beyond his current line of sight. But it was all the same – miles and miles of the same ruins, garbage heaps and daydreaming Volonans, no matter which way he looked. A hill could be seen in the distance, atop which stood several massive towers shaped like lighthouses. They looked like foreboding shadows, not to be approached under any circumstances whatsoever by any mortal who valued his or her life.

After an hour of fruitless walking, Marc began to feel very tired. The gravitational pull on this world was much stronger than that back on Earth, requiring him to consume much more energy for every step. Not sure what else to do, he decided to try to talk to one of the Volonans. He approached one of them, sitting on a boulder and gazing dreamily at the sky.

"Hello!" he said, trying to sound cheerful.

The Volonan didn't look at him.

"I am Marc," he continued, pointing at himself. "You are?"

No response.

"Can you hear me? Hello?" He gathered enough courage to poke the alien on one of its long arms.

The Volonan didn't budge. Marc tried the same thing with a couple of other Volonans, but it was the same result every time. This was a useless exercise, he soon realized. Back to the aimless wandering it was.

He didn't get very far, however, before he began hearing a deep whirr. It was far away behind him, but getting louder by the second. He turned around nervously. At first, he saw nothing, but then it became visible, flying through the air at a low altitude and at high speed. Another one appeared to the left, then another to the right.

They looked like bats, he thought, except that their wings weren't flapping. Evidently, these were no living creatures, but flying machines of some sort. And they were heading straight toward him.

Suddenly one of the machines fired a laser-like streak of light. Before he had any time to react, the streak landed several feet away from him. A powerful explosion followed, shaking the ground and causing him to lose his balance and fall. Then came another explosion in front of him, and another behind. It was obvious what, or more precisely, who the target of those machines was. Luckily for him, their aim wasn't the best.

He got up and ran as fast as he could. It wasn't easy, though, given the strong pull of gravity and the rockiness of the terrain. Several times he stumbled and fell, hurting one of his knees, legs or ankles. But thanks to the adrenalin rushing through his body, he got up every time and kept on running.

As they quickly caught up with him, the machines kept firing more frequently, and they eventually chased him onto a bridge over a deep gorge. Before he was able to reach the other side, one of the machines flew ahead and turned around to face him. With his escape path cut off on both sides, all he could do was stop and stare at the machines. They looked menacing, with their dark bodies and wide, curved wings. The tips of the wings carried the guns that were firing those deadly shots.

Marc stood still and awaited his fate, for he knew that death was staring him in the face. But as he heard the machines fire, a figure suddenly jumped onto the bridge from the depths of the gorge below, grabbed him, and jumped off the other side with him. It all happened in the flash of a second. And as both of them fell into the gorge, the shots hit the exact point he had been standing on, causing the center of the bridge to blow up in a big explosion.

It was a free fall. "Haaaaaaaaahhhhhh!" Marc yelled. Out of fear, he did not dare look into the depths of the gorge below. Instead, he kept his gaze focused on the mystery figure that was holding him tightly with one of its long arms. It was a Volonan.

With its free arm, the Volonan suddenly grabbed onto a ledge on one side of the gorge. With a violent jerk, they immediately stopped falling. Then, with just that one arm, the Volonan pulled both itself and Marc up onto the ledge.

Marc was surprised at the amount of strength those flimsy looking arms contained. A human would never have been able to pull off such an acrobatic stunt.

The ledge led to the opening of a cave. Still holding Marc, the Volonan rushed into the opening. And none too soon, for the debris from the destroyed bridge above came thundering down the gorge. Some large chunks of rock crashed onto the ledge they had just landed on, sending off plumes of dust that chased after them into the cave.

Marc coughed in the darkness, while trying to brush the dust from his eyes.

The Volonan let go of him and propped him up against the wall of the cave. It laid its four-clawed paw on his mouth, motioning to him to stay absolutely still. Then it took up position next to him, flattening itself as much as it could against the wall.

It soon became obvious why. Through the settling dust, Marc could see the flying machines outside, hovering around in the gorge. One of them came right near the entrance to the cave, shining a light inside. The light moved around, and at one point shone directly on his face.

"This is it," he thought, "the end!"

Surprisingly, the light kept on moving around. Eventually, the machine flew up and away. The other two machines also took off.

The Volonan stranger relaxed and turned to face him. Opening its mouth, it began making some high-pitched whines that sounded somewhat like the siren of a police car.

"I'm sorry, I don't understand," he said, shaking his head.

The Volonan took something out of its pocket and pressed a button.

"How does that sound?" a lively female voice said in English.

Marc nodded approvingly. "Much better! Is that a translator?"

"Why, yes, that's what it is," the Volonan said, looking at the small device she was holding. "And it detected both our languages! That's not too bad, not too bad at all."

"Who are you?"

"Who am I? I'm not the stranger here. Who are you?"

Marc wasn't sure whether to trust this individual. After all, she was a Volonan, one of the enemy. On the other hand, she had saved his life. After some hesitation, he said, "I am Marc Zemin, a human from the planet Earth."

"Human? Earth? Never heard of either. Where is this 'Earth'?"

"It's a part of the, uh, Mendo-Biesel star system."

The Volonan smiled. "The Mendoken Republic? Well, young human, you're certainly a long way from home! That does explain a few things, though."

"What do you mean?"

"Why those drones were after you, for one. Let me guess, you broke out of your virtual world?"

"Yes, I did. Are you, uh, not virtual?"

The Volonan laughed, making a screeching sound that almost pierced Marc's ears. "Nope, I'm the real thing!" she said. "But believe me, I'm the only Volonan you'll find who is, on this planet anyway."

He stared at the Volonan, confused.

"It's a long story," she continued, flapping her big ears and letting out a sigh.

An uncomfortable silence followed, during which the Volonan peered closely at him from top to bottom. Finally, she touched his forehead with her hand. "Zorina is the name. Pleased to meet you."

Marc picked up her hand with his and gave it a shake. "Pleased to meet you too. Thank you for saving my life!"

"No worries. Just remember – the way to dodge those drones is to stay absolutely still when they are close by. They can only sense abrupt motion, not bodies that are stationary or moving very slowly. That's how I always evade them."

"Is that how they distinguish between those in virtual worlds and those that aren't?"

"Hmm, smart these humans are. I like it!" Zorina sat down on the floor of the cave, and leaned back against the wall. "Well, time for a little nap."

"A nap? Now?" Marc was surprised. "What about those drones?"

"Oh, they won't be back for a while. Besides, I have to take a nap every couple of hours. Otherwise, my body tires out and I get very irritable. You wouldn't want that, would you now?"

Marc wasn't sure what to say.

"Nothing unusual for us Volonans, I assure you," she said, closing her eyes. "Real life is a lot more tiring than virtual life."

Before he could open his mouth again, she was already snoring heavily through her trunk.

He sat down as well, opposite her on the other side of the cave. There was nothing else he could do at the moment, other than wait for her to wake up again. Whoever she was, she seemed his only hope for any chance to get out of here alive. And she would probably be able to answer some of the many questions he still had.

What a strange individual she was, though! She definitely seemed to have a lot more emotion and temperament than any Mendoken he had met. As he watched her sleeping in peace, he wondered whether all Volonans were like this. If they were, then they were clearly a far cry from the evil, treacherous monsters he had imagined them to be.

He closed his eyes and tried to relax, but couldn't. He was too worried that those drones might come back at any moment. But as the minutes passed and nothing happened, his worries began to subside. Finally able to think again after all the commotion he had just been through, he began recalling the time he had spent in the virtual realm. It had been like a dream, a very lifelike, long lasting dream of a perfect life. As wonderful as it had been, his own mind had eventually rejected that perfect world, because as a human he wasn't made for that kind of life.

It had been a learning experience, though, that much was for sure. He now knew how wonderful life with Iman might have been like, had things worked out between them. He now knew how much he had lost by letting her go. He now knew that after all these years, deep in his heart he was still in love with her. Cheryl had just been an attempt to get over Iman, an attempt to get attention during a very lonely and depressing phase of his life.

Did he ever have any hope of getting back together with Iman, he wondered, even if he ever made it back to Earth some day? She was surely married by now to somebody from her own culture, just like her family had wanted. Traveling back in time to mend things was not an option – that much was certain now. His experiments had failed, and for good reason. As the Mendoken had shown him, real space was not quite as relativistic as humans believed it to be. If he traveled faster than the speed of light, even through other dimensions, Einstein's theory of relativity would no longer apply, and the clock would just keep ticking forward at its normal rate. He would just get to his destination very quickly, that was all.

Besides, traveling back in time to change things – wasn't that just escaping from reality? Wasn't it similar in concept to living in a virtual world, a world of lies? It would possibly have a similar outcome in the end too. Somehow, whatever events he tried to prevent or alter by going back in time would end up happening anyway, because they had already happened in his past. No matter how hard he tried to prevent his parents' deaths, they would end up dying at some point. Maybe not on that particular day or location that he remembered, but soon enough and by a similar cause. The breakup with Iman would similarly be inevitable.

There was, he realized, only one way out of his predicament – to face it, to deal with it, and to learn from it. That was the only way to solve problems, the only way to get over things and to move on. Trying to escape would just cause the unattended problems to grow bigger over time, just like his ghost in the mirror had said. It wasn't necessary for everything to be solved right away, nor was it necessary for everything to be perfect. In fact, life for him as a human could never really be perfect. The way to live his life was to face reality and to take charge of his life. He would learn to hope for the best, but plan to be ready for the worst.

A half hour passed. The dust from the falling bridge debris had completely settled now, giving a clear view outside through the mouth of the cave. Marc could see the far wall of the gorge, only about 30 feet away, and was reminded of the fall from the bridge. What a frightening experience! Good thing he hadn't looked down towards the bottom of the gorge during the fall.

He turned his head to look the other way into the depths of the cave, but all he could see was darkness. He began wondering if there were any strange creatures lurking about inside. But before those thoughts turned to irrational fear, he was delighted to see Zorina stir awake.

"That was nice," she said sleepily, letting out a big yawn. She blinked and looked at him, apparently taking a moment to remember who he was.

"I'm glad you got some rest," he said, hoping he would now finally get some answers.

She took something out of her pocket, broke it into two pieces, and handed a piece to him. "Hungry?"

He stared at the dark green bar in his hand, and realized how hungry he was. All those tasty dishes that Iman had fed him in his virtual world – that seemed so long ago already. And who knew what the Volona had really been feeding him all that time to keep him alive? It was probably better he didn't know.

"Come on, it's just *sparli*," Zorina said, apparently sensing his hesitation. "It's very nutritious. Contains all the necessary nutrients for survival, it does."

He analyzed the bar closely. It actually felt like bread, though it had a more pungent smell. Taking a chance, he bit into it. It was surprisingly soft, and tasted a little bitter, kind of like solid beer. The inside was yellow.

"There you go!" she said, chomping away. "Isn't so bad, is it?"

"No, it's actually quite good!" He gulped it all down quickly.

Next, she took out a bottle from another pocket, causing him to wonder how many other pockets she had and what else she had in them.

"Here, some ale to wash it down," she offered.

Feeling more at ease now with Volonan cuisine, Marc took a swig. He expected it to be bitter, just like the few times in his life that he had drunk ale back on Earth. But this was sweet, very sweet indeed, with a fruity taste. He liked it.

"Now, can you tell me where we are?" he asked, handing the bottle back to her.

"In a cave, obviously," she said, glancing around between swigs of ale.

He frowned. "I mean this place, this planet!"

"Ah, well say so! This is Nopelio, the fourth planet in the Volo-Gaviera star system. We are in the city of Krasia. Well, one of its suburbs anyway."

"This is... a city?" Marc felt it was more like a collection of trash heaps.

Zorina didn't seem to take offense. "We Volonans don't care what our real world looks like anymore, because we never spend any time in it. Our cities haven't been maintained at all since we began moving into the virtual realm."

"I figured as much. But you – why exactly aren't you sitting out there in a daze, like the others?"

She flapped her ears. "As much as I'd love to return to the virtual world of my dreams, doing so would immediately result in my detection."

He raised his eyebrows. "So you're out here because you're... hiding? From whom?"

"Let's just say I've upset some powerful Volonans. So it's better I lie low for a while, out of sight."

"And they can't find you here, because now you're disconnected from the virtual realm, right?"

"Hmph, these humans really are smart!" Zorina said, bobbing her head up and down in apparent content. "All Volonans are connected to the Virtual Translation Grid. It's a central system that functions across the Empire, keeping track of the individual choices of all Volonans and letting them live whatever lives they choose to in their own virtual worlds. Some choose to just do nothing in the real world and live out their virtual lives in daydreams, like all the Volonans you probably saw earlier on the streets. Others actually perform real jobs, like the troops that brought you here and those that man our ships. The Grid takes care of all the necessary translations between what they do in their virtual worlds and what they actually end up doing in the real world.

"Now that's all very nice, but one of the unpleasant side effects is that any single Volonan connected to the Grid can be located at any time by the imperial authorities."

"But if that connection is severed, then you're free?"

"Freedom is a relative term, my friend. You've seen the state of the real world here. You call living in this dump freedom, when I could be lying in a virtual, perpetual state of bliss in a beautiful garden of blue ice, sipping heavenly *vintenza* and being tended to by hunky males on all sides?"

Marc had a thing or two to say about that, but before he could open his mouth, she went on. "But yes, you're technically correct. If the connection is severed, the Empire loses track of me. They might have a general idea of where I am, but they have no way of pinpointing my exact location at any moment. The most they can do is to send those drones with hopeless firing aim after me, same as they did for you."

"Why don't they just send some troops into the real world as well, to come and find us?"

She laughed. "Volonans will never voluntarily come into the real world, no matter how high the stakes."

He guessed that it was like asking humans to voluntarily go to hell.

"It's also not an easy process to break out of a virtual world, believe me," she added.

He smiled. "Oh, I believe you. I just went through it!"

"True. It can be very taxing on the mind, eh?"

Marc was silent for a moment. He was taking a liking to Zorina, and he felt quite comfortable talking to her. He had this instinctive feeling that he could trust her, even after all the horrible things he had heard about Volonans from Sibular and the other Mendoken. Why he felt that way, he wasn't sure. It was the same way he had felt upon meeting Sibular for the first time.

"Why did you save my life?" he finally asked.

She looked at him and smiled. "Any enemy of those drones is a friend of mine. Besides, it's not often that I get to meet another non-virtual individual. Life can get quite lonely in these parts, you know?" After a short pause, she asked the question he had hoped she wouldn't ask. "Now tell me, how did you end up here?"

He was silent.

Once again, she seemed to sense his hesitation. "I'm no friend of the authorities, if that helps," she said. "I have some fundamental differences with Adrelina."

"The ruler of the Empire?"

"The same. The main reason I'm here."

"Who exactly are you?"

Zorina flapped her ears again. "You first, young human!"

"Very well," he said, taking a big chance. "I was on board a Mendoken vessel that was destroyed by Volonan ships."

"By a triangular formation?"

"Yes – your ultimate weapon, from what I've heard. 'Ultimate' is quite the word, believe me! It was by far the most frightful thing I've ever seen. The entire ship just exploded around me! But what I don't understand is how I'm still alive."

"Oh, that's easy enough. The triangulation weapon generates a spatial anomaly – that's where it gets its destructive power from. Problem is, it often generates unwanted smaller spatial anomalies on the side. You were probably pushed into one of those during the impact of the main anomaly, and its shield protected you from the explosion."

"You mean like a bubble?" Marc asked, astonished. "Filled with what – air?"

"Well, whatever atmosphere was on your ship. And after the explosion, one of the Volonan ships probably picked you up, had you connected to the Grid and dropped you off here. My question, though, is why were you attacked? Where was your ship?"

"We were right here, in this star system."

She looked very surprised. "Inside the Empire? How did you cross the border?"

He hesitated. "By a consar," he finally said, realizing that he had no other way to explain it.

"A consar? The Mendoken have consar technology?" She looked even more surprised.

"They do now."

"And you were a prisoner of the Mendoken, I presume?"

"A prisoner? Oh no! I was on board voluntarily."

"What! And why, may I ask?"

"Well, in a nutshell, to respond in kind to your people's attacks on Mendoken worlds."

"Attacks! What attacks?"

"The ones using consars!"

"Consars? What nonsense!" Zorina laughed.

"You think this is funny, do you?" Marc said, starting to get annoyed.

"Young human, I've been living totally alone in this dump of a place for what feels like eternity. Considering the comfortable virtual life I left behind and where I am now, I can assure you that humor is far from my mind these days!" She was clearly annoyed too.

He tried studying the expression on her face, but realized he wasn't particularly knowledgeable about Volonan facial expressions. "You really don't know, do you?" he said.

"Know what? Will you kindly elaborate?"

"Your people have been using consars to bypass Mendoken defenses, to attack planets and space stations deep inside Mendoken territory."

She laughed again. "So these are the lies the Mendoken have been feeding you, eh? It's no different from the rubbish they keep claiming officially. That's how they justify their continuous attacks against our border defenses."

Marc's face flushed with anger. "They are not lies!" he shouted. "I saw a Volonan consar attack on an unprotected Mendoken planet with my own eyes! No matter what your Empire claims or denies, I already know the truth."

"Rubbish! The Mendoken probably showed you an act, just to convince you to help them against us."

"Now *that* is rubbish!" he yelled. He had to admit that the thought had crossed his mind, but he refused to believe the Mendoken were capable of such an act. They just didn't seem to have that kind of evil or deceptive nature in them.

Zorina sneered. "Are you the one who showed them how to travel through consars?"

In his fury, he opened his mouth right away to answer, but then he changed his mind and stayed silent. Regardless how trustworthy Zorina seemed, he couldn't imagine any Volonan appreciating the fact that he had helped the Empire's archenemy to such a large extent.

"Now you listen to me, young human!" she said, evidently sensing his guilt. "My people don't have the technology to use consars. Consar research was banned many years ago across the galaxy, and we have strictly honored that ban. Besides, consar capability would give us no benefit in maintaining or protecting our virtual worlds, the only purposes that we do any scientific research or development for. So what the Mendoken have been telling you is impossible."

"How can you be so sure of that? You're just a recluse and an outlaw – you admitted as much yourself!"

"I'm Adrelina's sister, that's how."

Chapter 21

When Sharjam came to, he couldn't immediately remember where he was or what had happened. The first thing he felt was a sharp pain on the back of his head, right at the spot where he had been hit. Then he felt an even sharper pain in his arms, and looking up, he realized why. His hands were pulled up above his head, attached to a latch in the ceiling with thick rope, and his feet were similarly fastened to the floor. With his body stretched out to its fullest, he couldn't move at all.

"Not a very pleasant situation we are in," Dumyan whispered, already awake. He was a few feet away from his brother, and in exactly the same position.

Sharjam groaned. "It hurts!"

"To put it mildly. The pressure on my hip is unbearable!"

Sharjam could still feel the tingling pain in his own wounded leg, so he could only imagine the agony his brother was going through. Their injuries from the landing on Droila were still far from healed. He tried his best not to think about it, and instead focused his thoughts on his surroundings.

It was dark all around, with only a tiny amount of light trickling in through an oval window. But the light was enough for him to identify the room they were in – the small prayer chamber located right at the front of the Boura-class ship. The window was located on the far wall, built into the only door to the room.

"It appears we are being watched," Dumyan said, gesturing towards the window with his head. Every now and then, a shadow passed by outside.

"Are you surprised?" Sharjam remarked.

"Not really."

"How long have we been here, hanging like this?"

"I am not certain. Several hours at least. At least, that is what the pain feels like. So how long did you last after me?"

"Back in the cockpit? No more than a minute."

"Did you notice any others?"

"Yes. A female."

"A female?" Dumyan tried to grin in between the throbs of pain. "Was she pretty?"

Sharjam scowled. "Considering our current condition, is that all you can think of?"

"What else should I do? We are stuck, after all."

Sharjam couldn't argue with that. Their situation was indeed hopeless, and light-hearted conversation was perhaps the best way to cope. "She was pretty, actually," he said, grinning sheepishly.

"She was the one who knocked you out?"

Sharjam was reminded of the splitting pain in the back of his head. "Yes, and she is probably the one watching us from behind that door, since Ozwin is piloting the ship. How do you know this Ozwin anyway? Did you meet him on one of your adventures?"

Dumyan sighed. "He is a most ruthless and vicious character. I had the misfortune of running into him in the Afta-Gouran star system."

"Where the Eelaks lived?"

"Yes. I was sent there on a mission by our father, when he was still in power. It was to understand the source of the Eelaks' discontent with his rule, before they began spreading all that slander about him across the Dominion."

"I remember you leaving for that journey. I was in the middle of my final clergy examinations. But I did not know that you met Ozwin there."

"I mentioned it to our father upon my return. Ozwin was living on Eelatan at the time, the home planet of the Eelaks. He was quite the champion in Eelak leadership circles. They refused to meet with me even once without him being present."

"How did he become such a hero?"

"By teaching them our way of life, our religion, and our scientific knowledge. They gladly scooped it all up, eager to learn from a people much more advanced than their own."

"But it is against the law to teach our ways to less advanced species!"

"It is only against the law to do that to any species that has not yet been accepted into the galactic community. We had already lifted the silupsal filter around Afta-Gouran, so the law no longer applied to the Eelaks. Ozwin knew that when he arrived on Eelatan."

"In hindsight, clearly a big mistake on our part to lift that filter."

"That is an understatement. The Eelaks had reached a certain level of technological progress, but intellectually they were still far behind the acceptable norm."

"Well, Afta-Gouran was strategically a very important location for us, as far as I remember. Right on the Phyrax border."

Dumyan nodded. "That was the reason. And the presence of the filter on that section of the border was preventing us from guarding it. It was, in fact, the only section of our entire border with the Phyrax Federation that was not fortified. Our father was very worried that the Phyrax would invade the Dominion through that system. So by lifting the filter, we were able to bring our ships there and guard that section of the border as well."

"But look at the horrible chain reaction that rushed decision caused."

"Who would have known? At that time, Wazilban was a nobody, just some monk on some remote world. We had no idea who he was, let alone how he and his band of thugs were plotting to topple our father. I had no knowledge that he was the one who had sent Ozwin to the Eelaks, with this elaborate plan to instill dissent across the Dominion with their help."

"Any idea how those two met?" Sharjam asked.

"Not really. Ozwin is a mercenary, and a member of the Raidamin clan, from what I have heard. I assume Wazilban found him and won his allegiance by paying him a lot of money."

"I notice a pattern with this Ozwin, taking advantage of less advanced species. First the Eelaks, now the Doolins."

"Yes, that is his expertise. Most likely that is why Wazilban hired him in the first place."

"But he did not teach the Eelaks to worship Aftarans, did he?"

Dumyan shook his head. "No, he did not. Once he had gained their trust, he showed them fabricated evidence about our father's rule and his supposed plans to destroy them. They believed him whole-heartedly, never once second-guessing him."

"Intellectually far behind the acceptable norm, as you said." Sharjam thought for a moment, and added, "Our people made a similar mistake, though."

"Yes, true, but they fell for a craftier trap. See, Wazilban knew what he was doing, and he picked the Eelaks for multiple reasons. For one, their location was right on the Phyrax border, an ideal spot for sparking trouble. For another, they were a species just introduced to the Dominion, eager to make friends amongst our people. And they were also an incredibly pious species."

"So I heard. I never actually met any Eelaks, but I read about them. Their concept of religion revolved around one almighty Creator, just like ours. A marked contrast from the polytheistic religions or atheistic ways of life we have usually found with emerging species on other worlds. I believe most of the Eelaks quickly converted to our religion after their first contact with the Dominion."

"Yes, thanks mostly to Ozwin. But believe me, he did not convert them because he was trying to show them the path to righteousness or redemption. He did it so that he could set the conditions for the perfect trap." A smirk appeared across Dumyan's face. "The perfect setting to accuse our father of the worst possible crime."

"Heresy!" Sharjam whispered, that horrible period in history still fresh in his memory.

"Yes, heresy! And the only reason the Eelaks got away with it was because our people let them."

"They fell prey to Wazilban, who took advantage of the situation. He was the one who suddenly appeared in the limelight, spreading the accusation of heresy across the Dominion. The Eelaks claimed our father was planning to attack them, much a lie as that was. And Wazilban argued that an attack like that against a vulnerable, backward species that had already converted to our faith amounted to heresy."

"Yes, but it was the Aftaran people who let Wazilban take advantage of the situation. They were only too eager to accept him, only too eager to hear his words of hate and warmongering, only too eager to rise up in arms into a massive revolt against our father's rule. And all at the mere sound of that one word – *heresy*."

Sharjam smiled, realizing where Dumyan was trying to go with this discussion. "What happened was not a fault of our religion or our way of life, Dumyan."

Dumyan looked directly at his brother. "Oh? Do you think this would have happened if the majority of our people were not so inflexible and blind about religion ruling every aspect of their lives? If they could just have used reason for once, then they would have seen how absurd this whole charge was."

Sharjam looked down, avoiding his brother's angry gaze. "It is the blind faith our people have that is at fault, not the religion itself."

"What is the difference?"

Sharjam thought a bit before answering. "The religion teaches us to live our lives a certain way, but it is a way of moderation. It teaches us how to be good and righteous, and above all, reasonable about everything. But it is the people who misinterpret the religion, who take it to one extreme or another. Religion can be a powerful tool, both for good and bad, because of the emotions it stirs in people. Unfortunately there are always those few extremists and fundamentalists who misuse it, who steer people in the wrong direction by offering a misguided, narrow-minded interpretation of the Scriptures. That is exactly what Wazilban did."

"And how is it that he was able to convince so many trillions, if not quadrillions, of Aftarans that his interpretation was the correct one? Surely there had to be something in our Scriptures that supported his arguments, something that was clear enough to begin with."

"It was the classic case of taking things out of context. The Scriptures are always misunderstood when specific verses are read by themselves and taken out of context of the greater meaning. That is why we need people who are learned in the Scriptures, such as established scholars and clerics, to interpret them and explain them to us. What Wazilban did was quote certain powerful verses by themselves, interpret them completely out of context in the most extreme way possible, and then sell the idea to the public."

"Well, how is it that he had such a massive success, and so quickly? Especially considering that Wazilban was a nobody from nowhere, with no scholarly credentials? Even his clan was unheard of before he appeared!"

"Because of his message and the way he positioned it. To the majority of people, the long and detailed academic sermons of our clerics could sometimes be bland and downright boring. Even though what the clerics taught was correct and just, it did not sound interesting or exciting to the average Aftaran. Much of the content many did not even understand.

"Suddenly, along came this fiery and outspoken Aftaran, with a powerful, new message. He appealed to the most basic of our emotions and instincts, using the right buzzwords and sound bites that he knew Aftarans would care most about. Phrases like 'freedom for anyone to pray anywhere, anytime', or 'defend the faithful against oppression', or even 'raise the lantern of truth in the darkest corners of the Dominion'.

"If you think about it, these phrases are all so incredibly generalized and over-simplified that they really do not mean much in real life. They might be good principles to abide by, but they can never be applied uniformly across the Dominion, at least not without destroying entire worlds, massacring billions of innocent lives, or forcefully converting different species to our religion and way of life. But they stir up powerful emotions in people, causing them to take sides, often irrationally and against their better judgment.

"Combine that with a few misinterpreted verses from the Scriptures, some fabricated evidence that conveniently supports the message, as well as general nervousness about growing hostilities with the Phyrax, and it creates an explosive mixture. It generates fear in the hearts of ignorant people, and fear breeds intolerance of others. It arouses people to join struggles they would otherwise never believe in. As more and more join the rising tide of belligerence, soon it becomes the accepted norm – the fashion of the times, so to speak. And before you know it, speaking out against it causes you to be branded as a heretic and a traitor to the Aftaran 'cause', because now there is a 'cause' worth fighting and dying for. And nothing is worse in our society than to be branded as a heretic or traitor.

"This was how our father was falsely labeled as a heretic and of being a weak, incompetent leader who didn't have the strength to confront the Phyrax. This was how our people fell prey to Wazilban's web of deceit and extremism. The High Clerics always warned us about the dangers of extremism. Unfortunately, their message has been forgotten by our people, just as the High Clerics themselves and all their noble principles of moderation that guided the Aftar for so many millions of years have also been forgotten."

Dumyan listened quietly to everything Sharjam was saying. He could see the sense in his brother's logic, but he wasn't totally convinced. He had never been a big fan of the tremendous religious focus in Aftaran society, or even of some of the things mentioned in the different religious texts. Of course, he had a deep respect for the sacred Scriptures and for the High Clerics. Nobody had done as much service to the Aftaran people as the High Clerics. But he just couldn't bring himself to agree with many of the laws or decrees that he knew about – they just seemed too narrow and too restrictive, far more than they needed to be. He couldn't understand why the all-knowing, all-merciful Creator would ordain such rules on the Created. Instead, he generally found his own principles, the ones he had developed as a result of his life's experiences, to better suit what he considered his more open-minded palate. And those were the principles he usually tried to live by.

"I have read some of the verses that Wazilban used in his public speeches," Dumyan said, once Sharjam had finished speaking. "They are quite lucid in their meaning, and do not need additional interpretations. They clearly support Wazilban's policies of belligerence and intolerance towards others."

"Have you read all the Scriptures from beginning to end?"

Dumyan laughed. "Of course not! That would take me years!"

"Did you ever attend clerical university, where they spend several days on each verse, trying to understand its meaning and relevant context in the Scriptures?"

"No! I followed a different career path from you. You know that!"

"Then how can you make such a statement?"

Dumyan opened his mouth right away to reply, but realized he didn't have a good answer.

Sharjam went on. "As I already mentioned, you have to understand the proper context of every verse. Our Scriptures are quite hard to comprehend! You can never understand them fully without the appropriate lengthy education and rigorous training under the qualified clerics. The majority of Aftarans do not have training to that necessary level, and Wazilban took advantage of that. He even killed off the High Clerics to make sure nobody would have access to the truth anymore. With the highest level removed, darkness and falsehood quickly trickled down the clerical hierarchy, spreading to the masses like wildfire."

"Regardless, at the end of the day, can you deny that this would never have happened if our society was not so deeply religious?"

Sharjam shrugged. "No, I cannot. But we do not really know what kind of crime-ridden, backward and corrupt society we would have ended up as, were it not for our religion and all the guidance it has provided us for the entirety of our existence."

The topic of conversation ended abruptly, for the door opened and light from the corridor brightened the prayer room. A figure walked in.

"Both of you, keep your mouths shut," the figure said in a stern voice.

"Or else what?" Dumyan demanded.

"Or else you get another blow on your heads, only this time it will be twice as hard." She brandished her boryal in a show of strength.

"She certainly does not mince her words," Dumyan thought, knowing not to test the sincerity of her threat. He wondered what she looked like, but couldn't see her face because it was veiled.

The figure turned around and stepped out of the room without another word. The door closed behind her with a heavy thud.

After a brief period of silence, Sharjam whispered, "Dumyan, we have got to get out of here."

"Considering our current situation, that might be a very hard thing to do," Dumyan whispered in return.

"We have to try. We cannot just stay like this and wait to be handed over to Wazilban's gloating hands."

Dumyan smiled, surprised at how action-oriented his brother had become over the past few days. But he could see no hope of escape this time.

Sharjam appeared to be reading his mind. "The Creator is with us and will guide us," he said softly. "The Creator is always on the side of the righteous."

Dumyan shook his head, looking down and feeling defeated. "Nay, Sharjam, this time the Creator appears to have left us in the lurch. I see no way out."

"You lose faith too quickly. With the Creator on our side, there is always a way."

Dumyan lifted his head and looked at his brother. It wasn't like Sharjam to speak so optimistically without a valid reason. "Meaning?"

"This is a prayer room, after all. Obviously our guard is not very religious, otherwise she would not have been silly enough to lock us up here. Or perhaps she has no knowledge of my educational background."

Dumyan was confused. "What is so special about a prayer room?"

"Ah! I see you share the same ignorance. Well, that is not a terrible surprise, given your lack of interest in all things religious. You see, every prayer room contains copies of the Scriptures."

"I know that!" Dumyan whispered. "But how does that help us at the moment?"

"You think all we were taught in clerical university was how to interpret the verses in the Scriptures?" Sharjam said.

Dumyan's eyes opened just a tad wider. "I am listening."

"We were also taught their power, power that goes well beyond the common enchantments known to most Aftarans." With that, Sharjam closed his eyes and began uttering something quietly.

Dumyan watched and waited, wondering what his brother had in mind.

He didn't have to wait long. The wall behind him suddenly began lighting up. He turned his head to see, and noticed seven small, bright circles forming on the wall. They were spread along a horizontal line, about a foot apart from each other, and they were silver in color. Once their shapes had solidified, they moved a few inches out of the wall, floating magically in thin air.

Dumyan realized right away what they were. They were scripture coins, a key foundation of the Aftaran religion, and the primary way the seven sacred Scriptures were read and revered across the Dominion. Made of an ultra-light metallic compound, each coin could store an entire copy of a single Scripture, the largest of which contained over 19,000 verses. When commanded to do so, a scripture coin could magnify and display any of the Scripture's verses in the open air, in clear view for everyone to see. Every prayer room or chamber across the Dominion had to have seven coins, one for each scripture. Otherwise, it was not considered a proper prayer chamber.

The eighth sacred Scripture, known as the Hidden Scripture, was never included in any prayer chamber, since it was not available to the public. Only the High Clerics, the chief order of the clerical hierarchy, officially had access to the Hidden Scripture. There were only three carefully guarded coins in the entire Dominion that held the Hidden Scripture, and it wasn't possible to make copies of them. One of them had been handed by Ouria to Autamrin in secret, shortly before his escape into exile. This was completely against Aftaran religious law, but desperate conditions had called for desperate actions. Dumyan could only guess what had happened to the other two copies after the murder of the High Clerics. Most likely Wazilban had both of them now.

Sharjam stared at the coins, and began speaking loudly. "O sacred Scripture of Conducts, arise and shine!"

As he said these words, the second coin from the left came further forward, and aligned itself horizontally in midair. Its color turned a brilliant golden, and bright golden symbols began forming in the air above it.

Sharjam's voice was booming now. "Unveil your power, for your haven has been tainted!"

The symbols crystallized into glowing Altareezyan text, clearly displaying a verse from the 12th chapter for both brothers to see:

> *The prayer room, a chamber of worship,*
> *A place of peace and sanctity,*
> *An icon of hope in a sea of despair,*
> *Remains forever watched and protected*
> *By the very words of truth it shelters.*

Dumyan was amazed. He had never seen this verse before, although he had to admit that he did not know the Scripture of Conducts or any of the other Scriptures too well. He wasn't sure what to expect next, but he was starting to feel that something major was about to occur, something completely beyond his control.

"Make right the grievous wrong you see before you!" Sharjam commanded the scripture coin.

The verse vanished, and was immediately replaced by another:

> *A sanctuary for the just and righteous,*
> *A refuge for the oppressed and persecuted,*
> *Freedom for the faithful shall never be lost herein,*
> *For as long as these words are called forth within.*

As soon as Dumyan had finished reading the last line in the verse, the words exploded in a loud bang. A dazzling ball of flame spread across the room, hitting him and Sharjam at the same time. He felt a wave of heat tear through his body. Fearful at first, he soon realized that it actually felt comfortable and warm. He almost began hoping that it wouldn't go away.

But within a couple of seconds, the bright flame was gone, and along with it the pleasant warmth. The room was dark and cold again. The scripture coin was still there in midair, but it wasn't displaying any verses. More importantly, though, Dumyan noticed that the bonds on his hands and feet had disappeared. He was free! The blood rushed back into his arms as they dropped to his sides, and the pain began subsiding right away.

"Sharjam, how did you...?"

But Dumyan wasn't able to finish his question. The door burst open at that moment, and their guard stormed in.

"What is going on here?" she yelled, looking confused when she saw the scripture coin hanging in the air in the middle of the room.

"Payback time," Sharjam said calmly.

The guard, standing right in front of the coin, noticed that both Dumyan and Sharjam were free. She immediately took out her boryal and aimed it at Sharjam. "Do not move, or I will fire!" she threatened.

"Your threats have no meaning in this chamber," Sharjam said, his voice steady and authoritative.

Dumyan wasn't sure what to do. His instincts told him to lunge at the guard and to try to take her boryal, but he knew he wouldn't be fast enough. She would clearly have enough time to fire at Sharjam before he even reached her. He wondered how Sharjam could be so calm in a situation like this, but he guessed his brother still had another trick up his sleeve. Something else was clearly about to happen.

And it did. A new verse appeared above the scripture coin, the big, bright words completely startling the guard:

> *Their evil subjugators and captors*
> *May wield their deadly weapons*
> *And try their utmost to harm and kill.*
> *But fail they shall, and miserably,*
> *For the power of the blessed Scriptures*
> *Has no equal in the worlds of mortals.*

"What is...?" the guard began, but before she could get any further, the verse exploded, sending off a ball of fire in her direction and quickly engulfing her entire body. She screamed in pain, letting go of the boryal and falling to the floor.

After several seconds, the flame around her vanished. She lay motionless on the floor.

Dumyan immediately stooped down and picked up the boryal. "Is she... dead?" he asked, still in shock.

"Dead? Oh no!" Sharjam shook his head. "She is just unconscious, but will remain so for many hours."

They picked her up, and subjected her to the same fate they had endured – arms stretched above her head and attached to a latch on the ceiling, and feet fastened to the floor.

Dumyan lowered her veil and stared at her face. "You were right, she is attractive!" he said. "What a pity she is with the bad guys. Otherwise she could have been a good match for you, eh?"

Sharjam didn't answer, instead quietly uttering some words with his eyes closed. Soon after, the scripture coin that had freed them glided silently back into the far wall and faded away. The other coins also retreated and faded away. Sharjam bowed before them as they disappeared.

Dumyan bowed as well. He had just developed a newfound respect for the Scriptures. Clearly there was a lot more to them than met the eye. Perhaps, when this adventure was all over, he would spend some more time studying them. Perhaps he did have a lot to learn from his younger brother, more than he had ever cared to admit.

"Come on," Sharjam said, turning to Dumyan and looking more determined than ever. "We have got a ship to commandeer."

Chapter 22

"Wait for me!" Marc shouted. He was trying his best to catch up with Zorina, who was more than 30 yards ahead, prancing forward with her strong hind legs. Her baggy, crimson colored outfit fluttered in the wind as she moved. It had big yellow spots all over, and was torn in multiple places. She looked like a clown, he felt, a clown who couldn't afford to buy new clothes.

"We haven't got all day, you know?" Zorina yelled back. "Those drones could be back any minute!"

Marc knew she was right. They were in the open air, darting across the disheveled streets of the city of Krasia, and would be easy targets for drones. But he was having a hard time keeping up with her fast and surefooted pace across the rugged terrain. Not only was this planet's gravitational pull much stronger than that of Earth, the searing heat was also exhausting him. His clothes were totally drenched in sweat, and he could feel the sweat beads continuously trickling down his forehead and cheeks. The nauseating smell everywhere wasn't helping much either, constantly making him want to throw up.

Nevertheless, he was trudging along with high hopes. Back in the cave, he had learned that Zorina was of royal blood and an extremely important individual in the Volonan Empire, and furthermore that the translator device she was holding was actually not her own. The day before, she had discovered a number of dead Mendoken bodies scattered all over a public square in another section of the city. Among them, there had been one living Mendoken, standing dazed and unaware of his surroundings, his mind engrossed in his own virtual world. The translator had been lying on the floor near him. She had tried giving it back to him, but he had shown no reaction. So she had taken it, hoping that it might come into use for her some day. And it sure had, the very moment she had met Marc.

Marc, his heart pounding upon hearing this news, had immediately asked her to take him to that living Mendoken. As far as he knew, there had only been one Mendoken on board any of the three ships carrying a translator with human language encoding, and that was Sibular. Perhaps he was still alive!

Zorina had been reluctant to venture out into the open again. She had wanted to relax and take it easy for the rest of the day, but Marc had convinced her otherwise. When she had learned that Sibular was one of the top space travel engineers in the entire Mendoken Republic, she had suddenly begun bobbing her head up and down in excitement, and had hastily led the way out of the cave.

It had been a calculated risk on Marc's part to tell her about Sibular's background. The Mendoken and Volona were still bitter enemies, after all. But he had learned a little about her and her own background while sitting in the cave, and had figured there were more pros than cons in taking this step.

Zorina, it turned out, had an engineering background herself. As the Empress's sister, she had held the title of Chief Imperial Defender, the highly prestigious and important post of overseeing the Empire's border defenses. She had commanded millions of ships and billions of troops, and had personally designed many of the protective systems currently in place around the borders. She had been a highly respected and admired Volonan, and her life had been just wonderful. It had been so wonderful, in fact, that her virtual life had almost been identical to her real life.

A time had come, however, when she had fallen out of grace with her sister. Stripped of her position and dishonored, she had been charged with treason and was to spend the rest of her life in a virtual prison. But after a couple of years of imprisonment under incredibly harsh conditions, she had found a way to break out of the virtual realm and out of the Virtual Translation Grid altogether. Since then, she had been a fugitive out here in the real world. It was a miserable life, all by herself in this mess of a place, constantly in hiding from drones. But it was still better than the prison she had left behind.

Unfortunately, she had no means at her disposal to go anywhere else. Going back into the Grid was not an option, even if it was technically possible, for she would be imprisoned again right away. Leaving this planet and the Empire altogether was not an option either – there were no docked ships nearby, and she definitely didn't have the technical knowledge to build a ship by herself. Her area of expertise was defense, after all, not space travel. In short, she was stuck.

Marc had reasoned, therefore, that if he could give Zorina even a glimmer of hope in escaping from her current predicament, then she would jump on the opportunity. Enemy or not, she would realize that one of the best space travel engineers from the most technologically advanced society in the galaxy would be a useful asset for her to have in finding a way off this planet. His reasoning had worked.

"So would you care to tell me how you fell out of grace with the Empress?" he asked, puffing as he finally caught up with her. She had stopped in the middle of the street, as if to survey the landscape of ruins around her.

She lifted her hand, motioning for him to be silent. "Hear that?"

"Hear what?" He stood still and strained his ears, but he really couldn't hear anything.

"Drones. Approaching from that direction." She pointed to her left.

Sure enough, several seconds later, he saw three specks emerging from the dark clouds in the gray sky, heading towards them at high speed. "What do we do?" he asked nervously.

Zorina seemed calm. "Nothing, don't move at all. Not even to scratch your nose, not even when they come right near you. It is our best hope of survival."

Marc did as he was told – he froze. As he soon discovered, however, it wasn't easy. As the drones came closer, he had to fight extra hard against his natural instinct to run and look for cover. He could feel the adrenalin rushing through his body, raising his alertness and making him sweat even more profusely in the heat and humidity.

The drones stopped right in front of Marc and Zorina, and began circling around them. The humming noise of their engines was deafening to Marc's ears. But just as it seemed like they were about to fire, they turned and sped off into the distance.

Zorina's strategy had worked! She had undoubtedly done this many times before. Waiting until the drones were out of sight, she relaxed and said, "Okay, we can move now."

"Only too gladly," he thought, thankful to have escaped death once again.

They began walking again.

"See those towers on top of that hill?" she said, pointing at the huge structures in the distance that he had seen earlier.

"Yes, I was going to ask you about them," he said, once again trying his best to keep up with her fast pace. "What are they?"

"They are the Grid's local transmission towers for Krasia. They transmit energy waves to all Volonans in the city connected to the Grid, waves that contain both the data about their individual worlds and the necessary nourishment to keep them alive and healthy."

"Must be some kind of waves!" He was stunned by this technological marvel that could carry both information and food invisibly across thin air. "So these towers exist everywhere?"

"Absolutely everywhere – around this planet, around all other inhabited planets and moons, all the way to the furthest corners of the Empire. Volonan ships traveling across space have their own local transmitters as well, even when they're outside the Empire."

Several minutes later, she stopped again, this time at the entrance to what had probably once been a public square. Up ahead, he saw a structure, or at least what was left of it. Its base was still there, a gigantic hemisphere made of a bluish stone, with the flat side facing up. But laid out across the flat surface was nothing more than an untidy heap of colorful pebbles.

Whatever this thing had once been, it must have been very pretty, he thought. It seemed like the Volonans had once lived quite well in the real world, with nicely constructed buildings, streets and other structures. But for some reason, they had one day decided to leave it all behind and move into the virtual realm, leaving everything they had built to fall apart over time and rot.

"This is where I last saw your Mendoken friend, in front of this monument," Zorina said. "I have to warn you, though. The sight isn't pretty."

Marc strained his eyes to look around the monument, and understood right away why she had warned him. He was shocked to see a number of dead Mendoken bodies on the ground. As he slowly walked up to them, his shock soon turned to horror. There weren't just a few bodies, there were hundreds of them, scattered all over the large square. There were flies in the air, buzzing around the rotting corpses, as well as vulture-like birds flying low in the sky. The stench was unbearable, far worse than the already horrid smell hanging everywhere in the air.

His horror soon turned to anger. "This is mass murder!" he screamed. "Why would anybody do this?"

She walked up behind him, not looking too happy about what her people had done. "This is where the imperial authorities must have brought all the Mendoken who survived the attack, including you. They probably hooked all of you into the Grid and left. Then they began monitoring your activities in your virtual worlds. Once they realized that most of these Mendoken weren't of any use to them, however, they killed them all. All, that is, except for you and your friend. You must have wandered off from this area at some point while still in your virtual world, but your friend stayed behind."

"But why kill them?" he cried. "What crime could they possibly have committed against the Empire as unarmed, helpless prisoners connected to the Grid?"

"The Empire never keeps foreign prisoners. For security reasons, to make sure no foreigner ever gets hold of our virtual technology."

He shook his head in disbelief. "This is terrible, it's barbaric!"

"It might seem barbaric to you, but if I tell you of our history and how we've become like this, you might have a little more understanding for our actions. I'm not trying to defend what's happened here – I think it's horrible too. But I'm just telling you that there are reasons for our highly protective and suspicious nature."

Marc was feeling anything but understanding. But he knew he couldn't hold Zorina responsible for these deaths, as she hadn't killed them. His spirits were also lifted when he noticed one figure standing among all the dead bodies. "Sibular!" he yelled with joy, running up to the figure.

It was Sibular alright. His thin eye and wide mouth were clearly identifiable, and he was still wearing his brown hat. More importantly, he was alive!

"He can't hear you," Zorina said, catching up with Marc. "His mind is far away."

Sure enough, Sibular looked dazed and sleepy, like all the Volonans with their minds in their virtual worlds.

"How come there are no guards anywhere?" Marc asked, surprised.

"No need," she said. "Once he's attached to the Grid, he has no means of escape. And if he needs to be killed, the Grid takes care of it in the virtual realm. If his mind is shut down, his body dies soon after."

"But I got out of the Grid."

"And you're one of the very few I've ever heard of that have. The imperial authorities would never have imagined that you could break out by yourself, so they wouldn't have bothered guarding you either. Little did they know they were in for a surprise!" She stared at Marc. "There must be something unique about you humans."

"Yes, our so-called 'imperfect nature'," he said sarcastically. He definitely didn't feel so bad about human nature anymore, after all the death and destruction he had witnessed since his takeoff from Earth. This latest mass murder had further confirmed his growing impression that cruelty was not a uniquely human trait. It was, in fact, widespread across the galaxy, and present on much larger scales than humans would ever have imagined possible.

She laughed. "Imperfection? Far from it! It takes tremendous amounts of willpower and inner strength to break out of the Grid, far beyond those possessed by most of my people or even your Mendoken friends here. You humans are obviously mighty creatures!"

"Are we really?" he said, almost growling. "My world is still shrouded in one of those silupsal filters, because you all think my people are so primitive and backward compared to all of you Mendoken, Aftar, Volona, Phyrax, and whoever else in this galaxy I haven't heard of yet."

"Ah, those silupsal filters! You know, somehow I've always thought of them as virtual worlds of their own. But anyway, the reason we use silupsal filters is to give less advanced species the time they need to evolve by themselves, until they're ready for the rest of us."

He was about to retort, but she cut him off.

"We're not any better than you, you know," she said. "We've just been around a lot longer."

He fell quiet after that statement. She had just said what he wanted to say. The fact that she felt the same way, and that she had the courage to say it, made him feel a little more at ease.

"What about you?" he asked her after a short pause. "How did you get out of your virtual prison?

"Well, in my case, as a Volonan, I consciously knew that I was in a virtual world. And given my unique position among the imperial authorities, I had detailed knowledge of the Grid's architectural limitations. I used it to my advantage to find a way out. But it still wasn't easy, I can assure you. I'm not sure I'd be able to get out a second time, if I were once again connected."

"Then how will *he* get out?" Marc asked, staring at Sibular.

Zorina looked pensive. "He won't be able to by himself, that much I can tell you. The Mendoken may be our enemies, but in many ways they're like us. We both love to be complacent and accept things without question, as long as everything appears fine and taken care of. So your friend here won't want to leave his perfect surroundings of his own accord. The fact that he has no idea he's connected to the Grid or how it works won't help him either."

"So what can we do?"

"There's only one way. Going into his virtual world and convincing him to get out. And you're the one who's going to do it."

Marc was alarmed. "Why me and not you? Won't they find me if I reconnect to the Grid?"

"Same is true for me, isn't it? But given your track record, I'm pretty sure you will have a better shot than me at staying focused and remembering your goal, once you're in the Grid. Besides, Sibular already knows you. He has no idea who I am. Furthermore, you two were brought here at the same time, and for the same reasons. His virtual world is likely very similar to the one you were in. Since you convinced yourself to get out of yours, you have a better chance of convincing him to do the same."

Marc thought about his own virtual world experience, vivid in his memory as if it had all been real. "But I was back on Earth. Why would Sibular...?"

"Details such as location are not important, young human! It's the bigger picture that is. If you two were the only prisoners from those Mendoken ships that were kept alive in the Grid, it could only have been for an important reason. They wanted some critical information from both of you, information that they figured out only the two of you had."

"So they were monitoring our activities in the Grid to learn something from us. But what?"

"Based on what you've already told me, I think I might have a good idea."

He raised his eyebrows questioningly.

"They wanted to find out how you could possibly have penetrated our border defenses," she said. "In other words, they wanted to get their hands on your consar technology, so that they could retaliate in kind against the Mendoken."

He shook his head.

"Oh, come on!" she exclaimed, looking irritated. "You still think that we already have it?"

"Some proof that you don't would be nice. I've already seen the proof that you do. Very dramatically too, I might add."

"Proof, eh?" she said, flapping her ears. "You don't need proof. Just use your common sense. Tell me this – what is it you were doing in your virtual world? Other than living in harmony in the home of your dreams and making love to your mate, of course. That's just the standard stuff to keep you happy and complacent."

He thought about it. "I was working as a professor, at a university on Earth," he said. He thought some more, then added, "Yes! I was famous, and successful."

"In what?" she asked right away.

"In, uh, wormhole research."

"And what exactly are 'wormholes'?"

Marc could see what she was getting at. And, he had to admit, he could see the logic. The Volonans had kept him and Sibular alive, but had killed all the other Mendoken. He and Sibular had probably known more about consar technology and its intricate details than any of the other Mendoken on board the three attacking ships. Surely that was no coincidence.

Zorina went on. "The imperial authorities let you live in your perfect virtual world, and lured you into working on your favorite topic of research. They observed you closely, hoping to learn about consar technology. Any one of the individuals you interacted with in your virtual world might have been an imperial spy, appearing to you as a loved one or a friend, while others may just have been figments of your imagination. Virtual worlds are usually comprised of both real and imaginary characters, and to the untrained eye it's impossible to tell one from the other."

Marc dreaded to think that the virtual Iman he had repeatedly made love to might actually have been a Volonan spy, or that his virtual parents might have been spies.

"In any case," she added, "tell me why the imperial authorities would go to such trouble, against all known prohibitions about keeping foreign prisoners, all to try to discover something they already know and have?"

He was silent, trying to figure things out in his head. If not the Volona, then who could possibly have been behind the consar attacks on Mendoken territory? Might it really all have been an act by the Mendoken? But why? The Mendoken just didn't seem capable of that kind of deception – they were so straightforward and logical about everything. None of this made any sense. Something strange was afoot here, he just didn't know what. He was reminded for a moment of his visions of death and destruction across the galaxy, but couldn't understand how they might be related to any of this.

"What I'm wondering is how far the imperial authorities got in their quest before you escaped," Zorina said.

Marc snapped out of his thoughts. "Probably not very far in my case. I was already rebelling against my virtual status before I had spent much time revealing the details of my research. But what I'm wondering is how far they've gotten with him." He nodded his head towards Sibular.

"Well, the longer we wait, the further they'll get. Chances are they'll kill your friend here as soon as they have all the information they're looking for." She paused. "You wanted proof, right? You'll see for yourself what he's up to, once you go into his virtual world. Then you'll have your proof, I guarantee you."

Soon after, Marc was ready. He and Zorina lifted Sibular onto the base of the hemisphere, and laid him flat and face up on the surface. Marc then laid himself down facing the opposite direction, the tip of his head almost touching Sibular's.

As Marc had learned from Zorina, the way the Volona connected an individual to the Grid was through a small connector implanted at the top of the head. He had felt the top of his own head, and had found a slight bump there. Sibular's head also had one, beneath his hat. Sibular's connector, of course, was still active. Marc's was not – it had shut off the moment he had broken out of the Grid.

There were only two ways to reactivate a connector that had been shut off. One was by direct reconnection to the Grid, which could only be done by imperial authorities with the relevant devices. The other way was to bring it into very close contact with another active connector. The latter way would allow an individual to join another's virtual world and be a part of it. This technique had been used a lot in the past when the Volona had first been experimenting with virtual technology, but was hardly ever used anymore. Nowadays, every Volonan was already in his or her own virtual world, and privacy laws also prohibited one Volonan from directly entering another's virtual world without that Volonan's express consent.

"Now remember, you can't afford to spend too much time in the Grid, or the imperial authorities will detect you and imprison you once again before you know it," Zorina said. "And this time, they'll probably take more precautions to make sure you don't break out again. But I have full faith in your strength, and I'm sure you'll get out just fine."

Marc wasn't so sure, and he definitely didn't have her faith. But he also knew there was no other option. He had to bring Sibular back to reality, and not just because he liked him or because he felt loyalty toward him. Sibular was probably his only hope of ever making it out of this horrible planet and out of the Volonan Empire altogether.

"Ready?" Zorina asked.

"Ready as I'll ever be," he said, closing his eyes.

She lifted both Marc's and Sibular's heads, and gently pulled them towards each other until their tips touched.

Marc felt the tip of his head suddenly turn cold, very cold. Like a thick liquid, the biting cold spread all over his head, and then down the neck to the rest of his body. The sensation was almost identical to the one he had felt when crossing from his virtual world to reality through the mirror earlier that day. Zorina had told him to stay absolutely calm and stationary during this phase, and that was exactly what he did. The cold liquid eventually drained out through his legs and feet, and only after it was all gone did he open his eyes, ready to face Sibular's virtual world.

He found himself standing in the center of a huge circular hall. The domed ceiling was transparent, letting in the brilliant sunlight from above through the cloudless blue sky. The air was cool and dry, and above all, smelled good – a welcome change from the hot, humid air in the world he had just left behind. The hall was filled, not with humans or Volonans, but with Mendoken. Thousands and thousands of them, standing in rising rows against the wall, completely surrounding the arena in the center where he stood.

But he wasn't alone in the arena. Standing in between stacks of various types of equipment was the one Mendoken he was looking for. Sibular was the center of attention in the hall, presenting something to the crowd of spectators all around him. There was also a group of seven Mendoken standing in a line in the arena in front of Sibular, facing him and listening intently to his presentation. Marc recognized the third one from the left as Osalya, the Imgoerin's top aide. Which could only mean that the figure standing in the middle, with his black hat and shining armor, was the Imgoerin himself. This presentation was obviously very important!

Marc tried to listen to the speech, but heard nothing other than the soft humming tone that the Mendoken used to communicate with each other. He walked slowly towards Sibular, trying to pay no attention to the crowd. None of this was real, he kept telling himself. Those thousands of Mendoken weren't really there, nor were the Imgoerin or Osalya.

But as he walked, he suddenly felt very drowsy, the same way he usually felt before falling asleep. His thoughts began to wander, trying to make him lose focus and just accept that his surroundings were real. Zorina had warned him that this was going to happen, and that it would happen repeatedly. Once the Volonan authorities detected his presence, this was how they would try to imprison him again in the Grid.

As soon as Marc felt the wave of sleepiness coming, he slapped and pinched himself a few times, just as Zorina had told him to do. This made him alert again, reminding him of where he was, and that he was here for a specific mission. As he came closer to Sibular, he recognized the stacks of equipment. They were consar travel instruments, most of them Mendoken, but some of them also looking awfully similar to the instruments from his own lab at Cornell.

"No doubt, this is the proof that Zorina wanted me to see," he thought. Here was Sibular, living the Mendoken definition of a perfect, blissful life. He was doing the ultimate service to the entire Mendoken civilization – teaching his people how to defend themselves, with the very weapon they believed their archenemy had successfully been using against them. For a Mendoken like Sibular, there could be no greater accomplishment, no greater pride, than to selflessly benefit his people in so major a way.

But what Sibular didn't realize was that none of this was real. It was all a trick, a plot by the Volonan imperial authorities to learn his secret. They were watching him closely in his virtual world, recording every move he was making, every word he was uttering, and wouldn't stop until they had the complete formula for consar travel.

Now Marc knew for sure that Zorina was right. The secret to consar travel was the only reason the Volona had kept him and Sibular alive. They had failed with Marc, but were about to succeed with Sibular. And as Zorina had explained, they would most likely kill Sibular once they had obtained all the information they needed. Marc had to act now, and had to act fast before the Volonan authorities detected him here and came after him!

"Hey, Sibular!" Marc called, waving as he walked straight up to him.

Sibular stopped presenting and looked at Marc.

"Hey, it's me, Marc, remember me?"

Sibular made some humming sounds in response.

Marc put his hand in his pocket, and out came the Mendoken translator device. Zorina had shown him how to carry an object from the real world into the virtual realm, just by holding the object and focusing his thoughts on it.

He switched the device on. "Can you understand me now?"

"Yes, who are you?" Sibular said in his usual monotone, robot-like voice. "I am in the middle of an important presentation."

"I am Marc Zemin, from the planet Earth," Marc said. "Don't you remember me?"

"Should I?"

"Yes! This place, all these Mendoken, none of this is real! You're actually a prisoner of the Volona, stuck in your own virtual world. And you need to get out, as soon as possible!"

Sibular's face was expressionless, in typical Mendoken style. "How can that be?"

Marc felt the drowsiness hitting him again, so he slapped himself a couple of times to snap out of it. "Don't you remember? I helped you figure out how to travel through consars! We were on a ship that went through a consar into Volonan territory. We attacked the Volo-Gaviera system, but we couldn't get out again, and our ship was destroyed. Then you and I ended up as Volonan prisoners. I managed to get out of my virtual world, but you're still stuck in yours."

Sibular was quiet for a few seconds, and then said, "I do not know what you are talking about. I discovered consar travel by myself." Then he turned to continue presenting to the Imgoerin and the rest of the Mendoken crowd.

Marc felt distressed. He knew he was running out of time. "Listen to me!" he shouted. "We have got to get out of this prison!"

Sibular broke off his presentation again. "Why do you call this a prison?"

"Look around you!" Marc pleaded, pointing at the Imgoerin and his aides, as well as all the other Mendoken in the spectator rows. "Do you see any of them moving or reacting to my intrusion? They're all just standing there and listening, as if your presentation is continuing undisturbed. Is this normal? Would this really happen in real life?"

Sibular looked around. "No, that is strange," he admitted.

"I'm telling you! They are not real! And what about these instruments?" He pointed to some of his own lab apparatus. "Do these look like Mendoken creations to you?"

Sibular floated over and took a closer look at the equipment. There was an obvious contrast between the small, cylindrical and transparent Mendoken devices, and the much bulkier and more primitive looking human lab instruments with LED lights blinking on their surfaces.

"These are not your creations," Marc said. "They are human devices! From my lab, on Earth! Don't you remember?"

Sibular was quiet again. He floated around the arena for a while, and eventually returned to where Marc was standing. "You fainted," he said.

Marc scowled. "I beg your pardon?"

"You fainted, on the moon Ailen. In front of Osalya." Sibular pointed at the virtual Osalya, standing no more than 40 feet away. "You were asleep for 7.6 Earth hours."

"Why yes, you're right! So you remember!"

"Earth – third planet of Mendo-Biesel, enshrouded by a silupsal filter that is monitored by station Selcher-44328."

"Yes! Yes!" Marc was ready to jump with joy. But he was starting to feel very weak now, as the repeated attacks of drowsiness kept intensifying. The Volonan authorities had undoubtedly discovered him in the Grid by now, and were trying hard to lure him into a virtual trap.

"The attack – our ship – it exploded," Sibular said. "How did we survive and end up here?"

"It's a long story. I'll explain it to you. But first, we need to get out of here, and quickly!"

"How?"

"Leave that to me. Just follow my instructions to the letter."

Chapter 23

Marc and Sibular rushed to get out of the Grid. Marc was feeling fainter by the second, as the attempts by the Volonan authorities to lock him in the Grid intensified. But Sibular, now convinced that Marc had spoken the truth, kept pushing him to lead the way out.

Per Zorina's instructions, they were to make their way to the nearest mirror. Mirrors, as she had told Marc, were the gateways from the virtual realm to reality. The only problem was that the Mendoken never used mirrors, so there were none in Sibular's virtual world. After some thought, Marc decided on the next best thing, something there was no lack of in Mendoken worlds – water. The many artificial lakes spread across all Mendoken cities were always filled with absolutely still, purified water, providing highly reflective surfaces that almost looked like mirrors.

Sibular pointed out that there happened to be just such an artificial lake right outside the hall. They hurried out to it and, after staring at their own reflections and focusing their thoughts on the transition, took their chances and jumped into the water.

The water felt quite warm and comfortable, which was not at all what Marc had been hoping for. He wanted it to be freezing cold and heavy, just like the way it had felt during his previous transitions between the virtual and real worlds. As Zorina had explained to him, this icy, heavy liquid was a very special substance. It automatically appeared during a transition, and its purpose was to desensitize the body from the shock it experienced as it went from one realm to the other.

Fortunately, the temperature of the water dropped dramatically as they sank further into the lake, and the water became heavy. It was working! The freezing liquid seeped into Marc's head and into the rest of his body, cooling down all his vital organs. Then it drained away again, out through his legs and feet.

Once the liquid was gone, he opened his eyes and found himself back in the real world. He was lying on the base of the large monument, exactly at the same spot he had departed from. The searing heat and humidity hit his face instantly, as did the stench. Feeling dazed, he got up, and noticed Sibular was already standing. They had both made it!

"This is a most disgusting place," Sibular observed. "Where are we?"

Marc couldn't help smiling in agreement. "Welcome to Nopelio, the fourth planet in the Volo-Gaviera system. This is the city of Krasia."

Sibular surveyed the ruins around him. "This is a city?"

"I had the same reaction when I first saw it." Marc proceeded to explain why the Volona lived this way in real life.

Sibular appeared to notice the dead Mendoken bodies for the first time. "They were on our ships. Why are they all dead? Did the Volona kill them?" His voice was calm and robotic as always, even after this dreadful sight.

"Yes," Marc said sadly, "I'm afraid so."

"Why? Is that individual responsible?" Sibular pointed to Zorina, who was lying on the ground several feet away, snoring loudly through her trunk.

"No! She had nothing to do with it."

"Is she... a Volonan?"

"Yes, that's what they look like in real life." Marc told Sibular who Zorina was, how he had met her, and how she wanted to get off this planet as much as they did.

"So this is Zorina herself?"

"Yes! Have you heard of her before?"

"But of course. She is well known among the Mendoken. She is primarily responsible for the Volonan Empire's impenetrable borders. A brilliant engineer, from what I know, and a ruthless tyrant like most Volonans."

Marc scowled. "I don't believe she's a ruthless tyrant at all. She saved my life, you know?"

"The Volona are masters of deception, Marc," Sibular said. "You should never trust them. Look at how they killed all these Mendoken."

"This was horrible, no doubt. But don't forget, we were all captured by the Volona as we tried to attack them. They had no reason to show us any mercy. Besides, this wasn't Zorina's doing! In fact, she explained to me what she thought happened here, and why we were left alive as prisoners, much against Volonan practice as that is."

Sibular was silent for a few seconds, then said, "I am listening, Marc."

Marc explained his whole understanding of the situation to Sibular, including how they had survived the attack on their ships, how they had ended up on this planet, and how and why they had been connected to the Grid.

"It cannot be," Sibular said calmly after Marc had finished. "It is impossible."

"You had better believe it! How else can you explain that we are the only ones still alive, and why in both our virtual worlds we were pursuing consar travel as the ultimate crowning achievement of our careers? That has to be what the Volonan authorities were after."

"It could also be because they wanted to find out how we discovered consar travel capability."

"Why would that be so important? If they already had the technology themselves, why would they go through all this trouble just to find out how we got it?"

"Perhaps it is all a trick," Sibular suggested. "They might just want us to believe that they do not have consar capability, so that we return to the Republic and report that they do not have it."

Marc shrugged. "For what purpose? The Mendoken government would never believe us, and the war would just continue without any interruption. Surely the Volonan imperial authorities would know that, if they really were behind the consar attacks on your worlds. So what would such an elaborate hoax accomplish?"

"I do not know."

"I'm telling you, Sibular, there's something very strange going on here. Your people claim the Volona have been repeatedly attacking them through consars, yet the behavior of the Volona clearly indicates they don't even have consar capability. In fact, they've been trying to use you and me to get their hands on the technology. The reason, I would imagine, is so they can strike back against the Mendoken Republic in retaliation for our strike against them. We may have viewed our strike as a retaliation against their consar attacks, but they appear to have viewed it as a completely unprovoked, unexpected first strike against them deep inside their own territory. None of this makes any sense! Who is telling the truth, and who is pulling wool over our eyes?"

"What is the purpose of putting wool on one's eyes?"

Marc groaned. "It's a human expression, never mind! Do you see what I'm saying, though?"

"I understand what you are saying, but it will take a lot more than your experiences here to help me overcome centuries of distrust and enmity between my people and the Volona."

"Well, I think this distrust is exactly what has been fueling the fire. The war continues because neither side believes what the other is officially claiming. And nobody is interested in negotiation, it seems."

"The hostility and distrust run far too deep, Marc," Sibular said. "The days of negotiation ended a long time ago."

In the silence that followed, Zorina stirred awake, letting out a high-pitched yawn. She rubbed her eyes and stared at both of them. Bobbing her head up and down in content, she said, "So you made it back, in one piece!"

"Two pieces, to be precise," Marc said, grinning. "Zorina, I'd like you to meet Sibular. Sibular, this is Zorina."

"Pleased to meet you," Zorina said, reaching up to touch Sibular's forehead with her hand. "Regardless of the enmity between my people and yours, I want you to know that I have nothing against you personally. I also want you to know that I had nothing to do with the killings that took place here, nor do I in any way condone them."

"Thank you, I appreciate that, Zorina," Sibular replied.

"Okay!" Marc said after a short, awkward silence. "Now that we're all here and the formalities are over with, let's figure out a way to get out of this God-forsaken place!"

Still on top of the base of the monument, the trio spent close to an hour deliberating what to do next and how to do it. Sibular remained standing, since Mendoken never sat down, while Marc and Zorina were both seated on the edge of the base. It wasn't a very constructive or pleasant conversation, however, mainly due to the constant tension between Sibular and Zorina. The two kept getting into arguments, especially because of Sibular's polite but stubborn refusal to believe anything Zorina was saying, in addition to Zorina constantly raising her voice and accusing the Mendoken of being the aggressors in the current war.

Marc was astonished to see how two highly intelligent, well educated beings from such advanced civilizations could engage in this kind of mindless arguing, and particularly how they could use blatant stereotypes to justify their assertions. The hatred and prejudice clearly ran very deep, so deep that logic and reason had long ago lost their roots in the wide chasm between the two species.

"Human nature obviously isn't uniquely human," he thought.

After a while, the lack of cooperation and progress was starting to get on his nerves. "Now both of you listen to me!" he shouted, standing up and making no attempt to hide his agitation. "Those drones will be back any minute now. And while you two continue your inconsequential bickering, they'll keep coming back until they succeed in killing the three of us. Meanwhile, the war is escalating, with both sides accusing each other of the exact same thing. Call me crazy, but something doesn't add up here – either one side is lying, or perhaps both. Either way, if we don't get out there and somehow stop this madness, there soon won't be a Mendoken Republic or Volonan Empire left worth bickering about!"

Both of Marc's companions were instantly quiet, seemingly taken aback by his sudden outburst. But before either of them had any chance to respond, the all too familiar sound of drones filled the air.

"You see what I mean?" Marc pointed out. "Here they come again! We can't afford to stay here a minute longer than is absolutely necessary." He almost welcomed the arrival of the drones, as he knew it would drive his point home.

"Stay absolutely still, both of you," Zorina whispered. "Don't even make the slightest sound, Sibular. The drones only react to sudden movements."

Sibular did as he was told. In spite of his distrust for Volonans, it seemed he had chosen to trust her on this matter.

The three drones, now visible below the thick clouds in the gray sky, approached at high speed. Marc could feel the sweat trickling down his forehead. Just like the last time he had seen the drones, his mind fought hard against the urge to run away. Standing absolutely still, he only allowed his eyes to move as they followed the motion of the drones.

The drones circled around the monument several times, evidently sensing the presence of something suspicious. They slowed down and descended, exploring every inch of the gigantic structure. Their sensors, sending out wide rays of red light, crossed over the trio's motionless bodies several times. But, finding nothing worth firing at, they gave up after a while and flew off again.

Marc heaved a sigh of relief. Once the drones were out of sight, he said softly, "So, my friends, can we please agree that we'll work together to leave this planet?"

"Yes, Marc," Sibular said.

"You have my word," Zorina said, flapping her ears.

They began deliberating again, but this time much more constructively. Zorina told Marc and Sibular about her failed attempts in the past to get off the planet. There was a big scrapyard several miles away, she explained, where parts of old Volonan ships lay scattered among many other kinds of junk. She had tried several times to assemble a simple ship there with some of those parts, but had not been successful due to her lack of expertise in ship design. The constant attacks by drones hadn't been much help either, always preventing her from making any reasonable progress.

"Perhaps you'll have better luck, Sibular?" she said, eyeing him with a look of anticipation.

"I can take a look, but I have to admit my knowledge of Volonan ship technology is quite limited," Sibular replied.

Zorina bobbed her head up and down with delight. "Oh, I hate to admit it, but our ships are not nearly as sophisticated as yours. Our advancement efforts are always focused on enhancing the Grid and defending our borders, not on traveling through space. So you should be able to figure it out with ease."

They trudged over the rough terrain, Zorina leading the way, followed by Sibular, and Marc taking up the rear. Zorina, as sure footed as ever with her strong hind legs and long arms, had no problem prancing from rock to rock. Sibular had an even easier time, floating smoothly through the air above the ground. The story was very different for Marc, however, who kept tripping and falling, with the hot, steamy weather just wearing him out. He was having a very hard time keeping up with the other two, so much so that he frequently had to call out for them to slow down.

After several such calls, Zorina began to express her annoyance. "We'll never get there at this rate," she grumbled. "Humans may be smart, but they certainly aren't very fast."

Sibular noticed how far behind Marc was, and stopped. "Zorina, keep going, we will catch up."

Zorina flapped her ears, and strutted on without looking back.

Sibular waited for Marc to reach him. "Since you are having trouble keeping up, perhaps you should hold onto me."

"What, really? How?" Panting with exhaustion, Marc was only too happy to accept the offer, but wasn't sure whether Sibular would be able to carry that much additional weight.

Sibular lowered himself to the ground and helped Marc climb onto him in a piggyback fashion. The extra weight, as soon became clear, would be no issue for his strong mechanized limbs and solid body armor. Cautioning Marc to hold on tight, he lifted from the ground and sped off.

Marc gasped in surprise, tightening his grip around Sibular's shoulders. Sibular was accelerating fast, very fast. Before long, they were racing through the air at high speed. The ground below turned into nothing more than a blur.

"Holy smokes!" Marc shouted above the roaring wind. "How can you possibly go so fast?"

"Our armor shells have small engines built into them," Sibular replied. "They can come in handy sometimes."

In less than half a minute, they had caught up with Zorina. She watched with astonishment as they zoomed past her.

Marc laughed when he saw the expression on Zorina's face. "Okay, we'd better slow down now!" he said to Sibular.

Sibular decelerated, came to a stop and allowed Marc to get off his back.

Zorina joined them shortly, and eyed Marc's wide grin with disdain. "No need to rub it in!" she muttered, and then looked at Sibular. "What in the Grid's name do you have inside you, my man?"

"Just a small engine," Marc said, before Sibular could open his mouth. "They do come in handy sometimes, you know?"

She threw her hands up in the air and sighed. "These Mendoken and their machines! Anyways, here we are."

Sure enough, they had reached the edge of what looked like a wide canyon. The other side was at least a mile away, perhaps more. The entire floor of the canyon below was covered with all kinds of junk. It was indeed one big scrapyard, just as Zorina had described.

As Marc surveyed the landscape, he began losing hope. "How are we ever going to build anything from this huge pile of garbage, let alone a ship that can travel through space?"

"Hey, don't lose faith before we've even started!" she said in a reprimanding tone. "There are a lot of useful spare parts down there, believe it or not." She turned to Sibular. "What do you think, my man?"

Sibular, who was intently observing all the different pieces of junk in the canyon with his magnifying vision capability, said, "Yes, I believe it is possible to build a ship from the materials present. But it will take time."

"See?" Zorina said to Marc. "I told you! Have more faith in our brainy friend!"

With that, they began their descent to the canyon floor. Zorina led them down a steep path, one she had been on many times before. At the bottom, they set up camp in the same spot that she had used in the past, under the shelter of what had once been the wing of a drone.

Marc sat down on a section of broken pipe. He was feeling exhausted, and was certain that any moment now he would die of thirst in the scorching heat. Much to his delight, Zorina revealed a bag full of food supplies that she had stored in the corner of the wing during her last stay. She sat down next to him, and together they drank some ale and shared a few pieces of sparli. He instantly felt better.

"Hey, my man, want some sparli, with some ale to wash it down?" she called out to Sibular.

"Thank you, but I do not require any nourishment," Sibular replied. He was analyzing a number of ship parts a short distance away.

"What the...? How does he survive?"

"You don't know?" Marc said. "The Mendoken don't eat or drink. I was surprised too when I first found out. Their brains are mostly organic, but their bodies are half organic and half mechanized, and each half fully supports the functions of the other half. When they were first evolving, they used to eat a plant called Torteg, but once they incorporated the mechanized parts into their bodies, they no longer needed nourishment in the form of food. Their mechanized parts are designed to continuously absorb energy from the electromagnetic waves that surround them. That's one thing there's certainly no lack of in the universe. The mechanized parts then provide the necessary energy to sustain the organic parts. The organic parts in turn are responsible for intelligence and overall consciousness."

"Amazing! Although I suppose it's not too different from the way the Grid nourishes all Volonans who are connected to it. We obviously don't have such extensive mechanized body parts like the Mendoken have. The only things we do have are those connectors on the top of our heads to receive the Grid's transmissions and convert them into the energy our bodies need to survive. Volonans have to be connected to the Grid, though, in order to obtain energy like that. Otherwise, it's down to traditional food and drink.

"You know, the only time I've interacted with Mendoken in the past was in the virtual realm. And, believe me, the details of their bodies were somewhat altered by the Grid. Although their heads and faces were quite close to reality, their bodies were always shown to me as ugly and slimy, with lots of tentacles that they used to pick up and consume anything in their sight. I was quite surprised to see how normal the Mendoken really looked when I came across your friend here."

Marc was reminded of his own perception of aliens as a child, thanks to all the science fiction movies and books he had been exposed to. As he thought about this, he wondered how much difference there really was between humans and Volonans. Humans generally saw what they wanted to see and believed what they wanted to believe. That was just their nature. Humans felt better about themselves by believing that any aliens out there had to be uglier and more evil than they were. Those kinds of stories always found widespread appeal with the public, no matter how far-fetched from any kind of verifiable reality they actually were. The Volona had just taken this concept to the next level, where they actually lived in worlds of their own imagination, where everything they believed or wanted to believe physically appeared as reality, as fundamental truth.

Zorina yawned. "Well, time for a nap." She glanced at Sibular. "Let me guess, he doesn't sleep either?"

"Nope, none of them do."

"Ah! Hopefully he'll make some progress in the meantime then." With that, she lay down on the ground and rested her head on the pipe. Within seconds, she was fast asleep.

As Marc finished his last mouthful of sparli, he decided to follow her example. Given how tired he was, he knew he wouldn't be of any help to Sibular at the moment. He felt a lot more at ease now, knowing that the three of them were here together, with a plan to get off this planet that just might work. He didn't know why, but he felt as if he was with two long lost friends, both of whom he had found again after a very long time.

He lay down on the ground next to Zorina. Gazing up at the sky, he wondered why it was that there appeared to be no day or night on this planet – the sky was always the same dismal gray. Perhaps the days were just really long here, he thought. Before any other possibilities came into his head, he drifted off to sleep.

When Marc awoke, he wasn't sure at first where he was. For a moment, he thought he was back in his dream house on the cliff, with Iman lying by his side. But that happy thought faded away as soon as he opened his eyes. The sky was the same dismal gray, the air still terribly hot and humid, and the surroundings nothing more than the same messy piles of junk.

"How long have I been asleep?" he wondered. He sat up, and noticed Zorina was no longer lying next to him. In fact, neither she nor Sibular were anywhere in sight.

He stood up in alarm, and began looking for them in between the piles of junk. He feared the worst. Had the two of them fought and killed each other? Or had they left without him?

In the distance, he could hear the sounds of drilling and metal clanking. Hoping for the best, he followed the direction the sounds were emanating from. After passing by the ruins of an old spaceship, he finally saw what the source of the noise was.

Just ahead, standing in front of what looked like one of the ship's engines, were Sibular and Zorina. Rather than fighting each other, they were hard at work, attaching pieces of machinery to each other. They were working at an incredibly fast pace, much faster than Marc had ever seen any humans perform construction work. And they had clearly made a lot of progress during the time he had been asleep.

"Who says Mendoken and Volonans can't work together for a better future?" he thought, smiling. He walked up to them and offered a helping hand.

The three of them worked all day long, trying to restore the old ship engine to its original state. Every couple of hours, Zorina stopped to take a short nap, while Marc drank some ale to replenish his body with all the water he was losing in the intense heat. The two of them also ate carefully rationed sparli for lunch and dinner. Sibular kept working continuously, never once wavering or stopping for a break, never once complaining about anything.

And so the days passed, and bit by bit the ship they were constructing began to take shape. Zorina showed Marc a natural spring right in the center of the canyon, where they were able to bathe and get fresh drinking water from. She also went back to her living quarters on the outskirts of Krasia at one point, baked enough sparli to last them for several weeks, and brought it all back to the canyon in neatly packed rations.

While Sibular toiled away nonstop on building the ship, Marc and Zorina set up a detection system around the entire perimeter of the canyon which gave early warnings of any approaching drones. This system provided them with ample time to stop whatever they were doing and stay absolutely still whenever any drones came flying over the canyon.

For the most part, Marc and Zorina followed Sibular's instructions while working on the ship, since he was the most knowledgeable about ship technology. They discussed many topics while they worked, and although squabbles periodically erupted between Marc's two companions, squabbles which were either quickly put down by Marc or abruptly stopped due to visits by drones, each of them ended up gaining a better understanding and appreciation for each other in the process. Marc learned quite a bit about Volonan history from Zorina, the highlights of which included the following:

Over 2.5 billion Earth years ago, the Volona lived in the real world, and had big, thriving cities spread across their home planet of Barenoa. Volonans always had a hedonistic culture, enjoying living in comfort, partaking of good food and spending all their skills and assets on entertainment and pleasure. As their population grew, the Volona consumed all of the planet's natural resources. While a select few warned of the ramifications of what was happening, the majority paid no attention. They were too engrossed in enjoying their lives to the fullest. But eventually, the planet's ecological system collapsed, and the once beautiful world of forests, oceans and blue skies turned into a complete wasteland. Mother Nature had taken enough environmental abuse, and was no longer willing to cooperate. And once Mother Nature had had enough, no amount of power or technological sophistication could fight her wrath or calm her down.

During that time, one cataclysmic natural disaster followed the next, and millions of Volonans died on Barenoa. Those that remained worked frantically to develop space travel technology, and built ships with which they escaped from their home world. Some of the ships made it to other livable planets and moons in nearby star systems, where the survivors settled and started new societies. Although all of these worlds had flora and fauna of many different kinds, not too many actually had intelligent civilizations. Those which did were so backward that the Volona had no trouble colonizing them and pushing them into small, isolated enclaves.

Initially, the Volonan settlers were more environmentally conscious, vowing to never repeat the same mistake again. But as one generation replaced the next, history was soon forgotten, and the Volona reverted to their old ways of pleasure seeking and limitless consumption. Within a few million years, they had once again depleted the natural resources of all their new home worlds, and once again had to leave to look for other livable planets and moons.

This cycle continued, with newer generations leaving their homes every few million years and settling on other worlds. But after a couple of hundred million years of such activity, this cycle abruptly came to an end. One of the planets the Volona landed on was already inhabited by an intelligent species. Although seemingly behind the Volona in science and technology, they were still far more advanced than any other species the Volona had ever encountered before. Known simply as the Sak, they appeared to be very friendly and welcomed the newcomers with open arms, allowing the Volonans to live on their planet in exchange for technical knowledge and training.

But once the Volona began settling down on their new home world, the Sak revealed their true nature. They were actually a highly belligerent, parasitic species, and preyed on unsuspecting visitors from outer space. They were also a lot more technologically advanced than was previously thought. Out from huge underground bunkers came highly sophisticated weapons, with which the Sak quickly overpowered the unsuspecting and unprepared Volonan settlers. Then they began mass-murdering their new prisoners.

After the Volonan settlers were wiped out, the Sak boarded the ships the Volona had arrived on and headed off into space. They began attacking and invading other Volonan worlds with tremendous ferocity, massacring many millions of Volonans and taking over their worlds. Within a few years, they became a major threat to the very survival of the entire Volonan race.

Extinction, however, was not in the Volona's fate. Among the demoralized survivors spread thinly across the different worlds emerged a new leader called Simorina, who united what was left of the Volonan people and led them to war against the Sak. After many years of bitter fighting and unfathomable death and destruction, the Sak were finally defeated.

Under Simorina's leadership, the Volona resolutely decided never to repeat their mistakes of the past. They would never again trust any other advanced alien civilization, no matter how friendly they appeared to be, and would never again colonize other inhabited worlds. Instead, they would build a society that could sustain itself forever on the worlds they already inhabited, and protect themselves with might and main against any attacks by outsiders. So they formed an integrated, united Empire, spread across all their star systems and surrounded by secure borders. And they moved into the virtual realm, where they would be able to perpetually live in ultimate luxury and comfort, consuming as much as they wanted without having to worry about affecting the environment.

In over a billion years that have passed since then, the Volona have perfected their virtual technology and made their borders impenetrable. The Virtual Translation Grid, the heart of their virtual technology, is an ingenious system that not only takes care of the virtual worlds of all Volonans, but with the help of the dense material purania also sustains itself perpetually through energy from the radiation of close to 300 billion stars across the Empire, never once wasting any natural resources or emitting any pollutants.

The Volona have remained in their virtual worlds ever since Simorina's time, and never intend to return to reality. They have no reason to, as the virtual realm has not only provided them with all the pleasures they ever wanted, the stability and shelter it has given them has also enabled them to become one of the four most advanced and powerful civilizations in the galaxy.

"Well, that certainly explains the Volona's distrustfulness of other species," Marc thought, as he finished listening to Zorina's long account of Volonan history. "Although it still doesn't justify it."

One night, as they lay down near each other before falling asleep, Zorina told Marc the story of how she had had fallen out of grace with the Empress Adrelina:

Zorina and Adrelina are identical twins, the only daughters of Yulandina, the previous ruler of the Empire. Her reign lasted for over 100 Earth years, and ended about 50 years ago. At her deathbed, Yulandina faced a quagmire. In female dominated Volonan society, the youngest daughter is traditionally chosen as the next Empress, because she will most likely outlive the oldest and will therefore have the longest rule. In this case, however, because there was no youngest, Yulandina arbitrarily handed the throne over to Adrelina. As always, these events were depicted somewhat differently to everyone by the Virtual Translation Grid, depending on the relevant context in each individual's own virtual world. And, as always, each individual could choose to find out the real truth by specifically requesting that information from the Grid.

Zorina was never happy with this decision by her mother, mainly due to her continuous and sometimes bitter rivalry with Adrelina ever since her childhood. To pacify Zorina and to make sure that she didn't begin a rebellion, the new Empress appointed her as Chief Imperial Defender, one of the most prestigious posts in the whole Empire.

This strategy seemed to work. For over 30 years, the relationship between the two sisters remained relatively peaceful. But then, an anomaly in the Grid occurred – they both fell in love with the same male, a Volonan by the name of Rudoso. The

Grid made it appear to Zorina as if Rudoso was exclusively in love with her in her own virtual world, and similarly with Adrelina in hers. Meanwhile, Rudoso had the impression in his virtual world that he was only in love with Zorina.

Such anomalies in the Grid hardly ever happen, and it is ironic that it happened to the two most powerful Volonans in the Empire at the same time. Whenever these anomalies occur, they are impossible to detect until after the Grid has already corrected the anomaly by itself. Unfortunately, this process usually takes a long time, due to the tremendous complexity of the Grid and the number of activities it manages on a daily basis for 4.5 quintillion Volonans. It took 12 years for the Grid to recognize and correct the Rudoso anomaly, probably the costliest anomaly in its history.

Although Volonans freely engage in sexual relations with multiple partners, often at the same time and frequently swapping their partners with other Volonans, they do place tremendous importance on exclusive, monogamous relationships between males and females when it comes to love and family. So when the Rudoso anomaly became public knowledge, all hell broke loose. Rudoso decided to stay with Zorina, which made Adrelina absolutely furious. She accused Zorina of orchestrating the anomaly, with the ultimate goal of overthrowing her with Rudoso's help. She had both Zorina and Rudoso charged with treason, and imprisoned them for life. They weren't even given an opportunity to prove their innocence. Zorina was physically transferred to the Volo-Gaviera system, far away from the seat of imperial power in the Volo-Maree system, while Rudoso was taken to another location purposely kept secret from Zorina.

Zorina spent 2 years in captivity, before eventually breaking out of the Grid and finding herself here on the planet Nopelio. Now, 6 years later, she has no idea what happened to Rudoso or how to find him, though she often thinks of him. Most likely he is on some remote planet somewhere, imprisoned in his own virtual world.

The night Marc heard this story, he didn't fall asleep till very late. He couldn't help thinking of his own experience with Cheryl, particularly how she had been stuck between him and another, and how she had chosen the other over him. As he gazed at the gray skies above, he wondered how much more intense Adrelina's pain would have had to have been than his own, considering how much in love she had been with Rudoso for so long a period of time, and how important such loving relationships apparently were for Volonans. He also wondered whether he would have reacted as harshly as Adrelina did, had the circumstances been that severe for him.

"Somehow I doubt it," he thought.

Chapter 24

It took a total of 15 days for Marc, Sibular and Zorina to finish assembling the ship. Not that it was much of a ship by anyone's definition, but its makers weren't worried about looks, sophistication or comfort. Their primary goal was to build something big enough to hold the three of them and fast enough to help them escape from the Volonan Empire. The Aftaran border was much closer to Volo-Gaviera than the Mendoken border, so their plan was to head in the direction of the Aftaran Dominion. Sibular was confident that, given the good relationship between the Aftar and the Mendoken, they would find easy passage to the Mendoken Republic once they reached the Dominion.

After much initial reluctance, Zorina had agreed to accompany Marc and Sibular all the way to the Republic. As afraid as she was of traveling into the heart of what she considered enemy territory, she had eventually been persuaded that her presence and testimony would make it much easier for Marc and Sibular to convince the Mendoken government that the Volonan Empire was not behind the consar attacks on their worlds. Sibular had also given her his word that if she helped put an end to this war, then the Mendoken government would undoubtedly protect her and grant her asylum.

The three of them now stood in front of their completed ship. Overall, it was no larger than an average sized helicopter. In appearance, it was more like a random collection of different shapes and colors, with a central transparent hump that housed the cockpit, two wings of unequal length and width, and three uncovered kilasic engines mounted just behind the hump.

"She's definitely no looker," Zorina observed.

Marc couldn't agree more. If this ship were to enter a competition for aesthetic value, it would come dead last, that was for sure. There was no mistaking its meager origins from stray pieces of junk.

He also wasn't feeling particularly confident about its reliability or safety. Forget consar travel – that wasn't even an option for this vessel. Not only were the necessary materials and precise measuring instruments for consar technology not available in this scrapyard, a contraption coupled together so loosely would never be able to withstand the tremendous multidimensional forces during consar entry and exit. The ship's occupants would literally be pulled apart, atom by atom. But even with its conventional kilasic engines, he wasn't convinced the ship would hold together during takeoff, let alone fly through space.

"You're, uh, absolutely sure it won't be easier to stop this war by just telling the Volonan authorities what we know, right?" he asked Zorina.

She looked surprised. "By reconnecting to the Grid? Are you nuts, young human? I'll be back in prison and you'll be dead before we get anywhere near any imperial authorities to tell them anything. That's what I'm absolutely sure of."

And so the course of action was clear. Sibular climbed into the cockpit first, and Zorina followed.

Marc felt his heart rate jump as he climbed on board after them. "This could very well be the last flight I ever take," he thought. Regardless of the risks, however, he knew all too well what was at stake, and that staying back on this hell of a world would not allow for a life worth living anyway.

It was snug inside the cockpit, with barely enough room for the three of them, but the full 360 degree view of the outside actually gave the cockpit a spacious feel. The few instruments and screens across the front dashboard looked archaic, especially compared to the sophisticated systems Marc had seen earlier on board the big Mendoken ships.

Sibular stood in the front, as he was the main pilot, while Zorina took a seat as the flight navigator to his right. Marc took up the rear of the cockpit, where he had a small seat all to himself. His task was to monitor the function of the engines and to make sure they were always running smoothly. Sibular had given him a crash course on how kilasic engines worked, and had shown him how to correctly interpret the data from the eight gauges connected to the engines.

Sibular sealed the cockpit door shut. "Are you both ready?"

Zorina bobbed her head up and down with excitement, while Marc gave a reluctant nod. The only inviting thing about this small cockpit, he felt, was that its oxygen supply and air conditioning system provided somewhat of an improvement over the hot, humid air outside.

With that, Sibular touched an icon on one of the illuminated screens on the dashboard. The engines lit up right away, springing to life with a deafening roar. He pressed several other icons on the screen, and then rested his front hands on two handles that protruded from the dashboard.

As the ship lifted straight up from the ground, heavy vibrations tore through its chassis, and Marc could have sworn he heard clanking sounds coming from below. But all the engine gauges showed normal readings, and his fellow crewmembers seemed unconcerned.

After the ship had reached a height of about 50 feet from the ground, Sibular pulled on the two handles, and the ship began moving forward. He then took it for a short test flight around the canyon, pulling and pushing each handle to control tilts, turns and speed. No test flights had been conducted earlier, in case drones spotted the ship's movement and shot it down before it had even had a chance to clear the atmosphere. This was to be both the ship's first test flight and its maiden voyage through many light years of hostile space.

Fortunately, Marc's fears of the ship's stability appeared to be unfounded. It certainly was noisy and it did rattle a lot, but it flew effortlessly through the air. After a couple of more laps around the canyon, Sibular tilted the vessel upwards and flew it into the gray sky.

Nevertheless, their exit from Nopelio wasn't going to be quite that easy, as they very well knew.

"Here they come!" Zorina exclaimed, pointing to the navigation screen in front of her.

Sure enough, as Marc looked over her shoulder at the screen, he could see a few blips approaching from the right. Several seconds later, he saw the real things outside, as the silhouettes of drones broke through the clouds and headed towards the ship. And this time, there weren't just the standard three, there were nine of them.

"Should we come to a standstill?" Sibular asked.

Zorina flapped her ears. "No! There isn't enough time. We have to outrun them!"

Sibular pressed a couple of icons on the panel screen and pulled on the handles. The ship sped up and entered the thick clouds with full force. Visibility instantly dropped, and heavy turbulence began tossing the ship about.

"Where are they?" Marc asked frantically, feeling the nausea rise in his head.

"They're coming up behind us!" Zorina shouted, staring at the navigation screen. "They'll fire any sec...!"

Before she could finish her sentence, a bright light zoomed right past the ship from behind, missing its left wing by inches. Other bright lights followed on both sides, above and below. The drones were firing shot after shot.

"We've got to go faster!" Marc yelled.

Sibular made some adjustments on the dashboard, and pulled harder on the handles. The ship accelerated, clearing each layer of clouds and entering the next more and more quickly.

The drones followed as best as they could and kept firing with their horrible aim, but fell further behind. As Zorina had explained, Volonan drones were not constructed for travel at high altitudes or in space – their primary purpose was to fly low above the ground, looking for and killing any fugitives that had somehow been able to disconnect from the Grid. The maximum speed any drone could reach was no more than 2,000 miles per hour, a far cry from the interstellar speeds this ship could reach with its kilasic engines.

Finally, the ship broke through the last cloud layer, without getting hit even once by the drones. The sky above was clear and deep blue, a sight that gave Marc a sense of liberty he hadn't felt in a long time. He looked back to see if the drones were still following, but there weren't any.

As the ship cleared Nopelio's atmosphere and headed off into deep space, he began to relax. Glad to finally leave that hellhole of a world behind, he also felt more at ease about the ship's reliability. So far, it was doing just fine, with all the engine gauges showing normal readings. There clearly was something to be said for Mendoken technical prowess and Volonan creativity, especially when combined with the help of a neutral, uniting human hand.

"The closest point along the Aftaran border is 204 light years away from here," Zorina said, pressing some icons on the navigation screen.

Marc did the math in his head. At the vessel's projected maximum speed of 20,000 times the speed of light, it would take almost 4 Earth days to get there, and that was assuming everything went smoothly. Then he remembered something which made him very uneasy. "Zorina, isn't there a barrier of ships around the Volo-Gaviera system to protect the sources of purania here? That's what we attacked when we arrived. How are we going to get past it?"

She smiled. "Not to worry, my friend! The barrier here at Volo-Gaviera doesn't cover the whole star system like a silupsal filter does. Such a project would be too costly for the Empire, and, frankly, unnecessary. The barrier only protects specific sections of this star system where the purania is, mostly around the planet Lupomo and its moons. As the furthest planet in the star system, Lupomo is quite far from our current position and our path out of here, I can assure you."

"Well, that's a relief!"

"Oh, it is! Otherwise this would be a very short flight with a most unfortunate ending."

"What about other ships that might be looking for us during our journey? If one of them spots us, we're finished!"

"That's highly unlikely. See, within the borders of the Empire, Volonans can't really track anybody or anything that has disconnected from the Grid. So they have no way of finding us, unless we first provoke a ship or attempt to cross a barrier. That's why our borders need to have such strong barriers, because if any outsiders happen to cross through it successfully, then they're free to roam around inside the Empire with a very low risk of being detected." She paused. "So the only thing for us to be concerned about is crossing the barrier at the border. That's a real barrier – it's quite different from the one you attacked here. It's a lot more sophisticated, covering the entire perimeter of the Empire without a single gap or hole anywhere. And, believe me, it's very difficult to penetrate, whether you're coming in or going out."

Sibular laughed. "Brrrrrrrrrrrrrrrrrr. Considering your background as Chief Imperial Defender, Zorina, your knowledge should help us."

"Yeah, you were responsible for the border defense system yourself, weren't you?" Marc added. "Know of any vulnerabilities?"

Zorina looked hesitant at first. "Well, I trust you both enough by now. Promise me you'll never reveal these secrets to anyone else, even under the harshest of tortures or the direst of circumstances, especially not to any foreign power. Sibular, that includes the Imgoerin and the rest of the Mendoken government."

Marc and Sibular both gave her their word. By now, Marc had a fairly good understanding how important the impenetrability of the Empire's border was for Volonans.

Zorina cleared her throat. "The original barrier that was set up around the perimeter of the Empire was very secure, but had a number of major problems. Over time, enhancements were added to fix those problems. Some of them were added by none others than yours truly.

"Anyway, there's one fix that was added long before my time that I believe we can take advantage of. See, there are several nebulae along the border with the Aftaran Dominion that are hyperactive hotbeds for comets, asteroids and stardust. The trajectories of many of these comets lead right through the border, and in the past, comets used to repeatedly crash with the barrier as they tried to pass through it. This kept causing considerable damage to the barrier, and continuously generated false intrusion alarms for the defense system. Eventually, the barrier was reprogrammed to let such natural phenomena pass through freely."

"Don't silupsal filters do the same thing?" Marc asked.

"Yes! Except that silupsal filters aren't designed to be defense systems. They don't destroy everything that attempts to pass through them without prior authorization."

"But this ship looks nothing like a comet or any other natural phenomenon,"

Sibular said. "We will immediately be detected and destroyed when we attempt to cross the barrier."

"A direct, simple crossing wasn't quite what I had in mind, my man! We're going to try something a little more adventurous."

As expected, they easily exited the Volo-Gaviera star system without having to pass any barrier. And by sticking to some of the less traveled routes in the Yuwa highway system, they avoided encountering too many Volonan ships along the way to the border region. Those which they did encounter they kept a safe distance from, in order to avoid provoking them in any way whatsoever. The ship's instrument clusters gave minor trouble a couple of times, but they were corrected without much effort. The engines ran smoothly throughout the journey, not once coughing or losing thrust.

Although conditions onboard were cramped for the three occupants, the mood remained positive and upbeat. On the fourth day, they reached a nebulous region near the border commonly referred to as the Hurling Mist among Imperial Guards, a name it had earned due to the high volume of comets and meteoroids it continuously generated in its midst and flung towards the border.

Marc was mesmerized by the view. There were brightly colored clouds of gas all around, many of them with surprisingly familiar shapes. Some looked like flowers, while others looked like raging herds of different kinds of animals. Scattered between these clouds were large chunks of icy rock, most of them stationary, others moving in random directions. Back on Earth, he had seen pictures of nebulae taken by the Hubble telescope. But, as he could now see for himself, pictures didn't come anywhere close to witnessing the real thing.

As he kept looking ahead, he remembered something he had learned in his college astronomy classes – nebulae were the birthplaces of stars. All the stars in the universe had once been born in gas clouds similar to the ones he was now staring at, and hence all forms of life in the universe owed their existence to such clouds. It was truly a humbling experience to be able to see them so close.

Sibular slowed the ship down to maneuver it through the rock fields. "Well, Zorina?"

"Hold on, my man, just hold on." She kept looking at the navigation screen and performing calculations, then out at the sky, and then back at the screen.

Suddenly she stood up, just as a group of five comets emerged from one of the clouds. "There, see, I told you so! Comets come out of this area all the time. Alright, aim for the second one from the left. It appears to be headed straight for the border."

Sibular increased speed to catch up with the comets, swaying hard to the left and right to avoid colliding with the rocks in the ship's path.

"Careful, Sibular!" Marc shouted, just as the ship's right wing almost hit a rock.

After a highly turbulent ride, the ship caught up with the comets. Having cleared the vast array of rock fields, each of the comets was starting to head off in a slightly different direction. With far easier maneuverability now in open space, Sibular steered the ship towards the second comet.

As they approached the comet from above, Marc was able to get a good look at the icy mass that made up its core. It was a not a big piece of rock, perhaps no more than 3 or 4 miles across, but behind it lay incredibly long trails of dust and ionized gas. It wasn't glowing much, mostly because comets only glowed brightly when they heated up. That usually happened when they approached stars, and there wasn't a star nearby in this region of space. This particular comet was probably heading for some distant star on the other side of the border, which it would orbit around before returning to its point of origin. That was just the nature of comets, at least those in this part of the galaxy.

"Okay, get ready to land," Zorina said. "Easy does it now."

Sibular slowed the ship down to match the velocity of the comet, and then gently lowered it onto the rough, uneven surface. Dust particles gathered quickly on the cockpit's windows, blocking much of the outside view. Fortunately, Zorina's navigation screen provided Sibular all the help he needed in setting the ship down on its target landing point – the bottom of a deep, narrow gully barely wide enough to fit the wingspan of the ship.

Once the ship had reached the bottom of the gully, Sibular turned off the engines and all the lights. The surroundings immediately turned pitch dark, with only a tiny amount of light seeping in through the opening of the gully above. It was so dark, in fact, that Marc had to wait for more than a minute before he could see anything. He could tell that this was an ideal spot on the comet to rest the ship, as the depth and narrowness of the gully would hopefully conceal its presence at the border.

"I guess all we can do now is to wait," he said, stretching his arms and leaning back in his seat.

Since comets generally moved at only a small fraction of the speed of kilasic powered ships, it took them almost 9 hours to reach the border.

"There it is!" Zorina finally said, breaking the long silence in the cockpit. She was pointing at a solid line that had appeared on the top of her navigation screen, a line that the comet they were on had an intercept path with.

Marc immediately got up from his seat and looked out the ship's window, hoping to catch a glimpse of the border barrier through the opening of the gully far above. Although the dust of the comet's trails made it difficult to see anything at all, he was still able to make out the familiar twinkle of stars in the distance. There didn't seem to be anything unusual or new out there.

But then, the ground shook violently for a couple of seconds, and the sky above lit up all of a sudden in a dim red color.

"That's it, we've entered the barrier!" Zorina said, bobbing her head up and down with excitement. "It's working!"

Through the dim red hue, Marc could make out the shadows of large, pin-shaped objects in the distance. They had flat tops resting on long stems that thinned out towards the bottom, and were spaced apart in a never-ending grid-like pattern.

"Those are the barrier's monitoring nodes," Zorina explained, following Marc's gaze. "They are spread out across the entire perimeter of the border. Not to worry, though, because they are unmanned. They only take action if they spot an alien intrusion or attack."

"What action do they take?" Marc asked.

"Oh, they destroy the targets right away. But if they fail, they alert nearby Imperial Guard ships that an intrusion is taking place. You see, due to the humongous size of the border, manned ships have to be few and far between at any given point along the barrier. Otherwise, we Volonans would end up with our entire population just guarding the border!"

As she spoke, a white flash passed by over the surface of the comet.

"Was that a scan?" Sibular asked.

"Yes, and there will be plenty more, but they are unlikely to penetrate this deep into the gully. We're safe, don't worry."

"Well, I certainly hope you're right," Marc said, looking up at those eerie, pin-shaped nodes. Somehow he wasn't convinced that crossing the border was going to be quite as easy as she was making it out to be.

Much to his chagrin, his intuition was correct. Although the entire 3 hour journey through the barrier was uneventful, even after multiple scans from different nodes, something went horribly wrong at the very end. Just as the comet was about to exit the barrier, one of the last nodes performed a scan. This node was directly above the comet, and extremely close. Its scan penetrated the gully from above, reached all the way down to the bottom, and swooped over the ship with its brilliant white light.

Right away, Zorina yelled out several swear words that Sibular's translator wasn't able to translate into English, and then added, "Quick, Sibular! Get this ship out of here! Hurry!"

Sibular immediately sprang the engines to life, and pulled the ship out of the gully as quickly as he could without hitting the walls. Just as the ship sped away from the comet's surface, the node began firing at the comet with laser-like streaks of light. It took only a few such streaks to hit the comet, before the entire mass of rock blew up in a gigantic explosion.

Sibular accelerated the ship as fast as he possibly could, trying to keep ahead of the emerging cloud of fire and debris. Several large pieces of debris barely missed the ship, mostly thanks to his skillful maneuverability. But as the ship finally exited the barrier, one piece of debris hit the left rear wing and the leftmost engine. The impact caused the ship to spiral out of the barrier into open space.

"Is anybody hurt?" Sibular asked, as he desperately tried to bring the ship's spiraling under control.

Marc and Zorina both motioned that they were fine.

But the ship definitely wasn't. The engine gauges were showing haphazard readings, and as the spiraling continued, parts of the damaged engine and wing broke off and floated away into space.

"Sibular, the left engine is gone, and the middle engine is overheating!" Marc shouted, staring at the gauges with alarm.

Sibular shut the middle engine down right away, before it had a chance to blow up. With only one functioning engine remaining, it took him a while to stop the spiraling and finally resume a normal, straight course away from the barrier.

Gazing back out of the ship, Marc could clearly see the wall of the barrier they had just passed through. It looked like a colossal canvas of dim red paint, covering the entire view of the rear sky. The nodes could still be seen, looking like black pins evenly distributed in neat rows all across the canvas.

It was a phenomenal sight, he thought, and downright scary. "So are we finally out of the Volonan Empire?"

"We certainly are!" Zorina said excitedly.

"They're not going to attack us anymore?"

"Nope, they can't. We're out of the Empire's jurisdiction. Imperial Guards aren't allowed to follow us here. We have just officially entered the Aftaran Dominion."

Marc felt highly relieved. "The Aftarans don't have any barrier like that, right?"

"Nobody else in the galaxy has a barrier like that. Nobody cares about border protection as much as we Volonans do."

"That is because nobody is as hopelessly paranoid as you Volonans are," Sibular said.

Zorina flapped her ears in annoyance. "Thanks to constant provocations from Mendoken troublemakers!"

Marc scowled at both of them. "Hey! Now isn't the time to argue."

"You are right, Marc," Sibular said, and paused for a moment. "To answer your question, the Aftarans generally do not have too many ships, and they have fairly loose border controls. They do have some ships that periodically patrol their borders, and the side that faces the Phyrax Federation is significantly more fortified due to their current war with the Phyrax. But this side is relatively quiet. The Aftar and Volona may be enemies, but because the Volonans do such an outstanding job in guarding the border on their side, the Aftarans do not feel compelled to waste resources on fortifications themselves. So the chances of us actually coming across an Aftaran ship in this area are quite slim."

"Quite slim, eh, my man?" Zorina said with a smirk. "Then how do you explain that?" She nodded towards the navigation screen.

Marc got up from his seat to take a look. Three blips had just appeared on the top part of the screen, and they were rapidly closing in on the ship. "Aftaran ships?"

"Evidently," Zorina said, looking somewhat smug that Sibular's prediction had just been proven wrong. "That's what their identity signature says."

"Interesting, and surprising," Sibular said. "It appears a reception committee has been waiting for us."

"Well, hopefully they can help us repair our ship!" Zorina said enthusiastically. "Or maybe even help us get to your Republic. The Aftarans are your friends, aren't they?"

"Yes, but I do not understand how they could be expecting us," Sibular said, slowing the ship down in preparation for the encounter. "That is quite strange."

Chapter 25

The Afta-Raushan star system had a total of 4 planets and 9 moons. Right in the center of the Dominion, Afta-Raushan was one of the oldest living stars in the entire galaxy, and also one of the smallest. Its small size, in fact, was the key to its longevity. Stars sustained themselves through the process of nuclear fusion, where their cores continuously joined hydrogen atoms to generate helium and release energy. Once their internal supplies of hydrogen fuel ran out, stars would eventually die. Since small stars burned up only small amounts of hydrogen, their fuel supplies lasted much longer than those of big stars. Afta-Raushan, less than one tenth the size of Earth's Sun, was actually almost as old as the beginning of the current expansion wave of the universe – close to 13 billion Earth years. And Aftaran scientists estimated that it would continue to burn for at least another 10 billion years, if not more.

Meenjaza, the desert world that the Aftar had originated from, was the second planet in orbit around Afta-Raushan. To this day, it remained the seat of the Dominion's power. The first planet was a small, hot and rocky world called Humdira, the third a gas giant called Fultafa, and the fourth another desert planet by the name of Soondaza. Apart from Fultafa, all the planets and moons in the system were inhabited by Aftarans. There were no space stations in this system or anywhere else in the Dominion, as the Aftar did not possess the level of technology needed to build and sustain such structures. And, just like the rest of the Dominion, ship traffic here was very light.

The Boura-class vessel that Dumyan and Sharjam were on had encountered no other ships on its way into the Afta-Raushan system. Lord Wazilban, while aware of their coming, had apparently chosen not to send any fleet to intercept or attack them, since the messages he had received had led him to believe that Ozwin was bringing the vessel to Meenjaza with the two brothers as captives. But little did Wazilban know that those two captives were now the masters of the ship, and that Ozwin and his companion had in turn become the captives, both securely tied up and rendered completely immobile for the remainder of the journey.

Contrary to his original plan of trying to reach the Mendoken Republic, Dumyan had changed his mind, and, after much discussion and argumentation, convinced Sharjam that it would be more effective to fight Wazilban in the heart of the Dominion. Even if the Mendoken could somehow be persuaded to help overthrow Wazilban, the Aftaran people might rise up to defend him because he was still their elected leader. They might view the Mendoken as an occupation force and not as a helping hand. The better way to fight Wazilban, therefore, was to turn the Aftaran people against him, by revealing to them what a deceiver and charlatan he really was, by showing them how his policies of belligerence and tyranny against the Phyrax and the rest of the galaxy were bringing about an ever-growing vicious cycle of violence, death and destruction. In short, Dumyan had argued, the only way to defeat Wazilban was to lead a rebellion against him by his own people, not by getting help from outside.

And so here the two of them were, at the doorsteps to the seat of Aftaran power, the same power that was eagerly awaiting their arrival in chains, eagerly waiting to torture them to death. Any normal individual who had escaped Wazilban's brutal clutches at least once before would clearly consider it madness to voluntarily return to his lair. But these two brothers weren't normal individuals, nor was their cause normal. They had more at stake here than most Aftarans, significantly more.

"There it is," Sharjam said, pointing ahead at a bright blue sphere in the distance. He was sitting in the cockpit, next to his brother who was piloting the ship with his thoughts. They were heading towards Medonis, the only moon around the fourth planet Soondaza. Sharjam was very familiar with Medonis, since it housed the university he had graduated from years earlier. Officially known as the Raushan Clerical Academy, it was the oldest, the most famous, and widely accepted as the best clerical school in the entire Dominion. It had established such popularity, in fact, that over time its campus had grown to cover most of the livable land on the moon.

"You are certain your old teacher is still there?" Dumyan asked.

"I am not certain, but I cannot imagine where else he would be. When I graduated, he told me he would soon retire to the monastery at Mt. Lina. He was getting old, and wanted to spend the rest of his years there in solitude and prayer."

"How can you be so certain that you can trust him?"

"He was very fond of our father, and held the highest contempt for Wazilban and his rising to power."

"But a long time has passed, and we do not know how things have changed here in the meantime."

"Well, that is precisely why we should see him. We need to find out how things have changed before we can take any action. If nothing else, the sacred bond between clerical masters and their students should prevent him from selling us out."

"Yes, assuming Wazilban has not abolished those bonds as well."

Sharjam certainly hoped that was not the case. He had very warm memories of his old teacher, Master Heeran of the 654th generation of the Zuljibah clan, under whose wise guidance he had spent many years studying the Scriptures and the age-old ways of Aftaran history's great spiritual leaders.

The submarine-shaped ship began its descent, cutting through the moon's blue atmosphere like a sharp knife. Once it had cleared the thin and patchy cloud layer, Sharjam was able to gaze at the landscape below. He remembered how he had never much cared for Medonis's lush greenery, deep blue seas or snow-capped mountains. Like most Aftarans, he felt more at home in dry desert environments, thanks to his upbringing on Meenjaza's sand dunes. Yet now, after being away for so many years, and particularly after spending the past two years in the underbelly of a mountain on an inhospitable ice world, he felt a wave of nostalgia towards this place. This time, the world below looked downright beautiful, and he was glad to be back.

Dumyan guided the ship over the university campus, spread far and wide between wooded areas, rivers and rolling hills. A few small vessels could be seen flying in the distance, and other vehicles were moving about between the campus buildings. But none paid any attention to the approaching Boura-class ship.

Up ahead, Sharjam could see the mountains that he once used to see everyday from his dorm room window, the mountain range that split up the north side of the vast campus from the south. The nearest mountain, rising to a lower height than the ones behind it, was Mt. Lina. Perched atop its wide, flat peak was a magnificent, tan colored structure. Like many prominent Aftaran buildings, it was adorned with spiked domes and wide, sweeping arches, giving it both an elegant and somber look. Four tall towers stood upright near the center of the structure, spaced evenly apart from each other in a square formation. This building was one of the official monasteries of the university, a place where teachers and students alike went to meditate and pray whenever they wanted. It was also the destination point for Sharjam and his brother.

"Where can we land this ship?" Dumyan asked.

"There is a landing platform just behind the monastery building. It is not very big, however, since it is primarily meant for short range vessels. You may find landing there a little difficult."

The landing platform was small alright, but turned out to be no problem for Dumyan's outstanding flying skills. He slowed the ship down to a standstill and gradually brought it down to rest on the ground. It fit snugly on one side of the tarmac, leaving enough space for other, smaller ships to land and take off with ease. Luckily there were no other ships about at that moment.

"Nobody seems to be expecting us, and that is a good thing," Sharjam said, surveying the deserted platform. "We need to remain as inconspicuous as possible, and not reveal our identities to anybody but my old Master. Fortunately, monasteries in the Dominion operate on the basis of anonymity. It does not matter who you are or where you come from. As long as your intentions are pure, you are welcome inside. So hopefully it will not be too difficult for us."

"Yes, but let us get moving," Dumyan said, getting up from his seat and veiling his face. "The more time we waste, the higher the chances one of Wazilban's spies here will notice us."

After making sure the two prisoners in the prayer room were adequately cared for, Dumyan followed Sharjam out of the ship. Medonis's sweet smelling breeze instantly hit his face as he descended onto the tarmac. It was a very welcome and refreshing feeling for him to breathe such good air again, as it was to see a blue sky above and a brilliantly shining sun.

Sharjam pressed the buzzer next to the large, wooden door at the entrance to the monastery building. A few seconds later, the door slid open. The two brothers entered cautiously, looking down to avoid anyone's gaze.

"May the Creator protect you from harm, strangers!" a voice called out, as the door shut behind them.

"And you!" Dumyan and Sharjam replied in unison.

"This is a sanctuary for all who seek closeness with the Creator." The voice seemed to echo off the walls of the corridor they had entered.

It took several seconds for Dumyan's eyes to adjust to the dim lighting inside. The corridor was long, its ceiling high, and, like the interiors of many Aftaran buildings, supported by vaulted archways. The walls were covered with colorful symmetric patterns and beautiful works of calligraphy from the sacred Scriptures. Outside light shone in directly at steep angles through small windows high up on the walls. The floor was made of brilliant white stone, commonly found in Aftaran buildings.

Dumyan turned around to face the door, and saw the Aftaran sentry who had let them in. Dressed in a black robe, he was short and stocky, and in his right hand he held a scepter of some kind. His head was covered and his face veiled, as was customary whenever Aftarans met for the first time.

Dumyan decided to keep his mouth shut and let his brother do all the talking. The last time he had set foot inside a monastery... well, he couldn't even remember when that had been. Sharjam, on the other hand, knew this place like the back of his own hand, and was well versed in all its rules and customs.

Sharjam spoke, raising the pitch of his voice and changing his accent slightly to avoid recognition. "We accept your hospitality with gratitude." He bowed before the sentry. "May the Creator's blessings be showered upon you for eternity."

"And upon you both," the sentry replied, bowing as well.

"We are travelers from afar, who seek naught but the road to solace in life and in death."

"May the Creator increase your solace with every step you take in your journey."

"Thank you for the kind words. Can you take us to Master Heeran? We have come a long way for his renowned knowledge in the matters of the faith."

The sentry was silent for a moment, apparently startled by the request. "Master Heeran is no longer with us," he whispered, glancing nervously up and down the corridor. "But I can lead you to his apprentice. She is still here in the monastery."

Dumyan found the sentry's reaction intriguing. Obviously something bad had happened to Master Heeran, something the sentry was afraid of. It was clear that he and Sharjam would have to tread very carefully here. Danger could be lurking behind the ornately decorated walls of this house of sanctity.

"Yes, that will do fine," Sharjam said.

"Please follow me." The sentry led the way down the corridor, up a flight of stairs and through a series of chambers.

Dumyan noticed a number of Aftarans in the different rooms, perched in front of visual displays, studying the Scriptures and other texts. Others were sitting quietly, praying or meditating. Others still were huddled together in groups, engaged in earnest conversation. A few glanced briefly at him and Sharjam, and some appeared to eye the two of them with suspicion, or maybe that was just his imagination. The majority seemed to pay no attention to them at all.

Dumyan and Sharjam followed the sentry into the residential wing of the monastery, along a passage with doors leading to private rooms on either side. The sentry finally stopped in front of one door, and waved his hand in front of a small screen on the wall.

"May the Creator protect you from harm," a female voice said through the speaker below the screen. The screen itself remained blank.

"And you," the sentry said. "Two visitors wish to see you."

"I am expecting no visitors. You must be mistaken. Please go away." She sounded calm and polite, but firm.

"They have come for Master Heeran," the sentry said.

Silence. Seconds later, the door slid open just a couple of inches.

"I will leave you here," the sentry said. "May the Creator help you find that which you seek." He bowed and walked off in a hurry.

Dumyan slowly pushed the door aside and walked in. The first thing he noticed was the open window on the far side of the room, giving a clear view of the bright sky above and the university campus below. The room was very small, furnished with only a thin mattress on the floor and a prayer corner next to the window. Such austere simplicity was typical for Aftaran monasteries, allowing residents to focus on spiritual thoughts without any distractions.

Sharjam followed Dumyan into the room, and heard the door shut abruptly behind him. He spun around immediately, just in time to see the nose of a boryal staring directly at him. The Aftaran holding it was just over 7 feet tall, with her head covered and her face veiled.

"Who are you and what do you want from me?" she demanded sternly.

Sharjam was shocked and surprised. "That voice," he thought. "That voice, it is... so familiar. But it cannot be!" He opened his mouth to speak, but words failed him.

"We are looking for Master Heeran," Dumyan said, stepping in for Sharjam's silence. "Where is he?"

"What business have you with him?"

"No, there is no doubt," Sharjam thought. He knew that voice like no other. Without any further hesitation, he dropped his veil and revealed his face to her. "Raiha! It is me, Sharjam!"

"Sharjam? But what... how?" The sternness in her voice had disappeared, and she appeared not to notice the boryal slipping from her hand and falling onto the floor.

Sharjam walked up to her and dropped her veil. She still looked as stunningly beautiful as ever, with her twinkling brown eyes and soft, auburn colored feathers.

"Oh, Sharjam, I thought you were dead!" Raiha said with joy, embracing him with open arms.

"And I thought you had left this place for good!" Sharjam said gleefully, as he hugged her tightly. "Why did you return?"

"I changed my mind after a couple of years, and decided to return to finish my studies. You had already left by then. Master Heeran agreed to take me on as his apprentice."

"Alright!" Dumyan said, lowering his own veil. "Dear brother, when will you find your manners and introduce me to your attractive friend here?"

"I am sorry! Raiha, this is my older brother Dumyan. Dumyan, this is Raiha, my close friend from our days of study here at the academy."

"I am very pleased to meet you, Dumyan," Raiha said, bowing her head. "I have heard many a tale about you from Sharjam."

"Really? And yet my brother has conveniently kept your existence completely hidden from me and the rest of the family. I wonder why?" Dumyan grinned mischievously.

Sharjam felt embarrassed. "Raiha and I had a romantic relationship for several years. I did not inform anybody in the family because, well, I did not want my reputation of piety and solemnity to be tarnished. It would not have done wonders for the status of our family with the public either, especially while our father was ruling the Dominion."

Dumyan laughed. "While everyone called me the loose, wild one. You sly devil, you! I should have learned to keep my activities under wraps, like you! Would have saved me a lot of grief with our parents."

"It was not just for him," Raiha said. "I wanted to keep our relationship totally secret as well."

"Why?"

"I joined the academy as a Kerberat nun," she said quietly, sounding very embarrassed. "I was sworn to celibacy."

Dumyan laughed again. "Kerberat, Ferberat, Merberat or whatever – I could not care less about these things, Raiha, as Sharjam probably has told you before. I am just glad to hear that my brother is more like me than he has ever cared to admit in his whole life! Now, tell me, what happened to your relationship?"

"We were getting too close, too involved with each other," Sharjam said. "It was interfering with our studies, and it was also becoming increasingly difficult to hide our relationship from others."

"So we broke it off," Raiha added. "It was very hard. So hard for me, in fact, that I decided to leave the university altogether and return to my family."

"What!" Dumyan's surprise showed clearly on his face. "You gave up the relationship just for that? That is ridiculous!"

"Ridiculous for you, maybe," Sharjam said. "But you have to respect that Raiha and I have very different lifestyles and priorities from you. You do not know how strict rules and customs are in these clerical schools."

"That may be, but I still think it is ridiculous that you gave up your relationship because of what others might think. You can never be happy if you live your life that way. Especially if there is nothing to be ashamed of in the first place. What is wrong with a healthy relationship between two consenting adults?"

Sharjam wasn't sure what to say. He had missed Raiha terribly these past few years. If he were faced with the same situation again, he wasn't sure he would give her up a second time. He gazed at her, wondering if she felt the same way.

"Honestly, Sharjam, some day I will have to tell you what Birshat and I have been through," Dumyan continued. "Then you will understand what sacrifices couples sometimes have to make in order to stay together. Nothing outweighs the happiness that results from a loving, caring relationship." He paused. "But at the moment, we have more urgent things to worry about. Raiha, can you tell us what happened to Master Heeran?"

"That is a long story, and I will tell you," Raiha said. She motioned to both brothers to sit down on the mattress, and then sat down on the floor opposite them. "But first, you must tell me how you survived Lord Wazilban's attempts to kill you, and why in the Creator's name you have taken such a risk to return to the heart of his power base."

Sharjam gave Dumyan a slight nod, indicating Raiha could be fully trusted.

They spent close to an hour talking in Raiha's small room. Dumyan and Sharjam related to Raiha how they had escaped with their father and those loyal to him to the planet Tibara, and how they had remained in hiding there all this time. They also told her how the noose around their father was tightening, and how conditions were getting worse for him by the day. This was why they had come back. They were going to take the fight right back to Wazilban in his own courtyard, in his own comfort zone. They were going to rouse the Aftaran people, and show them what kind of villain Wazilban really was. They would take back what was rightfully theirs, and return their father to the throne.

Raiha listened intently to the whole story. "A very noble and commendable plan, and very, very bold," she said at the end.

Sharjam frowned. "You do not believe we can succeed?"

"With the Creator's help, you surely will. But it will not be easy. Wazilban's powers grow stronger and more absolute by the day. Any last remnants of democratic governance eroded when he disbanded the Council of Elders."

"He did not!" Dumyan sounded enraged.

"Yes, he did. But that is nowhere near the worst of it, Dumyan. Things have been progressively worsening over the past couple of years. Ever since you all escaped from right under his clutches, Wazilban has dramatically tightened his grip on the Dominion. He has replaced all regional governors and key positions in the military with Aftarans of his own choice, and significantly increased the size and power of the armed forces. Secret police now actively monitor all activity in public institutions like this one, with spies planted in virtually all religious and social organizations of any reasonable size. No public dissension is allowed anywhere, no freedom of speech, and all supposedly for the security of the Aftaran people. Anybody who dares to speak out against Wazilban or his policies is taken away, accused of being a terrorist and a heretic, and publicly executed after a short, staged and totally unfair trial. And anyone who doesn't condemn those executed in the strongest possible terms is accused of being unpatriotic and a terrorist sympathizer."

"This is horrible!" Sharjam exclaimed. "How is he getting away with this? Why is the public not reacting? Why are they not rebelling en masse?"

"Shhh, keep your voice down, Sharjam," Raiha said quietly. "You never know who might be listening in the next room. The spies are everywhere."

"You are right, sorry," Sharjam whispered.

"There are pockets of resistance across the Dominion," Raiha explained. "There are some rebels here on this moon. Fouzil, the sentry who let you in, is one of them. There are even a few rebels in hiding on Meenjaza, right on Wazilban's doorstep. But by and large, the public is very afraid to attempt anything. Ordinary Aftarans are staying home and keeping their heads low, lest they get picked up by the secret police. That is what happened to Master Heeran – he was made an example of at this academy."

Dumyan frowned. "What do you mean?"

"In a lecture he gave at the academy seven months ago about religion and peace, he dared to criticize our war with the Phyrax. I was there, Dumyan, and I know what he said. All he said was that our religion teaches us to promote peace and understanding, and that violence should only be used as a last resort if nothing else works. He then questioned whether that principle was always being applied under Wazilban's rule. That was all it took! The next day, he mysteriously disappeared from the campus, and appeared a couple of days later as a prisoner of the Dominion on Meenjaza. Four days later, he was executed, after a staged trial accusing him of being a traitor and a heretic."

"He was... executed? Oh, my goodness!" Sharjam couldn't believe his ears. His old, beloved teacher, dead! And for such a trivial reason. His head began spinning in shock.

"I know, Sharjam, I am so sorry," Raiha said. She got up and sat next to him on the mattress to comfort him. "He was so kind and tolerant, so knowledgeable and so brilliant. Rarely do you find a single Aftaran with all those qualities. I still miss him terribly every single day.

"But do you see now why everyone is so scared to say or do anything? The other problem is that there is no strong leadership to take charge of an organized rebellion. Our last hope was your father, and of course you two, but Wazilban led us all to believe you had perished at the hands of his forces." She sighed. "He took control of the media first, spreading his messages like wildfire across the Dominion. The public paid no heed to your father's wise warnings, finding much more interest and excitement in Wazilban's radical rhetoric. So they swept Wazilban into power with much fanfare and hope. They fell for his lies and empty promises, and now they are paying the price for it. Only the Creator knows how much worse things will get before they start getting better."

"That is precisely why we have returned," Dumyan said. "To make things better. Hopefully the public will listen to us this time!"

Raiha smiled. "Oh, they will. The tides have turned amongst the public. Even with the constant propaganda being dispersed by the heavily regulated news broadcasts, ordinary Aftarans have become absolutely fed up with this tyrannical regime that violates every basic right of freedom that they used to enjoy. The war with the Phyrax is completely out of control, with the death and destruction on both sides rapidly increasing by the day. Aftarans are dying daily by the thousands! Yet Wazilban refuses to negotiate or seek a diplomatic solution to the conflict, and instead continues to intensify his hateful rhetoric against the enemy. He is using up all of the resources in the Dominion to continue this war, drafting young Aftarans to join the military and sending them to the frontier to die, and even forcing priests and monks to work on building weapons and military ships. And all for what, I ask you? Does he not see that we cannot win this war by force? The Phyrax are far too big and powerful an enemy. And the more we fight them, the more their resolve grows to fight back. Wazilban is blinded by hate and pride, it seems, and his blindness is driving our people and way of life to the ground."

"And yet it is unpatriotic to speak out against those who are leading our nation to the brink of destruction," Dumyan said, smirking. "How ironic."

Raiha nodded. "So the public will listen to you. But listening by itself will not accomplish the job. Wazilban needs to be overthrown, and his stooges across the Dominion need to be brought to justice. None of that will be easy, considering the might of the military and the reach of his secret police."

"Ah, but the Creator is on our side," Sharjam said defiantly. "And the Creator is more powerful than all others combined." He thought of mentioning the coming of the Sign in the Hidden Scripture to Raiha, and how he and Dumyan might have seen the Sign back on the planet Droila. But he decided against it, for now at least. There was a reason it was called the Hidden Scripture, after all. Even he wasn't really supposed to know about its content.

"Why not join us in our mission, Raiha?" Dumyan said. "We need all the help we can get."

Sharjam froze for an instant. "Dumyan! We cannot ask her to put her own life in danger like that!"

Raiha smiled again. "Sharjam, is that not my decision to make? And yes, Dumyan, I will gladly join you. With the Creator's help, we most definitely will succeed."

"But Raiha, the perils are far too great! You just told us yourself how dire the situation is – Wazilban's powers and his reach are overwhelming."

"And that is precisely why I want to join you, Sharjam. It is no longer the life of an Aftaran that I lead here under Wazilban's reign. It is like living in a cage, a cage of fear and despair, of hate and anger. Ever since Master Heeran was executed so mercilessly, I have been dying to do something. So many endless nights I have lain awake, trying to devise a plan to fight back, to take revenge against those who killed him. So many days I have prayed to the Creator to show me a way. But what could one lowly Aftaran like me do against such a powerful enemy? Yet now, the Creator has finally answered my prayers." She gazed at both brothers with a combined look of determination and contentment in her eyes. "I am coming with you, whether you like it or not."

Sharjam didn't know what else to say. She had always been a headstrong individual, something he had always admired in her, and she had just spoken with such conviction that he knew it was unlikely he could get her to change her mind. Besides, although he was worried for her safety, he was also secretly happy that they wouldn't have to part ways again so soon.

"You should know," Raiha added, "that there are rumors floating around that Wazilban did not kill the High Clerics, but has them imprisoned on Meenjaza and is using them for his own benefit."

"Really?" Sharjam was stunned. "That would be incredible! If it is true, we must free them right away! They will have the foresight and the wisdom to tell us how to defeat Wazilban."

"Well, we shall have to find out for sure if they are alive or not," Dumyan said. "And I believe there is only one way to do that. Raiha, can you get us in touch with the rebels on Meenjaza?"

"Yes, I can, although it will not be easy."

"Good! We will definitely need their help. To begin with, we have some precious cargo they will need to watch over while we search for the High Clerics on Meenjaza."

"What kind of cargo?"

"Two prisoners – associates of Wazilban's. I believe they may yet come in quite handy."

Chapter 26

The ship that Marc, Sibular and Zorina were on was badly damaged after being shot at during its passage through the Volonan border barrier. With just one functional engine left, it had almost no chance of reaching the nearest Aftaran star system in any reasonable amount of time. And that was assuming the last engine wouldn't overheat and die as well.

The three friends were, therefore, more than happy that help had arrived at so opportune a time, help in the form of three Aftaran vessels. Sibular brought the ship to a complete standstill as the vessels came into view ahead. Spread apart in a horizontal line, they were flashing green and yellow lights.

"They almost look like police cars with those flashing lights," Marc thought. "Very large police cars, though." In contrast to the tiny ship he was on, they were massive – at least a couple of thousand feet long, a few hundred wide and another few hundred tall. Nowhere near the size of Mendoken Euma or Kril vessels, of course, but still quite big. They had the basic shape of submarines, with long, thin snouts that widened towards the middle and then thinned out again towards the end. Each ship had a hump above its middle section, which Marc assumed served as the cockpit or bridge. The hulls had a dim orange color.

"Gyra-class vessels," Sibular explained. "Designed for long distance travel from one end of the Dominion to the other and beyond. The green and yellow lights indicate that they come in peace. If the lights were red and blue, we would not be stopping right now."

The Aftaran captain hailed them over their ship's rudimentary communication link, and upon hearing that a Mendoken was on board, graciously offered to help them repair their ship and give them whatever other supplies they needed to continue their journey.

"We will lock onto your ship with a tracking beam and pull it inside one of our vessels," the captain announced over the link.

Seconds later, a beam from the middle Aftaran vessel locked onto the hull of the tiny ship, and the ship instantly began moving towards the Aftaran vessel.

"Feels like an invisible rope pulling us in," Marc thought. He glanced at Sibular, sensing a slight uneasiness in the Mendoken's expressionless face. Or maybe it was just uneasiness that he was feeling himself. Either way, he didn't feel totally comfortable with what was happening. He tried to brush it aside, dismissing it as fear or nervousness about meeting another alien race for the first time. He also reminded himself that he and his friends were extremely lucky to have found somebody to help them out of their current predicament.

Zorina, who had been silent for a while, spoke. "So how do you think they knew we were coming, my man?"

"That is a mystery," Sibular said. "But they might not necessarily have known we were coming. Perhaps the Mendoken government just asked the Aftarans to keep their eyes open for survivors from the attack on Volo-Gaviera."

"You think the Mendoken government would actually publicize the news of that failed consar attack to the Aftarans? Seems highly unlikely to me."

"They may have, in order to save the lives of any Mendoken who managed to escape across the border into the Dominion."

Marc was also skeptical about Sibular's explanation, but decided to stay quiet. He didn't know enough about the details of the alliance between the Mendoken and the Aftar to pass judgment on this question.

The tracking beam pulled the small ship through a gate into the belly of the Aftaran vessel, laying it to rest in the middle of what appeared to be a landing bay. Several small, short-range transports were parked nearby.

Even though he was clearly inside an interstellar spaceship, Marc felt the landing bay looked more like the inside of an ornate medieval mansion. Not that he had ever set foot in one, but he had seen plenty in pictures and movies. The floor was made of polished white stone, and the ceiling comprised of multiple rows of arches. The ceiling sections in between the arches were covered with elaborate decorations, as were the pillars that supported the ends of the arches. He focused his eyes on the decorations, and noticed how they were covered with different forms of calligraphy in a text he had never seen before.

"Here they come," Sibular said, getting up and opening the hatch to the cockpit. He climbed out of the ship and floated gracefully down to the floor.

Marc came out last after Zorina, barely avoiding slipping and falling to the floor with a thud. He inhaled deeply, savoring the fresh, cool air inside the landing bay. He hadn't breathed air this good since back on Earth, and felt thankful that Aftaran preferences for air quality were so close to those of humans. Even the air on Mendoken worlds and ships, while fresh and very rich in oxygen, was a tad too cold and dry for the average human.

Unfortunately, he could see that the story was quite different for Zorina, who was shivering with cold. Not surprising, he thought, considering the hot and humid air her kind was used to on worlds like Nopelio. He came close to her and put his arm around her, hoping to transfer some heat from his own body to hers. He glanced at Sibular, who was standing upright as usual, not at all affected by such changes in air temperature or pressure.

Up ahead, he saw two shadowy silhouettes approaching from between the pillars of the dimly lit landing bay. As they came closer, the first thing he noticed was how tall they were – both of them had to be nearly 8 feet in height. Their bodies were covered in loose brown robes, and their heads and faces wrapped in cloth of the same color. The only exposed parts of their entire bodies were their eyes.

Marc felt a rising wave of apprehension. He wasn't sure why, but his feeling of uneasiness about these Aftarans was intensifying, and it wasn't just because of their mysterious looks. Something just didn't seem right about them, even though he couldn't quite place what it was.

One of the Aftarans stepped forward and bowed. Sibular bowed back. Marc and Zorina followed Sibular's example.

"May the Creator protect you from harm, friends," the Aftaran said in a low, crackling voice, keeping his face covered.

"And you," Sibular replied, obviously somewhat familiar with Aftaran customs.

"I am Thorab, of the 438th generation of the Fourian clan, and the Captain of this fleet. This is my High Officer Rulshanim, of the 312th generation of the Shufra clan. This ship is your home for as long as you desire, as are all our ships for our Mendoken friends." Once again, Sibular's translator was working flawlessly, instantly performing the correct translations for everyone.

"We appreciate your hospitality," Sibular said. "I am Sibular Gaulen 45383532, Senior Space Travel Engineer from Lind at Mendo-Zueger. This is Zorina, and this is Marc." He pointed at both of them respectively.

The Aftarans looked stunned at first, then alarmed. "Zorina?" Thorab said. "You are not...?"

"Yes, yes, I am a Volonan," Zorina said, flapping her ears as she cut him off. "This is what we really look like. And yes, I am the same Zorina who used to be Chief Imperial Defender."

"In the name of the Creator!" Thorab shouted. He took a step back and his hand slipped into his robe, as if he was about to take out a weapon.

Marc was alarmed. He wondered if it had been wise for Zorina to mention who she really was, but realized that Thorab would probably have figured it out sooner or later.

"Zorina is no longer affiliated with the Empire," Sibular said quickly. "She is now as welcome there as you and I. She has escaped with us to seek refuge in the Mendoken Republic. I personally vouch for her, and assure you she poses no threat to you."

Thorab apparently wasn't convinced, as he kept his hand inside his robe. He turned to Marc. "And where might you be from?"

Marc swallowed hard before opening his mouth. "I am a human from Earth, a planet in the Mendo-Biesel star system."

Thorab's eyes lit up. "I have not heard of your species before. You are from inside the Mendoken Republic?"

"Yes."

Thorab relaxed all of a sudden, and took his hand out of his robe. He then whisked his hand past his face, and the veil over his face magically slid away into the rest of his robe. Rulshanim did the same.

Marc could clearly see their faces now, and was instantly reminded of the pictures of Aftarans HoloMarc had shown him and the ones he had seen in his visions. They had big, round brown eyes, and beaks for mouths. Their skin was covered with small feathers.

"Kind of like big owls," he thought. It was obvious these Aftarans didn't look half as threatening with their faces uncovered. He wondered if that was why they kept them covered when meeting strangers who could potentially be enemies.

Thorab bowed again in front of the three visitors. "It is my honor to have you on board. Rulshanim will show you to quarters where you will be able to rest, freshen up and partake of nourishment."

As relieving as Thorab's sudden change in behavior was, Marc found it to be highly suspicious. Hoping to have some light shed on the mystery, he gathered the courage to ask the question he was sure both of his friends were also asking in their heads: "Were you expecting us, Captain?"

"Expecting you?" Thorab's beak widened slightly to indicate a sly smile. "No, we were not expecting the three of you in particular. But we have recently stepped up our patrols of the Volonan border, due to some, shall we say, irregular events on the other side." With that, he turned around and began walking away.

Marc was not at all pleased with the response. Not only did it not answer any of his outstanding questions, it opened up additional ones. After finding out where Marc was from, why was Thorab no longer concerned about Zorina and the fact that she was a Volonan? And why didn't he ask what Marc and Sibular had been doing in the Volonan Empire to begin with? The answer was far from clear. The only clear thing at that moment was that Marc and his friends needed the Aftarans' help, both to fix their ship and to get some much needed food and rest.

"Please follow me," Rulshanim said to the visitors. He led the way out of the landing bay and into the depths of the ship.

Aftaran cuisine was a marked improvement from the dry and bitter sparli Marc had been surviving on for over 2 weeks. It was all vegetarian, and incredibly hot and spicy. He had always been a fan of spicy food, but he had to admit that nothing he had ever eaten in his life before came anywhere close to the spiciness of the thick curry he was currently eating. Much as he enjoyed its taste, every bite seemed to put his tongue on fire.

As he and Zorina gulped down their second helping of vegetable curry, Sibular floated into their quarters. It was a medium sized room, with no windows and the same ornate décor of the landing bay. Beautiful calligraphy covered the walls and the ceiling, and the floor was made of the same white stone found across most of the ship.

In contrast, the furniture in the room was very simple. There were just two thin mattresses on the floor, and a rug with several cushions in one corner. Marc and Zorina were sitting on the rug, leaning back on the cushions as they ate. They had taken warm showers, and were now dressed in gray Aftaran robes. Marc was surprised by how comfortable his robe was. He had also watched with interest when Rulshanim had shown Zorina how to magically wrap her robe around her body several times for additional warmth.

"What news, Sibular?" Marc asked between mouthfuls of spicy curry.

"Captain Thorab has offered to not only help repair our ship, but to also take us through a large part of the Dominion on board this vessel."

"Why would he do that?"

"He says they are already headed in the direction of the center of the Dominion, and can take us as far as the Afta-Raushan star system."

"Afta-Raushan?" Zorina asked. "The system the Aftar originated from?"

"Yes. It will actually save us a lot of time, as we will have to traverse the entire Dominion to get to the Mendoken border anyway. If we reach Afta-Raushan on board this vessel, we will be halfway there in less than half the time."

"In far more comfort too, I might add!" Zorina said, bobbing her head up and down enthusiastically. She took in another mouthful of curry, as if to drive the point home.

But Marc wasn't feeling at all enthusiastic about the offer. "You both feel this is a good idea?" he asked, keeping his voice low in case the Aftarans were monitoring the conversation. "Don't you think there's something strange going on here? Captain Thorab – he seems like a highly suspicious character to me. Didn't you see how he changed his behavior as soon as he found out where I was from?"

"Yes," Sibular admitted. "But to what end, I do not know. What I do know is that as an Aftaran he is unlikely to cause any harm to a Mendoken. That would cause an interspecies incident between allies."

Marc shook his head. "I don't know. I just don't trust him. And I don't feel comfortable staying on this ship a minute longer than we absolutely need to."

Zorina flapped her ears, looking somewhat incredulous. "You would rather get our little ship repaired and cross the Dominion in those cramped conditions, with only dry sparli to eat for days on end? If it doesn't break down again and leave us stranded in empty space, that is. And I doubt we'll be lucky enough to have another Aftaran ship pick us up again at that point. In that contraption of a transport, chances are we'll be dead long before we reach Afta-Raushan, let alone Mendoken territory."

Marc got up and began pacing around. "Yes, I would rather take my chances with friends I trust than with strangers I don't, regardless of the odds. I'm telling you both, something is not right here. I can feel it. I..."

To his surprise, he was not able to finish the sentence. The rest of the words just refused to come out of his mouth. Instead, a wave of weakness suddenly overcame him, causing his head to spin and forcing him to close his eyes. Losing all control over his muscles, he collapsed and fell to the floor. He lay there motionless, his face touching the cold stone surface, unable to utter a sound or move a muscle. Far away, he thought he could hear Sibular's and Zorina's voices, but he wasn't sure. As his mind separated from his body, he remembered where he had felt this way before – on the moon Ailen, in front of Osalya, the Imgoerin's aide. If he wasn't mistaken, he was about to have another group of visions, and he was powerless to do anything about it.

Sure enough, the first vision came within a few seconds, and was followed by another several minutes later. Then came another, and another, just like the last time. And just like the last time, most of the visions were the same ones, at least the ones that he could remember. First came the view of Earth, looking quite at peace from a distance, and then blowing up in a massive explosion. Then he saw other planets blowing up, whole star systems disappearing into oblivion, and finally the entire Milky Way galaxy crumbling to dust. After that came the dead bodies everywhere – first humans, then Mendoken, followed by Aftarans, Phyraxes and Volonans.

The visions continued for what seemed like many hours, perhaps days. Sometimes there were long periods of emptiness between visions, during which he could neither see nor hear a thing. Like the last time, darkness and cold eventually began to engulf him, and despair kicked in next. He shivered in the darkness, and could hear the sinister laughter of that evil shadow far away.

But then, light replaced darkness once again. A sparkling star appeared in the distance and moved closer, followed by another, then four more. The six stars brought warmth and light, glowing brightly as they came closer. He stopped shivering, and felt stronger. Hope began to replace despair, as the shadow's laughter faded away in the distance. He smiled at the stars, feeling happy and reassured that they were there with him.

Then he heard a voice. "He is waking up."

And, just like that, his eyes opened up back to reality.

"Where... where am I?" Marc croaked, blinking and rubbing his eyes. Sibular and Zorina were standing right in front of him.

"Still on board the Aftaran vessel," Sibular replied.

Marc looked around, and realized he was in the same room he had collapsed in. He was lying on one of the two mattresses on the floor. His Aftaran robe had been wrapped around his body a couple more times to keep him warm. "How long was I asleep?"

"3 days, in your units of measurement," Sibular said.

"3 days!" Marc was shocked. Last time, it hadn't even been 8 hours.

"We couldn't leave this vessel, since you were in no condition to travel in our little ship," Zorina said. "So we stayed here."

Marc looked at Zorina. She actually seemed to have gained a little bit of weight, probably from all the tasty food she had been eating here for the past 3 days.

"We have almost reached the Afta-Raushan star system," Sibular said. "Our ship has also been fully repaired. Some enhancements have even been added with the help of the Aftaran crew on this ship."

"You see, young human, your doubts about these Aftarans were in vain!" Zorina said, grinning.

Marc sat up slowly, wincing due to the throbbing pain in his head. He was glad, though, that things had been progressing so smoothly. Had his intuition about the Aftarans on this vessel been wrong? Everything seemed to indicate that it had, and yet every corner of his mind wanted to shout out that Captain Thorab was not to be trusted.

"So what happened to you, Marc?" Zorina asked, flapping her ears. "You had us really worried for a while!" She offered him a mug filled with a thick yellow liquid. "Here drink this. It's called *rauka*. The Aftarans say it has magical healing powers."

Marc took a sip. It tasted extremely bitter, but he was surprised at how quickly the strength began flowing through his veins. "These... these visions," he said, "I had all these visions. It's happened once before."

"On Ailen," Sibular said.

"Yes, on Ailen." He gulped down the rest of the rauka. 3 days of no nourishment had left him famished.

"Sibular mentioned that incident while you were asleep," Zorina said. "Tell me about these visions."

Marc hesitated. Not only was he suspicious that the Aftarans might be eavesdropping on their conversations, he also figured that both Sibular and Zorina would laugh at him and think he had totally lost his wits. But as he thought more about it, he realized he needed help. These horrible visions made no sense, and he felt a rising concern about having seen them again. Perhaps sharing all he knew with his trusted friends would help him figure out at least a part of this mystery. Sharing with his friends would perhaps also help lower his seemingly unjustified suspicion of the Aftarans on this ship.

Keeping his voice down, Marc told his friends everything he had seen in his visions, both this time and the time before, and mentioned how he had repeatedly seen some of the same images in his dreams. He added that he had first seen the image of Earth blowing up in a dream back on Earth, the night before his fateful pickup by the Mendoken. He also pointed out how strange it was that he had seen images of Volonans in his visions before he had even known what Volonans looked like.

"Hmm, very strange, very strange indeed," Zorina said once Marc had finished. "You appear to have some kind of psychic power."

"Either that, or I'm simply going bonkers." Marc smiled, feeling a little better that he had gotten everything off his chest.

She flapped her ears. "I doubt it. If you really were going crazy, then you wouldn't have seen things in your visions that turned out to be true. Like what we Volonans look like, for example. It's very strange. I definitely think there's something supernatural at work here. Though what, why, and who, if anyone, is behind it I have no idea. What do you think, my man?"

"I do not believe in supernatural phenomena, Zorina," Sibular said. "We Mendoken do not acknowledge the existence of anything that cannot be substantiated by scientific evidence."

She looked annoyed. "How do you explain this then?"

"I cannot. But if I understand the pattern of the visions correctly, they are painting a picture that a major calamity is about to befall our galaxy, where most of the major civilizations will be destroyed. That is, unless Marc foresees it and prevents it, with the help of some other force or forces of 'light'."

Marc shook his head in disbelief. "But how could I possibly foresee such a catastrophe?"

"That I do not know, Marc," Sibular said. "But it may not be wise to ignore your visions altogether, especially if any of them turn out to be true. They may somehow be tied to the discovery we have already made about Volonan consar travel capability."

Zorina corrected him right away. "You mean lack thereof."

"Yes, lack thereof. That discovery was largely thanks to Marc's involvement and intuition, not only because he helped my people develop consar travel capability that allowed us to mount the attack inside your Empire, but also because he was able to break out of his virtual world, meet you and trust you, and then get me out of mine. Otherwise, this information would have remained hidden while the war between my people and yours continued to spiral out of control. So, as much as Marc's visions defy all forms of logic I am familiar with, I am not ready to discount them quite yet."

Marc was relieved his friends didn't think he had lost his mind, even though their analysis was just raising more questions instead of answering any.

"One other interesting thing appears to be the timing of your visions," Zorina said. "The first time it happened, you were about to return to Earth. Instead, you changed your mind and stayed with Sibular. This time, you were adamant about taking off in our own little ship instead of staying here on the Aftaran vessel, but your collapse forced us to stay here anyway."

"Almost as if I'm being steered to go to certain places and do certain things," Marc thought. Could it perhaps be God speaking to him? But he didn't even really believe in God the way religious people did. If God really did exist, why would God choose an unbeliever like him? That didn't make any sense. Perhaps some other spiritual or supernatural entity then, like Zorina had suggested. But who or what, and above all, why? Something told him he wouldn't know for a while yet, if ever.

After a warm shower and a spicy meal, Marc felt much better. As he sat with his friends in their room, the screen next to the door suddenly lit up with a bell-like chime. Captain Thorab's image appeared.

"Dear guests, we... ah, Marc, you have awoken! All praise to the Creator! How do you feel?"

Marc got up and walked to the screen. "I'm better, thanks. You were saying?"

"We have reached the entrance to the Afta-Raushan system. You are welcome to leave with your ship now, or continue with us into the system."

Marc glanced briefly at his friends, and turned back to the screen. "We will leave now, thanks. You have been most kind with your hospitality."

"It has been our pleasure. I will send a couple of crewmen to escort you to the landing bay, where your ship is ready and waiting."

Minutes later, the three friends were walking back to the landing bay, accompanied by two Aftaran crewmen dressed in black robes. When they reached the entrance to the landing bay, one of the crewmen pressed the latch to open the gate. "After you," he said in a gruff voice.

Finding their behavior a little strange and unfriendly, Marc stepped first into the landing bay, and froze in shock. The shock soon turned to fear, once it became clear to him that his initial intuition about Captain Thorab and his crew had been correct all along.

Their little ship was nowhere in sight. Instead, all he could see in between the bay's pillars was a cohort of 12 Aftaran soldiers, all dressed in black robes with their faces covered, and all standing in a wide semi-circle around the entrance. In their hands, they held strange looking weapons, all pointed directly at him.

Sibular floated slowly into the landing bay. "Stay still, Marc," he said quietly. "Those are boryals they are holding, highly lethal Aftaran weapons."

Marc was still too stunned to move. For a second, he thought about turning the other way and running as fast as he could, but he knew better than to doubt Sibular's advice. He heard Zorina gasp and, out of the corner of his eye, saw her being pushed into the landing bay by the two crewmen. Seconds later, he heard the gate he had entered through shutting behind him. The three friends were completely trapped inside the landing bay.

One of the Aftarans in the center spoke, his booming voice echoing in between the pillars of the wide hall. "With the authority vested in me by Lord Wazilban, the three of you are hereby arrested."

Marc's jaw dropped in astonishment. Arrested? By Lord Wazilban, nonetheless, the supreme head of the Aftaran Dominion.

"Under what charge?" Sibular asked, staying as calm as ever.

The Aftaran leader laughed. "You have the nerve to ask, you crafty, treacherous conspirators?"

"What in heaven's name are you talking about?" Marc demanded.

"Take them away!" the Aftaran leader bellowed to his soldiers, paying no attention to Marc's protests.

Chapter 27

"Meenjaza certainly lives up to its name as a desert world," Marc thought. As he stared out the window of the short-range Shoyra-class vessel at the golden surface of the planet below, he wondered what undesirable fate awaited him and his two friends amidst those wide, sandy dunes. For the first time in his life, he was a prisoner, shackled in electronically controlled restraints on his wrists and ankles.

He had already been a prisoner of the Volonan Empire, of course, but that had been a very different experience. There, he had lived a virtual life of dreamlike oblivion, whereas this time, he was a real prisoner, in mind and body. And it was a feeling he didn't like at all.

Captain Thorab had tricked them and had led them right into a trap. By the time he had announced their arrival in the Afta-Raushan system, the Gyra-class ship had already arrived in front of Meenjaza and had docked with a smaller Shoyra-class vessel carrying a cohort of Aftaran soldiers. Thorab had purposely kept Marc and his friends in windowless quarters to prevent them from witnessing this event.

After being put in restraints, they had been transferred to the Shoyra-class ship, where they now stood with their faces pressed against the far window of the ship's cabin. The Aftaran soldiers stood behind them, holding boryals pointed directly at their backs.

"What do you think they want from us?" Zorina whispered, breaking the silence. She was standing in between Marc and Sibular.

"I have no idea," Marc whispered back. It was the exact question he kept asking in his mind again and again. Conspirators! They had been labeled conspirators. But why?

"It was our mistake to doubt your intuition, Marc," Sibular whispered. "About Captain Thorab."

"Silence, you infidels!" one of the Aftaran soldiers behind them thundered. "One more word out of any one of you, and it will be the last word you ever utter!"

The three friends fell quiet right away. Marc felt afraid, as he noticed just how ruthless these Aftarans appeared to be. He and his friends were being called "conspirators" and "infidels". Given what he already knew of conservative Aftaran society, he cringed at the thought of the harsh treatment that likely lay in store for them.

The ship descended over a city, full of majestic structures spaced far apart from each other among the sand dunes. Marc was stunned at the architecture of the buildings – almost all of them looked like gigantic houses of worship, similar to pictures he had seen of ancient cathedrals, mosques and temples across Europe, Asia and the Middle East. Some of them had spires, while others had domes. Almost all of them had tall pillars with sweeping arches in between, and their overall shapes were either rectangular or pentagonal. A few of the larger structures had six sides. Even from a distance, he could tell that despite their classical appearance, the exteriors of these buildings were clearly well maintained and kept in tiptop shape. It was a marked contrast from the shabby ruins of the Volonan world of Nopelio.

In between the buildings lay gardens of sand sculptures, organized in neat, symmetric patterns. It took him a moment to understand their real purpose – to an observer from high up in the sky, they spelled out words in beautiful calligraphy. He was amazed to see such large writing sprawled across a planet's surface like that, writing whose religious meaning evidently bore a constant reminder to traveling Aftarans where their priorities lay, and served as a warning to visitors from other civilizations to respect the Aftaran religion during their stay. Without a doubt, religion was a major part of Aftaran life.

The pilot maneuvered the ship in between other Shoyra-class vessels and small ships flying through the air, and brought it to land on a circular open-air strip. Several other small ships were already parked on the strip. Three large, identical looking buildings stood around the circle, each one with tall pillars, spiked domes and sweeping arches.

Once the ship had come to a standstill, Marc saw Aftaran soldiers dressed in black rushing out of all the buildings, on foot and on floating platforms. In less than a minute, the ship was totally surrounded. The soldiers inside the ship opened the door, and roughly pushed the three prisoners out onto the strip.

As the dry desert wind hit his face, the first thing Marc noticed was not the large number of Aftaran soldiers waiting to take him into custody, nor was the first thing he felt fear at the sight of all those weapons pointed at him. No, the first thing he noticed was the bright sunlight shining down on him through the cloudless blue sky. It had been a while since he had seen such clear sunlight from the ground. And, despite the hopelessness of the situation he was in, the first thing he felt was hope. For he could somehow sense that the world he had landed in had plenty of good and compassion in it, as farfetched from reality as it seemed at that moment. And, considering how his feeling about Captain Thorab had been correct, he hoped this new feeling would turn out to be correct as well.

So Marc kept his head high, as several Aftaran soldiers on the ground grabbed the three of them and dragged them onto one of the floating platforms. Glancing over at Zorina, he noticed that she didn't look happy at all. Obviously she was not feeling the same glimmer of hope, surrounded and being shoved around by these towering creatures with their black robes and covered faces. No, this clearly wasn't the life of liberty she had been hoping for beyond the borders of the Volonan Empire. Sibular, of course, was his usual expressionless self, although he had to be wondering how these Aftarans could possibly be treating a Mendoken ally like this.

The platform sped off like magic towards the nearest building, entered through a gate that slid open on the ground level, and glided down a long, dark tunnel. Less than a minute later, it reached the other end of the tunnel. Another gate slid open automatically and let the platform pass through unhindered.

The view that lay beyond the gate left Marc breathless in awe. The hall they had just entered was magnificent. The arched ceiling was so high up that he could barely see it, and lines of stone pillars shot up to it along the walls and across the hall. The ornate decorations and calligraphy everywhere were a significant step up, both in size and grandeur, from those on Captain Thorab's Gyra-class ship. The spotless white stone floors gleamed in the light trickling through the colored windows on the walls, as well as the light from hundreds of flickering lamps in front of a huge altar-like setup on the far side of the hall.

The floating platform came to a stop at the entrance to the hall. The three prisoners were motioned by their Aftaran guards to descend to the ground, and were then led on foot towards the altar along an aisle down the middle of the hall. Both Marc and Zorina tripped on their ankle restraints and fell a couple of times, but were abruptly pulled up and instructed to keep walking forward.

Perhaps this walk wouldn't have been half as hard or embarrassing, Marc felt, were it not for the hundreds of silent Aftarans in the hall, all with their eyes focused on him and his two friends. Most of them were sitting on the floor in rows that faced the altar. As he walked past each row, he could hear the Aftarans whispering to each other, some of them making strange croaking noises while others just shook their heads. All of them had their faces fully covered, so he couldn't make out their expressions.

After what felt like an eternity, he reached the altar and climbed up its short flight of steps. The altar was truly beautiful, with gold inscriptions on the stone partitions around it shining in the radiance of the hundreds of lamps that lay in front. A single column made of solid brown stone stood in the center, no more than 5 feet in height. Atop was a flat, glowing silver surface, probably made of a luminescent compound. The prisoners were told to stand in a line behind the column.

Staring at all the inscriptions on the partitions in front of him, Marc hoped with all his heart that the words contained messages of peace, compassion and reason, messages that these Aftarans would adhere to in dealing with him and his friends.

"Turn and face the audience!" one of the Aftaran soldiers commanded, sounding far from peaceful or compassionate.

Marc hesitated, but knew he had no choice. Taking a deep breath, he turned towards the crowd. Looking past the brown stone column at the uncountable pairs of eyes below, he tried to suppress his fear with the feelings of hope he had felt upon landing on this planet, hope that whatever suspicions these Aftarans were harboring towards him and his friends, the good in them would ultimately lead them to the truth. They would understand that the three of them were innocent of these horrible accusations, and would set them free. Little did he know, however, that these feelings of hope were about to be crushed.

"Fellow citizens, arise for the righteous, enlightened leader of our beloved Dominion, Lord Wazilban!"

The words echoed across the large hall. A door on the right side of the hall slid open, and in walked a procession of Aftarans. It was a square formation of bodyguards protecting a single individual in the middle. The bodyguards all wore red robes and had their faces covered, while the Aftaran in the middle wore a bright, flashy green robe. He was taller than the others, and had no head or face cover. Instead, his robe had a high collar that circled all around his neck.

As he stared at Wazilban, Marc could feel a rising wave of fear and despair, and pain suddenly spread throughout his body. He began shivering, and sweat beads began forming on his forehead. He couldn't understand it, but the very sight of Wazilban made him feel terrified, even though there was nothing particularly terrifying about Wazilban's appearance. His face had the typical features of an Aftaran – owl-like eyes, ears and beak, and feathers covering the skin. Sure, his face was somewhat elongated, and his feathers and eyes were green, but that certainly wasn't enough to warrant such irrational terror.

The procession approached the altar, right past the bowing crowd of Aftarans. Wazilban climbed up the steps to the altar and stood in front of the prisoners. One of the soldiers guarding the prisoners bowed in front of him, and whispered something into his ear. He then walked up to Marc and stared at him closely.

Marc closed his eyes in fright. He just couldn't bear the sight of this horrible, evil individual.

Without a word, Wazilban moved on to inspect both Sibular and Zorina. Then he turned to face the crowd of Aftarans. Standing in front of the stone column, he placed a coin-like object on the silvery surface and whisked his hand over it. Both the coin and the surface of the column immediately lit up in a golden color. Seconds later, large, brightly lit golden letters appeared in the air above the column, clearly visible for everyone in the audience to see. From what Marc could tell, it looked like some kind of verse, and it was written in the same character set and style as the inscriptions on the walls. Everybody in the audience immediately bowed their heads in front of the floating verse.

Wazilban read aloud from the text, in a mysterious, chanting tone. The words, translated into English by Sibular's translator, caused Marc to gulp with fear:

> *Those who wage war against the righteous*
> *Shall ultimately conquer naught but their own fortunes.*
> *Nowhere shall they find solace for their crimes,*
> *And never shall they escape the justice they are due.*

The verse faded away after Wazilban had finished. Then he addressed the audience directly in his loud, booming voice. "My dear fellow Aftarans, may the Creator protect you from harm."

"And you!" the crowd replied loudly in unison.

"I stand before you here today as I often do. But today I serve neither as your humbly appointed leader, nor as your spiritual guide. Nay, today I stand here as an impartial judge to try these three alien conspirators. For the magnitude of the crime they have committed deserves no less than the attention of the highest office in the Dominion."

His words echoed across the large hall, its well designed acoustics easily carrying his loud voice to the farthest corners. The audience was dead silent, listening to him intently.

Wazilban went on. "The crime they have committed knows no equal, except perhaps the treachery of Autamrin and his followers. Fortunately the grace of the Almighty Creator has once again saved us, and brought these transgressors to justice before they could inflict any harm on us.

"These three individuals conspired to infiltrate our beloved Dominion from enemy space, with caches of powerful, deadly weapons and detailed plans. And detailed plans for what, I ask you? To attack us, to overthrow me and the rest of the Aftaran leadership. To overthrow us who all of you chose as your leaders, and to replace us with enemies of the Dominion. Enemies who hate us and our way of life, who believe neither in the Creator nor in the ways of the righteous, who speak nothing but blasphemy and commit nothing but sacrilege.

"The sins of terrorist infidels such as these know no bounds, and surely the Creator shall deal with them appropriately at the appointed time. It would normally not be our duty to judge them, nor would it be our duty to enforce the path of righteousness upon them. Indeed, we have always abided strictly by the principle of 'live and let live'. We have done nothing to them. But these terrorists chose to declare war on us, and that has changed everything. They have declared war on the Aftar, on the only ones who follow the righteous ways the Creator has laid down for all mortals. In so doing, they have declared war on the Creator. There is only one word to describe such individuals." He pointed a menacing finger at the prisoners and raised his voice. "They are heretics! Heretics in the eyes of the Creator!"

The audience, silent up till now, began cheering and booing at the same time – cheering at Lord Wazilban and booing at the prisoners.

Marc heard Zorina gasp in shock, and out of the corner of his eye saw her wildly flapping her ears. Indeed, he couldn't believe his own ears. What in the blue blazes was Wazilban talking about? What conspiracy? What heresy? And who was Autamrin? What kind of "impartial judge" was Wazilban anyway, directly accusing them of these crimes before even showing any evidence? This whole thing was absurd!

"Lord Wazilban, this appears to be a mistake," Sibular said. "We are no conspirators or enemies of the Dominion. I am a Mendoken space travel engineer, these are my companions, and we merely seek safe refuge to the Mendoken Repub..."

"Silence!" one of Wazilban's bodyguards bellowed. "You shall only speak when ordered to speak! You should be thankful that you are even being given the opportunity to defend yourselves. Considering the crimes you have committed, you should be executed right away!"

The audience's jeering now turned into a deafening roar. They obviously seemed to agree with this statement.

"Come now, all present, we must be fair!" Wazilban said, raising his hands in a conciliatory gesture. "This is an impartial trial, and these individuals, no matter how horrible their crimes, must be allowed the opportunity to defend themselves. We are believers, after all, and must not stoop to the level of morality and justice of infidels such as these."

The audience's roaring and jeering continued. Evidently they did want to stoop to that level of morality and justice, whatever level that was.

Marc felt rising alarm at what was happening. This hall was obviously a court of some sort, and this event was a trial. A laughable, staged trial with no impartiality or legal representation whatsoever, but a trial nonetheless. And considering how things were going so far, it was quite obvious that the outcome wouldn't be in favor of the defendants.

"I call forth the primary witnesses in this case!" Wazilban announced.

The door to the side of the hall opened, and in walked Captain Thorab and his High Officer Rulshanim. A platform floated in behind them, carrying all kinds of paraphernalia that Marc couldn't identify.

"I should have guessed," Marc thought. The same two Aftarans he had never trusted were now going to provide false testimony about him and his friends to the court. As disturbing as this new development was, he actually felt intrigued to see what kind of fabricated evidence they would come up with.

Thorab and Rulshanim climbed up to the altar, and bowed in front of Wazilban.

"This is Captain Thorab, one of the best Gyra-class captains in the Dominion," Wazilban said, addressing the audience. "And this is his High Officer Rulshanim. Both have selflessly served our people for years." He then turned to Thorab. "Captain Thorab, do you recognize these three individuals?"

"I do, my Lord. This is Sibular Gaulen, a Mendoken. This is Marc Zemin, of the species known as 'Humans' from a planet inside the Mendoken Republic. And this here is Zorina, once the Chief Imperial Defender of the Volonan Empire, and the one and only sister of Empress Adrelina."

The audience gasped in amazement at the mention of Zorina's identity.

"You see, my fellow Aftarans?" Wazilban said. "The ideal makings of a terrorist conspiracy! Our belligerent neighbor, the Volonan Empire, in collaboration with our archenemy the Phyrax, sent their top military defense specialist into the Dominion. Her assignment? To analyze our defenses and verify our vulnerabilties, so that the Volona and Phyrax could together follow with a full-scale invasion of our beloved Dominion. And how did she attempt to disguise her mission? By traveling with this Mendoken and his Human friend, to make it look like she is a friend of our Mendoken allies. Such craftiness, such twisted treachery – it sickens both my body and soul to even think of it!"

"This is outrageous!" Zorina yelled, violently flapping her ears. "These are all barefaced lies, I assure you! I..."

"Silence! How dare you call our righteous leader a liar!" That was the same bodyguard who had earlier silenced Sibular.

The crowd roared again. Marc felt certain that if they were allowed to, they would probably start throwing things at him and his friends.

"These are indeed the conspirators we caught crossing over from the Volonan Empire," Thorab said. "And I have plenty of evidence to verify your statements, Lord Wazilban."

"Indeed? Please present the evidence, we are all listening."

Captain Thorab proceeded to give a detailed account of how Marc, Sibular and Zorina had infiltrated the Dominion aboard a small but heavily armed Volonan spy ship. Luckily they had been intercepted by Thorab's fleet before making it very far into the Dominion. After deadly exchanges of fire and heroic maneuvers on the part of Thorab's crewmen, the enemy ship had finally been rendered immobile and its crew captured. A subsequent search of the enemy ship by Thorab's crew had revealed not only stashes of highly sophisticated weapons, but also detailed plans of the Aftaran defenses and of a massive Volonan conspiracy to invade and take over the Aftaran Dominion by force. The Phyrax were repeatedly mentioned by name in the plans as an important ally in this conspiracy.

As Thorab recounted this fantastic story, he and Rulshanim displayed several items from the floating platform that had accompanied them into the hall, items that had supposedly been found on the enemy ship. There were fancy looking weapons Marc had never seen before, as well as small devices that projected large 3D screens in the hall for everyone to see. The screens showed intricate details of the Volonan invasion plans, with full-blown diagrams of attack patterns and vulnerabilities to be searched for in the Aftaran defense systems. The names of different Phyrax and Volonan military leaders were also listed in the plans.

There was so much detail, and the information so well presented, that Marc himself almost began to have doubts about Zorina's true intentions for coming with him and Sibular. But one glance at his friend caused him to brush away any suspicion. Zorina looked totally puzzled, and at the same time horrified beyond belief. No, he had no doubt that she was totally innocent of these charges, and all this evidence clearly was fictitious. In any case, there was no way she could have packed all those weapons and plans onto that tiny contraption of a ship they had traveled on. Nor would she ever have had the time or privacy to load all that stuff on board – Sibular had almost never left the ship during its construction back on the planet Nopelio.

Once Thorab had finished his testimony, Lord Wazilban addressed the audience again. "And there you have it, my dear fellow Aftarans! All this evidence proves beyond a shadow of doubt the guilt of these three terrorists. They took advantage of our innocent nature, good grace and love of freedom to enter the Dominion. But their intention was far from good, it was evil. They planned to infiltrate our worlds, and prepare the scene for a massive invasion by the enemy. An enemy that would surely leave no single Aftaran alive, that would surely burn to the ground every building and place of worship our ancestors built for us. An enemy that would destroy our civilized way of life and replace it with nothing but dirty decadence and decay. A heathen enemy that believes not in the Creator or the ways of the righteous, but worships its own shortcomings and vices. An enemy that has no morals to speak of and thrives on deceiving others. That, my dear fellow Aftarans, would have been our fate, were it not for the many patriotic, heroic Aftarans like Captain Thorab defending our beloved Dominion!

"Recall the verse I quoted earlier from the Scripture of War. For enemies such as these, there is no pardon or second chance. Nay, for such heretics, there is only one punishment worthy of their crimes!"

The audience roared once again, this time much louder than ever before. Most of them were standing now, and many had even removed the veils around their faces. Marc could see their eyes glowing with anger, anger directed solely at him and his friends.

Wazilban turned to the prisoners. "Have you anything to say in your defense?"

Marc winced, and looked again at Zorina. She seemed too flabbergasted to speak. Sibular was quiet too, probably trying to calculate in his head all the possible scenarios that could have led to such an unbelievable situation.

Marc realized it was up to him to say something. Hoping that Sibular's translator would correctly translate his words into the Aftaran language, he began speaking. "We..." He paused and cleared his throat, trying to stay calm and keep his nervousness under control. "We are innocent of all these charges." He cleared his throat again, trying to make his voice more audible across the large hall. "I don't know what your motive is for going to such lengths to accuse us of things we haven't done, but none of this evidence is true. It's all fabricated."

Wazilban laughed, with a deep, croaking sound. His laughter echoed loudly across the hall, and the laughter of the audience soon joined in chorus.

What was said after that, Marc no longer heard, for the sound of Wazilban's laughter brought time to a standstill for him. His jaw dropped in astonishment, and he asked himself repeatedly if it could really be true. But it soon became clear to him that there was no mistake – the sound of that laugh was too deeply engrained in his memory. It was, without a doubt, the same laugh he had heard in his visions, the sinister laughter of that evil shadow far away, the one who had laughed nonstop at all the killing and destruction everywhere and at the wiping out of all life in the galaxy.

Bewildered, he closed his eyes. Lord Wazilban, the evil mastermind behind such a gigantic calamity? How could this be? Why would the leader of the Aftaran

Dominion want to do such a terrible thing, something that included the total annihilation of his own people? Did this explain why Wazilban was framing Marc and his friends? And where were these visions coming from anyway? As more and more questions crept into his head, Marc found himself sinking into a sea of confusion.

When he finally opened his eyes again, however, what he saw before him suddenly cleared up a lot of his confusion.

Chapter 28

The view in front of Marc had changed. It was still the same hall, with the same high ceiling and rows of pillars, the same stone floor and the same walls covered with calligraphy. It was the same altar he was standing on, just behind the stone column. Even the crowd of Aftarans was still there, filling up most of the hall.

And yet, something clearly had changed. It was Wazilban – he no longer looked the same. Nobody else seemed affected by or even to have noticed this change, not even Sibular or Zorina. They were all still fixated on Wazilban's stern speech. To Marc, however, the difference was as clear as the cloudless blue sky outside.

He blinked repeatedly, incredulous at what had just happened. But there was no doubt about it – Wazilban was now a completely different creature. He had grown to about twice his original size, and his upright posture had swooped down to an almost horizontal spine. The head, now pointing slightly downwards at the end of the neck, no longer had any soft, owl-like Aftaran features. Gone were the feathers and the round eyes, gone were the beak and the pointed ears. Instead, the head and face now looked like those of a menacing reptile, with alligator-like eyes and brightly glowing, rubbery green skin. The open snout was long and pointed, displaying wide jaws and shiny, sharp teeth.

Wazilban's robe was also gone, allowing Marc to see the whole body. It was large and muscular, with two short limbs facing the front and a long, heavy tail in the rear. Perhaps the most noticeable thing about the body, apart from its glowing skin, was that it had no legs or feet. It was, in fact, floating in a stationary position in midair, with the support of two wide wings that constantly flapped in a slow, sweeping motion. The motion reminded him of manta rays and how they swam through water, something he had witnessed many years earlier as a child at the Vancouver Aquarium.

The Mendoken also floated above the ground, of course, but they used mechanical anti-gravity mechanisms in the bottom of their armor shells to do so. This creature, whatever type of alien creature it was, was floating through the natural capabilities of its own body. But as graceful as its wing motion was, Marc could find no grace in the alien's ominous face. It had a constantly angry and scornful expression, as if it was ready to strike at anyone or anything that dared to cross its way.

"This is more what I would expect someone with Wazilban's personality to look like," he thought. The alien's appearance certainly was a sharp contrast from the innocent looking faces of most Aftarans.

His surprise grew when he noticed that Wazilban wasn't the only one who had changed shape. So had Thorab and Rulshanim, and so had a couple of Wazilban's bodyguards. Even several Aftarans in the audience had changed shape, all of them strategically dispersed throughout the hall. They were all floating in the air, just like Wazilban. He blinked again, then closed his eyes for several seconds and opened them, hoping this disturbing sight would go away. But it didn't.

His attention returned to Wazilban's voice, just in time to hear the end of the speech.

"There is no other path for these terrorist conspirators, these infidels, these heretics," Wazilban was saying. "They have declared war on the righteous and on the Creator, and thus the Creator has declared war on them! It is the will of the Creator that they be executed! Take them away!"

The crowd roared fiercely in support of Wazilban's order. The soldiers grabbed the prisoners and hustled them down the steps of the altar. Marc heard Zorina gasp and Sibular protest in his usual composed manner, but it was all to no avail. There seemed to be no way for them to escape. These big soldiers with their powerful weapons had them totally surrounded and were dragging them away. Yet Marc felt a sense of urgency that something had to be done, not just to save his own life and those of his friends, but to warn the Aftaran public that they were being misled. For it had finally dawned on him what was going on.

These creatures – Wazilban, Thorab, Rulshanim and those others among Wazilban's bodyguards and the audience – they had to be aliens from another civilization. They had infiltrated Aftaran society and had disguised themselves as Aftarans, taking over key positions of importance. If Marc's visions had any shred of truth to them, then the ultimate goal of these aliens was clear – the destruction of all life in this galaxy. But why? Where were they from?

The Aftarans were obviously blind to the fact that some of their own, including their leader, was an alien. For sure, nobody else in the hall had noticed how these individuals had suddenly changed shape into different creatures. So why was Marc the only one bestowed with the ability to see through their disguises? Was this simply another vision, then, or was it real? Perhaps it was both?

Either way, things now made more sense. There was clearly a massive conspiracy at play here, and it seemed that Marc, Sibular and Zorina were convenient scapegoats of this conspiracy. Contrary to the false accusations that the three of them were conspirators, the actual conspirators were the accusers themselves. And the three of them were being rushed to death before they could reveal the true conspiracy.

The prisoners were led along the main aisle out of the hall, past the hundreds of cheering and booing Aftarans in the audience. Marc looked at some of their faces, and decided it was now or never. The alien conspirators had to be stopped at all costs before it was too late.

"Stop!" he suddenly yelled at the audience, trying to make himself heard above all the commotion. "You must listen! We are innocent, we are not your enemies! Lord Wazilban – he isn't an Aftaran! Nor are Captain Thorab and Rulshanim. They are aliens! They have somehow infil..."

That was as far as he got. One of the floating aliens nearby in the audience suddenly leaped into the air and dived straight at him, clasping one of its limbs over his mouth before he could utter another word. He struggled to get the rough-skinned, rubbery hand off his mouth, but the alien, more than twice his size, was far too strong. Sibular and Zorina both tried to rush to his rescue, but were abruptly apprehended by the other Aftaran soldiers.

Keeping its limb over Marc's mouth, the alien joined the procession of Aftaran soldiers leading the prisoners out of the hall. "Move faster!" it ordered the soldiers in front with a raspy voice.

The soldiers complied. To them and to all other Aftarans in the hall, this alien was obviously just appearing as another Aftaran, possibly an Aftaran of high rank whose commands were to be followed without question.

As they exited the hall, Marc was able to catch one last glimpse of Wazilban back on the altar. Even from that distance, there was no mistaking the sly look of content in the glowing alien's reptilian eyes.

The execution center that the prisoners were led to was an open air stadium-like structure, several miles away from the hall where they had been sentenced. They were transported there on board a floating platform, heavily guarded on all sides by Aftaran soldiers. Their mouths now gagged with small electronic devices, none of them were able to say anything at all. Once the device had been planted inside Marc's mouth, numbness had quickly spread through his jaws, tongue and even down his throat. He could no longer open his mouth or even make a humming sound.

The majority of Aftarans that had been in the hall followed them on floating platforms of their own. Marc could see Wazilban on board one of the floating platforms in the distance, accompanied by Thorab, Rulshanim and his bodyguards. They still looked like the same alien creatures.

During the short trip, he paid little attention to the scenery around him. The brilliant sunshine through the cloudless blue sky was pleasant, providing just enough warmth to make the dry, somewhat cool air feel comfortable. The buildings everywhere were majestic in size and appearance, and the streets they crossed had many curious Aftarans staring at them. Most of the Aftarans on the streets looked concerned and fearful upon seeing the prisoners, quite unlike the cheering Aftarans back in the hall.

But none of that concerned him. What he was worried about was imminent death, both his own and those of his two friends. He felt pangs of guilt, thinking that his visions, intuitions and actions had been responsible for leading Sibular and Zorina into this dangerous trap. Certainly Zorina's death would be on his conscience, as he had urged her to join him and Sibular in their quest to leave the Volonan Empire. But then again, he had warned both of them not to trust Captain Thorab. And in hindsight, there was no doubt whatsoever that his feelings about Thorab had been correct.

He also felt completely powerless to stop the grand conspiracy of these mysterious aliens, who he was now convinced were planning to destroy all life in the galaxy. He had failed to warn the Aftaran public what was happening, and there was no room for a second chance. A feeling of quiet resignation overcame him, a feeling he had not had since the days of his mother's battle with kidney cancer. Just as he had helplessly watched her die a slow and painful death, he was now helplessly witnessing his own death, and letting these aliens continue unhindered with their evil grand scheme.

The platform arrived at the execution center, a cylindrically shaped building that reminded Marc of the historical Colosseum in Rome. Certainly what was going to happen inside was not too different from what the ancient Romans had used the Colosseum for – public executions and other barbaric acts involving prisoners and slaves.

The platform floated past the main gates, into a tunnel through the inside of the building, and out into the open air arena in the center. The rows of spectator seats surrounding the arena had just started filling up with Aftarans arriving on their own floating platforms.

Up ahead, Marc could see a stage, right in the middle of the arena. On it were a number of poles, spread evenly apart in a straight line. He didn't need a second glance to figure out what the poles would be used for.

"We're going to be burned at the stake," he thought, "in front of these bloodthirsty Aftarans. Or perhaps eaten alive by monstrous animals." He found it hard to believe how a civilization as advanced as the Aftar could stoop to such barbaric behavior. Had they always been this way, he wondered, or had Wazilban and his alien cahoots sufficiently blinded them to this level of hate and savagery, to this level of excitement in observing the misery and pain of others? Not that it really mattered, of course. Either way, he was about to die.

The prisoners were dragged up onto the stage, and each one of them securely tied to a pole. Marc felt pangs of pain as the new restraints cut into the flesh of his neck and belly, but the total numbness of his mouth and throat did not even allow him to cry out. He felt horrible and exhausted, helpless and utterly defeated. It was all over now, and there was no stopping the inevitable. All those spectators would soon get the spectacle they were eagerly waiting for.

"Bring forth the executioners!" Wazilban ordered, his words echoing through loudspeakers mounted around the perimeter of the arena.

Marc strained his eyes and saw Wazilban in the distance, high up in the spectator rows on a special podium, surrounded on all sides by his bodyguards. He was still a glowing reptilian alien, one of several spread out among the Aftaran spectators. Marc also noticed that most of the spectator rows were actually empty. The stadium could easily house several thousand, but the total number of spectators could not possibly be more than a few hundred, probably the same few hundred that had earlier attended the sentencing back in the hall. Perhaps most Aftarans did not support this kind of barbarism after all.

The spectators cheered as three Aftarans entered the arena on a floating platform and approached the stage. They were dressed in brown robes, and their heads and faces were veiled. When Marc saw what they were holding in their hands, his eyes bulged out in horror.

"They're not going to burn us!" he thought. "They're going to behead us!"

There was no mistaking it. Each of the three Aftarans was brandishing a long, curved blade made of a shiny silver colored metal. They jumped off the platform and onto the stage, quickly positioning themselves in front of the prisoners. Turning towards Wazilban in the distance, they bowed their heads before him.

"In the Creator's name, proceed with the execution of these heretics!" Wazilban commanded. "And let this be a warning to all others who dare to conspire against the righteous and against the Creator!" His words thundered across the open air stadium.

All the other soldiers still on the stage abruptly jumped off and hurried away. The only ones left on the stage now were the three prisoners and the three executioners, one executioner standing in front of each prisoner.

Marc stole one last glance at Zorina to his right. She was quivering in fear and horror, tears rolling down from her large eyes onto her short trunk and cheekbones. He would never forgive himself for bringing her into this mess, and he just hoped she would have the heart to forgive him. Then he turned to look at Sibular, who stood motionless and expressionless as always. He envied Sibular, wishing he also had that kind of strength to extinguish his emotions.

He looked up at the deep blue sky and the brilliantly shining sun. How many times he had looked at the sky back on Earth, hoping for a cloudless day of sunshine and warmth after endless days of rain and snow. His state of mind had always been greatly affected by the weather. Sunny days had always lifted his spirits just a little, even in the worst of times. And yet, today, on this brilliantly sunny day, his spirits had never been lower. His whole life began flashing before him, his lonely childhood days, his mother's bouts of depression, his many daydreams of being a superhero, then onto his happier college days and the love of his life.

If only he could see Iman just once more, if he could only tell her how much he still loved her and how he would do everything he possibly could to win her back. But she was gone from his life, as was his mother. And all his efforts to go back in time to change things had failed. Even with his tremendous gift of intelligence, all his efforts to make something of his life, to somehow accomplish something major, had all failed. His short-lived feelings of self-importance, thanks to his visions that he was destined to prevent the galaxy from imploding, had all been for nothing. Now his own life was about to end, and with it his hopes of saving not just those he knew or cared about, but all of humanity and, in fact, all the countless other forms of life in the galaxy.

As the executioners turned to face the prisoners, Marc lowered his gaze from the sky and stared at the one in front of him. The executioner was just over 7 feet tall, with the round, brown eyes that were intently staring at him the only part of the Aftaran's body he could see.

The executioners lifted their blades together, ready to slice the prisoners' necks with one swift blow. "In the name of the Creator!" they cried in unison.

Marc closed his eyes and waited for death. He had miraculously escaped death more than once before, but this time he knew there was no escape. He heard the swooshing sound of the blade approaching his neck, and sensed a shadow engulfing him. And then, all was dark.

*   *   *

The spectators in the stadium looked shell-shocked. This certainly was not the show they had been expecting. The three prisoners and their three executioners had simply vanished into thin air, just as the executioners had swung their blades at the prisoners' necks. The stage in the center of the arena was totally deserted now, with the prisoners' restraints lying scattered on the stage around the poles.

The initial shock soon turned to chaos, as Aftarans began getting up and asking each other what had happened. Many began hurrying towards the exits, prophesying that this was an intervention by the Creator, and the Creator's wrath would be upon them for trying to execute those who were innocent. Others figured the executioners had simply performed a magical enchantment, since enchantments once used to be so commonly practiced among Aftarans. Others still countered that the practice of such enchantments was banned under Lord Wazilban's rule, and no Aftaran on Meenjaza would dare to perform such an act in his or her right mind, especially not in front of the mighty Wazilban himself.

Located up high in the spectator rows, Lord Wazilban was worried about what had happened, but kept his calm. As far as he was concerned, none of these Aftarans had figured out who he really was or why he was here, and that was all that mattered. To them, he still looked like the same tall Aftaran, with his flashy robe, high collar, green feathers and green eyes. His associates, planted in key locations here in the stadium, still appeared as the same Aftarans as well. He glanced at a couple of them near him among the spectators. Like him, they were keeping their calm, mingling and blending in perfectly with the crowd. Yes, he had definitely trained them well. Good training was, after all, key to their success, training that had already allowed many more of his associates to take over key positions of influence across the entire Aftaran Dominion.

Nevertheless, something troublesome had just happened, something he had not expected or planned for in his master plan. This was the third unexpected event within a span of 30 days, and that was not good at all. The first event had been the disappearance of a Boura-class ship and its occupants on its return from the planet Droila. On board had been two of his associates, Ozwin and Ruminat, as well as two highly precious prisoners – both of Autamrin's sons. He would have been only too happy to get his hands on them, and to torture them until they revealed the location of their father's hideout. Then he would have had them publicly executed for treason and heresy. But now they were gone, free again to cause whatever mischief they desired in the Dominion.

The second unexpected event, the Mendoken consar attack on Volo-Gaviera, had taken him completely by surprise. The Mendoken were not supposed to have consar technology, not just because it was forbidden in the galaxy, but also because his spies in the Republic had always destroyed any consar research labs the Mendoken had attempted to build in order to gain an upper hand in their war against the Volona.

Upon hearing the news of the attack, Wazilban had surmised that some other powerful force had suddenly stepped in to help the Mendoken construct consar capable ships, a force that had thus far eluded his spies in the Republic. He had, therefore, decided to take action, using one of the many principles engrained in his mind:

Unexpected or unplanned events will always occur. It is a part of life. Success lies in taking advantage of those events to turn things in your favor.

So Wazilban had immediately alerted his associate Thorab, already assigned to patrol the Volonan border, to keep his eyes open for any fugitives from the failed attack attempting to escape the Volonan Empire.

Once again, Wazilban's principle had prevailed. Thorab had indeed been able to capture three such fugitives, and, just as Wazilban had figured, an alien from a hitherto unknown species known as Humans had been among them. The Human definitely did not look particularly advanced, sophisticated or powerful, but as Wazilban well knew, looks could often be deceiving. A quick search of the Aftaran chronicles had also revealed no useful information about these Humans. The Mendoken had evidently kept the existence of this species well hidden, possibly by concealing them under a silupsal filter.

Nevertheless, that Human had undoubtedly been responsible for helping the Mendoken build consar enabled ships. That Human, with all its powers, would become a major danger to the master plan if allowed to freely roam in the Dominion. If Autamrin and his insurgent scum got wind of the Human's presence, they might take him to be that absurd "Sign" mentioned in the Hidden Scripture, and would then seize the opportunity to launch a full scale rebellion against Wazilban. Considering how sour the general mood among the Aftaran public already was these days, it wouldn't take much for such a rebellion to lead to dour consequences for his master plan.

If, on the other hand, Wazilban were quickly able to sentence this Human and its companions to death for crimes these highly religious Aftarans considered unpardonable, then he could prevent the rebellion from launching anytime soon. The execution would also send another clear warning message to any would-be rebels to continue to lie low and never dare to rise up in arms against his rule.

So Wazilban had decided to frame the three fugitives with fabricated evidence and a well-crafted story. As soon as he had learned that Zorina, the Volonan Empress's sister herself, was one of the three, he had come up with the idea to label them as enemy conspirators working for the Empire. The majority of Aftarans didn't know or care about the intricacies of Volonan dynasty politics or the recent anomalies of the Virtual Translation Grid. Few of them knew, therefore, that Zorina actually was an outcast in her own land, and unlikely to currently be operating in the interests of the Empire.

The framing had worked flawlessly, and in hindsight, none too soon. For this Human had exhibited powers well beyond what Wazilban could initially have imagined. During the trial, the Human had somehow seen through the Aftaran disguises Wazilban and his associates had successfully adorned in front of everyone for all these years. Luckily one of his associates in the audience had jumped on the Human in the nick of time, just as the Human had begun exposing the truth to the public. Otherwise, a major disaster would have erupted right there and then.

But now the third unexpected event had just occurred. The three prisoners had vanished along with their executioners, and that could only mean one thing. Those executioners were insurgents, and they had used forbidden enchantments to take the prisoners to safety, enchantments Wazilban had forbidden specifically for reasons such as this. How the insurgents had managed to penetrate his tight security apparatus and pose as the executioners, he didn't know. But he certainly was going to punish those responsible, and severely. The harshest of torture methods would have to be used, and some heads would have to roll, literally. This kind of breach would not be allowed again, that was for sure. Just as alarming was the fact that the insurgents had been freely wandering through the public buildings, right here on Meenjaza. They must have attended the trial in secret, heard the accusations against the prisoners, and then decided to act.

Furthermore, the insurgents now had the three prisoners. They would undoubtedly take the Human to be the "Sign", especially if Autamrin's sons had joined them, and would also learn the startling truth that Wazilban and his associates were actually not Aftarans. They would soon launch their rebellion against Wazilban and his forces, possibly with consar technology that the Human would show them how to use. And that was something Wazilban definitely could not afford, not at this critical moment when everything else was going so well and according to plan. No, this Human and its companions would have to be found as soon as possible and killed. The rebellion would have to be crushed before it could even begin. He would have to act now, and quickly.

Wazilban stood up, and addressed everyone in the stadium with a confident smile on his face. "My dear fellow Aftarans, there is no need whatsoever to panic!

This was all planned! The infidels are dead, with their heads cut off. I decided to let the executioners put on a little enchantment, just to entertain you and to show you something different from the usual gory scenes. But you can all rest assured that justice has been done." He paused. "May the Creator reward you for coming to witness this important execution. And may the Creator continue to protect us from such heretics and conspirators."

The level of noise among the spectators instantly dropped. Most of them seemed satisfied with Wazilban's explanation, although some questioned loudly whether he was lying in order to save face.

Wazilban looked around him, and wondered for a moment whether to be concerned about the isolated ranks of dissent in the crowd. These few hundred handpicked Aftarans were, after all, his most fervent supporters, and he had always been able to count on their unanimous backing. If even they were beginning to show opposition, then times really were turning bad.

"No, no matter," he thought. "The insurgents and their latest acquisition are far more important at the moment." As always, he would stick to another principle of his:

Success lies in the prioritization of all things, combined with the focus only on those that are of the highest priority.

Accompanied by his bodyguards, he began moving away from the spectator rows and out of the stadium, leaving the spectators to disperse of their own accord.

Chapter 29

The fragments of what had once been planets and stars looked like specks of dust scattered across the sky. Marc could hear cries for help all around him from uncountable numbers of Mendoken, Aftarans, Phyraxes and Volonans. The cries were of deep pain and immense suffering, all amidst Wazilban's evil laughter. The darkness was blinding, the cold unbearable, and Marc's despair absolute.

But the cries, evil laughter and darkness eventually subsided, soon to be replaced by light from six sparkling stars. The stars came closer and surrounded him, bringing much needed warmth and hope. His despair faded away, and strength returned to his heart. He smiled at the stars, feeling happy and reassured that they were there with him. Then he heard a voice.

"He awakes!"

He heard the words, but didn't recognize the voice. He wondered if he was dead.

"Can you hear us, Marc?" another voice said.

He instantly recognized the second voice as Sibular's. "Yes, I can hear you," he mumbled, slowly opening his eyes.

Once the blurry image around him had come into focus, he found himself staring up at three Aftarans. He was lying on a blanket spread on the ground, and the Aftarans were seated in crouching positions around him. Looming over him, they were intently studying his face. Their own faces were uncovered, allowing him to notice that two of them looked very similar, with their tan colored feathers, pointed beaks and round brown eyes. Perhaps they were siblings, he surmised. The other one had auburn colored feathers, and the facial features were softer and prettier – undoubtedly a female. He recognized her eyes as those of his executioner in the stadium.

No, evidently he wasn't dead. He had just had another one of those wretched dreams, the dreams that constantly reminded him of his visions. Nearby, he could see Sibular's familiar physique, standing in his usual upright, floating posture.

"Your other companion is fine too," one of the two identical looking Aftarans said. "She is still sleeping."

"Who are you?" Marc asked.

"My name is Dumyan, of the 1238th generation of the Subhar clan." He spoke quickly, his voice full of life and energy. Pointing at the identical looking Aftaran sitting next to him, he said, "This is Sharjam, my younger brother. And that is Raiha. She is of the 789th generation of the Fuzia clan."

Marc was not surprised at the mention of clans. He had already encountered this Aftaran custom upon meeting Captain Thorab and Rulshanim. Sibular had also explained to him how much importance Aftarans placed on their clan heritage.

Dumyan went on. "We were your three 'executioners'. We intervened in the nick of time, taking the place of the actual executioners as they were entering the stadium. Then we carried you through the desert and brought you here."

"I am glad to see you survived your execution," Raiha said, with a twinkle in her eyes.

"But how did you do it?" Marc asked in amazement, slowly sitting up and looking at Raiha. "You swung that blade at my neck, didn't you?"

"The power of illusion can be overwhelming," Sharjam said, leaning back to give Marc more space. He sounded very similar to Dumyan, although his pace of talking was slower. "Especially when that power finds its strength in verses of the sacred Scriptures themselves."

"That is just my brother's humble way of saying that he has a number of enchantments up his sleeve," Dumyan said, widening his beak to reveal a smile.

Marc wasn't totally sure what either of them meant, but decided not to press on it. The main thing was that he and his friends were alive and free, and in good company. Even though he had just met them, he could feel that these Aftarans were good-hearted. It seemed the goodness he had sensed during his landing on Meenjaza had finally decided to reveal itself.

"Where are we now?" he asked.

"We are on Meenjaza, under the floor of the Furish crater in an unpopulated part of the desert," Raiha said. "We are safe from Wazilban's soldiers and surveyors here, at least for the time being."

Marc looked around, and noticed that they were inside a dimly lit cavern with a low, rocky ceiling. There were several other Aftarans in the cavern as well, most of them busily attending to various types of monitoring equipment that he didn't recognize.

"This is a local rebel base," Sharjam explained. "Rebels against Wazilban and his tyranny, that is. Unfortunately there are very few rebels scattered across the Dominion, thanks to the wide reach of Wazilban's forces and the harsh punishment for those who dare speak their minds against him, let alone take up arms. You just escaped that punishment yourself."

"This base is also not permanent," Dumyan added. "The reason we are safe here for the moment is due to a uniquely powerful and dynamic magnetic field in Meenjaza's mantle. It constantly moves around, and periodically causes high amounts of geomagnetic radiation to be emitted at deep craters such as this one. The radiation is so strong that military vehicles scanning the area cannot see through it, and it also repels surveyors before they can get close enough to be harmful. But because the field is constantly in motion, the radiation at this crater will soon disappear, and we shall have to move before our presence is detected."

Marc understood now what all the monitoring equipment was for. He also wondered what surveyors were, but a more pressing question was already on his mind. "Why did you rescue us?"

"I asked them that too," Sibular said. "But they wanted to wait until you woke up before they answered."

Marc was about to respond, but began feeling lightheaded. He closed his eyes and lay down.

Sharjam abruptly got up and walked away, soon to return with a mug in his hand. "Here, drink this," he offered, giving Marc the mug. "It is called rauka, and it will give you strength."

Marc slowly sat up and looked at the yellow liquid. He had drunk it once before on Captain Thorab's ship, and knew how effective it was. Without hesitation, he lifted the mug to his mouth and gulped all of the rauka down in one swig. It worked like magic, just like the last time. He felt strong again, and the lightheadedness disappeared right away.

"We have been looking for you for a long time," Dumyan said, watching the color return to Marc's face. "Although we did not know it was you we were looking for until very recently."

Marc shook his head in confusion. "What do you mean? Looking for whom? The three of us? Or me?"

"Well, we intended to rescue you and whoever else was accompanying you, but we were specifically looking for you alone. That we came across Sibular and Zorina, both such highly skilled individuals from their own civilizations, is an added bonus."

"Why me?"

"This may be difficult for you to believe or accept in one shot, but perhaps there is no better way to tell you," Sharjam said. "Your coming is prophesied in one of our sacred Scriptures, and you are needed for us to defeat Wazilban and restore peace and prosperity to the Dominion."

Marc's jaw dropped in amazement. "Prophecy! In your sacred Scripture? Me? How is that possible? I am not an Aftaran, and I don't even know anything about your religion, let alone believe in it!"

"Be that as it may, there is no doubt that you are the one," Sharjam said. "Our High Clerics have told us so."

"Your who?"

"The High Clerics are the supreme authority of our religion, the ones who interpret the sacred Scriptures for all of us and guide us along the path of righteousness," Sharjam explained. "For the longest time, we thought Wazilban had killed them after taking control of the Dominion. But we recently discovered that he has kept them as prisoners all along, right here on Meenjaza. We were able to visit them in secret, but did not have enough time to free them and bring them back with us. They are all old, and do not have the physical strength to withstand travel through harsh conditions. By the will of the Creator, we shall free them when our mission is over." He paused. "Marc, we need your help. Will you please help us?"

Marc couldn't believe what he was hearing. In bewilderment, he stared at Sibular, who was just standing there in silence. This whole situation reminded him somewhat of his first encounter with the Mendoken, when a powerful alien civilization had sought his help, the help of a single human. Now, it seemed, the Aftar were doing the same thing. But this time, his arrival was already mentioned in a prophecy!

His gaze returned to the three Aftarans sitting around him. He couldn't help wondering if this whole thing was some kind of practical joke. But why the Aftarans would go to such lengths just to humor themselves, he couldn't imagine. Was he really someone special after all? That would certainly explain his visions and his growing sense of intuition.

"I can try my best to help you," he said. "But first, you must explain to me what exactly the High Clerics told you."

All three Aftarans looked highly relieved, and Marc noticed Sharjam whisper a short prayer of thanks with his eyes closed.

"It is a long story, and all has to be explained in the proper context," Sharjam said after opening his eyes again. "But come, you must be hungry. I know I am. Let us all eat something, and we will tell you more during the meal."

*   *   *

"Rebels or shipmates, it seems all Aftarans know how to cook!" Zorina exclaimed, gladly taking in a second helping of spicy vegetable curry. After waking up, she had joined the others.

They were all sitting in a circle in a corner of the cavern – Marc, Zorina, Dumyan, Sharjam, Raiha and a few other Aftaran rebels. The curry was still simmering inside a large pot that stood over a portable stove in the center of the circle. Raiha kept offering more curry to everyone, along with fresh pita-style bread from a small oven next to the pot.

Sibular, who of course never ate, stood nearby, discussing Meenjaza's magnetic field fluctuations with a couple of Aftaran rebels. Marc had no doubt that Sibular would have some useful technical advice for the Aftarans. Mendoken technological know-how was just so far ahead of the Aftar, it was almost like the difference between a fancy sports car and a child's tricycle.

Marc had to agree with Zorina, though, that these Aftarans certainly knew how to cook. The food was simple and unglamorous, both in the way it was prepared and the way it was presented, but it was delicious. It also helped to know that there were just vegetables in the curry, since Aftarans were strict vegetarians. He definitely wouldn't have been nearly as amenable to eating meat from animals he had never seen or heard of before. He just wasn't the adventurous type when it came to trying different kinds of food.

There was something uniquely quaint about the atmosphere as well, especially in the dim lighting. As a child, Marc had always longed to go out into the woods around Vancouver with his best friends, camp around a fire at night and exchange made-up stories about heroism and adventure. He had, however, never had any best friends to share such moments with. Now, all these years later as an adult, it seemed that longing was finally being satisfied. That he was thousands of light years away from Vancouver's woods on another planet, with a group of aliens fighting a war against a powerful galactic conspiracy, was a different story altogether.

Zorina was brought up to speed on how the three of them had been rescued, and also why. "Marc mentioned in the Aftaran sacred Scriptures?" she exclaimed, bobbing her head up and down in amazement. "Unbelievable! In which text?"

"The Hidden Scripture," Sharjam said between mouthfuls of curry.

"The what? I thought I've heard the names of all seven of them before, and that name doesn't sound familiar. Mind you, what we learned in the Grid about you folks and your religion might not have been entirely accurate or objective."

"I would have been surprised if you had heard of it," Sharjam said. "There are only seven Scriptures available to the public. But there is also an eighth, and it is called the Hidden Scripture for a reason. Only the High Clerics have the authority to see it."

"Why is it hidden?" Zorina asked. "And how do you know what it says if it is hidden?"

"It is hidden because its content is far too difficult and vague for common Aftarans to understand. It contains prophecies, mostly of events in the Dominion, but only the High Clerics know how to interpret the prophecies correctly. The High Clerics gave our father one of the only three copies of the Hidden Scripture when Wazilban took over the Dominion, to safeguard it in case he killed them. During our time in hiding, we read all of it, from beginning to end. That is how we came across the prophecy, but we did not understand it properly or recognize its true relevance until we visited the High Clerics this time."

Marc shrugged. "But what is it about me that's so unique? I'm just an ordinary being, from a species way behind all of you. My world still has a silupsal filter around it, for heaven's sake!"

"Therein lies the brilliance of the prophecy," Dumyan said. "The perfect cover, keeping you hidden out of everyone's sight until the appointed time."

"And now, that time has finally come!" Sharjam said excitedly.

Dumyan and Sharjam went on to explain who they really were. Taking turns, they told of their father Autamrin, the previous ruler of the Dominion, and how Wazilban had come from nowhere and tricked the public with lies into rising up against Autamrin. Autamrin and his followers had had no choice but to go into hiding on a remote world, hotly pursued by Wazilban's forces but always staying one step ahead. With their father, Dumyan and Sharjam had spent the last two years in seclusion.

Since then, the Aftaran people had learned their lesson, watching with increasing alarm as Wazilban's autocratic regime had solidified its power base and spread its policies of belligerence across the Dominion. Over time, Aftarans had gotten more and more fed up with the continuous loss of both their basic civil liberties and the lives of their loved ones to the pointless and brutal war against the Phyrax. Now only a handful of extremist Aftarans remained as Wazilban's supporters. The masses, though ready to revolt, were being kept at bay by Wazilban's constant shows of military strength and well publicized harsh punishments for those who dared oppose him. The swiftly conducted trial and public execution of Marc, Sibular and Zorina was intended as yet another reminder to those who were contemplating dissent.

Dumyan and Sharjam, after these past couple of years in hiding, had finally decided to take their chances and return to the heart of the Dominion, to gain the support of the masses and to take up the struggle against Wazilban. The two brothers had met up with Raiha by chance on a nearby moon, and had then joined forces with the other rebels here on Meenjaza. Together, they were going to overthrow Wazilban and his evil regime.

Marc listened intently to the whole story. He was very glad to learn that the majority of Aftarans were nothing like the bloodthirsty, jeering crowds he had seen in Wazilban's court and in the stadium. Those radical Aftarans had, as he was told, been handpicked to attend from the steadily shrinking number of Wazilban's diehard supporters, supporters who with all the mounting information around them about their leader's ways still chose to live in denial and blind conviction. The majority of Aftarans were actually much more moderate, much kinder and far more reasonable individuals. The majority of Aftarans, as their religion taught them to be, were tolerant, compassionate, just, and very hospitable to guests from other worlds.

"So where do I fit in to all this?" Marc asked after the two brothers had finished talking.

"You are the Sign," Sharjam said, taking a sip of water. "The one who has the ability to see that which the rest of us cannot, that which we need to know in order to defeat Wazilban. Without your help, we cannot succeed – the prophecy says so. One of the reasons we came back was to look for the Sign. It was not until we faced the High Clerics that we understood what it really was and how to find it."

"Him, rather," Raiha said, nodding in Marc's direction. "How to find him."

"Indeed, him," Sharjam agreed.

Marc felt as if he had been struck by lightning. The "Sign" was someone who had the ability to see things others could not. And that individual was none other than him. Now it was starting to make sense. He wasn't insane after all!

"So, Marc, can you tell us if you have seen anything so far, regarding Wazilban or anything else about the Aftaran people or the Dominion, that seemed peculiar or out of place?" Dumyan asked, staring directly at Marc. "Something that nobody else has noticed?"

Marc returned the stare. "Yes. As a matter of fact, I can."

"Aliens!" they all exclaimed in unison. The look on the face of every single Aftaran in the circle was one of total shock. Zorina looked astonished as well, and Sibular floated over to them after hearing the commotion.

"Yes," Marc said confidently, "Wazilban is an alien from another species, as are a number of others. They appear to have completely infiltrated your society and established themselves in key positions." He then told everyone the whole series of events since his departure from Earth, focusing on his visions, his growing feelings of good and bad about select individuals and places, and finally his ability to recognize Wazilban and the others as aliens.

For a long moment, there was complete silence. The Aftarans in the circle exchanged uneasy glances with each other.

"Do you... do you see any of the aliens here?" Sharjam asked.

Marc looked around the cavern again, just to make sure. "No," he said. He then proceeded to describe what the aliens looked like, and also explained what he thought their intentions were, based on what he had seen in his visions.

"This is unbelievable!" one of the other Aftarans sitting in the circle said, shaking her head. "To have been tricked like this for all these years! Where are these aliens from? I have heard of no species looking like that in the entire galaxy."

"I don't know," Marc said, shaking his head as well.

"Do you have any evidence of this?" Dumyan asked.

"Evidence? No, I have no evidence. I'm just telling you what I saw with my own eyes."

Dumyan was silent for a moment, and then suddenly got up. "I have an idea. Marc, come with me." He began walking off towards an exit on the far wall of the cavern.

Marc got up and followed, wondering where Dumyan was going. Sharjam, Zorina and Sibular accompanied him.

"So they're aliens!" Zorina whispered into Marc's ear as they walked. "Is that what you tried to tell all those Aftarans in the hall, when we were being led away after the sentencing?"

"Yes," Marc whispered back. "Before I was abruptly hushed by one of those aliens in the audience."

"Amazing! And to us, they all looked just like Aftarans! Eh, Sibular?"

"It certainly is most peculiar," Sibular said quietly.

Dumyan led the way out of the cavern and down a narrow, dark tunnel. After less than a minute of walking, they reached a dead end, marked by a lamp perched on the far wall. In front of the wall, Marc could see an Aftaran standing guard next to a big cage with thick metal bars. The guard moved out of the way as Dumyan approached.

Dumyan pointed at the cage. "Now, Marc, tell me what you see."

Marc looked beyond the bars of the cage, and a familiar feeling of terror instantly shot through his body. His face turned pale, sweat beads appeared on his forehead, and his legs began shivering. His first instinct was to run away as fast as he could, to get as far away from the evil in front of him as humanly possible. But as he turned, he found the way out of the tunnel blocked by Sharjam, Sibular and

Zorina.

"Marc, what do you see?" Zorina asked, grabbing hold of his arms.

"I see two of those aliens!" he whispered, turning to look at the cage once more.

There was no doubt about it. The aliens were there inside the cage, staying afloat in midair with the slow, sweeping motions of their wings. They didn't have a lot of space, though, as the cage wasn't very big. One of the aliens was larger than the other, and also looked meaner and tougher. Not that the other had a sweet appearance by any standards – both of them had their long snouts open, displaying their shiny fangs and looking ready to pounce on anything that came within their reach. And both of them had their threatening, alligator-like eyes focused on Marc.

"What do *you* see?" Marc asked Zorina in return.

"I just see two Aftarans," Zorina said. "Sibular?"

Sibular agreed with Zorina, as did Dumyan and Sharjam.

"They are two dangerous mercenaries who work for Wazilban," Dumyan said. "Ozwin and Ruminat. We crossed paths with them on another star system."

Sharjam walked up to the cage and addressed the prisoners. "Your disguise has finally been exposed! We know you are not Aftarans. Tell us who you are, where you are from, and what your purpose is here in the Dominion."

The prisoners looked stunned but remained quiet, avoiding everyone's gaze.

"Speak!" Sharjam thundered. "You can no longer hide the truth."

The larger alien looked up. "I have no idea what you are talking about. We have nothing to hide. We are Aftarans, like you. The only difference is that we are not traitors to Lord Wazilban, the chosen leader of the Dominion!"

Sharjam pretended to ignore what the alien had just said, and turned towards Marc. "Marc, reveal to us that which they refuse to admit."

Marc hesitated. Even though they were behind thick bars, he was terrified of those creatures.

Sharjam walked over and whispered into Marc's ear. "You need not fear them. Evil and dangerous they may be, but once they hear what you have to say, they will be more afraid of you than you of them. Fear them less, and they will fear you more. It is the nature of Creation that truth shall always prevail when it directly confronts falsehood, for the Creator always sides with the righteous. Trust me, and have faith."

Marc didn't feel any more confident after hearing this statement, but realized that he had no choice. All the others had their eyes on him, waiting for him to begin speaking. Trying his best to swallow his fear, he slowly took a few steps towards the cage. He took a deep breath, and began describing the appearance of the creatures. He went on to explain how these aliens were planning to exterminate all the civilizations in the galaxy. As he spoke, the prisoners' faces began to show increasing alarm.

Dumyan was closely observing the aliens. "Why are you so afraid, Ozwin, if you have nothing to hide?"

Ozwin looked very uncomfortable, evidently not at all prepared that anyone would be able to see through his disguise. "This... ah... individual... is mad!" he said, his voice sounding panic-stricken. "He knows not what he says!"

"Tell us who you are!" Dumyan insisted.

The prisoners were quiet.

Sharjam motioned to Marc to move closer to the cage, and to continue speaking.

Marc, now feeling more confident about Sharjam's predictions, moved all the way up to the bars. He repeated everything he had just said, but this time with a louder voice and with more vivid detail.

The aliens retreated to the rear of the cage as much as they could, the terror in their reptilian eyes now clearly showing.

"Tell us from where you have come!" Sharjam cried, his voice full of anger.

"Leave us alone!" Ruminat suddenly shouted, her face cowering behind Ozwin's. "You cannot stop us anymore!"

"Be quiet!" Ozwin snapped at his companion.

"Quiet for what?" Ruminat said, sounding distressed. "They are all doomed anyway! What does it matter?"

"You fool!" Ozwin yelled, clasping his limb over Ruminat's snout. "She is... delirious, do not listen to her!" he said to the others, trying to cover up the damage she had done.

But it was too late. Dumyan looked at Sharjam, revealing a big grin on his face.

"Satisfied?" Sharjam asked his brother.

"Indeed, indeed I am. You know, I suppose this explains why those Doolins on Droila thought we ate meat. They were unknowingly dealing all the time with these aliens, thinking they were Aftarans."

"Yes," Sharjam agreed. "Based on Marc's description of their appearance, these aliens certainly do not seem to be vegetarians."

Dumyan turned to Marc. "My friend, you now have my full conviction."

Chapter 30

The surge of geomagnetic radiation through the Furish crater abruptly came to an end. Two days had already passed since the arrival of Marc and his friends at the Aftaran rebel base, and now it was time to move. Without the protection of the radiation, Wazilban's soldiers would probably soon locate and destroy the base, if a surveyor didn't blow it all to smithereens first. And after hearing a detailed description of surveyors and their awesome destructiveness, Marc, Sibular and Zorina had been quick to agree with the Aftaran rebels that leaving the crater as soon as possible was indeed the wisest decision.

There was also another reason to leave without delay. On the evening of the second day, the two prisoners Ozwin and Ruminat had suddenly vanished. According to the Aftaran guard, they had not physically broken out of the cage. Instead, their bodies had simply vaporized into thin air. It couldn't have been done with an enchantment, for they had had no scripture coins at their disposal, and possession of the appropriate scripture coin was always needed before any enchantment could be enacted. So evidently these aliens had other powerful capabilities not known to any Aftaran. With their alien origins already exposed, these two had obviously decided to use their native capabilities to flee. No doubt, they would quickly make contact with Wazilban and inform him where the rebels were located. It was imperative for the rebels, therefore, to be far away from the Furish crater by the following morning.

For the rebels, moving between the many thousands of craters dotting Meenjaza's surface was always one of their most difficult and perilous tasks. It was so perilous, in fact, that when hiding under Meenjaza's craters had been suggested as an option to Autamrin and his followers during their escape into exile, it had not even been given a second thought.

With their antiquated and inaccurate monitoring equipment, it usually took the rebels a long time to figure out where the geomagnetic radiation would blast through next. There was just no easily predictable pattern that the radiation followed. Furthermore, the trek across the desert to the next crater always left them vulnerable to attack, especially if the trek turned out to be a long one. Digging into the sand and hiding was often the only option when enemy ground vessels or surveyors passed by. But this method was far from safe, and many a time entire rebel processions traveling across the desert had been spotted and destroyed.

Everyone was more than happy, therefore, to this time have access to Sibular and Zorina's advanced technical knowledge. It took Sibular only a couple of hours to recalibrate the monitoring equipment, so that it could track the path of the geomagnetic radiation far more accurately. Zorina, once she had been briefed on the scanning mechanisms of surveyors and ground vessels, was able to use her extensive expertise in defense to devise a protective shielding system that would render everyone invisible to enemy scans during the journey.

And so, on the next day, early in the dawn hours after the Aftarans had held their morning prayers, they all began their journey across the desert. Their destination: the Gaufaltin crater, 170 miles north from their current position. They would steer clear of all urbanized areas along the way, and would as much as possible travel under the shadows of tall sand dunes and rocky hills. For the 21 travelers, the biggest issue was that they had no real means of transportation – no ship, vehicle or floating platform. Even if they did have one, traveling at that speed would increase the risk of their detection, with or without Zorina's protective shield. So their only option was to move on foot, and in single file like a procession, in order for the shield to be most effective.

Well, not quite on foot, as it turned out. Much to Marc's delight and fascination, Sharjam enacted an enchantment that would allow everyone to float over the sand.

"This is amazing!" Marc exclaimed, gliding effortlessly over the ground as if he was on invisible, jet-powered rollerblades. Even the heavy load of supplies and pieces of monitoring equipment he was carrying on his back no longer felt like a burden.

"Isn't it?" Zorina agreed, bobbing her head up and down in approval. "Now we're all like you, Sibular!" She was right between Marc and Sibular in the procession, and, like everyone else, was carrying a load on her back. In her hand was a small device she had built herself. Its purpose was to keep the invisible protective shield operational whenever the presence of enemy ground vessels or surveyors was detected.

Sibular followed quietly, choosing not to comment. He also chose not to rely on Sharjam's enchantment, but on his own Mendoken-built floating mechanism instead.

Raiha was right in front of Marc in the procession. "This is how we were able to carry the three of you here across the desert," she explained, "using this enchantment."

Zorina looked puzzled. "Wait, if you Aftarans can perform such magic tricks all the time, why can't you just make us invisible to those surveyors and scanners during our journey? Why do you need this shield mechanism I designed?"

"Enchantments are not easy to enact, and are even harder to sustain for extended periods of time or for large numbers of individuals," Raiha said. "The vanishing act is one of the hardest, and impossible to sustain for the duration of this journey."

"How do you guys even perform these enchantments?" Marc asked, as the procession began moving forward with Dumyan leading the way and Sharjam taking up the rear.

"Many Aftarans can perform simple enchantments," Raiha said. "We use the miracles of Nature itself to transform small things from one form to another, such as creating a small plant from air, for example. But bigger enchantments, such as making you vanish in the stadium or keeping all of us afloat for an entire journey, require a much deeper knowledge and understanding of the Holy Scriptures."

"You mean this magical power comes from the Scriptures themselves?"

"But of course! The power lies in the words of the verses. Simple enchantments are based on simple, well-known verses. But only those who have a deep knowledge of more difficult and obscure verses, as well as the necessary training to really understand their meaning, can use the power they contain for larger, more elaborate enchantments. Sharjam is one such individual."

She paused, and the expression on her face turned to one of sorrow. "I also have knowledge of the Scriptures, but I am not yet trained in enacting much of their power. My great master Heeran, the same master that Sharjam had and one of the Dominion's most highly regarded teachers of religion, was taken away and killed by Wazilban before he could teach me those skills."

"I am very sorry to hear that," Marc said, although he wasn't very surprised to hear it. It sounded just like the kind of thing Wazilban was not only capable of, but would actually enjoy doing. "I hope all the efforts you are putting into this rebellion will one day lead you to victory over Wazilban, and to justice for all the crimes he has committed against your people."

Raiha smiled. "For the longest time, I believed there was no hope. I was living a life of seclusion and shame. But then, Dumyan and Sharjam suddenly appeared one day at my doorstep. Sharjam, the one who I deeply loved for many years and the one who I thought was dead, came back into my life just like that. And then, just like that, you arrived." She looked at Marc. "The prophecy from the Hidden Scripture that Sharjam told me about after we met the High Clerics, that in the midst of this darkness a light would finally come, has come true. You are the Sign, Marc, and we have found you. With you, and with the Creator's help, we shall surely find victory."

Marc was taken aback by how much faith Raiha had in him, and it made him feel both honored and worried at the same time. Sure, he seemed to have some unexplained ability to see certain things that others couldn't, and he had helped these rebels see through the alien conspiracy that had taken hold of their Dominion. But how was he going to help a handful of rebels defeat this alien species that was not only extremely cunning and resourceful, but had also completely fooled many billions of well-armed Aftaran soldiers into unconditional servitude?

It just seemed so incredibly foolish that he began wondering what he was doing here, and why he had even bothered to tell these rebels everything he had seen. All he had done was create an even more impossible situation for himself, for Sibular and for Zorina. And yet, he knew that he had to do it. He had to help these rebels, even though their chances of success were ludicrous at best. Not just because they had saved his life, not just because they were fighting an enemy intent on destroying all life in the galaxy, but also because they had placed their trust and faith in him. And that was more than could be said for anyone he had known back on Earth.

They glided along silently over the sand, under the dim lighting of the dawn sky. A crimson hue soon appeared to their right over the horizon and spread upwards, chasing away the darkness of the night. The sunrise of Afta-Raushan followed, the old, small sun responsible for the birth of the mighty Aftaran civilization.

Marc was mesmerized by the beautiful, golden brilliance of the sun, its rays spreading quickly across the cloudless atmosphere. The sand dunes lit up one by one in their own golden color, as if an invisible hand of light was sweeping across the land.

"It is beautiful!" Raiha remarked. "Meenjaza's sunrise is something I can never get enough of."

Marc welcomed the warmth of the sun's rays after the cold night. "I don't remember the last time I ever saw a sunrise. Back on Earth, I usually woke up after the Sun had already risen. And on those winter days when the Sun rose late, the sky was either covered with clouds or I was too busy getting ready to go to school to notice. I have seen many a sunset, mind you."

"Ah, but sunsets do not compare to sunrises! The sky is much clearer after a quiet night."

Marc had to agree. It truly was a spectacular sight, and he felt that just being able to witness it had made this trek through the desert worthwhile.

But that feeling was abruptly brought to an end by Sibular, who, with his razor-sharp 360 degree vision, had been watching the rest of the horizon all around him at the same time. "Is that a sandstorm approaching, Raiha?" he asked.

Marc immediately turned the other way to look. At first, he saw nothing. That direction was still fairly dark, and his eyes had been partly blinded by staring at the rising sun for so long. But then, as the blindness disappeared, he saw it. A vast, white cloud, covering one end of the horizon to the other and rising up high into the sky, was creeping over the sand dunes and heading straight towards them.

"No," Raiha said, almost whispering, "that is no sandstorm." Raising her hands to her mouth, she yelled out, "Alarm! A surveyor approaches from the left!"

Marc froze in his tracks. A surveyor – the deadly weapon used by Wazilban to seek out and destroy his enemies in the remotest places. And now one was heading straight for them!

"Well, let's just hope the shield works," Zorina said, adjusting some controls on the device she was holding. "Tell everyone to stand absolutely still. Nobody should move or open their mouths." She looked surprisingly calm, seemingly confident in her own work.

Raiha yelled the order out to everyone else. They all immediately stood dead in their tracks, their eyes focused on the rapidly approaching terror.

Marc felt the same way he had felt when Zorina had told him to stand still in front of the drones on the Volonan planet Nopelio. Every instinct in his mind and body told him to turn and run away as fast as he could. But he reminded himself that Zorina had been right the last time, and he had every trust in her that she would be right again.

Within a few minutes, the surveyor reached them, passing effortlessly over the nearest sand dunes. He could now see thousands of globules of yellow light inside the cloud, dancing around in all directions. Upon closer scrutiny, he noticed that the globules actually represented Aftaran faces, with their eyes wide open as they searched every corner of space for anything suspicious. The faces looked innocent enough, but as he had been told, as soon as any one of them found the target they were looking for, the bulk of the surveyor would explode, indiscriminately obliterating everything within a 10 mile radius.

The first globules approached him. He closed his eyes in apprehension, hoping for the best, but expecting the worst. A second went by, then two, then three. Nothing happened. He opened his eyes again, and to his amazement saw how the globules were simply flying by over his head. Straining to look out of the corner of his eye, he could see them flying over everyone else's head as well. The surveyor, unable to penetrate or see through the protective shield, was simply passing over it as if it was just another sand dune.

Marc heaved a sigh of relief. Once again, Zorina's genius had saved the day! He eyed the surveyor passing overhead, and felt as if he was inside a narrow tunnel with transparent walls, a tunnel barely high enough to fit the tallest Aftaran, yet long enough to protect the entire procession.

It took a long time before the surveyor's last globules made their jump over the shield. And, just like that, the vast cloud was gone, heading off in the direction of the rising sun.

After offering Zorina their heartiest congratulations and thanks, everyone began moving again. Fortunately, the rest of the journey was fairly uneventful. They stopped once for a quick meal, and a couple of times spotted convoys of military ground vessels in the distance. But Zorina's shield turned itself on automatically every time, rendering the entire procession invisible to both the soldiers' scanners and their naked eyes.

A few hours later, they arrived at their destination. As they amassed at the edge of the Gaufaltin crater, Marc got a good look at the depths of blown out rock below. The crater was huge, easily over twice the size of the crater they had left behind. The other side had to be at least a couple of miles away.

"The largest crater in this hemisphere," Dumyan pointed out, standing next to Marc. "The impact, billions of years ago, is recorded in historical chronicles to have spread volumes of ash over the whole globe."

"Why does Meenjaza have so many craters?" Marc asked. "Shouldn't the atmosphere burn up most meteors on a collision course with the planet?"

"The craters were actually not caused by meteors," Dumyan replied. "They were caused by bombs. It was during a time when our civilization was still in its infancy, and we still had not united as a people or traveled out into space. There were several nations of Aftarans here on Meenjaza, constantly battling each other for supremacy and control of the planet.

"The craters have been preserved by the Aftar ever since. To serve as a reminder of the horror and destruction in times of war." Dumyan sighed. "Not that it has done much good since Wazilban came to power. Within the span of a few years, he has single-handedly destroyed all the ethics and morals our civilization developed before that over billions of years."

Dumyan led the way down a steep, narrow path to the bottom of the crater. At the bottom, he made straight for a narrow opening in the wall of the crater, hidden behind a column of rock. He disappeared inside, and popped out again shortly afterwards to signal that the coast was clear.

Minutes later, they were all inside a cavern under the crater, similar to the one they had left behind. To Marc's surprise, several other Aftaran rebels he hadn't met before were already there. They had arrived less than an hour earlier, after scouting several different cities on Meenjaza to keep track of Wazilban's activities. Dumyan and Sharjam spoke to them quietly for a while, and then came back to the others.

"Some important updates," Sharjam announced. "Wazilban is frantically looking for you everywhere." He pointed at Marc, Sibular and Zorina. "He has been sending scores of surveyors and millions of soldiers, not just all over the planet, but into the rest of the star system and beyond. He is bent on catching and killing you."

"That is no surprise, considering what is at stake for him," Sibular remarked.

"No it is no surprise, but here is what you will find interesting, Sibular," Dumyan said. "The wars on both fronts are spiraling out of control – ours against the Phyrax, and yours against the Volona. The Mendoken in particular appear to be suffering due to continuous waves of Volonan consar attacks. So Wazilban has apparently convinced the Mendoken Imgoerin to join forces with him in a coalition, to fight both the Phyrax and Volona together. He is inviting the Imgoerin to visit the Dominion. They will meet at the Bara Dilshai resort in five days, where they will publicly sign a covenant."

Marc thought he actually saw Sibular's single eye flicker in a faint show of astonishment. It was the highest amount of emotion he had ever seen in Sibular's face.

"That is not all," Sharjam added. "Wazilban has somehow found out that the Mendoken also have consar technology now, and he has convinced the Imgoerin to use it in all joint battles against the enemy."

"What!" Zorina shouted, violently flapping her ears. "This is a hoax, right? Tell me this is a hoax! The Volona don't have consar technology! Why doesn't anybody understand this? We are not behind those consar attacks on Mendoken territory! For the Mendoken to strike again with consar technology against the Empire will be pure one-sided aggression!"

Sharjam shook his head. "I do not know who really is behind the consar attacks, but I am afraid what I am telling you is not a hoax."

"This is unacceptable," Sibular said. "This will dramatically escalate the wars, and will ultimately spell disaster for all."

Marc was not terribly surprised by this development. "This is exactly what I've been on about! It's what Wazilban wants – for the major civilizations in this galaxy to wipe each other out. That leaves the path clear for whatever he and his alien cahoots want to do next."

"The timing also makes sense," Dumyan said. "The meeting will receive much publicity and fanfare. Wazilban wants to bolster waning support for the war against the Phyrax in the Dominion, by showing everyone that he now has a powerful ally joining forces with him. And he probably also wants to speed up his grand scheme, whatever that is. Now that you are on the loose, Marc, he knows it is only a matter of time before his secret is unveiled to the masses."

Zorina was still angry. "But how can a handful of aliens possibly expect to wipe out all the civilizations in this galaxy? Even if the Mendoken and Aftar succeed with their aggression and defeat the Volona and Phyrax, that still leaves the Mendoken and Aftar for the aliens to deal with, doesn't it?"

"Yes, but the Mendoken and Aftar will be severely weakened by the war," Marc said. "And we don't know yet how many of those aliens are already here, or how much military power they have at their disposal."

"Actually, Sharjam and I already have an idea just how Wazilban intends to take care of whoever is left in the galaxy at the end of the war," Dumyan said.

Everyone turned to stare at Dumyan. And, from the expression on Dumyan's face, Marc knew the answer wasn't going to be pretty.

"How?" Zorina asked.

"During our journey out of the planet Tibara, we landed on the neighboring planet Droila. There, in the depths of its oceans, we discovered vast fields of Starguzzlers. Th..."

Zorina interrupted him. "Starguzzlers?"

"That was what the Doolins called them."

"The who?"

"Zorina, I will explain it all, not to worry," Dumyan said, looking slightly irritated.

Zorina flapped her ears and kept quiet.

Without any further interruptions, Dumyan described everything he and Sharjam had witnessed on Droila, including meeting the Doolins, inspecting the Starguzzler fields, and finally encountering Ozwin and Ruminat. He described what the Starguzzlers looked like, with their spherical shells and glowing red sparkles within.

"They were not very big," Sharjam added. He displayed a diameter of 3 feet with his hands. "But there were millions of them. And they were being tended to by the Doolins like crops."

"You believe these Starguzzlers are weapons?" Sibular asked.

"Of some sort, yes," Dumyan said. "The very name the Doolins gave them –

Starguzzlers – suggests their purpose is far from peaceful. We have no idea what kind of weapon or how they will be used, but I have no doubt they are meant for mass destruction."

"Starguzzlers." Marc uttered the name silently several times, trying to make sense of it. The literal meaning would be: "something or somebody that consumes a star". But what did that really mean? What could possibly have the ability to consume an entire star, especially something that was only 3 feet in diameter? Then again, they were growing like crops. But how big could they possibly get? And what good would it do to consume a star anyway?

"In any case, there is no doubt Wazilban is behind it," Sharjam said. "That was why his subordinates Ozwin and Ruminat were there – he sent them to monitor the growth of those Starguzzlers."

Raiha frowned. "I dread to find out how many other such Starguzzler fields there might be across the Dominion."

Silence followed, during which everyone appeared to be deep in thought.

Marc thought too, trying to make sense of it all and to figure out what to do. And, after a while, he was the one to end the hush. "We must stop this as soon as possible!" he cried out.

Sharjam shrugged. "Marc, that much is already certain. But the question is how."

"We must stop the meeting between Wazilban and the Imgoerin. No, better yet, we must show up at the meeting, and expose the truth in front of the Imgoerin!"

"You mean publicly reveal to the Imgoerin that Wazilban is an alien?" Dumyan said.

"Yes! We will convince the Imgoerin not to combine forces with Wazilban, and simultaneously reveal the conspiracy to both the Mendoken and Aftaran people!"

Raiha didn't seem convinced. "But how can we possibly do that? The meeting will be heavily guarded by Wazilban's forces. Wazilban will take no chances, since he knows you are still on the loose and with us. And even if we do get in by some miracle, how do we show the Imgoerin and everyone else what only you can see?"

Sharjam looked pensive. "There may be a way. I will have to do some research in the Holy Scriptures first."

"Can't we just do something similar to what we did with your two prisoners?" Zorina asked. "Confronting them directly with the truth? It worked with those two, after all."

Sharjam sighed. "Direct confrontation of truth over falsehood only works on minds that are weak to begin with. I doubt we will find Wazilban's mind to be as weak as those of Ozwin and Ruminat. He is the leader of these aliens, after all. It will undoubtedly require a lot more strength in us to confront him directly."

"Furthermore, showing the Imgoerin the truth does not necessarily mean that he will believe you," Sibular pointed out. "He may think you are performing a magic trick, something you Aftarans seem to be quite adept at."

"Ah, but that's where you come in, Sibular!" Marc said. "Given your function in the Mendoken hierarchy, I presume the Imgoerin knows who you are, right?"

"Yes. I have met him on several occasions."

"And he trusts you?"

"Naturally. We Mendoken never lie. It is not in our nature. All Mendoken trust each other without question, and help each other out without fail."

Marc grinned. "Well then, my friend, it looks like you'll have some storytelling to do at the meeting of the Titans."

Chapter 31

Bara Dilshai was the most famous holiday resort in the entire Aftaran Dominion. Not that there were many resorts in the Dominion to begin with, considering how Aftarans generally abstained from entertainment or leisurely activities. Whatever resorts there were usually catered not to Aftarans, but to tourists or official visitors from other species. Bara Dilshai, however, was different. Aftarans and others alike flocked to this location every year.

There was a valid reason for the resort to be so popular, and it was not the size of its facilities, the variety of amenities it had, or the fact that it was perched atop the rocky surface of a large asteroid. No, its claim to fame rested solely on one criterion – its location in the Glaessan galaxy. Situated right in the heart of the Aftaran Dominion, it provided the closest, completely unhindered, crystal clear view of the very center of the galaxy itself. Specifically, it provided the closest view of the supermassive black hole that made up the center of the galaxy.

Black holes had always been revered by Aftarans as gateways out of the known universe, perhaps even to the realm of the Creator. That was why so many Aftarans came to Bara Dilshai, to witness this wonder for themselves. Of course, nobody had ever dared to travel into a black hole or even get close enough to one to determine if that was really true or not. Anyone trying to do so would have ended up with a very painful death, for the tremendous gravitational pull of the black hole would have literally ripped that individual's atoms apart as it sucked the body into its dense mass.

Efforts by Mendoken scientists to send probes into black holes had always resulted in failures. The probes had without exception ceased to communicate upon nearing the black holes, and had never been seen or heard from again. So, while a number of scientific theories did exist, the exact nature of black holes still remained a mystery to this day across the galaxy.

From a distance, it was not easy to see a black hole with the naked eye. The only way to really spot one was to look for a dark patch in the sky. Its gravitational pull was just so strong that not even light could escape from its clutches. In fact, the most significant measure of how large a black hole was, a quantity known as the event horizon, was the distance from its core within which light could not escape. On Earth, humans called this radius around a black hole the Schwarzschild radius, named after the famous German scientist who had worked extensively on the theory of black holes.

The supermassive black hole at the center of the Glaessan galaxy was called supermassive for a reason. It had a mass about 10 million times that of Earth's Sun, and a Schwarzschild radius of about 19 million miles. Most other black holes in the galaxy, of which there were no small number, averaged a Schwarzschild radius of only 3 miles. This was by far the largest black hole in the galaxy, dwarfed only by supermassive black holes in the centers of other, larger galaxies in the universe.

Marc stared at the center of the Glaessan galaxy through the cockpit window of the Boura-class vessel he was on. One of the few interstellar spaceships the rebels had in their possession, it was the same ship Dumyan and Sharjam had snatched from Ozwin and Ruminat during their journey from the planet Droila. Marc was standing right behind Dumyan, who was sitting in the pilot's seat and controlling the ship's functions with his mind. On board were also Sibular, Zorina, Sharjam, Raiha and three other Aftaran rebels. They had all slipped away from Meenjaza with a short range Shoyra-class vessel stolen from the Aftaran military, and made it to the moon Medonis around the planet Soondaza. There, they had transferred over to the Boura-class ship, dutifully watched over by Raiha's friends at the monastery of Mt. Lina ever since Dumyan and Sharjam had left it there earlier.

Four days later, they had arrived in the center of the galaxy. The supermassive black hole, more than 125 million miles away from their current position, was a huge ball of darkness covering much of the sky ahead, like a gigantic circle that had been cut out from the middle of a starry canvas and thrown away. The space around the outer edges of the ball appeared warped, and multiple jets of matter appeared to emanate from the ball in different directions.

"Incredible!" Marc whispered. It looked both beautiful and foreboding at the same time.

"That is nothing," Sharjam said, standing next to Marc. "Try this." He handed Marc a pair of goggles with large lenses, clearly made for the large eyes of Aftarans.

"What are these?"

"Spectacles that make electromagnetic waves of all frequencies visible to your eyes. We use them on Meenjaza to track the planet's magnetic field as we move from crater to crater. Try them."

Marc brought the goggles up to his face. They immediately snapped over his eyes, and automatically adjusted to his vision and focus. What he now saw caused his jaws to drop in amazement. The whole sky around the black hole was awash with brilliant colors, displaying waves that stretched out in concentric rings in all directions. Blue, purple and white were the dominant colors of the rings. It was an absolutely terrific sight.

"This is why so many come here to witness this wonder for themselves," Sharjam said, smiling as he saw the look of astonishment on Marc's face.

"It's unbelievable! It's a... a rotating black hole, isn't it?" Marc had studied black holes quite extensively in college, and knew about the theory behind them. The moving patterns of the waves seemed to indicate that the dark mass in the middle was rotating.

"Yes," Sibular replied, as he entered the cockpit. "All supermassive black holes in the cores of galaxies are rotating black holes."

Marc was about to ask Sibular what current Mendoken science said about why these supermassive black holes existed in the cores of galaxies, but was interrupted by Dumyan from the pilot's seat.

"There!" Dumyan raised his hand and pointed out the cockpit window towards a cloud of tiny specks to the left. As he pointed, a section of the cockpit window automatically zoomed in on the cloud, magnifying the image several hundred times.

Marc took off the goggles from his eyes, and saw that the cloud was actually an asteroid field. One of the asteroids, the one the window was focusing on, was larger than its neighbors, and had a number of buildings spread across its surface.

"That's Bara Dilshai?" he asked. It looked like a surprisingly vulnerable spot to have so famous a resort.

"Yes," Sharjam said. "It is as close as you can get to the black hole. Go any further than that and you run the risk of being sucked into its gravitational field, with no hope of ever returning."

Marc didn't need any further convincing that it wasn't safe to go past that point. The dark mass beyond looked anything but inviting.

"But look!" Dumyan pointed out. "Just as we feared."

Just as they had feared indeed. The asteroid was completely surrounded by Aftaran military ships, mostly long range Gyra-class vessels, but also a number of smaller Boura-class and Shoyra-class vessels. They were spread apart in a gridlock fashion, allowing no access to the resort without a direct confrontation.

But this Marc and his rebel friends had been expecting. No doubt, Wazilban was going to take no chances with this meeting. He would have arranged for the tightest security possible around Bara Dilshai. The rebels had already come up with a plan to avoid this security dragnet. Upon arriving at the resort, they were going to try to make direct contact with the Mendoken delegation, which, according to well publicized Dominion news transmissions, had just arrived a few hours earlier. Once the Mendoken delegation found out that Sibular was on board the rebel ship, they would undoubtedly listen to the rebels and offer them protection. This much Sibular had assured the others – no Mendoken would ever turn his or her back on another Mendoken, regardless of the circumstances.

The plan, however, had one flaw. It relied on the assumption that the Mendoken delegation's ship would be parked in space outside the wall of Aftaran ships, giving the rebels direct access to the Mendoken ship. Sibular had pointed out that the Mendoken never depended on the protection offered by foreign hosts during their visits to worlds of other species, and therefore always parked their ships at a fair distance from the meeting points. But now, as the rebels gazed upon the asteroid in front of them, it was all too clear that the Mendoken vessel at Bara Dilshai was well inside the wall of Aftaran ships, parked very close to the asteroid's surface. With its inverted mushroom shape, the Aima-11 transport liner was a giant compared to the much smaller submarine shaped Aftaran ships in front of it, but direct access to it was cut off nonetheless.

"This is most peculiar," Sibular said, keenly eyeing the barricade around the asteroid. "The Mendoken never do this."

"It can only mean one thing," Sharjam said. "Wazilban must have insisted the Mendoken comply with his security arrangements. He is obviously expecting that we will show up and will try to get help from the Mendoken."

"I can't say I'm terribly surprised," Marc said, frowning. He felt frustrated that their primary plan was ruined, and could only hope that their backup plan would work. He also began wondering how long it would take for their presence to be detected by the Aftaran vessels.

He didn't have to wonder for too long. A hailing sound suddenly blared through the cockpit, followed by a message read aloud by the ship's computer:

Rebel heretics, surrender immediately and prepare to be boarded. Attempt to attack or even move from your current position, and you will be destroyed immediately.

The message was clear and to the point. But nobody on board was in any mood for surrender.

Dumyan turned from his seat to look at Sibular. "Did you make all the necessary adjustments?"

"Yes," Sibular said, "your communication controls are ready."

Dumyan closed his eyes and focused extra hard on the ship's controls. Seconds later, a message written by Sibular went out from the ship towards the asteroid through a bosian layer, encrypted using technology only decipherable by advanced communication equipment on board Mendoken ships. It was short and sweet, stating the following:

This is Sibular Gaulen 45383532. I am alive and on board a Boura-class Aftaran vessel, with a group of Aftaran rebels and the Earth human Marc Zemin who helped us develop consar technology. We have critical information about Lord Wazilban that the Imgoerin should know before signing the covenant. Wazilban's forces will try to prevent us from reaching you. Please open the lower gates on the Aima-11 vessel to permit entry.

Dumyan then sent out another message, unencrypted and intended for the Aftaran ships in the barricade. It was shorter, but not quite as sweet:

Greetings, puppets and mindless submissives of Wazilban the tyrant. Your ignorance is only surpassed by your stupidity.

"Did you have to send the second message?" Sharjam exclaimed. "It will only further inflame the situation!"

"Does it make a difference?" Dumyan said with a smirk. "As if our chances of survival are better one way or the other?"

Within seconds of the transmission, several Aftaran Gyra-class vessels began moving out of the barricade and accelerated rapidly towards the rebel ship.

Sharjam moved to the wall of the cockpit and pressed on an intercom button. "Zorina, are you ready? We are progressing with the backup plan."

"Yes, Sir!" Zorina's voice crackled over the intercom speaker. "But just remember, we can only zap enough power from the kilasic engines to do this once for a ship this size, and the effect will last no more than a few minutes." She was located in the ship's engine room, along with Raiha.

"Hopefully that will be all we need," Marc thought. He knew it was going to be tight.

*   *   *

The Aftaran ships closed in on the rebel ship. Watching through the cockpit window, Marc could count 20 of them, but perhaps there were more behind the front line. The ships began flashing red and blue lights, the colors of battle. No quarter would be given, that much was for sure.

Everyone in the cockpit was dead silent, intently watching the ships approach. It was so quiet that Marc could hear his own heart beating, and it was definitely beating harder and faster than usual.

Just as the approaching ships began firing their first shots, Dumyan raised his hand. Immediately, Sharjam yelled into the intercom, "Zorina, now!"

Marc noticed a wave flash over the surface of their Boura-class ship. Then Dumyan maneuvered the ship to avoid the onslaught of enemy fire.

"It appears to be working," Sibular observed calmly.

Marc heaved a sigh of relief. Zorina's cloaking mechanism was indeed working. The enemy ships, evidently having lost all sight of their target, began firing blindly around them.

Dumyan skillfully piloted the ship around the armada of approaching enemy ships and headed straight for the asteroid. More Aftaran ships dislodged from the barricade around the asteroid and started blanket firing every which way. The Aftarans were obviously hoping that at least one of the shots would hit the rebel ship and break the cloak.

The Mendoken vessel was still a good 3 to 4 minutes away. Dumyan accelerated the ship as much as he could, while trying to avoid the barrage of deadly shots. But it kept getting progressively more difficult. The enemy ships they had bypassed were turning around and firing from the rear. Evidently the Aftaran military had guessed the trajectory of the rebel ship, even though they couldn't actually see it.

"Why aren't the Mendoken doing anything?" Marc said in frustration, watching as the view outside was completely lit up by continuous streaks of weapons fire. "Surely they can blast all these Aftaran vessels to smithereens with their superior power! Have they even responded to our message?"

"No," Sibular said, "and I would not expect them to. They are on foreign territory, and thus have no authority to interfere on our behalf. They will not reply, and will take no action until we actually enter their territory. Only once we are inside one of their ships can they protect us."

"The principle of non-interference applies, since the Mendoken and the Aftar are not at war with each other," Dumyan added.

The rebel ship edged forward silently, passing the Aftaran military barricade and closing the gap to the Mendoken vessel. As the massive Mendoken Aima-11 ship appeared ever closer, Marc noticed that the ship's lower gates had been opened, just as Sibular had requested. So the Mendoken had received and accepted the message! His hopes began to rise. It was so close now, literally no more than a mile away.

But then the inevitable happened. One of the blindly fired shots hit the rebel ship, causing an explosion in the rear of the craft. The cloak immediately collapsed, and the ship was once again visible to the enemy. Within seconds, the first direct shot hit, followed by another, and another. The ship shook violently, causing both Marc and Sharjam to lose their balance and fall to the floor.

Sharjam immediately got up and rushed to the intercom on the wall. "Is anybody hurt? Is anybody hurt?"

"No!" Zorina replied, her voice crackling through the intercom. "Nobody here in the engine room. But I'm not sure how many more shots we'll be able to take. One of them barely missed the rear left kilasic engine."

"Nobody in the prayer room either," one of the other rebels announced over the intercom.

More shots hit, a couple right in front of the cockpit. Dumyan tried firing back a few times, but there were just too many ships closing in on them.

"We cannot stay on board," Dumyan finally said, getting up from his seat.

Sharjam agreed. "Everyone, abandon ship!" he shouted into the intercom. "I repeat, abandon ship!"

"What!" Zorina yelled back. "Are you nuts? We'll all die!"

"As we will if we stay on board! Zorina, take refuge under Raiha's robe."

"What in the blue blazes are you talking about?"

"Just trust me! Get under her robe, and both of you get out of the ship through the nearest exit. Geershan, you and the others in the prayer room also get out. Remember to wrap your robes around your faces."

Sharjam then walked over to Marc. "Marc, get in here, quick!"

Without waiting for Marc to react, the towering Aftaran lifted his robe and wrapped it around Marc's face and body. Dumyan did the same with Sibular. Then Sharjam took out his boryal, aimed it at the cockpit window, and fired.

The sound of shattered glass filled the cockpit, and then Marc heard the air in the cockpit being sucked out of the broken window. He couldn't see anything in between the layers of robe wrapped around him, but he could feel that he and Sharjam were being pulled out of the ship into space. None too soon either, for the very next thing he felt was the tremor and heat of a massive explosion nearby. Evidently their Boura-class ship had just been annihilated.

Marc was amazed to find that he could breathe just fine inside Sharjam's robe. It was yet another of the many miracles these Aftarans seemed to have up their sleeves. He hoped to high heaven that everyone else had made it out of the ship in time. For the first time in his life, he closed his eyes and uttered a silent prayer asking for help. He wasn't entirely sure who he was praying to, and as far as he was concerned, it didn't matter. He just wanted the prayer to reach whoever had control over everything that was happening.

Hot flashes of fire continued to ignite nearby. The Aftaran Gyra-class vessels were still trying to destroy the crew of the rebel ship, but the targets were now probably too small for their heavy weapons.

What happened next, Marc didn't know. Maybe it was Sharjam using another enchantment to gather the others and propel everyone towards the open gate of the Mendoken ship. Or maybe his prayer really had been answered and divine intervention was somehow taking place.

Either way, all he knew for sure was that a minute or two after their exit from the ship, he and Sharjam crashed onto a surface. The impact caused both of them to roll over several times. He felt the jolts, but Sharjam's robe somehow magically shielded him from any pain. Then the robe unwrapped by itself, tossing him out onto the floor and causing him to roll a few more times before he came to a full stop.

He sat up, and once the dizziness had subsided, looked around and realized he was in a hangar inside the Mendoken vessel. They had made it! The gate they had entered through was closing, and through the gap he could see the enemy Aftaran ships pulling away in the last second to avoid a diplomatic incident with the Mendoken. To his delight, everyone else had arrived as well, safe and sound – Dumyan with Sibular, Raiha with Zorina, and the three other Aftaran rebels by themselves.

To the other side, Marc could see the reception committee – a number of Mendoken standing in a straight line. And in the middle was none other than Osalya Heyfass, top aide to the Imgoerin. Her dark skin color, white hat and gleaming metal armor covered with symbols were unmistakable.

With a tremendous feeling of exhilaration, he closed his eyes and uttered a silent whisper of thanks. He addressed it to the same one he had prayed to earlier, whoever that was.

Chapter 32

"We have never liked Lord Wazilban," Osalya said, "especially not his oppressiveness towards his own people or his belligerence towards others. The Imgoerin, however, has had no choice but to deal with the elected leader of the Aftaran people. As you know, our policy is to never interfere in the internal affairs of other civilizations. The reason the Imgoerin has accepted Wazilban's invitation to join forces is that our war with the Volona is spiraling out of control, and we are not faring well at all. While the Aftar are not that strong militarily, their wisdom, experience and political reach can benefit us." She paused. "But now you bring me this surprising news about Wazilban, and you even tell me that the Volona are not behind the consar attacks on our worlds. Do either of you have any evidence to support your allegations?"

Marc said nothing, choosing instead to stare out the window at the neighboring tall buildings. Like the very first Mendoken vessel he had traveled on, this Aima-11 transport liner had an entire modern city built inside its hull. The view of this high-tech metropolis was a marked contrast from the craters, caverns and ancient buildings of Meenjaza, as well as the ruins of the Volonan planet Nopelio. Yes, it felt good to be back inside a Mendoken ship again. The Mendoken were without a doubt a people he felt comfortable with and knew he could rely on.

"We have no physical evidence, Osalya," Sibular said. "But I offer you my word that everything Marc has just told you is true. It is imperative that the Imgoerin not sign the agreement with Lord Wazilban."

Osalya stood silent for a moment. She, Sibular and Marc were the only ones in the room. "And you assure me that neither the Aftaran rebels nor Zorina are in any way forcing you or blackmailing you to present this story?"

"Once again, I offer you my word," Sibular said, his face totally expressionless.

"Then that is all I need, Sibular," Osalya said, her face just as expressionless.

Marc was astonished. Although Sibular had already explained that no Mendoken would ever doubt the words of another Mendoken, he had never expected convincing Osalya to be this easy. He wondered what it would take for humans to ever reach this level of mutual trust.

"I will contact the Imgoerin," Osalya said, "even though he specifically requested for no interruptions during his meeting with Wazilban."

"How much time do we have?" Marc asked.

"Very little, Mr. Zemin. He is due to sign the covenant in front of the public and the media in 29 minutes."

Osalya waved one of her front limbs in the air, and a large 3D screen instantly appeared in front of her. She tried several times to execute commands on the screen, but no image appeared.

"What's going on?" Marc asked.

"This is most peculiar," Osalya said. "I cannot reach the Imgoerin, even on his private channel. This never happens."

She then contacted a communications engineer on board the ship, who ran some tests and verified that nothing was wrong with the communications equipment. The link to the Imgoerin had evidently been manually cut off.

Marc didn't need any extra moment to figure out what was going on. "Wazilban must have had the link cut to prevent us from getting through. Who else is there with the Imgoerin?"

"His seven bodyguards," Osalya said, "and three aides."

"Any other Mendoken?"

"A contingent of media representatives from across the Republic."

Marc was not impressed. "We've got to get to the resort, now!"

Minutes later, a group of shuttles took off from one of the hangars on the Aima-11 ship. On board one of the shuttles were Marc, Sibular, Osalya, Dumyan, Sharjam and a number of heavily armed and shielded Mendoken special troopers. The other shuttles were carrying more troopers. Zorina, Raiha and the three other Aftaran rebels stayed behind. Zorina and Raiha had both been hurt during the crash landing in the hangar, and needed medical attention. There was also universal agreement that having a Volonan show up at a well publicized meeting where the heads of the Mendoken and Aftaran civilizations were about to declare a joint war on the Volona probably wasn't the brightest of ideas, as it wasn't to have too many Aftaran rebels show up in front of all that media fanfare.

The Mendoken troopers on board Marc's shuttle offered spare guns to everyone else. Dumyan and Sharjam politely declined, opting to stick to their boryals instead. Marc had no choice but to accept, since he had no weapon of his own. He had never held a gun in his life before, much less used one.

One of the troopers showed him how to use the gun. It was called a *ganvex*, a weapon that blasted the target with an invisible shock ray, instantly rendering the target unconscious and immobile for hours. While purposely not as deadly as the Aftaran boryal, the ganvex's rays could travel through walls, floors, ceilings, pretty much any barrier made of any material, until they found the specific target they were meant to hit. The ganvex could also hit multiple targets at the same time. It was an extremely accurate weapon, and came with a virtual visor that allowed its user to see through walls to locate targets.

"Remember, Mr. Zemin," the trooper said, "if you see an Aftaran soldier about to fire his or her boryal at you, you must target the soldier and fire first. Do not hesitate. Otherwise the blast from the boryal will propel your body asunder into stray molecules."

Marc didn't like the way that sounded, but now was not the time to lose courage. "I'll try to remember," he said with a thin smile.

He held the black weapon in his hand, and was surprised at how light it felt. It didn't look anything like a pistol or a rifle, or even like any of the fancy laser guns he had seen in sci-fi movies. Instead, it had the simple shape and size of a small horseshoe magnet. It was important to hold the ganvex right in the middle, he was told, as the lethal ray emanated simultaneously from both ends when the weapon was fired. The virtual visor also appeared automatically in front of his eyes as he held the ganvex, giving a clear view of possible targets all around.

The shuttles landed on the asteroid, and docked with entry ports outside Bara Dilshai's main reception building. Since the asteroid had no atmosphere and very low gravity of its own, such ports were necessary to provide direct access to the resort. Through the window, Marc could see a few Mendoken shuttles and many Aftaran Shoyra-class vessels already parked at other ports.

Once the port's docking doors had opened, the Mendoken troopers exited the shuttles and floated onto passageways that led to the building lobby. Marc and the others followed along the passageway leading from their shuttle. They were all, however, abruptly stopped by a horde of Aftaran soldiers blocking the way into the lobby. Civilians in the lobby began hurrying away through other passages, evidently realizing that a confrontation was about to take place.

"Please return to your shuttle and to your ship," the commander of the Aftaran forces said in a harsh, unfriendly tone, addressing the Mendoken contingent.

Marc was not surprised to see that the commander was an alien like Wazilban. There were also a few more of the aliens among the soldiers. By now he knew only too well, however, that he was the only one who could see through their disguises.

"Under what order, Commander?" Osalya demanded, floating to the front in between the Mendoken troopers. "We are here to see the Imgoerin. We have every right to see him."

"The Imgoerin specifically requested for no interruptions during his meeting with Lord Wazilban. You must go back to your ship and await his return."

Osalya seemed perfectly calm and level-headed, in true Mendoken style. "I am the Imgoerin's top aide. Such requests always contain the caveat that I may contact him if the situation so requires."

"The situation does not so require at the current time," the alien commander replied with a sneer. "Everything is progressing smoothly as planned."

"Smoothly for you maybe, but not for us. You will now let us pass. Failure to do so will put you in direct violation of the diplomatic charter between our two civilizations. I trust you know what that will mean for you and your career."

The commander didn't seem the slightest bit intimidated, and also appeared to notice Dumyan and Sharjam for the first time. "Your party includes rebels who are wanted criminals in the Dominion!" he said angrily, raising his voice. Then he pointed at Marc. "And a foreign terrorist who conspired to overthrow Lord Wazilban! That puts you in direct violation of the diplomatic charter as well. You will hand the three of them over to me, and then you will return to your ship. You have no other business here."

Osalya remained firm. "Those three individuals have sought asylum with us. They are now under the protection and legal jurisdiction of the Mendoken Republic. This, as I suspect you know, is fully supported by the diplomatic charter. You now have as much a right to arrest them without our consent as you do to bar me from contacting my leader. You shall make way for us. This is your last warning."

"And this yours!" The alien commander signaled to his Aftaran soldiers to brandish their boryals. "By the will of the Creator, leave or be forced to leave!"

For several seconds, the two sides stared at each other, weapons at the ready, nobody moving or making a sound. Marc knew the inevitable was about to begin, and tried to prepare himself mentally as much as he could. His hand clutched tightly onto his ganvex, with the visor over his eyes allowing him to zoom in on the Aftaran soldiers. As he had been told to do, he firmly blinked his eyes once for every target he could identify. This step registered the targets with the ganvex, and when he pressed the trigger, shock rays would be fired at all of the registered targets at the same time.

The sound of the first shot rang across the lobby. It was a boryal, making a sound like a wheezing firecracker, followed by a clasp of thunder. And, unfortunately, it was not a warning shot. It hit one of the Mendoken troopers in the front, and although her protective shield deflected much of the blast, her left front limb was blown away. The impact of the explosion caused her to lose her balance and fall to the ground with a thud. Immediately two of her comrades moved in front of her to protect her, as others pulled her away to the side.

Then the battle began. Shots flew in both directions, and everyone ran or floated for cover behind the lobby's many pillars. Hiding behind a pillar himself, Marc pointed his ganvex right through the pillar at the nearest Aftaran soldier he could see with the help of the visor, and pulled the trigger. There was absolutely no sound or vibration, but almost immediately he saw the soldier fall unconscious to the ground. And, just like magic, all the other soldiers he had earlier picked as targets by blinking his eyes also fell to the ground at the same time.

Emboldened by his success, he picked new targets with the visor and pulled the trigger again. Again a number of Aftarans fell. But then several boryal shots whizzed past his ears, causing him to pull back in fright.

He took a brief moment to look around and take stock of the situation. Dumyan was standing behind one of the adjacent pillars, firing his boryal repeatedly at the Aftaran soldiers.

Marc noticed how the boryal was never aimed directly at the target. The boryal's ray shot in the direction the weapon was pointed at first, but then curved in a slightly different direction. He supposed the reason for this curved trajectory was to give the target a false sense of security until the ray actually hit.

He also noticed Sharjam and Sibular nearby, firing away at the enemy. At one point, he saw one of the aliens posing as an Aftaran soldier fire multiple times at Sharjam. Without hesitation, he targeted the alien soldier with his visor, and fired the ganvex. The alien fell right away, and Sharjam immediately gave him a nod of thanks. Shortly thereafter, another one of the aliens began shooting at him. But Sibular quickly took care of that individual with his ganvex.

The enemy soldiers in the lobby outnumbered the Mendoken landing party at least 5 to 1. But the sheer technical superiority of the ganvex in being able to target multiple individuals at once, as well as the better protective shielding the Mendoken troopers were wearing, allowed the Mendoken to keep edging forward to the far side of the lobby. The Mendoken lost several of their troopers to deadly boryal rays, but the number of Aftarans who fell was much higher, most of them unconscious but some of them dead thanks to the boryals of Dumyan and Sharjam.

As Marc hopped forward from pillar to pillar, he saw the Aftaran forces draw back further, until the alien commander signaled a formal retreat and they all fled through multiple corridors on the far side of the lobby. He felt relieved, but he also knew they would be back soon, and in greater numbers. There wasn't a moment to lose.

Osalya, who had been here earlier to inspect the resort before the Imgoerin's arrival, pointed the Mendoken troopers towards one of the corridors the Aftaran forces had retreated through. "This way to the grand hall," she said.

A number of Mendoken troopers entered the corridor first, securing the way for everyone else. As Osalya, Marc and the others followed, another huge horde of Aftaran soldiers came into the lobby from the other side. They began firing their boryals at the Mendoken contingent, just as the last batch of Mendoken troopers was entering the corridor.

Marc looked back at the lobby with alarm. "They're going to cut us off from both sides in this corridor!" he yelled.

"We have no choice but to press on through the corridor," Osalya said. "The grand hall is not far now."

Indeed, the grand hall wasn't far, but its entry was closed by a heavy metal door and blocked by more Aftaran soldiers. The fighting continued, with the Mendoken contingent now stretched thin fighting Aftarans on both sides. Marc and Sibular focused on the Aftarans blocking the door to the grand hall, while Dumyan and Sharjam aimed their boryals at the rear. There were no pillars to hide behind in the corridor, which left everyone more vulnerable to getting hit.

More Mendoken troopers fell, as did many Aftaran soldiers. Then Marc heard a loud bang to his left.

"Sibular!" he cried, watching his friend fall to the ground. He jumped over to catch Sibular before he toppled over, but didn't get there in time. Sibular's whole body crashed to the floor with a thud, and then lay still. A bluish liquid began seeping out from what was left of the lower section of his armor casing, directly hit by a boryal ray.

"Oh, my God!" Marc cried in shock, ducking to avoid getting hit by the heavy fire exchange in both directions. "Oh, my God! Sibular, are you... are you alive?"

Sibular turned his head ever so slightly to face Marc. "Yes," he whispered. "I... will... be alright. I... think."

Marc cried out frantically for help. A Mendoken trooper came over and helped pull Sibular to the side of the corridor, propping him up against the wall. Then the trooper quickly analyzed Sibular's wounds.

"He will survive," the trooper said, taking out a small device and spraying something from it over Sibular's broken casing to stop the bleeding. "Provided we can get him back to our ship quickly. His organic-mechanical balancing system has been damaged." Without another word, the trooper went back to fighting.

Marc sat in a crouching position next to Sibular. He wondered how he could possibly help Sibular stay alive. If only he had more knowledge of Mendoken anatomy!

"Marc... you must... continue fighting. Time... running out... Imgoerin." Sibular's voice was getting fainter by the second.

"But I can't leave you here like this!"

"Nothing... you can do... for me here." Sibular's right front limb lifted off the floor and pointed at the door to the grand hall. "Imgoerin... you... must... show him... truth. My life... everyone's life.... depends... on it."

Marc realized with horror that Sibular was right. He wasn't sure how many minutes were left before the signing was to occur, but it couldn't be too many.

"Go... Marc. Take... this." Sibular pointed to the translator device clipped to his shoulder. "Will... need."

Marc reluctantly picked up the translator, but refused to get up. It took Osalya, who had seen what was happening, to come over and change his mind.

Osalya took a quick look at Sibular. "Not to worry, Mr. Zemin. Sibular will be fine. Once we break through that door, all fighting will stop, as the Aftarans will not dare fight in front of all the prominent political figures and media representatives inside the grand hall. And then we will be able to take Sibular back to our ship for treatment."

It was clear, then, that the only way to save Sibular really was to get that door open. So Marc got up and began firing again at the Aftaran soldiers blocking the way. As he kept firing, anger developed inside him, anger directed at those Aftarans and their alien overlords for what they had done to Sibular. He shot harder, faster, taking down as many of the enemy as he could, all the while counting the minutes his friend probably had left to live.

Lord Wazilban stood inside the grand hall of the Bara Dilshai resort, completely unimpressed by what the hall had to offer. As far as he was concerned, what made this hall grand was neither its large size nor the fact that its transparent walls gave a magnificent, unhindered view of the supermassive black hole in the distance. No, the only thing grand about this hall was what was taking place inside it at the current time.

Wazilban had just finished giving his speech to an audience of many important figures. There were media representatives from most of the major news carriers in the Dominion and the Mendoken Republic, as well as leaders of the Aftaran military and regional governors from across the Dominion. The key Aftaran positions of authority he had, of course, replaced with associates of his choice after rising to power, most of them members of his own kinfolk in disguise. Such a move had been necessary to keep advancing the master plan. Otherwise even the simplest of steps would have required fabricating a whole story around, just to keep these righteousness and virtue obsessed Aftarans from raising questions.

The most important figure in the hall for Wazilban today, however, was no Aftaran or anyone of his own kind. It was the leader of the most populous and technologically advanced civilization in the galaxy, the Mendoken Imgoerin himself. His eyes were keenly focused on the Imgoerin, who was now speaking on the stage. He wasn't particularly concerned about the content of the Imgoerin's speech, though. Like his own carefully crafted speech praising the benefits of this new military coalition, the Imgoerin would likely have similar words to say, albeit probably more fact-filled and less emotional.

What Wazilban was more concerned about was the Imgoerin's body language, especially his facial expressions and limb movements, as difficult as such language was to discern on the robotic Mendoken. Although Wazilban had purposely arranged for a complete blockage of all information transmission into and out of the grand hall during this meeting, he was still worried that the technically savvy Mendoken might find a way to get through to the Imgoerin from their ship. And if they did, then any disruptive news would possibly cause the Imgoerin to stomp on his speech or at least show some flicker of uncertainty in his single, 360 degree vision eye.

The last thing Wazilban wanted or needed after all this planning and preparation was for the Imgoerin to feel uncertain about this coalition. At the slightest sign of hesitation on the Imgoerin's part, Wazilban was prepared to insist on and accelerate the signing procedure. He knew only too well that once the Imgoerin willingly signed the covenant, the Mendoken would be bound by law to uphold the terms of the coalition, regardless of whatever information the Imgoerin were to receive after that. Given Mendoken nature to abide by the rule of law no matter what, the Imgoerin would have to keep honoring the covenant until both sides reached a consensus to break it off. And Wazilban had no intention of ever providing the Imgoerin that consensus.

But Wazilban also knew he had good reason to be worried about disruptive news. His army had so far been unable to capture the fugitives who had escaped from his clutches, or any of those pesky Aftaran rebels they had likely joined forces with. That individual from the hitherto unknown, advanced species known as Humans, with his unique ability to see through the carefully designed disguises Wazilban and his associates had adorned for so long, was clearly too much of a danger to remain alive and free. The repeated failures of the Aftaran military commanders to catch this Human and the other fugitives had been intolerable, and he had personally decapitated the heads of several of them to send a clear message to the rest that such failure was no longer an option they could live with. There simply was no greater motivator than fear, as he and his associates well knew.

Since a Mendoken was among the fugitives, Wazilban had deemed it only logical that they would try to make contact with the Imgoerin and his crew during his visit to the Dominion. The visit had, after all, been widely announced well ahead of time, something Wazilban himself had felt compelled to arrange for the sake of rallying the wavering Aftaran public back onto a solid war footing. So now, at the meeting, he was taking no chances. Not only had he taken extra security precautions to tightly restrict all access to the resort, including banning any Mendoken troopers from setting foot on the asteroid, he had also seen to it that all communication into and out of the grand hall was blocked during the event. That did mean no live media broadcasts of the ceremony, but that was a price he was more than willing to pay. Once again, he had applied his principle of prioritization. A couple of hours delay in getting the news out to the public wasn't nearly as critical as preventing any news about the fugitives or rebels getting to the Imgoerin's ears before the signing of the covenant.

There was, however, one major drawback to this total communication blockage. The event had been going on for a good hour and a half, first with a reception welcoming the Mendoken delegation, followed by detailed reports from both the Aftaran and Mendoken sides on how badly their individual wars were progressing. Then Wazilban had taken the podium for a while to explain why this coalition was necessary. And now, finally, the Imgoerin was delivering the very last speech before the actual signing. But during this whole time, Wazilban had not been able to communicate with anyone outside the hall, not even his own forces guarding the resort.

This was a major bother for him, because he hated to be kept in the dark about anything. He had no idea if the fugitives and Aftaran rebels had attempted to make it to the resort or make contact with the Mendoken ship, or whether they had been able to break the barricade his forces had erected around the perimeter of the resort. He thought it unlikely they would be able to pass through the barricade, but even if they did make it to the Mendoken ship, he thought it even less likely the rational thinking Mendoken would attempt to risk landing on the resort or forcibly try to gain entry to the event while their leader was there inside the grand hall, exposed and defenseless. But then again, nothing could be discounted. The Mendoken had surprised him before with their consar attack on Volo-Gaviera. Fortunately he had successfully turned that event into his favor, unleashing a series of events that had eventually led to this meeting today. But the Mendoken could easily surprise him again, and this time with less desirable consequences.

Wazilban had also made it clear that no Aftaran soldiers were to enter the grand hall during the event, nor were any boryals or other weapons to be allowed inside. Broadcast images of firearms, armed guards or any conflict at what was supposed to be a meeting between two friendly allies would send the wrong message to the masses. In any case, there was only one main door into and out of the hall, which, surprising as it was for a hall this size, was necessary to maintain the clear view of the black hole through the transparent walls. That door was going to be well guarded from the outside, so he had felt comfortable with this decision to keep the guards out of the hall.

But now, during the event itself, he felt anxious, counting the seconds as the Imgoerin's speech came to an end. A couple of times, he thought he heard muffled noises behind the main door. But he dismissed the idea, attributing the sounds to his own nervous imagination. The walls and doors of the hall were far too thick to allow any noise to pass through anyway.

Finally, the Imgoerin uttered his last words, and a brief applause rippled through the audience. Relieved, Wazilban walked up to the stage to stand next to the Imgoerin. All those years of thoughtful deliberation and tactful, secret execution were about to result in a major step forward for the master plan. It was going to be a great moment for him and his people.

Both leaders faced the audience together, as two large screens appeared above them in the air. Both screens scrolled through the text of the covenant, one displaying it in the Mendoken language and the other in the Aftaran language of Mareefi.

One of Wazilban's aides addressed the audience. "Fellow Aftarans and Mendoken, we will now proceed with the signing."

The audience applauded as Wazilban lifted his hand, allowing his face to be scanned by rays from the screens. A holographic image of his face then appeared in the lower right corner of both screens, indicating that he had signed the covenant.

The time had come. "Franzek, your turn," he said to the Imgoerin.

The Imgoerin got ready to raise one of his front limbs. But at that very moment, a powerful explosion suddenly rocked the grand hall. The ground shook violently, causing many in the audience to lose their balance and fall to the floor.

Struggling to keep his own balance, Wazilban turned to look at the main entrance. As the smoke and dust around the entrance gradually dispersed, he realized to his dismay that the large, heavy metal door blocking all access to the grand hall had been blasted away. Despite all the precautions he and his associates had taken, his worst fear was about to turn into reality. It was clear now that the time had come to prepare for the inevitable.

Chapter 33

Marc followed Osalya into the grand hall, only too glad that the fighting had come to an end. After a long, raging battle, the Mendoken contingent had overpowered the Aftarans blocking the entrance, and had then blasted the door open with explosives. Almost immediately, the Aftaran soldiers advancing from the rear had stopped shooting and had retreated out of sight. Just as Osalya had predicted, the Aftarans would no longer fight once the door to the grand hall was opened. A battle scene with the Mendoken would be too major an embarrassment for their leader in front of the Imgoerin, especially while their two civilizations were about to embark on a new alliance of military cooperation.

Some of the Mendoken troopers had then carried their wounded to the shuttles and transported them back to the mother ship. Marc had felt the strong urge to go back with them and make sure Sibular received adequate medical attention, but he knew he was needed far more urgently here, now.

"How many of them do you see?" Dumyan whispered into Marc's ear. Both he and Sharjam were right behind Marc as they entered the grand hall.

"The aliens?" At first, all Marc noticed was the mesmerizing view of the supermassive black hole through the transparent walls on the far side. He forced his eyes to focus on the inside of the hall, and found a wide seating arrangement similar to that of a semicircular amphitheater. He had just entered at the very top level of the amphitheater, and a long flight of steps in front led the way down to the main stage. The audience rows were filled, mostly with Aftarans, some Mendoken, and a surprisingly large number of the aliens. Different kinds of equipment were spread across the hall, probably being used by media representatives to record this historic event.

Marc could see two figures standing on the stage. One was an alien, undoubtedly Lord Wazilban, and next to him was a Mendoken who had to be the Imgoerin himself. Above their heads were two large screens suspended in the air with no visible supports, displaying text for everyone in the hall to see.

"The aliens are everywhere!" Marc whispered to Dumyan. "I've never seen so many of them in one place before."

"I am not surprised," Dumyan replied. "We are surrounded by the cream of Aftaran leadership. These aliens have clearly gained hold of all the key positions of power in our society."

Osalya was already floating towards the stage. Marc began walking down the steps behind her, followed closely by Dumyan and Sharjam. The Mendoken troopers stayed back, guarding the entrance to the hall.

All the members of the audience seemed stunned, turning their heads to look at the four individuals descending towards the stage. Some of them quietly whispered questions to each other, while others just stared in apparent confusion.

Lord Wazilban was the first to break the deafening silence in the hall. "What is the meaning of this unwelcome, unauthorized interruption?"

Osalya ignored Wazilban, speaking directly to the Imgoerin instead as she floated up onto the stage. "You must not sign this covenant, Franzek."

Her words echoed across the hall through its inbuilt sound propagation system, and members of the audience gasped right away in surprise.

"I beg your pardon!" Wazilban exclaimed. "Leave the stage immediately! Our two societies are about to embark on a historic journey. This is no time for games! Leave, or be forced to leave!"

Osalya didn't budge, so Wazilban called for the guards.

In the meantime, Marc, Dumyan and Sharjam had reached the stage, but were waiting at its edge. Marc's eyes met Wazilban's, and the familiar fear shot through Marc's body right away. He noticed a slight waver in Wazilban's usually confident expression, as if Wazilban was a little afraid himself.

The Mendoken troopers were evidently doing their job holding the entrance. Wazilban called again, but no Aftaran guards came into the hall. He then called on the audience to help remove the intruders.

Several of the aliens in the audience got up to rush to Wazilban's aid. The Imgoerin's bodyguards, who had been standing at the base of the stage, immediately got up onto the stage to protect the Imgoerin and Osalya. Marc raised his ganvex in anticipation of the upcoming conflict, and Dumyan and Sharjam did the same with their boryals.

"Stop!" the Imgoerin ordered. "All in the audience, please stay in your assigned positions." His voice was deep and authoritative, but monotonous like those of all Mendoken.

Everyone froze in their tracks, not only due to the Imgoerin's command, but also because a number of armed Mendoken troopers had just entered the hall and were rapidly advancing to secure the stage.

Marc looked at the Imgoerin, a tall Mendoken, who, like Osalya, was wearing shiny metal armor with symbols written over it. His skin, however, was lighter in color. On his head was a black hat, the one and only black hat in the entire Mendoken Republic, its unique color signifying the very top of the Mendoken hierarchy.

Wazilban seemed astonished. "But Franzek, you cannot be serious! These are criminals, terrorists! They are trying to sabotage the creation of our coalition because they want our enemies to destroy us. Surely you cannot allow that to happen!"

The aliens in the audience began shouting slogans in support of their leader, and called on the Imgoerin to ignore the intruders and to sign the covenant.

But the Imgoerin was unmoved by the commotion. "Whoever the other intruders may be, Osalya is my trusted top aide, no criminal or terrorist. I will listen to what she has to say before I sign the covenant. Considering all that is at stake here for our two peoples, you will surely offer me that courtesy, Wazilban?"

Wazilban did not look happy at all, but obviously knew he could not force the Imgoerin to sign the covenant, especially not in front of the armed Mendoken troopers and all the media luminaries in the audience. The media would report the coercion to both the Mendoken and Aftaran populations, voiding the effectiveness of the coalition before it had even begun. So, despite all the booing and jeering from his kinfolk in the audience, he moved out of the way and allowed Osalya to approach the Imgoerin.

Osalya and the Imgoerin hummed silently with each other for a while, barring anyone else's translators from picking up their words. Marc waited anxiously, keeping an eye on Wazilban and the other aliens to make sure none of them attempted any sudden movements. Luckily none of them did. Perhaps they were all too tense themselves, wondering what was going to happen next.

Finally the Imgoerin spoke. "I request the Human and his two Aftaran companions to join us on the stage."

The aliens in the audience now were roaring in protest. Wazilban pleaded with the Imgoerin, but to no avail.

"Please, Wazilban, you will honor us as your guests in the Dominion," the Imgoerin said calmly. "You will extend to us the courtesy the Aftaran people have always been renowned for."

Wazilban, evidently at a loss of words, shook his head and motioned to the audience to stay quiet.

"This is it, showtime!" Marc thought, climbing up the five steps to the stage.

"This is preposterous!" Wazilban exclaimed, letting out a nervous laugh. "Complete, utter lies, Franzek! These are lunatic terrorists, who will stop at nothing to spread any slander they can come up with to prevent us from defeating our enemies!"

Marc had just finished describing that Wazilban was actually an alien in disguise, as were many others in the audience, all holding key positions of power in the Dominion. He had also explained what he believed the agenda of these aliens was.

The aliens in the audience protested loudly as Marc made his claims, while many of the Aftarans whispered to each other in surprise. The Imgoerin, however, remained silent.

"They have no evidence to support these laughable allegations!" Wazilban continued. "We all know that I am an Aftaran in flesh and blood, my whole life dedicated to the good of the Aftar. The Aftaran people have chosen me to lead them, to defend them and everything they cherish. All I have done since I became their leader has been in their interests and for their security. I would never deceive my own people like the way this... this nobody from an unknown species is claiming." He paused. "Franzek, would you take the word of these terrorists over that of mine? They should be taken away and executed for their crimes and their lies!"

The Imgoerin waved Wazilban aside. "Have you any evidence, Human?" he asked Marc.

Marc swallowed hard. "Yes, we most certainly do." He felt more than grateful for the question, as risky as he knew the procedure he was about to submit himself to was. Sharjam had left little doubt about that.

Marc turned to face the audience, while Sharjam walked up to stand beside him. Sharjam took out a scripture coin from inside his robe and placed it flat on his palm. He then ran a finger from his other hand around the edge of the coin, causing the coin to glow brilliantly in a golden color.

"O sacred Scripture of Truthfulness, unveil your power, for your laws have been broken!" Sharjam's voice boomed across the grand hall, catching the undivided attention of every member of the audience.

Bright golden symbols appeared above the coin in the air, large enough for everyone in the audience to see. The symbols took the shape of the ancient Altareezyan script, displaying the following verse:

There is no place for treachery amongst the righteous,
No room for deceit amidst the truthful.
Harsh is the crime committed by those who deceive,
And harsher still if they deceive the righteous.

Many Aftarans in the audience appeared to recognize the verse, and began murmuring to each other in excitement. Wazilban tried to advance towards Marc, but was stopped by the Imgoerin's bodyguards.

"Silence, please!" Dumyan shouted. He was standing at the edge of the stage, right in front of the audience. "The next step requires acute concentration."

The hall fell into a hush right away.

Sharjam now moved behind Marc, and placed the glowing coin on Marc's head.

Marc felt the warmth of the coin spreading slowly down his head and neck to the rest of his body. The time had finally come to release his burden, the burden of a secret that had haunted the entire galaxy for so long.

"Reveal the truth!" Sharjam thundered. "Expose the treachery you see before you!"

The verse disappeared, and was instantly replaced by the next one:

Glory and fame they may find for a while,
But fear them not, nor lose hope.
For while they strive with might and main
To mask their faces and hide their tracks,
Never shall they escape the words of truth.

The audience began to murmur nervously again, but Marc paid no attention to that. He was far more concerned with the searing heat that was now rippling through his body, as if every part of him was glowing like the scripture coin on his head. Suddenly the words of the verse melted into a single ball of fire in the air above him. Then the ball shot straight into his chest. A sharp pain tore through his heart, causing him to scream in agony. He would have collapsed to the floor, were it not for some invisible force holding him upright.

Seconds later, a brilliant circle of light burst out from around his heart with a loud bang. The circle spread out rapidly to the edges of the entire hall, slicing right through the hearts of everyone on the stage and in the audience.

As the light faded away, so did the pain in Marc's heart and the heat in his body, and so did every last shred of his strength. Falling backwards as his legs gave way, he would have hit the floor with a thud if Sharjam hadn't caught him in the nick of time.

"It worked!" Sharjam whispered into Marc's ear. "The deed is done. My, are those aliens ugly!"

The hall was filled with shrieks. Not shrieks of pain, but shrieks of astonishment and realization, for everyone could now see what Marc had been able to see all along.

Sharjam pulled Marc off the stage and to the side, away from the main focus of everyone in the hall.

Dumyan addressed the audience from the stage. "Fellow Aftarans and Mendoken guests, the mighty conspiracy is at last exposed! You see before you the extent to which these aliens have infiltrated our society and taken over all the key positions." He pointed at select aliens in the audience. "Including the position of the supreme leader himself!" he added, pointing at Wazilban, now clearly visible as an alien to all. "They are single handedly responsible for all the damage caused to our civilization and to our relations with other civilizations over the past several years."

Wazilban laughed nervously again, and many of the aliens in the audience joined him in a chorus of laughter. "Very nice, sons of the heretic Autamrin! An entertaining show of ancient magic! Fortunately our people and our Mendoken friends are not silly or gullible enough to fall for such childish pranks. Enough games for now, however. The Imgoerin and I have much urgent business to attend to. Leave the hall immediately! Your treason shall be dealt with later."

A number of Aftaran soldiers had been allowed by the Mendoken troopers to enter the hall in the meantime. But they did not interfere, choosing instead to silently watch the spectacle from a distance.

"Childish pranks?" Dumyan said, sounding incredulous. "If that is all this is, then why not try undoing what we have just done?"

"The practice of such magic is strictly forbidden in the Dominion," Wazilban replied. "Only criminals like you would have the nerve to maintain the skills necessary for these tricks!"

"Forbidden since you came to power!" Sharjam retorted. "Obviously to prevent anyone from revealing your true nature."

Wazilban pretended to ignore Sharjam's comment. "This magic trick is no proof of anything!" he implored to the Imgoerin. "Please, we should not let this nonsense interfere with our plans for the coalition."

Before the Imgoerin could reply, Dumyan spoke again. "So you want more proof? Then you shall have it!" He jumped down from the stage and faced one of the aliens in the first row of the audience. "You, what is your name and clan?"

The alien seemed unsure what to do. "My name is Jarez, of the 852nd generation of the Lemshar clan," he said in a hesitant tone.

"Thank you, Jarez. An honor to meet a member of the famous Lemshar clan! Can you tell me who the first member of your clan was?"

"Of course! It was Yusabir, the legendary philosopher."

"Very good! And who was his wife?"

"Fairah, of the 103rd generation of the Sumidin clan," the alien replied, starting to appear more confident.

"Is there a point to these questions?" Wazilban demanded from the stage. "This heretic terrorist is making a mockery of every Aftaran!"

"Excellent, Jarez!" Dumyan continued. "Now, tell me, which verse of which Scripture did Yusabir and Fairah decide to put on the seal of the Lemshar clan?"

The look of confidence on the alien's face was abruptly replaced by one of confusion. "Seal? What seal?"

Dumyan seemed to look confused as well. "Why, the seal given to you when you were born, by your parents! Every Aftaran has one of his or her own clan. It is a prized possession, one each of us holds dear and hidden, a personal secret always kept locked away safely in our homes. Surely you know that?"

"Oh, *that* seal!" the alien said, trying his best to recover from his blunder. "Yes, of course. I, ah, just do not remember which verse is on it."

The Aftarans in the audience began murmuring to one another.

"You do not remember? Well, that is a shame!" Dumyan looked up at the rest of the audience. "Anybody else here from the Lemshar clan?"

A couple of Aftaran hands went up, and Dumyan picked one of them.

"Madam, please tell our forgetful friend here which verse is on the seal of the Lemshar clan."

The Aftaran hesitated at first, reluctant to reveal such a cherished secret.

Sharjam spoke out. "It is permissible to reveal the verse on your seal, if it is necessary to do so for the sake of justice."

"Very well. It is verse 373 from the Scripture of Faith."

"Indeed!" Dumyan said. "Would you concur?" he asked the other Aftaran who had put his hand up.

"Yes. I have known this since before I could speak."

"As you should have! We have been raised to never forget the verses on our seals. It is a part of who we are as Aftarans, even though we never speak of this practice in public. The question I have is: what has this alien done with the real Jarez? Did he kill him and take his place? Or did Jarez really ever exist in the first place? Given the large sizes and the widespread distribution of some of our clans, it may prove difficult to hunt down the true answer. And that is something these aliens clearly knew and took advantage of."

Dumyan then repeated the same procedure with three other aliens. None of the aliens knew which verses were on the seals of their clans they claimed to be a part of, but other Aftarans of the same clans knew them just fine.

The audience was in uproar. Aftarans, now convinced that this whole thing was no magic trick, were hurling insults at the aliens. The aliens in turn began moving away from the rest of the audience, gathering up on one side of the stage next to their leader.

"You see?" Dumyan said, addressing the whole audience. "They are clearly not Aftarans! They do not even know one of the most basic tenets of who we are. Do you need any more proof?"

"No!" was the unanimous roar of a reply, coming from Aftaran civilians and soldiers alike.

"And how about you, sir?" Dumyan asked, turning back to the stage to face Wazilban. "Need any more proof?"

But Wazilban was nowhere to be found, and nor were any of the other aliens. They had all vanished into thin air, in one big flash.

The five Shoyra-class vessels that pulled away from the Bara Dilshai resort were clearly visible through the transparent walls of the grand hall.

"They all disappeared in front of our eyes, just like your two prisoners back on Meenjaza!" Marc said to Sharjam, staring at the ships carrying the aliens away from the asteroid.

"Yes, those aliens obviously have powerful capabilities," Sharjam said angrily.

The ships headed off in the direction of the supermassive black hole. Marc wondered for a moment if they were actually going to go into the black hole. "That would be suicide!" he thought.

The hall was in total chaos. Prominent Aftarans and Mendoken in the audience were engaged in loud debate with each other, trying to make head or tail of all that had happened. Dumyan was speaking to the Imgoerin, explaining who he and his brother were and how they had ended up here, as well as Marc's ability to see through the aliens' disguise and how Sharjam had used the power of the Scriptures to uncover it. Aftaran soldiers and Mendoken troopers alike were scrambling out of the hall towards their own ships, vowing to pursue the aliens until they were caught. The soldiers had also contacted the crews of the Aftaran vessels surrounding the asteroid, instructing them to block any ships attempting to break out through the barricade.

"We must go after them!" Marc said, just as the first vessel took off in pursuit of the ships carrying the aliens.

Sharjam agreed. He was about to follow Marc up the aisle and out of the hall, when his eyes seemed to notice something in the sky. "Marc, look at that!"

Marc turned around to look back. "Holy smokes!" he yelled. "It can't be!"

But it was. Five blue specks had appeared in space in the path of the escaping ships, right before the barricade of Aftaran vessels. The specks quickly grew into circles, just as each ship came to a stop inside one of the circles. The circles then increased in thickness, becoming spheres that completely engulfed the ships.

"You know what is happening, Marc?" Sharjam asked, as everyone in the hall fell quiet and began watching the scene outside.

"Yes! The aliens are about to escape into a consar!"

A single tunnel leading off into a different dimension appeared behind the spheres. Then, with bursts of energy, the spheres catapulted one by one into the tunnel and disappeared, barely escaping the fire from the vessels in hot pursuit.

"That's it, we've lost them!" Marc said, shaking his head in dismay. He couldn't believe it. These aliens had consar technology! They had probably been the masters of consars all along. If they could travel through consars, perhaps they had come from very far away, maybe even another galaxy. That would certainly explain why nobody had so far been able to identify their kind.

But now, there would be no way to find out for sure. Since their cover had been exposed, the aliens had decided to leave, probably returning to wherever they had come from. They had most likely alerted all the other aliens scattered across the Dominion to immediately leave as well. There would be no way to find out anymore who these aliens really were, or the reasons for their agenda of annihilation. They had disappeared without a trace.

Or had they? Marc's eyes focused again on the spot where the ships had disappeared. The tunnel was still open! What was going on?

Osalya floated over to where Marc was standing. "It appears we are in luck, Mr. Zemin," she said.

"How so?"

"The strong gravitational pull of the supermassive black hole is preventing the consar entrance from closing."

Chapter 34

The Mendoken shuttles returned safely to their Aima-11 mother ship, and landed in one of the ship's many hangars. Sharjam waited eagerly as the shuttle he was on came to a complete stop. He stood by the door, and as soon as it slid open, was the first to step out. Standing there on the hangar floor was Raiha, the one he so dearly loved. He ran to her and embraced her, his heart filled with joy.

"Oh, Sharjam, I am so glad!" Raiha said, tears welling in her eyes as she hugged him tightly. "I prayed nonstop to the Creator to bring you back to me, alive and well."

"The Creator has listened to you," Sharjam said, smiling and struggling to hold back his own tears. "How are you feeling now?" He took a step back to gaze at her. As always, she looked absolutely beautiful.

"Like new! These Mendoken doctors are amazing with their skills and medical technology. They not only healed my wounds, but also smoothed the skin and feathers. I guarantee you will not be able to find a single scar anywhere on my body."

"Well, maybe I should do a detailed search then, just to make sure," Sharjam said mischievously.

Before Raiha could respond, Dumyan approached them. "Sharjam, I am supposed to meet shortly with the Imgoerin to discuss what to do next about the aliens. You should come with me."

"Go ahead, Dumyan," Sharjam said. "I want to spend some time with Raiha before we go off again."

Dumyan looked surprised. "You are actually willing to let me make a decision for the both of us?"

"My brother, I have never had more faith in you and your often hasty, irrational decisions as I do now."

Dumyan's face slowly broke into a smile. He winked at Raiha and walked away.

"Well!" Raiha said, raising her owl-like ears. "I wish your father were here to see how far you two have progressed. Remember the horror stories you used to tell me before, how you and your brother constantly argued about anything and everything?"

Sharjam nodded. "I think that was my father's whole intention in sending Dumyan and me off by ourselves to confront Wazilban." He paused. "And on the topic of my father, there is something I need to talk to you about."

The two of them walked to the transparent wall on the far side of the hangar, and admired the clear view of the ship's internal city in the distance. Sharjam first related to Raiha everything that had happened at the Bara Dilshai resort. She had already heard the summary report, but now wanted to hear all the details.

"News reports are also coming in that other Aftarans in key positions across the Dominion have suddenly disappeared," Raiha said after Sharjam had finished.

Sharjam frowned. "All of them aliens, no doubt, heading back to wherever they came from. Wazilban must have broadcast the message before disappearing through the consar."

"So what will happen next?"

"We will follow Wazilban and catch him! We cannot let him get away with what he has done."

"How? By going into the consar?" Raiha didn't seem to like that idea too much.

"What other choice is there? It is risky, I know, but we must find him and his alien associates before they strike us again."

"If you are going, then I am going with you!"

Sharjam knew this was coming. "No! You are not. It is too dangerous."

"If it is not dangerous enough for you, then it is not for me either," Raiha said defiantly. "I am not going to lose you again."

Sharjam shook his head. "Listen to me, Raiha! This mission is not going to be anything like our playful adventures on Meenjaza. No Aftaran has ever traveled through a consar before. We will have to rely on the Mendoken, who themselves have not yet perfected consar technology. If we ever make it to the other side, wherever that might be, we have no idea what awaits us there. There may be trillions of those aliens with sophisticated weapons, waiting to pulverize us the moment we show our faces. From a statistical point of view, it is a downright foolhardy mission."

"So why are you going, then?"

"Because I have to. After what Wazilban did to our father, Dumyan and I have to defend the honor of our family and our clan. We must bring Wazilban to justice, or die trying."

Raiha's expression turned both sour and sad. "And what about my honor? If I go with you and help you bring Wazilban to justice, I can finally establish a good reputation in front of your family and clan. Then they will be more inclined to accept me one day as your wife."

"Of course! And that is precisely why I need you to take on another mission yourself, one that is just as important for my family and clan. Considering the upheaval that will undoubtedly rock the Dominion now that Wazilban has been exposed, you are the only one Dumyan and I can trust to take this on while we are gone. And if anything should happen to Dumyan and me, our family and clan will always remain in good hands as long as they are in yours."

"You sure you want to come along? I think you need more time to recover."

"I will be fine, Marc," Sibular insisted, his voice back to its old self again. "I just needed a new balancing system."

"Well, that and this shiny new armor you have, my man!" Zorina chimed in.

The three friends were back inside the Mendoken Aima-11 ship. Like Raiha, Zorina was fully recovered now, and Sibular was well on his way to getting better. He had been brought back to the ship in the nick of time, just as his consciousness had begun fading for good. The doctors had spent a good hour operating on him, which in the world of Mendoken medicine was an eternity. Fortunately, as it usually was with Mendoken medical interventions, the operation had been completely successful.

A couple of hours had passed since the disappearance of Wazilban and his alien associates through the consar, but the consar's entrance still remained open. Due to the strong gravitational pull of the black hole behind, it was now bent back at its edges and stretched into more of a square shape.

"Wazilban clearly didn't take the black hole's presence into account when he planned his escape," Marc thought, as the three friends left the medical facility on a vehicle and headed towards one of the hangars on the outer edge of the ship. "But then, Wazilban probably didn't expect to have to escape at this time and at this location." This was good news, because it probably meant that Wazilban didn't know the consar entrance on this side was still open, and thus wasn't expecting anyone to follow him.

Of course, nobody had a clue where the consar led to or what was waiting at the other end. Mendoken scientists on board the ship had already tried using their sophisticated tracing instruments to plot the entire path of the consar, but so far had failed. None of the probing signals sent by the instruments had been able to make it back out of the consar. The conclusion – the only way to find out where this consar led was for someone to travel through it.

The Aftarans did not have any consar technology, nor did they have much scientific knowledge of what consars were really about. After consultation with the Aftarans, the Imgoerin had therefore taken the decision to send a Mendoken scout ship through the consar for a reconnaissance mission. Fortunately the Aima-11 vessel was carrying a number of scout ships and fighter vessels equipped with consar travel capability. This was something the Imgoerin had insisted on before leaving the Republic for the Dominion, just in case they were attacked by the Volona en route. The technology, while still far from perfect, had recently been enhanced to avoid a repeat of the tragic incident at Volo-Gaviera.

In order for the mission to remain inconspicuous and agile, however, only one scout ship was to go through the consar. And Marc, Sibular and Zorina were determined to be on it. This journey would perhaps be their most perilous yet, but none of them were deterred by the dangers that lay ahead.

The vehicle arrived in the hangar and stopped in front of the consar equipped ship. It was a standard Sil-5 scout ship, shaped somewhat like a supersonic jetfighter with a sturdy wing on each side, two slanted tails in the back, and a main tube-like body. Overall, it was probably no bigger than a Boeing 737 airplane, Marc guessed, although it definitely looked a lot sleeker.

The three friends descended from the vehicle and joined a group of individuals standing in front of the craft. Several Mendoken troopers and Aftaran soldiers were there, as were Dumyan, Sharjam, Osalya and the Imgoerin himself.

The Imgoerin greeted the three newcomers. "Welcome. Both my people and the Aftar owe you tremendous gratitude for exposing this conspiracy in the nick of time, a conspiracy that has haunted the Dominion and the whole galaxy for so long. I do not fully comprehend how you were able to see through the disguise of these aliens, Mr. Zemin, nor do I understand the enchantment that Sharjam enacted to give the rest of us that same vision. What I do know is what I saw and heard, and it is clear to me that these aliens are highly organized and committed to their cause. Whatever their intentions, they have a long term agenda, and I think it unlikely they will have given up so easily. They will be back, and likely in greater numbers. We must figure out when, how and why, so that we can defend ourselves and perhaps even strike first. That is the purpose of this mission."

The Imgoerin paused for a moment, before continuing. "I can understand why the Aftarans here want to risk their lives for this mission. They have personally suffered immeasurable losses because of these aliens. But why you three?"

Zorina spoke first. "Respected Imgoerin, I want this war and enmity between my people and yours to end, once and for all. My people are not behind the consar attacks on the Republic. I am convinced these aliens are behind it, and I plan to prove it."

"I am beginning to feel the same way," the Imgoerin said. "And I look forward to the evidence you bring back."

"Respected Imgoerin, I just want to see this conspiracy completely unveiled, especially considering my somewhat inexplicable involvement in unveiling its top layer," Marc said.

"Understood, Mr. Zemin," the Imgoerin said. "What about you, Sibular? I would hate to lose such a fine engineer as you to this dangerous mission. You have demonstrated remarkable skill and courage over the past few weeks. The entire Republic is in your debt."

Marc was happy to see Sibular get so much recognition from the Imgoerin for his contributions to the Republic. For a Mendoken, there was no greater honor. Sibular's virtual world experience back in the Volonan Empire had finally come true, even if not quite in the same way as he had originally imagined.

"I thank you for the kind words, respected Imgoerin," Sibular said. "I am the resident space travel and consar expert. I believe it only makes sense for me to join my friends on this mission, in case they encounter issues getting into or out of the consar."

"He used the word 'friends'!" Marc thought. For a Mendoken to use that word was downright unreal. Perhaps all the time Sibular had spent with a human and a Volonan had caused a few of their traits to rub off on him.

Marc then walked up to Dumyan and Sharjam, who were getting ready to enter the scout ship. "Where's Raiha?" he asked. "Is she alright?"

"She is fine," Sharjam said. "But she will not be joining us on this mission. Instead, she is leaving for the remote system of Afta-Johran, to bring our father and his followers back to Meenjaza. She will also free the High Clerics from their prison on Meenjaza."

"You're certain they'll all be safe on Meenjaza?" Marc asked.

"Certain? No. Everything lies in the hands of the Creator. But now that the public knows the truth about Wazilban, we are starting to get reports from the nearest star systems that many Aftarans want our father reinstated as their supreme leader. All the Aftaran soldiers here have already pledged their allegiance to him." Sharjam grinned. "By the will of the Creator, after all this time, the honor of our family and our clan will finally be restored!"

*   *   *

The scout ship took off and sped out of the hangar, leaving its Aima-11 mother ship and a well wishing Imgoerin and Osalya behind. On board were the Mendoken pilot, six Mendoken troopers and six Aftaran soldiers, all of them handpicked due to their high ranks and noteworthy reputations. Accompanying them were Marc, Sibular, Zorina, Dumyan and Sharjam.

Due to their knowledge of and experience in flying through consars, Marc and Sibular had been chosen to accompany the pilot in the cockpit, where they watched over the consar instruments. Everybody else was in the main cabin behind, in between the stacks of surveillance equipment. Seats had been made available for all the non-Mendoken on board.

Marc watched as the pilot fearlessly maneuvered the ship toward the consar. He eyed the tunnel entrance ahead, now no more than tens of miles away. Its shape was almost completely square, with the four corners pulled way back and its middle section bulging out. Inside, the tunnel was ablaze in a big whirlpool of different colors, all flowing into the gaping hole in the middle. It looked quite scary, but he reminded himself that he had been through a consar once before.

As the ship approached the consar entrance, Sibular pressed an icon on the 3D screen above the consar instruments. The ship's surface lit up right away in brilliant white, and a wide blue circle began forming around the ship. The blue circle grew in thickness, soon encompassing the entire ship in a sphere. To Marc, it was all too familiar.

Sibular and the pilot both dropped from their floating positions and locked the bottom of their encasings to the floor.

Marc held on with all his strength to his seat. "This is it, no more turning back," he thought.

The sphere lunged forward into the tunnel. Marc instantly felt a tremendous force pushing him back into his seat. Like the last time, he could barely keep his eyes open, and felt he would pass out at any moment. Like the last time, however, he didn't. The gravitational pull quickly subsided, allowing him to relax and open his eyes again. They had successfully entered the consar!

Through the lightly transparent sphere, he could see the wall of the tunnel, filled with random shapes of different colors, constantly changing shape and size. Bands of thin matter from a different dimension drifted through the tunnel, right through the sphere and through the ship, without causing any physical damage.

"Well, Sibular?" he asked.

"Unfortunately there is no more information than what we had before entering," Sibular said, closely monitoring the data readouts on his screen. "The signal probes sent from our mother ship could have failed to return for a number of reasons, including interference from radiation from the supermassive black hole, or significant attenuation during consar entry or exit. But now that we are inside the consar, there is no reason why the signal probes I am sending out should not be able to return. Yet they are attenuating to negligible levels before reaching the end. This is surprising, because the signals are designed to easily traverse up to 2 million light years of equivalent space in our regular 3 dimensions."

"You mean...?"

"We appear to have entered a very long consar, Marc."

The minutes ticked by as the scout ship traveled through the consar. The minutes soon turned to hours, the hours to days. Outside, the tunnel had turned totally dark, and the bands of matter floating through the ship had become much thicker and more numerous. Still, there was no end in sight.

Marc, Zorina and the Aftarans on board tried to make the best of their cramped living conditions, taking advantage of little corners in the main cabin to set up camp where they could sit or sleep. Marc and Zorina were only too glad that the Aftarans had brought plenty of spicy food rations with them, just in case the journey turned out to be a long one. The two of them regularly joined the Aftarans every few hours for a meal in the rear of the craft.

The Mendoken troopers stayed alert and busy throughout, regularly monitoring the surveillance equipment for any activity. Sibular and the pilot remained in the cockpit, never once coming back to the main cabin.

As the days passed, the occupants of the ship grew more and more concerned about the distance they were covering. It soon became clear that, in the equivalent of their own 3 dimensions, they had traveled much farther than the entire width of the Glaessan galaxy and even the distance to the neighboring Andromeda galaxy. Nobody from the Glaessan galaxy had ever traveled this far before, nor had anyone spent this much time inside a consar. Some began to question if their bodies would somehow get permanently altered by the consar's different dimensions, while others wondered if they would ever make it back home alive.

The uncertainty only kept growing, because nobody knew how much further the end of the consar was. Not a single one of Sibular's signal probes had so far returned, and he was still sending out a new one every hour. Yet through it all, not a single one of the ship's occupants expressed doubt about the mission or whether it was better to turn back. Everyone's dedication to the cause was absolute.

And so was Marc's. Regardless of the uncomfortable conditions on board, the length of the journey through unexplored dimensions or the possible dangers that lay ahead, he was determined to get to the bottom of this conspiracy. He was determined to find out why this had all happened, who was ultimately behind it, and what his role in all of it really was. Sure, he was the 'Sign' who had unveiled the conspiracy, but how deep did this conspiracy really run? Why had he of all gazillions of beings in the galaxy been picked for this cause? Who had picked him anyway? And how had he been given this capability to 'see' that which others couldn't?

Dumyan and Sharjam had not been able to provide him with the answers to these questions. Both of them had instead suggested that it would be best to ask the High Clerics directly upon their return. The High Clerics would most likely know some of the answers, but not all. The rest Marc would have to discover for himself, and the best way to do that would be to follow the conspirators until all was revealed. And so here he was, on that very quest.

During the meals, Marc spent a lot of time conversing with the Aftarans. The same soldiers he had earlier been battling with for his life were now sitting next to him, sharing food and friendly stories. All signs of enmity were gone.

"It's amazing what a difference knowing the truth makes, especially when truth is on your side," he thought.

He generally found the Aftarans on board to be very warm individuals, easy to talk to and get along with. While they were very religious and firm in their convictions, they were also highly knowledgeable, tolerant and understanding of others. The suspicions he had always had of religious people back on Earth, of being ignorant, narrow-minded zealots with hidden agendas of conversion or extermination, clearly didn't apply to these Aftarans. He found the time he was spending with them to be quite refreshing and educational.

Over the days, Marc noticed that Sharjam seemed a little sad, spending a lot of time in solitude and often engaged in lengthy periods of meditation or prayer. On the seventh day, Marc finally mustered the courage to ask him what was wrong.

"It is nothing," Sharjam said, as Marc sat down next to him. "I am apprehensive of what lies ahead, like everyone else here."

Marc smiled. "I think I know you better than that by now, Sharjam. You're not the kind to be afraid of danger, and definitely not the kind to be saddened by it."

Sharjam sighed. "Ay, I suppose you are right." He was silent for a long moment, and then spoke softly. "But I am afraid. I am afraid of what will happen to me and..." He paused again. "Let me ask you something, Marc. Have you ever had to give up something you truly treasured, something that meant everything to you, something without which you thought life would no longer have any meaning? Something you were forced to give up because you had no other choice?"

Marc was taken aback by the question. "Do you mean something, or...

someone?"

Sharjam grinned, somewhat sheepishly. "Someone, I suppose."

"Yes, I have."

"And if you had the chance to turn back the clock, would you let it happen again?"

Marc couldn't help chuckling to himself, thinking how hard he had once tried to literally turn back the clock. "No, most definitely not! I would do everything in my power to keep that special someone with me."

"Why? The circumstances would still be the same, would they not?"

"The circumstances maybe, but not my point of view. If I went back in time, I would know how lonely my life would be in the future without that individual, because I would already have lived that lonely life. Clearly I wouldn't want to go through that life again, or else why would I have chosen to go back in time in the first place?"

"But if I changed the course of events to be with that someone, it would negatively affect many other things of importance, many of them beyond my control."

Marc raised his eyebrows. "Ah! But it's all about priorities, isn't it? And considering what you know now, would you still give everything the same order of priority as you did back then?"

"No," Sharjam admitted. "Probably not. But if I choose to be with that individual, it might hurt others who care about me and that individual. It could have societal repercussions for the reputations of both our families."

"But wouldn't the others who care about you and the other individual just want you both to be happy? Wouldn't they understand if you two took a decision for your own happiness? If they really cared about you, wouldn't they eventually learn to forgive you and learn to live with your decision? I mean, how bad can it be? You're not torturing or killing anyone, or breaking any laws for that matter. Right?"

Sharjam said nothing. Instead, he stared out the window at the wall of the consar tunnel, seemingly deep in thought.

Marc sat there silently next to the tall Aftaran. This conversation was reminding him just a little too much of his own relationship with Iman, especially how he had lost her to her family and culture. Of course, for him there was no turning back the clock, no second chance. Iman was gone, and even if he did ever make it back to Earth one day, there was next to no hope of ever getting back to together with her. And he most certainly didn't want Sharjam to share that same fate.

So Marc spoke, somewhat forcefully. "You know, I once gave up my chance to be with the love of my life, because I didn't fight for her as much as I should have. I backed away from confronting those who opposed our union, never even trying to address their grievances or gain their acceptance. So they won. Had I stuck it out and fought, I might have won. Or perhaps both sides could have won. But I just gave up and walked away. Years have passed since then, and I still miss her terribly. My life has never been the same since.

"Sharjam, there's obviously a lot I don't know about Aftaran customs and traditions, but I truly believe Raiha is a very special individual. For what it's worth, all I can say is that you'd be a fool to let her go a second time."

Sharjam looked into Marc's eyes and smiled. "Thank you for the thoughtful advice, my friend. I will pray that the Creator one day leads you back to your home world, back to the arms of the love of your life."

Marc smiled back, and stood up to return to his own corner in the cabin. At that moment, the door to the cockpit slid open, and Sibular floated into the cabin.

Marc suddenly felt a wave of excitement. "Any news?"

"Yes," Sibular said. "One of the signal probes has finally returned. This means the end of the consar is now less than 2 million light years away."

Chapter 35

It took another 24 hours for the scout ship to reach the end of the consar. In all, it had spent a full 8 Earth days inside the confines of the tunnel, covering a distance of over 16 million light years of equivalent space in regular 3 dimensions.

According to Sibular, the exit point was inside the heart of a galaxy known to Mendoken astronomers as LG65325. Human astronomers knew it as galaxy M94 in the CVn I Cloud, a group of galaxies at a distance of between 14 and 20 million light years from the M81 group that the Milky Way (Glaessan) and Andromeda galaxies belonged to. As with all visible galaxies, however, humans on Earth could only see a small percentage of M94, thanks to the silupsal filter that surrounded their solar system.

The Mendoken did not know much about this galaxy, other than that its shape, size and age were similar to those of the Glaessan. Needless to say, no Mendoken or any other beings from the Glaessan had ever traveled to this galaxy before.

"So this is where Wazilban is from," Marc said, sitting in the cockpit beside Sibular.

"We can only assume so," Sibular replied. "We shall hopefully find out for certain soon enough."

Outside, the consar tunnel's walls were lighting up again in a mix of different colors, and the bands of matter passing through the ship were thinning out. A hole opened up ahead, marking the exit point. Then, in one big burst of deceleration, the ship flew through the hole and broke free from the consar. The protective blue sphere shriveled up and vanished, as did the opening to the consar behind. The ship was once again back in regular space.

Or was it? Marc jaw dropped in surprise as he looked out through the cockpit window. "Sibular, didn't you say this galaxy is similar to ours? What's going on here?"

"I do not know, Marc. This does not at all conform to the coordinates I have. We should be right in the center of LG65325."

But they were staring at a pitch black sky, with hardly a star in sight. Marc thought he could probably count the total number of stars by the fingers on his hands.

"The charts our astronomers have of LG65325 may be outdated," the Mendoken pilot suggested.

"Yes," Sibular agreed. "The charts are outdated by 16 million years, or the time it takes for the light of the stars in this galaxy to reach ours. Something significant has evidently happened to this galaxy in the past 16 million years."

Dumyan stepped into the cockpit. "By the power of the Creator!" he gasped, seeing the empty sky outside. "What is this?"

Marc shrugged. "Well, it seems that galaxy LG65325 doesn't really exist anymore."

"How can that be? Any sign of Wazilban? Any ships nearby? Planets or moons?"

"Nothing within a 500 million mile radius," the pilot said, eyeing one of the navigation screens beside her.

Dumyan shook his head. "We must not be in the right place. Something is wrong. Could the consar have shifted its path while we were traveling through it?"

"No, that is physically impossible," Sibular said confidently. "A consar path, once created, will remain as it is for eternity, even after its openings have disappeared and it is no longer accessible. We are in the right place, without a doubt."

"Then how do we explain this?" Dumyan pointed at the sky outside.

Everyone was silent, trying to make head or tail of the situation. A couple of minutes passed before a small dot suddenly appeared in the rear corner of one of the navigation screens.

"What is that?" Dumyan asked.

Sibular tried to identify the dot with the help of the ship's computer. But the computer returned no matches from its extensive database.

"The unidentified object is heading our way," the pilot announced, pointing at the navigation screen. "It is approaching from behind."

Sure enough, the dot was moving towards the center of the screen, advancing a few millimeters every minute. It was also growing in size as it moved.

"Why is it growing?" Marc asked, starting to get worried.

"It is not growing, Marc," Sibular replied. "The computer is continuously recalculating the size of the object as it obtains more information about it."

As the minutes passed, the dot, now grown into a full-blown sphere, was moving ever closer.

Marc felt a rising apprehension. "Uh, guys, we should move out of this thing's path."

Sibular and Dumyan both agreed. The pilot moved the ship to the left by a million miles, and then resumed the course forward.

"The object should come into visual range in 5 minutes," Sibular said.

Exactly 5 minutes later, Marc heard several cries from the cabin. He stepped out of the cockpit, and saw Sharjam, Zorina and everyone else in the cabin huddled around one of the windows on the rear right side of the craft. He ran up to them, and once he could see what they were looking at outside, cried out in shock himself.

A gigantic white sphere, easily the size of a large planet, was approaching rapidly from the rear. Over a million miles away, it was passing by the ship along a parallel course. It had an outer spherical shell that looked like a transparent balloon, and inside was a glowing red sparkle. The sparkle seemed to have no fixed shape. Instead, it just kept dancing around inside the shell, sometimes looking like a star, at other times like a cube or a series of disconnected lines.

It was an eerie sight, and easily the largest moving object Marc had ever seen in his life. It was larger than any ship, planet destroyer, space station or anything else. This thing was, simply put, humongous!

Sharjam looked at Dumyan, who had just arrived in the cabin. "Dumyan, you will not believe this!" he cried, his eyes wide open in amazement. "That is a Starguzzler out there!"

Dumyan looked out the window, and also cried out in surprise. "This is unbelievable! It must be, what, maybe a hundred million times larger than the ones we saw on Droila?"

"At least! The resemblance is unmistakable, though. It clearly is a Starguzzler, without a doubt. This must be the size they can grow to."

"Grow from a tiny sphere to something *that* size? That thing is larger than any planet you are suggesting it could have originated from. It is impossible!"

"That would depend on the material they're made of and how they're grown," Zorina said.

Dumyan's eyes narrowed. "What do you mean?"

"Well, it's simple, really. How different would this be from, say, a silupsal filter? We create a small amount of the membrane, and then let it self-replicate. A small amount that fits in the size of my palm is all that's needed to eventually cover an entire solar system. We just have to keep providing the membrane with a constant energy supply while it grows, then shut off the supply once the growth is complete.

Perhaps that monster out there uses a similar mechanism to grow that big. The only question is, where does it get its energy from? And why would anyone create something that big to begin with?"

"Weapons," Sharjam whispered. "At that size, those Starguzzlers could surely be very powerful."

Marc nodded. "Exactly what Wazilban needs to destroy all life in our galaxy. I dread to find out how it actually works." He then walked back to the cockpit, along with Dumyan, Sharjam and Zorina.

The giant Starguzzler kept on moving, seemingly oblivious to the tiny scout ship nearby. Its gravitational force, however, was not at all oblivious to the ship's presence. The force began pulling on the ship as soon as the massive body had passed by and moved on ahead.

The Mendoken pilot reversed the ship's kilasic engines, trying to break free from the Starguzzler's gravitation pull.

"Wait!" Dumyan said, raising his hand. "Perhaps we should not break free completely, but just maintain enough thrust in the opposite direction to keep a safe distance. That monster does not seem to have noticed us, or even if it has, does not care. So following it might make more sense than blindly searching through empty space. It might even lead us to what we are looking for."

Marc stared at the looming giant through the cockpit window. "I couldn't agree more."

The scout ship followed the Starguzzler silently through dark, empty space, at close to 100,000 times the speed of light. Several hours passed before something else finally appeared on one of the cockpit's navigation screens.

"A star system, 300 million miles ahead," the pilot announced.

"Any planets?" Dumyan asked, awakening from his slumber. He was seated on the floor of the cockpit, propped up against the wall.

"Yes, two on the far side. It is still too early to tell how large and what types. But there are also several other large objects in close proximity to the star."

"More Starguzzlers, it seems," Sibular said, doing a quick check on the ship's computer. "Five of them surrounding the star."

The Starguzzler they were following slowed down as the star system came into visual range, and it seemed to be heading straight for the sun to join its five counterparts. In order to avoid a meltdown from getting too close to the sun, the pilot broke the ship free from the gravitational pull of the Starguzzler, and took it along a different course toward the planets on the far side.

The ship passed by the sun at a distance of 10 million miles, allowing everyone on board to see with their own eyes what the Starguzzlers surrounding it were doing.

"Hence their name," Sharjam whispered, breaking the stunned silence in the cockpit.

"Indeed, hence their name," Marc thought. And hence their size. The Starguzzlers were literally sucking plasma out of the sun, through long tubes emanating from the surfaces of their spherical shells. The bright gas could be seen traveling through the tubes and into the inner layers of their transparent bodies. Their red sparkles seemed to dance around with delight, thankful for the energy that was steadily flowing in.

Marc was amazed. He could never have imagined consumption on so grand a scale. An entire star was slowly being eaten up by huge, sentient objects. The stars themselves were evidently the energy sources these objects tapped to grow so big and sustain themselves.

"This is likely how the majority of stars here have disappeared over time," Sibular said, "due to these Starguzzlers."

"Which means there are probably many of them in this galaxy," Dumyan said. "I cannot understand how even Wazilban would be crazy enough to build such a catastrophic creature or weapon."

"We may find out soon enough," Sibular said, pointing to one of the screens beside him. "The computer is saying there are ships in orbit around the nearer planet."

As the scout ship approached the nearer planet, the Mendoken troopers began using the sophisticated surveillance equipment on board to study both planets and their surroundings, and to try to locate Wazilban or any of the other aliens who had escaped from Bara Dilshai. To their surprise, they found both planets to be hospitable for life, but empty of any signs of it. Just as surprisingly, there seemed to be no security grid or any other defense system protecting either of the planets.

"These aliens may have consar technology, but they seem to lack basic protection infrastructure," Sibular observed.

"Well, either that or they just don't care enough to set it up," Zorina said. "They may not have any real enemies in this galaxy, or at least what's left of this galaxy. And it sure doesn't seem like they're expecting us."

No, the aliens really didn't seem to be expecting the visitors, nor did they seem particularly concerned about their presence. There were a number of ships orbiting the nearer planet, none of which bothered to budge or hail the approaching Mendoken scout ship. In fact, none of them seemed to register any life signs on board. And what turned out to be most surprising of all was that all the ships orbiting the planet were carrying identification signatures of Aftaran, Mendoken and Volonan vessels.

"Impossible!" Dumyan and Sharjam exclaimed in unison.

"Maybe not," Zorina said, pointing at the cockpit window's magnification system.

The first alien ship came into view. It looked like a Volonan warship, red in color, with its familiar rectangular shape and overhangs at its edges. But the ship was still under construction, its entire upper half no more than a mesh of foundation rods. Other Volonan ships nearby were already completed. In the vicinity were a large number of Aftaran Gyra-class vessels and a few Mendoken battlecruisers, most of them whole but some under construction. And they all had one thing in common – they were deserted.

Zorina bobbed her head up and down in excitement. "You see, my man?" she said, addressing Sibular. "Just as I kept telling you! These ships are replicas, built by the aliens. They used these ships to attack your worlds, and then blamed it on my people."

Marc studied the scene outside intently. "Their goal was obviously to start a war between your two civilizations, so that you would eventually annihilate each other." He paused and stared again at the ships. "It's funny, you know. There doesn't seem to be a single ship out there that isn't a replica. Don't these aliens have any ships of their own?"

Nobody knew the answer.

Marc went on. "The aliens must have used these Gyra-class replicas to travel freely into and out of the Dominion. The presence of Mendoken replicas seems to indicate they also traveled to the Republic. I wonder to what extent they infiltrated Mendoken society."

"I doubt to the same extent as ours," Dumyan said. "The Mendoken are far more difficult a species to infiltrate. I hate to admit it, but it is the truth. They are a lot more rational and not as easily swayed by words of emotion as my people are. Wazilban would not have gotten very far in the Republic with his ornate speeches."

"You are probably right," Sibular agreed, as the scout ship flew right between two partially completed replicas of Mendoken Kril-2 battlecruisers. "But there definitely was some level of infiltration. Since the beginning of our current war with the Volona, we repeatedly tried to research and master consar technology. But our research facilities were always mysteriously destroyed before we could make any reasonable progress. We never found the culprits, but I now believe these aliens were behind it. They probably kept a close watch on our scientific work across the Republic, and always made sure that we did not master consar technology. But they ultimately failed, because they did not anticipate Marc's emergence and were not able to stop him in time."

"Why would these aliens go to such pains to ensure your people didn't develop consar technology?" Zorina asked, frowning.

"To avoid being detected, obviously," Dumyan said. "They would not have wanted anyone to trace their paths back here to their home worlds."

Marc nodded. "And once Wazilban realized the Mendoken had gained hold of consar technology anyway, he decided to use this fact to his advantage to form an alliance and accelerate the wars between the different civilizations!" He smiled. "I have to say, these aliens are obviously very smart, and quite adept at strategizing."

"Combined with their evil nature, that makes them one dangerous enemy," Sharjam added.

"No doubt," Marc thought. The aliens had gone to great lengths to plan for the destruction of the Glaessan's civilizations. But the fundamental question still remained – why? He didn't know, but he was fairly certain these Starguzzlers had something to do with it. And if there was anywhere in the entire universe to find out the answer, this had to be the place. But then, there was also the other big question – where had the aliens all disappeared to, leaving these replica ships behind?

One of the Mendoken troopers from the cabin floated into the cockpit. "We have located the signatures of the Aftaran Shoyra-class vessels that the aliens used to escape from Bara Dilshai," she announced. "They are parked on the surface of the planet, in a clearing in the midst of a dense forest. But there is no sign of Wazilban or any of the other aliens."

Without a word, the Mendoken pilot flew the scout ship directly towards the midsize planet. As the ship got closer, Marc noticed that the surface of the planet was mostly grayish-green with isolated patches of blue, indicating the presence of large masses of land and smaller seas of water. In some ways, it looked like the reverse of Earth, which had smaller sections of land and wide expanses of ocean water covering its surface.

"What if this is a trap?" Zorina suggested. "They may be luring us to this planet to destroy us."

"Why go to the trouble?" Sibular said. "They could easily use one of their large replica ships out here to fire at us right now and blow us apart with one shot. A scout ship this size is no military match for any of those vessels. I think it is more likely the aliens may all be communing somewhere in secret. Perhaps deep below the surface of the planet, which is why our scanners cannot detect them. They must be preoccupied with bigger things at the moment, and are therefore paying no attention to us."

"Bigger things like those, maybe?" Dumyan said, pointing at a series of blips that had just appeared on one of the cockpit's navigation screens. The blips soon became visible to the naked eye through the cockpit's wide window.

"What are they?" Marc asked, sensing trouble.

The entire sky was suddenly lighting up with uncountable numbers of those bright spots, instantly transforming itself from a black mass into a starry sky. It looked a lot like the sky Marc had grown up seeing on clear nights back on Earth. Except for one major difference – the stars seemed to be growing in size, and rapidly.

"More Starguzzlers, many more," the pilot said, eyeing the navigation screen closely. "They are all converging on this location."

Zorina flapped her ears. "I don't like this, not one bit. We've got to get out of here as soon as possible!"

"Yes, but not until we have obtained the necessary information we came here for," Dumyan said firmly. "We will have to take our chances with the Starguzzlers. Too much is at stake for us to turn back now."

The scout ship descended effortlessly through several layers of clouds, its outer shell made of a sophisticated material impervious to the tremendous heat generated during entry into planetary atmospheres. After the ship had passed through the lowest cloud layer, the dense forests below that covered much of the planet's surface became visible to the naked eye. According to the surveillance equipment on board, there wasn't a single town, city or settlement of any kind on the entire planet, nor were there signs of the aliens anywhere. In fact, there were no signs of life whatsoever on the planet.

The scout ship landed in a tiny, empty clearing a couple of miles away from the much larger clearing where Wazilban's Shoyra-class vessels were located. All on board had agreed that this was the right thing to do in order to remain as inconspicuous as possible. The rest of the journey would then have to be made quietly on foot through the forest.

"It is deceptively cold outside," Sibular warned everyone, as he opened the exit door in the ship's cabin.

Marc wrapped the Aftaran robe he was wearing around his body a couple more times to stay warm, and whisked the robe's veil over his face. By now, he had quite mastered the use of the magical robe, and greatly enjoyed its comfort and convenience.

They stepped out into the clearing, a Mendoken trooper and Aftaran soldier leading the way, followed by Sibular, Dumyan, Sharjam, Marc and Zorina, who in turn were followed by four more troopers and soldiers in the rear. The pilot remained inside with the rest of the contingent to guard the ship.

It was cold alright, freezing cold. Even with the robe tightly wrapped around him, Marc could feel the icy air trying to edge its way through to his skin. The lighting in the clearing was dim, but there was enough of it to let him see his surroundings. The ground was covered with what had probably once been something similar to grass, but was now all shriveled up and frozen. The trees surrounding the clearing were tall, but lifeless. They looked like evergreens, yet their leaves were all gone. The air was absolutely still, and there was total silence, unusual silence for a place out in the open.

Regardless of its current morbid conditions, Marc realized this was obviously a world that had once been full of life. At some point, however, temperatures must have dropped to unbearable levels and killed everything on this planet. He wondered whether the Starguzzlers were somehow responsible for this change in climate. Perhaps their gradual consumption of the sun's gases had reduced the amount of light and warmth the star could radiate, resulting in a slow and painful extermination of all wildlife on its surrounding planets. "What a tragic outcome," he thought.

The group made its way cautiously through the forest. Sibular and the Mendoken troopers floated easily over the wide roots of the trees, while the others had to watch their steps to make sure they didn't fall. It soon became obvious to Marc that the roots weren't the only obstacles to watch out for. There were skeletons of strange looking animals scattered all over. Some seemed as large as the dinosaurs of prehistoric Earth, with bulky bodies, long, swooping necks, and pointed snouts. Others were much smaller, with birdlike bodies and wide wings, while some were more insect-like, with long tentacles and multi-eyed faces. The only thing they all had in common was that they were dead, the flesh of their bodies long gone like the leaves on the trees. The entire forest was one big, natural graveyard.

After close to an hour of trudging through the forest, the group arrived at the larger clearing where the five Shoyra-class vessels were parked. Hiding from behind the trees, they peered out into the clearing. A couple of the Mendoken troopers used their portable surveillance devices to scan the clearing and its surroundings. There was no sign of the aliens.

After a few minutes of surveying, one of the Mendoken troopers slowly ventured from his hiding place into the clearing, his two front limbs aiming his ganvex weapon straight ahead. He was followed by one of the Aftaran soldiers, and then by the rest of the party.

Marc's hands clutched tightly onto his own ganvex, as he nervously walked out into the clearing towards the nearest vessel. His eyes darted suspiciously to the left and right, looking for the slightest movement in between the trees or between the parked ships. But there was none, and a quick check of all five ships revealed no aliens on board.

"Where can they all be?" Marc wondered aloud, walking out of the last ship with Sibular.

"We must look for a gate of some kind in the ground," Sibular replied quietly. "I am certain they are all below us in the planet's crust."

"How can you be so sure?"

"That is the only logical conclusion. We know there are no aliens anywhere in this forest, yet their ships are here."

Everyone combed the entire clearing for a hidden gate or door that might lead to an underground passage, but over a half hour of searching revealed nothing. The Mendoken surveillance devices could not locate any secret gate or opening in the ground either. In fact, for some odd reason they weren't able to scan more than a few feet below the surface.

Marc began to feel frustrated. They had come all this way unhindered, through a consar across many millions of light years and then on the tail of a gigantic Starguzzler, only to reach a dead end now in the midst of a dead forest on a dead planet.

"I give up!" Zorina said, wiping her forehead as she walked over to the edge of the clearing. "Time for a quick nap." She sat down on the ground and leaned back against a tree. But just as she closed her eyes, the tree suddenly began swaying. She yelled out in fright and jumped up, flapping her ears violently as she ran back out into the clearing.

Marc turned to look at the swaying tree. Its tall trunk creaked and groaned, and a few of its branches broke loose and came crashing to the ground. Then the rest of the branches magically folded up into the trunk, turning the entire tree into a long, smooth pole. The ground surrounding the base of the tree caved in, and with a thud and a whoosh the whole structure descended into the ground and disappeared out of sight.

"What in the name of the Creator is going on?" Sharjam exclaimed, looking stunned.

Sibular floated over to the gaping hole left behind by the tree, and cautiously peered down. "It appears we have uncovered what we were looking for," he announced, looking up again at the others.

"An underground passage?" Dumyan asked.

"It appears so."

"Wait a minute, not so fast, my man!" Zorina said, still visibly shaken by the whole experience. "What are the odds that I coincidentally leaned against the one tree that serves as a secret gate to an underground world? It could be a trap!"

Without answering, Sibular floated over to the next tree at the edge of the clearing, and pushed with his two front limbs against the base of the trunk. The tree began swaying right away, folded up its branches and disappeared into the ground below with a whoosh, leaving behind a hole identical to the first one. Sibular then repeated the process with three more trees at the edge of the clearing.

"As you can see, Zorina, it was no coincidence," he said calmly, watching the last tree vanished out of sight.

Zorina grunted and muttered something under her breath that Marc couldn't understand. It certainly didn't sound like anything nice.

But Marc wasn't terribly concerned at that moment about yet another skirmish between Sibular and Zorina. He was far more worried about what awaited him and his friends under the planet's surface. Crouching over the edge of one of the holes, he gazed into the depths below. The hole was perfectly circular, had a diameter of about 15 feet, and was no more than 30 feet deep. There appeared to be a rudimentary elevator on one side, consisting of a small ledge supported by vertical tracks. At the bottom, he could barely make out a dimly lit passage. The tree that had slid through this hole was nowhere to be seen, probably resting somewhere below the floor of the passage.

As Marc watched the first Mendoken trooper float into the hole and onto the ledge, he tried to prepare himself for whatever dangers lay below. He could only hope that they would all make it out of this planet again alive.

Chapter 36

Marc and the others had entered a labyrinth, heading in single file down one passage after another. At the first passage crossing, they made a left. Then a few crossings later, they made a right. Then another left. On and on this went, with no end in sight.

Marc felt totally lost. The only thing he knew for sure was that every passage they were turning into was tilting downwards, leading them deeper into the planet's crust. He also knew he had no choice but to rely on the surveillance devices the Mendoken troopers were holding. The devices had calculated the shortest path through the labyrinth to what they simply called the "destination point". They weren't able to provide any additional information on what the destination point actually was, except that all passages in the labyrinth eventually led to it.

From above the surface, the surveillance devices had not been able to penetrate more than a few feet into the soil. But now that they were below the surface, they had successfully plotted maps of the entire passage network. The Mendoken troopers attributed this anomaly to some invisible surveillance jamming mechanism surrounding the planet's surface, preventing anybody outside from being able to scan the inside of the planet.

"Do you still think these aliens have no enemies in this galaxy?" Sibular asked Zorina, as they turned into yet another passage.

"Fine, fine, you win again!" Zorina said with a sigh. "You happy?" She paused before speaking again in a more composed tone, as if to regain her reputation as the resident defense expert. "Obviously their defense system is different from the ones we're used to back home. It seems to be geared more towards staying hidden, rather than explicitly thwarting invaders."

"And towards protecting what's below the planet's surface, instead of the space around it," Marc added.

The passages all looked exactly the same. They were oval in shape, with a width of about 20 feet and a maximum height of 15 feet at the center. The lighting was dim, thanks to tiny lamps fixed to the ceiling every 30 feet or so, revealing bare, uninteresting walls made of solid rock. Marc felt the only positive thing about the passages was that it was much warmer inside them than it was back on the surface.

A half hour passed, then another half hour. They had descended deep into the belly of the labyrinth, without coming across a single alien. The surveillance devices claimed the destination point was close now, very close. And then, there it was. There was no door, no gate, no wall at the end, just an abrupt end to the passage. What lay beyond was solid darkness, both to the naked eye and to the surveillance devices.

Huddled around the end of the passage, they all stared at the darkness beyond. Pointing flashlights ahead did no good – the light just faded away into the distance, revealing absolutely nothing.

"What do we do now?" Marc whispered.

"Why are you whispering?" Zorina asked.

"I... I don't know," he said uneasily. "I feel as if someone is out there in the dark, watching us."

"You can feel it?" Sharjam asked. "What exactly do you feel?"

Marc was unsure how to answer. He had been feeling a growing level of anxiety during the hike through the labyrinth. "Well, I feel that we have reached the end of our quest. Whatever answers we have been seeking lie in wait for us out there, ready to pounce on us. And I feel fear of that which awaits us, for all of us may not make it back out alive."

"We came here with that risk in mind, my friend," Sharjam said in a reassuring tone. "If the Creator has decided that the time has come for you, me or anyone else in this group to die, then there is nothing we can do to change the Creator's will. But I can assure you that there is no nobler cause to die for than the defense of our homelands and our loved ones."

"Can you see anything, Marc?" Dumyan asked.

Marc focused his eyes as best as he could and stared ahead into the darkness. Several seconds later, he gave up in frustration and shook his head. "Nope, I can just feel the same..."

But he wasn't able to finish the sentence, for at that moment a deafening sound of laughter erupted in his ears, a deep, resonating laughter easily recognizable as that of Lord Wazilban. He tried to cover his ears to block out the sound, but to no avail. The others all asked him what was wrong, but he couldn't find his voice. The laughter kept getting louder and louder, eventually becoming so unbearable that he closed his eyes and fell to his knees in despair.

He tried hard to pull himself together. He reminded himself that this was similar to his visions, where darkness and evil laughter had threatened to encompass him and destroy him. He reminded himself that if he stood firm, then they would eventually subside and be shooed away by light and hope.

And so they did. The laughter did eventually die down, and once he opened his eyes, the darkness ahead was gone. In its place was an entrance to what seemed like an underground world.

"Can you see?" he whispered to his friends.

"Yes, we can see everything," Dumyan said. "It is unbelievable! Somehow you appear to have breached this defensive barrier for all of us."

"Wow! I don't know how. It was like... one of my visions. Darkness, hopelessness, loud laughter..."

"Indeed," Sharjam said, nodding. "Your visions obviously had many a purpose, not just to help you see through the conspiracy and to guide you throughout your journey, but also to train you to handle obstacles like this barrier."

"That's all very good, but we'd better get moving before someone out there notices us!" Zorina said, pointing to the steep path downwards that lay beyond the entrance.

Nobody could disagree with that. The group cautiously made its way in single file down the path, which leveled off after a few hundred feet and led straight into a huge underground settlement carved out of the planet's crust. There were houses, hundreds of them, situated in a grid-like pattern around a central square. The houses were made of rock and seemed fairly rudimentary in design and construction, leading Marc to wonder how aliens of such technological sophistication could live in such primitive conditions.

And there the aliens were, gathered in the square. There had to be thousands of them, all facing the center, their eyes fixated on a bright, moving 3D image suspended in the air above their heads. The image was so bright that it provided enough light for the entire settlement, the rest of which with all its narrow alleys seemed to be deserted.

"What are they all staring at like that?" Marc wondered aloud.

"Images of Starguzzlers, it seems," Dumyan said. "Looks like they are somehow communicating with those monsters."

"This indicates the Starguzzlers are beings of intelligence," Sibular said. "And they evidently have some form of influence over the aliens."

"To say the least!" Marc added. "They all seem completely captivated by the images."

"Shhh!" Zorina hissed. "We must tread carefully and quietly. We don't know what's going on down there yet, and the aliens could turn their heads and spot us at any moment."

Several minutes later, Marc and the others reached the floor of the underground settlement. They slowly began edging their way towards the central square, hopping from behind one house to the next in order to stay out of sight. Once they had reached the last row of houses around the square, they stopped and waited.

Peering out from behind one of the houses, Marc was now able to get a clear view of what was happening in the square. The aliens were keenly gazing up at the image from all sides of the square, as if mesmerized by what they could see. And what the image displayed were hordes of Starguzzlers, flying through space with their large spherical bodies and dancing red sparkles within. Every few minutes, loud sirens wailed through the underground settlement.

As Marc watched the scene, he realized that Dumyan was right. The aliens were indeed communicating with the Starguzzlers, and the haunting sirens were the sounds the Starguzzlers were making when they "spoke". Several of the aliens were right in the center of the square, speaking among themselves and to the Starguzzlers in between the sirens. Their language sounded harsh, and it wasn't understandable to him at all. His Mendoken translator obviously didn't recognize their native tongue.

"Not surprising," he thought. No Mendoken would ever have heard this language before, as the aliens would never have exposed their identity or their language to anybody in the Glaessan. But here, on their own turf, the aliens had no reason to hide anything. They were all in their native reptilian garb, brandishing their menacing eyes, long snouts and sharp teeth, their shiny skin and muscular bodies, their heavy tails and wide, sweeping wings with which they constantly stayed afloat. Without a doubt, their aura was vicious and far from friendly.

One of the aliens standing in front of the others Marc would recognize anywhere – Lord Wazilban. He seemed to be doing most of the talking with the Starguzzlers, and was issuing orders to the other aliens around him.

Marc also spotted Thorab, Rulshanim, Ozwin and Ruminat in the crowd, as well as a number of other faces he had seen on Bara Dilshai. The aliens were clearly all here. The big question was why they were all so mesmerized by the presence of the Starguzzlers, so much so that none of them had noticed him or any of his companions encroaching upon their settlement.

Or, at least, that was what Marc and his companions thought. And that was why what happened next took them completely by surprise.

Wazilban suddenly stopped talking to the Starguzzlers, and turned to look in the direction where Marc and his companions were hiding. A hush fell over the entire square, as all the other aliens also turned their heads to follow his gaze.

"Welcome, friends, or should I say, enemies!" Wazilban said in Mareefi. His loud, booming voice reached easily across the square and into the settlement's alleys.

Before Marc or any of his companions could make a move, aliens suddenly appeared out of thin air all around them. Within seconds, the aliens had completely surrounded the intruders in a tight circle, leaving no room for escape. Their eyes were full of anger and hate, void of any signs of mercy. Several of them revealed their reptilian instincts by lunging forward to bite their new prisoners with their sharp teeth. Luckily they were pulled back by their comrades in the nick of time. With their front limbs, all the aliens were holding weapons shaped like hollow poles, pointed straight at the intruders.

Marc felt like he was surrounded by a pack of hungry wolves, ready to pounce on their prey. Only that these were much larger, more dangerous and far more intelligent creatures than wolves. And whatever kind of weapons those hollow poles were, he felt fairly certain they could inflict far heavier damage than just blow air. While he and his companions briefly pointed their ganvexes and boryals at the aliens, it was painfully clear they were heavily outnumbered and that any fight would be futile. Without further ado, he and the others followed Dumyan's lead and dropped their weapons to the ground. Almost immediately, a couple of the aliens came forward and took the weapons away, after which the rest of the aliens in the circle lowered their poles.

Then Wazilban appeared with a flash inside the circle. His face bore a scowl, with his snout open and his sharp teeth glistening in the dim light. Facing the intruders, he spoke. "You have interrupted a most critical discussion. We are not at all pleased. Did you really think we were not aware of your arrival in this star system and on our planet? What kind of idiots do you take us for?"

Nobody responded. Marc knew he and his companions had taken a lot for granted, but he also knew they had had no other choice but to keep pushing forward until they got to the bottom of this alien mystery.

Wazilban went on. "This is our world, our space. You have no business here."

"And what business did you have in ours?" Dumyan demanded. "What business did you have creating so devious a scheme to take over our Dominion and instigate wars between the civilizations of our galaxy? We most certainly have plenty of business here. We have the right to know the reasons why, and the right to seek retribution for all the harm you have caused us."

Wazilban broke out in laughter. Marc shuddered as he heard it – it was a laugh he knew far too well.

"Retribution!" Wazilban thundered. "How do you propose to so much as lift a finger now without getting your head blown off, Dumyan? I can see your reputation of foolhardiness is clearly justified." He paused. "I must admit I do not know how the lot of you managed to follow us here to this galaxy, nor am I certain how you crossed the barrier at the entrance to our settlement. I can only assume it has something to do with this individual." He pointed a menacing limb at Marc. "I never did quite figure out who you really are and what species you are from, Zemin. You have been a most annoying thorn in our master plan. But it matters no more. As intelligent and resourceful as your species might be, you were dumb enough to lead your little band of adventurers here right into our hands!" He laughed again. "You can rest assured that none of you will ever make it out of here again alive."

Marc tried hard to keep his wits together. He reminded himself that regardless of all the evil things Wazilban had done, a higher power had consistently protected him and helped him come this far. That power had helped him see through Wazilban's conspiracy, and had helped him bring the civilizations of the Glaessan together to unveil it. Whatever this higher power was, it was far greater and more insightful than Wazilban, that much faith he already had. Whatever this higher power was, it had brought him this far for a purpose, all the way from Earth. He couldn't imagine that power would abandon him now at this critical juncture.

So he felt strong enough to speak out. "Kill us if you will, Lord Wazilban, but we are only the first ones to arrive here. Others will soon follow. Your conspiracy has already been unveiled, your grand scheme already thwarted. Whatever additional plans you have, they are all futile now."

"Empty threats!" Wazilban gloated. "Nothing can stop us anymore. Nothing can stop *them* anymore." He pointed at the image of the Starguzzlers looming above the square.

"Who... what are those things?" Marc asked.

"Those 'things', as you call them, are the Masters. Those very same 'things' are about to invade your galaxy in droves and destroy everything in their paths. They shall all be arriving shortly in the vicinity of this star system to prepare for consar entry. It is only a matter of time before your civilizations will be reduced to stardust." He laughed again. "And now I must excuse myself. The final preparations require my attention. As you might imagine, setting up a consar large enough to fit a Starguzzler is a difficult task, as is the sheer number of consars we will need. Wishing you all a pleasant death!"

"Wait!" Sharjam insisted. "At least give us the satisfaction of knowing why before we die. Why invade our galaxy, why destroy it all? To what end? How does this all help you and your people?"

"I would love to indulge you, Sharjam, but thanks to you lot and your, heh, valiant activities at Bara Dilshai, you have left us with no choice but to accelerate our invasion plans." Wazilban turned to the aliens surrounding him and said something in his harsh sounding native language.

The aliens pointed their weapons again at the intruders, as Wazilban's body swiftly faded away from sight.

Marc felt his hopes fading away just as swiftly. He closed his eyes, waiting for imminent death. He couldn't believe that this was how it would all end. He couldn't believe that all his efforts and those of his friends had been in vain, that the higher power he had begun placing his faith in was going to let him down like this.

Then, just as he thought he heard the triggers being pulled, he heard the wailing sirens of the Starguzzlers blast through the settlement. Opening his eyes, he saw the aliens lowering their weapons once again. Something, it seemed, had just happened.

Chapter 37

Wazilban, or Jaegor as his real name was, was becoming increasingly agitated. The Masters were once again unnecessarily wasting time, thanks to their annoying curiosity and stubbornness. He had already explained to them the risks of delaying like this, but as usual they had failed to grasp all the implications. No, the Masters were not the quickest in making decisions or taking action – that much he knew. Regardless, they were the Masters, and their wish was his command.

"Might I request the Masters to consider that these intruders from the Glaessan are highly dangerous," he said, staring up at the moving image of the Starguzzlers as he appeared again in the center of the square. "They should be executed right away before they attempt to escape. Some of them have powerful magical capabilities, and they may all vanish in an instant. It is not like the transference mechanism my people use – if they vanish, we may no longer be able to locate them."

The lead Starguzzler wailed away in response, its sirens perfectly understandable to Jaegor. "We want to know how they arrived here from the Glaessan. You assured us none of them would ever make it here, yet here they are. Were it not for one of us spotting their presence and leading them to this star system so they could be interrogated, we would not even have known they were here. We need to make sure no more of them are coming. This is a bigger risk to our survival than anything else, especially if our invasion of their galaxy fails. Bring them before us. We will interrogate them ourselves."

"But we do not have time!" Jaegor insisted. "We need to complete preparations for the invasion right away."

"Time that we have lost thanks to your bungling things in the Glaessan. We shall no longer rely on your scheming and strategizing. Bring them forward, Jaegor! We shall not ask again."

Jaegor sighed, and signaled to his guards to call off the execution and bring the prisoners forward instead. He knew this was a mistake. It was no easy matter to get Aftarans to talk against their will, and to get the robotic Mendoken to talk was downright impossible. Volonans he didn't have enough experience with. That other alien Zemin with the supernatural powers – well, the chances of getting that one to talk would probably be even slimmer. So perhaps the only way to do this would be to torture an Aftaran or two. In other words, it would all take time, time he didn't have. Every second counted right now, every second that passed was another second given to the civilizations of the Glaessan to spread word of the conspiracy, to stop fighting each other and to unite against the common enemy. His whole master plan was falling apart. If he could only make the Masters understand! But, as he well knew, disobeying the Masters always led to far more serious consequences.

The prisoners were brought into the center of the square in front of Jaegor, carefully watched on all sides by guards holding their weapons at the ready.

"Here they are, Masters, as you commanded," Jaegor said, looking up at the Starguzzlers.

"Translate for us, Jaegor," the lead Starguzzler said. "How did you enter this galaxy? Did you follow Jaegor?"

Jaegor couldn't help chuckling to himself. The Masters really had no idea how to deal with beings of other species. They were just too used to always getting everything their way with his people. Nevertheless, he went ahead and repeated the questions aloud in Mareefi.

There was a short period of silence, during which the intruders exchanged glances with each other. Then Dumyan spoke. "Considering what you are about to do to our people, the least you can do is tell us who or what you are and why you intend to invade our galaxy. Then we will tell you whatever you want to know."

Jaegor was a little surprised at Dumyan's willingness to reveal any information whatsoever, but realized it was probably a delaying tactic of some kind. He translated Dumyan's words for the Masters, and then protested to them again to not waste time with the prisoners.

"Tell them whatever they want to know, Jaegor," the lead Starguzzler said. "And have one of your subordinates translate everything for us as you speak."

Grinding his jaws in frustration, Jaegor began telling the intruders the story of his people and the Starguzzlers. He tried his best to keep things brief, but was repeatedly interrupted by Dumyan and a couple of the other intruders to provide more details. Overall, he stuck to the following outline:

My real name is not Wazilban, it is Jaegor. Wazilban is the Aftaran name I adopted. My people are known as the Ungha. We are a very old civilization, our origins dating back to the very beginnings of the universe's current oscillation. This galaxy, or what is left of it, is our home. It was once a galaxy as big and populous as yours, and it was filled with stars, planets and moons. Life flourished in every region and in the farthest corners, and many an intelligent civilization found its roots here. Ours was one of the first such civilizations, sprung forth from the jungles of a planet called Konasum in the heart of the galaxy. We learned early on that the only way to survive in the jungle, in a world of ferocious predators, was to be both the strongest and smartest, the most advanced and the most powerful. Survival of the fittest, at all costs and regardless of the costs of others – that is the law of the jungle, and that is the motto we have always followed.

In the beginning, our people were not physically the biggest or strongest species on our planet, and perhaps not even the most intelligent. Often our ancestors were attacked by other species on Konasum and many were killed. But we were the only ones who strove to be the strongest and most intelligent, the only ones with the ambition to be greater than who we already were. Bit by bit we fought the others, bit by bit we conquered and took over the whole planet. In order to defeat our powerful enemies, we developed a strategy known as <u>implosion</u>. Some of us would disguise ourselves as the enemy and infiltrate them from within, restricting our capabilities only to those that they possessed in order to avoid arousing suspicion. We would rise to key positions of power over time, and then take steps to cause the enemy society to weaken from inside. Instigating infighting among various factions of the enemy was usually the most effective method. Eventually this led to the society's implosion, after which we were able to defeat them effortlessly.

After taking over the entire planet, we became a prosperous and developed nation. Soon we grew advanced enough to travel through space, and began colonizing other habitable worlds in nearby star systems to meet the needs of our growing population. Most of the time we encountered species far more primitive than our own, and we subdued them with ease. But ever so often we had to use our implosion strategy to defeat another advanced civilization. Over time, we truly perfected the techniques of disguise and implosion. We also assimilated many great technologies from the civilizations we conquered. Examples include shape-shifting for disguises, consar travel and transference (the ability to instantly transfer our bodies from one location to another over short distances).

Our expansion regime did not always remain so successful, however. We eventually came across other civilizations more advanced and militaristic than our own, and we found it impossible to infiltrate them using our implosion strategy. They began striking us with their sophisticated weapons, massacring billions of our people and pushing us out to the very edges of the galaxy. It was then that we decided to alter our military strategy and invest all our resources in weapons development instead. We came out with more and more advanced weapons, with which we were able to strike back and regain our lost worlds. In the process, we also regained our stature as a force to be reckoned with.

But our enemies were not the kind to back down. An arms race began, with each side coming up with more and more destructive ways to kill as many of the other as possible. In the end, we prevailed, for we came up with the ultimate weapon, a weapon so large and so powerful that it could eliminate an entire star and all surrounding planets by itself. A weapon so intelligent that it could collaborate with others of its own kind to conduct an entire war. And it won our war for us in no time. With the Starguzzlers, we not only defeated and eradicated our enemies, but soon established ourselves as rulers of the entire galaxy.

"How did you come up with the name 'Starguzzler'?" the Volonan Zorina asked, interrupting Jaegor once again.

"Is it not ironic that the most advanced weapon ever created is made up of the most basic elements?" Jaegor said proudly. "They are composed of the same simple gases you see in stars, combined with large amounts of pure energy. They obtain the nourishment they need to sustain themselves by consuming gas from the stars. Their intelligence they get from a red nucleus that is comprised of a sophisticated neural network."

"So in your race to develop the ultimate weapon, you became blinded and you did not stop to think of the consequences of your actions," Dumyan said. "You succeeded in building your weapon, but failed to foresee the environmental and sociological disaster that would unfold if you lost control over it. And lose control you did, for it became more powerful than you."

Jaegor had to agree. "Not only more powerful than us, they learned how to sustain themselves without our help. Initially, we fed them with the natural gases found inside the bedrock of our own planets, but they later adapted to consume the gases of stars by themselves. That was when we decided to give them the name 'Starguzzlers'. They multiplied manifold, and their bodies and neural networks grew in size. They grew more intelligent and independent, far more than we had ever intended them to be. They began communicating with us and placed demands. They threatened to destroy us if we didn't comply, and made an example out of many of our planets and moons to prove they were serious. We had no choice but to give in to their demands. Slowly but surely, they became our masters, and have been so ever since."

"Is it correct to assume that the Starguzzlers eventually multiplied in such great numbers that they consumed most of the stars in this galaxy?" the Mendoken Sibular asked.

"Yes. And with the stars gone, so were all our worlds that completely depended on them for light, warmth, gravity... well, pretty much everything. Our entire civilization was destroyed and the majority of us, many quadrillions, were dead. All that is left of us now is what you see here. Once we had huge cities with tall skyscrapers and beautiful gardens spread across many planets, but now all we can claim as ours are a few disheveled houses in this one underground settlement on this one planet."

"Why are you all huddled up in this one place?" Dumyan asked. "Even your disguised ships under construction out there are all empty." He pointed up in the direction of the sky.

Jaegor hesitated at first, but knew what he was about to say was no secret in front of the Masters. "I recalled everyone to the settlement upon our arrival, in order to make preparations for the invasion. But in general most of us stay together like this below the surface of the planet, with no easy access by outsiders. That way, the Masters cannot punish us anymore for any of our infractions without destroying all of us. Their firepower is so big that they cannot target anything smaller than an entire planet. If they destroy this last planet of ours, our civilization will be completely extinguished, and they will no longer have anyone to help them accomplish their goals."

"They are running out of stars here, so now their goal is to emigrate to another galaxy in order to survive?" the same Mendoken asked. "And they are using you to make all the preparations for them? That is why you infiltrated our galaxy, to cause our civilizations to implode, so that the Starguzzlers face no resistance when they invade?"

"And that is why you have been raising infant Starguzzlers inside our galaxy in hiding, to increase their number and create an element of surprise during the invasion," Dumyan added. "Although those Starguzzlers are probably not ready or big enough for battle yet, since you did not anticipate executing the invasion so soon."

"It appears you have figured it all out," Jaegor said with satisfaction. "Now it is time for you to answer the Masters' questions."

"Not so fast, Wazilban, or Jaegor or whatever your name is!" Dumyan said. "One more question. Why our galaxy? Are there not many others closer to your own?"

Jaegor knew Dumyan was trying to buy as much time as possible, but a glance up at the Masters made it clear that they wanted him to keep answering until the intruders were satisfied. Reluctantly, he went on. "We did our research, Dumyan. Your galaxy is large and has an abundance of stars. And, believe it or not, your galaxy is the only one we know of where consar travel is forbidden, thanks to the religious beliefs of you Aftarans. We purposely chose your galaxy because our traveling into and out of the Glaessan through consars would not be noticed and our routes would not be traceable."

The intruders looked dumbstruck, as if lightning had hit them.

Jaegor went on. "We also made sure that nobody succeeded in developing consar travel capability in the Glaessan. Although somehow we overlooked this species." He pointed at Marc. "The Mendoken did a good job of hiding it from us."

The intruders remained silent.

Jaegor felt an overwhelming sense of triumph. Seeing just how shocked these representatives from the Glaessan were was an excellent indication of how well his master plan had been working, all the way until the final snag. Perhaps reminding the Masters of that would earn him a good standing with them again.

"We studied all your societies, and decided it would be easiest to infiltrate the Aftar first," Jaegor said, pointing at the Aftarans among the intruders. "You lot were just so gullible and so easy to sway any way we wanted, just as long as we pretended to follow the ways of your 'Creator'. You have your own religious zealotry and holier-than-thou attitude towards others to thank for that. Then, once we had the Dominion fully in our grasp, we moved to rekindle old wounds between the Aftar and the Phyrax, and between the Mendoken and Volona. We purposely picked confrontations that would hit on the values held most dearly by each civilization and confirm its prejudices of the others, thereby generating the maximum amount of distrust and anger on all sides.

"Take the Mendoken, for example. They have strong ethics of truth and honesty. They believe the Volona to be the exact opposite – lying and deceitful. So we decided to strengthen that belief. We built replicas of Volonan warships, after months of studying their designs in secret. The replicas were identical to the actual ones right down to the last detail, including all weapons systems. We then traveled with the replica ships into the Mendoken Republic, straight from here through consars. We destroyed targets inside the Republic, and came right back here again. The Volona vehemently denied that they had performed the attacks, of course, or that they even had consar technology. But the Mendoken, given their prejudices towards the Volona, did not believe them. Their distrust of their age-old enemy just intensified, and led to the beginning of a new war. It was a similar situation between the Aftar and Phyrax, archenemies just waiting for any reason to strangle each other. We simply edged them on towards the battleground.

"Our goal was to have the Mendoken and Volona, the two more technologically advanced civilizations in the Glaessan, destroy each other completely. With the advanced military technology both of them left behind, we were going to equip the Aftar to easily wipe out the Phyrax. That would just leave the Aftar standing, which for the Masters would be a cakewalk to take care of during their subsequent invasion of your galaxy. Now the task will be harder for the Masters, thanks to your meddling, but it is of no consequence. In the end, all your societies will be eradicated, the Masters will take over the Glaessan, and my people will finally be free!"

A period of silence followed, during which Jaegor watched the prisoners. They all seemed far too stunned to say anything. Yes, the master plan certainly had been ingenious, and it had worked almost to the very end. He turned his gaze up to the Masters with a look of content on his face. But the Masters remained quiet – they were clearly much more concerned about the present situation.

Finally, the alien Zemin spoke. "You are evil, Jaegor, pure evil. Your thirst for power and domination has turned your people into slaves of your own creations. And now you are willing to destroy an entire galaxy, with all its civilizations and forms of life, all innocent of your transgressions, so as to gain your freedom? You want others to pay the price for your inexcusable mistakes?"

"Like I said, we live by the law of the jungle," Jaegor said. "We are out to protect our own interests, as are you."

"I don't know what kind of jungle you grew up in!" the alien Zemin exclaimed angrily. "But where I come from, the basic law of the jungle is to maintain a perfect balance between all forms of life, from small to big, from weak to strong. Each species lives within its own boundaries and only consumes that which it needs. Nowhere is there any sanction for eradicating another species altogether to suit your own ends, let alone all other species in the jungle!"

Jaegor was starting to get annoyed, and his patience really was running thin. "Spare me your morality, Zemin! You have no knowledge of our suffering, no idea what we have been through! Whatever species you are from, chances are you would do far worse if you were slaves to such overbearing Masters for as long as we have been. We have studied the major civilizations in your galaxy. I dread to think what your beloved Aftar or Mendoken would have done in our place, or the Volona or Phyrax, for that matter."

"We would never stoop to such levels of morality!" Dumyan cried. "Our way of life and code of conduct prevent us from committing such horrible acts of evil."

"Nor would we have ever developed a weapon we could not control," the Mendoken Sibular added.

The crowd of Unghans in the square began jeering, many of them itching to lunge forward at the intruders with their long snouts.

"You lot have no right to judge us!" Jaegor rasped, his face green with anger. "And even if you did, it would not matter. Whatever you think of us, it will make no difference to the outcome, for the strong shall always prevail." He pointed at himself and the other Unghans around him.

"And the weak shall always die!" one of the other Unghans added, pointing at the prisoners and laughing loudly. Other Unghans joined in a chorus of laughter.

Before anybody else could say anything, the Starguzzlers began wailing again.

"Stop the arguing, and get us our answers now, Jaegor," the lead Starguzzler said. "We are running out of time."

"That is what I have been saying all along," Jaegor thought, clasping his long jaws together in frustration. His reptilian eyes narrowed as he stared at the prisoners, wondering who to torture first if they refused to cooperate, or even kill a couple right away to make a point.

Chapter 38

Sharjam stood still, listening intently to Jaegor's fantastic story about the history of the Unghans and the Starguzzlers. It was incredible to think how low a level of morality and ethics an entire society could stoop to, to do all the things the Unghans had done. He closed his eyes and issued a prayer of thanks to the Creator for always guiding the Aftar along a path of relative enlightenment.

It was also incredible to think that a small band of reptilians, hiding deep underground on a remote world millions of light years away from his home, held the key to the survival of his people and that of all other species in the entire Glaessan galaxy. And right now, it was up to him and his companions to figure out a way to stop these reptilians from carrying out the inevitable.

Actually, as he well knew, it was up to just him. He was the only one with enough knowledge of the Scriptures and the enchantments they contained, enchantments whose powers were the only chance he and his companions had to get out of this quagmire.

Dumyan, it seemed, knew this too, for he was trying to buy as much time as possible by continuously asking Jaegor more questions. Every now and then he was stealing a glance at Sharjam, as if trying to gauge if Sharjam had figured out which enchantment to use.

Sharjam hadn't figured anything out, however. He had only brought two scripture coins with him – the Scripture of Faith and the Scripture of War, since those were the only ones he had thought he would need. His mind was racing now, trying to sift through pages and pages of those two Scriptures from memory. But he couldn't concentrate. Too much was happening around him, too much new, frightful information coming out of Jaegor's mouth. Enacting an enchantment always required total concentration, patience and careful preparation. He had none of those luxuries at the moment, nor did he even know which enchantment to try.

As Jaegor's account came to an end, Sharjam knew he and his companions only had minutes left to live. Now they would be forced to reveal whatever the Starguzzlers wanted to know, and as soon as that was over, they would be blown to bits by those pole-like weapons. He tried his best to calm his mind and his nerves, praying to the Creator to give him strength and guidance. Then he focused his thoughts on the task at hand.

He thought first about repeating the disappearing enchantment he had orchestrated on Meenjaza to rescue Marc, Sibular and Zorina, but realized it wouldn't work here in the same way. Not unless he had the time to transport one individual at a time out of here and come back to get the next. No, it would have to be a different enchantment that required him to stay put and send his companions one by one to the surface of the planet. The question remained whether he would have enough time to get everyone out before the Unghans realized what was going on and fired at him, but it was better to save at least some of his companions than none at all. He had never tried such an enchantment before, so he didn't know for sure how quickly he would be able to get everyone out.

There was also another issue. It was clear that the Unghans had this so-called *transference* capability of their own, which they probably regularly used to travel between this settlement and the replica ships in orbit around the planet. That explained why there were no ships parked on the surface, except for the ones Jaegor and his cahoots had used to escape from Bara Dilshai. Jaegor had probably been in such a rush to call this meeting that he had landed straight on the planet, and had then used transference from the surface to reach the underground settlement. Using the same mechanism, some of the Unghans could easily transfer from here to the surface and pursue Sharjam's companions as they tried to escape. The Unghans could blow the Mendoken scout ship apart before it even had a chance to take off.

No, the only way for Sharjam to do this was to first get his companions out, and then use some other enchantment to destroy the Unghans. Leaving even one Unghan alive could pose a risk for his companions' escape. Leaving even one Unghan alive would permit the preparations for the Starguzzler invasion to continue, thereby initiating a far more cataclysmic destruction of life in the Glaessan. And it also meant one other thing – he would have to sacrifice his own life.

As this realization dawned on him, he began to feel afraid. Not afraid of death itself, for no devout Aftaran feared death, but afraid of leaving behind the ones he held dear. His thoughts went to Raiha, the one who he had decided to finally propose to if he ever made it back home. The one who he was ready to spend the rest of his life with, regardless of what anyone else thought or said. The one he had finally found again after all these years, only to lose her once more now, and this time forever. He thought about Autamrin, his kind and loving father, who had always protected him and guided him with words of wisdom. He remembered how his father had ruled the Dominion with a just and benevolent hand for so many glorious years. Yet the last living memory he would have of his father would be in that underground cave on the ice world of Tibara, hiding from those deadly surveyors. He would not live to see his father ever retake the throne, to see honor returned to his family and his clan, to see peace and happiness once again reign over the Aftaran people.

Sharjam turned to look at Dumyan, who had just started explaining to the Starguzzlers how he and his companions had gotten here. Dumyan had not given Jaegor the opportunity to threaten coercion, and had instead voluntarily begun talking. Spending a lot of time on details, he was giving a vivid description of how they had followed the escaping Unghans through the consar.

But Sharjam wasn't really listening to what Dumyan was saying. His mind was wandering, remembering all the adventures he and his brother had endured since their departure from the cave on Tibara. He could still hear his father's words of wisdom, saying that their mission together would make them begin to appreciate and understand each other. Well, that had certainly happened. After all they had been through, Sharjam finally felt he had a brother that he truly loved and a friend he could trust with his life. But now, just as they had finally attained the relationship their parents had always longed for, fate would tear them apart for good.

Lastly, Sharjam turned to look at Marc, and was instantly reminded of the reason they were all here. Marc Zemin, an alien from a small, unknown world, was the Sign, the Sign mentioned in the Hidden Scripture who would lead the Aftar to victory over the darkness that had befallen the Dominion. Sharjam and his brother had followed the prophecy to the letter. They had not hastened Marc's advent, and had not waited upon his arrival.

And indeed, Marc had not failed them – he had fulfilled the prophecy to the letter. He had lifted the curtain of deception and blindness cast over the eyes of the Aftaran people for so long, and had led them here to the very source of that darkness.

The Creator's ways were certainly strange, Sharjam knew, but in the end good did always triumph over evil. The Aftar and the other civilizations of the Glaessan would stand up to the Unghans and put an end to the Starguzzler invasion plan.

Sharjam just needed to execute his part of the Creator's will to make sure that was going to happen. He needed to get his companions out of here to return to the Glaessan and report what they had seen, and he needed to stop the Unghans from proceeding with their grand scheme. In other words, he was an integral part of the prophecy, a key player in the series of events that would lead to victory of the righteous over the unjust.

As Sharjam realized this, the fear in him subsided and hope took its place. He reminded himself that those who followed the paths of righteousness and faith were always the ones who prevailed in the end. The Creator was always on the side of the righteous, and the Creator was the most powerful of all. The Creator would protect him, in life and in death, and the Creator would also protect the loved ones he was leaving behind. His sacrifice was the Creator's will and a part of the Creator's plan.

Time was running out. Dumyan had just finished answering the Starguzzlers' questions. As expected, Jaegor was now giving the order to his guards to fire on the prisoners. While everybody's eyes were focused on Dumyan, Sharjam quietly slid his hand into his pocket and pulled out the scripture coin representing the Scripture of Faith. He held it tightly, feeling its warmth flow to his palm and up his arm. As the warmth spread over his entire body, he suddenly felt a surge of strength. Closing his eyes, he quickly whispered the following verse:

> *When evil seizes upon you from all sides,*
> *When all chances of survival have faded*
> *Like the light of the sun at dusk,*
> *Lose neither hope nor faith,*
> *For through thick and thin shall you be led*
> *Back into the light of the sun.*

He opened his eyes after uttering the last word, and blew a puff of air in Marc's direction. Marc instantly disappeared from sight. Without waiting, he blew another puff of air towards Sibular, followed by Zorina, and then the Aftaran soldiers and Mendoken troopers. One by one, they all vanished into thin air.

Sharjam's performance was so quick that by the time Jaegor and the other Unghans realized what was going on, only Dumyan was left. The Unghans began screeching in anger, and several of them jumped on Sharjam. They pulled his robe apart with their teeth as he fell to the ground, but not before he had successfully blown out one more puff of air towards Dumyan.

Dumyan, obviously realizing that Sharjam was in trouble, yelled out in anguish. "Sharjam, wait, do not...!" But it was too late. Dumyan faded away like the others, and was gone.

The Unghans held Sharjam firmly on the ground, keeping his arms and legs spread apart. Jaegor approached and stood over Sharjam, his face seething with rage.

"Your dratted magic will get you nowhere in our world, Aftaran!" he hissed. "We can instantly transfer anywhere ourselves, to the surface of the planet or beyond. Your pestilent companions will never escape. They will all be hunted down like prey and killed before they reach your ship. There will be nobody left to come back for you." He then addressed the Unghans holding Sharjam. "Take the coin away from him. Then let him die a most painful death."

Sharjam screamed in agony as the Unghans tore into his flesh with their sharp teeth. They left no part untouched – the stomach, chest, legs, arms, even the head. More and more of the other Unghans in the square crowded around to witness the spectacle and cheer their support for the killers. He could never have imagined such savagery from a species so advanced and intelligent.

Sharjam tried his best to keep his mind as focused as possible, to shut out all the distractions and the unbearable pain. The Unghans tried desperately to wring open his hand and grab the scripture coin from him, but he kept his fist clenched as tightly as he could. With whatever strength was left in his body, he whispered the next two verses from the Scripture of Faith:

> *Should evil engulf you and tear you asunder,*
> *Still lose neither hope nor faith,*
> *For the evil shall itself be torn asunder*
> *By the power of the blessed Scriptures.*
>
> *And as the sparkle of life in your heart fades*
> *Release your burden and rejoice,*
> *For you are of the righteous and just,*
> *And forever after shall you find naught but peace.*

Sharjam opened his eyes and stared Jaegor calmly in the face. "Surely the Creator watches over us in life and in death," he said, and broke into a wide smile. Then he opened his hand and let go of the scripture coin. The coin, now glowing brightly in a golden color, hit the ground with a soft tinkle.

Jaegor yelled to one of the guards holding a pole-like weapon to fire at Sharjam right away. But before the guard could break through the crowd and even aim the weapon, the scripture coin suddenly exploded with tremendous force, instantly pulverizing the bodies of Sharjam and all the Unghans around him. The shock wave spread to the edges of the underground settlement within seconds, obliterating everything in its path and leaving nothing but a cloud of fire and dust behind.

The ground shook with ferocity, causing Dumyan to fall onto the dead, frozen grass. He had just magically appeared on the surface of the planet, seconds after vanishing from the underground settlement. He was back in the very clearing from which they had earlier entered into the labyrinth. The others were all already there, dazed like he was. All, that was, except for Sharjam.

It took a moment for Dumyan's mind to clear, for him to realize what had just happened. And as soon as he did, he cried out, "Sharjam! What have you done! What have you done!"

There was no doubt what Sharjam had done. He had sacrificed himself to save his companions. He had first gotten them out to the planet's surface, and had then destroyed the underground settlement and all within.

Dumyan couldn't believe it. Although he had expected Sharjam to try to initiate some disappearance enchantment, he had expected him to come with the rest of the group. The Unghans would have chased them, of course, but at least there would have been a chance for escape. Dumyan had not in his wildest dreams imagined that Sharjam would stay behind and sacrifice himself like that. That was not the Sharjam he knew. The Sharjam he knew was never impulsive, never hasty or reckless, not like he was. And yet the same Sharjam had taken the most impulsive, daring action of all, far more so than he could ever have done.

As Dumyan lay there in shock, the ground shook again. The others, all visibly stunned by what had just happened, came close to him.

"Sharjam...?" Marc began. "What did he...?" His words trailed off. The look of horror and dismay on Dumyan's face was too obvious.

"Ay, he must have sacrificed himself for our sake," one of the Aftaran soldiers said sadly. "May the Creator grant him peace and happiness for eternity."

"Surely the Creator watches over us in life and in death," the other Aftarans added in unison, bowing their heads in reverence for the fallen one.

But there was no time for mourning. "We must get out of here, Dumyan," Sibular said in his usual emotionless tone. "The explosion has made the ground unstable."

Sibular was right. The ground wouldn't stop shaking, and the tremors were getting more violent by the second. The explosion had probably ruptured some fault line in the planet's crust, setting off a series of violent quakes.

Dumyan heard Sibular's words, but felt no strength to get up. His mind was filled with the haunting image of his brother being eaten alive by those savage

Unghans. He was the one who had hinted at Sharjam to take action. He was the one who had always prodded Sharjam to become more spontaneous and adventurous. Without a doubt, he was the one responsible for his younger brother's death, nobody else. Sharp pangs of pain hit his heart, and his breath grew shallow. He felt like he was drowning in a stormy sea of guilt and regret.

"Dumyan!" This time it was Zorina, and her voice sounded a lot more urgent than Sibular's. "We must get out of here! Come on! Now!"

Dumyan didn't budge.

"Dumyan!" Marc cried. "If we don't get out of here now, then your brother will have sacrificed himself for nothing!"

Dumyan knew Marc was right. But where was his strength? He just couldn't move. Then he felt several hands grab him and lift him up. They held him up until he was strong enough to stand on his own, and then pushed him to start walking through the forest. The walking soon turned to running, then to frantic fleeing.

His senses began to come back. He could now feel the ground shaking under his feet, and could see the trees swaying around him. He thought he heard branches and even entire trees crash to the ground nearby, but he wasn't sure. A couple of times he fell when the ground shook, but he just got up and kept on following the others.

Eventually they reached the other clearing where their scout ship was waiting. It was hovering in the air above the trees, to avoid being damaged by the shaking ground and falling branches. As soon as they appeared in the clearing, the ship lowered several steel-like ropes to the ground. The ropes immediately snapped around the waists of all of them, and effortlessly lifted them up into the air and into the belly of the ship. It was none too soon, for the ground under them shook again and suddenly cracked open, splitting the clearing into two and sending many of the uprooted trees into the growing crevasse below.

With all on board, the Mendoken pilot pointed the ship upwards and accelerated into the sky as quickly as possible.

The mood on board the scout ship was dour and sad. Nobody said a word, as the ship exited the planet's atmosphere and headed out into space. Marc knew he and his friends were lucky to have escaped at all, and with so few casualties. But none of that changed the fact that Sharjam was dead. Sharjam had done the ultimate noble, selfless thing – he had sacrificed himself to save the others. He had evidently also eradicated what was left of an entire civilization, but there had been no choice. Showing mercy here would have resulted in a much larger eradication of all civilizations in the Glaessan.

These Unghans had all been directly responsible for the great conspiracy over the civilizations of the Glaessan, Marc told himself. They had either participated in or at least actively supported the massacre about to take place across the galaxy, all of it to further their own ends. So none of these Unghans could really be called innocent. Furthermore, he didn't recall seeing any children among the Unghans. Perhaps the Starguzzlers hadn't allowed them to have any, in order to maintain tight control over their population growth.

Marc remembered how well he had gotten to know Sharjam over the past several days. It was Sharjam who had saved his life on Meenjaza and revealed the Unghan conspiracy to all, and it was Sharjam who had opened his eyes to his unique role as the Sign the Aftar had been waiting for. That same Sharjam was now dead.

As sad as he felt about what had happened, Marc didn't even want to imagine how Dumyan was feeling. It was just too horrible to think about. Instead, he tried to focus his thoughts elsewhere. Sitting in the main cabin, he stared out one of the windows at the abandoned replica ships hovering above the planet. Those were the only ships the Unghans seemed to have, no other ships of their own. Perhaps it was because the Starguzzlers had not allowed the Unghans to have any, thereby ensuring that the Unghans did not escape from their clutches. The only ships allowed were those constructed specifically to infiltrate the Glaessan for the purposes of the grand scheme.

It was amazing, he thought, to what lengths the Unghans had gone with their scheme. They were true masters of the arts of disguise and deception, and combined with their total lack of morals or compassion for others, had perfected their strategy of implosion. They would almost have succeeded with their plan to cause the major civilizations of the Glaessan to implode, were it not for the unexpected turn of events after his own arrival in the Dominion. Instead, their strategy of implosion, successful again and again for billions of years, had finally turned on them. In a sense, the Unghans had just been forced to implode themselves, by the very victims they had been targeting for implosion. And it was the last implosion any Unghan would ever live to see.

Or was it? He wondered if there were more Unghans still left in the Glaessan. Considering how far they had infiltrated the Aftaran Dominion and all the spies they had planted across the Mendoken Republic, it was only logical to assume that there were still many of them left. They would hopefully all be caught and dealt with in a just manner.

Right now, however, there was something far more critical to worry about – getting back to the Glaessan. And as he gazed out at the sky behind the replica ships, he knew it wasn't going to be easy. The Unghans were gone, but there was still another threat looming.

"Obviously Jaegor wasn't kidding when he said they were all coming here," Zorina said. She had just joined him by the cabin window.

Marc couldn't agree more. They had already seen the Starguzzlers in approach during their earlier descent to the planet. Back then, however, the Starguzzlers had just been tiny specks in the dark sky. Now that they had arrived, each of them appeared bigger than the very planet Marc and his companions had just left behind. Their massive bodies blocked the view of anything behind, and the light they emanated brightened up the sky like a million suns. Millions of them there had to be, for every direction the eye turned, they were there, and so close to each other that they were almost touching. The scout ship, the two planets and this whole section of the star system was completely surrounded by them.

Zorina scowled. "How are we going to get past them? I doubt they'll just give us free passage. Especially after what we did to their beloved Unghans."

Marc and Zorina walked up to the cockpit, where Sibular and the pilot were engaged in deep discussion.

"Can we enter a consar before we reach the Starguzzler blockade?" Marc asked Sibular.

"We were just discussing that," Sibular replied. "It will be difficult, considering the length of trajectory needed to enter the consar. The gravitational pull of the Starguzzlers will also be an issue, given their size. For ideal conditions, we need to be well past them before we can attempt any entry."

The less than ideal conditions, however, were about to get even less ideal. Some of the Starguzzlers, their red sparkles dancing viciously with anger, began spewing out hot flames. The flames looked like huge sun flares, each about the size of a whole moon, and quickly sped across vast expanses of space. Fortunately the aim of the Starguzzlers was hopelessly inaccurate. Just like Jaegor had said, they could not target anything smaller than an entire planet. But more and more Starguzzlers from all sides began shooting flames in the general direction of the scout ship, reducing the amount of free space left for it to move through.

"What are we going to do?" Marc wondered, feeling a tinge of panic as he saw the edge of one flame reach awfully close to the ship's left side. The path ahead was already blocked by several other flames, as was the path behind.

Zorina was flapping her ears in fright, and Marc thought he could hear her teeth chattering as well. She obviously had no idea what to do.

The pilot tried her best to maneuver the ship to dodge more incoming flames, swaying to the left and right, up and down. But it was getting increasingly difficult.

"Sibular!" Marc shouted, noticing how his Mendoken friend seemed to be standing still, as composed as ever. "Any brilliant ideas? All it will take is for one of those flames to hit us, and we'll all be fried in an instant!"

"Remember Volo-Gaviera, Marc?" Sibular replied calmly. "Perhaps we should try the same thing here."

"Volo-Gaviera? What's that got to..." Marc's eyes lit up, for he suddenly remembered how the Mendoken battlecruisers had shrunk to a tiny, untraceable size while trying to escape the onslaught of Volonan ships. "Why, yes! Is this ship equipped?"

"Yes, it is. We made sure of that before leaving on the mission. The technology has also been significantly improved in the meantime." Sibular pressed some controls on a screen, and the scout ship with all its contents began shrinking instantly.

"Sit back and enjoy the ride, Zorina!" Marc said, smiling. "You're about to have your socks blown off."

"I don't wear socks," Zorina replied, but then gasped as soon as she noticed the Starguzzlers and their flames outside growing infinitely larger. "Wha... what's happening?"

"Mendoken technology at its finest. I'd better inform the others in the cabin what's happening, before they freak out like you."

The Mendoken shrinking technology worked flawlessly. At a millionth its original size, the scout ship was easily able to maneuver around the Starguzzlers' flames, like a tiny fly evading the waving hands of a crowd of people. The Starguzzlers continued to spew their flames in all directions, but no longer had a clue where the ship was. The ship soon passed through the blockade unhindered, along a path right between the colossal bodies of two neighboring Starguzzlers.

"Free at last!" Zorina shouted, as the ship emerged on the other side of the blockade. A clear view of dark space lay beyond.

Marc stood next to her in the cockpit, and felt highly relieved as well. They had just passed what was hopefully the last of a series of insurmountable barriers.

"Free at last, yes, but look over there." Sibular pointed at a long series of blue circles in formation to the left, on the far side of the Starguzzler blockade. They were big, but very far away and only faintly visible to the naked eye.

Marc strained his eyes to see, and frowned as soon as he realized what they were. "Consar openings!"

"Yes," Sibular said, "it appears the invasion is going ahead. The Unghans must have left enough preparations already in place for the Starguzzlers to carry on by themselves."

Marc felt heavily disappointed. Sharjam had sacrificed himself for two reasons

– to save his companions and to prevent the invasion from happening. He had succeeded with the former, but regrettably not with the latter. Now it was up to his companions to make sure the latter was also successful.

"We've got to get back as soon as possible!" Zorina said. "We can no longer prevent the invasion. All we can do is to prepare everyone in the Glaessan for all out war. And it's going to be a war against an enemy more powerful than anything we have ever encountered before."

Everyone agreed. And so, after gaining a fair distance from the Starguzzler blockade, the ship regained its original size and entered a consar. The plotted destination: the Afta-Raushan system in the heart of the Glaessan galaxy, over 16 million light years away.

Chapter 39

The dry desert winds blew with gusto across Meenjaza's golden, sandy landscape. The cloudless sky was a clear blue and the sun shone brilliantly, just like the last time Marc had been here. But the last time he had been here, he had landed in chains. This time, he was landing as a hero.

The scout ship, escorted on both sides by Aftaran Shoyra-class vessels, landed safely on a circular open-air strip in between a number of Dominion administration buildings. The buildings were large and majestic looking, no different than other buildings on Meenjaza Marc had seen before. Their spiked domes and sweeping arches sat atop their pentagonal shapes, and tall pillars marked the many entrances on each side.

The journey through the consar had been largely uneventful, a most welcome change after the uninterrupted series of adventures the ship's occupants had faced with the Unghans and Starguzzlers. During the 8 days on board, Marc, Zorina and the other Aftarans had consoled Dumyan on his loss. They had pointed out how Sharjam had sacrificed himself for the most important of causes – the survival of the entire Aftaran race and of all other civilizations in the Glaessan. Sharjam would always be remembered as one of the greatest Aftarans in history for his contribution to his people. And now it was up to Dumyan to carry forward Sharjam's memory and make sure he had not died in vain, for the struggle was far from over. The main battle for survival still lay ahead.

News of the scout ship's safe return to the Glaessan had reached Meenjaza a few hours earlier, and a large crowd of Aftaran well-wishers and curious onlookers had already assembled around the landing strip. As the ship's doors opened, a number of floating platforms emerged from the gates of one of the buildings and came forward into the strip.

Marc stepped out into the open air, and saw several Aftarans and Mendoken descending from the floating platforms. Among them were Osalya and the Imgoerin. The two of them had evidently either stayed in the Dominion all this time, or had returned from the Republic for this event. Either way, their presence indicated just how important the Imgoerin considered this mission to have been.

There was another Aftaran accompanying the Imgoerin, one who Marc didn't recognize. He looked old, very old, and tired, as if he had not slept in many nights. His uncovered face showed tearful eyes. Dumyan ran up to him and embraced him, and the two held each other for a long time. No doubt, it was Autamrin, the father of Dumyan and Sharjam, the long time ruler of the Dominion before the advent of the Unghan conspiracy. This was a reunion of father and son, under what should have been very joyous circumstances. But the circumstances were far from joyous, for the other son was dead.

Marc then noticed Raiha standing nearby. She looked completely devastated. Her eyes were red from all the crying, the feathers on her face soaked with tears. All the short-lived hopes and dreams of a blissful life with Sharjam as her husband were now shattered forever. As he watched her, he felt a sudden surge of sorrow, and his own eyes began to moisten. For sure, he knew what it was like to lose a loved one so prematurely. It was something he would never want anyone to suffer through, not even his worst enemy.

Dumyan hugged Raiha, and whispered what must have been kind and soothing words into her ear. It was a stirring moment, and many in the crowd began to shift uneasily.

Another female Aftaran came forward and hugged Dumyan, then tried to console Raiha. Marc guessed this had to be Birshat, Dumyan's long time love. It was good, he thought, that Dumyan had someone to share his life with. Times were going to be tough for him for a while, having to cope with the loss of his brother and the associated feelings of guilt. Having someone he loved to support him during that period was going to be critical.

"Hail to Sharjam, our hero!" somebody suddenly yelled.

"Hail to Sharjam!" the crowd roared in response. "Hail to Sharjam!" Their voices sounded raw and full of emotion, like an army of soldiers crying out their readiness for battle.

"Hail to Autamrin, our true, just leader!" somebody else shouted.

"Hail to Autamrin, hail to Sharjam, hail to Dumyan!" was the unanimous roar. "May the Creator bless them!"

Marc watched the spectacle around him with wonder. There was so much

energy, so much excitement in the air. The alien conspiracy that had haunted the
Aftaran people for so long was gone, and the just, fair ways of old would once again
flourish across the Dominion. The Aftaran people were learning from the grievous
mistakes they had made, and would hopefully never repeat them.

Yet all he could feel was conflicted and uncertain. Not only was he worried about
the upcoming battle with the Starguzzlers, he couldn't stop thinking about all the
inexplicable things that had happened to him and all the supernatural capabilities
he had been given. And somehow, all seemed to have been magically foretold. Did
this prove the existence of some kind of higher power? Then again, if such a higher
power really did exist, and if that power really was as benevolent as its believers
seemed to think it was, why would it let all these horrible things happen in the first
place? Why would this power let good individuals like Sharjam die, and why would
it choose to ruin the lives of those who loved him so dearly?

As Marc wrestled with these thoughts, he overheard one of the Aftarans in the
crowd saying to Dumyan, "Mourn, Dumyan, but do not regret. Your brother did the
right thing. And do not forget that despite his suffering, he still killed all his
tormentors before they were able to kill him."

And that, Marc realized, was perhaps one way to rationalize the existence of a
higher power – justice was usually done in the end, in one form or the other.

According to Aftaran religious tradition, a burial ritual had to be enacted by the
nearest of kin as soon as any Aftaran was pronounced dead. If the body was not
present, a ritual still had to be held. The ritual for Sharjam, however, would have to
wait due to the unique urgency of the situation. After quick formal introductions
and a trip into one of the nearby administration buildings, the travelers were only
given a half hour to freshen up and have a quick meal. After that, they were to join
Autamrin and the Imgoerin in a conference. Sibular, who of course needed no
freshening up or nourishment, went off to the meeting right away.

After the meal, Marc, Dumyan and Zorina were ushered into the conference
room. The décor was standard Aftaran, with ornate foundations but sparse
furnishings. The white floor was shiny and spotless, with stone pillars on the sides
that shot straight up to the arched ceiling. The walls were covered with colorful
patterns and beautiful works of calligraphy, and small windows near the top of the
walls passed sunlight in at steep angles.

The room was filled with Aftaran and Mendoken dignitaries, and a number of
security guards. Among them were the Imgoerin, Osalya, Sibular, Autamrin,
Birshat and Raiha. They were all huddled around a collection of 3D screens floating
in midair. The screens were flashing through lists of data and graphical charts,

with reports constantly appearing from across the Dominion and the Republic.

"Mendoken equipment behind the scenes, no doubt," Marc thought. The Aftar just didn't have the level of technological sophistication needed to pull in data simultaneously from so many disparate sources over so vast a region of space.

Having heard the account of all that had happened in the other galaxy from Sibular, everybody in the room was eager to discuss how to handle the impending threat. So far, there were no reports of any Starguzzler sightings anywhere. But everyone knew it was just a matter of time before the reports began coming in. Autamrin had already ordered the destruction of all infant Starguzzler fields inside the Dominion, including the one on the planet Droila. The Imgoerin had instructed the Mendoken to do the same inside the Republic, if any Starguzzler fields were found there. It was also agreed upon that the caretaker Doolins were innocent of the Starguzzler conspiracy and had simply been tricked by the Unghans into submission. The Doolins were therefore to be told the truth about their former masters, and then to be freed to live their lives as they chose.

The discussion then began in earnest. There was unanimous agreement that the Starguzzlers would have to be confronted as soon as they began arriving in the Glaessan, before they could inflict much damage. The big question, however, was how to confront them.

"We cannot defeat them with our existing weapons," Sibular pointed out. "Even our planet destroyers are no match for their size and firepower."

"They can eradicate entire star systems at a time," Dumyan added. "They shoot long flames that burn up everything around them in an instant."

Marc nodded. "I'm certainly no expert on all the weaponry you have at your disposal, but I don't think there's any way you can fight the Starguzzlers by attacking them head-on with battleships. They're just too big. You'd need thousands of ships for each Starguzzler."

"What if the Volona join us in the battlefield?" Autamrin suggested, casting a quick glance at Zorina. His old voice seemed to quiver ever so slightly.

Zorina flapped her ears. "It would certainly help. My people are experts in defense, after all, and have a large armada of powerful warships. But to be honest, even if I had enough time to convince our headstrong Empress to join forces with the Volona's archenemies, it still wouldn't make enough of a difference for us to win. Like you, my people don't have the kind of weapons needed to tackle the Starguzzlers. Their size is definitely an issue, but it isn't the only issue. If we use conventional firepower, my guess is the Starguzzlers will just absorb the heat and energy from the shots and become even stronger. The Unghans told us the Starguzzlers are made mostly of hot gases and pure energy. So firing at them will pretty much have the same effect as hurling a boost of hydrogen into the center of a burning sun."

"That is what we have observed," Osalya said. "While you were gone to the other galaxy, we had several infant Starguzzlers transported from Droila to one of our ships for study. We were curious about their nature, after we had heard about the fields from Dumyan and Sharjam. Extensive tests conducted by our scientists revealed that these entities only grew bigger and stronger with every attempt to destroy them."

"That does not sound promising," Autamrin said. "I pray to the Creator that *someone* has an idea? I believe we are all painfully aware of what will happen if we have none."

Silence filled the room.

"You Volonans always pride yourselves in being at the forefront of defense research, Zorina," the Imgoerin finally said. "And you were their Chief Imperial Defender. What would you have done if the Starguzzlers were at the gates of your Empire?"

Zorina seemed a little taken aback by the directness of the question, but she didn't hesitate in responding. "Well, I would first try to figure out whether we had the necessary means at our disposal to counter the threat."

"And if not?"

"Then I would seek the help of somebody who did have the means, or at least the knowledge of how to acquire the means."

"And do you know who might have the means or the knowledge? Do not restrict yourself only to those you currently see around you." It almost seemed like the Imgoerin knew where this conversation was headed.

Zorina looked puzzled for a moment, but then broke into a wide grin. "Why, yes, as a matter of fact, I do."

"I thought you might, Zorina," the Imgoerin said calmly. "I thought you might. They are your friends and allies, after all."

"That they are!" The excitement on Zorina's face was starting to show, especially once she began bobbing her head up and down with delight. "You obviously are the Imgoerin for a good reason! I could kick myself for not thinking of this myself." Then she looked thoughtful. "You know, I'm kind of surprised the Unghans didn't think of them as a potential risk for the Starguzzlers."

"They probably did," the Imgoerin said. "Remember, the Unghans had planned to have them destroyed before the Starguzzlers arrived. But that plan was muddled and accelerated after our intervention. The Unghans and Starguzzlers may have seen no alternative, and just decided to take their chances with beginning the invasion right away."

"Who are you talking about?" Autamrin asked.

"Friends of my people, but enemies of yours," Zorina said. "The Phyrax."

Everyone in the conference room began talking to each other excitedly at the mention of that name.

The Phyrax, the Glaessan's fourth major civilization, and the only one Marc had not yet encountered. He recalled some of the facts that HoloMarc had given him on his first journey from Earth. Archenemies of the Aftar and enemies of the Mendoken by association, the Phyrax were the galaxy's only major civilization with no system of government, laws or sense of community. They lived as hermits in the clouds of their gaseous home planets. They were the only species with no gender and with no eyes, noses or ears. Their bodies were huge, growing up to 20 feet in height and 8 feet in width.

"Zorina, how do we know the Phyrax will be able to defeat the Starguzzlers?" Dumyan asked.

"We don't. But their physical nature suggests they may have a better chance than we do. Their bodies are made from the gases found in the atmospheres of their home planets. If anybody has a chance of not immediately getting pulverized to ash by the flames of the Starguzzlers, it's the Phyrax. They may actually be able to get close enough to put up a reasonable fight."

"Given their nature, they will likely also have a better chance of figuring out if the Starguzzlers have any vulnerabilities we can take advantage of," the Imgoerin added.

One of the prominent Aftarans in the room spoke. "Regardless, we cannot possibly join forces with old enemies who have done us so much harm throughout our history. We cannot trust the Phyrax."

Some of the Aftarans in the room began murmuring in agreement. Autamrin and Dumyan eyed them closely.

"With all due respect, can any of you offer an alternative solution?" Osalya said, putting an abrupt end to the murmurs.

Silence filled the room for a short while.

"Now is not the time for squabbling," Autamrin finally said. "We have done too much of that for too long. We may have plenty of differences with the Phyrax, but if we do not all unite against this new, deadly threat, none of us will be around much longer to carry on the squabbles. The Starguzzlers will not distinguish between Aftaran or Phyrax, Mendoken or Volonan – they will destroy us all."

Again a few murmurs among the Aftarans, this time most agreeing with Autamrin.

"But how do we get them to join us?" another Aftaran asked. "They will never believe what we have to say, and will accuse us of concocting some scheme to trick them. They do not trust us or the Mendoken, just like we do not trust them."

"No, but they'll trust me," Zorina said with an air of confidence. "I happen to know some of them personally. Besides, when the Starguzzlers begin arriving and destroying their worlds, they won't need much more convincing."

"Perhaps if we take one of the remaining infant Starguzzlers here as a sample, the Phyrax might have a chance to find a vulnerability in those monsters," Dumyan suggested.

"Yes, good idea," Zorina agreed.

"I shall go with you to the Phyrax. And we shall also take a cohort of soldiers for safety on the journey."

"No, Dumyan! You know the Phyrax – they're a little on the, ah, eccentric side. They will refuse to even talk to me if they see an Aftaran or Mendoken accompanying me."

"But you should not go alone! Too much is at stake for just one individual to carry this responsibility."

"Don't worry," Zorina said, smiling and casting a glance at Marc. "I won't."

A few hours later, a Mendoken scout ship took off from a Kril-3 battlecruiser above Meenjaza. Its destination: the Phyra-Keldax system inside the Phyrax Federation, over 100,000 light years away. On board were just two individuals, Marc and Zorina, sitting in seats installed for them in the cockpit. On board was also an infant Starguzzler, carefully sealed in a special container.

Both Marc and Zorina had been given a crash course on how to operate and pilot the ship. There had, however, been no time for practice runs. Reports of Starguzzlers arriving through consars in different parts of the galaxy were already coming in, so there wasn't a moment to lose. The scout ship was consar equipped, so luckily the journey wouldn't take more than 75 minutes. At standard kilasic speeds, it would have taken over 2 months.

Zorina, who sat in the pilot seat, led the ship out of the Afta-Raushan system. Marc, who was manning the consar instruments, plotted the consar trajectory and set up the entry point in a quiet region just outside the star system. The ship entered the consar without any problems, surrounded by the standard protective blue sphere and pulled straight into the tunnel by a powerful, invisible force.

As they watched the consar tunnel's familiar bands of thin matter fly by them, the two of them talked about what lay ahead.

"I'm sorry I volunteered you for this mission, Marc, but I had no choice," Zorina said, relaxing into her seat.

"Not at all," he replied. "I would have volunteered anyway. Anything I can do to save our galaxy. I'm also very curious to finally meet the Phyrax."

"Yeah, well, let me tell you, they aren't a very nice bunch."

"You mentioned to Dumyan that they're eccentric."

"Very! You should definitely leave all the talking to me while we're there. You'd be surprised at how strongly a Phyrax might react to something you unwittingly say. Before you know what's hit you, you'll be cast out of the Phyrax's home in the clouds. And since Phyraxes live on gas giants, the planet's dense, poisonous atmosphere will slowly eat up your insides as you fall to the core far below, rendering your prolonged experience of death most unpleasant."

Marc cringed at the thought, and wondered what he had gotten himself into. "So, uh, who are we meeting?" he asked, trying to sound cheerful.

"An old Phyrax friend of mine by the name of Jinser-Shosa. We worked together on a number of defense initiatives over the years, back when I was Chief Imperial Defender."

"So your people really are close to the Phyrax, then."

Zorina bobbed her head up and down. "You can say that again! The alliance isn't always fine and dandy or easy to maintain, but we generally get along. The Phyrax may be eccentric, but they're also very easy going and a lot of fun once you get to know them and earn their trust. Can't say the same for your robotic Mendoken and ultra-religious Aftaran buddies." She smiled. "In my virtual world inside the Grid, I always pictured Jinser-Shosa as a handsome male Volonan. I'm curious to see what it looks like in real life."

"It?"

"Yes, 'it'. Phyraxes have no gender, remember?"

"Ah, yes, what a strange concept." Marc had never heard of an intelligent, sentient being without gender. He then remembered the other unique thing about the Phyrax. "So if they have no sense of community and are so individualistic, then how will convincing one of them to help us get more of them to help?"

She laughed. "They're individualistic alright, but that doesn't mean they have no sense of responsibility or compassion for each other. The Mendoken and Aftar like to think they don't, one of the many prejudices your buddies have about others they don't understand. The Phyrax actually have this unwritten code of conduct and honor among themselves, where they respect each other's boundaries and preferences. They also help each other out if asked, especially if they can be convinced that there's something in it for them too. How else do you think they've become such a powerful civilization over time?"

Marc considered this point, and realized it was true. A completely individualistic society, where each member did his, her or 'its' own thing without any regard for anyone else, could never function as a society. It would just never evolve – nobody would ever work together with anyone else to accomplish anything. Instead, everybody would just keep stepping on and fighting each other to get ahead. Any attempts at construction would be doomed for destruction.

Both of them remained quiet for a while. The consar walls outside were pitch dark now, indicating the ship was deep inside the tunnel.

Zorina finally broke the silence with a big sigh. "You know, I really miss my life back in the Grid."

He turned to look at her. "I'm not surprised. That's where you spent most of your life. And your days since you left the Grid have not exactly been the rosiest, first living as a lone scavenger on the planet Nopelio, then getting pulled into this series of life threatening adventures because of me."

"Oh, don't get me wrong. I don't regret for a second having joined you on this quest. Anything was better than the lonely life I was leading on Nopelio. And it certainly has been a most eye opening and exciting experience for me. Not just because of the criticality of our mission and what's at stake for all of us, but because of everything I've learned about the Mendoken and the Aftar in the process. Like all Volonans, I grew up with hordes of prejudices about those two peoples. Now that I've interacted with them myself, I feel far more positive about them. Plus, I've made some good friends in the process, like you."

Marc felt a tingle of warmth in his heart. "So what do you miss, then? Or, should I say, *who* do you miss?"

She grinned. "It seems you know me too well, eh? I do miss the ease of life in the Grid, the ability to constantly experience all kinds of pleasure without really having to work to earn them. But you're right. What I miss most is a 'who'. I miss him a lot. Terribly, in fact. If there's a single wish I have, other than the defeat of the Starguzzlers, of course, it's to one day find Rudoso and be with him again."

"If we survive the Starguzzler onslaught, I'm sure you will."

Zorina shook her head. "You don't know my sister. She is so jealous and vengeful by nature that she will ensure I remain a fugitive from the Grid for the rest of my life. She could never bear to see me and Rudoso happy together."

"Even though that whole anomaly in the Grid was not your fault?"

"As I said, you don't know my sister."

"Well, I would place my hopes on just one thing then. If we succeed in our mission, the Empress might be so grateful to you for saving her Empire from destruction that she will forgive you. She might even let you back into the Grid as a free Volonan."

"I certainly hope you're right, Marc. But hope is all I have at the moment."

Marc noticed the tunnel outside beginning to light up. They were nearing the end of the consar. "Well, my friend, if that's all we have, then let's cling on to it with all our might."

Chapter 40

The Aftaran burial ritual was generally a very simple occasion. The nearest of kin of the deceased would wrap the body in the same robe that Aftaran had worn on the day of his or her passing. They would then take the body to a prayer hall and lay it flat on the ground. Sitting around the body, they would pray for that individual's peace and protection in death. This part of the ritual could last anywhere from a few minutes to several hours, depending on how long they wanted to keep praying. Afterwards, they would carry the body outside to the nearest burial site and lay it to rest in the ground.

Aftarans did not bother with elaborate coffins, tombstones or unique locations of choice to bury their dead. Any hole in the ground in a designated burial area was acceptable, and the only thing separating the body from the surrounding soil was the robe. According to Aftaran beliefs, the body was no longer of any value once the individual was dead. It was the spirit that remained sentient in death, the spirit that was set free. And the Creator did not distinguish between spirits by their wealth or appearance. The only thing the Creator cared about was how good that individual's character had been in life, and that was the only criterion the Creator used to determine how peaceful to render that individual's eternity in death.

Sharjam's burial ritual was held without his body, since his body had been blown to bits on a world millions of light years away. Inside the prayer hall, Dumyan sat in a large circle facing nothing more than a bare stone floor. But it mattered not, for the ritual was meant for Sharjam's spirit, not his body. It was his spirit that everyone was praying for.

Dumyan's father was sitting nearby in the circle, accompanied by a number of close relatives from the Subhar clan. Birshat and Raiha were there too. Dumyan also spotted most of the other Aftarans who had spent two years with him and Sharjam in hiding in the underground caves of Tibara, including Zeena and Kabur.

Dumyan closed his eyes and uttered prayer after prayer for his brother's spirit. It was strange how the words came so freely out of his mouth now, when for most of his life he had so strongly resisted the pressure to learn the verses of the Scriptures and follow their guidance. All his life he had been quite the rebel against the Aftaran traditions, all his life he had butted heads against his brother for being so religious and so conservative.

But thanks to Sharjam, Dumyan had at last begun to understand the virtues of living a life of piety, especially after witnessing firsthand the truths and powers hidden inside some of the verses of the Scriptures. Thanks to Sharjam, Dumyan had seen the merit of using prudence and taking the time to think something through before jumping into action. Yet thanks to Dumyan, Sharjam was now dead. Dumyan would never forgive himself for that, as much as others had tried to console him that it wasn't his fault.

Dumyan turned to look at his father, who was sitting some distance away in the circle to his right. The old Aftaran looked sad and defeated, rather than happy and proud to have retaken the throne over the Dominion. His eyes looked as though they had aged a hundred years since Dumyan had left him on Tibara, most of it probably in the last day and a half after hearing the news of Sharjam's death. He probably blamed himself for what had happened, for having sent his two sons into harm's way in the first place.

As he stared at his father, Dumyan silently pledged to himself, and to the Creator, that he would lead his life in a more balanced way from now on. The Creator willing, if the Starguzzlers were defeated, he would make it a point to find a Master under whom he could study the Scriptures. He knew he was a little old to start now and it would certainly take a long time to reach Sharjam's level of knowledge and power, but he was determined to do it. It was the very least he could do to honor his fallen brother. It was the least he could do to carry on Sharjam's legacy for the sake of his family and his clan, for nobody in the current generation of the Subhar clan was as well versed in the intricacies of the Scriptures as Sharjam had been. Indeed, it could be argued that there weren't too many Aftarans left in the entire Dominion who were as well versed as Sharjam had been, thanks to the persecution and eradication of many of the Aftar's great spiritual leaders during Wazilban's brutal reign.

After the ritual was over, the Aftarans in the circle got up and dispersed. Dumyan headed with his father over to one of the nearby landing strips, to meet with the Imgoerin and his contingent one last time. The Mendoken were preparing to leave and head back home, from where they would prepare their forces in the Republic for battle.

The Imgoerin and Autamrin had already had a lengthy discussion before the burial ritual, and had made some key strategic decisions. Given the close alliance between the two nations, the Mendoken and Aftar would combine forces wherever possible to combat the Starguzzlers. Obviously Mendoken military technology was far superior to that of the Aftar, and the Mendoken had more ships by several orders of magnitude. But the Aftarans, with their years of wisdom, experience and supernatural abilities, would provide valuable insight and help wherever needed. Ironically, the terms of the agreement were not too different from those of the covenant the Imgoerin had earlier almost signed with Lord Wazilban. The cause this time, however, was different and far nobler.

The Aftarans would also send a delegation to the Volonan Empire to persuade the Volona to join the war effort. In this war, all four of the major civilizations would have to unite and collaborate if they were going to succeed. For the first time in history, all four civilizations were about to face a single, common enemy that threatened their very existence.

The Volona were not exactly on good terms with the Aftar, but at least those terms were better than the ones they had with the Mendoken. The Aftar stood a better chance of persuading the Volona than the Mendoken did, especially considering that the Unghan conspiracy had been based in the Dominion. The Aftaran delegation would present tons of evidence about the conspiracy to the Volonan Empress, to help her overcome any suspicions and make her realize what was at stake for her own people.

"All is settled then, Autamrin?" the Imgoerin asked, just as he was getting ready to board his shuttlecraft on the landing strip. Most of the Mendoken in the contingent had already left on other shuttles and had boarded their mother vessels out in space. Apart from the Imgoerin and his bodyguards, Sibular and Osalya were the only Mendoken left on the strip.

"Yes, Franzek," Autamrin replied. "Dumyan will lead the delegation to the Volona. I am not happy to let him go, especially not now. But I know there is no better Aftaran to do the job."

"Good. My engineers have already equipped several of your Gyra-class ships with consar capability. So your delegation should be able to reach the Volo-Maree system within 2 hours, avoiding the infamous border barrier along the way as well."

Autamrin smiled. "I do not know how to thank you for everything, Franzek."

"Thank me when the battle is over and we have won," the Imgoerin said simply, as he boarded the shuttle with his bodyguards.

Sibular and Osalya both waved goodbye to the Aftarans and followed the

Imgoerin inside. Seconds later, the shuttle lifted off without a sound and flew straight up into the clear blue sky. It disappeared from sight in the blink of an eye.

Dumyan stood next to his father, deep in thought. The battle ahead was inevitable. Only a miraculous intervention by the Creator would prevent it, and that was unlikely to happen. The only question that remained was whether the Creator would help them gain victory over the Starguzzlers. He thought about the new task he had just been assigned, and knew it was not going to be easy. Luckily Zorina had given him specific instructions on how to travel within the Empire without being detected by Volonan forces, how to connect to the Grid and how to get a direct audience with the Empress. But Zorina had also made clear that trying to get out of the Grid after being connected to it was going to be no trivial task.

Autamrin put his hand on Dumyan's shoulder. "Well, my Son, all we can do now is place our hopes on a Volonan fugitive and a being from a silupsal-covered world none of us know anything about."

Dumyan sighed and nodded slowly. "May the Creator grant them success. Otherwise everything else we are doing will have been in vain."

The Phyrax Federation covered the largest region of space in the Glaessan galaxy, with over 580 billion star systems in its jurisdiction. Although the overall population of the Phyrax was lower than that of both the Mendoken and the Volona, their adventurous, conquering spirit had caused them to travel far and wide from the very beginnings of their civilization, colonizing vast expanses and the farthest corners of the galaxy in their name before anyone else.

Phyra-Keldax, a blue supergiant star with a diameter over 600 times, a mass over 70 times and a luminosity over 10,000 times that of Earth's Sun, was located in one of the galaxy's farthest corners, in a region humans on Earth believed was a part of the neighboring Large Magellanic Cloud galaxy. Humans, of course, had no idea that the size of the Milky Way was actually more than 10 times what they thought it was, easily engulfing both Magellanic Clouds. And, as with all inhabited star systems in the galaxy, Phyra-Keldax was completely invisible to human telescopes, even with its sheer size. Phyra-Keldax was so big, in fact, that if it were to take the place of Earth's Sun, its body would easily engulf the orbits of Mercury, Venus, Earth and even Mars.

Due to its fairly unique size and luminosity, Phyra-Keldax always shone brightly in the sky in its section of the galaxy, more so than most other stars nearby. Marc didn't know this, so when the scout ship he and Zorina were on emerged from the consar it had been traveling through, he was stunned by the dazzling splendor of the big sun that lay ahead.

"Guess I forgot to tell you," Zorina said, laughing at his reaction. "This is one of the largest stars in the entire galaxy."

"Incredible!" he whispered.

"Isn't it? Ironically, the largest stars also have the shortest lives. They can't sustain their sizes for too long and eventually collapse in on themselves by their own gravitational pull. The result is a supernova explosion, often further leading to a neutron star or even a black hole."

The scout ship headed directly for the 14th out of a total of 36 planets in the star system, a gas giant by the name of Devoreef. At 3 times the size of the planet Jupiter, it certainly was huge, though easily dwarfed by the sun it orbited around. There was a multitude of rings around it, like the planet Saturn.

"That's where Jinser-Shosa lives?" Marc asked.

"Yes. Now, how much do you know about gas giants?"

Marc tried to recall some of the things he had learned in his undergrad astronomy classes. "They're composed mostly of gas, obviously. A gas giant may have a rocky core, but the majority of its mass comes from gas, mainly hydrogen and helium. Essentially the entire planet is like one huge atmosphere."

"A very hot and inhospitable atmosphere, mind you, and it's also filled with ammonia and methane. The Phyraxes love it, of course. For them, the atmospheres on our worlds would be totally inhospitable. Anyways, we'll have to wear protective suits with oxygen supplies the whole time we're there. We'll also have to limit our physical movement. Because of the size and mass of the planet, the gravitational pull on Devoreef is, ah, shall we say, several times higher than anything you've ever experienced in your life before. The good news is that we're going to be at a very high altitude, so the effects won't be as pronounced."

Devoreef appeared in the distance to the naked eye. It was orange in color, like Jupiter and Saturn, with the many colorful lines and patches spread across its surface indicating a very stormy atmosphere.

"Definitely looks far from inviting," Marc observed.

"You can say that again! Back when I was connected to the Grid, I always saw this planet as a paradise of lakes and pastures whenever I visited Jinser-Shosa. Certainly looks a lot worse in real life."

"Wait, so you've never actually seen any of this with your own eyes?"

"Oh, I saw it alright. Just that the Grid translated everything I saw into what my mind wanted to see. And the Grid took care of all my body protection needs automatically, of course, because it sensed where I was going."

Marc shook his head in wonder. Even though he had heard so much about Volonan virtual technology by now, he never ceased to be amazed at how the whole thing worked.

As they approached the planet, Zorina began slowing the ship down, and used the onboard communication system to send out a greeting signal to Jinser-Shosa. She also explained to Marc how the Phyrax had no coordinated system of defense or communication within the Federation, and only very loose border controls along the Federation's perimeter. Phyraxes did communicate with each other individually and also shared information, but each individual was on its own for the most part. And if any individual had guests from outside, that was that individual's business and not anyone else's.

It took almost a minute for a response to come through. The voice sounded raspy and full of excitement, and Marc couldn't place whether it was male or female. It seemed to fall right in the middle. "Zorina! Old pal! What a pleasant surprise! See you in a few."

"In case you're wondering, Jinser-Shosa is one of the few non-Volonans who physically saw me when I was still connected to the Grid," Zorina said to Marc. "We Volonans generally don't allow outsiders to see us."

"So I've heard. Although it seems you have single handedly changed all that. Now we all know what you Volonans look like. Personally, I think that's a good thing."

She chose not to respond, focusing instead on carefully leading the ship through Devoreef's rings and into the thick, poisonous atmosphere. The view outside was instantly filled with dark, stormy clouds on all sides. Their reddish and orange colors became visible whenever a periodic flash of lightning shot through the sky. Tiny droplets of rain kept landing on the cockpit windows, but were instantly squeezed out of sight by the ship's high speed.

"How can anyone live in a place like this?" Marc wondered. The only consolation he had was that this Mendoken scout ship was specifically designed to travel through hostile atmospheres on unexplored worlds. Its heavy hull was made of a totally impervious material, and it could remain perfectly steady even in the stormiest and windiest of environments. Ingenious Mendoken technology constantly kept adjusting the ship's motion to compensate for external turbulence.

After several minutes of descent through the thick clouds, Zorina pointed at an approaching blip in the navigation screen. "There it is! Jinser-Shosa's home."

Another couple of minutes later, Marc could see a dark shadow ahead through the cockpit window, even darker than the clouds it was surrounded by. It almost looked like a cloud itself, but its edges were a little sharper and straighter, and there were lights glistening over its surface.

As the scout ship came closer, it soon became clear to him how massive the structure was. The difference in size between it and the ship he was on was like that between an oversized elephant and a tiny ant. It was also amazing to think that the entire thing was made of gaseous material.

Zorina slowed the ship down as a gate opened on the surface of the structure. "Jinser-Shosa is waiting for us inside," she announced.

The ship passed through the gate. Inside was a bizarre world that Marc wasn't sure at first what to make of. The place was foggy but well lit, with windows along the surface providing views of the outside. There were no walls, no floors and no ceilings, just vast emptiness. It was like being inside the belly of a huge whale, a cloudy, misty belly. There were brightly colored objects floating around everywhere, however. Most of them looked somewhat like furniture items, and many kept changing shape. Some looked like comfortable reclining seats one moment and beds the next, while others switched between bizarre looking tables and shelves. There were also other devices floating around, some of which looked like weapons and different types of machines. They all had one thing in common, though – they were enormous, many almost as large as the scout ship itself. Zorina didn't bother maneuvering the ship around them, choosing to fly right through them instead. They were made of gas, after all, and posed no threat to the ship's hull. She finally brought the ship to a standstill in front of a red, blinking light.

Behind the light, a figure became visible. At first, Marc thought it was just another item of furniture changing shape. But he quickly recognized the shape from his own visions and the pictures HoloMarc had once shown him. It had the overall resemblance of a fluffy cloud, but it did have a distinct head, main body and a couple of long, wavy limbs. Without a doubt, it was a Phyrax.

"Must be taller than a giraffe!" he thought. It had to be close to 20 feet in height. The giraffe was also the right animal to compare to for another reason, thanks to the Phyrax's yellow color and big brown patches all over its body. The body, however, was much wider than that of a giraffe, perhaps 7 feet in the middle. The face was also nothing like that of a giraffe. It was devoid of any features whatsoever – no eyes, nose or mouth, no ears or hair. It was, in fact, a perfectly expressionless face.

"Come on, let's go!" Zorina said, getting up from the pilot's seat.

They both put on protective suits supplied by the Mendoken. Several properties of the suits, including their heights, had been specially adjusted for Marc and Zorina before their takeoff from Meenjaza.

As Marc sealed the transparent helmet over his head, he felt like he was looking out from inside a fishbowl. Three small screens appeared in his line of vision, displaying data about the current status of the suit's internal and external environment. To his surprise, the Mendoken had even remembered to make sure his suit displayed data in English. "That's what you call attention to detail," he thought.

Marc and Zorina tested the communication link between the two suits, and then Zorina opened the door to the outside. As they both expected, gaseous fumes immediately burst into the cabin of the ship. But the suits were not affected at all, allowing them both to breathe from the supply of compressed oxygen stored in slim tanks on their backs.

"Now remember," she said, as she got ready to step out of the ship, "leave all the talking to me. Under no circumstances should you open your mouth!"

"What if I get asked a direct question?"

Zorina tried to flap her ears inside her helmet. "Which part of my instructions didn't you understand?" With that, she operated her suit's controls and floated out into the gas and vapor filled world beyond.

Marc followed a couple of minutes later, once he had figured out how to operate his own suit's controls and had tried taking a few steps inside the ship. With the planet's strong gravitational pull, every move he made would require a lot of energy. "This is definitely not going to be fun," he thought.

"How are you?" Zorina asked Jinser-Shosa. Her suit was working to keep her suspended in a stationary position in the gas filled emptiness of the Phyrax's home.

Jinser-Shosa was flying freely around her. "How? Horrible, that's how!" Its voice was loud and rough, and translated into perfect English for Marc by his unfailing Mendoken translator. Its face remained completely blank and still while it spoke, as if somebody else altogether was speaking. Then it suddenly flew off into the depths of the cloud, sat on one of the moving seats for a few seconds, and flew back. "Life is disgusting!"

"Disgusting? Why is it disgusting?"

"Because you brought this, this... thing with you!" Jinser-Shosa pointed one of its limbs in Marc's direction.

Marc swallowed hard, wondering how the Phyrax could see without any eyes.

Zorina laughed. "You mean Marc? He's a good friend of mine."

"But not of mine. I want him dead, right now!" Jinser-Shosa lunged forward to attack Marc.

"Stop!" Zorina shouted with defiance, immediately blocking the way. "You will not touch him!"

The Phyrax pulled back, much to Marc's relief. "I hate strangers," it grumbled, "especially in my home."

Zorina seemed unperturbed, as if she had been expecting this. "Jinser-Shosa, we've been friends for a long time now, haven't we?"

"Why, yes, we have," the Phyrax admitted.

"And do you think I'd bring a stranger to your home without a valid reason?"

"No, no, I suppose not." Jinser-Shosa flew away again, and returned several seconds later lying on a bed.

"What a bizarre individual!" Marc thought. Jinser-Shosa clearly was eccentric, and not just because of its appearance.

"So what does bring you here, my friend?" Jinser-Shosa asked Zorina.

"Well, it's a long story. We come from the Aftaran Dominion, where..."

"The Dominion!" Jinser-Shosa screamed. "How dare you! You are herewith a sworn enemy of mine!" This time it lunged forward at Zorina, brandishing a weapon that had floated onto one of its limbs.

But Zorina stood firm. "Stop this!" she shouted back. "Listen to me first, will you, before jumping to conclusions like this for no reason?"

Again the Phyrax pulled back, and let go of the weapon. It flew off once more, only to return on a seat again.

Marc realized Zorina had been wise to tell him to keep his mouth shut. Talking to Phyraxes obviously required a certain amount of skill and experience, both of which she seemed to have. If he had spoken, he would probably have been burned to ashes by now.

Zorina proceeded to tell Jinser-Shosa the whole story of the Unghan conspiracy and the Starguzzler invasion. She also explained who Marc was, how they had met on the planet Nopelio, and related the series of adventures they had experienced together. Throughout the narration, Jinser-Shosa kept charging at Marc whenever the Mendoken and Aftar were mentioned by name, only to be pushed back again by Zorina every time. It also asked a lot of questions, especially whenever the Starguzzlers were mentioned. And at least once every few minutes it abruptly flew off. Every time it did this, Zorina stopped her account, after which it would come rushing back to hear more. Then she would patiently continue with her story.

"Some attention span this Phyrax has," Marc thought. He was starting to wonder how a creature as crazy and inconsistent as this could possibly help them defeat the Starguzzlers, and he hoped to high heaven Zorina knew what she was doing.

Zorina finished telling her story, and Jinser-Shosa flew off again. This time it was gone for almost a minute, during which Marc cast uneasy glances at Zorina. To his surprise, however, Zorina seemed perfectly calm.

The Phyrax flew back, holding what appeared to be a screen of some sort. "Well, Zorina, you know, those, those... things you mentioned."

"The Starguzzlers."

"Indeed! Nasty, aren't they? Do they look anything like this?" Jinser-Shosa nodded at the screen, and suddenly a crystal clear image sprang to life.

Marc's jaw dropped in amazement, and any doubts he had about the Phyrax dropped as well. The image displayed a Starguzzler, spraying fire at a brown colored planet.

"Yep, that's them!" Zorina replied excitedly, trying to bob her head up and down inside her helmet.

"These revolting monsters! That picture was taken an hour ago in the nearby Phyra-Roidax system. They've suddenly begun popping up everywhere across the Federation and wreaking havoc. I've been picking up reports and requests for assistance from other Phyraxes all morning, and I was just getting ready to go out and try to help my neighbors in Phyra-Roidax when you called."

"I am not surprised," Zorina said. "The Starguzzler invasion has begun. And believe me, they will leave no corner of the Federation untouched. It's only a matter of time before they arrive here at Phyra-Keldax."

"Horrible! So do you know how to fight these behemoths? I hear they destroy everything in their paths in one sweep, and many Phyraxes have already been killed. It's just ghastly! What to do? What to do?"

Jinser-Shosa was about to fly off again, but Zorina stopped it short. "We are here because of the Starguzzlers, Jinser-Shosa, but we were hoping you would be the one to figure out how to fight them. No Volonan, Aftaran or even Mendoken will be able to, that much is for sure."

The Phyrax let out a deafening laugh. "Me? How could I? I've never seen them or fought against them before."

"Well, the renowned courage of your people aside, because the Starguzzlers are made of gas, like you. If anyone can find a way to destroy them, it's you."

"But I don't even know their chemical composure! And I couldn't possibly get close enough to one of them to figure it out. I would be instantly destroyed, and then what good would that do any of us?"

"Not to worry, my friend. I wasn't thinking of putting you in harm's way like that, not just yet anyway." Zorina chuckled. "It just so happens that we have a solution to your dilemma. But first, I need you to promise me something."

Chapter 41

Jinser-Shosa did make the promise, but only after a lot of arguing and numerous attempted charges at both Marc and Zorina. In the end, Zorina made Jinser-Shosa realize that the challenge ahead was far too big to waste time fretting over old grudges the Phyrax had towards the Aftar and Mendoken. After all, it was the Unghans who had instigated the current wars, not the Aftar or Mendoken, and their agenda couldn't be allowed to succeed. She explained that the only way to defeat the Starguzzlers was to eradicate them across the entire Glaessan, not just in the Federation. Destroying only the ones in the Federation would result in more of them continuously coming into the Federation from other parts of the galaxy and wreaking more havoc. Jinser-Shosa therefore had to give Zorina its word that if she provided the Phyrax with the means to find a way to destroy the Starguzzlers, the Phyrax would in turn help the Volona, Mendoken and Aftar destroy the Starguzzlers in their sections of the galaxy.

With that, Zorina and Marc went back into the scout ship and brought forward the container housing the infant Starguzzler.

"Here you go!" Zorina said. "Analyze away."

Jinser-Shosa's first reaction, once it realized there was an infant Starguzzler inside, was to lunge at the container and destroy it. But Zorina quickly convinced the Phyrax not to, explaining how samples of the Starguzzler could be taken to perform tests and find a potential vulnerability.

Marc was amazed at how impulsive Jinser-Shosa was. It seemed to always react first and think later. If the Phyrax were like this in general, that certainly explained why they didn't function as a community and chose to live such independent, individual lives. They would all end up killing each other if they spent too much time together.

Jinser-Shosa picked up the container and flew off without another word.

The two friends waited, and waited. They could hear strange noises in the distance, like saws buzzing and metal chains clanking against each other, followed by wailing sirens and howling winds. Then all was quiet. Finally a flash of brilliant light appeared ahead, followed by a loud thud.

A few minutes later, the Phyrax returned. Parts of its face and body seemed to be covered with ash, and one of its limbs was blown away.

Marc was about to open his mouth to ask what had happened and if Jinser-Shosa needed help, but Zorina quickly motioned to him to keep quiet.

"What news?" she asked.

Jinser-Shosa's limb magically began growing back as it spoke, and its voice gave no indications of pain. "Well, I took a look at that mini-monster. And fortunately it is no more!" It laughed. "I have to say, it felt wonderful to destroy that thing!"

"But not before you...?"

"Hmm? Oh, yes, yes, the reason you brought it here. I think we may have something. But it will be risky."

"Pray, tell us."

"I will, but along the way."

"To...?"

"Phyra-Roidax, where we can try out my theory for real."

Every Phyrax's home was also an interstellar ship, and Phyraxes simply called them *homeships*. The vast, irregularly shaped gas formation that constituted a Phyrax's typical homeship had an invisible, impenetrable seal around its perimeter, allowing it to travel through the vacuum of space without losing its structural integrity. A number of kilasic engines were usually anchored right in the heart of the homeship, controlled by a series of instruments that randomly floated around within the perimeter.

Phyraxes, in keeping with their hermit lifestyles, generally traveled alone. Although each homeship had plenty of empty space inside to hold a decent population, Phyraxes preferred total solitude. Even in battle, every Phyrax charged ahead with its own homeship. There was no coordinated army or leadership that gave the orders. Somehow, however, the Phyrax as a species were always very successful in battle. Their enemies attributed this phenomenon to a number of factors, including their individual bravery, their ability to innovate under the harshest of circumstances, as well as their unbending spirit of adventure and burning desire to conquer.

It was an exception for Jinser-Shosa, therefore, to be traveling with guests on board its homeship, and it made no secret of its displeasure in having to do so. Both Marc and Zorina remained quiet during the barrage of insults and threats of destruction they kept receiving. Marc was definitely getting quite used to the Phyrax's irrational behavior by now, and tried hard not to take the harsh words personally.

With its powerful engines, Jinser-Shosa's homeship lifted effortlessly out of Devoreef's atmosphere and headed out into space. The Mendoken scout ship that Marc and Zorina had arrived on was still inside, securely parked in one of the lower corners of the homeship's belly. The two of them joined Jinser-Shosa near a set of windows and controls on one edge of the ship, keeping a clear distance behind the Phyrax so as not to encroach upon its sense of space. Phyraxes generally needed a lot of space for themselves, since they tended to aimlessly fly about a lot. The controls kept flying about randomly as well, and had to be followed wherever they went.

The maximum speed this homeship could reach was close to 200,000 times the speed of light, allowing it to travel to the neighboring Phyra-Roidax system in just under a half hour. And when the homeship arrived at its destination, its sensors indicated that the local scene was far from pretty. A miniaturized rendering of the star system showed that 3 of its planets and 10 of its moons were no more. They had just been blown away and completely erased from the map.

Jinser-Shosa cursed away. "You murderous, brainless blobs of hot air! Just you wait, your time is coming!"

"Their time is coming," Marc thought. He certainly hoped so anyway. He had absolutely no idea what Jinser-Shosa was planning to do. Along the way, it had abruptly decided not to tell him or Zorina anything, just because it hadn't felt like doing so.

The culprits were spotted just outside Phyra-Roidax, four of them, happily sucking plasma from the star's core. Phyra-Roidax was a small star, far smaller than the supergiant Phyra-Keldax and significantly smaller than Earth's Sun as well. At the rate it was losing its gas to these Starguzzlers, it didn't have too long to live.

As the homeship approached the star, several surviving Phyrax homeships were spotted nearby, bravely trying to bombard the Starguzzlers with the weapons at their disposal. It was all to no avail, of course. All shots fired just disappeared inside the Starguzzlers' bodies with no effect, probably attenuated to nothingness by the dense plasma layers. The Starguzzlers weren't even paying any attention to the attackers, well aware that nothing and nobody was powerful enough to harm them.

"Those fools!" Jinser-Shosa shouted. "They have no idea what they're up against." It immediately made contact with the other Phyraxes, telling them to stop firing and to pull away. This homeship was going in with a plan, and it needed no help.

"You are sure about what you're doing, right?" Zorina asked.

Jinser-Shosa turned from the ship's controls and leaped towards Zorina. "You doubt me after all these years of knowing me?"

"No! I, ah, don't doubt you. I just want to make sure you've taken everything into account. We're only going to get one chance at this. And if we fail, then all is lost."

"Hmph! In that case, stop bothering me and let me make sure I get it right!" The Phyrax went back to making adjustments to the ship's controls.

After several minutes, Jinser-Shosa finally spoke with its raspy voice. "If you must know, I'm planning to fly the homeship directly inside one of those heinous beasts!"

Marc jumped in surprise, and had to try extra hard to keep his mouth shut.

"What!" Zorina exclaimed. "*That's* your plan?"

"Well, yeah! What else did you think I had in mind?"

"But that's suicide! We'll surely be vaporized the moment we collide with it!"

"Hah! To the contrary, my friend. Your years as Chief Imperial Defender have definitely made you too cautious. We'll fly right through its surface and into its heart. The tests I did on your sample showed that the surface has only a very thin protective shell. Those Starguzzlers seem to mostly maintain their spherical shapes by nothing more than their own gravitational pull. Kind of surprising that so powerful and sophisticated a weapon has so rudimentary a defense mechanism!"

"Probably because their creators knew that nobody would be daft enough to try to fly into one! Wouldn't the heat and radiation instantly kill us? It would be like flying into a burning sun!"

Jinser-Shosa laughed. "Nothing this homeship won't be able to handle. All Phyrax homeships are built from the same basic ingredients found in stars and gas giants, and made to withstand very high heat and radiation. Besides, my homeship was specially designed to fly into the cores of stars. Or did you forget what my favorite hobby was?"

Zorina nodded cautiously. "Will the homeship protect Marc and me too? Our bodies and suits are clearly not made for that kind of temperature or radioactivity."

"Who? What?" Jinser-Shosa seemed to hesitate. "Oh, yes, yes, it should. You're inside the homeship, after all. In any case, do you have a better idea?"

Zorina was silent.

"We'll simply take out its central neural network," Jinser-Shosa continued. "Without the core energy and sentience that holds it together, the whole thing will collapse. That will set off a chain reaction, resulting in a massive explosion in the end. Given the vast gas and energy reserves it has, you can only imagine the fireworks we will witness." It laughed again. "That's how I destroyed the sample you brought. Very gladly too, I might add!"

"You, ah, sure that we won't get caught in the explosion ourselves, right?" Zorina asked. "We'll get out in time?" She was obviously very aware of the tendency Phyraxes had to get carried away with adventure, often foregoing their own safety in the process.

"What? Oh, yes, yes. Good point. I forgot about that."

"This is crazy!" Marc thought. They were being led into a scorching furnace by a nutcase that always acted first and thought later. Not knowing what else to do, he closed his eyes and prayed. Yet again, he was about to stare death in the face, and it had to be only a matter of time before his luck finally ran out. But as he prayed, he began to relax a little. For whatever reason, his instincts were telling him that he could trust Jinser-Shosa. And given how far his instincts had gotten him already, he could only hope they wouldn't fail him now.

The Starguzzlers seemed to take no notice of Jinser-Shosa's approaching homeship. They were too busy sucking plasma out of the star, and obviously did not feel threatened by something as insignificant as a miniscule cloud. And even if they did, as Zorina explained to Jinser-Shosa, they would never be able to aim directly at something that small anyway.

"Gas-thirsty fiends!" Jinser-Shosa exclaimed, speeding up the ship as it neared the surface of the nearest Starguzzler. "They'll get what they deserve!"

All Marc could see through the windows now was the Starguzzler's massive body, covering the entire horizon like a planet he was about to land on. But this was no planet. The shining white, almost transparent body made that painfully clear. The dancing sparkle within was so close now that its bright red haze would blind anyone who stared at it directly.

He braced himself for impact. All he ended up feeling, however, was a slight tremor emanating through the homeship's chassis. Jinser-Shosa had evidently been right – the protective shell around the Starguzzler really was very thin. The ship had entered the Starguzzler's body without encountering any resistance, and seemed to be holding fine as it headed straight for the core.

Through the ship's windows, Marc could see nothing but a white glow outside, with the red sparkle ahead coming ever closer. "Perhaps this won't be so bad," he thought.

But he was wrong. After having traveled well into the Starguzzler's body, the homeship suddenly came to a stop. It began shaking, first softly, and then violently.

Jinser-Shosa seemed far from happy as it analyzed the data on a couple of displays nearby. "Hmph! The Starguzzler has realized we've entered its body, and is trying to get rid of us. It's trying to dissolve us with waves of high energy radiation."

"We'll hold, right?" Zorina asked.

"Hold, yes, but not indefinitely. These waves are not letting us move forward."

"So we're stuck?"

"Seems so! That leaves us with only one option. Not one I particularly like, though. I was hoping to get much closer to the center."

Jinser-Shosa began firing freezer missiles towards the red sparkle. The freezer missile, a weapon as deadly to gaseous life forms as a thermonuclear bomb was to beings made of solid mass, instantly lowered the temperature of the surface it came into contact with to absolute zero. The gaseous target would condense, freeze and die within seconds.

The problem here, however, was that the homeship was still quite far from the core, and the density of the Starguzzler's body was very high. The missiles were also made of a very light material. The chances of any one of them making it all the way to its target was very slim.

The shaking began to get more violent, and warnings of cracks forming in the homeship's perimeter seal appeared on the displays. Jinser-Shosa cursed away and fired missile after missile, but every one of them came to a stop before reaching the sparkle.

"We've got to give the missiles more thrust!" Jinser-Shosa shouted, and abruptly flew off into the depths of the homeship.

More reports of growing cracks were coming in. Sirens were wailing across the homeship now.

Marc stared at the homeship's controls and felt totally helpless. He knew nothing about this ship, nothing about how to get it out of the jam it was in. And Zorina didn't seem to either. They were both completely at Jinser-Shosa's mercy.

"Don't worry, my friend," Zorina said reassuringly. "I know Jinser-Shosa seems thoughtless and reckless. But through all their thoughtlessness and recklessness, Phyraxes have a remarkable knack for survival and ultimate triumph. You'll be amazed at what they can do under the most ominous of circumstances."

An ominous circumstance this undoubtedly was, and its knack for triumph Jinser-Shosa displayed within a few moments. Marc suddenly saw another series of missiles take off in the direction of the core. Seconds later, white flashes appeared inside the red sparkle. All the missiles had hit their target.

Jinser-Shosa returned through the cloudy mist of the homeship's belly. "Success! Success!" it exclaimed gleefully.

The red sparkle collapsed and vanished, like a sea of water disappearing into a giant whirlpool. The hold on the homeship was instantly gone as well. The ship was free again, but its perimeter seal was about to give in altogether.

"Get us out of here, Jinser-Shosa, now!" Zorina yelled.

Jinser-Shosa reversed the ship's engines and began pulling it out of the Starguzzler's body. The hull shook fiercely, but by some miracle seemed to be holding together. On one of the 3D displays, Marc tensely watched the path of the ship as it edged its way towards the surface of the Starguzzler.

But then it happened – the chain reaction. It started off as a small flash at the point where the sparkle had been. The flash disappeared, and was followed by a shockwave that swiftly expanded in all directions. The wave looked like a bright red balloon that was being blown up far too quickly, and it was quickly catching up with the ship.

Jinser-Shosa floated frantically from control to control, trying to get the ship to go as fast as possible. "Come on, baby!" it kept saying. "Give me all you've got! Don't let me down now after all these years!"

Marc watched with horror as the shockwave closed in on the ship. But just as the growing balloon was about to touch the edge of the ship, the ship broke free through the Starguzzler's outer shell.

"Hoooorrrraaayyy!" Jinser-Shosa howled with excitement.

The homeship, now back in regular space, accelerated as fast as it possibly could to get away. And none too soon, for the Starguzzler, now completely engulfed by the balloon, exploded with a massive burst of energy. The colorful ball of fire that spread across the night sky would easily be visible up to hundreds of light years away, appearing to the untrained eye as something similar to a supernova.

It took every ounce of thrust in the homeship's kilasic engines to try to stay ahead of the impact of the explosion. And stay ahead it did, for as fast as the ball of fire was, it couldn't possibly expand faster than the speed of light. Jinser-Shosa's ship had already accelerated to speeds beyond that. The other Starguzzlers nearby also scrambled to get away from the explosion as fast as they could.

Albeit its dangers, the plan had worked. Marc, Zorina and Jinser-Shosa were still alive, and the ship they were on, although damaged, was still intact. And, most importantly, the Starguzzler was dead.

*   *   *

Jinser-Shosa sent communiqués to the other Phyraxes in the area, gloating about its accomplishment and giving them detailed instructions on how to destroy the Starguzzlers. It also warned them to fortify the perimeter seals of their homeships, and to increase the range of their freezer missiles before attempting to enter the Starguzzlers' bodies. Then it began flying happily around Marc and Zorina, and even spoke to Marc for the first time.

"It worked! It worked! What do you think, eh? Am I a genius or what? My name will forever be engraved in Phyrax history!"

Marc glanced at Zorina, who nodded back at him. He then cautiously spoke his first words to the Phyrax. "Yes, you are a genius, a very courageous genius. We are very, very proud of you."

"I like this individual, Zorina! Why didn't you introduce me to him before? Now come, let's have a blast. No pun intended!"

"You did it, Jinser-Shosa!" Zorina said, bobbing her head up and down with delight. "But remember your promise. This is not yet the time to celebrate."

Chapter 42

The great battle for the survival of the Glaessan had begun. Starguzzlers were appearing all over the galaxy through consars, causing death and destruction everywhere. Entire planets and moons were being blown up, with their big, bright stars consumed and reduced to nothing more than red dwarfs. Countless ships, Mendoken planet destroyers and space stations were being eliminated, none of them any match for the size and firepower of the Starguzzlers. This was by far the greatest threat the galaxy had ever faced.

The Mendoken, Aftar, Volona and Phyrax had all set aside their differences to communicate and collaborate with each other on countering the Starguzzler onslaught. They had also already notified all other members of the galactic community living within their jurisdictions of the impending doom, and had instructed them to prepare for the worst possible scenario. Those species living under silupsal filters had, of course, been excluded from any of the communiqués.

Under Dumyan's lead, the Aftaran delegation traveling to the Volonan Empire had met with success. It had been a tough sell, but the Empress had eventually seen enough evidence to be convinced. She had pledged her forces to join the Mendoken and Aftar in the fight against the new, common enemy, and had then helped the delegation exit the Grid and return to the Dominion.

The Phyrax had been brought into the game with the help of Marc and Zorina. Jinser-Shosa, a Phyrax and a friend of Zorina's, had been the first to destroy a Starguzzler, and the news of how it had been done had spread quickly across the Federation. Other Phyraxes had begun destroying Starguzzlers using the same technique, but the Starguzzlers had eventually caught on and were now steering clear of Phyrax homeships, avoiding them like the plague.

After leaving Jinser-Shosa's homeship, Marc and Zorina had entered a consar on board their Mendoken scout ship and had headed directly to the Mendo-Zueger star system. At the planet Lind, they had met with the Imgoerin and had reported the success of their mission. As agreed upon between the four advanced civilizations, the Imgoerin had then sent millions of Kril, Euma and Aima vessels to all sections of the Phyrax Federation through consars. The Mendoken ships had attached themselves to Phyrax homeships, and had escorted them through consars to all corners of the galaxy. Jinser-Shosa's homeship had been escorted directly to the Mendo-Zueger system, as a result of Jinser-Shosa's desire to join Marc and Zorina for the remainder of the conflict.

Across the galaxy, the plan now was for Mendoken, Aftaran and Volonan ships to attack the Starguzzlers head-on and distract them as much possible, while the Phyrax homeships secretly entered the Starguzzlers' bodies and destroyed their neural networks. This was because the Phyrax ships were the only kind capable of entering the Starguzzlers' bodies without instantly being vaporized by the tremendous heat and radiation. Many ships and many more lives would be lost in the process, but there was no alternative.

Standing on a platform on board one of the space stations around Lind, Marc, Sibular and Zorina were about to see this plan in action. They were keenly watching the spectacle outside through the station's transparent walls. Five Starguzzlers had just arrived in the Mendo-Zueger star system through consars, and one was making its way directly towards Lind. Its goal, evidently, was to destroy the very seat of power of the Mendoken Republic. An entire armada of Kril battlecruisers and planet destroyers was amassed in front of the planet, blocking the Starguzzler's trajectory. Some of the Kril ships began flying ahead, firing torpedoes at the approaching giant. Then several planet destroyers flew out in arcs and bore down on the Starguzzler from both sides, releasing their annihilative energy beams in its direction.

As expected, the Starguzzler was not affected at all. It seemed to gladly absorb all the energy. But in response, it sprayed a huge flame around itself. The flame shot out to the front and to the sides, instantly engulfing and blowing up the Kril ships and planet destroyers that had dared challenge its supremacy.

"Thank goodness those ships were unmanned!" Zorina exclaimed.

"Yes," Sibular agreed, "remote control definitely has its uses."

Jinser-Shosa's voice crackled over a small speaker device Zorina was holding. "I'm inside the Starguzzler! Just entered from the rear."

"Good luck, Jinser-Shosa!" Zorina said.

"Hah! I don't need it."

This time, Jinser-Shosa made no mistakes. Its homeship had been repaired and strengthened, and the stock of freezer missiles replenished. The Starguzzler's sparkle went out within a couple of minutes, and a shockwave formed in its place. Just as the homeship emerged from the giant's surface, the entire Starguzzler exploded in a dazzling display of fireworks.

"Hoooorrrraaayyyy!" Jinser-Shosa yelled through the speaker.

"Congratulations, my friend!" Zorina yelled back. "You did it again!"

Without another word, Jinser-Shosa took off to help the other Phyrax homeships present in the star system destroy the remaining four Starguzzlers.

The great battle, as great as it was, did not last long. It didn't last longer than a few days, in fact. During that time, the Starguzzlers destroyed many worlds and killed trillions of individuals. In some cases, home worlds of entire species were wiped out altogether. But the Phyrax demonstrated incredible prowess in carrying out and perfecting the technique Jinser-Shosa had pioneered. Although the Starguzzlers kept learning how to evade the Phyrax attacks by communicating with each other, the Phyrax always stayed a step ahead with more and more sophisticated attack methods. And while many Phyraxes perished in the process, every single Starguzzler across the Glaessan was eventually found and destroyed.

The Mendoken, Aftar and Volona all worked hard to support the Phyrax, giving them the necessary cover with armadas of ships and tons of firepower. In many star systems, particularly those along the border regions, Mendoken, Aftaran and Volonan ships stood side by side and fired together on the Starguzzlers. It was truly a historic and monumental display of united resolve, and it paid off in the end.

Marc was overjoyed to hear the report that the last Starguzzler had fallen. He was also overjoyed to hear that his own home star system had not been touched. The Starguzzlers, it seemed, hadn't known what to make of silupsal filters and had steered clear of them.

Celebrations and parties abounded across the Glaessan, particularly among the Volona and Phyrax. The Mendoken did not celebrate on any occasion, and just went about their daily business. The majority of Aftarans spent their time in prayer and reflection, thanking the Creator for saving the galaxy and restoring peace to the Dominion.

Marc and Zorina were invited to a private party on Jinser-Shosa's homeship, still parked outside the planet Lind. They dragged Sibular with them as well, after getting approval from Jinser-Shosa to bring a Mendoken on board. Jinser-Shosa was so pleased with its recent accomplishments that it no longer cared for centuries of animosity between the two civilizations.

Sibular had initially protested that he had a lot of work to do, but eventually gave in. After some convincing by Marc and Zorina, he finally saw the logic that taking a break every now and then to spend time with friends wasn't such a bad thing. So donning protective suits, the three of them entered the homeship. There, amidst a dazzling display of gas powered fireworks, they were entertained by Jinser-Shosa's stories of its many adventures and exploits across the Federation.

"Jinser-Shosa clearly doesn't know what modesty means," Marc thought, as he listened to the tales of heroism and bravery. But he also had to admit that, exaggerated or not, some of the stories were quite fascinating.

Marc's thoughts eventually began to wander, leading him back to his own series of adventures since he had left Earth over a month earlier. It had certainly felt a lot longer than a month. Nobody on Earth would ever believe what he had been through. Nobody on Earth ever could.

He thought about his visions and feelings of intuition, and how they had steered him in different directions throughout his journey. He thought of the prophecies in the Aftaran Scriptures that had somehow identified him as the "Sign", and of his unique ability to see through the Aftaran disguises of the Unghans. He had somehow been chosen to have these powers to see and feel, but he didn't know why he had been picked out of the gazillions of beings in the galaxy. Nor did he know who had chosen him. Was it God, the Creator, or whatever the name of the supreme deity was?

It didn't take long for him to realize that if he didn't want these questions to haunt him for the rest of his life, he still had one more trip to make before he finally headed back home.

"You seem deep in thought, Marc," Sibular said, just as Jinser-Shosa finished telling another of its stories.

"I am. Hey, Sibular, I know the Imgoerin must be really busy at the moment, but do you think I can get an audience with him in the next few days? I need to ask him for a favor."

"Considering all you have done for us, I doubt that will be a problem. I will see to it as soon as this event ends."

Marc did receive an audience with the Imgoerin, the very next morning in fact. It turned out the Imgoerin had already wanted to speak to him, Sibular, Zorina and Jinser-Shosa. Jinser-Shosa, however, had already left in the early hours of the morning, heading back home to the Federation. It hadn't wanted to stay a day longer than absolutely necessary, since it was dying with eagerness to fly across the Federation and brag about its recent accomplishments to other Phyraxes.

The remaining three friends arrived on board a shuttle at the Imgoerin's palace, nothing more than a small apartment atop one of Lind's countless skyscrapers. Osalya ushered them past the security guards and into the Imgoerin's private office. The furnishings were functional but not at all decorative, and the highlight was the stunning view of the outside. At the very top of the skyscraper and with completely transparent walls all around, it was possible to see miles and miles of the tops of tall black, cylindrically shaped buildings. There seemed to be no end of them, no matter in which direction Marc looked.

The Imgoerin was standing in the midst of a series of 3D screens, analyzing different kinds of data and maps from across the Republic. "Welcome," he said, floating out of the array of screens to greet them.

Sibular bowed his head slightly, and Marc and Zorina followed his example.

"It is I who must bow to you," the Imgoerin said, and did so. "The three of you have done far more for the Republic and for the whole galaxy than I could ever have done. I would like to thank each of you again."

"Thank you for the recognition," Sibular replied.

"And as a show of gratitude, Sibular, the Mendoken people have raised your status in the Hierarchy 1,000,000 levels up to the head of the entire Space Travel Research Center. Your level designation is herewith no longer 45383532 but 44383532. The vote was unanimous among all affected individuals in the Hierarchy."

Sibular bowed slightly again. "I am truly honored, respected Imgoerin."

"I have good news for you too, Zorina," the Imgoerin continued. "You are, of course, welcome to stay here. But I doubt you will want to. The Empress sent me a message stating that she was very pleasantly surprised to hear of your role in saving the galaxy, and that you are herewith 'forgiven for your transgressions'. I do not know what she is referring to, but you are free to return to the Empire and rejoin the Grid. You will be reassigned to your position as Chief Imperial Defender. A certain Rudoso will also be forgiven."

Zorina couldn't hide her joy. She jumped up and down with delight and even hugged the Imgoerin, much to his surprise. Then she hugged Marc, Sibular and Osalya as well. "Thank you, respected Imgoerin, thank you so much! You have no idea what this means to me!" She bobbed her head up and down so far that it almost touched the ground.

"A Euma-9 vessel is waiting outside Lind to take you home," Osalya said. "You may board it whenever you are ready."

"I'll be ready right after this meeting!"

The Imgoerin turned to Marc. "Now, Mr. Zemin, you came from a silupsal

S.W. Ahmed

covered world, but have demonstrated more intelligence and maturity during your time with us than perhaps most of us. This has caused us to reevaluate our entire silupsal strategy, and raises the question of whether we should lift the filter around your home world. Your people are clearly more advanced than we thought."

Marc was astonished by the Imgoerin's statement. "You're serious?"

"Yes, certainly. It appears we could learn a lot from your civilization, as yours undoubtedly could from us."

Marc thought about this for a long moment. In the end, he surprised even himself with what he said. "No, I don't think that's a good idea."

"Why do you say that, Marc?" Sibular asked. "This would be a unique opportunity for your people."

"Because my people aren't ready yet. Fundamentally, I don't think there's anything wrong with your silupsal strategy. When I first heard about it, I was shocked and felt it was immoral to hide the truth from others like that. But the more I've thought about it since then, the more I've begun to realize that it actually is the best solution. Every society does need a certain level of maturity and experience before it joins the galactic community, otherwise it will not be able to survive."

"You do not believe your people have reached that level of maturity?"

"No, and let me tell you why. No doubt, a lot of the bad traits of my people exist out here as well. In the past month, I have seen a lot of distrust, prejudice, hate and cruelty. These traits seem to be universal, and that is why this galaxy has never been a very peaceful place. Perhaps no galaxy in the entire universe is.

"But there is a huge difference of scale between what happens out here and what happens on my home world. You Mendoken are united as a people. The Volona are united as a people. So are the Phyrax, and the Aftar as well now that the Unghans are gone. Regardless of the differences between your civilizations, within each civilization you live in relative peace and prosperity, peace and prosperity that are very well distributed to every corner of your territories. And that is why you are able to not only survive in this vast ocean of civilizations, you are able to thrive and lead others."

Silence filled the room, and Marc felt all eyes intently watching him. But he didn't feel the slightest bit nervous or hesitant. After all the fearful, near-death experiences he had been through over the past few weeks, fear of speaking his mind and fear of standing up for his beliefs no longer had any place in his heart. He drew a deep breath and kept going.

"On Earth, my people have no unity. There is no unity between countries, between cities, between neighbors or often even within the same family. We steal from each other, hurt each other, and even kill each other. There is little tolerance for or understanding of other people, other cultures, religions, social habits, laws, you name it. People only believe what they've been raised since childhood to believe, beliefs that are riddled with the most nonsensical prejudices towards others. As they grow up, they refuse to bridge those glaring gaps in their knowledge, choosing instead to live in their own shells of ignorance. Even when shown volumes of evidence that clearly contradict their narrow minded views, they refuse to acknowledge the truth and somehow brush it all aside with a shrug. And guess who takes advantage of that ignorance and those prejudices – the leaders and politicians. That's how entire wars have been fought because of disagreements over the smallest of things, entire races wiped out because they didn't share the same identities or beliefs as their conquerors.

"On Earth, there is no such thing as equality. The richest person lives right next door to the poorest person, and has no qualms about doing so. The rich live in mansions, drive fancy cars, and use up and waste all of the planet's resources. At the same time, the poor have no idea under which roof they'll find shelter the next night or where they will find a few scraps of food to avoid starvation. The rich have all the power, and that power corrupts them to gain more power. They continually implement policies to make themselves richer and more powerful at the expense of everyone else. To satisfy their greed, they develop more and more deadly weapons with which to terrorize, kill and enslave the poor and powerless, to invade their countries and steal their possessions. They do so with smiling faces, selling their actions to the masses at home by denying any wrongdoing, twisting the facts, and claiming it's all for noble causes like the advancement of freedom, human rights, global peace and prosperity. And, thanks to the ignorance of the masses, they get away with all of it. They are often even celebrated as heroes. The poor and oppressed retaliate, of course, fighting back with whatever means they have at their disposal. Some of them even terrorize and kill innocent people who live in the rich and powerful countries, since the innocent are usually the most vulnerable and the easiest targets. But all that does is intensify the policies of oppression they are subject to. That's how the vicious cycle of violence steadily worsens.

"Oh, we may think we've become more civilized over time, and maybe we have. But definitely not to the extent that our leaders claim we have. Every now and then, one of them will give a grandiose speech on how humanity has progressed so far in the last few years or few centuries. We claim to have learned from our previous mistakes, and vow to never repeat them. But somehow we always do. Perhaps not to the same group of people, perhaps not on the same scale, perhaps we don't even call the atrocities by the same name. But, in the end, they are still atrocities.

"No, respected Imgoerin, my people are not ready. We first need to learn how to trust each other and to treat each other with respect, tolerance and understanding. We first need to learn how to live in peace with each other, to overcome our individual greed and to share our wealth so that everyone is adequately provided for. We need to learn to take care of our planet, to not incur Nature's wrath by polluting it and wasting all of its precious resources. We need to become self-sufficient and not self-destructive, we need to become united as a society. Then and only then will we be ready to meet other, far more advanced societies like yours.

"Otherwise different nations, different groups of people on Earth will have their own agendas and will try to use you to further their own ends against others. Some may even try to acquire your weapons with which to destroy their enemies. Others whose hearts are filled with distrust may try to fight you directly. Some will worship you as gods, others will cast stones at you for being devils. Most will be occupied with using your presence to gain more wealth and more power. Only a handful of educated, intelligent people will truly understand the implications of what your existence and the existence of countless other alien civilizations means for the human race. But their voices will be drowned out by the inferno that will sweep over the globe due to your presence. In the end, we will likely implode as a civilization by completely destroying ourselves. We almost did that by ourselves several times already, without any contact with outsiders.

"So I humbly ask you, respected Imgoerin, to keep the silupsal filter in place until my people are ready. It will likely be a while, if ever. Either way, we need to learn from our own mistakes and our own experiences, the same way that your people did billions of years ago. Otherwise we will never become a great civilization."

The Imgoerin was silent for a moment, and then spoke. "Well, Mr. Zemin, you know your people better than we do. But if you as an individual are any indicator of the maturity of your people, then I can assure you that the human race has nothing to worry about. As you have requested, however, for now the silupsal filter around your star system will remain in place."

"I would suggest the topics of trust and tolerance are very relevant for us too," Zorina said to the Imgoerin. "It is clear the Unghans took advantage of the distrust and intolerance between my people and yours, for example. Same thing between the Aftar and Phyrax. I grew up believing that you Mendoken are the most sadistic, tyrannical despots the universe has ever seen. In the Grid, we Volonans always saw you as the ugliest creatures, with slimy skin and lots of tentacles and the desire to devour everything in your sight. How far from the truth is that? You don't eat or drink at all, let alone devour everything in your sight." She nodded at Sibular. "Now that I've spent time with some of your people, it's obvious to me you are nothing like what we grew up believing. You're not perfect, obviously. Nobody is.

But you're a far cry from being sadistic or tyrannical."

"Likewise, Zorina," Sibular said. "We also had many misconceptions about Volonans that you have cleared up for me."

"This actually brings up a very important point," Marc said. "I've now had the opportunity to learn about each of the four advanced civilizations of the Glaessan, and to a greater or lesser extent have interacted with members of each of them. I feel that each civilization has become so great because, through many trials and tribulations, it eventually chose to follow a specific path of principles and guidelines. Once chosen, it stuck to that path through thick and thin, never once swaying or compromising. It is this combination of conviction and dedication to a worthy cause that always leads to success, and it clearly has for all four civilizations."

"What do you consider the issue to be then, Mr. Zemin?" Osalya asked.

"Well, strangely enough, each civilization chose a path that was completely divergent from the other three! You Mendoken went in the direction of science, logic and a strong, hierarchical community focused on selfless participation and contribution. The Aftar buried themselves in religion and spirituality, shunning all forms of worldliness and choosing to live lives of asceticism instead. The Volona, on the other hand, shunned all forms of spirituality to live lives of hedonism and physical enjoyment, choosing to exist in an alternative, virtual domain to be able to continuously satisfy their desires. And finally the Phyrax, who value individual liberty and independence more than anything else, decided to have no sense of community or laws whatsoever. Each Phyrax was completely free to pursue its own goals, to travel and to conquer, to test its bravery and to show off its skills.

"With success comes complacence and arrogance, and with arrogance comes ignorance and intolerance of ways different from your own. Ignorance and intolerance, in turn, lead to downright distrust and hatred of others. And that's what happened to each of your civilizations. The Mendoken and Aftar gravitated naturally to one side because they shared many core principles, and so did the Volona and Phyrax to the other. Between the two sides, the distrust and hatred grew to staggering levels. The wars that followed were a natural result. You did achieve peace finally, but it was a fragile peace."

"But then came the Unghans," Zorina said. "They studied our societies and the chemistry between them, then came up with a strategy to pit us against one another. Because each civilization went to an extreme in one way while disregarding other ways of life, it became weak in the other areas and thus became vulnerable to exploitation. You Mendoken, for example, are such a hierarchical community with very little individuality that you do not question the assumptions made by your leadership. Please don't take that personally, respected Imgoerin."

The Imgoerin nodded and stayed silent.

Zorina went on. "You all just blindly assumed that we Volonans were behind the consar attacks because you believed we were deceptive by nature, without questioning if it really was the case."

Marc agreed. "Similarly, the Aftar are so engrossed in their religious ways and what they believe to be the path of the righteous that they were easily rallied up to take extreme, fundamentalist stands against 'infidels' and 'hypocrites'. That's how the Unghans convinced the Aftar to choose Wazilban as their leader, and to support his cause in fighting the Phyrax and quashing those Aftarans who stood in his way. It was his narrow minded, extremist way or the highway, so to speak."

"The Unghans also exploited vulnerabilities in the Volona and Phyrax," Sibular said. "The high amount of suspicion the Volona have towards outsiders, thanks to their zealous protectiveness of their virtual worlds, led them to distrust every step we Mendoken made to negotiate with them or reach a deal with them on a particular issue. That was how every war between us and them began, including the most recent one. And the Phyrax..."

"The Phyrax's uncompromising desire to be free and independent to do whatever they want," Zorina said, interrupting him. "They would never tolerate the Aftar imposing any kinds of religious dogma or code of conduct on them. That has always been a major source of tension between the two societies. The Unghans took advantage of that by disguising themselves as Aftarans and forcefully attempting to convert a group of Phyraxes near the border to the Aftaran religion. That was how the most recent war between the two began."

"Are the three of you suggesting that we change our way of life to be more balanced, so as to avoid these kinds of situations?" the Imgoerin asked.

Marc raised his eyebrows. "Change your way of life? Heavens, no! You have become so great because of your way of life. I think what we, or at least I am suggesting is that you should never become arrogant or complacent in your views as you live your way of life. Regardless of your own success, you should always keep a balanced view of other ways of life and other societies, and give others the benefit of doubt before jumping to conclusions about them. Every society has both virtues and shortcomings, including yours. No civilization is perfect. So you should never be extreme in your views, for extremism in any form blinds good judgment. Moderation is the key to maintaining healthy, long lasting relationships with others."

"You are right in principle, Mr. Zemin," the Imgoerin said. "But there are also billions of years of history, countless wars and confrontations that have formed these opinions of each other over time. It will not be easy by any means for us to suddenly begin trusting the Volona, or for them to begin trusting us."

"No, it certainly won't be easy. But look at how all four civilizations came together to fight the Starguzzlers. In the face of a deadly external threat, you all shunned your differences and fought together against a common enemy. In other words, given the right motivation, you were able to unite. Given the right motivation, you *can* unite."

"Could the same not be said for your people on Earth, Mr. Zemin?" Osalya asked.

Marc had guessed this question might come. It was only too logical a deduction, one a Mendoken would be unlikely to miss. "It could, Osalya. My people, however, will only unite for as long as the threat exists. As soon as it subsides, they will return to their old ways. They are not yet mature enough to fully learn from such an experience.

"In your case, you have already demonstrated that you can learn from your past experiences. After a violent history, you Mendoken eventually united under a single banner many years ago, and ever since then your civilization has been unstoppable. Similar events happened with the Volona, Aftar and Phyrax. So you all *know* what the benefits of learning from your mistakes are, since you have seen the fruitful results of doing so. And now that you have seen what the benefits are of working together for a greater good, you won't go back to the status quo of the past." He paused. "At least, I hope you won't. Because one thing I know very well from human history is that the same things keep happening to those who don't learn from their mistakes."

"Well articulated, Mr. Zemin," the Imgoerin said. "We will certainly take advantage of this opportunity to extend hands of friendship to the Volona and Phyrax. I can only hope they will reciprocate."

"I will see to it that my people do, respected Imgoerin," Zorina said. "And Jinser-Shosa already promised me this morning before it left for the Federation that it would talk to other Phyraxes about this as well."

"I am glad to hear it, Zorina. Mr. Zemin, I would also like to extend an invitation to you to stay here with us on Lind as an advisor to our administration. We could surely use your insight on many an occasion."

Marc's jaw dropped in surprise. He had not at all been expecting this, and it took him a moment to grasp its full implications. Nevertheless, he had no doubt about how to answer. "That is truly an astounding honor, respected Imgoerin, and one I am not at all worthy of. I would like to wholeheartedly thank you for the offer. But I think it is time now for me to go home. Given all I have learned out here, I feel I can put my skills to better use by helping humans reach the maturity they need to eventually face the truth of what lies in the cosmos beyond their doorstep."

S.W. Ahmed

"A worthy cause, no doubt. I am certain you will excel in it. The only thing I ask, then, is that you never reveal any of what exists outside your silupsal filter to your fellow humans. At least not until you think they are ready."

"That you can be sure of. I do have one final favor to ask of you, respected Imgoerin. I would like to visit Meenjaza before I head home. Would you be able to provide me with a ship?"

"Brrrrrrrrrrrrrrr," the Imgoerin said. "It is amusing to hear that, Mr. Zemin. It just so happens that this was the final reason I called you here this morning. I received a request from Dumyan yesterday, asking for you to join him on Meenjaza before you head home."

Marc was startled again. "Why?"

"All he said was that there is someone there who really wants to meet you."

Chapter 43

It was an emotional farewell, at least for Marc and Zorina. Sibular seemed indifferent as usual, although Marc could have sworn he saw a hint of sadness in the Mendoken's single eye. The three of them were standing on a platform on one of the space stations around Lind, getting ready to board their respective ships. Zorina was about to head directly into a Euma-9 vessel docked nearby. The vessel's destination was the Volonan border, in a narrow section of the galaxy where the Republic and the Empire actually had a common border. There, a Volonan ship would pick Zorina up and transport her home to the Volo-Maree system. Sibular was about to get on a small shuttle that would take him to a far closer destination – the nearby moon Ailen, where the Space Travel Research Center was located. And Marc was going to board a small scout ship that would take him straight to Meenjaza in the Aftaran Dominion.

Consar travel, it turned out, would once again be banned across the galaxy. Regardless of the significant timesaving benefits of consar travel, the Aftarans had specifically asked for the ban to be re-enforced by all four civilizations as a part of any upcoming peace treaty. This was not just because traveling into other dimensions was forbidden in their religion, but because they insisted that consar travel posed the risk of disturbing the domains of unknown civilizations in other dimensions. How those civilizations would react was anyone's guess, but it was unlikely to be particularly friendly. And if they turned out to be far more advanced than the civilizations of the Glaessan, then the whole Starguzzler invasion might pale in comparison to what the Glaessan would face next. Everyone could only hope that with all the consar travel that had recently occurred, the damage had not already been done.

The small scout ship Marc was about to travel on would be the last ship in the galaxy to undertake a consar journey – once to Meenjaza and back. Marc was to be given this honor, because of his unique role in helping the Mendoken attain consar technology and all that had happened since then. Then he would head home to Earth on board a Euma-9 vessel, traveling at standard speeds through regular dimensions.

As he got ready to say goodbye to Sibular and Zorina, Marc realized he had never had such close, loyal friends in his whole life. Even though the three of them were from such divergent backgrounds and had only known each other for just over a month, they had stuck with each other through thick and thin, trusting each other unconditionally and supporting each other every step of the way on their quest. If that wasn't true friendship, he didn't know what was. Sibular and Zorina had never abandoned him, even during the most trying of times. That was more than could be said for anyone who had meant anything to him back on Earth.

He knew it would be impossible to stay in touch with either of them, for he would not be allowed to keep any communication equipment or any other form of evidence of where he had been once he passed through the silupsal filter to return to Earth. But he certainly hoped that somehow, somewhere he would see them again one day.

"Remember to lighten up once in a while, my man!" Zorina said to Sibular, and hugged him.

"And you remember to occasionally face the real world, Zorina," Sibular replied. A short "Brrrrrrrr" followed.

"Marc, my friend, take care of yourself," Zorina said, hugging him for a long moment. "Remember to follow your heart too, not just your mind. Especially for the things that matter to you the most." With that, she waved and got on a vehicle that whisked her away towards the gate of the waiting ship.

The two remaining friends were silent for a while. Marc wasn't sure what an appropriate way to say goodbye to Sibular would be.

"I would like you to have something, Marc," Sibular finally said.

"Wait, I thought I'm not supposed to take anything from here back to Earth?"

"This is not something anybody else on Earth will ever see. It is for your eyes only, it will always remain with you and it will die with you."

"What is it?"

"Just a small token to always remind you of your time here with us. Close your eyes for a moment."

Marc closed his eyes, wondering what Sibular could possibly give him that nobody else would be able to see. He thought he felt a slight puff of air over his face, but he wasn't sure. Then all was still. He opened his eyes, looked at his hands and his body, and also felt his face. There didn't seem to be anything different or peculiar anywhere. In the distance, he could see Sibular floating away.

Marc thought of calling out to Sibular and asking him what he had done, but decided against it. Perhaps what had just happened was simply Sibular's way of avoiding an emotional goodbye, something he clearly wasn't accustomed to.

With a sigh, Marc headed towards his scout ship, wishing that the farewell with his Mendoken friend had been a nicer one.

A couple of hours later, Marc's scout ship exited a consar and landed on Meenjaza outside a group of Dominion administration buildings. The Mendoken pilot promised to wait for him on the landing strip while he went about his business, however long it took.

He stepped out into the gathering dusk. The sky on this desert planet was crystal clear as usual, with the setting sun sending out streaks of crimson from one horizon to the other. It was truly a beautiful sight.

Dumyan was the only Aftaran standing on the landing strip. "Glad you could make it!" he said, smiling and putting a hand on Marc's shoulder.

Marc smiled back. "It's good to see you again, Dumyan! How are things going here?"

"Celebrations abound! Aftarans across the Dominion are spending their time praying in large gatherings and thanking the Creator for granting them victory."

Marc chuckled silently at the solemnity of the Aftaran celebrations. "And how are you holding up, my friend?" he asked.

"It has been tough, I can tell you. Even more for my father than for me. I think of Sharjam all the time, and I still cannot believe he is gone. But there is so much happening here right now that needs our attention that we are not even getting the time to mourn. The one consolation we have is that all the things happening are things that Sharjam would have been happy about and very proud of."

"And how is Raiha?"

"She has been very sad, but with the help of the Creator, she will be alright in time. In memory of Sharjam, our family will watch out for and support her for the rest of her life, as if she were a member of our clan."

"I am glad to hear it," Marc said.

The two took off on a floating platform, away from the administration buildings and into the wide streets. Sure enough, there were gatherings of Aftarans everywhere out in the open, all sitting quietly and praying.

Along the way, Dumyan informed Marc that the Ungha as a species were not quite extinct. A number of Unghans had been found in the Dominion and had been arrested. Some Unghans had apparently also been found in hiding in the Mendoken Republic, Volonan Empire and Phyrax Federation. They had been acting as spies for Jaegor, providing him with vital information for his grand scheme and carrying out his orders in every section of the galaxy. The surviving Unghans were now to be given a small corner of the galaxy where they could live by themselves and get a new chance to build a society. They would, of course, be closely monitored by all four major civilizations to make sure they never posed a threat to anyone again.

Marc felt the cool nighttime desert air hit his face, as the floating platform raced past more buildings and crowds of praying Aftarans. "I know why I wanted to come back one more time," he said to Dumyan. "But why did you want me to come back? I hear there's someone here who wants to meet me?"

"Yes. But how about you tell me first why you wanted to come back."

"To find out more about my role as the Sign. I want to know why I was chosen, who was behind my visions, and how my existence could possibly have been foretold in any Scripture."

"That does not surprise me. The whole experience must have been quite eye-opening for you."

"Eye-opening! I could think of a lot more descriptive words than that."

"Well, let me just say that this individual, or group of individuals, rather, will be able to answer your questions."

The building they eventually entered only had one large dome as a roof, instead of several smaller ones as most of the other nearby buildings did. It also had six tall towers, one on each corner of its six sides.

Dumyan led the floating platform through a corridor and brought it to a stop in front of a tall door. "I will wait for you here. What you see and hear inside is for your eyes and ears alone."

Marc nodded and stepped off the platform. The door instantly swung open by itself. Glancing briefly back at Dumyan, he walked in.

"Please step forward, Marc Zemin," a female voice said. The voice sounded old, very old.

The room was dimly lit, but Marc's eyes soon grew accustomed to the darkness. He could see five figures sitting on the floor in a semi-circle, all dressed in white robes.

"Do you know who we are?" the voice asked. It came from the figure sitting in the middle. She looked as old as she sounded, with white and gray feathers and faded eyes. She was undoubtedly much older than Autamrin. So too, it seemed, were most of the others in the room. They all had their heads covered but faces unveiled.

"I think I have a fairly good idea," Marc replied. "You must be the High Clerics of the Dominion."

"Indeed. My name is Ouria. I am the lead High Cleric. We were imprisoned by Wazilban, or Jaegor as we now hear his real name was, during his reign. Officially, he claimed we were dead. But he kept us imprisoned in secret, in case he needed us for anything. Finally we were freed by Raiha after the Unghans fled the Dominion. That is why we did not meet you earlier, as much as we wanted to. Please sit."

Marc sat down on the floor, facing the semi-circle. He felt a sense of humility to be in the presence of such devout figures.

"It is an honor to finally meet you," Ouria said. "You were given a tremendous burden to carry on your shoulders. And with the Creator's help, you led all of us to victory." She paused. "We called you here because you have fulfilled your destiny, and now it is time to release you of your burden."

"Why was it *my* destiny? Who assigned me this destiny? Was it the Creator?"

Ouria smiled. "The Creator's ways are truly strange, and as much as we strive to understand them, we mortals never really do. The Creator knows what the destiny of every individual is, even before the individual is born. We all have the choice to pursue our lives the way we want to, but whatever way we choose to live is ultimately our destiny as already known by the Creator."

Marc wasn't sure what to make of this answer. "So are you basically saying that I'm nothing special?"

Ouria smiled again. "Not at all. What I am saying is that your destiny was known by the Creator in the same way that everyone else's destiny is. Your destiny just happened to be as unique and special as it was."

Marc was still confused. "Sharjam told me that I was the Sign, as foretold in your Holy Scriptures."

"And indeed you are. That was why you were given the power to see that which nobody else could see."

"Did the Creator pick me to be the Sign, then, or not?"

"The Creator knew your destiny at birth, that you would one day become the Sign. But none of us mortals could ever have known that until we actually picked you to be the Sign."

Marc jumped in surprise. "You picked me to be the Sign? How? When?"

One of the other High Clerics got up and walked towards Marc. "I am Rayim, of the 349th generation of the Hayriah clan," he said, and sat down in front of Marc. "It is good to see you again. You have aged since we last met."

"We've met before?" Marc couldn't recall when. Rayim looked quite different from any of the other Aftarans he had met. His feathers were a dirty red in color and his beak unusually long. His eyes weren't quite as faded as those of Ouria.

"You will not recognize me. It was years ago, and I did not permit you to see me." Marc shook his head in disbelief. "Years ago? But I was on Earth!"

"Indeed. The third planet in the Mendo-Biesel system. It still feels like yesterday when I was there on my quest, a secret mission known only to us High Clerics. Even the Mendoken had no knowledge of it, nor did Autamrin or any of his followers. It was quite a journey, I can tell you, and passing unnoticed through the silupsal filter was a real challenge. I always knew I was taking a big risk by picking your planet, with all the ghastly things mentioned about your people in the Mendoken databases. But after all my searches from one end of the Glaessan to the other, it just felt right. In spite of all the faults you humans have, you are actually quite unique in the galaxy. You have the right balance of qualities and characteristics of all four advanced civilizations – the scientific, logical thought processes of the Mendoken, the ability to have faith and believe in the unseen like our people, the desire to seek pleasure and amuse yourselves like the Volona, and the drive for freedom, independence and adventure of the Phyrax. If there was anyone who could understand all four civilizations and bring them together to unite against a common enemy, it was someone from your society."

"It also had to be a society under a silupsal filter in the Mendoken Republic, one that the Aftaran chronicles would have no mention of because it was not in the Dominion and not yet a part of the galactic community," Ouria added. "This was so as to ensure that Jaegor would never suspect the Sign was in hiding there. If we had picked an Aftaran to be the Sign, Jaegor might have found out who it was and had that individual killed right away before the mission had even begun."

Marc was flabbergasted. All this time, he had thought he was somebody special, somebody who had been chosen for a mission by a higher power, perhaps by the Creator, by God. But now he was hearing that he had simply been chosen by a mere mortal.

"So you came to Earth to pick the Sign?" he asked Rayim. "Why did you end up picking me?"

"I needed to find someone who had the highest probability of making a specific scientific discovery, a discovery the Mendoken would take notice of because they desperately needed that technology to fight the Volona. So I picked the one person on the entire planet who was working on something that I knew would lead to the discovery of consars – you. You were working on building a time machine, but time travel is impossible. Your research was inevitably going to lead to the discovery of consar travel instead. It also helped that you were unattached and had no family.

You would have the fewest qualms of leaving your planet when the Mendoken came for you."

Marc smiled. "So you took a big gamble."

"The largest in my life and possibly in the history of the Aftar. I prayed many a night before I finally approached you, asking the Creator to make sure I was making the right choice. And with the Creator's help, I did."

"How did you actually 'pick' me? What did you do?"

"I had to give you something. Something that gave you the power to see all the things you have been able to see in your visions and dreams ever since, the power to guide you to make the right decisions so that you could fulfill your destiny as the Sign. And I had to make sure that the thing I gave you would never leave your possession, no matter where you went or what you did."

"When was this?"

"Less than 3 Earth years ago, well after your mother had passed away and you had already begun working on your time machine research. It was just before our imprisonment by Wazilban. I watched you for several days, totally invisible to you and all others on your world, of course. It did not take me long to notice there was one thing you never let go of."

Marc searched through his mind to figure out what Rayim was referring to. And as soon as he realized what it was, he felt his mouth dry up with excitement. He reached inside his pocket, and slowly pulled it out.

"There it is!" Rayim exclaimed.

There it was indeed. Marc's antique pocket watch, the family heirloom that he always kept with him, no matter where he went or what he did. It was all he had left of his family, all he had left of his heritage, and that was why it was so dear to him. It also always brought him luck, and that was why he often brought it out before doing anything important. His first time travel experiment was one such example. That experiment had failed, but it had opened doors for him that had completely changed his life and had brought him all the way here today.

He flipped open the golden timepiece and stared at it. The dials were still working perfectly, even though the time it showed obviously had no relevance here on Meenjaza. The small photo of his parents was still there on the inside cover, both of them smiling up at him with pride.

"Allow me," Rayim said, taking the pocket watch from Marc. He closed his eyes and uttered a prayer, then ran his finger around the edge of the cover. Suddenly the entire timepiece began shining brightly, and the watch section came loose. He lifted the watch section from its cover, and revealed what lay underneath to Marc.

"Behold, the third copy of the Hidden Scripture!" Rayim announced proudly, displaying it to the other High Clerics as well.

There it was, tucked away inside the cover of the pocket watch, hidden all this time under the body of the watch section – a shining, golden scripture coin.

Marc's jaw dropped in shock. "This... this coin was responsible for making me the Sign?"

"It guided you every step of the way to ensure you fulfilled your destiny. Whenever you swayed from the ordained path, its power pulled you back."

"My visions, my dreams!" Marc whispered. The collapse on Ailen as he had made up his mind to return to Earth had prompted him to stay with the Mendoken. His own mind rebelling against his virtual self on Nopelio had caused him to break out of the Volonan Grid. The collapse on the Aftaran Gyra-class vessel as he had wanted to leave that ship had made sure he stayed onboard and ended up on Meenjaza. Learning to cope with the visions had also helped him finally break through the barrier around the Unghan stronghold.

Finally, it seemed, the puzzle was starting to take shape, piece by piece. "So are you saying this coin made all the decisions for me?" he asked Rayim.

"Made the decisions? No. It just guided you in the right direction. The decisions you made were still yours."

"What about my feelings? I felt good and bad vibes about different individuals, way before there was any reason to think anything about them. Was that the coin too?"

"No, not entirely," Ouria said. "While the scripture coin did intensify the emotions you felt upon encountering individuals and situations, your basic intuition was still yours. The scripture coin never took over your personality or your thought process. It merely showed you the terrible things that would happen if you did not do what it wanted you to. It encouraged you to stay true to your destiny, by helping you clearly separate those who would help you in your cause from those who would do all in their power to hinder you. It never lied to you and it never turned you into somebody you were not."

"That is right," Rayim said. "I would never have picked someone who I did not think was up to the challenge of being the Sign."

Marc shook his head in disbelief. It did feel somewhat comforting to know, though, that his basic intuition was his own and not that of the scripture coin. It seemed he was a good judge of character after all, far better than he had ever had reason to believe during his entire life on Earth. All he needed was to have faith in his own judgment.

"Can you explain to me what I saw in my visions?" he asked. "I mean, I understand the warnings of darkness, death and destruction. But every time all that faded away, six lights that came to my side, lights that gave me hope and warmth.

What did those lights represent?"

Ouria seemed to think for a moment. "We cannot interpret everything you saw, since your visions are only for you to interpret. But I would guess that the lights represented those things that most helped you accomplish your mission. Do you know what they might be?"

Marc's eyes lit up, once he realized what Ouria was referring to. They weren't things, but individuals. And there were exactly six of them, from all four advanced civilizations of the galaxy – Sibular, Zorina, Dumyan, Sharjam, Raiha and Jinser-Shosa. Somehow the scripture coin had known all along that these six were going to help him in his quest. "Incredible!" he thought.

Then another thought came to his head. "So if you knew all about this disaster and this conspiracy ahead of time, why did you even need a Sign? Why not just expose Jaegor and the rest of the Unghans yourselves?"

"No, we did not know, Marc Zemin," Ouria replied. "All we knew was what the Hidden Scripture told us, which was that the calamity befalling the Dominion could only be removed with the help of the Sign. We just needed to choose the Sign, and the Scripture would take care of the rest. We had no idea that Jaegor was actually an alien from another galaxy, nor did we know what conspiracy he was plotting. We had never heard of the Starguzzlers or what they were capable of. You were the first to see through it all, and through you the rest of us were able to see it. Such is the power of the Scriptures."

"And such are the ways of the Creator," Rayim added. "They are truly strange. One mistake our ancestors often used to make was to try to understand the Creator and the Creator's agenda based on their logic and their definition of what was good and bad, right and wrong. But over time we have come to realize that the limited level of understanding and knowledge we mortals possess makes that impossible. Now we no longer make that mistake."

Marc wasn't fully convinced. "If the Scriptures hold so much power, then, why didn't you use that power to break out of your imprisonment?"

"You think logically, Marc Zemin," Ouria said, smiling. "That is a good thing, and one of the reasons you were chosen. Wazilban took away all our scripture coins, without which we were powerless. No enchantment can ever be enacted without the correct scripture coin in your possession. All our powers lie in the Scriptures and not in ourselves, for the Creator has blessed the Scriptures with these powers."

"Does that mean the Creator wrote the Scriptures?"

Ouria smiled again. "Actually, we do not know if the Creator wrote them. We do not know who did. Nowhere in any of the Scriptures does it say that they are the Creator's own words. Very few of the verses even mention the Creator by name. The Scriptures have been there as long as our people have existed, and over time we have come to treat them as sacred truth. In many ways, it does not matter who wrote them."

"But why would you religiously follow laws that are not from the Creator as if they were from the Creator?"

Ouria was silent for a moment. "Do you have religious texts on your world, Marc Zemin?"

"Yes. A number of them, actually."

"Do their followers believe them to be the words of the Creator, even if it is impossible that all the different texts could have been written by the same Creator because of their opposing decrees and rituals?"

"Generally, yes, but not in all cases. We call the Creator 'God', though."

"That is but a name. We once used to have different names for the Creator too. Some of our ancestors even worshipped multiple creators, but eventually they came to the realization that there has to be one, omnipotent creator who is responsible for all of creation. If there were multiple creators, there would have to be another creator who created those creators. You would always have to end up with one creator at the very beginning.

"Now, regarding the Scriptures, knowing who wrote them is not as important as believing in what they say and following what they teach. And if they teach us to be better individuals and live better lives, then what is the harm in believing? I doubt any of the followers of the different religious texts on your world can physically prove that the Creator actually wrote any of them, just like they cannot physically prove that the Creator exists. We cannot either. The Creator chooses to remain unseen. We do see clues of the Creator's handiwork everywhere. All of Creation is the Creator's handiwork, after all. But as much as they may or may not coincide with current science, they are still just clues, not hard, factual evidence, as the Mendoken keep telling us time and again. In the end, it all boils down to one thing – faith."

"The magic word," Marc thought. He had heard that plenty of times before. "But no scriptures on my world can perform miracles like yours," he said to Ouria. "If they could, my world would be a very different place."

"Can they not? How did they ever gain acceptance over your people without showing miracles?"

"Oh, they claim to have shown miracles in the past. There were prophets who revealed the scriptures to people throughout history, and they supposedly performed miracles. So did many saints who followed the teachings of those prophets. But there is no way to verify any of those claims today. All the eyewitnesses have been dead for centuries."

"Neither will there be any way for anyone several centuries in the future to verify the miracles you have witnessed with our Scriptures. All they will be able to do is take your word for it. All they will be able to do is have faith, similar to how your people have faith in your prophets and saints of the past."

"But how can you live your whole life based on faith? What if the faith isn't true? Isn't it all in vain then?"

"We all live our lives based on faith, whether we believe in the Creator or not," Ouria said. "Faith in our children, our parents, our friends, our careers and our future. Everything is based on faith, for none of us know what will happen tomorrow. The worst possible things could happen to us at any time. We may lose our loved ones, lose our jobs, or even die ourselves. Yet we always maintain the faith to carry on and hope that everything will be fine. Faith makes us live our lives better. Faith makes us feel that life is worth living.

"It is the same with having faith in the Creator. It gives us a feeling of meaning, of purpose, a feeling of hope that there is more to life than a fleeting few years of consciousness between birth and death. It gives us the assurance that we do not cease to exist the moment we die, but that we remain conscious in death as well. As the Scriptures tell us, death is just a different form of life, and it lasts for eternity. Without such faith, life has no value. Without such faith, life would be unbearably lonely."

"So you're suggesting faith is the same thing as hope?"

"Faith is much stronger than hope. Faith lasts through thick and thin. It never withers and it never dies."

Another of the High Clerics spoke. "Faith also gives us a basis for organized religion, with laws, morals, ethics – all the things that are needed for a society like ours to be a society. There is no greater source of motivation to be good, just and kind to others than faith in an all-knowing, all-powerful Creator."

"But organized religion can often lead to blindness and narrow-mindedness," Marc insisted. "In its extreme form, it can lead to fundamentalism and militancy. On my world, many highly religious people believe their way is the right way and everyone else's way is wrong. They try to force their beliefs on others, and often turn violent in order to impose their will. Our history is filled with wars fought over differences in religious beliefs."

"Your people are young, Marc Zemin," Ouria said. "As a species, you have not existed for even a couple of million years, let alone billions like us. We were like you once. It took many periods of war and peace for us to learn how to turn religion into a tool for compassion and tolerance, not bigotry and violence. In time, your people will also learn the same thing. You will learn how to interpret your religious texts in their correct contexts and how to always pick the moderate middle ground, never swaying to one extreme or the other. You will learn when to supplement your interpretations with logic and reason, and where to draw the boundaries to never cross. You need not focus solely on religion like we have chosen to do, and given the balanced nature of your species, it is unlikely you will be able to. But you will eventually see that some level of religion and faith is needed and can actually help in the advancement of your society. It will give your people the necessary discipline to treat each other with respect. It will give you faith not just in the Creator but also in yourselves, faith to unite towards a common future that will eventually lead you to become one of the galaxy's great civilizations.

"The path ahead will not be easy, that I can assure you. Look at us. Even after all those millennia of solidifying our way of life, you sadly bore witness to how easily Jaegor was able to sway our people to darkness again. From time to time, your people will face such leaders with hidden agendas as well. The challenge will lie in countering their messages of hate and belligerence, and in remaining committed to the path of peace and righteousness."

Rayim took out the scripture coin from the pocket watch cover, put the timepiece back in its case and handed the watch back to Marc. "Your mission is herewith complete, Marc Zemin. If there is any way I could apologize for assigning you such a monumental task without asking you first, I would. But I am sure you will agree that there is no way you would have believed me or accepted the task if I had. Regardless, I hope you will appreciate as much as we do what an honor it is to have accomplished all you have. With the Creator's help, you have saved all of us. You have saved the whole Glaessan. And we shall never forget it." He bowed in front of Marc, and the other High Clerics followed suit.

Marc took this as an indication that the conversation was over. He bowed back and left the room.

After bidding Dumyan farewell, Marc headed back to the Mendo-Zueger system on board the Mendoken scout ship. The short consar journey was uneventful, and he spent it all in deep contemplation. He thought about everything the High Clerics had told him, and tried to decipher what it all meant. The one thing that had begun to give him a glimmer of hope about the proof of God's existence had just been just shattered. It was not God who had chosen him to be the Sign, it was an Aftaran. It had been a logical decision by a mere mortal. By selecting him as the "Sign", the Aftaran High Clerics had taken practical steps to ensure that their prophecy was going to be fulfilled. In a sense, his advent as the Sign had been a self-fulfilling prophecy.

Sure, he had experienced many inexplicable events, events that had allowed him to correctly foresee the future and to expose hidden truths to others. But none of that offered any clear evidence of the existence of God. No scientific panel would ever accept them as anything other than supernatural phenomena. In the end, he realized, the only way to believe in God was to rely on faith, just like Ouria had said.

He had to admit, though, that faith was something he now had. He just couldn't find any other way to explain everything he had witnessed. How many of those supernatural phenomena could have been magic tricks, how many of those foretold events just simply occurrences not explicable by science? How many of his narrow escapes from death could have been attributed to coincidence? And how else could he explain all the wonders of creation that he had seen from one corner of the galaxy to the other and beyond?

Most of his life he had been an atheist, and later on he had become an agnostic. But now, he knew, he had faith. He definitely wasn't ever going to be a follower of any religion or any set of rituals, that much was for sure. But he could sense that something was out there, some power that had created everything and was in control of it all, some power that had the ability to foresee, to destine and to intervene. And fundamentally, that power, while its motives and its methods seemed impossible to fathom, was good.

Chapter 44

The Euma-9 vessel that was to transport Marc back to Earth was waiting for him at one of the space stations around Lind. As he arrived on the ship's control deck, he was surprised to be greeted by Commander Maginder. It turned out this was the same ship and same crew that had picked him up from Earth a month earlier. It was no coincidence, for this crew was responsible for the region of space where Earth was located, and knew the area better than any other Mendoken crew.

Marc was pleased to see his old acquaintance Petrana piloting the ship. He spent some time talking to her as the ship took off, telling her about all the things he had been through since their last encounter. She went on to tell him how this ship had participated in the battle against the Starguzzlers at a star system not too far from Mendo-Biesel. The ship had been almost destroyed at one point, but had luckily made it through in the end.

After some time, Marc went down to his quarters, the same lavish quarters made especially for him that he had stayed in before. Since this was no consar journey, it would take over 2 days to reach Earth. "Might as well get some rest," he thought.

The journey home was uneventful. Just as the ship reached the entrance to the Mendo-Biesel system, he came back up to the control deck to witness the entry through the silupsal filter. Watching the massive gate open in the wall of darkness ahead, he thought about how he was willingly returning inside the shell he had lived his whole life in, the shell all humans were living in.

"Dark matter indeed," he said to himself. Humans believed that most of the matter in the universe consisted of dark matter invisible to the human eye, and the debate about the composition of dark matter still raged on in scientific circles today. There were numerous theories that it consisted of particles different from neutrons, protons and electrons, the baryonic particles that most of known, visible matter was comprised of. All kinds of interesting names had been given to these invisible particles, including axions, sterile neutrinos, SIMPs and WIMPs. Yet it had never once occurred to humans that this dark matter might consist of the very same baryonic particles they could already see. It was just purposely hidden from their view by beings far more advanced than them.

As the ship passed through the filter and began its approach toward Earth, Marc remembered one more thing that had been puzzling him for a while. Realizing that he only had minutes left with the Mendoken, he walked up to Petrana to ask her. Given her expertise on Earth and humans, he figured, she would most likely know the answer.

"Petrana, since you Mendoken actively monitor the silupsal filter and make sure there is no communication between us and those outside our solar system, why is it that we have had so many reports of extraterrestrial sightings on Earth throughout history? Who flies all those flying saucers and UFOs and what not?"

"That is one of the interesting qualities of your species, Marc," Petrana said. "Some of you appear to relish tricking others with acts of deception. Acts that are not harmful, but are nonetheless untrue and unproductive."

"So you're saying all the sightings are fake?"

"Not all. There may have been occasions where ships of other species in the galaxy managed to pass through the filter undetected, but generally we Mendoken do a thorough job in monitoring all traffic through the filter. Some of the sightings may also have been of advanced aircraft developed in secret by humans."

"I presume you mean military aircraft? Whose are they?"

"Of the country you live in, mostly – the United States. They are undoubtedly the current leaders in space and air travel technology on your planet, with aircraft already built and tested that are far more advanced than what the public is aware of. We have observed several of their recent developments with interest."

"Really!" Marc was surprised to hear this. "I suppose they keep these things secret in order to keep their edge over other countries."

"Yes. It is ironic that a species as creative and hard working as yours needs to have enemies in its own midst in order to keep advancing and progressing. You humans would be a lot more productive if you all worked with each other instead of against each other."

Marc watched the familiar blue planet appear in the distance. He was coming home at last! After all he had experienced out in space, his emotions about the decision he had taken were mixed, but his resolve was absolute.

Commander Maginder came over and asked him to give up his translator device. He was then to enter a transport cylinder that would take him down to the surface, the same way he had initially ascended from Earth.

"Where would you like to land, Mr. Zemin?" Maginder asked. "At the same location where we picked you up?"

"That depends on whether you can locate someone on Earth for me."

"We can locate any human being anywhere on the planet. We can also collect detailed information about that person for you, if you so require."

Marc had never been to Europe before, even though he had always really wanted to visit. During his senior year at MIT, he had planned to surprise Iman by inviting her to join him for a trip to Europe the summer after his graduation. Instead of heading to the most typical tourist destinations like London, Paris or Venice, he had planned on going just to Vienna and Prague, two cities out of the main limelight but with very rich histories and many beautiful sights. He had also planned to propose to her during that trip, in Vienna on the banks of the river Danube. But that trip had never occurred, because the two of them had broken up well before his graduation.

"Life can be so funny sometimes," he thought. He had never imagined he would actually ever make it here under such different circumstances. It was also a strange feeling to be back on Earth, a strangeness that was compounded by the fact that he had chosen to land in a location so foreign to him.

He was standing on top of a bridge over the Danube, staring at the water flowing silently under him, water that flowed all the way from the Black Forest in Bavaria to the Black Sea 1800 miles away. The city of Vienna was spread on both sides of the river, the older part to the west where all the historical landmarks were located, and the much newer section to the east where many of the modern structures lay. The afternoon winter sky was clear, with the Sun already beginning its descent over the western horizon. The air was cold, but he took no notice of the temperature. The jacket the Mendoken had made for him was keeping him plenty warm, and the shoes they had provided were very comfortable for walking. There was a decent amount of traffic on the bridge, with cars whizzing by in both directions. It was rush hour, after all, with people heading home from work on this Tuesday evening.

As he walked over the bridge to the eastern side of the city, crossing over a man-made island and an artificial waterway that ran parallel to the river for several miles, he wondered about the meeting that lay ahead. He had expected to be nervous, but he wasn't. He was surprisingly calm. After all he had been through, nervousness just didn't seem to be in his vocabulary anymore. He was no longer afraid of tough challenges or undesirable outcomes, no longer prone to spiraling depression. He had no fear of abandonment or rejection anymore, for he had experienced true, loyal friendship. He was a different person now, one who had confidence and faith, faith in himself and in a higher power to guide him and help him through thick and thin. He had learned to fight for what he believed in and what he wanted, to never to give up those things that mattered the most. He was determined never to repeat his mistakes of the past, nor would he ever try to escape into it again.

His destination was clearly visible now – a series of modern looking buildings not too far from the banks of the artificial waterway. A large triangular structure called "Austria Center" stood out in front. Built in the late 1980's, it was a modern conference center that could host close to 10,000 people at a time. But where he was headed was the complex of modern looking buildings behind the center – a number of curved structures that reminded him of the shape of the City Hall in Toronto, which he had once seen as a child.

These buildings were much larger, however, and there were many more of them. This complex also held a far more global function. It housed one of the four main United Nations offices of the world, along with New York, Geneva and Nairobi. Known as the Vienna International Center, it was home to the well known International Atomic Energy Agency (IAEA), the United Nations Industrial Development Organization (UNIDO), and a number of other, smaller UN organizations.

Marc arrived at the main entrance to the complex and walked into the security building. Security here was high, similar to that of international airports. Following a line of people, he walked through a metal detector and was then abruptly stopped by a stern looking security guard.

"Name?" the guard asked, in a voice commensurate with his looks.

"Marc Zemin."

"Identification?"

Marc produced his Canadian passport. The Mendoken had been gracious enough to fetch it for him from his room in Ithaca before he had left their ship. If things here went the way he was hoping, he wouldn't be returning to Ithaca himself anytime soon. There was just nothing there for him anymore to go back to.

The guard fumbled through the passport's pages. "Who are you here to see?"

"Iman Houry. She works at the CGTU."

The guard stepped away, made a call, and returned after a minute. "Ms. Houry will be down to meet you in a moment," he said curtly, handing Marc his passport back.

Marc walked up to the window and stared at the wide plaza between the curved buildings. There was a fountain in the center, surrounded by a circle of poles carrying the flags of the UN's member states.

"If she comes out walking," he said to himself, "there's no chance. But if she comes out running..."

She came out running.

Even from a distance, he could see how beautiful she was. She looked just like the way he remembered her, both from his undergrad years and his more recent virtual life experience in the Volonan Empire. Her long, auburn hair fluttered in the wind as she ran, her attractive figure well carried inside the gray suit she was wearing. As she came closer, he could see her brown eyes sparkling with excitement. And as soon as she saw him staring through the window, her lips broke into a smile.

She ran into the security building and hugged him tightly. "Marc! What are you doing here? How did you find me?"

He smiled, fighting hard to keep his emotions under control. "Oh, you know, information is freely available these days with modern technology. I thought I'd come by and surprise you."

"Surprise! Are you kidding me? I almost got a heart attack when I heard your name!"

Her voice still sounded as sweet as ever, but it had a hint of brokenness. She had obviously been through a lot. The Mendoken had already told him about her current relationship status, and that, of course, was why he was here.

"How long are you in town for?" she asked excitedly. "Do you have time now? Let me show you my office!"

"I don't have any set schedule, and I'd love to see your office."

Iman led him through the plaza, into one of the buildings and up the elevator. On the 27th floor, her office faced the Danube river and the city of Vienna beyond. It was a beautiful sight, especially in the gathering dusk.

She showed him the kind of work she was doing. The CGTU (Center for Global Tolerance and Understanding) was a new initiative at the UN, whose sole purpose it was to promote better understanding between different societies in the world, especially between nations, cultures or religions that were in conflict. Her area of specialty, of no great surprise given her identity and background, was bridging the gap between the Muslim world and the West. With current political events around the globe, this conflict was probably the biggest threat to world peace at the moment, fueled largely by prejudices and stereotypes on both sides. These prejudices had simmered over centuries of conflict and had most recently erupted to a boil. Her job, therefore, was to establish education programs for the public on both sides, programs that would break down the prejudices and help either side understand the other.

Marc listened to everything she was saying with keen interest. "World peace," he thought. It was such a cliché. And yet, cliché or not, it was the single most important thing humans had to accomplish. It was the most important thing humans had to attain before they could finally be ready for the shattering reality beyond their little world.

"You know, I would love to switch careers and move more into this kind of work," he said.

Iman looked startled. "What! You? I thought you were always the dedicated scientist!"

"People can change, Iman," Marc said with a grin. "What your organization is doing is critical for the future of the human race, I'm convinced of that. As critical as fighting global poverty and inequality, as critical as fighting famine, disease and global warming. Prejudices are usually based on complete distortions of facts, facts that are often untrue to begin with or are heavily generalized from specific events or circumstances. All you have to do is a little research or spend some time with somebody from the other side, and you'll soon come to see that most prejudices are baseless. Spend a little time with somebody from the other side, and you'll learn that everybody has his or her own story to tell. And in the end, you'll see that people across the globe have more similarities than differences.

"I used to hold prejudices myself once, against many societies around the world. I know I must have said many a nonsensical thing about your culture too, and I'm sure it played a role in our breakup. I know it's a little late now for an apology, but I truly am sorry for ever hurting your feelings. I was ignorant, foolish and immature. And I am none of those things anymore."

Iman blinked. "You're serious, aren't you? What's changed you so much?"

"Let's just say my eyes have been opened, in more ways than one. I've come to realize that science and technology will always progress with or without someone like me, because humans will always want to research, discover and build new things. But what never seems to progress is peace, unity, or understanding between people. People can have the most sophisticated computers, planes or rockets that they want, but all of it is meaningless if all they end up doing is using the technology to fight and destroy each other. The hardest science of all is social science, and that's the science I want to be involved in from now on.

"I agree with you that the biggest obstacles to peace across the globe are ignorance and prejudice. Politicians have their own agendas, of course, as do extremists. Politicians usually instigate wars for economic reasons, or just because they are power hungry. Extremists instigate strife because of their ingrained hate towards all who aren't exactly like them. But the only reason both are able to get away with their actions is because the masses who give them the authority to create turmoil and wage wars are ignorant. If the public had as much respect for people of other societies and cultures as they do for their friends and neighbors, politicians and extremists would have their hands tied and most conflicts across the globe would instantly evaporate."

She nodded excitedly. "That's exactly why this center was created!"

He stared at her, wondering how she had managed to stay so beautiful with all she must have recently been through. There was a hint of sadness in her face, no doubt, but it was only a hint.

"Iman, do you have plans for dinner?" he asked.

"No. I was just going to work a little more and then go home." She smiled. "But I can make an exception for you."

They ate at a local restaurant on the man-made island between the Danube and the artificial waterway. Marc paid no attention to the location or to what he was eating. All he cared about was the person he was with.

Iman told him about her life over the past few years since their breakup. She had finished her degree at Harvard a year after he had left Boston, and had then returned to Amman, Jordan where her family was based. Her parents had insisted right away that she get married, and had introduced her to suitor after suitor. After holding out for several months, she had eventually succumbed to the mounting pressure, not just from her parents but from the entire extended family.

"So you got married," Marc said.

"Yes, I had no choice. He was a young man from a very rich and well known family in Amman. The whole thing was completely arranged. I only met him a couple of times before our wedding date. He had studied in England, so somehow our two families thought we'd be right for each other because we had both lived and studied abroad. Were they wrong!

"I was determined to try to make the marriage work, but I found him to be indifferent towards me and quite uninterested. It didn't take long for me to figure out why. Within a week after our wedding, he confessed to me that he was actually deeply in love with someone else, someone his family hadn't allowed him to marry. He had been going out with an English girl during his time at Oxford. Same deal as what happened to you and me – his family wouldn't accept it, and had pressured him to marry someone from Jordan.

"The indifference soon grew to hate, hate towards me, my family, even our culture, our country, everything. He would pick fights with me on the smallest of things, leave home and not come back for days. Everyone in my family kept telling me to try harder to make him happy, since a young man from such a good family was a unique find. I tried, believe me, I tried. But nothing worked.

"One day, he told me he needed to go abroad on a long business trip. He was gone for a month. Then, a couple of weeks later, he took off again. He didn't call or write once during those trips. After a few more of those long trips, he came back home one day and told me he didn't want anything to do with me anymore because I wasn't pleasing him as his wife. That was when I totally broke down, and I finally gave up on him. I left the house and went back to my family. My brother did some research, and soon found out that my husband was spending all his time in England, having an affair with that same girl back in Oxford.

"That was when my family turned 180 degrees. They totally took my side and stood up for me against my husband, providing evidence to his family that he was the one at fault for the breakdown of our marriage. Then I filed for divorce.

"My family stood by me, but our community did not. All the blame fell on me for ruining the marriage. He could have done no wrong because his family was so respected, and also because he was the guy and I was the girl. His family, with all their wealth and power, went on a whole campaign to discredit my parents and spread slander about me. My father began to suffer mentally and physically. One day, he came home and collapsed in front of our eyes with a massive heart attack. He died on the way to the hospital, not even 60 years old."

"I am so sorry to hear that," Marc said. "I did not know."

Iman's eyes turned moist. "It was the hardest time of my life, Marc. I fell into a long period of depression. The slandering did not stop, even after the passing of my father. It soon became clear to my mother and my siblings that it wouldn't be easy to find any other respectable man who would want to marry me under those conditions. Not that I wanted to marry again! I just wanted to leave Jordan, to start afresh somewhere else and to build my career. After some persuasion, during which my younger sister actively supported my cause, my mother and brother reluctantly agreed. They also agreed not to pressure me into marrying again. I was finally free to do what I wanted."

"How did you end up coming to Vienna?"

"Well, you know how I've always had this thing about how there are no societies more misunderstood in the West than those of the Middle East. When I returned to Jordan, it became very clear to me that the misunderstandings went both ways. And with the rising tide of hate and anger on both sides since the horrors of 9/11 and the wars that followed, I decided to pursue a career in bridging the gaps. I began searching all over, and on the Internet found the links to this new UN organization in Vienna. I applied for a job and got accepted! I've been here now for over a year."

"And how has life been for you overall since you moved here?"

"The work has been great. It's exactly what I hoped it would be, and more. But I'll be honest – life here is lonely. I don't have any relatives here, which I suppose is both good and bad. But I don't have too many friends either."

"Have you been dating?"

"I went out on a few dates with a couple of different men I met at the UN. But things never clicked. We just didn't connect. I've never connected with anyone, not like I did with...." Her words trailed off as she looked away, and she remained quiet for a moment. "Then I gave up, and I've been single since."

The moment, Marc knew, had come. "Iman, I've been doing a lot of thinking for a while. And I know it's crazy to bring this up now after all this time. I'm not here because I've suddenly had an old crush rekindled, nor am I trying to relive our college years due to an early midlife crisis. I'm here because I've reached the realization that you and I actually can have a great future together. We were both young before and immature about a lot of things. But we've both learned from our mistakes since we last saw each other, and I think the kind of things we've learned are things that have brought us closer together, not further apart.

"I'm not saying that we should go make passionate love tonight to make up for all the time lost. Nor am I suggesting that we should run right away to the nearest church, mosque or courtroom to get married. But what I am saying is that perhaps we could try starting again from the beginning. We could try dating and see how things go. I think we'll both be surprised at how wonderful it could get."

Iman looked stunned at first, but then just stared for a long time at her half finished meal of turkey schnitzel and potato salad. Finally, she looked up at him. "If you actually are serious about what you just said, would you be willing to live here in Vienna? I really don't want to move from my current job at the moment, and you know how I've never been a fan of long distance relationships."

Marc's heart jumped with delight. "I've always wanted to visit here," he said happily. "So why not try living here in one shot?"

He reached over to give her a kiss. The whiff of perfume that filled his nose was all too familiar. Her favorite brand hadn't changed in all these years.

She didn't resist his advance. "Marc, I..."

They kissed. It was a brief kiss, but it lasted a sweet eternity for him. Her lips felt just as soft and warm as they used to.

He sat back down, and looked at her thoughtfully.

"What?" she asked, blushing.

He just shook his head. He couldn't very well tell her how much and for how long he had been waiting for this moment. Maybe one day he would, but not today.

He decided to change the topic instead. "So are there any job openings in your organization? I know the UN has got its inefficiency and bureaucracy issues, and there's a lot of ugly politics. But it's still the most encompassing body this planet has ever seen. If there's any organization that has a chance to bring the world together, it's the UN. Besides, I would love to work side by side with you. I think we could make quite a team."

Iman grinned, and a mischievous twinkle appeared in her eyes. "I'm sure we could work something out. But what if you have to end up working for me, instead of with me?"

"I'll take anything, as long as there's both you and global understanding in the picture." He had bigger plans for his future with the UN, of course, plans and ideas that would hopefully help shape and secure the future of the human race. Perhaps he and Iman would be able to do it together. For now, however, just being with her was all he could possibly ask for. It was all he wanted. And being able to work with her on a cause that would serve as a critical stepping stone for his future plans was simply a bonus.

They talked about many other things as they finished their meal. Then they went for a walk along the riverside.

Marc put his arm around her, and looked up into the night sky to thank his lucky stars for bringing him and Iman back together. But his eyes instantly widened with surprise. "Iman, what do you see up there?" he asked.

She looked up at the sky. "I see a clear night sky like any other. Why do you ask?"

"Hmm? Oh, nothing." He couldn't tell her, of course, what he could see, or that he had finally figured out what parting gift his Mendoken friend Sibular had given him. The sky was filled with billions of stars, all right next to each other, all shining brightly. The entire sky was like a giant sheet of bright white spots, far brighter and far more crowded than he had ever seen from Earth before. It was the same view as that of the night sky from Lind, from Meenjaza, from the many other planets and ships he had been on over the past month.

"Just a small token to always remind you of your time here with us," Sibular had said. Sibular had evidently injected something into Marc's eyes, some tiny, invisible piece of sophisticated Mendoken technology. Marc now had to be the only person on Earth who could see right through the silupsal filter surrounding the solar system, as if it wasn't there at all.

For the rest of his life, he realized, he would be able to look up at the sky every clear night and remember his journey through the heavens. For the rest of his life, he would constantly be reminded that it hadn't all just been a dream.

"Just a small token indeed," he thought, and smiled.

ABOUT THE AUTHOR

S.W. (Sajjad Waiz) Ahmed is an American science fiction writer of Bangladeshi origin. He grew up in Austria and moved to the United States at the age of 18, where he studied electrical engineering and pursued a career in computer software. A keen follower of science and an avid reader of science fiction since childhood, he now writes his own sci-fi stories as a hobby. Although his writing usually involves alien civilizations, it often draws strong allusions to contemporary issues and events in human society. He currently resides in the San Francisco Bay Area with his family. *Dark Matter* is his first novel.

The author's web site can be found at www.swahmed.com.

Printed in the United States
122998LV00003B/23/P